Anonymous

## The Rank and Talent of the Time

A dictionary of contemporary biography, containing one thousand interesting and

accurate memoirs of eminent living celebrities

.

Anonymous

**The Rank and Talent of the Time**
*A dictionary of contemporary biography, containing one thousand interesting and accurate memoirs of eminent living celebrities*

ISBN/EAN: 9783337030216

Printed in Europe, USA, Canada, Australia, Japan

Cover: Foto ©Raphael Reischuk / pixelio.de

More available books at **www.hansebooks.com**

THE

# RANK AND TALENT

OF

# THE TIME

A DICTIONARY OF CONTEMPORARY BIOGRAPHY

CONTAINING

ONE THOUSAND INTERESTING AND ACCURATE MEMOIRS
OF EMINENT LIVING CELEBRITIES

LONDON

GRIFFIN, BOHN, AND COMPANY

STATIONERS' HALL COURT

1861

# PREFACE.

THE utility of a Handbook of Contemporary Biography, if reliable, is so apparent, that the only use of a preface to this work is to give information as to the manner in which it has been prepared.

In the first place, the memoirs were compiled from every available general and special source,—and here we may express our obligations to Hachette's valuable French work—the "Dictionnaire Universel des Contemporains." It was found, however, that great discrepancies existed among statements derived from many authorities, and that, unless means were taken to verify the facts by communicating with the parties themselves, the hope of producing a *reliable* book must be abandoned. Accordingly, we took the liberty of addressing a communication to every individual whose name is introduced in the volume, with the exception of a few royal personages, whose actions and fortunes are matters of history. We stated that we wished to produce a trustworthy work, endeavouring to avoid, as far as possible, matters of opinion, seeing that until the whole career of a man is finished it is impossible fairly to estimate his character, and that we therefore respectfully requested replies regarding points of fact. Our communications have been generally responded to; and whatever may be the literary shortcomings of this work, we believe that it may be pronounced to be the most trustworthy Manual of Contemporary Biography yet published. Yet, as the volume contains nearly one thousand memoirs, it is impossible but that there are many errors both of omission and commission, and these we shall only be too happy to correct in future editions, if our readers will have the kindness to point them out, and to supply the information.

10, STATIONERS' HALL COURT,
*November*, 1860.

# INDEX OF NAMES.

| | PAGE |
|---|---|
| Aali Pasha . . . . . | 1 |
| Abbott, Rev. Jacob . . . | 1 |
| Abbott, Rev. John . . . | 2 |
| Abd-el-Kader . . . . | 2 |
| Abdul-Medjid, Khan . . . | 3 |
| Aberdeen, Earl of . . . . | 4 |
| About, Edmond . . . . | 6 |
| Adam, Jean Victor . . . | 6 |
| Adams, John Couch . . . | 6 |
| Agassiz, Louis Jean . . . | 7 |
| Ainsworth, William F. . . . | 8 |
| Ainsworth, William H. . . . | 8 |
| Aird, Thomas . . . . | 9 |
| Airy, George Biddell, M.A. . . | 9 |
| Albert, Prince . . . . | 10 |
| Albert, Martin . . . . | 11 |
| Alboni, Marietta . . . . | 11 |
| Alexander II., Emperor of Russia . | 12 |
| Alford, The Very Rev. Henry, D.D. | 12 |
| Alison, Sir Archibald, Bart. . . | 13 |
| Almodovar, Count of . . . | 14 |
| Alvarez, Juan . . . . | 14 |
| Ampère, Jean Jacques . . . | 14 |
| Andersen, Hans Christian . . | 15 |
| Andral, Gabriel . . . . | 15 |
| Anster, John, D.C.L. . . . | 15 |
| Anstey, Thomas Chisholm . . | 16 |
| Anthon, Charles, LL.D. . . | 16 |
| Antonelli, Cardinal . . . | 16 |
| Arago, Étienne . . . . | 17 |
| Argelander, Friedrich . . . | 18 |
| Argyll, Duke of . . . . | 18 |
| Argyropoulo, Pericles . . . | 18 |
| Aristarchi, Nicolas . . . | 19 |
| Arnold, Matthew . . . . | 19 |
| Arnott, Neil, M.D. . . . | 19 |
| Arthur, T. S. . . . . | 19 |
| Ashburton, Lord . . . . | 20 |
| Ashley, Lord. (See Shaftesbury) . | 353 |
| Astronomer Royal. (See Airy) . | 9 |

| | PAGE |
|---|---|
| Auber, Daniel F. E. . . . | 20 |
| Auerbach, Berthold . . . | 20 |
| Augier, Guillaume Victor . . | 21 |
| Austria, Emperor of . . . | 163 |
| Auzoux, Th. Louis . . . | 21 |
| Aytoun, William Edmondstoune . | 22 |
| Azeglio, Marquis d' . . . | 22 |
| Babbage, Charles . . . . | 23 |
| Back, Sir George, D.C.L. . . | 23 |
| Baehr, John Christian . . . | 24 |
| Bailey, Philip James . . . | 25 |
| Baily, Edward Hodges, R.A. . | 25 |
| Baines, Edward, M.P. . . . | 26 |
| Balfe, Michael William . . . | 26 |
| Bancroft, George . . . . | 26 |
| Baraguey, Marshal . . . | 27 |
| Barante, Baron de . . . | 27 |
| Barbès, Armand . . . . | 28 |
| Baring, Sir Francis, Bart. . . | 28 |
| Baring, Thomas . . . . | 29 |
| Baring, William. (See Ashburton) | 20 |
| Barlow, Peter . . . . | 29 |
| Barnes, Albert . . . . | 29 |
| Barnum, Phineas Taylor . . | 30 |
| Baroche, Pierre Jules . . . | 30 |
| Barrett, Miss. (See Browning, Mrs.) | 69 |
| Barrot, Odilon . . . . | 31 |
| Barry Cornwall. (See Proctor) . | 320 |
| Barth, Sir Henry . . . . | 32 |
| Barthélémy, Auguste-Marseille . | 33 |
| Bartlett, John Russell . . . | 33 |
| Bastide, Jules . . . . | 34 |
| Bauer, Bruno . . . . | 34 |
| Bavaria, King of. (See Maximilian II.) | 270 |
| Baxter, William Edward, M.P. . | 35 |
| Becquerel, Antoine Cesar . . | 35 |
| Bedeau, Marie Alphonse . . | 36 |
| Beecher, Miss Catherine . . | 36 |
| Beecher, Rev. Charles . . . | 36 |

| | PAGE |
|---|---|
| Beecher, Rev. Edward, D.D. | 36 |
| Beecher, Henry Ward | 37 |
| Beecher, Lyman, D.D. | 37 |
| Bekker, Emmanuel | 38 |
| Belcher, Sir Edward | 38 |
| Belgians, King of the. (*See* Leopold George Christian Frederick) | 242 |
| Bell, Henry Glassford | 39 |
| Bell, John | 39 |
| Bell, Robert | 40 |
| Bell, Thomas | 39 |
| Bendemann, Edward | 41 |
| Benedict, Julius | 41 |
| Bennett, William Sterndale | 42 |
| Berghaus, Henry | 42 |
| Berkeley, Hon. Francis, M.P. | 43 |
| Berlioz, Hector | 43 |
| Bernard, Claude | 44 |
| Berryer, Pierre Antoine | 44 |
| Bethell, Sir Richard | 45 |
| Bibesco, George Demetrius | 46 |
| Billault, Auguste | 46 |
| Binney, Rev. Thomas | 47 |
| Biot, Jean Baptiste | 47 |
| Black, Adam, M.P. | 48 |
| Blackwell, Elizabeth, M.D. | 48 |
| Blanc, Louis | 49 |
| Blanqui, Louis Auguste | 50 |
| Boeckh, Augustus | 50 |
| Bohn, Henry G. | 51 |
| Bonaparte, Jérome | 51 |
| Bonaparte, Louis Lucien | 52 |
| Bonaparte, Napoleon | 52 |
| Bonheur, Mademoiselle Rosa | 52 |
| Bopp, Franz | 53 |
| Bordeaux, Duc de | 93 |
| Borrow, George | 53 |
| Bosquet, Pierre François Joseph | 54 |
| Bosworth, Joseph, D.D., LL.D. | 54 |
| Botfield, Beriah | 55 |
| Botta, Paul Emilie | 55 |
| Bourqueney, Comte de | 55 |
| Boussingault, Jean Baptiste | 55 |
| Bowring, Sir John | 56 |
| Boz. (*See* Dickens) | 127 |
| Bravo-Murillo, Juan | 57 |
| Bray, Mrs. Anna Eliza | 58 |
| Bremer, Miss Fredrika | 58 |
| Brewster, Sir David | 59 |
| Bright, John, M.P. | 61 |

| | PAGE |
|---|---|
| Brodie, Sir Benjamin, Bart. | 63 |
| Broglie, Duc de | 64 |
| Brooke, Sir James | 64 |
| Brooks, Charles Shirley | 66 |
| Brougham, Lord | 66 |
| Broughton de Gifford, Lord | 68 |
| Brown, Miss Frances | 69 |
| Browning, Mrs. Elizabeth Barrett | 69 |
| Browning, Robert | 69 |
| Brunnow, Baron von | 70 |
| Bryant, William Cullen | 70 |
| Buccleuch and Queensberry, Duke of | 70 |
| Buchanan, James | 70 |
| Buckle, Henry Thomas | 71 |
| Buckstone, John Baldwin | 71 |
| Bulwer, Rt. Hon. Sir Henry Lytton | 72 |
| Bunsen, Chevalier von | 72 |
| Buol, Count | 74 |
| Buren, Van, Martin | 74 |
| Burgoyne, Sir John Fox | 74 |
| Burmeister, Hermann | 75 |
| Burnet, John | 75 |
| Burritt, Elihu | 76 |
| Burton, John Hill | 76 |
| Bustamente, Don Carlos Maria de | 76 |
| Caballero, Firmin Agosto | 76 |
| Cabet, Etienne | 77 |
| Cabrera, Don Ramon | 77 |
| Cailliaud, Frédéric | 78 |
| Caird, Rev. John, D.D. | 78 |
| Caird, James, M.P. | 78 |
| Cairns, Sir Hugh M'Calmont | 79 |
| Cambridge, H.R.H. Duke of | 79 |
| Campbell, Lord | 79 |
| Campbell, Rev. John, D.D. | 80 |
| Campbell, Sir Colin. (*See* Clyde, Lord) | 101 |
| Candlish, Rev. Robert, D.D. | 81 |
| Canning, Charles John, Viscount | 81 |
| Canrobert, François Certain | 82 |
| Canterbury, Archbishop of | 82 |
| Canterbury, Dean of. (*See* Alford) | 12 |
| Cantu, Cesar | 82 |
| Capefigue, Jean Baptiste | 82 |
| Cardigan, Earl of | 83 |
| Cardwell, Right Hon. Edward | 83 |
| Carey, Henry C. | 83 |
| Carlen, Madame Emilie | 84 |
| Carleton, William | 85 |

| | PAGE | | PAGE |
|---|---|---|---|
| Carlisle, Earl of | 85 | Cooper, Thomas Sidney, A.R.A. | 108 |
| Carlisle, Dean of. (*See* Close) | 101 | Cope, Charles West, R.A. | 108 |
| Carlyle, Thomas | 86 | Copley, John S. (*See* Lyndhurst) | 253 |
| Carnot, Lazare Hippolite | 87 | Corbaux, Miss Fanny | 109 |
| Carpenter, Wm. Benjamin, M.D. | 88 | Corbould, Edward Henry | 109 |
| Cary, Miss Alice | 88 | Cormenin, Vicomte de | 110 |
| Casabianca, Count of | 89 | Cornelius, Peter Von | 111 |
| Cass, General Lewis, LL.D. | 89 | Costello, Miss Louisa Stuart | 111 |
| Cattermole, George | 89 | Cousin, Victor | 111 |
| Caussidière, Marc | 90 | Coutts, Miss Burdett | 112 |
| Cavour, Count | 90 | Cowley, Lord | 112 |
| Cayley, Arthur | 91 | Craik, George Lillie, LL.D. | 113 |
| Celeste, Madame | 91 | Cranworth, Baron | 113 |
| Chadwick, Edwin, C.B. | 91 | Creasy, Sir Edward S., M.A. | 113 |
| Chambers, William and Robert | 93 | Cremieux, Isaac Adolphe | 114 |
| Chambord, Count de | 93 | Creswick, Thomas, R.A. | 114 |
| Chancellor, Lord. (*See* Campbell) | 79 | Croatia, Ban of. (*See* Jellachich) | 220 |
| Changarnier, General | 94 | Croly, Rev. George, LL.D. | 114 |
| Charles XV., Louis Eugène | 94 | Crosland, Mrs. Camilla | 115 |
| Cheever, George Burritt, D.D. | 94 | Crowe, Mrs. Catherine Stevens | 115 |
| Chelmsford, Lord | 95 | Cruikshank, George | 115 |
| Chesney, Major-General | 95 | Cullen, Paul, D.D. | 116 |
| Chevalier, Michel | 96 | Cumming, Rev. John, D.D. | 116 |
| Chevalier, Paul. (*See* Gavarni) | 171 | Cunningham, Peter | 117 |
| Chevreul, Michel Eugène | 97 | Cunningham, William, D.D. | 117 |
| Child, Mrs. Lydia Maria | 97 | Curtis, Benjamin R. | 117 |
| China, Emp. of. (*See* Hien Fung) | 208 | Curtis, George William | 118 |
| Chisholm, Mrs. Caroline | 97 | Cushman, Miss Charlotte | 118 |
| Christison, Robert | 98 | | |
| Clare, John | 98 | Dahlmann, Frederick Christopher | 118 |
| Clarendon, Earl of | 99 | Dale, Rev. Thomas, M.A. | 119 |
| Clark, Sir James, Bart. | 100 | Dalhousie, Marquis of | 119 |
| Clarke, Mrs. Mary Cowden | 100 | Dallas, George Mifflin | 120 |
| Clausen, Henri Nicolas | 100 | Dana, James Dwight, LL.D. | 120 |
| Close, The Very Rev. Dean | 101 | Dana, Richard Henry | 121 |
| Clyde, Lord | 101 | Danby, Francis, A.R.A. | 121 |
| Cobden, Richard | 102 | Danilo, Prince | 121 |
| Cochrane, Lord. (*See* Dundonald) | 140 | Dargan, William | 122 |
| Cockerell, Chas. Rob., R.A., D.C.L. | 102 | Darwin, Charles, M.A. | 122 |
| Codrington, Sir William, K.C.B. | 103 | D'Aubigné, J. H. Merle, D.D. | 123 |
| Cole, Henry, C.B. | 103 | David, Felicien | 123 |
| Coleridge, The Rev. Derwent | 104 | Davis, Sir John, Bart., K.C.B. | 123 |
| Collier, John Payne | 104 | Dawson, George, M.A. | 124 |
| Collin de Plancy, Jacques | 105 | Decazes, Elie Duc | 124 |
| Collins, Wilkie | 106 | De Grey, Earl. (*See* Ripon, Earl of) | 331 |
| Combermere, Viscount, G.C.B. | 106 | Delacroix, Eugène | 124 |
| Coningham, William, M.P. | 106 | Delane, John T. | 125 |
| Conscience, Henri | 107 | Delaroche, Paul | 125 |
| Constantine, Nicholæwitch | 107 | Demidov, or Demidoff, Anatol | 125 |
| Cook, Miss Eliza | 108 | De Morgan, Augustus | 126 |

| | PAGE | | PAGE |
|---|---|---|---|
| Denmark, King of . | 165 | Ellis, Rev. William . | 151 |
| Derby, Earl of . | 126 | Ellis, Sir Henry, K.H. . | 152 |
| Deschenes, Admiral Perceval | 127 | Emerson, Ralph Waldo . | 152 |
| Deville, Henry. (*See* Sainte-Claire) | 345 | Encke, Johann F. . | 152 |
| Dewey, Orville, D.D. . | 127 | Enfantin, Barthélémy Prosper | 153 |
| Dickens, Charles . | 127 | Eotvos, Josef . | 153 |
| Dickson, Samuel Henry, M.D. | 128 | Espartero, Don Baldomero . | 154 |
| Dilke, Charles Wentworth . | 129 | Espinasse, Esprit Charles Marie | 154 |
| Dilke, Charles Wentworth, junior. | 129 | Eugénie, Empress of the French | 155 |
| Dindorf, Wilhelm . | 129 | Evans, Lieut.-Gen. Sir De Lacy | 155 |
| Disraeli, Right Hon. Benjamin . | 129 | Everett, Edward, D.C.L. . | 155 |
| Dixon, William Hepworth . | 131 | Exeter, Bishop of . | 156 |
| Dobell, Sydney . | 132 | | |
| Doo, George Thomas, R.A. . | 132 | Faed, Thomas . | 156 |
| Doran, John, Ph.D. . | 133 | Fairbairn, William . | 156 |
| Douglas, General Sir Howard, Bart. | 133 | Fanny Fern. (*See* Parton, Mrs.) | 307 |
| Doyle, Richard . | 133 | Faraday, Michael, D.C.L. . | 157 |
| Drouyn De Lhuys, Edouard . | 134 | Fazy, Jean . | 157 |
| Duchâtel, Charles M. T., Count | 134 | Ferdinand IV. . | 158 |
| Dudevant, Madame . | 135 | Fergusson, James . | 158 |
| Dufaure, Jules Armand Stanislas . | 136 | Fields, James T. . | 158 |
| Duff, Alexander, D.D., LL.D. . | 136 | Fillmore, Millard . | 159 |
| Dufferin and Clandeboye, Lord . | 137 | Foley, John Henry, R.A. . | 159 |
| Duffy, Charles Gavin . | 138 | Fonblanque, Albany . | 159 |
| Dumas, Alexandre . | 138 | Forbes, Sir John, M.D. . | 160 |
| Dumas, Alexandre, junior . | 139 | Forrest, Edwin . | 160 |
| Dumas, Jean Baptiste . | 139 | Forster, John . | 160 |
| Duncombe, Thomas Slingsby, M.P. | 139 | Fortune, Robert . | 161 |
| Dundas, Vice-Admiral . | 139 | Fould, Achille . | 162 |
| Dundonald, Earl of . | 140 | Fox, W. J., M.P. . | 163 |
| Dunglison, Robley, M.D., LL.D. . | 141 | Francis Joseph I., Emp. of Austria | 163 |
| Du Petit Thouars, Admiral . | 142 | Francis II., King of Naples . | 164 |
| Dupin, André Marie Jean Jacques . | 142 | Francis V. . | 164 |
| Dupin, Baron . | 142 | Franklin, Lady Jane . | 164 |
| Dupont de L'Eure, Jacques Charles | 143 | Fraser, Alexander . | 165 |
| Dupont, Pierre . | 143 | Frederick VIII., King of Denmark | 165 |
| Dyce, Rev. Alexander . | 144 | Frederick William IV., K. of Prussia | 165 |
| Dyce, William, R.A. . | 144 | Freiligrath, Ferdinand . | 167 |
| | | Fremont, Colonel . | 167 |
| Eadie, John, D.D., LL.D. . | 145 | French, Emperor of. (*See* Napoleon) | 285 |
| Eastlake, Sir Charles Lock . | 146 | French, Empress of. (*See* Eugénie) | 155 |
| Edwardes, Sir Herbert B., K.C.B. | 146 | Frerichs, Frederic Theodore . | 168 |
| Egg, Augustus, R.A. . | 147 | Frith, William Powell, R.A. . | 169 |
| Eglinton and Winton, Earl of . | 148 | Frost, William Edward, R.A. . | 169 |
| Ehrenberg, Christian Gottfreid . | 148 | | |
| Eichwald, Edward . | 149 | Garibaldi, Joseph . | 169 |
| Elgin and Kincardine, Earl of . | 150 | Garnier Pagès, Louis Antoine . | 171 |
| Ellenborough, Earl of . | 150 | Gaskell, Mrs. L. E. . | 171 |
| Elliotson, John, M.D. . | 151 | Gavarni, or Paul Chevalier . | 171 |
| Ellis, Mrs. Sarah . | 151 | Gavazzi, Padre Alessandro . | 172 |

| | PAGE | | PAGE |
|---|---|---|---|
| Geefs, Guillaume | 172 | Grote, George, M.P. | 193 |
| Geefs, Joseph | 172 | Gudin, Théodore | 193 |
| George V., King of Hanover | 172 | Guizot, François | 193 |
| Georges Sand. (*See* Dudevant) | 135 | Guthrie, Thomas, D.D. | 195 |
| Gerhard, Edward | 173 | | |
| Gerstaecker, Frederic | 173 | Hagenbach, Charles Rodolphe | 196 |
| Gervinus, Georges Godefroid | 174 | Haghe, Louis | 196 |
| Ghika, Alexander | 174 | Hahn-Hahn, Countess von | 196 |
| Gibson, John | 175 | Halevy, Jacques-Elie Fromental | 196 |
| Gibson, Right Hon. Thomas Milner | 176 | Haliburton, Hon. Mr. Justice, M.P. | 197 |
| Gigliucci, Countess. (*See* Novello) | 295 | Hall, Mrs. Anna Maria | 197 |
| Gilbert, John Graham | 176 | Hall, Samuel Carter | 198 |
| Gilfillan, Rev. George | 177 | Hall, Sir Benjamin. (*See* Llanover) | 250 |
| Girardin, Emile de | 177 | Halleck, Fitz-Greene | 198 |
| Gladstone, Right Hon. Wm., M.P. | 178 | Halliwell, James Orchard | 199 |
| Gleig, Rev. George Robert | 179 | Hamilton, Rev. James, D.D. | 199 |
| Glencorse, Lord | 180 | Hampden, Renn Dickson, D.D. | 199 |
| Goderich, Lord. (*See* Ripon) | 331 | Hannay, James | 200 |
| Godwin, George | 180 | Hanover, King of. (*See* George V.) | 172 |
| Goldschmidt, Madame | 181 | Hardwicke, Earl of | 200 |
| Gomm, General Sir William, G.C.B. | 181 | Harris, James. (*See* Malmesbury). | 264 |
| Goodall, Edward, R.A. | 182 | Harris, Sir William Snow | 200 |
| Goodall, Frederick, R.A. | 182 | Hart, Solomon Alexander, R.A. | 201 |
| Gordon, Lady Lucy Duff | 183 | Harvey, George, R.S.A. | 202 |
| Gordon, Sir John W., P.R.S.A., R.A. | 183 | Hawthorne, Nathaniel | 202 |
| Gore, Mrs. Catherine Frances | 183 | Hayes, Mrs. Catherine | 202 |
| Görgei, Arthur | 183 | Hayter, Sir George | 203 |
| Gortchakoff, Prince Alexander | 184 | Head, Sir Francis, Bart., K.C.H. | 203 |
| Gortchakoff, Prince Michael | 184 | Headley, Joel Tyler | 204 |
| Gosse, Philip Henry | 185 | Helps, Arthur | 204 |
| Gough, Lord | 185 | Hengstenberg, Ernest William | 204 |
| Gough, John B. | 186 | Henley, Right Hon. Joseph W. | 205 |
| Gould, Augustus Addison | 186 | Herapath, William, F.C.S. | 205 |
| Gould, Benjamin Apthorp | 186 | Herbert, John Rogers, R.A. | 205 |
| Gould, John, F.R.S. | 186 | Herbert, Rt. Hon. Sidney, M.P. | 205 |
| Graham, Rt. Hon. Sir James | 187 | Hereford, Bishop of. (*See* Hampden) | 199 |
| Graham, Thomas, F.R.S. | 188 | Herring, John Frederick | 206 |
| Grant, Francis, R.A. | 188 | Herschel, Sir John F. W., Bart. | 206 |
| Grant, James | 188 | Herzen, or Hertzen, Alexander | 208 |
| Granville, Earl | 189 | Hien Fung, Emperor of China | 208 |
| Grattan, Thomas Colley | 189 | Hildreth, Richard | 209 |
| Gray, Asa, M.D. | 190 | Hill, Sir Rowland, K.C.B. | 209 |
| Greece, King of. (*See* Otho) | 300 | Hind, John Russell | 210 |
| Greeley, Horace | 190 | Hinds, Right Rev. Samuel | 210 |
| Grey, Earl | 190 | Hobhouse, Jno. Cam. (*See* Broughton) | 67 |
| Grey, Right Hon. Sir George, Bart. | 191 | Holland, Sir Henry, Bart., M.D. | 210 |
| Grey, Sir George, K.C.B. | 191 | Holmes, Oliver Wendell, M.D. | 210 |
| Griffin, John Joseph | 192 | Hook, The Very Rev. Dean | 211 |
| Grimm, Jacob Ludwig | 192 | Hooker, Sir William Jackson, K.H. | 211 |
| Grisi, Giulia | 192 | Hooker, Joseph Dalton, M.D. | 212 |

| | PAGE |
|---|---|
| Hope, George William, M.P. . | 212 |
| Horne, Richard Henry . . | 212 |
| Horsley, John Callcott, R.A. | 213 |
| Houdin, Robert Jean-Eugène . | 213 |
| Houssaye, Arsène . . . | 214 |
| Houston, General . . . | 214 |
| Howick, Lord. (See Grey) . | 190 |
| Howitt, Mary . . . | 214 |
| Howitt, William . . . | 215 |
| Hugo, Victor Marie, Vicomte | 215 |
| Hullah, John . . . | 216 |
| Hunt, Robert, F.R.S. . . | 216 |
| Hunt, Thornton . . . | 217 |
| Hunt, William Holman . . | 217 |
| | |
| Ingemann, Bernard Severin . | 217 |
| Ingersoll, Charles Jared . . | 218 |
| Inglis, John. (See Glencorse) | 180 |
| Ingres, Jean Dominique Auguste | 218 |
| Ireland, Lord Lieutenant of . | 85 |
| Isabel II., Maria Isabel Luisa | 218 |
| Isabey, Eugène Louis Gabriel | 219 |
| Ismail Pasha. (See Kmety) . | 228 |
| Isturitz, Don Xavier de . . | 219 |
| | |
| Janin, Jules Gabriel . . | 219 |
| Jasmin, Jacques . . . | 220 |
| Jellachich, Baron von . . | 220 |
| Jerdan, William . . . | 220 |
| Jerrold, William Blanchard . | 221 |
| Jewsbury, Miss Geraldine . | 221 |
| Johnston, Alexander Keith . | 221 |
| Jomini, Henri, Baron . . | 222 |
| Jordan, Sylvester . . . | 222 |
| Josika, Nicolas, Baron . . | 222 |
| Junghuhn, Frank Wilhelm . | 222 |
| | |
| Kane, Sir Robert, M.D. . | 223 |
| Karr, Jean Baptiste Alphonse | 223 |
| Kaulbach, William . . | 223 |
| Kavanagh, Miss Julia . . | 224 |
| Kean, Charles . . . | 224 |
| Kean, Mrs. Charles . . | 224 |
| Keble, The Rev. John, M.A. . | 224 |
| Kelly, Sir Fitzroy . . . | 224 |
| Kemble, Mrs. Fanny . . | 225 |
| Kern, J. Conrad . . . | 225 |
| Kinglake, Alexander William, M.P. | 226 |
| Kingsley, The Rev. Charles, M.A. | 226 |
| Kinkel, Gottfried . . . | 226 |

| | PAGE |
|---|---|
| Kinnaird, Lord . . . | 227 |
| Kiss, Augustus . . . | 227 |
| Kisseleff, Paul Dmitrevitch . | 227 |
| Klapka, General George . | 228 |
| Kmety, General George . . | 228 |
| Knight, Charles . . . | 229 |
| Knowles, James Sheridan . | 230 |
| Kobell, Franz von . . | 230 |
| Kock, Charles Henri Emmanuel | 230 |
| Kock, Charles Paul de . . | 231 |
| Kossuth, Lajos de Kossuth Falva | 231 |
| Kügler, Franz Theodore . | 234 |
| | |
| Laborde, Léon, Count de . | 234 |
| Lacordaire, Abbé . . . | 234 |
| La Marmora, Marquis de . | 235 |
| Lamartine, Alphonse de . | 235 |
| Lamoricière, General . . | 236 |
| Lance, George, R.A. . . | 236 |
| Landor, Walter Savage . . | 237 |
| Landseer, Sir Edwin, R.A. . | 237 |
| Langenbeck, Maximilian . | 237 |
| Lankester, Edwin, M.D. . | 238 |
| Lansdowne, Marquis of . . | 238 |
| Latham, Robert Gordon, M.D. | 238 |
| Lauder, Robert Scott, R.S.A. | 239 |
| Lawrence, Sir John . . | 239 |
| Layard, Austen Henry . . | 240 |
| Ledru Rollin . . . | 240 |
| Lee, Frederick Richard, R.A. | 240 |
| Lee, Rev. Robert, D.D. . | 241 |
| Lee, Mrs. A. Bowdich . . | 241 |
| Leech, John . . . | 241 |
| Lemon, Mark . . . | 242 |
| Lennep, Jacob Van . . | 242 |
| Leopold, King of the Belgians | 242 |
| Lepsius, Carl Richard . . | 243 |
| Lesseps, Ferdinand de . . | 244 |
| Lever, Charles . . . | 244 |
| Leverrier, Urban Jean Joseph | 244 |
| Lewes, George . . . | 245 |
| Lewis, John Frederick . | 245 |
| Lewis, Sir George Cornewall . | 245 |
| Liddell, Very Rev. Henry G., D.D. | 246 |
| Lieber, Francis, LL.D. . . | 246 |
| Liebig, Justus, Baron . . | 246 |
| Lind, Jenny. (See Goldschmidt) | 181 |
| Lincoln, Lord. (See N'castle, Duke of) | 291 |
| Lindley, John, M.D. . . | 247 |
| Lindsay, Lord . . . | 248 |

| | PAGE | | PAGE |
|---|---|---|---|
| Lindsay, William Schaw, M.P. | 248 | Maurice, Rev. Frederick D., M.A. | 268 |
| Linnell, John | 248 | Maury, Matthew F. | 270 |
| Liszt, Franz | 249 | Maximilian II., King of Bavaria | 270 |
| Livingston, The Rev. David, LL.D. | 249 | Mayhew, Henry | 270 |
| Llanover, Lord | 250 | Mazzini, Joseph | 271 |
| London, Bishop of | 250 | Mehemet Emin. (See Aali Pasha) | 1 |
| Longfellow, Henry Wadsworth | 251 | Meissonier, Jean Louis Ernest | 271 |
| Lough, John Graham | 251 | Melvill, The Rev. Henry, B.D. | 272 |
| Lover, Samuel | 251 | Melville, Herman | 272 |
| Lowell, James Russell | 252 | Menchikoff, Prince | 272 |
| Lucas, Hippolyte Julien Joseph | 252 | Menzel, Wolfgang | 272 |
| Lüders, General | 252 | Mérimée, Prosper | 273 |
| Lyell, Sir Charles, F.R.S. | 253 | Méry, Joseph | 273 |
| Lyndhurst, Lord | 253 | Metz, Frederick Auguste de | 274 |
| Lytton, Sir Edward Lytton Bulwer. | 254 | Meyerbeer, Giacomo | 274 |
| | | Miall, Edward | 275 |
| M'Culloch, Horatio, R.S.A. | 256 | Michaud, Louis Gabriel | 275 |
| M'Culloch, J. R. | 256 | Michelet, Jules | 275 |
| Macdowell, Patrick, R.A. | 256 | Mignet, François Auguste | 275 |
| M'Hale, Right Rev. John, D.D. | 256 | Mill, John Stuart | 275 |
| Mackay, Charles, LL.D. | 257 | Millais, John Everett, A.R.A. | 276 |
| Maclaren, Charles | 258 | Miller, Thomas | 276 |
| Macleod, Rev. Norman, D.D. | 258 | Milman, The Very Rev. Dean | 276 |
| M'Clintock, Sir Francis | 258 | Milnes, Richard Monckton, M.P. | 277 |
| Maclise, Daniel, R.A. | 259 | Minié, Claude | 277 |
| Maclure, Sir Robert Le Mesurier | 260 | Mitscherlich, Eilhard | 277 |
| Macmahon, Marshal | 261 | Mocquard, Constant | 278 |
| M'Neile, The Rev. Hugh, D.D. | 261 | Moffat, Robert | 278 |
| M'Neill, Sir John, G.C.B. | 261 | Montalembert, Comte de | 279 |
| M'Neill, Sir John, C.E. | 262 | Monteagle, Lord | 280 |
| Macready, William Charles | 262 | Monti, Raffaelle | 280 |
| Madden, Sir Frederick, K.H. | 262 | Morella, Count of. (See Cabrera). | 78 |
| Madoz, Pascal | 263 | Morny, Comte de | 280 |
| Magnan, Marshal | 263 | Morse, Samuel Finley Breese | 280 |
| Mahon, Lord. (See Stanhope) | 359 | Mulgrave, Lord. (See Normanby). | 295 |
| Malakof, Duke of. (See Pélissier) | 310 | Müller, Johannes | 281 |
| Malmesbury, Earl of | 264 | Muloch, Miss Dinah M. | 282 |
| Manteufel, Baron | 264 | Mulready, William, R.A. | 282 |
| Manzoni, Count | 264 | Munch, Peter Andreas | 282 |
| Mario, Joseph | 265 | Murchison, Sir Roderick, D.C.L. | 283 |
| Marochetti, Baron | 265 | Mushaver Pacha. (See Slade) | 355 |
| Marsh, Mrs. Anne | 265 | Musset, Paul Edmé de | 284 |
| Marshall, William Calder, R.A. | 266 | | |
| Marston, John Westland | 266 | Napier, Robert | 284 |
| Martineau, Miss Harriet | 266 | Napier, Admiral Sir Charles | 284 |
| Martinez de la Rosa, Francisco | 267 | Naples, King of. (See Francis II.) | 164 |
| Martius, Carl F. P. von | 267 | Napoleon III., Emp. of the French | 285 |
| Massey, Gerald | 268 | Narvaez, Don Ramon | 290 |
| Masson, David | 268 | Nash, Joseph | 290 |
| Maule, Fox. (See Panmure, Lord) | 306 | Nasmyth, James | 291 |

| | PAGE |
|---|---|
| Nees Von Esenbeck, Christian G. | 291 |
| Nesselrode, Comte de | 291 |
| Newcastle, Duke of | 291 |
| Newman, Rev. John Henry, D.D. | 292 |
| Newman, Francis William | 292 |
| Nichols, John Gough, F.S.A. | 293 |
| Niepce, De Saint Victor | 293 |
| Nightingale, Miss Florence | 294 |
| Noel, Hon. and Rev. Baptist, M.A. | 294 |
| Normanby, Marquis of | 295 |
| Norton, The Hon. Mrs. | 295 |
| Norwich, ex-Bishop of. (See Hinds) | 210 |
| Novello, Madame Clara | 295 |
| | |
| O'Brien, William Smith | 296 |
| O'Donnell, Marshal | 297 |
| Oliphant, Lawrence | 297 |
| Olmsted, Denison | 299 |
| Omer Pacha | 299 |
| Orbigny, Charles d' | 299 |
| Orloff, Alexis, Prince | 300 |
| O'Shaughnessy, Sir William B. | 300 |
| Otho I., King of Greece | 300 |
| Oudinot, Marshal | 301 |
| Outram, General Sir James | 302 |
| Overbeck, Friedrich | 302 |
| Overstone, Lord | 303 |
| Owen, Richard, F.R.S. | 303 |
| Oxenford, John | 304 |
| Oxford, Bishop of | 304 |
| | |
| Pakington, Sir John, G.C.B. | 304 |
| Palgrave, Sir Francis, K.H., F.R.S. | 305 |
| Palmerston, Viscount | 305 |
| Panizzi, Antonio | 306 |
| Panmure, Lord | 306 |
| Pardoe, Miss Julia | 307 |
| Paris, Count of | 307 |
| Parton, Mrs. Sara P. | 307 |
| Patmore, Coventry | 308 |
| Paton, Joseph Noel, R.S.A. | 308 |
| Paxton, Sir Joseph, M.P. | 309 |
| Payen, Anselme | 309 |
| Pedro V., King of Portugal | 309 |
| Peel, Frederick, M.P. | 310 |
| Peel, The Right Hon. Jonathan | 310 |
| Peel, Sir Robert, Bart. | 310 |
| Pélissier, Marshal, Duc de Malakof | 310 |
| Pelouze, Théophile Jules | 311 |
| Pennefather, Lieutenant-General | 311 |

| | PAGE |
|---|---|
| Pennethorne, James | 311 |
| Pepe, General | 311 |
| Pepe, Gabriel | 312 |
| Pepoli, Charles | 312 |
| Pepoli, Marchesa di. (See Alboni) | 11 |
| Persigny, Jean Gilbert Victor Fialin | 312 |
| Petermann, August Heinrich | 313 |
| Peto, Sir Samuel Morton, Bart., M.P. | 313 |
| Petty, Lord Henry. (See Lansdowne) | 238 |
| Phelps, Samuel | 314 |
| Phillips, John, M.A., LL.D. | 315 |
| Piccolomini, Maria | 315 |
| Pickersgill, Fred. Richard, R.A. | 315 |
| Pius IX. | 315 |
| Planché, James Robinson | 316 |
| Playfair, Lyon, C.B. | 316 |
| Poerio, Carlo | 317 |
| Poggendorf, John Christian | 318 |
| Pollock, Right Hon. Sir Frederick | 318 |
| Poole, Paul Falconer, A.R.A. | 318 |
| Pope of Rome. (See Pius IX.) | 315 |
| Portugal, King of. (See Pedro V.) | 309 |
| Potter, Cipriani | 319 |
| Potter, Louis Joseph | 319 |
| Pouillet, Claude S. M. | 320 |
| Powers, Hiram | 320 |
| Prince Consort. (See Albert, Prince) | 9 |
| Proctor, Bryan W. | 320 |
| Proudhon, Pierre Joseph | 320 |
| Prussia, King of. (See Fredk. Wm.) | 165 |
| Pulszky, Ferencz | 321 |
| Pulszky, Madame Ferencz | 322 |
| Pusey, Edward Bouverie, D.D. | 322 |
| Pyat, Felix | 322 |
| Pyne, James B. | 323 |
| | |
| Quinet, Edgar | 323 |
| | |
| Raffles, Rev. Thomas, D.D. | 323 |
| Ramsay, William, M.A. | 324 |
| Ranke, Leopold | 324 |
| Rankine, W. J. Macquorn | 324 |
| Raspail, François Vincent | 325 |
| Rauch, Christian | 325 |
| Raumer, Frederick von | 325 |
| Rawlinson, Sir Henry | 326 |
| Reade, Charles | 327 |
| Reboul, Jean | 327 |
| Redding, Cyrus | 327 |
| Redgrave, Richard, R.A. | 328 |

| | PAGE |
|---|---|
| Reed, Rev. Andrew, D.D. | 328 |
| Reggio, Duke of. (*See* Oudinot) | 301 |
| Regnault, Henri Victor | 329 |
| Reichenbach, Baron de | 329 |
| Reid, Captain Mayne | 330 |
| Rémilly, Ovide | 330 |
| Reschid, Pasha | 330 |
| Ribera, Count of. (*See* Almodovar) | 13 |
| Richardson, Charles, LL.D. | 331 |
| Richardson, Sir John, K.C.B. | 331 |
| Ripon and De Grey, Earl of | 331 |
| Ripon, Bishop of | 332 |
| Ristori, Adelaide | 332 |
| Ritchie, Leitch | 332 |
| Roberts, David, R.A. | 333 |
| Robson, Frederick | 333 |
| Roebuck, John, M.P. | 333 |
| Roger, Gustave H. | 334 |
| Rogers, Henry | 334 |
| Rogers, Henry Darwin, LL.D. | 334 |
| Roget, Peter Mark, M.D. | 335 |
| Rokitansky, Charles | 335 |
| Rolfe, Baron. (*See* Cranworth) | 113 |
| Rollin, Ledru. (*See* Ledru) | 240 |
| Ronge, Johannes | 336 |
| Rosas, Don Juan Manuel de | 336 |
| Rose, Gustave | 336 |
| Rose, Heinrich | 337 |
| Rosetti, Constantine | 337 |
| Ross, Rear-Admiral Sir James Clark | 338 |
| Rosse, Earl of | 338 |
| Rossini, Joacchino | 339 |
| Rothschild, Baron Lionel de, M.P. | 339 |
| Rudersdorff, Madame | 339 |
| Ruhmkorff, N. | 340 |
| Ruskin, John | 340 |
| Russel, Alexander | 341 |
| Russell, John Scott, F.R.S. | 341 |
| Russell, Right Hon. Lord John, M.P. | 341 |
| Russell, William Howard, LL.D. | 343 |
| Russia, Emp. of. (*See* Alexander II.) | 11 |
| Sabine, Major-General Edward | 344 |
| Sainte-Claire Deville | 344 |
| Saint Leonards, Baron | 345 |
| St. Paul's, Dean of. (*See* Milman) | 276 |
| Sala, George Augustus | 345 |
| Saldanha, Duke of | 346 |
| Salomons, David, M.P. | 346 |

| | PAGE |
|---|---|
| Sam Slick. (*See* Haliburton) | 197 |
| Santa Anna, Don Antonio Lopez de | 347 |
| Santini, Giovanni | 347 |
| Sardinia, K. of. (*See* Victor Emanuel) | 383 |
| Sartorius, Ernest William Christian | 347 |
| Saulcy, Louis Caignart de | 348 |
| Say, Horace Émile | 348 |
| Scarlett, The Hon. Sir James Yorke | 349 |
| Schamyl | 349 |
| Schnorr, Jules | 349 |
| Schœlcher, Victor | 349 |
| Schomburgk, Sir Robert Hermann | 350 |
| Schönlein, Johann Luk | 350 |
| Scott, George Gilbert, A.R.A. | 350 |
| Scribe, Eugène | 351 |
| Sedgwick, Amy | 351 |
| Sedgwick, Miss Catherine Maria | 352 |
| Sedgwick, Rev. Adam, M.A. | 352 |
| Senior, Nassau William | 352 |
| Seymour, Right Hon. Sir George | 352 |
| Shaftesbury, Earl of | 353 |
| Shuttleworth, Sir James Kay | 353 |
| Simpson, General Sir James, G.C.B. | 353 |
| Simpson, James Young, M.D. | 354 |
| Sinclair, Miss Catherine | 354 |
| Skoda, Joseph | 354 |
| Slade, Sir Adolphus | 355 |
| Smirke, Sir Robert | 355 |
| Smith, Alexander | 356 |
| Smith, Sir Henry, Bart. | 356 |
| Smith, Thomas Southwood, M.D. | 356 |
| Smith, William, LL.D. | 357 |
| Somerville, Mrs. Mary | 357 |
| Soulouque, Faustin | 357 |
| South, Sir James, F.R.S. | 358 |
| Spain, Queen of. (*See* Isabella II.) | 218 |
| Sparks, Jared | 358 |
| Spring Rice. (*See* Monteagle, Lord) | 280 |
| Spurgeon, Rev. Charles Haddon | 358 |
| Stanfield, Clarkson, R.A. | 358 |
| Stanhope, Earl of | 359 |
| Stanley, Rev. Arthur | 359 |
| Stanley, Right Hon. Lord, M.P. | 359 |
| Steell, John, R.S.A. | 360 |
| Stirling, William, M.P. | 360 |
| Stowe, Harriet Beecher | 361 |
| Stratford de Redcliffe, Viscount | 361 |
| Strauss, David Friedrich | 362 |
| Strickland, Miss Agnes | 362 |
| Swain, Charles | 363 |

| | PAGE | | PAGE |
|---|---|---|---|
| Sweden, King of. (*See* Charles XV.) | 94 | Veuillot, Louis . . . . | 382 |
| Syme, James, M.D. . . . | 363 | Viardot, Pauline Garcia . . | 382 |
| | | Victor Emmanuel II., K. of Sardinia | 383 |
| Taglioni, Marie . . . . | 363 | Victoria, Her Majesty the Queen . | 383 |
| Tait, Right Rev. Archibald . | 250 | Vittoria, Duke of. (*See* Espartero) . | 154 |
| Taunton, Right Hon. Lord . | 364 | Vigny, Alfred, Count de . . | 384 |
| Taylor, Alfred Swaine, M.D. . | 364 | Villemain, Abel . . . | 385 |
| Taylor, Bayard . . . | 365 | | |
| Taylor, Isaac . . . . | 365 | Waagen, Gustave Friedrich . . | 385 |
| Taylor, Isidore, Baron . . | 365 | Wagner, Richard . . . | 386 |
| Taylor, Tom . . . . | 366 | Wagner, Rudolph . . . | 386 |
| Tenerani, Pietro . . . | 367 | Wales, Prince of. (*See* Albert Edwd.) | 10 |
| Tennent, Sir James E., M.P. . | 367 | Walewski, Florian Alexandre . | 386 |
| Tennyson, Alfred, D.C.L. . | 368 | Walpole, Right Hon. Spencer, M.P. | 387 |
| Thackeray, William Makepeace . | 368 | Walter, John, M.P. . . . | 387 |
| Thalberg, Sigismund . . | 369 | Ward, Edward Matthew, R.A. . | 387 |
| Thesiger, Sir Fred. (*See* Chelmsford) | 95 | Warren, Samuel . . . | 388 |
| Thierry, Alexandre . . | 369 | Watt, James Henry . . | 389 |
| Thierry, Amédée . . . | 370 | Watts, Alaric Alexander . | 389 |
| Thiers, Louis Adolphe . . | 370 | Webster, Thomas, R.A. . | 389 |
| Thirlwall, Rt. Rev. Connop, D.D. | 371 | Wensleydale, Baron . . | 390 |
| Tholuck, Friedrich Gottreu . | 371 | Westmacott, Richard, R.A. . | 390 |
| Thompson, Rev. R. Anchor, M.A. | 371 | Whately, Archbishop . . | 390 |
| Thompson, Major-General Perronet | 372 | Wheatstone, Charles, F.R.S. . | 391 |
| Thoms, William . . . | 373 | Whewell, Rev. William, D.D. . | 392 |
| Thorneycroft, Mrs. Mary . | 373 | Whiteside, Right Hon. James, M.P. | 392 |
| Ticknor, George . . . | 373 | Whitty, Edward Michael . | 393 |
| Timbs, John, F.S.A. . . | 373 | Whitworth, Joseph . . | 393 |
| Tite, William, M.P., F.R.S. . | 374 | Wilberforce, Right Rev. Samuel . | 304 |
| Titiens, Teresa . . . | 374 | Wilkes, Charles . . . | 393 |
| Titmarsh, M. Angelo. (*See* Thackeray) | 368 | Wilkinson, Sir John Gardner, Kt. . | 393 |
| Todleben, Francis Edward . | 375 | William III., King of Holland . | 394 |
| Trench, Very Rev. Rich. Chenevix | 376 | Williams, Major-General Sir W. F. | 395 |
| Trollope, Mrs. Frances . . | 376 | Willis, Nathaniel Parker . | 395 |
| Troubridge, Col. Sir T., Bart., C.B. | 376 | Willis, Rev. Robert, M.A., F.R.S. | 396 |
| Tuam, Archbishop of. (*See* M'Hale) | 256 | Wills, William Henry . . | 396 |
| Tulloch, Rev. John, D.D. . | 377 | Wilmore, James Tibbits . | 397 |
| Tupper, Martin Farquhar, D.C.L. | 377 | Windham, Major-General C., C.B. | 397 |
| Turkey, Sult. of. (*See* Abdul-Medjid) | 3 | Windischgrätz, Alfred, Prince de . | 397 |
| | | Winslow, Forbes, M.D. . . | 398 |
| Uhland, Johann Ludwig . | 377 | Winterhalter, Franz Xavier . | 398 |
| Ullman, Karl . . . | 378 | Wiseman, Nicholas, Cardinal . | 399 |
| Urquhart, David . . . | 378 | Woehler, Frederick . . | 399 |
| Valencia, Duke of. (*See* Narvaez) | 290 | Wood, Right Hon. Sir C., M.P. . | 399 |
| Vandenhoff, John . . . | 378 | Wrangel, Ferdinand . . | 400 |
| Vaughan, Rev. Robert, D.D. . | 379 | Wright, Thomas . . . | 400 |
| Velpeau, Alfred Marie . . | 380 | Wurtemburg, King of, William I. . | 401 |
| Verdi, Giuseppe . . . | 380 | Wyatt, Matthew Digby . | 401 |
| Vernet, Horace . . . | 380 | Yendys, Sydney. (*See* Dobell) . | 132 |
| Véron, Louis Désiré . . | 381 | Young, Brigham . . . | 402 |

# COTEMPORARY BIOGRAPHY.

AALI PASHA, MEHEMIT EMIN, a Turkish statesman and legislative reformer, was born at Constantinople in 1815. At the age of fifteen he was admitted to the Translation Office of the Porte, on the recommendation of Reschid Pasha, the enlightened Turkish Reformer, who had the year before acted as Secretary to the Turkish Plenipotentiaries at Adrianople. In 1834 Aali Pasha was appointed Second-class Secretary to the Embassy of Ahmed Fethi Pasha to Vienna, where he spent two years. He visited Russia before returning to Constantinople, making no stay, however, in the empire of the Czar. In November, 1837, he became Chief Interpreter to the Divan, and in 1838 *Chargé d'Affaires* to London, in which post he remained till the following year. In 1841 he was appointed Ambassador to England, retaining that office until 1844. With the elevation of Reschid Pasha to be Grand Vizier, Aali rose to be Foreign Minister, and participated in all the political fortunes, good and bad, of his patron from 1846 to 1852. In 1852 he became Grand Vizier, and held the office for a few months, when he retired for some time from public life. In 1854, however, he obtained the post of Governor-General of Broussa, and in October of the same year was recalled to Constantinople, where he again became Minister of Foreign Affairs, and filled various other offices. After representing the Porte at

the Conferences of Vienna, he returned to Turkey to become Grand Vizier: an office which he held when a commission was appointed, over which he presided, to draw up, in concert with the representatives of the Western Powers, those measures favourable to the Christian population of the Turkish Empire which were confirmed in 1856. As Plenipotentiary of the Porte to the Paris Conferences, he took an active part in the deliberations, and signed the treaty of peace of 1856. In November, 1856, he resigned the office of Grand Vizier, and was succeeded by his old patron, Reschid Pasha. Three weeks after, he entered the council as Minister of Foreign Affairs, which post, however, he resigned immediately on the death of Reschid in January, 1858. He was then re-invested with the functions of Grand Vizier, in which he has manifested a sincere desire to reform Turkish abuses. From "A Biography of Aali Pasha," published in Turkish by Fatin Effendi, it appears that the former enjoys a high reputation among his countrymen for poetical ability. A small, modest-looking man, no one would conclude from his appearance that he possessed such energy and firmness of purpose as he has manifested in diplomatic negociations.

ABBOTT, REV. JACOB, an American author, and Congregational minister, was born at Hallowell, in the State of Maine, in 1803. He graduated at Bowdoin

B

ABB 2 ABD

College in 1820, and became a Congregational minister. In 1825 he commenced the publication of a series of moral and religious works, with which his name has now become identified, of which "The Young Christian," "The Corner Stone," "The Way to do Good," and his illustrated "Histories," are the best known. He has written besides a great number of juvenile works, which have had a wide circulation, especially in America. Among these are the "Rollo Books," the "Lucy Books," and the "Jonas Books;" the "Franconian Stories," "Marco Polo's Adventures," "Stories of the Rainbow," "The Florence Series," and "Harper's Story Books," each of these forming a series in an incredible number of volumes. These works are all intended for the use of the young, and have attained to great popularity, owing to the clearness and simplicity of the author's style, and the talent he possesses of infusing interest into his narratives. Many of his works have been reprinted in this country and translated into various languages.

ABBOTT, Rev. John, S.C., an American author, Congregational minister, and brother of the Rev. Jacob Abbott, was born in 1805 at Brunswick, in the State of Maine. He graduated at Bowdoin College in 1825, and at the Theological Seminary in Andover, Massachusetts, in 1829, where he was trained as a Congregational minister. His principal works are "Kings and Queens; or, Life in a Palace," "The Mother at Home," "The Child at Home," "The History of Napoleon Bonaparte," "The History of the French Revolution, as viewed in the light of Republican Institutions," and Memoirs of "Marie Antoinette," "Joséphine," "Madame Roland," "Henry IV.," "Cortes," "Hind Philip, Chief of Narragansett Indians." He is at present writing the Histories of the Monarchies of Continental Europe, those relating to "The Empires of Austria and Russia" having already appeared, and "The History of Italy" being on the eve of publication.

ABD-EL-KADER was born in the neighbourhood of Mascara in 1807. He was educated with his three brothers in the Guetna, a sort of seminary kept in the house of his father; the latter being a Saint, who claimed descent from the Prophet. He early distinguished himself by his learning and eloquence. An attempt of the Dey of Algiers to assassinate him induced him to seek an asylum in Egypt, whence he did not return till after the French conquest. His father, who had taken the lead in an insurrection of the Arab tribes near Oran, handed over his power to his son, who in 1832 attacked the city at the head of 10,000 mounted Arabs. They thought that the Turkish power being overthrown by the French at Algiers, they might achieve their independence. He was opposed, however, by General Boyer, who defended Oran with French troops, repulsing the Arab leader after a terrible engagement. Nevertheless, his influence continued to increase with the wild tribes of Barbary. In 1834 General Des Michels entered into a treaty with him, whereby the Chelif became the boundary between the French and native possessions. The result of this arrangement was, that a sort of small monarchy was formed for him, with Mascara for his capital, where he had ample leisure to prepare for a wide-spread resistance. The time came when he thought he might venture on a new attack. He crossed the Chelif, took possession of Medeah, and at the head of 20,000 mounted Arabs drove back the French from the course of the Macta. General Bugeaud was the first French commander who was successful in checking the resistance of the native population, and in breaking the prestige of Abd-el-Kader, who was of course looked upon by his countrymen as a prophet as well as a soldier. The French commander offered terms of peace to his vanquished enemy, and entered into the treaty of Tafna with him on 3rd May, 1837. Two years after Abd-el-Kader found a pretext in ill-defined clauses of the treaty for a fresh war. The campaign of 1840 followed. General Bugeaud was then appointed Governor of Algeria, and introduced a new system of attack. He organized razzias whereby French military operations being carried across the whole width of Barbary to the shores of the desert, he endeavoured to starve the Arabs into submission. The capture of Smala in February, 1842, forced Abd-el-Kader to retreat into Morocco; the emperor of that state having, it is alleged, subsidized him. In 1844 the combined troops of Abd-el-Kader and the Emperor of Morocco attacked General Bugeaud, who at Isly, on the 14th August, 1844, gained a decisive victory. The bombardment of the Moorish seaports by the French put an end to all overt interference on the part of the "Marocains," but it did not prevent the Arabs to the west of the Algerian frontier from joining the standard of insurrection. So late as 1845, he again menaced the great plain of the Metidja, the head-quarters of French colonization, which lies immediately behind Algiers. It was two years before the French troops, now acting with such part of the Emperor of Morocco's army as could be induced to fight against their countrymen, succeeded in crushing the Arab leader. Abd-el-Kader at last gave in his submission to General Lamoricière, on condition of being taken to Alexandria or St. Jean d'Acre. He was removed to France with his family, and afterwards confined at Toulon, the castle of Pau, and the castle of Amboise, with questionable respect to the pledge made him in Africa. The present Emperor set him at liberty in 1852, on the occasion of the proclamation of the Empire.

He afterwards settled at Brusa, where he lived in retirement until the town was destroyed by an earthquake. In 1853, and again in 1854, he visited Paris, and was quite a lion among the Parisians. He was anxious to take part in the Crimean war, but the state of his health forced him to remain at Constantinople; when last heard of he was in Damascus. He has lately (1860) taken the part of the Christians during the massacre perpetrated by the Druses, and his conduct in this respect would have done credit to one professing a higher degree of civilization. He protected to the utmost of his ability all the fugitives who arrived in Damascus, and he has received a decoration from the French Emperor in acknowledgment of his noble interference.

ABDUL-MEDJID, KHAN, Sultan of Turkey, was born 23rd April, 1823, and is the eldest son of Mahmoud II., whom he succeeded on the 1st July, 1839. His early education was conducted by mollahs and astrologers, and he has thus not had the advantage of a personal acquaintance with the customs and social life of Western nations. Abdul-Medjid ascended the throne of his ancestors at a most critical epoch in the history of Turkey. The battle of Nezib had just been gained by Ibrahim Pasha, who seemed to have beaten down the might of the Ottoman empire; and thus the Sultan commenced his reign in an unfortunate state of affairs in every respect, and at a very early age. In this critical juncture the leading European powers interfered, to prevent the dismemberment of the dominions of the Sultan. The Pasha of Egypt refusing to accede to the terms of the treaty of London, his obstinacy was ultimately brought to reason by British cannon. It had been anticipated that the reforms initiated under the stern rule of Mahmoud would be prevented under his somewhat facile successor. But in the

November of the year following his accession, the famous statute of Gulhani, or the Tanzimat or reforming ordinance, was proclaimed, which was to serve as the new basis of Turkish legislation. It had for its object the complete reformation of all the abuses which had converted Turkish rule into a perpetual state of anarchy. The Sultan thus vigorously prepared to follow out the dying requests of his parent. A conspiracy ensued, which was, however, speedily quelled. It is unfortunate that the reforms which the statute sought to introduce into Turkey have, practically speaking, been carried out nowhere except in Constantinople and its immediate vicinity. As connecting itself intimately with late important events in the career of the Sultan, it is worthy of note that religious liberty has been very fully enjoyed under his sway; indeed, neither of the powers that quarrelled over the guardianship of the holy places exhibits anything approximating to the same toleration of opinion. And his protection of the Polish and Hungarian refugees of 1848, even in presence of the menaces of Russia and Austria, evinced a resolution which ultimately America and England became emulous of seconding. The Sultan has been for some time past endeavouring, by reforming the executive, to introduce an economy to which the Turkish government has long been a stranger. He is, however, surrounded by ministers who have only their own ends in view. His personal expenditure is also of the most lavish kind, and unfortunately he lacks the energy required to give his reforms effect. The expenses of the Russian war have also tended to impoverish the nation. He has obtained loans through the guarantee of England and France, which, however, have only served to meet extraordinary expenditure, and which still leave him in an embarrassed state. Educated in the manner above referred to, the good in-tentions of the Sultan are to a great extent neutralized by the pernicious influence of early association.

ABERDEEN, George Hamilton Gordon, Earl of, was born in Edinburgh on 28th January, 1784. He received his early education at Harrow School, and afterwards entered the University of Cambridge, becoming M.A. in 1804. After returning from a lengthened tour in Europe, he published the results of some of his observations in a work entitled "An Inquiry into the Principles of Beauty in Grecian Architecture," which indicated the possession of an accurate and discriminating taste on the part of its author. Turning his attention to politics, Lord Aberdeen became Special Envoy to Vienna. This occurred at a time of great importance, and his mission was attended with success. Having entered the House of Lords, he was without office for many years, until he became Foreign Secretary under the Duke of Wellington in 1828, a post which he resigned towards the end of 1830. On Sir Robert Peel becoming Premier in 1834, Lord Aberdeen was chosen as Colonial Secretary. On the dissolution of this ministry, he remained without office for some years, and resumed the Foreign Department on Sir Robert Peel again becoming Premier. During his repeated official employments, Lord Aberdeen has been distinguished by an earnest attention to the duties of his position, and in political matters was generally opposed to liberal principles, until within the last few years, when Sir Robert Peel's conversion to Free-trade opinions made a breach in the ranks of the old Tory party. On Lord Derby resigning in 1852, Lord Aberdeen had assigned to him the difficult task of forming a new ministry, and his materials were of a most heterogeneous kind, inasmuch as he had to make his appointments from three different parties. Under such circumstances, it is a matter of surprise that the government thus formed lasted so long as nearly three years. This country, however, having declared war against Russia on account of the encroachments of that power on Turkey, in reference to the protectorate of the Greek Church, Lord Aberdeen was compelled to resign, owing to an adverse vote in the House of Commons, in 1855. This was occasioned by a general impression that he and his colleagues did not pursue hostile matters with the vigour and energy which were required in so serious a matter. It was alleged that both the army and navy were in a condition totally unfit to cope with the emergency. With respect to home matters, Lord Aberdeen was more successful, and during his tenure of office he introduced several bills which developed the resources of the country, and freed our public educational establishments from those trammels to which they had been tied for many centuries past. As a recognition of his great talent and acquirements, Lord Aberdeen has been elected Chancellor of King's College, Aberdeen, and also fills similar offices in other educational institutions. He has been twice married, and has one son living, Lord Haddo, who succeeds to the title on his father's decease. For the last few years Lord Aberdeen has taken no prominent part in public matters, and, comparatively speaking, has retired into private life.

ABOUT, EDMOND FRANÇOIS VALENTIN, a French writer and publicist, was born at Dreuze, in the department of Meurthe, in 1828. He entered the College of Charlemagne, at Paris, where he gained, in 1848, the highest honours in the class of philosophy. From the Normal School of Paris, he went as a teacher or professor to Athens. While in Greece he collected materials for a work of erudition, entitled "L'Isle d'Egine," published at Paris in 1854. He returned to France in 1853, and two years afterwards he published in the "Bibliothèque des Chemins de Fer," the book by which he was till recently best known, "La Grèce Contemporaine," which met with a brilliant success. The result was that the author found admission as a contributor to the "Revue des Deux Mondes," and published in that excellent periodical a romance entitled "Tolla." In 1856 he made his *début* as a dramatic writer, but was unsuccessful. He has since written "A Journey through the Paris Exhibition of 1856," in which he criticises the works of French artists then exhibited; a number of *feuilletons* contributed to the "Moniteur," under the titles of "Les Mariages de Paris," and three novels, entitled "Le Roi des Montagnes," "Germaine," and "Les Échasses de Maître Pierre." In 1857 he published his "Artistes au Salon," another criticism of the paintings of the yearly exhibition of Paris. His "Question Romaine" is the author's last important production.

ADAM, JEAN VICTOR, a French painter, was born in Paris on the 29th day of February, 1801. He was the son of Jean Adam, an eminent engraver. From 1814 to 1818 he was engaged in going through a course of professional study at the École des Beaux Arts. His first picture, sent in 1819 to the exhibition, was "Herminie secourant Tancrède." He continued to exhibit regularly as a painter till 1838, when he undertook a series of paintings for the Gallery of Versailles, among which may be enumerated "The Entrance of the French into Mayence," "The Battle of Montebello," and "The Capitulation of Meiningen." Since 1846 he has confined his attention to the lithographic department of art, in which he has attained to great success, and shown great fertility as an artist. Between 1821 and 1829 he gained several medals at Lille and Douay, and in 1826 and 1836 he obtained gold medals at Paris.

ADAMS, JOHN COUCH, an English

astronomer, was born in Cornwall, in 1817. Like Ferguson, he sprang from agricultural connexions, to attain a high position in the scientific world by the exercise of innate talent. He exhibited a decided taste for mathematics when very young, and fortunately was fostered in his choice by being sent to Cambridge to complete his education. In this university he was enabled to pursue his favourite study in its application to physical science, and paying great attention to astronomy, he soon distinguished himself by the profundity of his researches. He is chiefly known by his remarkable discovery, *à priori*, of the existence of a planet at the extremity of the solar system. For many years astronomers were at a loss to account for certain irregularities in the passage of Uranus round its orbit. Various theories had been proposed to explain these, but Mr. Adams, having suggested the idea of another and undiscovered planet existing, put his opinions to the test of mathematical investigation, and was thus enabled to assign a *possible position* for the supposed planet's place; which eventually, on its actual discovery, was found to be nearly true. This result is, perhaps, one of the most noble triumphs of modern science. By one of those inexplicable occurrences, in which two minds at a distance from each other are simultaneously engaged on the same subject, M. Leverrier, of Paris, had arrived about the same time at the same conclusion. A dispute of priority of discovery arose, similar to that which occurred between Leibnitz and Newton, but without any decisive result. The Royal Astronomical Society regarded each of these gentlemen as equally entitled to honourable distinction, and Mr. Adams has since become the President of that distinguished Society, and of which he forms a brilliant ornament. He also holds the Loundean Professorship of Astronomy in the University of Cambridge.

AGASSIZ, LOUIS JEAN RODOLPHE, a distinguished Swiss naturalist, now settled in America, was born in 1807, at Moitiers, Canton of Freyburg, in Switzerland. His ancestors were of French origin, and were among the number of those Protestants who, on the revocation of the Edict of Nantes, were forced to fly from France. His father was a Protestant minister, and intended him for the Church; but from an intuitive love for natural history, he preferred the study of medicine as affording a fuller scope for the bent of his genius. To carry out this design he entered the Medical School at Zurich, and subsequently the University of Heidelberg, where he devoted special attention to the study of comparative anatomy, gaining a high reputation among his compeers. From Heidelberg he went to Munich, where he remained four years. His great attainments brought him into connexion with the ichthyological department of the Natural History of Brazil, which made him known as a man of science. His parents remonstrated against this devotion to scientific study, and endeavoured by various means to cool his ardour. Fortunately, however, his indomitable perseverance and assiduity attracted the notice of the great German publisher, Cotta, who advanced him such money as he required for the successful prosecution of his researches. Having taken the degree of Doctor of Medicine and Philosophy, he repaired to Vienna, where he entered upon the study of fossil fishes. Visiting Paris in the prosecution of his studies, he gained the friendship of Cuvier and Humboldt. On returning to Switzerland he was appointed Professor of Natural History in the University of Neufchâtel, where he remained until 1846, when he embarked for America. Soon after his arrival in the United States he was appointed Professor of Zoology in the Lawrence Scientific School, and since then Professor of Comparative Anatomy in the University of Charleston. At the early age of thirty Agassiz was a member of nearly every scientific society in Europe. The Glacial theory, with which his name is now so honourably identified, was first published by him in 1837. To collect the facts relating to the subject, he spent eight summers upon the glaciers of the Aar, 8,000 feet above the level of the sea. The published contributions of Agassiz to the various departments of science are numerous and valuable. The best known of those are his researches on Fossil Fishes, his Natural History of the Fresh-water Fishes of Europe, and the "Principles of Zoology," by himself and Dr. A. A. Gould, and an "Essay on Classification," republished last year in this country. He is now engaged upon what promises to be his great work—"The Natural History of the United States." Two volumes of this work, which is to extend to ten, have been already published. The book is executed upon a grand and comprehensive scale, and when completed will form one of the noblest tributes to science of any age or nation.

AINSWORTH, WILLIAM FRANCIS, an English physician and traveller, was born at Exeter, in November, 1807. He studied the natural sciences and medicine, in the usual course, with the view of becoming a Doctor of Medicine, and obtained his diploma in 1827; starting in the same year on a geological excursion to Auvergne and the Pyrenees. On his return in 1828, he accepted the editorship of the "Journal of Natural and Geographical Science," published in Edinburgh, delivering at intervals a popular course of lectures on geology. The outbreak of the cholera in 1832 called him to London, where his skill in treating the hospital cases attracted so much notice, that on the abatement of the epidemic in the capital, he was sent to Ireland to pursue his system there.

In Dublin and Limerick he was equally successful. In 1835 he was appointed physician to Captain Chesney's Expedition to the Euphrates. After remaining for some time at Bombay, he went alone, in 1837, to Kurdistan and Asia Minor, these countries forming afterwards the chief object of a second expedition, which continued from 1838 till 1841. His investigations were not, however, limited to exploration from mere love of travel and adventure; he was charged with missions by the Royal Geographical Society to explore the course of the Halys; and by the Society for the Propagation of the Gospel to open up negociations with the Nestorian Christians. In the spring of 1840, he visited the country of the Nestorians, and returned to England the following year. Among the principal works Dr. Ainsworth has published are "Researches in Assyria," "Travels and Researches in Asia Minor," "The Claims of the Christian Aborigines in the East," and "Travels in the Track of the 10,000 Greeks," besides numerous papers contributed to scientific societies. In 1854 he became one of the Editors of "Bohn's Classical Library," to which he has rendered valuable service by his edition of Xenophon. Dr. Ainsworth is a cousin of William Harrison Ainsworth, the celebrated novelist and magazine conductor.

AINSWORTH, WILLIAM HARRISON, an English novelist, was born at Manchester, in 1805. He was destined for the legal profession, but Mr. Ainsworth preferred to devote himself almost exclusively to literary pursuits. His first attempt was a volume of poems, and after that Mr. Ainsworth published a romance called "Rookwood," which at once obtained great popularity. "Crichton" followed. In "Jack Sheppard," which next appeared, Mr. Ainsworth strove to exalt the virtues of a class of heroes who had till his time figured in the halter rather than in the pages of romance—the English highwaymen, whose adventurous lives and miserable fate had always invested them with a certain amount of popular sympathy. This work, which fostered a sentimentality by no means calculated to benefit public morals, had an immense success; the author, at the time of writing it, in all probability never speculated on its tendencies. He has not since written any work of the same kind. Mr. Ainsworth's numerous historical romances possess, in a high degree, all the best qualities of fictitious narratives; the plots are well constructed, the characters well drawn, great care being bestowed on the historical accuracy of the facts, and, what is also of great importance, the interest of the reader is sustained from beginning to end. The most remarkable of his romances are "Rookwood," "The Tower of London," "Windsor Castle," "The Admirable Crichton," "Old St. Paul's," "The Miser's Daughter," and "The Flitch of Bacon," His latest tale is "Ovingdean Grange." These works have been frequently reprinted in America, and translated into most of the continental languages, having met with a remarkable success abroad, more especially in France.

AIRD, THOMAS, a Scottish poet, was born at Bowden, Roxburghshire, on the 28th of August, 1802. After being educated in his native place, and the University of Edinburgh, in 1835 he was appointed Editor of the "Dumfries Herald," which he has since continued to conduct with much ability, taste, and success. In addition to his poetry, Mr. Aird has published several prose works of superior merit. The chief of these is his "Religious Characteristics," and "The Old Bachelor in the Old Scottish Village." Though not attaining the popularity that might have been anticipated, they both abound in passages of great power and beauty. The delicate discrimination with which he edited Moir's poems, and the admirable Life of the author prefixed to the poems, were the theme of general praise. Mr. Aird's poems have passed through two editions. With no trace of the spasmodic, and owing nothing to adventitious circumstances for popularity, they have won their way to a high place among the masterpieces of song.

AIRY, GEORGE BIDDELL, M.A. (Cambridge), D.C.L. (Oxford), LL.D. (Edinburgh), the English Astronomer Royal, was born at Alnwick, in Northumberland, on 27th July, 1801, and educated at the Grammar School of Colchester, in Essex. He entered Trinity College, Cambridge, in 1819; graduated, and was senior Wrangler in 1823; was elected Fellow of Trinity College in 1824; and in 1826 obtained the Lucasian Professorship of Mathematics (formerly held by Newton and by Barrow), which he exchanged in 1828 for the Plumian Professorship of Astronomy and Experimental Philosophy, which included the charge of the Cambridge Observatory. Besides giving great attention to the selection and accuracy of his observations, he has published their results in such a form as to render them immediately useful to science, a practice which by degrees has been followed in every important observatory. In discharge of the other duties of the chair, he instituted a course of experimental lectures on several subjects connected with applied mathematics, which (especially those on optics) attracted much attention. In October, 1835, he was appointed Astronomer Royal, and took charge of the Royal Observatory of Greenwich. Since that time, the Greenwich Observatory has been maintained in a state of great efficiency, and has been completely remodelled. Every new discovery has been at once adopted which was calculated to facilitate observation. One of Mr.

Airy's most laborious works was "An Abridgment of the Planetary and Lunar Observations from 1750 to 1830," published in 1846, and perhaps the most extensive individual work ever undertaken in astronomy. Among his scientific labours, we may mention his examination of the cause of the disturbance of the compass in iron ships, as the result of which he has given rules which are now universally followed for its correction. He has published treatises on the "Undulatory Theory of Light;" "The Tides on the Coast of Ireland, and in other places;" "Observations to establish the Longitude of Valentia;" and "Experiments to ascertain the Force of Gravity in the Colliery of Harton, near South Shields;" which, by the accuracy and care taken in the experiments, have been exceedingly valuable in the study of physical astronomy. Mr. Airy has been called on to assist the Government in the commission on the railway gauge; in the restoration of standards of length and weight (destroyed at the fire of the Houses of Parliament); and in the astronomical operations for defining the boundaries of our North American provinces. His principal Treatises on scientific subjects are the article in the Penny Cyclopædia, on "Gravitation," his "Mathematical Tracts," and "Ipswich Lectures," with the articles "Trigonometry," "Figure of the Earth," and "Tides and Waves," in the "Encyclopædia Metropolitana." He is also the author of numerous papers (frequently under the signature A. B. G.) in the "Athenæum" and the "Philosophical Magazine." Mr. Airy is a Fellow of the Royal Society, Member of the Prussian Order of Merit, and a Correspondent of the French Academy, of those of St. Petersburg and Berlin, and is well known throughout Europe and America as one of the most eminent cultivators of physical science.

ALBERT, FRANZ AUGUST KARL EMANUEL, Duke of Saxe Coburg Gotha, heir presumptive to the Duke of Saxe Coburg, and Consort of Queen Victoria, was born 26th August, 1819. He is descended from a long line of eminent ancestry in Germany. Prince Albert was educated with his elder brother, the present Duke regnant of Saxe Coburg Gotha, under the Consistorial Councillor, Florchutz, and at the University of Bonn. His studies there included ancient and modern languages, history, the physical and natural sciences, music, and painting. In 1838 he visited England with his father, and in two years afterwards was married to Queen Victoria at St. James's Palace. Prince Albert has ever taken a warm interest in all social questions, and has devoted himself to various pursuits which have given him a high character amongst all parties. He has paid great attention to agriculture, and has often carried off the highest prize offered for live stock. He has a model farm near Windsor, in the management of which he avails himself of every scientific appliance and improvement. As head of the Fine Arts Commission, and as chairman of the Council of the Great Exhibition of 1851, his services were invaluable, and to his exertions the nation is indebted for the promised exhibition of 1862, Prince Albert having offered to guarantee its success to a large pecuniary extent. The Prince holds a large number of official positions. But of all his titles the one which he seems most to value is that of President of the British Association for the Advancement of Science, to which he was elected in 1850. He opened the proceedings of the Association, at Aberdeen, with an address which was applauded by all parties in the empire for its earnest and graceful eloquence, as well as for its tact and knowledge. The public appearances of his Royal Highness are always judicious, and he has played with rare discretion the difficult and elevated part assigned to him in this country. He has avoided all connexion with politics, without any sacrifice of his dignity, or any concealment of his opinions on the social duties of life; and of such great questions as the education and advancement of the people, and the encouragement of art, science, and literature, he is an eminent patron. The peculiar perils that beset him, as the Consort of the Queen, were to attempt either too much or too little in public life. Any error in this respect might have subjected him to the charge of ambition or meddlesomeness on the one hand, or of insensibility or indifference on the other; but from these and other dangers his heart and his intellect have aided in preserving him, and he has gained the respect of all parties in the state, and the general approbation of the people. Scandal has never once breathed upon his name, and he has fulfilled all the duties of a gentleman and a citizen in such a manner as to set an example to all around and beneath him, and to make the most illustrious home in the country among the most exemplary and the most happy in every relation of life.

ALBERT EDWARD, PRINCE OF WALES, heir apparent to the British throne, was born 9th November, 1841. After receiving his preliminary education from tutors, his Royal Highness studied at Edinburgh and Oxford, and pursued the usual course of study at those universities. His progress and excellent qualities were thus spoken of by Lord Brougham on a late occasion at a public meeting in Glasgow:—"Of the Prince of Wales I have only to say that—as my learned friend Sir David Brewster, the principal of that university, can attest—he gained universal respect and esteem among all his teachers and all his fellow-pupils. I will only add that, soon after leaving Edinburgh, upon a late occasion in last May, I found that at Oxford he held precisely the same place in the esteem of his teachers and in the esteem of his fellow-pupils." The Prince left England in the summer of 1860, accompanied by the Duke of Newcastle, for the purpose of visiting Canada and the United States. In both countries his reception has been most enthusiastic. Carrying with him the prestige of his august mother, her Majesty Queen Victoria, the loyalty of the Canadians and the generosity of the Americans have at once been evidenced in every stage of his progress. On his return it is intended that he should enter the University of Cambridge.

ALBERT, properly called ALEXANDRE MARTIN, a French mechanic, Member of the Provisional Government of 1848, was born at Bury (Oise) in 1815. The son of a small farmer, he served an apprenticeship as a mechanical modeller at the house of one of his uncles; he went to Paris, and was present, when fifteen years old, at the revolutionary outbreak of July, 1830. He founded in Lyons the republican journal, "La Glaneuse," which indulged in severe attacks on the Government. He took an active part in the insurrection of Lyons, and was one of the chiefs of the "Society of the Rights of Man," in that city. In 1840 he founded a popular journal, "L'Atelier." When the revolution of February, 1848, broke out, Albert, who was working as a button-maker, took an active part in the contest. In his double capacity of revolutionary writer and mechanic, he formed a friendship with Louis Blanc, seconding the propositions of the latter by his speeches, writings, and influence. By Louis Blanc's means he was placed on the Provisional Government, and all the proclamations which bore his name had attached to it "Ouvrier," to identify him with the class whom he was supposed to represent. Albert was named representative for the department of the Seine to the Constituent Assembly. Arrested as an accomplice or instigator of the attempt of the 15th May, he was arraigned for the crime, but declared the tribunal incompetent, and refused to plead; condemned in consequence, he was sentenced to banishment, but has, instead, been sent to the Penitentiary of Tours.

ALBONI, MARIETTA, a well-known vocalist, was born at Forli, in the Romagna. She received a superior musical education, and made a very considerable progress in music in her native town; afterwards studying under Bertollotti and Rossini, at Bologna. She made her *début* at the Communal Theatre of Bologna, whence she went to the La Scala of Milan; she afterwards visited Germany, Russia, and Hungary. She made her first appearance before an English audience in the spring of 1847, and astonished those who had scarcely heard of her powers, by her superb voice, her careful training, and her accomplishments. Since then she has professionally visited Paris, and nearly all the continental cities of note, gaining literally "golden" opinions. Her appearances in this country have been frequent. The success of Alboni is of course chiefly to be attributed to the character of her voice and her talent as a singer. Her voice is a contralto of the greatest possible extent, flexibility, and purity, and the richness and facility of her vocalization are wonderful. There is no trace in her performances of labour or study; she seems to sing by inspiration; but as an actress she is not so remarkable. By marriage, Mddle. Alboni, although she retains her maiden name, has become Marchesa di Pepoli.

ALEXANDER II. ALEXANDER NICOLAEWITCH, Emperor of all the Russias, was born on the 29th of April, 1818, and succeeded his father, Nicholas Pavlowitch, on the 2nd of March, 1855.

Having received the military education always given to the heirs apparent of the great military monarchs and autocrats of the Continent; and having, moreover, been adequately instructed in all the branches of polite learning, forming the usual education of European gentlemen, he visited all the provinces of his future empire. He also made several tours in Italy. As hereditary prince, he enjoyed the entire confidence of his ambitious father, the late Emperor Nicholas I., and was familiarized by that monarch with all the details of his policy and system of government. At one period this hereditary prince was upon unfriendly terms with his next brother, the Grand Duke Constantine. Nicholas had not failed to perceive the difference of disposition in his two sons, and so forcibly did the possible results impress themselves on his mind, that he took every means to effect reconciliation between them. On the sudden death of the Emperor Nicholas—a death hastened by the vexation and grief consequent upon his foiled ambition in the attempt to seize upon the Ottoman empire—Alexander was peacefully proclaimed in his stead. One of his first acts was to end the hopeless war in the Crimea, before it assumed still more formidable dimensions, and to ratify the peace of Paris. His next act of domestic policy proved him to be a humane and enlightened man, as well as a prudent sovereign, who could see and measure the dangers of the future—an act no less beneficent than the emancipation of the serfs of his empire. In this he has had to contend with the prejudices of the higher classes; his firm but conciliatory demeanour has, however, effected the change gradually, and it is hoped that the opposition hitherto shown will be eventually overcome, and that his kind intentions may be shared by their present opponents. Alexander has taken no active part in the recent struggle of

Western Europe, consequent upon the policy and pretension of the Emperor Napoleon, but has contented himself with watching the current of events. He married, in 1841, the Princess Marie Alexandrowna, daughter of Louis IV., Grand Duke of Hesse, by whom he has had five sons and one daughter. Nicholas Alexandrowitch was born on September 8th, 1843. The other sons are Alexander Alexandrowitch, Wladimir Alexandrowitch, Alexis Alexandrowitch, and Sergius Alexandrowitch. The only daughter is Marie Alexandrowna, Grand Duchess of Russia, born in 1853.

ALFORD, THE VERY REV. HENRY, D.D., Dean of Canterbury, a poet and Biblical critic, was born in London in 1810, and educated at Ilminster Grammar School and Trinity College, Cambridge. He has published several poetic productions, which have been well received, has held several University appointments, and various preferments in the Church. His Greek Old and New Testaments have been carefully prepared. He is also the author of several papers contributed to serials and other periodical publications; and his work entitled "The Poets of Greece" exhibits an intimate and correct knowledge of the language. He has published many volumes of sermons, and critical memoirs on matters pertaining to ancient history. Owing to his eminent talents as a preacher, he was appointed by Lord Palmerston, Dean of Canterbury in 1857.

ALISON, SIR ARCHIBALD, BART., an historian, of Scotch parentage and education, was born at the Parsonage House of Kenley, in Shropshire, and highly distinguished himself during his connexion as a student with the Edinburgh University. In 1814 he was called to the Scotch bar, and in 1823 appointed an advocate-depute, an office which he held until 1830, when the Whigs came into power. On the return of the Tories to power he was appointed Sheriff of Lanarkshire, an office corresponding as nearly as may be to that of County Judge in England, if the jurisdiction of the latter had extended to all classes of judicial proceedings without regard to the amount in dispute, or to the distinction of law and equity, and to criminal as well as civil business. It was originally intended, doubtless, that the judicial business of Scotland should be divided fairly among the local judges, but Scotch institutions, particularly those connected with the law, rejoice in an immunity from legislative interference, which perpetuates many abuses. Thus the jurisdiction of some Scotch sheriffs is confined to a population of little more than 20,000, while that of the Sheriff of Lanarkshire includes a city of nearly 400,000 inhabitants. He has, however, the assistance of Deputy Sheriffs; his court being often one of appeal from their decisions. The consequence of this is that Sir Archibald Alison, since the date of his appointment as sheriff, has gone through an immense amount of work in his capacity of judge. Sir Archibald is popularly known as an historian, and his work on the "History of Europe" has been extensively read, and has brought its author into a world-wide reputation. It has been reprinted in America," and translated into many foreign languages. Sir Archibald Alison has published other historical and political works, and is the author of numerous contributions to "Blackwood's Magazine," collected and republished under the general title of "Essays." He is firmly attached to the principles of the Conservative party. Sir Archibald belongs to the most vigorous and masculine type of Scottish intellect. Going through an amount of business far beyond the powers of an ordinary man, his literary works are thrown off, *currente calamo*, without revision, without condensation, and without a due amount of attention to consistency, symmetry, and elegance of diction. Before recent changes in the civil procedure of the Scotch courts, Sheriff Alison's merits as a lawyer were not known, from the circumstance that errors in his decisions regarding matters of fact, arising from haste in disposing of the inordinate amount of business thrown upon him, were at that time attributed to defective knowledge of legal principles. His powers as a writer have been underestimated from the same cause. He must not be judged of by the slipshod pages of the "History of Europe," but by some of his minor productions, which entitle him to a place among the best and purest cotemporary writers of English prose. Sir A. Alison has received many public recognitions of his eminent literary services. He was created a Baronet in 1852, is a D.C.L. of Oxford, and he has held the office of Rector in the Glasgow and Aberdeen Universities. Amongst his miscellaneous works not mentioned above are his "Principles of the Criminal Law" (1832), "The Practice of the Criminal Law" (1833), "Free Trade and Fettered Currency" (1847), "The Life of the Duke of Marlborough" (1847), and subsequent editions in 1852 and 1855. In 1852 he published a continuation of his "History," being the "History of Europe from the fall of Napoleon to the Accession of Louis Napoleon in 1852," and in the early part of this year (1860) Sir Archibald published another edition of the entire work.

ALLEN, WILLIAM, D.D., an American author, was born at Pittsfield, Massachusetts, 2nd January, 1784. He entered Harvard College, and graduated there in 1802. He was President of Bowdoin College in 1820, but resigned in 1839. He succeeded the celebrated Dr. Channing as Regent in Harvard College. Whilst filling that office he prepared his "American Biographical and Historical Dictionary," which contained notices of about seven hundred Americans, and was published in 1809, being the first book of general biography issued in the United States. It passed through a third edition in 1857, and was enlarged so as to include no less than seven thousand names. He prepared the lives of American ministers for the Rev. David Bogue's "History of Dissenters." He also made a collection of many thousand words not found in the English Dictionaries, most of them being added to the edition of Webster published in 1854. He is the author of various other works of a miscellaneous character, but his reputation in America rests chiefly on his biographical and philological researches and labours.

ALMODOVAR, DON ILDEFONSO DIAS DE RIBERA, COUNT OF, a Spanish general and politician, was born at Valence about the end of the last century. He entered as a pupil of the School of Artillery, at Segova, but had scarcely joined the army when he was thrown into the dungeons of the Inquisition by the retrograde party. For his deliverance he was indebted to the revolution of 1820, the cause of which he embraced with ardour. In 1823, when absolutism was again rampant, he sought safety in exile, and did not return to Spain until after the death of Ferdinand VII. When he did return he rapidly rose to the first ranks of the liberal party, and was elected president of the Cortes; at the same time he re-entered the army (1834) with the rank of Field Marshal. In 1836 he became Minister for Foreign Affairs, under his friend Espartero, the Regent, and lost this office on the fall of that statesman in 1843. Since then he has remained faithful to the liberal cause, but has taken no active part in public affairs.

ALVAREZ, JUAN, a Mexican general, was born in 1780, in the state of Guerrero, of an Indian family, and educated in the midst of a population scarcely influenced by the habits of civilized life. In the southern provinces of Mexico he has succeeded in forming an influence among the half-civilized population, which almost resembles that of an independent monarch. In 1854, when it was asserted that Santa Anna aspired to the Presidency, Alvarez mustered his troops and raised the standard of insurrection. He was joined by other leaders, and Santa Anna in the following year was obliged to leave the country. On the 16th of September following a provisional government was formed, meeting in October at Cuernavaca, in the midst of a village protected by bands of Indians. Alvarez was appointed President, and Comonfort Minister of War. A few weeks later Alvarez, in spite of a prediction that he would perish in Mexico, proceeded thither. His first measures were aimed at the excessive privileges of the army and clergy, the most important of which he abolished by a decree dated 24th November of the same year. This was his most important act while President. Shortly afterwards he handed over the office to Comonfort, on being paid the sum of 200,000 piastres. He now resides at Acapulco in a state of complete independence.

AMPÈRE, JEAN JACQUES ANTOINE, a French writer, traveller, and Member of the Institute, was born at Lyons, on the 12th August, 1800. He is son of the celebrated scholar and physicist. He studied under the eye of his father. At an early age he was one of the principal contributors to the "Globe," and the "Revue Française," established by Guizot to oppose the government. In 1830 he acted as assistant and successor at the Sorbonne to M. Fauriel and M. Villemain. In 1837 he obtained the chair of French Literature at the College of France. In 1831 he published the "History of Poetry;" in 1839, "The Literary History of France before the 12th Century;" in 1841, "The History of the French Literature of the Middle Age;" at the same time he furnished a great variety of articles to the "National" and "Revue des Deux Mondes." M. Ampère is one of the best writers of travels of the day. His tours in Germany, Italy, Egypt, and North America have supplied him with observations which his extensive erudition and general knowledge have enabled him to work up into admirable articles for the "Revue des Deux Mondes." His contributions have been collected and published in 1833 and 1850, under the title of "Littérature et Voyages."

ANDERSEN, HANS CHRISTIAN, a Danish poet and novelist, was born on the 2nd of April, 1805, at Odense. His position in early life was by no means calculated to foster the talent which he subsequently exhibited. His parents were in very poor circumstances, and on the death of his father, young Andersen was left almost destitute. He, however, evinced an early taste for the drama, and even in his childish amusements would compose little plays, in which he and his companions were the juvenile actors. His mother was desirous of bringing him up to a trade, but the bent of his mind would not permit him to bear such trammels. By an accident he became connected with some players, who gave him a very humble part in a play they were performing. This circumstance fixed the future destiny of Andersen, and in 1819 he went to Copenhagen to seek his fortunes in any position which accident might open out to him. Like many other geniuses, he found that it was difficult to rise from obscurity on slender means. He, however, was fortunate in at last attracting the notice of a musician, who, having taken a fancy to Andersen, obtained sufficient influence to place him in a gymnasium, where his abilities soon brought him many friends, and thus laid the foundation of his future fame and success. After many struggles he turned his attention to literature, and having been successful in his first production, he obtained a sum from the Danish Government, which enabled him to take an extended tour through Central Europe. The publication of his "Improvisatore" at once gained him great reputation, and his position as a literary man was made. The limits of this sketch preclude the possibility of naming all his works, but amongst the most popular, beside the "Improvisatore," are the following, most of which have been translated into the German, Dutch, English, French, Swedish, and Russian languages, namely, his "O.T.," "Only a Fiddler," "The Two Baronesses," and "To Be, or Not to Be," "The Glory of my Life," "Fairy Tales," "A Picture Book without Pictures," "New Stories and Fairy Tales," "A Poet's Bazaar," "Rambles in the Hartz Mountains," and "In Sweden." A complete edition of his works was published in Copenhagen in 1854-55; and in Leipzic a translation of his collected works has appeared in thirty-six volumes. He has lately published a work entitled "The Sand Hills of Jutland."

ANDERSON, WILLIAM, LL.D., a Scottish divine, was born in 1799, at Kilsyth, and studied at the Glasgow University. When about twenty-two years of age he became pastor of John-street Church, Glasgow, and in this position has obtained great popularity as a preacher. The church has lately been pulled down, and a remarkably fine edifice erected in its place, in which Dr. Anderson now officiates, attracting the attention of his hearers as much by the vigour of his discourses as by the eloquence of his appeals. As a platform speaker he greatly excels, and in that position is often the advocate of justice and freedom for the oppressed. He has published several theological works, which have been well received by the reading public.

ANDRAL, GABRIEL, a French physician, was born at Paris on the 6th of November, 1797, and was the son of a Doctor of Medicine, who destined him for his own profession. After passing through the usual course of study, he took his degree in 1821. In 1828 he was called to the chair of Hygiène, and in 1830 elected Professor of Medical Pathology. In 1839 he was unanimously selected by his colleagues to succeed M. Broussais in the chair of General Pathology and Therapeutics. As a professor M. Andral is highly successful. The style of his lectures is peculiarly precise and clear. Notwithstanding the time devoted to the duties of his chair, and the practice of his profession, he has written a number of papers and works on special and general subjects connected with his favourite science. Among his publications are the "Clinique Médicale," "Cours de Pathologie Interne," "Traité de l'Auscultation Médiate et du Cœur," and a treatise on the treatment of typhus fever by purgatives. M. Andral's works have been extensively translated, and frequently republished.

ANSTER, JOHN, D.C.L., a distinguished poet, was born at Charleville, in the county of Cork, in 1793. He studied and took his degrees in Trinity College, Dublin, was afterwards called to the Irish bar, and for several years went the Munster circuit. In 1814 he was elected a scholar of Trinity College, and in the same year closed a session of the Historical Society with a speech from the chair, which was honoured with their gold medal for oratory. He has published some poems, which were well received, and gained the praise of accurate critics. In an early number of "Blackwood's Magazine," Dr. Anster published an account of Goethe's "Faust," with translated extracts. This was, we believe, the first English translation of any part of Goethe's great poem. The complete translation was published in 1835. His "Faust" has also been highly admired. A small volume of poems by Dr. Anster appeared at Dublin in 1837, entitled "Xeniola." Latterly he is understood to be exclusively occupied with professional studies and duties; and he is in receipt of a pension from Government. He holds an important office in one of the Irish law courts, and is Regius Professor of Civil Law in the University of Dublin. In 1851 he published "Letters Introductory to the Study of the Roman Civil Law."

ANSTEY, THOMAS CHISHOLM, a lawyer and politician, was born in London in 1816. He was admitted to the bar of the Middle Temple in 1839. He was tolerably well known by his political writings when he contested the representation of Youghal in 1847, and was returned to Parliament for that burgh, holding the seat until 1852. He was afterwards appointed Attorney-General at Hong Kong, from which post he has been lately recalled. He has published works entitled "British Catholics and the New Parliament" (1841), "A Guide to the Laws affecting Roman Catholics," "A Guide to the History of the Laws and Constitution of England," and has contributed political papers to various periodicals. He has recently been admitted to the Bombay bar.

ANTHON, CHARLES, LL.D., an American classical scholar, was born in the city of New York in 1797. In 1811, after receiving an excellent preliminary training, he proceeded to Columbia College, where he became Professor of Languages in 1835. Professor Anthon has edited a series of the classics, and also an edition of Lemprière's Classical Dictionary. He is now Professor of Greek in Columbia College, and Rector of the Grammar School attached to that institution. In this country he is best known by his edition of Horace, but he has not confined his attention to editorial labours. He has published a number of original works, chiefly on classical geography, Roman and Greek antiquities and mythology, which enjoy a great and well-merited reputation in America.

ANTONELLI, GIACOMO, CARDINAL, an Italian statesman, Secretary of State to his Holiness Pope Pius IX., was born near Terracina, on the 2nd of April, 1806. His father was a woodcutter. Antonelli was educated at the Seminario Romano. He was named successively Prelate, Assessor to the Superior Criminal Tribunal, and Delegate to Viterbo and Macerata. In 1841 he was appointed Under Secretary to the Minister of the Interior; in 1845 Grand Treasurer of the two Apostolic Chambers—that is to say, Minister of Finance. As a liberal politician he at this time found favour with the Pope. In the Consistory of June, 1847, he received the Cardinal's hat from Pius IX. As Minister of Finance he was member of the councils established by the Pope, and was besides named President of the extraordinary commission appointed to inquire into necessary reforms. Alarmed at the serious nature of the revolution, and the consequences of the liberal policy he had hitherto followed, he resigned his office, and was succeeded by Mamiani, who in turn gave way to Rossi. When Pius IX. fled to Gaeta, Cardinal Antonelli was appointed Pro-Secretary of State, and after the arrival of the French at Cività Vecchia, was placed at the head of a special commission charged with the reform of the administration of the States of the Church. Pius IX. having returned to Rome, April, 1850, the faithful cardinal was appointed Minister of State for Foreign Affairs, an office which he still continues to hold. He is also President of the Council of Ministers. An active and energetic man, he exercises complete control over the Pope, the real character of his in-

fluence being disguised under a careless and affable manner, which seems incompatible with firmness and energy of purpose.

ARAGO, ÉTIENNE, a French journalist, and brother of the late eminent astronomer, was born at Estagel, on the 7th February, 1803. He studied at the colleges of Perpignan and Sorèze, and afterwards proceeded to Paris, where, through the celebrity of his brother, he became a teacher of chemistry in the Polytechnic School. His tastes, however, pointed more to literature than to science. In his first undertakings he was associated with Balzac, and published conjointly with him "The Heiress of Birague," a history extracted from the papers of Dom Rago, ex-Prior of the Benedictines, and brought to light by his two nephews (Paris, 1822). This work did not answer, and the partners separated. M. Arago devoted himself to dramatic literature, and soon, without adventitious aid, took his place among the principal vaudevillistes of the day. He wrote incessantly for years, his pieces being, with very few exceptions, received well by the public. They consisted chiefly of vaudevilles and comedies, interspersed with couplets, among which may be mentioned, "A Day of Troubles" (1824), "To-morrow is the 13th, or Sentiment and the Almanac" (1826), "The Misfortunes of a Fine Young Man" (1834), "Just in Time" (1836), and "An Invasion of Grisettes" (1844). He has besides composed several melodramas of great merit. His masterpiece, however, is a comedy in five acts, entitled "Les Aristocrates," performed in 1847 at the Théâtre Français. As director of the Vaudeville Theatre, he did not succeed, and in 1840 was obliged to abandon the speculation. He then became a contributor to the "Siècle," under the assumed name of Jules Ferney. Entertaining very decided liberal opinions, he was afterwards a leader-writer for the "Réforme," a revolutionary newspaper. M. Arago joined the revolutionary movements of his times, and more particularly those of 1830 and 1848. After the revolution of 1848 he was elected to the Constituent Assembly, and took his seat on the left. He vehemently opposed the interference of France with Rome, and having stood out against the acts of the President, now the Emperor Napoleon, he was condemned for contumacy, and sought refuge in Belgium. He has since travelled much, and written several poems, among which may be mentioned his "Eaux de Spa," published at Brussels in 1852.

ARGELANDER, FRIEDRICH WILHELM AUGUST, an eminent German astronomer, was born at Memel on the 22d of March, 1799. He at first turned his mind to the study of economical questions, whilst he was studying at the University of Königsberg, but subsequently departed from that path to enter the more congenial field of astronomical science. His progress was such that in 1822 he was appointed assistant in the Königsberg Observatory. He afterwards was attached to the observatory at Abo, in Finland, where he succeeded Waldeck, the principal astronomer; and on its removal to Helsingfors in 1832, Argelander followed it. In 1837 he was appointed principal astronomer at Bonn, which post he still retains; and here he superintended the erection of an observatory, which was completed in 1845. He has published several valuable works on astronomy. Continuing the labours of Bessel, he determined the positions of the stars lying between 45° and 80° of declination. He published his observations in 1846, in a work which contains the position of 22,000 stars. For many years back Argelander has been engaged in observing the variations in the apparent brilliancy of the stars, a phenomenon never before his time carefully investigated, although indicated so early as the time of Tycho Brahe.

ARGYLL, George John Douglas Campbell, Duke of, a British statesman, was born in 1823. He entered the arena of ecclesiastical controversy in 1842, by publishing a "Letter to the Peers, from a Peer's Son," discussing the question of non-intrusion, in which he advocated the independence of the Church. In the same year he published his "Letter to Dr. Chalmers," in which he approves of some, but not all of the measures which were adopted by the secessionists from the Establishment. In 1847 the Marquis of Lorne succeeded to his father's titles and offices. In 1848 he published "An Essay on the Ecclesiastical History of Scotland since the Reformation," a production originally meant as a contribution to one of the "quarterlies," but which, having grown too bulky for its original purpose, was published as a separate treatise. The work is a good defence of the Presbytery. In 1851 he was appointed a Member of the Privy Council, in 1853 Lord Privy Seal, and in 1855 was Postmaster-General; and again in 1859 Lord Privy Seal under Lord Palmerston. In 1844 he married the eldest daughter of the Duke of Sutherland, Lady Elizabeth Georgina Gower. As a popular lecturer the duke is much esteemed. His varied attainments and knowledge of the great principles of natural science were evinced at the meeting of the British Association at Glasgow, over which he presided. He speaks frequently in the House of Lords, has shown considerable talent as a debater, and exhibited qualifications which may yet secure for him a leading place among the statesmen of the day.

ARGYROPOULO, Pericles, a Greek lawyer and statesman, was born about 1810, at Constantinople. He is the son of the late Jakovaki Argyropoülo, Grand Interpreter to the Porte, who published a translation of Montesquieu's "Spirit of the Laws" into modern Greek, and a "Life of Catherine" into Turkish, which are much esteemed. He studied law for some time in Paris, and then settled at Athens, where he was appointed Professor of Constitutional Law in the University. In 1853, having been appointed Rector of the University, he chose as the subject of his opening address, the praise of the great Alexander Mavrocordato, one of the most remarkable men of modern Greece. A member of nearly all the legislatures since 1843, he has been constantly in the ranks of the Constitutional opposition, of which his brother-in-law, another Mavrocordato, was the chief. In 1854 he held the portfolio of Foreign Affairs, but after a year's fighting against all manner of intrigue and animosity, he ceded his office to Boulgaris, without losing the respect of his bitterest enemies. His great work on municipal institutions entitled τα Δημοτικα, published at Athens in 1843, placed him at the head of the philosophical lawyers of the modern Hellenic race.

ARISTARCHI, Nicolas, a Greek statesman in Turkey, and Chief Interpreter to the Patriarch of Constantinople, was born in that city in 1800. He obtained, at the age of eighteen years, the situation of Keeper of the Seals to Prince Alexander Soutzo of Wallachia. Included in the disgrace of his family in 1821, he accompanied them in their exile to Asia Minor. His father, the last Phanariot Greek who held the office of Head Interpreter to the Porte, was murdered by order of the favourite Khalet Effendi. The latter having lost favour, Aristarchi, under the protection of the pashas who had replaced Khalet, returned to Constantinople, and has filled several public offices, and obtained the titles of a functionary of the first class. In his various capacities as a functionary and diplomatist his name has been mixed up with all the great events in Turkish politics, domestic and foreign, for the last quarter of a century.

ARMSTRONG, SIR WILLIAM GEORGE, C.B., an engineer, was born at Newcastle-on-Tyne on the 26th of November, 1810, and was destined for the legal profession; but, preferring mechanical studies, became partner in the Elswick works, near his native town. He was one of the earliest discoverers of the electricity of steam, which was first observed during the escape of steam from a locomotive safety-valve. He has lately been brought prominently before the public in consequence of his improvements in the manufacture of rifled ordnance, but has long been known in his profession through his general scientific attainments. Sir William has, after wearisome and costly experiments, succeeded in producing cannon of extraordinary range. In some instances a shot has reached the astonishing distance of nearly six miles, and was wonderfully true in its direction to the target. He has been engaged by the Government to superintend the manufacture of cannon at Woolwich, and also manufactures a large number of guns at his own factory. Many of these have been despatched to China, where their value has been tested in the contest which, unfortunately, has had again to be commenced with the "Celestials." Mr. Armstrong was knighted in 1854, is a Fellow of the Royal Society, and a member of the Council of the Civil Engineers' Institute of London.

ARNOLD, MATTHEW, a poet, eldest son of the late Dr. Arnold of Rugby, was born on the 24th December, 1822. After being educated at Winchester and Rugby, he went to Oxford as a scholar of Balliol College, becoming Fellow of Oriel College in 1845. In 1857 he was chosen Professor of Poetry in the University of Oxford, and two years afterwards Foreign Assistant Commissioner to the Royal Commission on Education, in which capacity he visited France, Holland, and Switzerland. His principal works are the "Strayed Reveller, and other Poems," and "Empedocles on Etna, and other Poems."

ARNOTT, NEIL, M.D., an eminent writer on physics, was born at Dysart, in Fifeshire, in 1788. He is the author of several scientific works. He gained the first prize of his class in 1801, at the Grammar School of Aberdeen, and then entered the University, where he took the degree of M.A. in 1806. He pursued his professional studies in London, under Sir Everard Home, Surgeon of St. George's Hospital. His chief work, "The Elements of Physics; or, Natural Philosophy, General and Medical, explained in Plain and Non-technical Language" (1827), is one of the best written productions of its kind, and has been translated into nearly all the European languages.

ARTHUR, T. S., a voluminous and highly popular American author, was born at Newburgh, in Orange County, in the State of New York, in 1809. He received an imperfect education at Baltimore. In 1833 he became connected, as agent, with a banking company in the Western States, but the company failing, he returned to Baltimore, and subsequently settled in Philadelphia as a writer of fiction. Among his principal works are, "Sketches of Life and Character," "Lights and Shadows of Real Life," "Leaves from the Book of Human Life," "Tales for Rich and Poor," "Ten Nights in a Bar-Room," "Anna Lee," "Orange Blossoms," &c.

ASHBURTON, WILLIAM BINGHAM BARING, second baron, was born in 1799. After having studied at Oxford he entered the House of Commons in 1826, and remained a member until 1848, when, on the death of his father, he was called to the Upper House. During Sir Robert Peel's Ministry, from

1841 to 1846, he was by turns Secretary to the India Board and Paymaster-General of the Forces. Louis Napoleon conferred on him, in 1855, the Cross of Commander of the Legion of Honour, for his services to the two great Exhibitions of National Industry in London and Paris.

AUBER, DANIEL F. E., a French composer and Member of the Institute. His father was a printseller in Paris, who was with his family in Normandy, engaged in his business, when the subject of this notice was born. At an early period in life Auber had been taught music. The death of his father leaving him at liberty to choose his own profession, he, in 1813, produced his first opera, a piece in one act, entitled "Le Séjour Militaire." It proved so unsuccessful that he was quite disheartened. In 1820 he produced an opera in three acts, entitled "La Bergère Châtelaine," which was well received. Then followed a long series of successes. In 1823 he became associated with M. Scribe, with whom his name is now indissolubly connected. "Le Timide" and "Fiorella" placed Auber among the most successful composers for the Opéra Comique. On the 29th February, 1828, his "Muette de Portici," or "Masaniello," was performed at the Grand Opéra, the words by M. Scribe and M. G. Delavigne. It took its place at once beside the greatest works of Rossini and Meyerbeer. M. Auber, however, soon found that the Opéra Comique was his proper field, and brought out a succession of pieces which are household words with the lovers of music, such as "Fra Diavolo," "Le Cheval de Bronze," "Les Chaperons Blancs"—which has long been the most popular of French comic operas,—"Le Domino Noir," and "Manon Lescault," which, the last of his works, although less widely appreciated, has met with most praise from the critics. Some of his incidental airs have had

a wonderful influence, beyond the world of musical amateurs. The "Amour Sacré de la Patrie," sung by Nourrit, gave the signal, at Brussels, for the Belgian insurrection of 1830. M. Auber is now. the most popular French musical composer of the day. His music is light and easy; it is graceful, and often marked by originality. He possesses all the movement and clearness of Rossini, without, perhaps, all his subtilty and depth in the representation of passion.

AUERBACH, BERTHOLD, a German writer, was born at Nordstetten, on 2d February, 1812, of Jewish parents. Abandoning theological pursuits, which he had followed at different universities, he gave his attention to literature on the termination of his studies. He lived at first on the Rhine, but in 1845 he removed to Northern Germany, and has since resided, alternately, at Leipsic, Dresden, and Breslau. His earliest work was "The Jewish Nation, and its Modern Literature" (1836), which was followed in 1837 by "Spinoza," a romance containing very interesting pictures of the social and religious life of the Jews. In 1839 he published "The Poet and the Merchant;" in 1842, "Educated Citizens, a Book for the Thinking Middle Classes." His reputation had become fully established in 1843, when he gave to the world his "Village Tales from the Black Forest," which has been translated into several foreign languages. In 1848 he published the "Professor's Wife," and soon after a new series of the "Village Tales." For some years previously he had published an almanac, addressed to the people, and intended for their instruction, in which he advocated moderate democratic opinions and the cause of popular education with much zeal. His next work was a "Journal of Events in Vienna, from Latour to Windischgrätz." He published, in 1850, a tragedy, "Andreas Hofer" a work which narrates the events of the

German revolution, as they appeared to the democratic politicians of the Continent. In addition to the romance of "Spinoza," already mentioned, M. Auerbach has published a translation of the whole works of the great Jewish philosophers, from the Latin into German, with long biographies prefixed to them.

AUGIER, GUILLAUME VICTOR ÉMILE, a French dramatic poet, was born at Valence on the 17th September, 1820. He studied at several universities with marked distinction. Rejecting the advice of his friends, who urged him to enter the bar, he adopted literature as a profession. In 1844 he presented to the committee of the Théâtre Français a piece in two acts, entitled "La Ciguë." It was rejected. M. Augier was not repulsed, however, by this failure. He presented the same drama to the committee of the Odéon, who, with more discernment than their rivals, at once saw its merit and accepted it. Its success was gratifying to the young author. "La Ciguë" had a run of three months, and indeed its popularity restored the backgoing fortunes of the theatre. The following year he produced "Un Homme de Bien," and subsequently "L'Aventurière;" following up these lighter pieces with "Gabrielle," a comedy in five acts, which has been pronounced by competent critics to be his best constructed and most finished work, whether as regards plot, poetry, or the delineation of character. At the solicitation of Mdlle. Rachel he wrote "Diane," a piece in five acts; but as all the interest was concentrated upon one character, it failed to command the applause bestowed on "Gabrielle." A number of pieces, of from one to five acts, proceeded from his fertile pen. The style of M. Augier is at once classic and easy, dignified and yet pictorial, never heavy, and always interesting. He may be said to have founded a new school in French dramatic literature, and his works, partly by their originality and partly by intrinsic merits, of a kind possessed in common with other dramatic productions, have acquired very great popularity.

AUSTRIA, EMPEROR OF. (See FRANCIS JOSEPH I.)

AUZOUX, TH. LOUIS, a French physician and anatomist, was born at St. Aubin d'Écroville, in the department of the Eure, about 1797. He took his degree of Doctor in Paris in 1822. From the very commencement of his studies he devoted himself to the improvement of anatomical models. At great expense he prosecuted experiments to discover a paste which had the requisite softness to receive the most delicate impressions, and the quality of afterwards hardening into a substance resisting moisture and insects. He succeeded; and published in 1839 the results of his inquiry in a work entitled "Elementary Lessons in Anatomy and Physiology, or Brief Descriptions of the Physical Phenomena of Life, by Means of Anatomie Clastique," (the word clastique from κλαω, to break, referring to the fact that his models can be broken, or taken down into pieces.) He explains the application of his invention to the fabrication of models, which serve to render dissection, to a great extent, unnecessary. He established at St. Aubin an extensive manufactory of models, illustrative of anatomy and physiology, which is not only remarkable for its products, but for the admirable way in which the moral condition of the workmen has been attended to. For his successful labours in facilitating anatomical studies, M. Auzoux has had many honours conferred on him, including various gold medals at the Paris Exhibition, and the Cross of the Legion of Honour.

AYTOUN, WILLIAM EDMONDSTOUNE, a poet and essayist, was born in 1813, and educated in Edinburgh. He comes of an ancient Scottish family, the Aytons of Ayton, from whom sprang the old poet Sir Robert Ayton. In 1840 he was admitted to the Scottish bar, and in 1845 was appointed Professor of Rhetoric and Belles Lettres in the University of Edinburgh. He is a principal contributor to "Blackwood's Magazine," in the pages of which first appeared his "Lays of the Scottish Cavaliers," the twelfth edition of which was published in 1859. Besides the "Lays," his other principal works are, "Bothwell, a Poem," a vindication of the character of Queen Mary; "Firmilian, a Spasmodic Tragedy;" and "The Ballads of Scotland." He is also part author of "The Book of Ballads, edited by Bon Gualtier," and of a volume of admirable translations of the poems and ballads of Goethe, published in 1859. In 1852 he received the legal appointment of Sheriff and Vice-admiral of Orkney, which he still holds, its duties only implying an occasional visit to the islands. In 1853 he delivered a course of lectures in London on "Poetry and Dramatic Literature," which were well received. Professor Aytoun is a conservative of the old school.

AZEGLIO, MASSIMO TAPARELLI, MARQUIS D', an Italian novelist and statesman, and late Sardinian Minister to England, was born at Turin in 1801. At the age of fourteen he was excommunicated for an assault upon his teacher, who was an ecclesiastic. In 1816 he accompanied his father to Rome, occupying his time principally with painting and music. He returned to Turin in 1829, and marrying the daughter of the great novelist Manzoni, he wrote several romances. The earliest of these was "Ettore Fieramosca," published in 1833, which, conceived in the style of Manzoni, and full of patriotic sentiments, was received with great enthusiasm. His next romance, "Niccolo di Lappi," published eight years afterwards, became equally popular. Deeply imbued with the spirit of Italian nationality, in 1842 he abandoned his favourite pursuits, and with his friends Balbo and Gioberti he made a tour through the provinces of Italy, exciting the revolutionary movement which troubled the last years of Gregory XVI. After the revolution of 1848 he supported the cause of the King of Piedmont, and, at the head of the Papal troops, fought against the Austrians at Vicenza, where he served as a colonel in the Venetian army, and was badly wounded by a ball in the thigh. Elected deputy to the Sardinian National Assembly, and nominated President of the Council of Ministers, he resigned the latter office in 1852 to his political adversary Count Cavour. Massimo d'Azeglio is brother of the Marquis Roberto d'Azeglio, and uncle to the Sardinian Minister at the Court of St. James's. Another brother is Padre Luigi Taparelli, lately Provincial of the Jesuits for the kingdom of the Two Sicilies.

BABBAGE, CHARLES, a mathematician and mechanical inventor, was born on the 26th of December, 1792. He entered at Trinity College, Cambridge, and devoted himself chiefly to mathematics and mechanics. The laborious calculations necessary in constructing tables of logarithms early called his attention to the value of any invention which should substitute for mental calculation the more precise principle of mechanism. Having obtained Government assistance, he commenced observations and experiments on the subject, and made a tour to the Continent, with the view of studying the various pieces of mechanism employed in the arts. On his return he published his "Economy of Manufactures," as the result of the inquiries he had made. This work Blanqui, the French Economist, has described as a hymn to machinery. It shows how the division of labour is carried out in manufacturing industry, and how the greatest results are to be obtained by the smallest expenditure of means. In 1828 Babbage obtained at Cambridge the mathematical chair of Trinity College, to which he had earned his title by numerous contributions to scientific periodicals and transactions. In 1825 he wrote a paper on the use of calculating machines, and in 1833 the apparatus, which was made in accordance with the views he had published, was found to be so far perfect in its construction as to produce every result which its ingenious inventor could have desired. It was at once a calculating and printing machine, and its value may be better estimated from the fact, that a table of logarithms of all natural numbers, ranging from 1 to 100,000, was produced, free from error, by its agency. Being manufactured on unerring mechanical principles, those mistakes incident to mental exertion were entirely done away with. Its value and bearing on even the practical work of navigation and engineering was greater than those engaged in practical details have any conception of. At the outset, Government, on the recommendation of the Council of the Royal Society, sanctioned grants for the construction of the machine; but from an injudicious economy in respect to expenditure of public money, its operations were ended when apparently reaching a triumphant issue. Mr. Babbage is a Fellow of the Royal Society of London, of the Royal Society of Edinburgh, of the Royal Irish Academy, and of the Cambridge Philosophical Society, besides being associated with the chief scientific societies of Europe and America. He has been a voluminous author. His "Reflections on the Decline of Science in England" appeared in 1830, in which the author seemed to apprehend that scientific research had seen its best days in Great Britain, an idea which he has without doubt withdrawn since the publication of that work. He had previously published several treatises on various subjects, but his great work is "The Economy of Manufactures and Machinery," already referred to, which has reached five editions in this country, been translated into most European languages, and reprinted in America. His writings embrace an extensive range of learning and research, but the principal works and papers from his hand relate to mathematics and mechanics. He was one of the founders of the Royal Astronomical Society, and of the British Association for the Advancement of Science.

BACK, Sir George, D.C.L., F.R.S., an English navigator, was born at Stockport, Cheshire, on the 6th of November, 1796. He commenced his naval career as midshipman in the Arethusa, and was present in several naval engagements, in which he never failed to acquit himself with distinction, but did not display his peculiar aptitudes until he was employed in various expeditions to the Arctic regions. Early in 1818 he was selected to accompany Captain Beechy, Captain Buchan, and Lieutenant (afterwards Sir John) Franklin, on the first modern voyage of discovery beyond Spitzbergen. In 1819 he again joined Franklin in the expedition from Hudson's Bay, and coastwise, east of the Copper Mine River. The journey being performed in winter, gave Sir George Back an opportunity of displaying a courage and endurance under fatigue, of inestimable service to his party. On his return in 1825 he was made commander. He accompanied Franklin beyond the M'Kenzie river in 1825, on a special mission of discovery, during which his great abilities were again exhibited by his having undertaken an exploration on his own account. In 1833 he commanded an expedition in search of Sir John Ross. He published an account of the expedition, under the title of "Narrative of the Arctic Land Expedition to the Mouth of the Great Fish River, and along the Shores of the Arctic Ocean in 1833-5." After being made post-captain, he proceeded in H. M. S. Terror, on an expedition to Frozen Strait and Repulse Bay, with a view of prosecuting discovery in the Arctic seas from Regent's Cape to Cape Turn-again, from which he came back in October, 1837. The expedition did not prove successful. After being for a long time shut up in the ice, he and his crews returned in a most miserable plight, from the effects of cold and hunger. He wrote a narrative of the voyage, which is clear, elegant, and interesting. It is entitled "Narrative of the Expedition of H. M. S. Terror, undertaken with a view to Discovery on the Arctic Shores in 1836-7." It was published in 1838, and he was knighted in the same year. He attained the rank of Rear-Admiral in 1857. He is a member of several foreign societies, and has received for his geographical discoveries the gold medals of the Geographical Societies of Paris and London.

BAEHR, JOHN CHRISTIAN FELIX, a distinguished scholar and philologist, was born at Darmstadt, on the 13th of June, 1798. He studied in the University of Heidelberg, where he was Assistant Professor, and afterwards Titular Professor, of Classic Literature. Subsequently (1833) he was appointed Custodier-in-Chief of the Library, Head Inspector of the Lyceum or College, and lastly, in 1845, Director of the Philological Seminary. The Grand Duke of Baden conferred on him the title of Private Aulic Councillor. He is a most voluminous author of historico-philological works, the most remarkable of which are his edition of "Herodotus," published in 1832 and 1833 at Leipzig; "A History of Roman Literature," of which the third edition was published at Carlsruhe, in 1844; "A History of Roman Literature during the Carlovingian Period;" a work on "Romano-Christian Theology," published in 1837,

&c. Since 1847 he has been the editor of the periodical entitled "Annals of Heidelberg," to which he has contributed valuable papers. Some of his contributions to the "Universal Encyclopædia of Ersch and Grabes," have been published separately.

BAILEY, PHILIP JAMES, an English poet, was born at Nottingham, April 22, 1816. After receiving the education afforded by the public schools of his native town, he proceeded to Glasgow, to study at the university of that city. His first poetic production was entitled "Creative Imagination," which was highly creditable to him, considering his youth. Having followed the legal profession for some time, his taste for literature, and the promptings of innate power, impelled him to abandon it for the thorny path of letters. While keeping "terms," and studying in the chambers of a conveyancer, he spent much of his time in the libraries of Lincoln's Inn and the British Museum, and there matured the tastes which were to determine his future career. He returned to Nottingham, where his father was a proprietor of a local paper, in the literary management of which he assisted for many years. His "Festus," published in 1839, was highly successful. It was considered one of the most daring poems of the age when it first appeared. His thoughts were remarkably original, and his imaginative clothing of them bold and graceful. Mr. Bailey has since published the "Angel World," "The Mystic," and the "Age," a satire.

BAILY, EDWARD HODGES, R.A., an English sculptor, was born at Bristol, 10th March, 1788. Although intended for commercial pursuits, he seemed from an early age to have had a taste for modelling, and the fact of his father being an eminent ship carver may possibly account for this. Having been introduced to Flaxman, that artist rendered young Baily every assistance in his power; and so rapid was his progress, that he obtained a prize from the Royal Academy, and soon became a successful candidate for popular favour. His "Eve at the Fountain" has been universally admired, and its reproduction in plaster has made it a familiar object in most parts of the kingdom. After engaging as modeller for Messrs. Rundell and Co., the goldsmiths, Mr. Baily produced his "Hercules casting Lycidas into the Sea," by which he secured the high opinion of competent critics. His works have been very numerous, and without detailing the whole, the following may be specially mentioned:—"Apollo discharging his Arrows," "Maternal Love," "The Three Graces," "Psyche," "The Girl preparing for the Bath," and his various public statues of eminent men.

BAINES, EDWARD, an English journalist, politician, and M.P., was born at Leeds in 1806. He is second son of the late Mr. Edward Baines, who may be said to have founded the "Leeds Mercury" newspaper, and who represented Leeds in Parliament for many years. The subject of this notice was educated at the Protestant Dissenters' Grammar School, Manchester. At an early age he became his father's assistant in the management of the journal, then his partner (1827), and ultimately the chief proprietor. One of the leading principles of the paper has been opposition to all schemes for State interference with the education of the poor. For twenty-two years he has been President of the Yorkshire Union of Mechanics' Institutes. In politics he is a decided liberal, advocating Free-trade, the Ballot, an extension of the franchise in counties and boroughs, complete civil and religious liberty, the total abolition of Church rates, voluntary and religious education, and the principle of non-intervention in continental wars. Mr. Baines has published "The History of the Cotton Manufactures;" "The Life of Edward Baines," his father; "A Visit to the Vaudois of Piedmont;" "The Woollen Manufactures of England;" and some minor works. He is a Justice of the Peace and Deputy-Lieutenant for the West Riding of Yorkshire. He was returned to Parliament by his native town at the general election of 1859.

BALFE, MICHAEL WILLIAM, a composer, was born in Dublin in May, 1808. At a very early age he showed a great talent for music. He received some preliminary instruction from Mr. Meadows, band-master of a regiment stationed at Wexford, which was followed by lessons from his father, and C. E. Horn, the celebrated composer. During a brief course of study he made wonderful progress as a violin player, and when sixteen years of age appeared at the theatre of Drury Lane in the opera of "Freischütz." He remained there only one year. In 1825 he set out for Italy, where he made his first attempt as a composer, writing for the opera of La Scala a piece entitled "Lapeyrouse." In 1827 he removed to Paris, where, under the name of "Balfi," he met with great success as a bass singer, with Malibran and Sontag. He returned again to Italy, and wrote a long series of operas for Milan, Paris, and London. In 1845 Mr. Balfe became director of the Italian Opera in London. It is a curious fact that the operas of this composer have succeeded better in Germany than in any other country. "The Bohemian Girl," and the "Quatre Fils d'Aymon," had an immense success at Berlin. Mr. Balfe is a disciple of Paër and Rossini, and to some extent resembles Auber in his productions. His principal operas are "The Bohemian Girl," "The Siege of Rochelle," "The Daughter of St. Mark," "The Enchantress," "The Maid of Honour," "Les Puits d'Amour," "The Jewess," "Les

Quatre Fils d'Aymon," "The Rose of Castile," "Satanella," &c.

BANCROFT, GEORGE, was born at Worcester, Massachusetts, U.S., in 1800. He graduated at Harvard College. He then travelled in Europe, studied at Göttingen and Berlin, under those eminent scholars Heeren and Schlosser, and in 1820 had conferred upon him the diploma of Doctor in Philosophy. After making the "grand tour," he returned to America in 1822. He was originally destined for the pulpit, but a love for literature proved the stronger attraction. For a brief period he held the post of Greek Professor in Harvard College. After publishing a volume of poems, and a translation of "Heeren's Reflections on the Politics of Ancient Greece," Mr. Bancroft devoted himself to the duties of an instructor of youth, opening a great public school at Northampton, to which he attracted a very eminent staff of professors from Germany. The intervals saved from professional duties were devoted to superintending and publishing a translation of "Heeren's Histories of the States of Antiquity, and the Political System of Europe and its Colonies." Between the years 1834 and 1855, Bancroft's great work, "The History of the United States," was published, in which the subject was treated in the spirit of that advanced criticism which has reformed the style of modern historical narratives. It placed its author at once among the great writers of the age. Having given efficient assistance to the political party to which he belonged, in 1838 he obtained a post in the Custom House. In 1846 he was appointed Minister to Great Britain, and in consequence of this appointment he resided in London until 1849. In that year he again returned to the United States, having received the most gratifying testimonials of esteem from all with whom he had come in contact. Mr. Bancroft has published poems, and has contributed to the "North American Review." His articles inserted in that periodical have been collected and published at New York, in 1855, under the title of "Miscellanies, Essays, and Reviews."

BARAGUEY, D'HILLIERS ACHILLE, COMTE, Marshal of France, was born at Paris on the 6th September, 1795. In 1812 he entered the army, attaining in 1815 the rank of captain, when he embraced the party of the Restoration. In 1827 he became a lieutenant-colonel, and in 1830 took part in the expedition to Algeria. His success against the Arabs gained him the confidence of the government of Louis-Philippe, and as the reward of his valour he was made a lieutenant-general. Attached in 1832 to the School of St. Cyr, as second in command, he repressed the republican movement, and acted with an energy which met with the approval of government. He was promoted to be field-marshal on 29th September, 1836, and took command of the school and of the guards towards the end of 1840. In the following year he filled the situation of Governor-General of Algeria, and headed many expeditions against the Arabs, under the orders of the Duc d'Aumale. He was Inspector-General of Infantry from 1847 until the revolution. On the fall of the citizen king in the revolution of 1848, the Provisional Government appointed him to the command of the military division of Besançon. He replaced Changarnier in the command of the army of Paris, and concurred in the accomplishment of the *coup d'état* on the 2nd December, 1851. For this service he was nominated a member of the "commission consultative." In the war with Russia, as Commander-in-Chief of the Baltic expedition, he was for his services elevated to the dignity of a Marshal of France, and received the Grand Cross of the Legion of Honour. He took an active part in the campaign of 1859, when France leagued with Sardinia to free Italy from the domination of Austria.

BARANTE, AMABLE PROSPER BRUGIÈRE, BARON DE, a French statesman and historian, a member of the French Academy, and formerly a peer of France, was born at Riom, in Auvergne, on 10th June, 1782. After studying in the Military School of Effiat he entered the École Polytechnique, where he remained for three years. In 1802 he entered upon his administrative career, as assistant to the Minister of the Interior, and subsequently became auditor to the Council of State. In 1809 he published anonymously a work on "The Literature of France during the 18th Century," which was such as to excite Madame de Staël's enthusiasm for the author, and to call forth the eulogium of Goethe. He subsequently held various official appointments both on home and foreign service, and was elected a Member of the Academy in 1828. He is the author of a number of papers in the "Revue Française," and the "Biographie Universelle." In 1822 he published "The Commons and the Aristocracy," and subsequently his greatest work, "The History of the Dukes of Burgundy, of the House of Valois, from 1364 to 1477." In 1851 he produced a "History of the National Convention;" in 1858 the "History of the Directoire Exécutive;" in 1857 and 1858 two volumes of "Historical and Literary Studies," "The Parliament and the Fronde;" and in 1859 "The Life of Mathieu Molé."

BARBÈS, ARMAND, a French politician and revolutionist, was born at the Pointe-à-Pître, in the Island of Guadaloupe, in 1809. At an early age he was brought to the south of France. He went to school at Sorèze, in the department of Tarn, where the instruction given inculcated absolute submission to the powers that be, whether in church or state. Barbès, at an early age, rebelled against these precepts. In 1830, after his father's death, he went to Paris to attend the law classes, and had an opportunity of manifesting his political opinions at that period of excitement. He had inherited a considerable fortune from his father, and he had thus ample leisure to devote his attention to the business of secret societies. During the whole reign of Louis-Philippe he was constantly engaged in conspiracies. In consequence of an unsuccessful attempt to overthrow the Government, he was condemned to death, a sentence which was commuted to perpetual confinement. The revolution of 1848 found him in prison, and restored him to liberty. He then founded a club, which took his name, in which the doctrines of socialism were superadded to republicanism. The name of Barbès sounded in the ears of the people like the tocsin against monarchy and the bourgeoisie. On the occasion of the insurrection of May, 1849, Barbès was sentenced to "déportation." In October, 1854, a letter written to a friend, by no means intended for publicity, and expressing a desire that victory should remain with the French army in the Crimean war, happened to fall into the hands of the French Government. The Emperor, thinking that a mark of respect for such a man as Barbès might impart a character of popularity to the imperial policy, took advantage of the opportunity to set him at liberty. Barbès, wounded in his political feelings at receiving a favour uncalled for, hastened to denounce the secret meaning of the measure, publicly refused to take advantage of it, and after a most energetic protest, left France a voluntary exile. He is now a resident at the Hague.

BARING, SIR FRANCIS THORNHILL, BART., son of the late Sir Thomas Baring, and nephew to the founder of the celebrated banking-house which bears his name, was born in 1790. He was educated and graduated at Christ Church, Oxford. He entered the House of Commons in 1826, as member for Portsmouth. In 1830 he was appointed a Lord of the Treasury, which office he held till 1834. In June of that year he was promoted to be Joint-Secretary of the Treasury, but resigned with the ministry on King William IV. suddenly calling Sir Robert Peel to his councils in November, 1834. In April, 1835, he was again Joint-Secretary of the Treasury, performing the duties of this office till 1839. From that year to 1841 he was Chancellor of the Exchequer; and from 1849 to 1852, First Lord of the Admiralty.

BARING, THOMAS, a capitalist, statesman, and member of Parliament, was born in 1800. He is brother to Sir Francis Baring. He became member for Yarmouth in 1835, retaining his seat till 1837. He contested the representation of London in 1843, but was defeated by a small majority. In 1844 he was returned for Huntingdon. His political creed is conservative, but he never figured prominently as a politician, and he derives his chief reputation from his connexion with those financial transactions and mercantile speculations in which his family has long taken such an important part.

BARLOW, PETER, a physicist and mathematician, was born at Norwich in 1776. Educated exclusively in the schools of his native town, he applied himself zealously to the study of mathematics and physics, and soon obtained reputation as a man of science. He was Mathematical Master in the Royal Military Academy at Woolwich for a period of forty years. In 1821 Mr. Barlow wrote an article which was published in the "Philosophical Transactions," to which he afterwards became a regular contributor during upwards of fifteen years. In 1823 he was elected a Fellow of the Royal Society, from which,

in 1825, he received the Copley medal for his researches in magnetism. In 1829 he was admitted a member of the Astronomical Society of London, and a corresponding member of the French Academy. Among the most remarkable of his books is his "Mathematical and Philosophical Dictionary," which at the present time is very scarce and of great value. His "Treatise on Materials used in Construction" records a great variety of experiments he had made with various materials employed at the dockyard at Woolwich. He is also the author of several important articles in the "Encyclopædia Metropolitana," and of an elaborate and important work on the "Machinery and Manufactures of Great Britain," published in 1837; of a "Treatise on the Force and Rapidity of Locomotives," published in 1838, and of various Government reports on subjects of the same kind, of the highest value as contributions to the literature of applied science. His "Essay on Magnetic Attraction" was one of the first works in which the phenomena of magnetism were distinctly enunciated.

BARNES, ALBERT, an American divine, was born at Rome, in the State of New York, on the 1st of December, 1798. He graduated in Hamilton College in 1820, and afterwards pursuing his theological studies at Princeton, he was ordained to the ministry, and installed pastor of the Presbyterian church in Morristown, New Jersey, on the 25th of February, 1825. From this place he removed to Philadelphia in 1830, where he still remains as minister of the first Presbyterian church in that city. Mr. Barnes has a high reputation in America as an eloquent preacher. He is the author of a volume of "Practical Sermons;" a volume of sermons entitled "The Way of Salvation," first published in London, and edited by the late Dr. Henderson; and of a volume on "Slavery." Besides other similar works, he has published "Notes" on Job, Isaiah, and Daniel, and on the entire New Testament, in eleven volumes. These "Notes" have all been reprinted in England and Scotland. Of the "Notes" on the New Testament, more than four hundred and fifty thousand copies have been sold in the United States, and it is supposed an equal or larger number has been disposed of in this country and in France.

BARNUM, PHINEAS TAYLOR, a well-known American "Showman," was born in the village of Bethel, in Connecticut, in 1810. From an early period he exhibited an aversion to work of the ordinary kind. After an unsuccessful attempt in the newspaper line, he had a share in the management of a strolling theatre. Subsequently he obtained possession of an old negress, whose proprietors represented her as having been the nurse of George Washington; she was said to be 160 years of age. Barnum adopted the story, and by means of his tact as a showman, and by the dint of advertising devices, induced thousands in every city and chief town in America to flock to see the early guardian of the Liberator. On this side of the Atlantic, pathetic pictures were drawn by the anti-slavery orators of the degradation thus cast upon the memory of the great general of the Republic. After the death of his old negress, Barnum bought the American Museum, in New York, and soon brought it into high repute and prosperity. His next great "card" was General Tom Thumb; but his most successful enterprise was the engagement of Jenny Lind, for a series of concerts in the United States, Canada, and Cuba, by which he claims to have netted £70,000 sterling. On his return to the United States, he was elected president of a bank, became largely interested in real estate in Bridgeport and vicinity, and promoted agriculture and enterprising thrift generally, with all the zeal of a public-spirited and benevolent citizen. In 1855 he published his "Autobiography," a candid and amusing relation of the innumerable arts by which he attained his notoriety or celebrity as the "Prince of Humbugs." In 1856 his fortune was frittered away, or greatly imperilled, by disastrous business complications; and in 1857-58 he gave lectures in London and some of the provincial cities of England, on his methods of obtaining notoriety as a stepping-stone to making money, &c., drawing crowded audiences and replenishing his treasury. The last advices represent him as again in prosperous circumstances, with firm health and unflagging energy.

BAROCHE, PIERRE JULES, a French advocate, was born at Paris, 8th November, 1802. His father, who had realized a small competency in trade, died when he was seven years of age, and he was sent by his guardian to the Lycée Charlemagne, where he distinguished himself. He was called to the bar on the 1st of April, 1823, and soon acquired professional distinction. On the 27th November, 1847, he was elected member of the Chamber of Deputies for the Charente-Inférieure. He took, however, no prominent part in the debates of the period immediately preceding the fall of Louis-Philippe, but he steadily opposed the ministry of Guizot. He signed the Acte d'Accusation drawn up by Odilon Barrot on the 23d February, 1848, in which they were accused of violating the rights of citizens, and of systematic corruption. The purpose of this manifesto was to effect a change of ministry, not to precipitate a revolution, and M. Baroche may have regretted the step he took. He owed nothing to the revolution of February, and in opposing the radical party he was guided solely by his convictions. His active interference in political affairs dates from the 8th May, 1848, when the Provisional Government handed over its power to the National Assembly. At this period the struggle between the republican party and those who sought to obtain a strong government, had reached the greatest intensity. Appointed Procureur-Général of the Court of Paris, he used repressive measures against the democratic press, and conducted various state prosecutions with an energy and ability which have made him an object of intense dislike to the radical party. On the 2nd December, 1851, M. Baroche was nominated President of the Council of State, a position in which he has exhibited an ability, tact, and capacity for work, and a firmness of character not anticipated from his professional career, in which he certainly did not rise to the very highest distinction. In 1855 he was invested with the Grand Cross of the Legion of Honour.

BARROT, CAMILLE HYACINTHE ODILON, a French statesman, was born at Villepot, in the department of Lozère, on the 19th July, 1791. His father, a conspicuous French statesman, was a member of the legislative body in 1804, and the only deputy who protested against the establishment of the Empire. At the early age of nineteen, M. Odilon Barrot was called to the bar. At this stage in his career he manifested an attachment to the Bourbons, which he has since justified on the ground that Louis XVIII. was at the time the representative of constitutional government as opposed to the absolutism of the Empire. Dissatisfied with the policy of the government, he gradually passed over to the opposition, and soon found himself in the ranks of the liberals, headed by Dupont (de l'Eure) and La Fayette. The courts of justice were the arena in which he first displayed his political prepossessions. His marriage with the grand-daughter of Labbey de Pompières bound him still more closely to the liberal cause. He was appointed President of the Society "Aide-toi, le Ciel t'aidera." He took an active part in the revolution of July, 1830. He was secretary to the municipal commission, which for some days performed the functions of a provisional government, and is said to have had a powerful influence in preventing .any compromise being come to with the elder branch, and in placing the Orleans family on the throne. Under the patronage of Dupont (de l'Eure) and La Fayette, M. Barrot stood, in 1831, as representative for the department of the Eure, and at the age of forty entered the Chamber of Deputies, in which he was destined to distinguish himself as a speaker until the fall of the parliamentary system in France. His first speech was a reply to M. Guizot, who had just been succeeded in the ministry by M. Lafitte. He refused on this occasion to admit that property should be considered the only electoral qualification, and maintained that the objects of the government called into existence by the revolution of July, ought not to be to perpetuate the restoration, but to create liberal institutions, and, so far as possible, to absorb the republican party by widening the foundations of monarchical institutions. It would be impossible within our limits to present even a summary of the events in the active political life of Odilon Barrot. When the number and class of public functionaries returned to the Chambers in 1846 called general attention to the prevalent corruption, and to the necessity of electoral reform, he took an active part in getting up the demonstrations in which all shades of the liberal and democratic opposition joined. He was the hero of the "banquets réformistes" of 1847. He failed, however, to understand the nature of the tempest he had raised. He expected nothing more than a change of ministry, and was in perfect good faith when he spoke of his fidelity to constitutional monarchy. He thought he held the reins and could direct the movement as he chose. The revolution of February was a bitter disappointment to him. Under the new order of things he was returned representative of the Département de l'Aisne. On the 27th September, 1848, he made a speech on the question of two chambers, which was very warmly applauded, but which failed to convince the assembly. After the election of Louis Napoleon as President of the Republic, M. Odilon Barrot took office as Minister of Justice and President of the Council, in the absence of the President of the Republic. The resignation of the ministry on the 31st October, 1849, was the signal of the rupture between the Legislative Assembly and the adherents of Louis Napoleon. On hearing of the dissolution of the Assembly, he was one of the first to protest and proceed to the Mairie of the arrondissement to proclaim the fall of the President. Seeing, however, that his efforts were quite unavailing in averting the destruction of liberal institutions in France, he from that time ceased to hold any office under government, and, indeed, altogether abandoned public life.

BARTH, Sir Henry, a scholar, traveller, and author, was born at Hamburg, 18th April, 1821. After receiving instruction in Hamburg he studied at Berlin, where the natural sciences, general geography and history, classics, and the history of antiquity in its bearings on the development of modern nations, engaged his attention. He travelled in Italy and Sicily before taking his degrees at Berlin in 1844, on which occasion he wrote a remarkable thesis, on the Commerce of Ancient Corinth. He went to London in the following year to study Arabic. The same season he visited the Mediterranean coasts of Europe, and commenced those exploratory expeditions which have since so much increased our knowledge of African geography. The government of Morocco would not allow him to pass through its territory, and he therefore proceeded to Tunis, whence he penetrated into Sahara, and crossed the vast deserts of Northern Africa to the Nile. In 1846 he crossed into Arabia, Syria, and Asia Minor; in 1847, travelled through Greece; and in 1848, returned to Berlin. He then became a private teacher at the University, and delivered lectures on African geography and the history of the Greek colonies. In the same year he published his "Exploratory Expedition to the Coasts of the Mediterranean in 1845, 1846, and 1847." He had just completed his work when news reached him that the English Government were fitting out an expedition to Central Africa. Bunsen and Petermann recommended that he should join it. He did so, and with his countryman Overweg and Mr. James Richardson, he set out from London in December, 1849. The expedition lasted four years, during which Barth travelled 12,000 miles. On his return, in 1855, he drew up a narrative of his journey, under the title of "Travels and Discoveries in North and Central Africa," published in Germany in 1855, and in England in 1857. This work is one of the most important contributions to modern geographical science, and the researches it records have placed Sir H. Barth among the most illustrious of the geographical explorers of our times.

BARTHELÉMY, Auguste-Marseille, a French poet, was born at Marseilles in 1796. He first acquired a reputation in his native city by a satirical poem against the Capuchins. The satirical powers of Barthélémy frequently brought him into contact with the government of the Restoration, and the revolution of July, 1830, found him in prison. Restored to liberty, he sang the victory of the people, along with M. Méry, in a poem dedicated to the Parisians—"L'Insurrection," which became very popular. From Louis-Philippe he received a pension of 1,200 francs; which, however, he subsequently lost, from not in all things yielding to the inspiration of the government. The latest effusions of the poet's genius are war songs celebrating the triumphs of the Crimea. As a writer he is held by his admirers in France to exhibit the vehemence of Juvenal, the bitterness of Gilbert, and the causticity of Boileau; but the praise would seem rather exaggerated, for numbers of his productions bear evident marks of haste, though rarely deficient in pungent sarcasm and rhythmical exactness.

BARTLETT, JOHN RUSSELL, an American ethnologist, traveller, and author, was born on the 23rd of October, 1805, at Providence, in Rhode Island. He received his education at Laoville Academy, New York, and at various schools in Canada. On leaving school at eighteen, and after filling several mercantile situations and taking a prominent place in promoting literature and science in Rhode Island, he removed, in 1837, to New York. On taking up his residence in this city he entered a large mercantile firm as a partner, but the great commercial crisis which soon after crushed so many houses, and led to a suspension of specie payments by the banks, involved him in the general ruin. Three years after he determined to embark in the book trade, to which he was attracted by his taste for literature, and, in partnership with Mr. Welford, he carried on for ten years this business with success and éclat. Mr. Bartlett meantime devoted himself to historical and ethnological studies. He was for many years the Secretary of the New York Historical Society, and in connexion with Albert Gallatin founded the American Ethnological Society, of which he was also the secretary. In 1849 he finally relinquished business, and returning to Providence the following year, was appointed by President Taylor, the Commissioner on the part of the United States to survey the boundary line between the United States and Mexico, in conformity with the treaty of Guadaloupe Hidalgo. He organized a large corps of engineers, and with them sailed from New York in August, 1850. Landing on the shores of Texas, he fitted out his expedition, which, including the officers, assistants, and an escort under Colonel Crony, numbered more than 300 men. With this party he traversed the vast regions of prairie and desert between the Gulf of Mexico and the Pacific. In connexion with the survey, Mr. Bartlett explored a large portion of Texas, New Mexico, &c. His various journeys extended over a distance of 5,000 miles, and occupied nearly three years. The results, embracing observations in astronomy, physics, and natural history, were published first in 1854, and afterwards in a more extended form in 1857-8, at the expense of the American Government. On his return from this expedition in 1854, Mr. Bartlett took up his residence in Providence, and was elected Secretary of State of Rhode Island, which office he has since filled. His published works are "A Dictionary of Americanisms," 8vo, which has been translated into Dutch; "The Progress of Ethnology," 8vo; "Reminiscences of Albert Gallatin;" "Personal Narrative of Explorations and Incidents in Texas, New Mexico, California," &c., 2 vols., 8vo; "Official Despatches and Correspondence connected with the United States and Mexico Boundary Commission," 8vo, &c.

BASTIDE, JULES, a French author and journalist, was born at Paris in 1800. After studying at the College of Henry IV., he entered the school of law, but ultimately became a wood merchant. He took an active part in the opposition to the Restoration. In 1830, after making a conspicuous figure on the barricades, he protested against Louis-Philippe being raised to the throne.

Taking part in the disturbances of the 5th and 6th of June, 1832, on the occasion of the funeral of General Lamarque, he was obliged to seek an asylum in England. In his absence he was condemned to death, *par contumace;* but on his return to France, two years afterwards, he underwent his trial and was acquitted. He then became editor of the "National," an appointment which he held for several years. On the 6th of May, 1848, he was appointed Minister of Foreign Affairs by the Executive Commission; a post in which he was continued till the 10th of December, by his intimate friend General Cavaignac. While in office he advocated a temperate republicanism, opposed socialism, and did all in his power to promote the English alliance. After retiring from the "National" in 1844, Bastide, with several of his friends, started the "National Review," and about the same time he wrote an elaborate essay on the "Fortifications of Paris," published in English in the "British and Foreign Review," and a number of political, philosophical, and scientific articles for Didot's "Encyclopédie Moderne." He is the author of a treatise on "Public Education in France," a "History of the French Religious Wars," and a work published in Brussels in 1858, entitled "The French Republic and Italy."

BAUER, BRUNO, a German scholar, historian, and critic, was born at Eisenberg, in the Duchy of Saxe-Altenberg, on the 6th of September, 1809. He is the son of a painter on porcelain, who settled in Prussia in 1814. Having studied in the Colleges and University of Berlin, he was received as Doctor of Theology in 1834. In 1839 he was named Professor at Bonn; but having advocated opinions inconsistent with the purposes of the chair, and been prohibited from proceeding with his lectures, he returned to Berlin, and there entered upon a series of critical and historical labours which have placed him in the highest rank of German scholarship. At first he devoted himself chiefly to Biblical criticism. Like Fauerbach, and all the new philosophical school of Germany, he made an attempt to reconcile theology and philosophy. His most remarkable works written at this period were "Doctor Hengstenberg," published at Berlin in 1839; "The Prussian Evangelical Church and Science," published at Leipsic in 1840; "A Review of the Gospel Narrative," and a "Review of the History of St. John." The consequence of the views expressed in these works was an open rupture with the Church. A work which he meant to publish at Zurich in 1843 was seized by the Swiss Government on account of the peculiarity of views expressed in it. It was entitled "Christianity Unveiled," and contained a complete digest of his theological opinions. After this period Dr. Bauer, forsaking theology for a time, devoted himself to literary and historical studies, and produced several valuable works. The most remarkable of these were, "A History of Modern Times subsequent to the French Revolution" (1843 and 1844), "A History of the Civilization and Enlightenment of the Eighteenth Century" (1843, 1845), "A History of Germany during the French Revolution and the Reign of Napoleon" (1846), and several other works connected with recent politics. Within the last ten years he has returned to Biblical criticism, and published a long series of works, the most remarkable of which is his "Criticism of the Epistles of St. Paul," of which the second edition appeared in 1852, in which he vainly attempts to show that these writings are not the productions of the usually received canonical authors. He now holds a high rank among the thinkers of the new philosophical school in Germany.

BAVARIA, KING OF. (*See* MAXIMILIAN II.)

D

BAXTER, WILLIAM EDWARD, a member of the House of Commons, was born in Dundee in 1825. After being educated there, and at the University of Edinburgh, he became a partner of the firm of Edward Baxter and Son, foreign merchants in Dundee. At an early age he travelled over a great part of Europe and the United States. In 1855 he was returned to Parliament for the Montrose district of burghs, as successor to Joseph Hume. His political sentiments are of the advanced liberal class, embracing extension of the suffrage and vote by ballot; he also advocates unsectarian national education. He is chiefly remarkable as one of the few home-bred Scotch members who, understanding Scotch subjects, venture to take a part in the discussions of the House of Commons. He has written and published "The Tagus and the Tiber" (1848), and "America and the Americans" (1850), together with some minor works, all belonging to that light and amusing department of literature to which our French neighbours give the name of "Impressions de Voyage."

BECQUEREL, ANTOINE CESAR, a French chemist, was born at Châtillon-sur-Loing, in the department of Loiret. Having studied at the Polytechnic School, he became, in 1808, an officer of Engineers, and served in the Spanish campaign of 1810. In 1815 he left the army, and having a decided taste for experimental science, turned his attention to electro-chemistry, and other branches of electrical science. To him we are indebted for a vast insight into the action of electric forces in nature, and the science of chemistry has by means of his researches been greatly extended, and the cause of the production of mineral bodies to a large extent satisfactorily explained in his researches on the chemical action of electricity. The ideas first suggested by M. Becquerel have been since amplified by Mr.

Crosse of Taunton, who was enabled to reproduce in the laboratory some of those gems and other products which are found in nature, by means of weak but long-continued electric currents acting on mineral solutions. As a philosopher M. Becquerel has greatly contributed to an exact knowledge of the cause of electric phenomena being developed in the voltaic battery, and of the thermo-electric arrangements which have since been extensively employed for the purpose of ascertaining and measuring slight changes in the temperature of bodies. In 1837 he received the Copley medal, and was elected a corresponding member of the Royal Society of London. His scientific researches contributed to the Academy of Sciences at Paris have had an important influence both in an industrial and social point of view. Becquerel is the author of the following works:—"A Treatise on Electricity and Magnetism," in 7 vols., 1834, 1840, 1847; "A Treatise of Physics in its Connexion with Chemistry and the Natural Sciences," 2 vols., 1844; "A Treatise on Climate," 1 vol., 1845; "A Treatise on Mineral Manures," 1 vol., 1845; "A Treatise on Terrestrial Physics and Meteorology," 1 vol., 1847; "A Treatise on Electricity and Magnetism," 3 vols., 1856; "A Brief History of Electricity," 1 vol., 1858.

BEDEAU, MARIE ALPHONSE, a French general, was born in 1804. Having studied at St. Cyr, he entered the army, and distinguished himself greatly during the Belgic campaign in 1831-32. In 1836 he went to Algeria, and within little more than four years rose to the rank of General of Brigade. In Algeria he was engaged in a perpetual succession of combats with the Arabs. Being victorious, he organized the province, and as the reward of his services was named a General of Division. On the return of the Duke d'Aumale to France, he became Governor of Algeria. In 1851

Bedeau was one of the generals arrested by Louis Napoleon and confined in the prison of Ham. In common with his companions in arms, he was subsequently set at liberty. As he is known to be a devout Roman Catholic, it was reported not long since that he had taken orders, but he has contradicted the rumour. In the crisis at Neufchâtel he offered his services to the Swiss.

BEECHER, MISS CATHERINE ESTHER, an American authoress, the eldest daughter of Dr. Lyman Beecher, was born on 6th September, 1800, at East Hampton, in Long Island, where she resided for about ten years. Her early education was received at Lichfield. After leaving school she experienced a severe shock by the death of Professor Fisher, of Yale College, to whom she was betrothed. A life of activity was required to ameliorate her distress, and in 1822 she opened a female seminary at Hartfort, Connecticut, where she remained for ten years. During that period Miss Beecher published a "Manual of Arithmetic," and several elementary books of instruction in theology and mental and moral philosophy. In 1832 she accompanied her father to Cincinnati, and was for two years engaged in teaching; but failing health obliged her to resign her connexion with the institution of which she had been at once the ornament and the head. Miss Beecher soon after devised a plan for female Christian education, to be promoted through a National Board, with normal schools and competent teachers. For many years she has pursued this object with untiring energy; it has been the purpose of her life; it has induced her to write, to travel, and to exert all the influence of her active intellect throughout the United States. Her scheme has been often laid before the public in detached works, among which may be cited, "Domestic Servants," "The Duty of American Women to their Country," "The Housekeeper's Receipt Book," "The True Remedy for the Wrongs of Women," and a "Treatise on Domestic Economy." Recently Miss Beecher has published a work on "Physiology, and the Condition and Habits of American Women," and the first volume of a course on "Theology and Moral · Philosophy," in which she ventures to depart from the theology of Calvin.

BEECHER, THE REV. CHARLES, an American clergyman, is son of the Rev. Dr. Lyman Beecher, and pastor of a church in Newark, New Jersey. He has published a work entitled "The Incarnation; or, Pictures of the Virgin and her Son," with an introduction by his sister, Mrs. Beecher Stowe (1849); "A Review of the Spiritual Manifestations" (1853), and "Pen-Pictures of the Bible" (1855). When his sister visited England and the Continent, during the height of the popularity of "Uncle Tom's Cabin," he accompanied her, afterwards contributing largely to her work, "Sunny Memories."

BEECHER, REV. EDWARD, D.D., an American author and divine, the eldest son of Dr. Lyman Beecher, was born in 1804. He received the principal part of his education at Yale College, where he graduated in 1822. He studied divinity at Andover and New Haven, and was appointed a tutor in Yale College in 1825. Subsequently he was elected pastor of the Park-street Church, Boston,—an office which he filled for five years, and which he resigned in 1831, to discharge the duties of President of the Illinois College, Jacksonville. He retained the latter post for thirteen years, retiring in 1844. In 1846 he was called to the charge of Salem-street Church, Boston, where he ministered for ten years, and is now pastor of a church at Galesburg, Illinois. He has published the "Conflict of Ages," "Papal Conspiracy," and "Baptism, its Import and Modes."

BEECHER, HENRY WARD, an American author and divine, is another son of the Rev. Dr. Lyman Beecher. He was born at Lichfield, Connecticut, 24th, June 1813. He graduated at Amherst College, Massachusetts, in 1834, and studied theology under his father at Lane Seminary, Cincinnati. His first settlement as a minister was at Lawrenceburg, Indiana, in 1837, where he remained for two years, and then removed to Indianapolis. He continued in the latter charge for eight years, at the end of which, in 1847, he was invited to the pastorate of the church of which he still continues minister. He is said to have the largest uniform congregation in the United States; he is a popular lecturer, and is moreover determinedly opposed to the institution of slavery. Besides occasional addresses, he has published a volume of "Lectures to Young Men," which has attained immense popularity. He edited the "Plymouth Collection of Hymns," and was one of the founders of the "Independent," a religious newspaper, published in New York, to which he has been a constant contributor. Two volumes of his articles have been collected and published under the title of the "Star Papers," his contributions being well known by the signature of an asterisk. Since the spring of 1859 his morning and evening sermons have been regularly reported and published each week in the "Independent," and "Banner of Light." Many of his works have been reprinted in England, and, under the title of "Life Thoughts," have enjoyed great popularity.

BEECHER, LYMAN, D.D., an American clergyman, and father of the distinguished persons noticed in the preceding memoirs, was born at New Haven, Connecticut, 12th October, 1775. He graduated at Yale College in 1797, and studied theology under President Dwight. In 1798 he was ordained pastor of a church at East Hampton, Long Island, and in 1810 he removed to the charge of the first church at Lichfield, Connecticut. There he continued about sixteen years, a devoted and active minister. In 1826, at the time when Unitarianism was attracting converts in various districts of New England, Dr. Channing leading the way to desertion from the ancient Puritan faith, Dr. Beecher was chosen pastor of the newly-established Hanover-street Church, in Boston. Under the circumstances, his ministry was necessarily, to a considerable extent, controversial, and he entered upon it with a full sense of his responsibility, throwing himself into the conflict with equal ardour and ability. In 1832 a theological seminary was founded at Cincinnati, of which Dr. Beecher was invited to take the direction; a position which he accepted, and for ten years retained, adding to its duties the pastoral charge of the second Presbyterian church. His learning, decided views, and stirring eloquence, had a powerful effect on the population of the West; for he was thoroughly in earnest, and known to take an active part in the promotion of temperance and every great philanthropic movement of the day. In 1842 he removed to Boston. He has since remained there without fixed employment, although remarkably vigorous in mind and body for a person of his years. In the cause of temperance he has written very effectively. His collected works have been published in three volumes, under his own supervision. Mr. Beecher is the father of nine children, who have all distinguished themselves in literature, and by their exertions in the abolitionist cause. The best known are those whose memoirs immediately precede this.

BEKKER, EMMANUEL, a German scholar and philologist, was born at Berlin in 1785. He studied at Halle, under the celebrated Wolf, and in 1807 was appointed Professor of Greek Literature in the University of Berlin. Having spent some time in Paris, he returned to Berlin, and published the first of his works, an edition of "Plato," in ten volumes. In 1815 he visited France and Italy, with his colleague, Gœschen, to prepare a "Corpus Inscriptionum Græcarum," and to decipher the manuscript of Gaius, discovered by Niebuhr. He afterwards made a tour through the German and English Libraries. His researches were diligent, and his conclusions, when given to the world, were found eminently accurate. He has published various important editions of Greek works, among which may be enumerated his "Attic Orators" (Oxford, 1823), "Thucydides" (Oxford, 1821), and "Aristophanes" (London, 1825). More recently Bekker has devoted his attention to Provençal literature, and has published in the Berlin reviews a series of articles on the chief works in this and other cognate dialects of Southern Europe, which possesses the highest merit. New editions of Plato, of Homer, of Thucydides, of the Attic Orators, of Aristotle, and of Tacitus, and numerous other works, are the results of his learned labours.

BELCHER, Sir Edward, an English navigator and author, was born in 1799, of an old English family, which for many years occupied a high position in the administration of the affairs of the American colonies. Having joined the navy in 1812, he served with honour in several important naval actions, in 1819 became a Lieutenant, and in 1829 was made Commander. Having afterwards been engaged in various services on the coasts of Africa and Portugal, he commenced a long voyage in the year 1836, being absent for nearly six years. On his return he published a highly interesting account, entitled "A Narrative of a Voyage Round the World, on board the 'Sulphur'" (London, 1843). In 1842 he was promoted to the rank of Post-Captain, made a Companion of the Bath, and received the honour of knighthood for services rendered in the Chinese seas. In 1843 he returned to the Chinese seas, and was engaged with fearful odds against pirates off Gilolo, and wounded. He at this time visited Labuan, rendering Sir J. Brooke most valuable assistance against the pirates infesting the Malay Archipelago. He published an account of his labours during this period in a narrative of a "Voyage to the Eastern Archipelago during the years from 1843 to 1846." In 1852 Sir Edward commanded the Arctic expedition sent in quest of Sir John Franklin, which, however, turned out unsuccessful, and owing to the dangers which beset the vessels, he was compelled to abandon them. In 1855 he published an account of his expedition, under the title of "The Last of the Arctic Voyages;" an important work, of which the scientific part was entrusted to a number of able naturalists. In addition to the volumes referring to the voyages, which are of high scientific importance, Sir E. Belcher has published various works of more strictly professional interest, and of great practical value, among which may be mentioned a "Treatise on Practical Surveying" (London, 1835), and works on the navigation of the rivers Douro and Gambia.

BELGIANS, King of the. (See Leopold George Christian Frederick.)

BELL, Henry Glassford, a poet and Scottish lawyer and judge, was born at Glasgow on the 8th of November, 1805. He is the son of the late James Bell, an eminent advocate. He was educated at the University of Edinburgh, where he graduated, and was called to the Scottish bar in 1832. His taste for literature was early evinced, but he rendered it subservient to the practice of his profession. Before passing advocate, he published a "Life of Mary Queen of

Scots," which appeared originally in "Constable's Miscellany." This work grew rapidly in public favour, and edition followed edition until about fifty thousand copies were exhausted. The style is elegant, the narrative clear, the descriptions graphic. At an early age he published a volume of poetry entitled "Summer and Winter Hours," and a miscellaneous volume of prose and verse, with the title of "My Old Portfolio." Both these books have been long out of print. He likewise established, and for some years edited with marked success, the "Edinburgh Literary Journal," a weekly periodical which obtained a wide circulation. Mr. Bell was appointed First Sheriff-Substitute for Lanarkshire, at Glasgow, in 1839. He takes a warm interest in every movement calculated to improve his native city; and there is no effort made towards advancing the social well-being of the community which he is not found advocating with that truest of eloquence, the language of the heart. We need scarcely say that he is the author of poetical pieces which have found a place in every school•collection, but which have been so long familiar to us, that we are often tempted to think of the author as belonging to a past generation.

BELL, JOHN, an English sculptor, was born in Norfolk, in 1812. In his various productions Mr. Bell has evidenced a desire to strike out an original course by the exercise of his own inventive faculties. In 1837 he exhibited the "Eagle Slayer," which has been pronounced by competent critics to be his best work. Four years later he produced his "Dorothea," which has been copied in porcelain, and has met with very high praise from those who have not had the opportunity of studying the other productions of the author. Among his works are statues of "Lord Falkland," "Sir Robert Walpole," now in the Houses of Parliament, for which they were commissioned; the Monument of Wellington between Peace and War, in the London Guildhall; and the statue for "Armed Science," at Woolwich, all large works in marble. His latest productions are the "Guards' Memorial of Waterloo," consisting of four colossal bronze figures, on a granite pedestal; and the memorial to those officers and men of the Artillery who fell in the Crimea, to be erected on the parade at Woolwich. To his chisel we owe "The Babes in the Wood," and "Andromeda." Mr. Bell has not confined his attention exclusively to sculpture, but has also made designs for fountains, domestic objects, &c., which have met with high praise from Art critics.

BELL, ROBERT, an English author, was born at Cork in 1800. He is the son of an Irish officer. He resided at first in London, afterwards in Dublin. He is the author of the "History of Russia," in three vols.; of the concluding volumes of Sir James Mackintosh's "History of England," and "Southey's "Lives of the Admirals;" the "Lives of English Poets," two vols., in "Lardner's Cyclopædia;" of the "Memorials of the Civil War," two vols.; "A Life of George Canning;" and "Wayside Pictures through France, Belgium, and Germany." Mr. Bell has also written several tales and novels, of which the "Ladder of Gold," and "Hearts and Altars," are the best known and most widely popular, as well as numerous dramatic pieces, including three five-act comedies, "Marriage," "Mothers and Daughters," and "Temper." An erudite and accurate writer, Mr. Bell has been largely connected with current literature and criticism, and a constant contributor to the quarterly and monthly periodicals. Originally editor of the "Atlas" newspaper, and the "Monthly Chronicle Magazine," he is also editor of the "Annotated Edition of the British Poets," a work on which great labour and research have been expended.

BELL, THOMAS, an English naturalist and author, was born 11th October, 1792, at Poole, Dorsetshire. He was educated in his native town and at Shaftesbury. He entered the medical profession in 1814, at Guy's Hospital, was admitted a member of the College of Surgeons in the following year, and in 1817 he became a lecturer at Guy's Hospital. For eleven years he was a member of the Council of the Zoological Society, and for about eight years he acted as Vice-President. He was appointed Professor of Zoology in King's College, London, in 1836. In 1828 he became a Fellow of the Royal Society; in 1839, 1841, and 1847 was chosen one of the Council; in 1848 was elected Secretary, which office he held until 1853; and has subsequently been a Vice-President of the Royal Society for five years. He has been President of the Ray and Linnæan Societies, and an Honorary Fellow of the College of Surgeons since 1844. He is the author of a number of papers which have appeared in the Proceedings of those societies with which he has been so long identified. His larger works are on British Reptilia (1829), British Quadrupeds (1836), British Crustacea (1853), and the Fossil Crustacea of Great Britain (1858). A new edition of "White's History of Selborne," with numerous additional letters, is announced as being now in preparation by Mr. Bell.

BENDEMANN, EDWARD, a German painter, was born at Berlin, December 3, 1811. He received an excellent literary education, but art was his true vocation. In 1831 he exhibited in the Berlin Exhibition "The Mourning of the Jews," the subject being taken from the 137th Psalm —"By the waters of Babylon we sat down and wept." In 1833 he produced his "Two Young Girls at a Fountain," accounted one of the best works among those purchased for the Westphalian Society of Arts. His next, and perhaps his most perfect work, was "Jeremiah on the Ruins of Jerusalem," a colossal painting, which procured the artist a medal of the first class from Paris in 1837. This picture occupies a prominent place in the Gallery of the King of Prussia. Between 1835 and 1837 Bendemann painted the following pictures: —"Harvest," for the Society of Arts at Berlin; "The Shepherd and Shepherdess" (of Uhland's poem), for Count Raczenski's collection; and "The Art of Painting at the Font of Poetry" (Die Künste am Brunnen der Poesie). In 1838 he was appointed Professor in the Academy of Dresden. He there completed a series of wall-paintings in the halls of the Royal Palace; a third hall, which was projected by the king, not having been carried out. About the same time he produced "Nansikaa," an oil-painting, in the possession of the King of Prussia, and an aquarelle of the same for Mr. Thompson of Belfast. In 1859 he was appointed Director of the Academy of Dusseldorf. His last production is a small oil-painting, entitled "Ulysses and Penelope," which was only completed a short time ago. Bendemann in all his works exhibits the characteristic excellences of the Dusseldorf school, its accurate drawing and skilful composition, its wealth of invention and poetic feeling. But to these he superadds a profound acquaintance with nature, and a grace which are specially his own; and he is one of the few painters of the school to which he belongs who have been equally successful in tableaux or genre, and in the grand historical style.

BENEDICT, JULIUS, a German musical composer and pianist, was born at Stuttgardt in 1805. He is the son of a banker in that place. At an early age he showed a great taste for music, received lessons from Hummel, at Weimar, and when fifteen years of age became the pupil of the great Weber. He became afterwards musical director at San Carlo, in Naples. In 1830, after a short visit to Stuttgardt and Berlin, where he met with considerable success, he first went to Paris, and then returned to Naples. In 1835, at the instance of the late Mdme. Malibran, he visited London for the first time, and, having accepted an engagement by Barbaja at Naples, composed his "Anno ed un Giorno," for young Lablache's *début* in that town. This opera having been received very favourably, led to his engagement as conductor of the Opera Buffo in London, whither, after a few months' residence in Paris, he removed in 1836, and has ever since remained. In 1838 he produced his first English opera, "The Gipsy's Warning," which rapidly obtained a success for which it was indebted to its power, beauty, and dramatic excellence. "The Brides of Venice," and "The Crusaders," followed. In 1850 he accompanied Jenny Lind to America, as pianist and conductor, and shared in that gifted lady's triumphs. For many years Benedict has been the director of various musical assemblies and concerts, not only in London, but throughout the provinces. His musical abilities are of the first rank, and his qualifications as a leader unsurpassed. His most wonderful triumph is in the fact that, although a German, and educated exclusively in the musical schools of Germany, he has succeeded in writing operas for the Italian and English stage, which have met with the highest success.

BENNETT, WILLIAM STERNDALE, a pianist and composer, was born at Sheffield in 1816. He studied in the Royal Academy of Music, where he had the good fortune to receive instruction from two admirable masters, Dr. Crotch and Cipriani Potter. His progress was remarkable, and his talent for music was soon distinctly developed. In 1836 he went to Leipsic, to take part in the concerts the great composer Mendelssohn was conducting, and his compositions performed there were so highly applauded, that the name of young Sterndale Bennett became familiar throughout Germany as that of a learned, imaginative, and fertile musician. He afterwards returned to England, and has for nearly twenty-five years laboured incessantly in his art. He composes rapidly: overtures, sonatas, concertos, piano studies, songs, all flow with equal ease from his prolific mind, and as a performer and instructor he ranks among the foremost. His style of scoring is in one sense peculiar. He is simple in his construction of musical phrases, scholastic without pedantry, and produces effects where no effect could have been anticipated. His orchestral arrangement is remarkable for these qualities. Mr. Bennett is one of the professors of the Royal Academy of Music, and conductor of the orchestra of the Philharmonic Society, a body which owes much of its renown to his zeal, activity, and genius.

BERGHAUS, HENRY, a German geographer, was born at Cleves on the 3rd May, 1797. The son of John Isaac Berghaus, a well-known historical and scientific writer, he was educated partly under his father's immediate care, and partly at the Gymnasium Paulinum, at Munster, where he directed his attention chiefly to mathematics and engineering. At the early age of fourteen he was employed under the French administration in Germany as an engineer, in connexion with the great system of inland navigation projected by Napoleon, and meant to extend from Lübeck and Hamburg to Paris. This official appointment, of course, ceased with the battle of Leipsic, and the retreat of the French beyond the Rhine. After the treaty of Paris, he went to the University of Marburg, where he prepared, while engaged in other studies, various works for the Geographical Society of Weimar. After Napoleon's escape from Elba, Berghaus, entering the Commissariat department of the army, was quartered at Rennes, and took advantage of his residence in that part of France to study carefully the geography of the surrounding country. On his return to Germany he published his excellent Map of France, in which he laid down his personal observations. In 1816 he entered the Faculty of Philosophy at Berlin, as a student under the rectorship of Schleiermacher. In 1818 he was appointed Geographical Engineer to the second section of the War Department, and in this capacity he took part in the Government survey which began in 1810, had been interrupted by the war of 1813-15, and was recommenced after the peace of 1816. In 1821 he obtained a chair in the Academy of Architecture, and withdrew from his military employment. He now devoted himself with renewed zeal to geographical pursuits, bestowing immense labour on the maps constructed by him, and the geographical papers and works of which he is the author. His chief productions are his Map of the Spanish peninsula, which is considered the best yet produced; his large Atlas of Asia, consisting of fifteen maps, with notes, published at Gotha between 1833 and 1843; and his Physical Atlas, consisting of ninety-three maps with explanations, the first edition of which was published at Gotha, between 1837 and 1843, and the second edition between 1850 and 1852. Physical geography was raised to the high position it now holds as a science by this work, which has been largely pirated from, and almost copied in publications which fail to acknowledge the source of their information. An English edition of this work, incorporated with new matter, was published by A. K. Johnston,

of Edinburgh, in which the materials derived from Berghaus were duly pointed out. The geographical works written by Berghaus are very numerous; several others are at this moment in the press, or in course of preparation. In 1852, at the request of a society under the auspices of the East India Company and the Governor-General of India, he wrote a Manual of Geography, which, on being translated into the Hindustani, Tamil, and other dialects, was to be introduced into the Indian native schools. Among the students who attended the geographical school founded by Berghaus at Potsdam in 1839, were the well-known A. Petermann of Gotha, who is his foster-son, Henry Lange of Leipsic, and Hermann Berghaus of Gotha.

BERKELEY, THE HON. FRANCIS HENRY FITZHARDINGE, an English politician and member of Parliament, was born on the 5th of December, 1794. He is the fourth son of the Earl of Berkeley, the representative of one of the oldest and most distinguished families in England. Elected in 1837 for the city and county of Bristol, he has sat in Parliament for that constituency ever since. Among Mr. Berkeley's speeches, one on the Commons' Enclosure Bill, and a speech in seconding Sir John Bowring's motion for the abolition of corporal punishment in the army, and a defence of the conduct of his brother, Sir Maurice Berkeley, who resigned a seat at the Admiralty, because the Board, with Lord Minto, declined to increase the crews of Her Majesty's navy, were among his earlier efforts. A speech in moving for a committee on the Beer Bill, which he carried, and a motion to abolish the Yeomanry force, were a happy mixture of satire and argument; and one moving for inquiry into the conduct of Lord Lucan, was acknowledged to be extremely able. Mr. Berkeley, however, has chiefly acquired his reputation as the chief speaker on the Ballot question, his speeches in favour of which have always secured the ear of the House, from their happy combination of wit and argument.

BERLIOZ, HECTOR, a French musical composer, was born on the 11th of December, 1803, at La Côte St. André, in France. He was intended for the profession of medicine, but soon abandoned it for that of music. Proceeding to Paris, he was enabled to acquire from Reicha and Lesueur, at the Conservatoire, all the instruction within reach likely to fit him for the profession he had adopted. He went to Italy in 1830, and, on his return to France in 1832, produced various operas and symphonies, which were, however, more scholastic than popular in their character. His productions thoroughly combine the gentle and plaintive with the massive and sonorous elements in music, and his style is founded on that of Beethoven.

BERNARD, CLAUDE, a French anatomist and physiologist, was born at St. Julien, near Villefranche, 12th July, 1813. He studied medicine at Paris, was received into the Hospitals in 1839, and became assistant to M. Magendie in 1841. In 1843 he received his diploma as Doctor of Medicine; and his knowledge increasing with study and practice in his profession, he became Doctor of Sciences in 1853. As principal assistant, in the fullest sense, to M. Magendie, he was called, in 1854, to the Chair of General Physiology, founded by the Paris Faculty of Sciences, and in the same year elected Member of the Academy of Sciences. In 1855 he was appointed Professor of Experimental Physiology to the College of France, succeeding M. Magendie in that chair. M. Bernard struck out a new path in the science of which he was a brilliant teacher; his discoveries were important; and he recalled attention to physiological problems that had been regarded as definitely solved, but of which he proved the solutions unsatisfactory. His papers published in the "Gazette Médicale" and the "Comptes Rendus de la Société de Biologie," are considered admirable expositions of the effects of the secretions on animal organization; but his reputation as a physiologist was firmly founded by his "Recherches sur les Usages du Pancréas," inserted originally in "Comptes Rendus" to the Academy of Sciences. He has published various papers on physiological subjects, all striking for their minute investigation and close logic, establishing principles previously unknown or unheeded.

BERRYER, PIERRE ANTOINE, a French lawyer, Legitimist politician, man of letters, and member of the Institute, was born in Paris in January, 1790. The son of an eminent pleader, he was educated at the College of Juilly, and embraced the profession of the law. His first appearance at the bar was in 1811. In politics he was a Legitimist; but believing that clemency would best serve the throne, he joined his father and M. Dupin in defending Marshal Ney and others who had been devoted to the cause of Napoleon. "It is a disgrace in conquerors," said he, "to gather the wounded on the field of battle to lead them to the scaffold." In vain he recommended Ney to the clemency of the Royalists. Notwithstanding the Legitimist traditions of his family, he pursued a course quite independent of party tactics or feeling. In 1816 he attacked the Minister of Police—Decazes, and warmly advocated the rights of the press. In a professional point of view his upright and independent conduct proved of great advantage. His denunciations of all measures that appeared oppressive, brought him immense practice. Returned to the Chamber of Deputies by the department of Hante Loire, he became the most brilliant orator of the Legitimist party. On the

Revolution of July, 1830, taking place, M. Berryer, of all the Royalist party, alone remained in the chamber to advocate a fallen cause. His policy, when he could no longer resist a change, was to turn the altered circumstances to the best account. He disputed the right of the Chamber to give a new constitution to France, in every instance advocated liberal measures, and demanded a broad enlargement of political privileges. When the Duchess de Berri landed in France in 1832, M. Berryer endeavoured to induce her to pursue a course the reverse of that which she had proposed to follow, but his efforts were fruitless, and dreading being more deeply compromised he fled to Switzerland, but was arrested, and imprisoned at Nantes. Tried, however, by the Court of Assize at Blois, he was acquitted triumphantly of all the charges against him. In 1833 he spoke from the tribune on behalf of the Duchess de Berri, defended Châteaubriand, and otherwise engaged himself in the interest of the Bourbons; in all his speeches exhibiting the same candour and liberality. In 1834 he opposed the government in the attempt to proceed against two members of the Chamber for libel, and was equally hostile to further restrictions on the press. When Louis Napoleon, in 1840, was captured at Boulogne, M. Berryer boldly undertook his cause. In the same year he made one of his finest speeches on the Eastern question. He visited London some time afterwards, to lay his allegiance at the feet of the Duc de Bourdeaux. After the Revolution of 1848, he was assiduous in endeavouring to promote the Legitimist cause, but he afterwards perceived that France was not ripe for a second restoration of the Bourbons. He was, in 1848, returned by the department of Bouches-du-Rhône, but he confined himself in the republican assembly to questions of finance and administration. In conjunction with M. Thiers and other Orleanists, he opposed the pretensions of the Prince President, and in 1851 expressed himself as hostile to the extreme course which was adopted by Louis Napoleon in December of that year. Since then he has retired from public political life, and devoted his great talents to his profession. The political importance which M. Berryer had attained to, almost unsought, involved him in pecuniary difficulties, which compelled him, in 1836, to advertise for sale his estate of Agerville, but to the honour of the party to which he belongs, and for which he had made so many sacrifices, it was disencumbered of the debts he had contracted, and restored to him. In 1852 he was appointed Dean or Bâtonnier of the Faculty of Advocates at Paris. In 1854 he was elected a member of the French Academy; the customary visit to the Chief of the state, in his case, being dispensed with. He is still engaged in laborious practice at the bar, as all English readers of newspapers know from the reports of his speeches in cases which excite an interest in this country, such as the Jeufosse case in 1857, and the Montalembert case in 1859. His speeches are quoted in all French collections as models of forensic eloquence, and those for Seguin against Ouvrard, for Castaing, Dehors, &c., have long been considered masterpieces by those best able to judge.

BETHELL, SIR RICHARD, an English lawyer and law reformer, was born at Bradford, in Wiltshire, in 1800. His father, a distinguished physician in Bristol, was descended of an eminent Welsh family. He was educated at the Bristol Grammar School, and afterwards entered Wadham College, Oxford, where he took his degree of B.A. In 1823 he was called to the bar, and in 1840 became Queen's Counsel. In 1851 he was elected for Aylesbury, was nominated Solicitor-General in the Aberdeen administration, and knighted. He succeeded Sir Alexander Cockburn as Attorney-General in 1856. Though displaced by the retirement of Lord Aberdeen, it has been stated that he might have retained his office under Lord Derby. The oscillations of parties have again placed the Attorney-Generalship in the hands of Sir Richard Bethell, who has long been universally admitted to be the ablest and one of the most learned lawyers at the bar. It is not as a successful practitioner alone that Sir Richard Bethell has risen to distinction. His efforts in the cause of law reform have gained for him the esteem of all who are not interested in the perpetuation of the abuses he has attacked. It is to be hoped that what he has done is but a mere prelude to what he is destined to do. The Ecclesiastical Courts, and the present system of conveyancing, to which he has hitherto chiefly directed his attention, are merely parts of a great system of abuses which urgently call for reform. In his schemes for the improvement of legal education in the Inns of Court, he has perhaps not sufficiently adverted to elements in the present machinery which, clumsy as they are, serve to protect the honourable character of the English bar, and to insure in its members qualifications not tested by examination papers. During the late session (1860) Sir Richard introduced a most elaborate act, which was intended to effect a reform in the administration of the Bankruptcy Laws, but owing to the protracted length of the session, he was compelled to withdraw it from the consideration of the House.

BIBESCO, GEORGE DEMETRIUS, ex-Hospodar of Wallachia, was born in 1804. He is a younger brother of the Hospodar Barbo Stirbey. After being educated at home, he went to Bucharest and Paris, where he spent seven years in perfecting his studies. Before his elevation to the Hospodorat he held the office of Sub-Secretary of Justice, under General Kisseleff's administration; afterwards he resigned, and visiting France and Austria, contracted friendships with many of the most eminent statesmen of those countries. On his return to Wallachia he was elected Hospodar, the choice being confirmed by the Porte. Eight days after the election he was solemnly installed. Previously liberal in his principles, the constitutional party founded all their hopes on his administration, but he soon betrayed a tendency towards absolutism, and a desire to conciliate Russian influence. Opposition grew strong in 1849; measures were adopted to impede, if not end, the encroaching rule of the Hospodar; the once popular Governor was disliked when it was found that he temporized and wavered, until at length, abandoned by the populace and the army, he gave in his adhesion to a new constitution, and named as his ministers the leaders of the opposition. His proceedings were of no avail; in a few days after, notwithstanding the representations of the Russian Consul, he abdicated the Hospodarat, and set out by Transylvania to Vienna. Since this period Prince Bibesco has resided alternately at Bucharest, Constantinople, and Paris. He is not the author of a work attributed to him, entitled "The Rouman Principalities before Europe."

BILLAULT, AUGUSTE ADOLPHE MARIE, advocate and senator, was born at Vannes in 1805. After studying law at Rennes, he settled at Nantes, as an advocate, and rose rapidly to reputation and practice. In 1830 he became a member of the Municipal Council, and in 1834 member of the Council-General of the Department. In 1837 he was elected to the Chamber of Deputies by three constituencies, of which he chose that of Ancenis. He entered into political life with great zeal, his views being liberal. In 1840 it was expected that the portfolio of Commerce and Agriculture would be placed in his hands by M. Thiers; but instead, the then new functions of Under-Secretary of State were confided to him. He subsequently joined the ranks of a moderate though progressive opposition, in conjunction with M. Dufaure. He was much abused for accepting the law business of the Duc d'Aumale, but without any tangible reason. After the Revolution of 1848 he was elected representative for the Loire Inférieure, and took his place in the ranks of the moderate democratic party, to which he has since remained faithful, though acknowledging the force of circumstances which it was out of his power to control. In 1854, believing he could be useful to France, he accepted the appointment of Minister of the Interior, on the retirement of M. de Persigny; but in February, 1858, resigned in favour of General Espinasse. He is a Commander and Grand Officer of the Legion of Honour.

BINNEY, REV. THOMAS, an English Nonconformist clergyman, was born at Newcastle-on-Tyne, and educated for the ministry at Wymondley, Hertfordshire. He was first placed at Newport, Isle of Wight, from which he removed in 1829 to London, to become the pastor of the Weigh House Chapel, Little Eastcheap. The building was taken down in 1834, when Eastcheap was widened, and the present large and more commodious chapel built on Fish Street Hill, the old name being retained. Since then he has always been recognised as one of the leaders of the English Independents. He has both travelled and written, but the great source of his fame is the pulpit, where he has acquired immense popularity, by the clear and striking way in which he explains the meaning of Scripture, the wide and thorough grasp he takes of the subject under discussion, and the Christian love and charity which everywhere pervade his sermons. He has lately returned from a lengthened tour in Australia, whither he had proceeded for the benefit of his health, and where his ministrations were highly valued.

BIOT, JEAN BAPTISTE, an illustrious French *savant* and man of letters, was born at Paris in 1774. After studying at the College of Louis Le Grand, Biot joined the artillery; but, preferring scientific pursuits, he was eventually appointed Professor of Mathematics in the Central School at Beauvais. In the year 1800 Biot was appointed to the chair of Natural Philosophy in the College of France, and when only twenty-eight years of age was elected a member of the Academy of Sciences. In 1806 he was a member of the Bureau des Longitudes; and, in conjunction with Arago, continued a series of researches on the properties of gases, which had been commenced by Borda. With Arago he assisted in extending the French arc of meridian, and for this purpose visited Spain, and subsequently embarked for England. The "Investigator" brig of war was placed at his service. The "Investigator" sailed north to the little island of Uist, and in this bleak region of fogs and storms his observations were completed. In 1840 the Royal Society awarded Biot their Rumford medal for his researches on the polarization of light. He has conducted an immense number of researches in physical science; a few in conjunction with M. Pouillet, most of them independently. They are recorded in the "Mémoires" and "Comptes Rendus" of the Academy, the "Mémoires d'Arcueil" and the "Journal des Savants," of the mathematical section of which he was long the editor. He is the author of "An Analysis of the *Mécanique Céleste* of Laplace," published in 1801; a work on "Analytical Geometry, applied to Curves and Surfaces of the Second Order," of which an eighth edition was published in 1834; of "An Elementary Treatise on Physical Astronomy," of which a third edition was published in 1850; and of a great number of other scientific works of the highest merit. M. Biot is distinguished as a literary man as well as a man of science. He is the author of an *Éloge* of Montaigne, and another of Gay Lussac. His remarks on education in this country attracted much attention some years ago. As a *littérateur* he has been admitted a member of the Academy of "Inscriptions et Belles Lettres," and also the French Academy; a rare distinction for a *savant*, and this is perhaps the best evidence that can be adduced of the high estimation in which his literary qualifications are held. M. Biot is a Commander of the Legion of Honour.

BISHOP, MADAME ANNA, an English vocalist, was born in London in 1815. Her musical taste having been early evidenced, she entered the Royal Academy of Music, and soon distinguished herself. She had at first intended to devote her attention to instrumental music, but being strongly urged by her professional friends, who had not failed to notice the superior voice she possessed, she resolved to study with the view of becoming a vocalist. Having made considerable progress, she sang as *prima donna* in 1838, at the Philharmonic Concerts, and at the Gloucester, Worcester, and other festivals. At first she had chiefly sung the productions of Handel, Mozart, and Beethoven; but eventually devoting herself to the Italian school, she appeared at the Royal Italian Opera House, at a concert given there. She subsequently travelled through most parts of continental Europe, and in every city achieved astonishing success. In 1839 she visited Copenhagen, and in 1840 Stockholm, where, notwithstanding the presence of Jenny Lind, Madame Bishop created a complete *furore*. She next visited St. Petersburg, where she achieved an equal success. Proceeding southwards, she afterwards appeared at Novogorod, at Kasam in Tartary, singing in the Tartar language, at Odessa, and, eventually reaching Vienna, added still further to her laurels. Returning through various German cities, she sang at Munich. In 1843 she visited Italy, and sang at Florence, Venice, &c., becoming *prima donna* at Naples, at the theatre of San Carlo. At Rome she undertook the *rôles* of 'Amina' in "La Sonnambula," and 'Lucia' in "Lucia di Lammermoor," where, as also at Palermo, she was received with great enthusiasm. She afterwards appeared at several concerts in England, and in 1846 went to America and visited the United States, Mexico, and California. In 1853 she left America for Sydney, and appeared also at Melbourne and Adelaide. South America was her next destination, and after singing in Valparaiso, &c., she returned to England in 1858. After singing at various concerts, she gave her farewell one on 17th of August, 1859, and shortly afterwards sailed for America. From the above imperfect sketch it will be observed that Madame Bishop has sung in every civilized part of the world, a feat unequalled by any other vocalist, and in the prosecution of which her success has been as constant as it has been deserved.

BLACK, ADAM, M.P., publisher of the "Encyclopædia Britannica," was born in Edinburgh, in the year 1784. After completing his education at the University of Edinburgh, he commenced business as a bookseller in 1807. Meeting with success in trade, he erected extensive premises at the North Bridge, which connects the old and new towns of Edinburgh, where his place of business has ever since remained. He is publisher of many important works; the chief of which, however, is the recent edition of the "Encyclopædia Britannica." For many years he was also publisher of the

"Edinburgh Review." More recently, he has bought the copyright of Sir Walter Scott's works, of which he has issued many well-known cheap editions. Mr. Black's connexion with the "Edinburgh Review" brought him into close contact with the most intelligent and influential members of the liberal party in Scotland; and for the last half century he may be said to have taken a lead in every agitation for burgh and parliamentary reform, which has met with the approval of moderate Liberals, and has distinguished himself by his cordial and indefatigable attention to the affairs of his native city. The highest municipal office, that of Lord Provost, was held by him from 1843 to 1848. As an acknowledgment of his unwearied public services the honour of knighthood was offered him, which, however, he declined. In 1856 he was elected by a large majority of his fellow-citizens as their representative in Parliament. Throughout his parliamentary career he has been a supporter of every practicable measure of social reform, especially of an extended and unsectarian system of education, and he has always been an uncompromising opponent to all intolerance in Church or State.

BLACKWELL, ELIZABETH, M.D., was born in Bristol, February 3, 1821. Her father emigrated with his family to the United States, where his death threw the latter on their own exertions for support. Having assisted her elder sister in bringing up the younger members of the family, she determined to devote her attention to medical studies. With this view she spent several years in accumulating, as a teacher, the necessary funds for the prosecution of her plans; during which period she studied Latin, and went through a preparatory course of medical and anatomical reading. Refused admission to twelve medical schools, she was at length received as a pupil at Geneva (N.Y.), where, in 1849, she passed her examination, and obtained the first medical degree ever conferred upon a woman. Having completed her medical studies in the hospitals of Paris and London, she settled in New York as a physician for women and children only. On revisiting England in 1859, she met with a cordial welcome; was admitted by registration to the right of practising medicine in this country, and delivered lectures on Hygiène to ladies in London, Birmingham, Manchester, and Liverpool. She has a very large practice in New York, where she has founded an hospital for female patients, and has published a book on "The Physical Education of Girls."

BLANC, LOUIS, a Frenchman of letters and publicist, was born at Madrid in 1813, in which city his father held the office of Inspector-General, under Joseph Bonaparte. By his mother's side he is descended from the Corsican family of Pozzi di' Borgo, of which the celebrated diplomatist of the same name was also a member. At the age of seventeen, immediately after the Revolution of 1830, and the accession of the House of Orleans to the throne, he returned to Paris, and connected himself with the "Bon Sens" newspaper; and by his contributions to that and other journals, speedily succeeded in acquiring for himself a high reputation as a political writer. He was the founder of the "Revue du Progrès," in the columns of which he first published his ideas upon industrial economics; a subject of peculiar interest to the working-classes of a country like France, in which there is no legislative provision, as in England, for the support of the poor when in distress, or when, from age and infirmity, they have become incapable of earning their subsistence. In the still more important work, by which he established his claim to the rank of an historian, "L'Histoire de Dix Ans," he gave a description of the corruption of

Louis-Philippe's government so vivid, that he did more than any other writer —M. de Lamartine excepted—to produce that electrical state of feeling in the public mind which exploded in the Revolution of 1848. When that event took place, the party known as that of the Social Democratic Republic, looking upon him as one of its most prominent leaders, saw with satisfaction that he had courage enough to accept the risks and responsibilities incurred by being a member of the Provisional Government. He subsequently undertook the office of President of the "Labour Commission," and thus gave the guarantee of his name and character to the working-classes, that their interests would not be neglected in the great revolutionary conflict of the time. He was elected as one of the representatives of the city of Paris, in the National Assembly of 1848, by 120,000 votes; and in that capacity brought forward and carried the famous motion for a repeal of the law by which the Bourbons, both of the elder and the younger branches, doomed the family of the Bonapartes to perpetual exclusion from the soil of France. Neither the author nor supporters of this motion foresaw the consequences that would result—consequences no less startling than the destruction of the Republic, which the Assembly were anxious to consolidate, and the re-establishment of the Napoleonic dynasty. The creation of the National Workshops, or *Ateliers Nationaux*, shortly after the Revolution, has been attributed to the influence of M. Louis Blanc. But this is quite a mistake. The principles on which they were established are directly at variance with all the ideas expounded in his work, the "Organisation du Travail." He protested against them most emphatically, both in his place at the councils of the Provisional Government as well as in the National Assembly. Their inevitable

dissolution led to the memorable insurrection of June, 1848, and the invasion of the National Assembly by an armed mob. After the insurrection had been quenched in blood, it was asserted that M. Louis Blanc had been a party to the attempt, and the new Government demanded authority for the Assembly to institute a prosecution against him. The Assembly declared by its vote, without any discussion, that there were no grounds for the prosecution, and the matter dropped. But amid the fearful excitement of that period, when "Socialism" had become the enemy which the whole of the influential and moneyed classes of France thought it their duty to denounce and combat, the charge was again brought forward. This time it met with more success. The Assembly recalled its previous vote, and leave was given for the prosecution. M. Louis Blanc immediately proceeded to the railway station, and made his way unmolested to England—a step which saved the Government from some difficulty if not danger, and for good reason, no effort was made to prevent his escape. M. Louis Blanc has ever since resided in England, and devoted himself to the peaceful pursuits of literature. He has published ten volumes of his "History of the French Revolution," and is still engaged upon that work. During his exile in this country, M. Blanc has thoroughly mastered the difficulties of the English language, and speaks and writes it with as much ease and elegance as his own. He first wrote in English his work entitled "Historical Revelations in answer to the Marquis of Normanby's 'A Year of Revolution in Paris,'" and translated it from English into French, for publication on the Continent. The most successful of M. Louis Blanc's works is his "History of the Last Ten Years," from 1830 to 1840, the publication of which was begun at Paris in 1841. The work, which consists of six volumes 8vo, has gone through a great number of editions.

BLANQUI, Louis Auguste, a French politician and *révolutionnaire*, was born at Paris in 1805. He is the younger brother of Jérome Adolphe Blanqui, the celebrated economist. In his youth he studied both law and medicine, and entered into all the political agitations occurring at the period of his student life, having for their object the entire reversal of existing political and social institutions. He was wounded in 1827, in the affair of the Rue St. Denis. He was a combatant on the barricades of 1830, and decorated for his services on that occasion. Taking an active part in the conspiracies and *émeutes* of the early part of Louis Philippe's reign, he was condemned to various terms of imprisonment, which it would be tedious to enumerate. The Provisional Government of the 24th February, 1848, had no sooner been installed, than M. Blanqui formed the Club of the Central Republican Society, which created great popular excitement at that period. The last revolutionary manifestation in which he was concerned was the attempt of the 15th of May, the failure of which led to his flight. Apprehended and tried by the Court at Bourges, he was condemned to ten years' imprisonment.

BOECKH, Augustus, a German philologist and classical scholar, was born in 1785, at Carlsruhe, in the Grand Duchy of Baden. He was educated at the University of Halle, and in the Teachers' Seminary at Berlin. Subsequently he became Professor of the Greek language in the University of Heidelberg, and, since 1811, in the University of Berlin. The works of this great scholar form an epoch in historical criticism, and in philology and archæology. The object of Philology should be, he maintains, to reproduce the whole political and social life of a people within a certain period. Although the views adopted by Professor Boeckh have been opposed by scholars of the old school, who fear that they will lead to a neglect of grammatical studies, they have had a most important influence on classical education in Germany. Professor Boeckh's principal philological and critical works are his edition of Pindar, consisting of the Greek texts, with various readings, a Latin translation, and notes; "Die Staatshaushaltung der Athener," translated into English by Sir George Cornewall Lewis, under the title of "The Public Economy of Athens;" and the "Corpus Inscriptionum Græcarum, auctoritate et impensis Academiæ Regiæ Borussiæ." Professor Boeckh is a member of most of the learned societies of Europe, and holds a high position amongst living philologists.

BOHN, Henry G., an eminent London publisher and bibliopole, was born in London, of German parents, in the year 1796. He is favourably known as the editor of the "Bibliotheca Parriana," and as a translator from the German. He has translated various works of Schiller, including "The Robbers;" compiled a "Handbook of Proverbs," and a "Polyglot of Foreign Proverbs," from the French, Italian, German, Dutch, Spanish, Portuguese, and Danish; also a "Handbook of Games," and numerous other works of merit, published in his popular libraries. He has edited Addison's works, and also a new and enlarged edition of Lowndes's "Bibliographer's Manual;" but his great work is his "Catalogue," published in 1841, which consists of 1,948 pages, and contains the titles of about 300,000 volumes. It is a literary lexicon on the most extensive scale, and admirable as a work of reference. Mr. Bohn has done great service to the reading public of this country by republishing cheap editions of books which, previous to his time, were confined to the

E

great libraries. He has shown great discrimination in selecting the works which form his Scientific, Illustrated, Classical, Antiquarian, Philologico-philosophical, Historical, and Ecclesiastical Libraries; his Library of the British Classics; and his Cheap Series, which form, altogether, nearly 1000 volumes. To Mr. Bohn is due the first cheap edition of the "Cosmos" of Humboldt; a work which has had a remarkable influence in widely spreading a taste for the natural sciences in this country. In 1850 he added a translation of the "Views of Nature," by the same author, the English edition being the joint work of Miss Otté and himself.

BONAPARTE, JÉROME, the youngest brother of Napoleon I., was born at Ajaccio, on the 15th of December, 1784. On Napoleon becoming First Consul, he removed Jérome, then fifteen years of age, from college, and placed him in the naval service. When hostilities broke out between France and England, in 1803, Jérome cruised off the West India Islands. Forced to quit that station without doing anything either brilliant or effective, he took refuge in New York. In the United States he married Miss Elizabeth Paterson. The marriage was a misalliance in the estimation of his brother, and Jérome's wife was forbidden to enter France. Under this interdict the daughter of the Baltimore merchant proceeded to England, where she gave birth to a son, Jérome Napoleon Bonaparte. Napoleon, on becoming Emperor, caused the marriage to be annulled by a decree of the Council of State. The Pope, however, refused to ratify the divorce. As Jérome made no figure at sea, Napoleon transferred him from the naval to the military service, and in 1807 he entered the army with the rank of general. In the same year he married Frédérique Catherine, daughter of the King of Wurtemberg. Some time after, Napoleon I. erected Westphalia into a kingdom, and created Jérome king. Compelled to abandon his territories on the abdication of Napoleon, he lived in exile until the return from Elba, when he repaired to Paris, and distinguished himself at Waterloo. After the final abdication of his brother, he lived chiefly at Trieste, where he purchased a palace, until Louis Napoleon became ruler of France. Jérome was then recalled to Paris, and the old man who had witnessed so many changes of fortune was created a Marshal of France, President of the Senate, and, in failure of the direct succession, heir to the Imperial throne. All parties concur in pronouncing him a most estimable gentleman, and if not the most fortunate yet the most amiable of his race.

BONAPARTE, LOUIS LUCIEN, second son of Lucien Bonaparte, was born in Worcestershire, January, 1813, during his father's residence in England. He passed his childhood in Rome and his youth in Florence. He visited Italy in 1854. Though travelling under every disguise that could secure privacy, he was recognised by his likeness to the Bonapartes, and met with an enthusiastic reception. The science of chemistry has much engaged his attention, and he has written several works on the subject. On the establishment of the Empire he was made a member of the Senate of France. Of late years he has been busily employed in translating the Parable of the Sower from St. Matthew into seventy-two European languages and dialects. He has also translated portions of the Old and New Testaments into the various dialects of the north of England. It is understood that he contemplates giving a version of the Holy Scriptures in every dialect spoken in England; a work certainly of immense labour, and requiring no ordinary philological discernment.

BONAPARTE, NAPOLEON JOSEPH CHARLES PAUL, second and only surviving son of Jérome Bonaparte by his second wife, was born at Trieste, 9th of September, 1822. He passed his earlier days alternately at Vienna, Florence, and Rome, and occasionally in Switzerland and America. Elected a member of the Legislative Assembly in 1850, Prince Napoleon, supporting the Red Republic and Ultra-democratic opinions, was known as the "Prince Montagne." The elevation of Napoleon III., however, to the throne made Prince Napoleon a devoted adherent of the imperial policy. During the Russian war in 1854 he held a command in the Crimea, but did not gain any distinction, although present at the Alma. He married, in 1859, the Princess Clotilde, daughter of the King of Sardinia, in pursuance, it was supposed at the time, of a design upon the throne of Tuscany or of Central Italy, to be brought to completion by the war against Austria for the liberation of Italy. At the head of a division of the French army, the Prince landed in Italy to co-operate with the forces of his imperial cousin and his royal father-in-law, but no opportunity presented itself for his being of service; and the sudden peace declared at Villafranca forbade his indulging in further hopes of military glory. The Prince is understood to be a warm friend of the English alliance, and a staunch Free-trader.

BONHEUR, MADEMOISELLE ROSA, a French animal painter, was born at Bordeaux, 22nd March, 1822. She experienced considerable advantage in being the daughter of a French artist of some note, and from this circumstance her intense devotion to art may have arisen. She was in a great measure self-taught. At first she had few opportunities of studying from life the animals to the painting of which she specially devoted her attention. Her enthusiasm, however, was so strong that she has even repaired to the slaughter-houses of Paris in search of

subjects for her pencil. Her earliest productions were "Goats and Sheep," and "Two Rabbits"—paintings which attracted considerable attention; and from that time she advanced rapidly in public estimation, her position, however, not being attained without severe study and indefatigable labour. Her first great work, that which at once settled her position as the French female Landseer, was the "Labourage Nivernais," finished in 1849, and now in the Luxembourg. "The Horse Fair" is known over the world by engravings, and stamps her as among the foremost animal painters of this or any other age. Her subsequent productions, although of great merit, have not surpassed in their execution and finish this splendid painting. Since 1849 she has been directress of the Free School of Design for females at Paris.

BOPP, FRANZ, a German philologist, was born on the 14th September, 1791, at Mayence, in the Grand Duchy of Hesse-Darmstadt. He studied at Aschaffenburg, where he formed an intimacy with Professor Windischmann, a learned Sanscrit scholar, who held the chair of philosophy and history in the University, and eventually Bopp determined to devote himself to the literature of the East. Having obtained a small pension from the Bavarian Government, he went, in 1812, to Paris, where, under the great French orientalists, Chezy Silvestre de Sacy and Auguste Guillaume Schlegel, he pursued for some years a course of severe study. He proceeded from Paris to London, where he continued his studies. After his return to Germany he was appointed Sanscrit Professor at Berlin. The labours of Bopp form an epoch in the linguistic researches which have been prosecuted with so much success in our times. His great work, which indeed is the standard treatise on the subject of which it treats, is the "Comparative Grammar of the

Sanscrit, Zenod, Greek, Latin, Lithuanian, ancient Slavic, Gothic, and German languages." A second edition was published at Berlin in 1857. It is the most important contribution which has been made in our times to the science of comparative philology, which is indebted very much for its rapid growth to this clear summary of its principles. Professor Bopp is the author of several editions and translations of the old Indian poems; of important works on Sanscrit grammar; on the Celtic languages (1849); on the connexion between the Malay-Polynesian and the Indo-Germanic languages; and on the Caucasian members of the Indo-Germanic languages.

BORROW, GEORGE, an English author, was born near Norwich in 1803. His early education seems to have included a period of study at the University of Edinburgh. His father, as an officer in the army, was obliged to move about a good deal, and that may have given rise to those wandering habits, that love of adventure, and predilection for the study of languages to which we are indebted for some of the most agreeable accessions to our literature. He made himself familiar, when but a youth, with the habits, customs, manners, and dialects of the gipsy tribes who roamed through England. Leaving this country, he travelled in France and Spain—almost over the entire Continent,—associating with the gipsies as with familiar friends. The result was his first work, "The Zincali," which gave lively and faithful descriptions of the Spanish gipsies, with a collection of their songs and poetry, and a dictionary of their language. This was new ground, broken for the first time in 1841. The work became instantly popular, for it was fresh in subject and style. The Bible Society of London, discovering that he had a fitness for the task, despatched him shortly afterwards on a mission to distribute the Bible, printed in the Spanish language, wherever opportunity arose, in the Peninsula. He undertook the mission, and on his return in 1843, published his "Bible in Spain," wherein he recounts his adventures, his journeys, and his imprisonment,—the latter being the cause of a misunderstanding so serious between this and the Spanish Government as to nearly produce a rupture. His "Bible in Spain" was followed by "Lavengro," a work partly autobiographical and partly imaginative. He is a considerable landed proprietor in the county of Suffolk, but spends much, if not all his time, in rambling through foreign countries on foot. He was from his youth upwards a determined pedestrian, having, in 1825, walked from London to Norwich, a distance of 112 miles, in about twenty-seven hours. He has written several works which have not yet been committed to the press, amongst others one called " Wild Wales," said to be in many respects a counterpart of the " Bible in Spain."

BOSQUET, PIERRE FRANÇOIS JOSEPH, a French Marshal, was born at Mont-de-Marsan, Landes, 8th November, 1810. He entered the École Polytechnique in 1829, from which he passed to the École d'Application, at Metz, in 1831, becoming a sub-lieutenant of Artillery in 1833, and in 1835 he went with his regiment, the 10th Artillery, to Algeria, where he served until 1853. During that period his promotion was rapid, and after passing through various grades he was appointed colonel in 1848. In May, 1843, he distinguished himself, at the head of his corps, in a "razzia" against one of the Arab tribes. He was more than once wounded. Raised to the rank of general of division in 1854, he accompanied the French army to the Crimea, where, at Balaclava and Inkermann especially, his gallantry and military skill were conspicuous, acquiring for him the highest character for courage and military daring. In 1856 he was named Senator, and soon after received the highest honour that can be conferred on a French soldier—the *bâton* of a Marshal of France. He has received from the Queen the Order of the Bath; and the Emperor conferred on him the Grand Cross of the Legion of Honour, in acknowledgment of his valuable services.

BOSWORTH, JOSEPH, D.D., LL.D., F.R.S., an Anglo-Saxon scholar and Professor at Oxford, was born in Derbyshire in 1788. He studied at the University of Aberdeen, passing the examination for, and obtaining the degree of Master of Arts. He was ordained a clergyman of the Church of England; and that he might be enabled to fulfil the duties of his position efficiently, in addition to Latin and Greek, he at an early age acquired a knowledge of Hebrew, with its cognate dialects, Chaldee, Syriac, and Arabic. His success was soon acknowledged by various honours conferred on him by the Universities of Cambridge and Oxford, and he received the diploma of Ph.D. from Leyden. In 1857 he received the degree of D.D. from Christ Church, Oxford. Besides two Anglo-Saxon Dictionaries and three Grammars, he is the author of works entitled the "Origin of the Danish Language" (1834); "Origin of the English, Germanic, and Scandinavian Languages and Nations" (1836); an "Abstract of Scandinavian Literature;" "Origin of the Dutch, with a Sketch of their Language and Literature." He is editor of "King Alfred's Anglo-Saxon version of the Compendious History of the World, by Orosius, with an English translation," and a "Description of Europe, and the Voyages of Othere and Wulfstan," written in Anglo-Saxon by King Alfred the Great. An edition of King Alfred's works in Anglo-Saxon and Latin; and the Gospels in the version of Wycliffe, of the Anglo-Saxons, and of the Mæso-Goths, in parallel columns, have engaged

his attention. He is a member of the principal literary and scientific societies of England and the Continent.

BOTFIELD, BERIAH, M.P., F.R.S., F.S.A., an English author and man of science, is son of the late Beriah Botfield, Esq. of Norton Hall, Northamptonshire. He was born at Earl's Ditton, Salop, in 1807, and received his education first at Harrow and then at Christ Church, Oxford, where he graduated Bachelor of Arts in 1828, in 1847 taking the degree of Master of Arts. He entered Parliament, as representative for Ludlow, in May, 1840, and continued to sit for that borough until 1847, being again elected in 1857. Mr. Botfield has written a "Tour in Scotland," privately printed, and "Notes on the Cathedral Libraries of England," published in 1849, besides contributing various papers to the learned societies of which he is a member. The politics of Mr. Botfield are Moderate Conservative.

BOTTA, PAUL EMILIE, a French traveller and archæologist, was born in 1805. He is son of an eminent historian of the same name. After studying medicine, he made a voyage round the world in the capacity of surgeon. Between 1830 and 1833, as physician to Mehemet Ali, he visited Sennaar and other parts of Egypt. On his return to France he was appointed French Consul at Alexandria, and afterwards, on settling on the banks of the Tigris at Mosul, having learned that a mound in the vicinity was supposed to cover part of the seat of ancient Nineveh, he commenced excavating, but obtaining no great success he next examined a similar mound at Khorsabad, and there he commenced operations anew. In this instance his hopes were realized, for ultimately he had the gratification of laying open the apartments of an Assyrian palace, thus opening up the way to discoveries which have since been followed up with so much success by Mr.

Layard and others. Sculptures and other objects of interest removed from the edifice were transferred to the Assyrian Museum in Paris; thanks to the cordiality with which the French authorities seconded M. Botta's labours. In 1857 he was appointed Consul-General at Tripoli. He has published a "Narrative of a Journey to Yemen, undertaken in 1837, for the Museum of Natural History at Paris;" a work entitled, "The Monuments of Nineveh, discovered and described by M. P. E. Botta, and measured and sketched by M. E. Flaudin" (1849, 1850); and an abstract from the same work, named "Inscriptions Discovered at Khorsabad" (1848).

BOURQUENEY, François Adolphe, Comte de, a French diplomatist, was born at Paris in 1800. He entered on his diplomatic career under the Restoration. He was attached to the French embassy at London in 1822, with M. de Châteaubriand, and was afterwards Secretary of Legation at Berne. Employed on the editorial department of the "Débats" (under the direction of M. de Châteaubriand), he became a Councillor of State. After the Revolution of 1830 he was successively Secretary and Chargé d'Affaires to the French Embassy in London, under M. Guizot. He was afterwards appointed Ambassador at Constantinople. At the Conferences of Vienna, in 1854, he insisted on the "four guarantees" as necessary conditions of peace. He was next accredited as Ambassador to Vienna in 1856, after having taken part, as French Plenipotentiary, in the Congress of Paris. After the signature of the Treaty of Zurich, where he represented France, he retired from the public service of the state, and took his seat in the Senate.

BOUSSINGAULT, Jean Baptiste, a French chemist and agriculturist, and a member of the Institute, was born at Paris on the 2nd of February, 1802.

He became a pupil at the Mining School of St. Etienne, and gave indications there of his intelligence and laborious disposition. Having received an offer from an English company to go to South America, for the purpose of retracing old mines which had been left unworked for many years, he at once decided on accepting it, and proceeded to his destination. His extensive powers of observation were thus called into exercise; and in 1821 he was appointed Professor of Metallurgy at Bogota, in South America. The revolution in the Spanish colonies compelled him, for a time at least, to enter the military profession as an engineer, with the rank of Lieutenant-Colonel, on the staff of General Bolivar. In 1826 he was appointed Superintendent of Mines in New Grenada, and while holding this situation he prosecuted several important scientific investigations. His geological and geographical observations, his excursions to the volcanoes of Ecuador, and his exploration of Chimborazo, which he ascended to the height of 19,700 English feet, with the view of studying the law of the decrease of temperature in the higher regions of the atmosphere, attracted the notice of European men of science, and more particularly of Humboldt and Arago. On his return to France in 1833 he was named Dean of the Faculty of Sciences, at Lyons, and subsequently appointed to the Chair of Agriculture at the Conservatoire des Arts et Métiers, at Paris. He has devoted himself, with great energy and success, to the study of science in its application to agriculture, more especially in reference to the economical production of food for cattle, and his observations on this subject have been published in the "Annales de Physique et de Chimie," and in the "Comptes Rendus" of the Academy of Sciences. He has also published various works, the chief of which is a "Treatise on

Rural Economy." He has been a member of the National Assembly and the Council of State. He is a Commander of the Legion of Honour. He has, however, entirely withdrawn himself of late from political affairs, and has given himself to the pursuit of scientific research.

BOWRING, SIR JOHN, an English writer and colonial governor, was born on 17th October, 1792, at Exeter, where his father was engaged in the woollen trade. Belonging to a family of Dissenters, he early contended, both through the press and on the platform, against the laws which excluded from political authority persons holding similar religious principles. This did not prevent him from turning his attention to matters of more enduring interest. Trade, economics, literature, and languages engaged his intellect, until his qualifications as a linguist were recognised throughout Europe, not less, if not more, than his knowledge of commerce, extensive though that was. He became conversant with many modern living tongues, and, so to speak, "excavated" the literary treasures hidden in many of the nearly-forgotten dialects of Europe. The University of Groningen showed its appreciation of his acquirements by conferring on him the degree of LL.D. One of his earliest literary productions was published between 1821 and 1823, entitled "Specimens of the Russian Poets;" in 1824, "Bavarian Anthology;" "Ancient Poetry and Romances of Spain;" in 1827, "Specimens of the Polish Poets," and "Servian Popular Songs;" in 1830, "Poetry of the Magyars;" and in 1832, "Cheskian Anthology." His comprehensive views of commerce led, under various governments, beginning with that of Earl Grey, to his employment as a Commercial Commissioner to other countries. In that capacity he visited France, Italy, the states of the Zollverein, and the Levant. At this period of his career he drew up several reports of the highest merit, published as Government Blue-Books, among which the chief are: "On the Commercial Relations between France and England" (1834 and 1835); "On the Commerce and Manufactures of Switzerland" (1836); "On Egypt, Candia, and Syria" (1840); and "On the Prussian Commercial Union" (1840). He was appointed Secretary to the Commissioners of Public Accounts by Earl Grey, and from 1835 to 1837, and from 1841 to 1849, he sat in parliament. When the treaty of Sir Henry Pottinger had opened to our trade the five principal ports of China, and gave us a footing on the seaboard, Dr. Bowring was nominated British Consul at Canton in 1841, and afterwards Chief Superintendent of Trade in China, and Plenipotentiary to the Court of Pekin. Having performed his duties satisfactorily, he returned to England in 1853, was knighted, and appointed Governor of Hong-Kong and its dependencies, with the chief control of the naval and military power. In 1855 he visited Siam, concluded a treaty with the two kings of that country, and returned to his governmental post. About two years afterwards a serious matter occurred, which led to the nomination of Lord Elgin as Ambassador Extraordinary, without, however, displacing Sir John Bowring. By an ordinance of the Legislative Council of Hong-Kong, which had been confirmed by the Queen's authority, certain colonial vessels were recognised by licence as of British ownership, and, consequently, were entitled to the privileges of the treaties with China. In defiance of this ordinance, a lorcha, designated the "Arrow," which had been sailing under the Hong-Kong licence, was boarded by the Chinese authorities, who seized the whole of the crew. Protesting, but not obtaining any redress, Sir John referred the question to the British Admiral, who resorted to strong measures to enforce obedience to the treaties; but, owing to the small force at his disposal, failed to obtain satisfaction. It was said that the licence of the "Arrow" had expired; but such an averment was not put forward by the Chinese authorities, who stated she did not at the time carry British colours, and was amenable, as a Chinese vessel, to the law of China. Sir John Bowring was accused of wanton and barbarous conduct in bombarding Canton. Be these matters as they may, Sir John returned from his post in 1859. The most important of his recent works are, "The Kingdom of Siam and its People," which was published in 1857; and "A Visit to the Philippines," in 1857-8. At the meeting of the British Association at Aberdeen, last year, Sir John Bowring read a paper on the Opium Trade, which attracted much attention.

BRANDE, WILLIAM THOMAS, an English chemist, was born in London in 1788. Having received his early education at a school in Kensington, he afterwards proceeded to Westminster School, where his abilities soon gained him the respect of his tutors. After travelling on the Continent, he entered St. George's Hospital as a medical pupil. He here evidenced that devotion to chemistry which has since made him so eminent as a man of science. In 1809 he was chosen a fellow of the Royal Society, and became, in 1816, the secretary of that learned body. About this time Mr. Brande had become highly popular as a lecturer on chemistry, and through his scientific attainments obtained a post in the Mint in 1825. Connected with various scientific societies, both in England and abroad, he had the honour of D.C.L. of Oxford conferred on him at the time that Lord Derby was chosen Chancellor of that University. His fame as an author rests on two elaborate and masterly productions, his "Manual of Chemistry," and his "Dictionary of Science, Literature, and Art,"—works which rank at the present time among the best authorities on the subjects of which they treat.

BRAVO-MURILLO, JUAN, a Spanish statesman, was born at Frejenal de la Sierra, in the province of Badajoz, ou the 8th of June, 1803. Destined for the church, he studied theology at Seville and Salamanca. Abandoning theology, however, he became a student of law, and, in 1825, entered the College of Advocates of Seville, filling at the same time the chair of philosophy in the university of that city. His great oratorical powers soon gave him celebrity, and he was appointed Attorney-General at Caceres, in the province of Estramadura. This official position was held by him until the beginning of 1836, when, for various reasons, he proceeded to Madrid, and became the chief editor, in concert with Pacheco and Perez Hernandez, of the "Bulletin of Jurisprudence." In 1837 he was elected to the Cortes, and in 1838 he was twice offered the post of Minister of Justice, once by the Count of Ofalia, and again by the Duke of Frias, which, however, he did not accept. When the Cortes was dissolved, he established the "Porvenir" newspaper, in which he renewed his attacks on the Government, as he did afterwards in the "Pilot," and had done before in several other newspapers. He became involved in political affairs in 1840, was arrested, but escaped by some means, and at last fled to Paris. He afterwards returned to Madrid; and in 1843 he was appointed, by the Lopez Cabinet, member of a commission which was formed for the compilation of a code, and of which he became afterwards the president, fulfilling this charge gratuitously for a long time. In 1847 he became Minister of Justice. In the same year General Narvaez, Duke of Valencia, being at the head of affairs, he was appointed Minister of Commerce, and fulfilled this charge until August,

1849, when he passed to the Ministry of Finance, the Duke of Valencia being still President, until November, 1850, when he resigned. Two months after, in January, 1851, on the fall of Narvaez, he was charged with the formation of a new cabinet, and was appointed President and Minister of Finance; he discharged the duties of both of these offices, worked a great deal in Finance, and made the arrangement of the Spanish debt by the law of August, 1851. On the 14th of December, 1852, he resigned his office, and the counter-revolutionary measures of his successors resulting in the insurrection of 1854, obliged him to quit Spain, Espartero and O'Donnell being then at the head of affairs. He was recalled in 1856, and elected member of the Cortes and President of the Chamber of Deputies in the legislature of 1858. This Cortes was dissolved by the cabinet, O'Donnell calling another, in which he decided to take no part. He has since retired from public life.

BRAY, Mrs. ANNA ELIZA, an English authoress, daughter of the late John Kempe, Esq., was born in the county of Surrey, towards the end of last century. She was married in 1818 to Charles Stothard, author of "The Monumental Effigies of Great Britain," son of the eminent painter. Her first work, illustrated by her husband, was "Letters from Normandy and Brittany," published in 1820. In the following year Mr. C. Stothard was accidentally killed, and she published a memoir of his life. She subsequently married the late Rev. Edward A. Bray, vicar of Tavistock. From that period she has produced, in quick succession, "De Foix," a romance of the 14th century; "The White Hoods;" "The Protestant;" "Fitz of Fitzford;" "The Talba;" "Warleigh, or the Fatal Oak;" "Trelawny;" "Trials of the Heart;" "Henry de Pomeroy;" "Courtenay of Walreddon;"

"Trials of Domestic Life;" "Borders of the Tamar and the Tavy," in letters to the late Robert Southey, poet laureate; "The Mountains and Lakes of Switzerland;" "A Peep at the Pixies;" "Life of Thomas Stothard, R.A.;" "Sketch of the Life of Handel," &c., &c. Her style is graceful, and her works are alike remarkable for sound morality and interesting narration.

BREMER, MISS FREDRIKA, a Swedish novelist and poet, was born in 1802, at Abo, in Finland. At the time that Finland was ceded to Russia she was three years old. Her father then sold his estate and removed to Sweden, where she resided with her family, sometimes at Stockholm and sometimes at Asta, a property which her father had purchased, three miles from the capital. When eighteen years of age, Miss Bremer began to compose verses in Swedish, but it was not till a much later period in life that she committed any important production to the press. In 1828 she published at Stockholm the first volume of her "Pictures of Everyday Life." They were succeeded by a new collection of the same kind, published between 1844 and 1848. The striking descriptions of modern Scandinavian life contained in these works obtained for them a wide circulation in Germany, and subsequently in France and England, and even in Italy and Holland, they having been translated into the languages of all these countries. In 1831 she obtained the gold medal of the Academy of Stockholm. Miss Bremer, shortly after publishing two books, giving an account of tours in Sweden and Norway, undertook, in 1849, a journey to America. The letters which she wrote to her sister during her stay in the United States and in the island of Cuba, from October, 1849, to September, 1851, were published at Stockholm, London, and New York, in 1853-4, in 3 volumes 8vo, under the title of "Homes of the New World." In this work she gives a very interesting account of the manners and institutions of our Transatlantic cousins, who seem to have accorded to her a very warm and flattering reception. On her way home to Sweden she stayed for some time in England. She is at present engaged in carrying out philanthropic schemes connected with the education and elevation of children of the poorer classes. In 1842 Mrs. Howitt first introduced her to the literary world of Great Britain by a translation of "The Neighbours," which, on account of its vivid delineations of domestic life in Sweden, at once found favour. "The Home" followed, and afterwards appeared in English "The Diary," "The H. Family," "The Midnight Sun," "The President's Daughter," "Nina," and "Brothers and Sisters."

BREWSTER, SIR DAVID, M.A., LL.D., K.H.; a physicist and author, Principal of the University of Edinburgh, was born at Jedburgh, in Scotland, on the 11th December, 1781. He was educated for the Church of Scotland, and admitted a licentiate, but a decided bias led him to the study of natural science. In 1800 he obtained the degree of M.A. at the University of Edinburgh. Taking up his abode in the Scottish capital, he commenced his researches and experiments in physical science, meantime studying under Robison, Playfair, and Dugald Stewart, then Professors in the University. Having made important discoveries regarding some properties of light, he received, in 1807, the honorary degree of LL.D. from the University of Aberdeen, and in 1808 was elected a Fellow of the Royal Society of Edinburgh. He became editor of the "Edinburgh Encyclopædia," a great work, which employed many years of his life, and of which he remained editor till its completion in 1830. The attention of Dr. Brewster was more especially directed to optics, a science in which many of his discoveries have been of the highest scientific and practical value. In 1813 appeared his "Treatise on New Philosophical Instruments," in which, and in various papers and essays, he gave publicity to discoveries on the refraction, dispersion, and polarization of light, which placed him in the first rank of contemporary inquirers in physical science. In 1815 Dr. Brewster was awarded the Copley medal, by the Royal Society of London, in recognition of the value of his optical researches, and in the same year that learned body elected him a Fellow. In 1816 the French Institute decreed him 1,500 francs, being one-half of their prize for the most important discoveries in physics made in any part of the world during the two preceding years. About the same time he invented the kaleidoscope, on which he published a treatise in 1819, and in 1818 the Royal Society awarded him the Rumford gold and silver medals for his "Discoveries on the Polarization of Light." In 1819 he commenced, with Professor Jameson, "The Edinburgh Philosophical Journal," and in 1824, as sole editor, "The Edinburgh Journal of Science," of which twenty volumes were published, —these periodicals being the first established in Scotland devoted to scientific subjects. In 1821 he founded the Scottish Society of Arts, which was incorporated by Royal Charter in 1841. In 1825 the French Institute elected him a corresponding member, and he received the same honour from other continental scientific societies. He originally suggested the formation of, and, indeed, may be said to have founded, the "British Association for the Advancement of Science," which has since proved so successful in forwarding the objects for which it was intended. So early as 1811, Sir David Brewster had thrown out the suggestion that a powerful lens

might be constructed of zones of glass built up out of several circular segments, and had recommended the adoption of the instrument, as a means of brilliant illumination, to the Scottish Lighthouse Board. It was shown that by the use of this invention, the navigation of our coast would be freed from many of its dangers. The plan was not, however, adopted, until Sir David Brewster had published, in 1826, his "Account of a New System for the Illumination of Lighthouses," and urged its adoption in the "Edinburgh Review," and had obtained a parliamentary committee for inquiry into the management of our British Lighthouses. At last, however, the dioptric system, his invention, was introduced in 1825 into the Scottish lighthouses, and afterwards into those of England and Ireland. It is now in general use in our colonies, and in every part of the world. Sir David Brewster is also the inventor of the lenticular stereoscope, now to be found in every household throughout the whole civilized world. He was elevated to the dignity of knighthood in 1832 by King William IV., an honour well won and justly conferred. In 1831 he received the decoration of the Hanoverian Guelphic order. He is now Vice-President of the Royal Society of Edinburgh, having twice obtained its medals and long been its secretary. In 1833 he received the degree of D.C.L. from Oxford, and afterwards from the University of Durham. He is also an officer of the Legion of Honour, and in 1849, on the death of Berzelius, was chosen one of the eight Foreign Associates of the Paris Academy of Sciences. He is a Chevalier of the Prussian Order of Merit, a Fellow of the Astronomical and Geological Societies, and a Member of the Royal Irish Academy. In 1838 Sir David Brewster was appointed Principal of the United Colleges of St. Salvator and St. Leonard's, in the University of St. Andrews, a position which he retained until 1859, when he was invited to assume the duties of Principal of the Edinburgh University. He holds that office at present, enjoying at the same time a pension of £300 per annum from the Crown. Sir David has written extensively on scientific subjects. His principal works are a "Treatise on New Philosophical Instruments," published in 1813; "Memoirs of the Life, Writings, and Discoveries of Sir Isaac Newton;" separate Treatises on the "Kaleidoscope" and "Stereoscope;" "The Martyrs of Science;" "More Worlds than One;" and "Letters on Natural Magic." He is also the author of numerous articles in the "Edinburgh Review," the "Quarterly Review," and the "North British Review;" his contributions embracing a wide range of subjects, scientific and literary, and attesting the versatility of his talents and the variety of his accomplishments. To the "North British Review," in particular, he has contributed a series of articles, one of which will be found in almost every number of that periodical. The subjects are generally connected with astronomy, physics, optics, geology, and physical geography; but they treat of many purely literary and historical topics, in no way connected with science, and all are remarkable for elegance of diction. At the disruption of the Scottish Church, Sir David Brewster joined the Free Church; he has been uniformly a liberal in politics.

BRIGHT, JOHN, an English orator and statesman, was born at Greenbank, Rochdale, in Lancashire, on the 16th of November, 1811. He is the second son of the late Jacob Bright, a cotton-spinner and manufacturer at Rochdale. Having received an ordinary school education, he was transferred, at the age of fifteen, to his father's office, to be initiated into the detail and management of the business, which, in default of his elder brother, who died young, he was destined to inherit. In 1835 he spent some months on the Continent, and extended his travels as far as Egypt and Palestine; thus helping to complete an education which circumstances had somewhat restricted. In 1838, when the famous Anti-Corn-Law Association of Manchester was formed, Mr. Bright became one of its council; and when in the following year the agitation assumed larger proportions, and grew into the Anti-Corn-Law League, the public career of Mr. Bright received its final determination. He became intimately associated with Mr. Cobden and the other leading spirits of the most powerful political organization of our time, and by the force of his genius, perseverance, and eloquence, shook the ancient citadel of monopoly till it tottered to its fall. While Mr. Cobden lent his calm and unanswerable logic to the cause, Mr. Bright gave it the impetus of zeal and passion. The one sapped the foundations of economic error, the other battered at its walls. The one convinced his opponents, the other carried them away captive; and both rendered such efficient service as to make it difficult to say which was the most useful or the most powerful. The organization of the Anti-Corn-Law League was remarkably adapted to accomplish the object in view. Public meetings were held in every part of the country; newspapers were established in the interest of the agitation; wherever there was a chance of success, the country was deluged with pamphlets; eminent men entered the ranks, but towering high above them all were the names of Cobden and Bright. The speeches of Mr. Bright were of the most effective description, and thoroughly English in tone as well as phraseology. Powerful, impassioned, and convincing, he so carried his auditors with him, that even those who opposed his politics were com-

pelled to admire his genius. But the oratory of the platform, however useful, is of comparatively little influence unless its echo be heard in Parliament. The League was always aware of this fact, and lost no opportunity to find and make an opening for the admission of its most prominent members into the House of Commons. In 1841 Mr Cobden was returned for Stockport, and in April, 1843, a vacancy having occurred, Mr. Bright contested the city of Durham; but the influence brought against him was too strong, and he was defeated. Not deterred by the failure, his opponent, Lord Dungannon, having been unseated for bribery, he contested the city a second time, in the month of July, in the same year, and was successful. His general political profession was that of a Radical and Free-Trade Reformer— attached to no party, but willing to support either Whigs or Tories, if their measures were such as he could approve, and founded upon the wants of the country and the rights of the people. Mr. Bright, although the repeal of the Corn Laws was the one leading object of his political life, found time to originate and support the appointment of two select committees of the House of Commons. The first of these was a committee on the Game Laws, appointed in 1845. The evidence which it procured was printed in the usual Blue-Book form in 1846. The same year, through the instrumentality of Mr. Bright, an abridgment of this evidence was published in a volume more suited for general circulation, and containing, from his pen, an "Address to the Tenant Farmers of Great Britain," strongly condemning the existing Game Laws. The other committee was on the subject of cotton cultivation in India; and the bulky volume containing the evidence taken by it has been often since referred to in discussions on this question. On this point Mr. Bright has always been well informed; and it was chiefly through his instrumentality that the late Mr. Alexander Mackay was despatched to India, at the expense of some of the leading manufacturers of Manchester, to report upon the causes, fiscal, natural, or political, which prevented and impeded the cultivation of cotton in such quantities as to render this country less dependent upon the Southern States of the American Union. Mr. Bright continued to represent the city of Durham until the repeal of the Corn Laws, and the consequent final establishment of Free-trade principles as the policy of the British Empire. After the repeal of the Corn Laws, and the ministerial crisis that followed the break up of the Conservative party by the defection, or self-sacrifice, of Sir Robert Peel, Mr. Mark Philips, a Liberal and Free Trader, who had shared with Mr. Milner Gibson the representation of Manchester, announced his intention of retiring from parliamentary life. After some discussion, involving the claims of Mr. Cobden (who refused to stand), and an invitation to Lord Lincoln, now the Duke of Newcastle, who withdrew, however, before the poll was taken, Mr. Bright became a candidate for the city of Manchester. Although many were opposed to his claims, their opposition was fruitless, and the party of Free Trade, aided by the Ultra Liberals, carried his election triumphantly. During the interval between his election for Manchester and the accession of the first Derby Ministry to power, Mr. Bright's activity in Parliament and on the platform was varied and continuous. In the House of Commons he proposed to apply the remedy of free trade in land to the state of things which produced the Irish famine. He appealed, unsuccessfully, for the despatch of a royal commission to investigate the condition of India; and in

1849 he was appointed one of the members of the Select Committee of the House of Commons on official salaries. At Westminster, and still more in the provinces, especially at Manchester, he co-operated with Mr. Cobden in the movement which the latter sought to create in favour of Financial Reform, mainly with a view to the reduction of our naval and military establishments. In 1851 he added his vote to those who attempted to censure Lord Palmerston for his conduct towards the Government of Greece in the matter of the claims of Don Pacifico, a British subject; and in 1852 he took a prominent part in the welcome given to Kossuth by the Liberals of Manchester. On the formation of the first Derby Ministry, Mr. Bright aided in that temporary re-organization of the Anti-Corn-Law League which the acceptance of Free Trade by the new Government afterwards rendered unnecessary. At the general election which followed, the return of Mr. Bright, as well as of Mr. Gibson, for Manchester, was opposed. But the principle of Free Trade was supposed to be once more at stake, and Mr. Bright, with Mr. Gibson, were re-elected by a considerable majority. Soon after the accession to power of the Aberdeen Ministry, the Emperor of the French, then newly elected to the throne, began to develop designs upon the custody of the Holy Places in Syria, which alarmed the jealousy of the late Emperor Nicholas, and led to the mission of Prince Menschikoff to Constantinople to insist upon concessions to Russia, as the head of the Greek Church, which the Ottoman Porte could not with safety or with dignity agree to. The Porte being supported in its resistance by the Government, the people, and the Press of Great Britain, the Emperor of the French saw that he had made a mistake, and withdrew from a false position. Not so the Emperor of Russia: persisting in his claims, and being encouraged in the belief that under no circumstance whatever would the people of Great Britain consent to undertake a war to support the independence of Turkey, or of any other state—he marched his armies across the Pruth. The result was the immediate alliance of England and France, who were afterwards joined by Sardinia, in support of the rights of the Sultan and the integrity of the Turkish empire. Mr. Bright and his political friends protested against the war, but his health having become impaired, partly from over-work in the service of the public, he was ordered by his physician to seek change of scene in foreign travel. In the spring of 1857, during his absence from Parliament, Mr. Cobden proposed and carried a vote of censure on the Government of Lord Palmerston, for the origin and conduct of the Chinese war that arose out of the quarrel incident to the capture of the lorcha "Arrow," in the waters of Canton. This vote led to a dissolution of Parliament, and at the election for Manchester which ensued, Mr. Bright lost his seat. In the autumn of the same year, the death of Mr. Muntz caused a vacancy in the representation of Birmingham. Mr. Bright having been invited to offer himself as a candidate, was unanimously elected, and took his seat once more in the House of Commons, amid the general acclamation of the country, who valued his honesty too highly to see him without regret discarded from Parliament. He supported, but did not speak on the motion of Mr. Milner Gibson, hostile to the second reading of the Conspiracy Bill, brought in to satisfy the jealous fears of the French Government, and the result of which was the overthrow of Lord Palmerston's Government. During the remainder of the session he spoke occasionally, especially on the subject of India, and with every evidence of a

complete restoration to health. In the autumn and winter of 1858-9, Mr. Bright made a tour of the provinces, and published an elaborate scheme of change in our representative system. Although dissatisfied with the moderate liberalism of the Palmerston-Russell administration he has generally supported that ministry, and gave in his adhesion to the Reform Bill unsuccessfully introduced by Lord John Russell in the session of 1860.

BRODIE, SIR BENJAMIN COLLINS, BART., D.C.L., an English surgeon, was born in 1783, at Winterslow, Wiltshire. His professional education was received at an anatomical school in London, and at St. George's Hospital, as a pupil of Sir Everard Home. After having delivered lectures on anatomy (in conjunction with Mr. Wilson) and on surgery, he was, in 1808, elected assistant-surgeon to St. George's Hospital, and eventually surgeon. He was chosen a fellow of the Royal Society in 1810, having contributed a paper to the "Philosophical Transactions," on the circulation of the blood in a foetus without a heart, during the previous year. In 1811 he received the Copley Medal for papers published in the "Transactions." These contributions treated of the influence of the brain on the action of the heart, the generation of animal heat, the modes by which death is produced by vegetable poisons, and other physiological problems. In 1814 he published an account of his experiments and observations on the influence of certain nerves on the secretions of the stomach. Dr. Brodie then rose gradually in reputation, and in 1832 was appointed Sergeant-Surgeon to Queen Adelaide. In 1834 he was created a baronet, and in 1850 he received the degree of D.C.L. from the University of Oxford. He is President of the Royal Society, and a corresponding member of the Institute of France, and also a member of numerous learned

societies in Europe and America. Sir Benjamin has published works "On Local Nervous Affections;" "On various Subjects in Pathology and Surgery;" "Pathological and Surgical Observations on Diseases of the Joints;" "Physiological Researches;" "Psychological Inquiries;" and "Lectures on the Diseases of the Urinary Organs." He has besides contributed largely to the Transactions of the Royal Medical and Chirurgical Society.

BROGLIE, ACHILLE CHARLES LÉONCE VICTOR, DUC DE, a French statesman and member of the Institute, was born on the 28th November, 1789. His father was a nobleman who refused to emigrate, and was guillotined in 1794 for his adhesion to the cause of the Constitution. Under the Empire, M. de Broglie discharged duties in the administrative office he held with so much intelligence as to attract the notice of the first Napoleon, who entrusted him with missions in Illyria, Spain, and Poland, although he was well known to be unfriendly to the empire. He was appointed by Louis XVIII. a peer of France, but he soon opposed, as a liberal, the Government of the Restoration. In 1828 he founded the "Revue Française," contributing to it many articles, among which the most remarkable was one on Capital Punishments. After the revolution of July, 1830, he held office for a few days as Minister of the Interior, ceding it, however, to his friend M. Guizot, for the ministry of Public Instruction. He was Minister of Foreign Affairs in October, 1832, resigning the office in April, but resuming it in May, 1834. He retired "finally" from public life in February, 1835; but after the election of Louis Napoleon he returned again to the arena of active politics, as a representative to the Legislative Assembly. The coup d'état changed affairs once more, and the Duc de Broglie has not since been heard of as a politician. In 1856 he was elected

a member of the French Academy, his title to this distinction being founded on his contributions to reviews, and his parliamentary speeches. His reception was quite an event, as it gave him, a statesman respected by all classes of politicians, an opportunity of expressing his opinions on the political changes which had overthrown the great men of Louis Philippe's time.

BROOKE, SIR JAMES, the Rajah of Sarawak, and Governor of Labuan, in the island of Borneo, was born in the year 1803, near the city of Bath. His father was in the Civil Service of the East India Company, and the subject of this notice at an early age went out to India as a cadet. The corps to which he belonged being engaged in the first Burmese war, he was wounded in the chest so severely as to render it necessary for him to return to England on furlough. As soon as his health and vigour were restored he returned again to India, but found himself superseded in the service for undue length of absence from his duties. This was owing chiefly to his being shipwrecked on his voyage to India, and the lengthened period required for his convalescence. He determined to take a voyage to China, and on the passage he was very much impressed by the natural wealth and fertility of the great islands of the Malay peninsula, rich in minerals and in all the products of the tropics, to an extent unknown on the continent of India. He wondered even at this time that no attempt had been made to put down piracy in seas so much frequented by European vessels, and to introduce European civilization into countries so accessible by the great extent of their sea-board. On his return to England in 1838 he urged upon the attention of Government the schemes he had formed respecting the Malay Islands. He wrote a paper at this time, an abstract of which was published in the Journal of the Geological Society, in which he pointed out the importance in an industrial and commercial point of view of the Malay archipelago, and enforced the necessity of something being done to establish peace and civilization in one of the most fertile regions of the tropics. All his efforts proving unsuccessful, he determined to proceed to Borneo as a private adventurer. Purchasing a small yacht named the "Royalist," he set sail with a picked crew of twenty men; and, well provided with the munitions of war, he undertook the formidable task of extirpating piracy in the Indian archipelago, and founding a settlement on some part of it. Fixing upon Sarawak, in the island of Borneo, as his first scene of operations, he sailed for that place. On his arrival he found the Rajah Muda Hassim engaged in suppressing a rebellion in his territories, and being asked to assist him in the undertaking, willingly consented. With the aid of Mr. Brooke and his small band of followers, Muda Hassim easily put down the insurrection, and with the consent of the sovereign installed Mr. Brooke as his successor. The latter then vigorously applied himself to the reform of the most open abuses. In 1841 his domination was firmly established. In a paper which he wrote during the following winter, he claimed the assistance of the English Government, on the ground that his objects were "to call into existence the resources of one of the richest and most extensive islands of the globe, to relieve an industrious people from oppression, and to check, if possible to suppress, *piracy* and the *slave trade*, which are openly carried on within a short distance of three European settlements, on a scale and system revolting to humanity." He had received no assistance up to this time, and had expended £10,000 of his own fortune. It is impossible to give any account of the beneficent measures he carried out in his attempts to put an end, one after the other, to the barbarous customs of the country. In 1847 he returned to England, and was warmly welcomed by his friends and the public, created a Knight of the Bath, and invited to dine with the Queen. The Government of the day acknowledged his title of Rajah, sent him out in a man-of-war, and made him governor of the new settlement of Labuan, in Borneo, with an allowance of £1,500 a-year, and £500 more for his services as consular agent. In the meantime, however, his enemies had been at work. The late Mr. Joseph Hume, prompted, it is said, by persons who had an interest in putting down Sir James Brooke, arraigned him in the House of Commons, accused him of various malversations, and endeavoured to have him morally condemned as a reckless spiller of human blood. While these charges were being discussed, Sir James Brooke, forsaken by the government, was attacked at Kutchin, his head-quarters, by the Chinese settled in the colony, and only succeeded in quelling the insurrection at the imminent peril of his life. A most satisfactory reply to the calumnies brought against Sir James Brooke will be found in his "Private Correspondence," published in 1853, which fully establish his claims to be considered a man of genius, actuated by the purest and most unselfish motives in his attempts to reclaim from barbarism the races of the Malayan archipelago, and entitle him to our esteem and admiration as one of the most daring and heroic men of the age. We regret to add that the Rajah has been compelled by shattered health to return again to England.

BROOKS, CHARLES SHIRLEY, a dramatic author and journalist, was born in 1815. His father was the eminent architect, William Brooks, who built the London Institution and the Church Missionary College. Mr. C. S. Brooks was educated for the law, and admitted a solicitor; but abandoning the profession, he devoted his attention to the drama and journalism. A series of plays, including "The Lowther Arcade," "Our New Governess," and "Honours and Riches," produced by him at the Lyceum in 1845-51, made his theatrical reputation. Becoming connected with the "Morning Chronicle," he visited, as its special correspondent, Southern Russia, Asia Minor, and Egypt, with the view chiefly of inquiring into the condition of the labouring classes in those countries. He has written several novels, of which "Aspen Court" and "The Gordian Knot" are the best. Mr. Brooks is also a contributor to the "Quarterly Review," and other leading periodicals. He is one of the principal writers in "Punch." He has collected the greater part of his contributions to the "Morning Chronicle" in a work published separately, entitled "The Russians of the South."

BROUGHAM, HENRY, LORD BROUGHAM, a man of science, orator, statesman, and lawyer, was born at Edinburgh in 1778. He is the descendant of one of the oldest families in Westmoreland, which dates from the Conquest, and has title to the ancient peerage of Vaux. His education was commenced in the High School, and finished in the University of Edinburgh. His quick intelligence and extraordinary aptitude were not unobserved, and during his residence at the University he gave himself ardently to the study of mathematics and physical science. At seventeen years of age he wrote a paper which he forwarded to the Royal Society, entitled an "Essay on the Inflection and Reflection of Light," which was inserted in its "Transactions" in 1796. He contributed another on the same subject in 1797, and one on Porisms in 1798. Having left the University on the termination of his studies, he travelled for some time on the Continent, making Sweden and Norway the principal points

of his tour. On returning to Scotland he settled in Edinburgh as an advocate or barrister for a few years. During this period he was the friend and companion of Jeffrey, Murray, Sydney Smith, Horner, Thomas Brown, and the other young men of genius who at this period did honour to the northern capital. In 1802, when the "Edinburgh Review" was founded, he was one of its most indefatigable contributors. He removed to London in 1806, and in 1807 he was called to the English bar. In the short truce which followed the peace of 1814 he visited Paris, and as a savant became acquainted with Carnot and other eminent Frenchmen. Once fixed in London, his practice as a lawyer grew upon his hands, his first great appearance being before the House of Lords, as counsel for Lady Essex Kerr, whose family claimed the Dukedom of Roxburgh. In 1808 he was counsel for some British merchants in London, Lancashire, and Yorkshire, claiming a repeal of the Orders in Council which had been issued in retaliation of Napoleon's Berlin and Milan decrees,— orders which went to prohibit, under the pain of capture, neutral vessels from entering any port in France. For some weeks Mr. Brougham examined witnesses for his clients at the bar of the House of Commons, doing his utmost for the interests of his clients; but the "Orders in Council" were not rescinded until 1812, when he was in Parliament, and could as a member support the petitions of his former clients. He had in 1810 entered Parliament for the burgh of Camelford, and at once ranged himself with the Whig opposition. In 1811 he carried the Bill which declared participation in the slave trade a felony, and thereby put an end to that traffic. On the dissolution of Parliament in 1812 he presented himself to the electors of Liverpool as a candidate for their suffrages;

F

but Canning, whom he opposed, possessed the weightier influence, and Mr. Brougham was defeated. He did not re-enter Parliament for four years, when, in the recess of 1815, he was returned for Winchelsea, a close borough. He entered with spirit, energy, and consummate ability on the discussion of all the questions that then agitated the public mind. Slavery and the slave trade, agricultural distress, parliamentary reform, Catholic emancipation, the Holy Alliance, reduction of the army, the Corn-law monopoly, and other topics, occupied his attention, and elicited his most fervid oratory. It was during one of his impassioned speeches about this period that he accused Canning of "baseness," and designated Peel an "ignominious parasite." Popular though Mr. Brougham had become, as a member of Parliament, exposing and denouncing abuses in the State, he was destined to command a still higher degree of estimation. Queen Caroline came to England to claim her rights as Queen Consort and wife of George IV. Supported by Lords Eldon and Liverpool, and all the Tories of the day, the King not only repudiated the claim, but put her on her trial before the House of Lords for adultery. Mr. Brougham having been the Queen's legal adviser on previous occasions, was now appointed her Attorney-General, and it fell to him to vindicate her honour and chastity before the first Court of Judicature known to the constitution. His labours were incessant, his eloquence without parallel; and, eventually, the King felt constrained to withdraw his Bill of Pains and Penalties against his wife. Mr. Brougham's cause was the cause of the people, and thenceforth he became a popular idol, and continued to mix himself up with every prominent question of the day. When Parliament was dissolved, on the death of George IV., Mr. Brougham contested the representation of the most important seat in England, that of the West Riding of Yorkshire, and won it. In the new Parliament he gave immediate notice of various measures of parliamentary reform. Before, however, his motion could come on, Sir Henry Parnell applied to the House for an inquiry into the Civil List, which was resisted by the Wellington government, but carried. The Duke resigned, and Earl Grey was commanded to form a ministry, in which he appointed Mr. Brougham Lord Chancellor, with a peerage, the title being "Brougham and Vaux." In the House of Lords, Lord Brougham was mainly instrumental in carrying the Reform Bill, and for four years, from 1830 to 1834, he toiled without intermission on behalf of various measures of reform; but in the latter year, William IV. caused the Melbourne administration to retire, and called the Conservatives to office, the Duke of Wellington being *interim* dictator, while Sir Robert Peel was on his way from Italy. The Peel government having been defeated on the first motion of importance submitted to the House of Commons, the Irish Church Revenues Bill, Lord Melbourne returned to power, and nominated his ministers, among whom, however, Lord Brougham had no place, and he has never since been a servant of the Crown. When Louis Philippe was deprived of the throne and a republic established, Lord Brougham, who had purchased property and built a house at Cannes, where he went every winter, applied, along with other English residents having property there, for naturalization as a security for it, but the claim was unsuccessful, in consequence of the opinion of the French lawyers, that the applicants must, as a preliminary to naturalization in France, cease to be English citizens. As an orator, Lord Brougham has had few equals in or out of the Senate; no living statesman possesses the same versatility. As an author he is occasionally care-

less, but always clear; as Chancellor, he performed the greatest judicial feat on record: he retired from the Court of Chancery without leaving a single case which had been heard in arrear for judgment. It is impossible to enumerate in this place Lord Brougham's practical efforts in the cause of education; suffice it to say, that among his other undertakings he established the "Society for the Diffusion of Useful Knowledge," and was the founder of University College, London. The addresses delivered by Lord Brougham to the meetings of the Social Science Association at Bradford, on the occasion of the foundation of the monument to Newton, and of his installation at Edinburgh as Chancellor of the University on which he has conferred so much honour, show that his activity and intellectual vigour are unimpaired. He has again evinced his interest in social affairs in his presidential address to the Social Science Congress lately held at Glasgow (September, 1860), where, in a speech of great length, he reviewed some of the most interesting occurrences which had taken place since the previous meeting, and which had a bearing on the objects of the Association. These recent efforts would alone, could they be detached from his earlier career, give him a title to be ranked as a philanthropist, statesman, orator, philosopher, and savant, among the most illustrious men whom this country has ever produced. The title of Brougham and Vaux descends by a recent grant to his brother, who also inherits the old claim to the title of Vaux. A collected edition of Lord Brougham's works has been published by Messrs. Charles Griffin & Co. They consist of Critical, Historical, and Miscellaneous works, forming ten octavo volumes, including "The Lives of Philosophers of the Time of George III.;" "The Lives of Men of Letters of the Time of George III.;"

"Sketches of Eminent Statesmen of the Reign of George III.;" "Natural Theology," comprising a Discourse on Natural Theology; "Dialogues on Instinct, and Dissertations on the Structure of the Cells of Bees, and on Fossil Osteology;" "Rhetorical and Literary Dissertations and Addresses, with Discourses of Ancient Eloquence," &c.; "Historical and Political Dissertations," contributed to various periodicals; and "Speeches on Social and Political Subjects, with Historical Introductions;" "Contributions to the Edinburgh Review, Political, Historical, and Miscellaneous," in three octavo volumes, arranged under the heads of Rhetoric, History, Constitutional Questions, Political Economy, Finance, Commercial Law, Physical Science, and Miscellaneous Subjects; "Paley's Natural Theology, with Notes and Dissertations by Lord Brougham and Sir Charles Bell," in three volumes; "Political Philosophy;" and what may be termed his Lordship's *magnum opus*, "A Treatise on the British Constitution," which has just issued from the press.

BROUGHTON DE GIFFORD, JOHN CAM HOBHOUSE, BARON, an English statesman, was born in 1786. The son of a wealthy brewer in London, he was educated at Cambridge, and in 1809 travelled in the East, publishing his observations under the title of "A Journey into Albania and other Provinces of the Turkish Empire." Lord Byron dedicated the fourth canto of "Childe Harold" to him. Being in France during the "Hundred Days," he wrote, after Waterloo, his "Letters to an Englishman," the opinions expressed in which subsequently led to his incarceration in Newgate. This condemnation rendered him popular, and on his release he was returned to the House of Commons in 1820. He adopted at first radical opinions, but in a few years his liberalism became less extreme. In 1831 Lord Grey appointed him Secretary-at-War, and in 1833 he became Chief Secretary for Ireland; subsequently, Chief Commissioner of Woods and Forests, and Secretary to the Board of Control. He was elevated to the peerage in 1851.

BROWN, MISS FRANCES, a blind poetess, was born June, 1818, at Stranorlar, in Ireland, where her father was postmaster. She lost her sight by small-pox when only eighteen months old, so that education in the ordinary form she could not receive. But her memory was most retentive, and she learned, from listening to others, to read and repeat their lessons. She attempted verse at seven years of age, and continued to compose, her sister being her amanuensis, until 1841, when the "Athenæum" introduced her to the public. She is the author of a large number of poems and tales of considerable merit, and enjoys a small pension from the Crown.

BROWN, WILLIAM, a capitalist, donor of the Liverpool Free Library and Museum, was born at Ballymena, county Antrim, in 1784. His father, Alexander Brown, was a native of Ballymena. William Brown was early sent to England for his education, which he received at a private academy, kept by the Rev. J. Bradley, of Catterick, near Richmond, Yorkshire. His educational opportunities were slender. At the early age of sixteen he was summoned from his books to acquire a knowledge of men and things. An active business career awaited him, and he was thenceforward compelled to pursue his studies and self-improvement under disadvantages, and in the absence of aids and auxiliaries which he has generously supplied to his younger and more fortunate fellow-townsmen. In the year 1800 his father determined to emigrate to America, and to seek his fortune in that land of promise. His family accompanied him; and when the father had established himself in Baltimore as a linen merchant, William assisted in the counting-house. He soon became so useful, and manifested such aptitude for business, that his father took him into partnership. Mr. Brown, *père*, was a man of remarkable shrewdness and enterprise. He established one son at Philadelphia, another at New York, while a third remained in Baltimore to assist him in carrying on the parent or central business. William, the eldest, was sent to England in 1809. The young merchant lost no time in revisiting the scenes of his birth, and in 1810 he married Sarah, daughter of Mr. Andrew Gihon, of Ballymena. The young couple came to Liverpool, and here William established a branch of his father's Baltimore firm, in correspondence with his brothers in New York and Philadelphia. The name of William Brown soon became known upon the Liverpool Exchange, and henceforward he became identified with the unparalleled progress and prosperity of the port. And to so great an extent did his business increase that in 1836 his transactions for the year amounted to above ten millions. In 1844 Mr. Brown offered himself for South Lancashire, but was defeated; although eventually he took his seat in the House, in 1846, having been elected by that constituency without opposition. His political principles are liberal, and throughout his career Mr. Brown has been the earnest advocate in every way of the principles of Free-trade. He retired from active political life in 1859. Mr. Brown has always shown the deepest interest in the affairs of the town of Liverpool, and the last instance of his munificence has been the presentation of a Free Library and Museum to his fellow-townsmen, at a cost to himself of forty thousand pounds, an instance of princely generosity scarcely paralleled in any age.

BROWNING, MRS. ELIZABETH BAR-

RETT, an English poetess, was born in London, in 1809, of a family in affluent circumstances. She was educated with great care, and at the age of fifteen her powers as a writer were known to her friends. Owing to the bursting of a blood-vessel in the lungs, she was for a long time in very delicate health, residing, for the sake of the climate, at Torquay. There she experienced a shock which permanently tinged her character with melancholy. Her brother, and two young men, friends, took out a small sailing-vessel, for a few hours' trip. They had been but a few minutes on their voyage of pleasure, when the boat went down, and all on board perished, within sight of the house where Miss Barrett resided. She was married to Mr. Robert Browning in 1846, and immediately after accompanied him to Pisa, subsequently removing to Florence, which they made their permanent home, varied by an occasional visit to England. In 1850 the publication of her collected works increased her reputation in England and on the Continent. Mrs. Browning can boast of a rich mine of poetical ideas, but the diction in which she frequently indulges detracts from what would otherwise be appreciated as the result of unlaboured poetic impulse.

BROWNING, ROBERT, an English poet, was born at Camberwell in 1812. He was educated at the London University, where he was looked upon as a thoughtful and imaginative student. His first literary production, "Paracelsus," was published in 1835. In 1837 he brought out "Strafford, an Historical Tragedy;" and in 1840, a long poem, entitled "Sordello." Each of these works attracted much notice, from their originality, choice of subject, and style of treatment; but being more addressed to the minds of cultivated readers than to the million, none of them became extensively popular. From 1842 to 1846 he published a series of poems, which he entitled "Bells and Pomegranates." Many of these are very beautiful; though they all, more or less, partake of that intellectual subtlety which precludes all but highly intellectual readers from clearly and fully comprehending them. Still they tended generally to extend and confirm the reputation he had previously acquired. In 1846 there appeared a collected edition of his poems; and in the same year he married Miss Elizabeth B. Barrett, the celebrated poetess. In 1850 he published one of his finest compositions, "Christmas Eve, and Easter Day," and in 1855 his "Men and Women," a collection of miscellaneous poems which go further than all his other works to prove him a genuine poet, not of the merely intellectual and metaphysical order, but one who feels as deeply as he thinks. Mr. Browning has frequently been compared with Tennyson, but their ideas and their styles are widely divergent. Since his marriage he has resided principally at Florence.

BRUNEL, ISAMBARD KINGDOM, an English engineer, was born at Portsmouth in 1806. His youth was spent in France, receiving his education at the College of Caen. One of his earliest engineering attempts was that of forming a tunnel under the Thames, which has been completed at great cost, but has not afforded the results which its promoters at first anticipated. After various engagements in connexion with engineering affairs, Mr. Brunel was appointed, in 1833, the engineer of the Great Western Railway, and in this capacity introduced the broad gauge. His views in reference thereto were strongly opposed by many eminent engineers, but eventually he carried his point. Many of the bridges on that line are fine specimens of engineering talent. He has been connected with several foreign railways, and was one of the chief engineers engaged in erecting the Britannia and Conway tubular bridges. He was the first to propose building large vessels for long voyages, and the Great Western steam-vessel was constructed on plans furnished by him. The boldest effort of Mr. Brunel's genius, however, has been the construction of the Great Eastern, which is the largest vessel ever built. Mr. Brunel is a Fellow of the Royal Society, and a member of many foreign learned Associations.

BRUNNOW, ERNEST PHILIP, BARON VON, a Russian diplomatist, was born at Dresden, 31st August, 1796, his father belonging to an ancient family of Courland. After having studied at Leipsic, he was admitted in 1818, by order of the Emperor, to the ministry of Foreign Affairs. From 1820 to 1823 he was Secretary to the Russian Embassy in London. After serving in various subordinate diplomatic offices, in 1839, having fallen into bad health from too close application to business, he was appointed ambassador to Wurtemberg, and conducted, at Darmstadt, the arrangements relative to the marriage of the Grand Duke Alexander. In 1839 he was sent to London on special business, and the following year he returned as ambassador, and then it was that he displayed rare ability as a diplomatist in negociating the treaty of 18th of July, 1840. When the Russian war broke out in 1854 he was recalled, and sent, in 1855, as Plenipotentiary to the German Confederation, with instructions specially to secure the neutrality of the lesser states. Along with Count Orloff he was chosen by Alexander II. to assist at the Conferences of Paris, and in 1757 he was sent to Berlin as Minister Plenipotentiary. He has since been reappointed to his old post in London.

BRYANT, WILLIAM CULLEN, a poet and journalist, was born at Cummington, Massachusetts, on the 3rd of November, 1797. After receiving an excellent preliminary education, he entered William College, at the age of sixteen, where he soon reached a conspicuous position by his superior classical attainments. He afterwards entered the office of a counsellor-at-law, and pursued for some years the practice of the law. He early became known as a poet, by the publication in verse of some political satires. Giving up the profession of the law, he, in conjunction with a friend, founded the "New York Review," and with two others an Annual named "The Talisman," in which many of his poems appeared. Eventually, however, Mr. Bryant became editor of the "New York Evening Post," and to this journal he has devoted his chief attention for many years. The genuine feeling and quiet gracefulness of style displayed in almost all his poetic effusions have rendered them peculiarly popular, no less in England than in America. After Longfellow, William Cullen Bryant is perhaps the American poet best known in Britain. In addition to his poetical works, Mr. Bryant has published several tales and sketches, which have attained considerable popularity in America, but which have not been reproduced in England.

BUCCLEUCH and QUEENSBERRY, WALTER FRANCIS MONTAGUE DOUGLAS SCOTT, fifth Duke of Buccleuch, was born in 1806. After studying at St. John's College, Cambridge, he, on arriving at majority in 1828, took his seat in the House of Lords. In 1842 he was Lord Privy Seal under Sir Robert Peel, and in 1846 President of the Council. In 1842 he was nominated a Colonel of the Edinburgh militia, and in 1857 appointed one of Her Majesty's aides-de-camp. The Duke is a moderate conservative in politics, and takes considerable interest in agricultural and social improvements, and the amelioration of the condition of the Scottish peasantry.

BUCHANAN, JAMES, ex-President of the United States, was born 23rd April,

1791, in the county of Frauklin, Pennsylvania. His father was a native of Donegal, in Ireland. Mr. Buchanan studied law, but had a strong bias for politics. In 1814, and again in 1815, he was elected a member of the Legislature of Pennsylvania, but he found the labours harassing, and retired after two years' servitude. In 1821 he first took his seat in Congress, and again retired into private life; but in 1831 he proceeded on political affairs to Russia, remaining at St. Petersburg for about two years. On his return to America he was elected to the Senate, and in 1845 was appointed Secretary of State to President Polk. In 1853 he was sent by General Pierce as Ambassador to the Court of St. James's, resigning that post in 1856, when his friends had secured his election as president. Mr. Buchanan has been a successful politician, belonging to what is called the Democratic—in opposition to the Republican—party; he of necessity supports the Southern or pro-slavery cause, but the pith of his policy lies in his principles of annexation, and his desire to wrest from Great Britain every inch of territory capable of absorption into the Union. His term of office expired in 1860.

BUCKLE, HENRY THOMAS, an English thinker and historian, was born at Lee, in Kent, on the 24th November, 1822. His father was a well-known merchant in Mark-lane; his mother a Miss Middleton, of the Yorkshire family of that name. For a short time he attended Dr. Holloway's school at Kentish Town, but his health, when a boy, being delicate, he was not subjected to what is called a regular education. Dr. Birkbeck, whose advice had been taken, having recommended that he should not be tormented with task-work, or confined to the close atmosphere of a school-room, he was allowed to pursue his own course undisturbed; and that he did not mis-spend his time is abundantly appa-

rent in every page he has written. Mr. Buckle is the author of two papers published in "Fraser's Magazine;" one "A Lecture on the Influence of Women," the other "An Essay on Liberty," being a review of Mr. J. S. Mills' work on the same subject. But his most remarkable production is the first volume of his "History of Civilization in England," published in 1857. It is merely the first part of a great work, which is to embrace the whole history of English civilization, and which, if carried out with the range of learning, the ability and the capacity to arrange and systematize materials drawn from the most varied sources, displayed in every chapter of this introductory volume, will place Mr. Buckle's name among the foremost of those writers who have treated of the philosophy of history. It is not, however, as an original thinker on the transcendental questions of sociology that Mr. Buckle's claims to distinction rest. His histories of the English intellect from the middle of the sixteenth to the eighteenth century, and that of the French intellect during the same period, forming part of this volume, are warmly admired by some of those who denounce most strongly his philosophical ideas, and even by them placed among the most important recent contributions to our historical literature. The remainder of the introduction is yet unpublished, and will be devoted to the investigation of the civilization of Germany, America, Scotland, and Spain—and the study of their differences. Its appearance is looked forward to with great interest.

BUCKSTONE, JOHN BALDWIN, a comedian and prolific dramatic author, was born at Hoxton, Middlesex, 18th September, 1802. His connections were highly respectable, being descended from the Derbyshire Buckstones, members of which are now amongst the principal landed gentry of that county. When but a boy he was a great favourite because of his quickness of repartee and aptitude for study. Educated at Walworth Grammar School, when but eleven years of age he was placed on board a man-of-war; but, after a cruise, his grandfather objected to the little fellow's going to sea, and had him brought home and sent back to school. His family then intended him for the law, but he did not follow that profession. He was a very discursive reader, though a quick learner; the stage had its attractions for him. He contracted his first engagement in the provinces. He then came to London and appeared at the Surrey Theatre, then at the Coburg, then at the Adelphi, then at the Haymarket, then at Drury Lane. In 1853 he became manager of the Haymarket, on the retirement of Mr. Benjamin Webster. In this theatre he, for several years, has accomplished the remarkable feat of keeping the house open every lawful night throughout the year, and always commanding full audiences. As an author, Mr. Buckstone has produced more comedies, dramas, and farces than any man of the age, and all have been without exception successful. His style as a performer is removed from that of all others in the same line. It is quaint, easy, and highly comic. Being a great favourite with Her Majesty, he has on many occasions received the honour of appearing at court dramatic representations at Windsor Castle. Mr. Buckstone is treasurer and master of the Royal General Theatrical Fund; joint-treasurer of the Royal Dramatic College, and a member of the Dramatic Authors' Society and of the Garrick Club.

BULWER, THE RIGHT HON. SIR HENRY LYTTON, a diplomatist and author, was born in 1804. He is the elder brother of the novelist, Bulwer Lytton. In 1830 he was sent on a special service to Brussels, and on his return became member for Wilton. He represented Coventry in 1831 and 1832, and Marylebone from 1834 to 1838. In 1837 he was Chargé d'Affaires at Brussels, and in 1837 Secretary of the Embassy at Constantinople, filling a similar post at Paris in 1839. At the Court of Madrid he was the British representative for several years, and, subsequently, proceeded in the same capacity to Washington. In 1848 he married the youngest daughter of Lord Cowley. From 1852 to 1855 he was Envoy Extraordinary to Tuscany. In 1856 he was appointed a Commissioner for the Danubian Principalities, and thereafter successor to Lord Stratford de Redcliffe, as ambassador to Turkey, where he still remains. He is an author as well as a diplomatist, having published "An Autumn in Greece," "The Lords, the Government, and the Country," "France, Social and Literary," and the "Monarchy of the Middle Classes."

BUNSEN, CHRISTIAN CHARLES JOSAIAS, CHEVALIER VON, a German scholar, philosopher, and statesman, was born at Korback, within the principality of Waldeck, but not far from the frontiers of Rhenish Prussia, on the 25th of August, 1791. In 1808 he became a student at Marburg; whence, in 1809, he proceeded to Göttingen. In 1811 he obtained a professorship, and not long afterwards published a work, entitled "De Jure Atheniensium Hæreditario," which at once established his position as a scholar. He devoted his attention chiefly to philological and philosophical studies, although his works everywhere display an intimate acquaintance with the great results of the physical sciences, and more especially of those which have a bearing on philological researches. To complete his studies he visited various parts of the Continent. His first journey was to Holland; thence he repaired to Copenhagen, where he studied the Norse language and literature under Magnussen. In 1816 he proceeded to Paris, and there he devoted his attention to

Arabic, Persian, and Sanscrit, under the great French Orientalists. From Paris he went to Rome. There he had the good fortune to secure the friendship and confidence of Niebuhr, whom he had some years before known at Berlin. This distinguished historian and critic at once appreciated the high abilities of Bunsen, and in 1818 secured for him the appointment of Secretary to the Prussian Legation, he himself being at that time Ambassador to the Papal See. In 1822 King Frederick William visited Italy, and made the acquaintance of Bunsen, whose religious views were much akin to those entertained by the monarch, then intent upon the innovations afterwards introduced into the Prussian Church. After the departure of Niebuhr, Bunsen was appointed Prussian Ambassador in his stead. During the whole period of his stay in Italy, Bunsen continued his laborious researches in philology, not confining himself to mere grammatical studies, but carrying his investigations into the history of the philosophical literature and political institutions of antiquity, ecclesiastical and liturgical history, archæology, and every department of human knowledge which throws light upon the history of civilization. The visit of the younger Champollion to Rome, in 1826, directed his attention to the new field of research opened by the clue discovered to the interpretation of the hieroglyphics. It was he who induced Lepsius to turn his attention to this subject. Bunsen took the deepest interest in the foundation, in 1829, of the Archæological Institute of Rome, for which he erected a hall near his own house upon the Capitol. His duties as Minister and Chargé d'Affaires at Rome threw upon him some very delicate negociations between the Pope and the Prussian Government, more especially those relating to mixed marriages, or marriages between Catholics and Protestants;

which, although arranged to the satisfaction of the Court of Rome, could not be settled to the contentment of the zealous Roman Catholics of Rhenish Prussia. After the disturbances on the Rhine, and the apprehension of the Bishop of Cologne, Chevalier Bunsen found his position at the Papal Court disagreeable, and was recalled at his own request. In 1839 he was appointed Minister at Berne to the Swiss Republic, and in 1841 Ambassador to this country. In 1844, on the occasion of one of those frequent visits he made to Berlin, to give the Prussian Government the benefit of his advice, he is understood to have recommended to King Frederick William IV. a liberal policy, and an assimilation of the legislative system to that of England. He supported the German policy in Schleswig-Holstein. On this question he published, in April, 1848, a work, addressed to Lord Palmerston, entitled "A Memoir on the Constitutional Rights of the Duchies of Schleswig and Holstein." Having a strong bias in favour of constitutional government, he resigned his embassy in 1854, when he found that the Prussian Court had determined to lean towards Russia. His absence from this country, where he had been looked upon as an adopted citizen, was generally felt as a public loss. He now resides in the neighbourhood of Heidelberg. In the midst of his labours as a statesman and diplomatist, Chevalier Bunsen has never discontinued his philological and philosophical researches, by which he is so well known in this country. In 1845 he published his "Church of the Future;" in 1847, "Ignatius of Antioch, and his Times;" in 1848, "Egypt's Place in Universal History;" and in 1851, "Hippolytus and his Age;" followed, in 1854, by the "Outlines of the Philosophy of Universal History, applied to Language and Religion." The last is perhaps one of the most important books which our generation has produced, and may be said to stand towards philology and the cognate sciences in the relation which Humboldt's "Cosmos" bears to those departments of knowledge which have for their object the study of the material universe. The work is written in an English style, remarkable for elegance and brilliancy.

BUNSEN, ROBERT WILLIAM, a German chemist, was born at Göttingen, where his father was Professor of Literature. He studied at the University of that city, evidencing a decided taste for experimental science, and completed his education at Paris. He afterwards succeeded Wöhler as Professor of Chemistry at the Polytechnic Institute at Cassel. In 1841 he was titular professor at the University of Marburg, and subsequently director of the Chemical Institute. In 1851 he held an appointment at the University of Breslau. Mr. Bunsen is chiefly known to scientific circles through his extensive researches in chemistry, but more especially by his invention of the carbon voltaic battery, which is now so extensively used by electricians. He has been a large contributor to the "Annales de Chimie," and has also published works which chiefly relate to his discoveries in inorganic chemistry.

BUOL, SHAUENSTEIN CHARLES FERDINAND, COUNT, a German statesman and diplomatist, and Austrian minister, was born at Hamburg on the 17th May, 1797. He is a son of the celebrated Count Buol, who as Plenipotentiary of Austria presided for many years over the Frankfort Diet. In 1816 he was attached to the Legation at Florence, and was sent as Secretary to the Embassy at Paris in 1822, and to London in the same capacity in 1824. He afterwards held various diplomatic appointments, and was Plenipotentiary at Turin when the Revolution of 1848 broke out. In 1848

he went as Ambassador to St. Petersburg, returning in 1850 to Dresden, to act as second imperial Plenipotentiary in the settlement of the Holstein question. After acting for some time as Ambassador to England, he returned to Vienna to become Minister of Foreign Affairs in place of Prince Schwartzenberg, who had just died. He appeared with Baron Hübner, at the Congress of Paris, as imperial Plenipotentiary, and signed the Treaty of 30th March, 1856. Count Buol has not confined his attention to mere matters of diplomacy, but has endeavoured on all occasions to further the progress of internal improvements in Austria. The position of neutrality which Austria held during the war was in a great measure to be ascribed to his exertions; he having sought throughout his whole career to emancipate Austria from Russian control. In 1859 he retired from office.

BUREN, VAN, MARTIN, ex-President of the United States of America, was born at Kinderhook, in the State of New York, 5th December, 1782. Although receiving a limited education when young, he turned his attention successfully to politics and law, and was appointed Attorney-General of the State, and sent as a senator to the Legislative Assembly of New York in 1812. He was one of the most ardent supporters of the war against Britain. In 1817 he led the opposition against Clinton, elected Governor of New York, and was deprived of offices which he held; but after a long struggle he was appointed Senator of the United States' Congress, in which he served eight years. He was an active partizan of General Jackson's presidency, and on that gentleman's election he was appointed Secretary of State of the United States, and nominated Ambassador to London, but the Senate afterwards refused to ratify the appointment. He gained popularity by that opposition, and was elected Vice-

President. When Gen. Jackson's term of office expired Van Buren was nominated as his natural successor; and though he had to contend with Clay, Calhoun, Webster, and Harrison, he was elected, holding office till 1840, when his claims for re-election were rejected.

BURGOYNE, SIR JOHN FOX, an English general, was born in Ireland in 1782. As one of the corps of Royal Engineers, he commenced his military career August, 1798, and served in Malta, Egypt, Sicily, and Sweden in the early part of the present century. In 1809 he joined the army under Sir Arthur Wellesley, and remained in Spain till the end of the Peninsular war in 1814. He conducted the sieges of Burgos and Saint Sebastian, and received the Gold Cross and one clasp for Badajos, Salamanca, Vittoria, San Sebastian, and Nive; and the silver medal and three clasps for Busaco, Ciudad Rodrigo, and Nivelle. After passing through the various intermediate military grades he attained the rank of Lieutenant-General in 1852, and was then created a Knight of the Grand Cross of the Bath. In 1854 he was sent to Turkey, and as chief of the Engineering Department of the British army took part in the events of the Crimea till his recall in 1855. He was present at the battles of the Alma, Balaklava, and Inkermann. For his services he was raised to the rank of General, and created a baronet. Sir John was thirteen years Chairman of Public Works in Ireland, and since 1845 has held the appointment of Inspector-General of Fortifications.

BURMEISTER, HERMANN, was born in 1807, in Stralsund, in Prussia, where his father was a Custom-house officer. He studied medicine for four years in the Universities of Greifswald and Halle. Professor Nitzch, with whom he was on terms of friendship, cultivated his taste for zoology and entomology. On the death of Nitzch, at Halle, in 1842, Burmeister filled the zoological chair in his stead, and between then and 1848 produced several scientific works of high merit, which added to the fame he had previously acquired both as an author and an entomologist. In 1840, having been already well known for his liberalism, and his facility of expressing his political opinions, Burmeister was chosen representative for Halle to the National Assembly; but his health, broken down by incessant work, compelled him to seek a warmer climate, and he went to Brazil. On his return to Europe, after two years' absence, he resumed his functions in the University of Halle. He has published numerous scientific works, among which may be enumerated, "A Manual of Entomology," and a work on the animals of Brazil. He also wrote two popular treatises, "The History of Creation," and "Sketches of Natural History," which have been very successful with the general public.

BURNET, JOHN, a painter, engraver, and art-critic, was born at Fisher-row, near Edinburgh, in 1784. Apprenticed to Robert Scott, the engraver, he studied assiduously, devoting his little leisure to the cultivation of drawing under John Graham, at the classes of the Scottish Academy. Here he was the fellow-pupil of Sir William Allan and Sir David Wilkie, his engravings from the works of the latter artist first directing attention to his abilities. Wilkie removed to London in 1804, and produced such a sensation by his picture of the "Village Politicians" that Mr. Burnet resolved also to attempt success in the English capital. He arrived in London in 1806, and called on Wilkie, who received him cordially, and assisted to obtain him employment in book engraving; but aspiring to a higher walk in art, he requested liberty to engrave "The Jew's Harp." Wilkie granted permission, and in 1809 he published the work, which was very meritorious. He afterwards, by his plate from "The Blind Fiddler," became established in public opinion as an artist of unsurpassed power. "Reading the Will," "Chelsea Pensioners Reading the Gazette," "The Rabbit on the Wall," and other works, were successively engraved by him with equal firmness and delicacy. All these are now familiar to the world, and it has been asserted that Wilkie's present fame rests nearly as much on the hand of Burnet as on his own productions. He has engraved his own pictures, as, for example, "The Greenwich Pensioners." He has also engraved several of Rembrandt's and Raphael's pictures, and has published some works, the value of which to the art-student can scarcely be over-rated; among these are, "Practical Hints on Painting," published in 1812; "Landscape Painting in Oil;" and "Hints on Portrait Painting." These and other writings of a similar class are illustrated by himself.

BURRITT, ELIHU, known as the "learned blacksmith," was born in Connecticut in 1811. His early education was by no means extensive, but by perseverance and industry he acquired a knowledge of many languages and dialects, and he is a proficient in mathematics. Mr. Burritt has made himself well known in this country and in France by his untiring exertions to form and consolidate the league of Universal Brotherhood. He is also a strenuous advocate for the ocean penny postage. In the prosecution of these philanthropic objects, Mr. Burritt has had a principal share in convening congresses of representatives of peace societies in London, Brussels, Paris, and Frankfort. He was the first to put forth the idea of an electric telegraph around the globe *viâ* Behring's Straits, connecting St. Petersburg and San Francisco. He is now engaged in urging upon the people of the United States the peaceful extinction of slavery by compensating the Southern States out of the national treasury for the emancipation of their slaves. "The Bond of Brotherhood," a monthly organ for the promulgation of peace principles, is understood to be chiefly the production of the "learned blacksmith." "Sparks from the Anvil," "A Voice from the Forge," and "Peace Papers for the People," are his chief independent contributions to literature.

BURTON, JOHN HILL, an author and historian, was born 22nd of August, 1809, at Aberdeen. His father was an officer in the 94th Regiment, who dying, left his family but slenderly provided for. Mr. Burton, after studying at Marischal College, Aberdeen, in 1831 was called to the Edinburgh bar. At first he had to contend with the vicissitudes attached to the career of a young advocate without independent means, but he struggled through with a manly spirit, writing for the Westminster and Edinburgh Reviews, when briefs were scanty. As an author he is sound and practical, and every work he has written bears evidence of the care and research bestowed on its preparation. His "Life and Correspondence of David Hume," "Lives of Simon Lord Lovat, and Duncan Forbes, of Culloden," and the "Narratives from Criminal Trials in Scotland," are all excellent. "The Scot Abroad," a very interesting series of papers, which appeared in "Blackwood's Magazine" some short time ago, is the production of Mr. Burton. His "Manual of the Law of Scotland," and "Treatise on the Law of Bankruptcy," are clear and well digested. He wrote the articles "Parliament" and "Prison Discipline" for the "Encyclopædia Britannica," and a great part of the articles on law subjects for the "Penny Cyclopædia." His chief work, however, is "The History of Scotland, from the Revolution of 1688 to the Extinction of the Jacobite Insurrection of 1745." He has held since 1854 the office of Secretary to the General Prison Board of Scotland.

BUSTAMENTE, Don Carlos Maria de, a Mexican archæologist, was born in Mexico about the close of the last century. He has devoted himself chiefly to the study of the antiquities of Mexico. His first production was a "Topographical Memoir of the Country of Ouxuca" (1821), which was followed by a dissertation "On the Republic of Tluxucola." His writings, though not very numerous, have appeared at intervals from this period to 1842. They are distinguished for original information and accuracy.

BUTT, George Medd, Q.C., an English statesman and lawyer, was born in 1797. He is the son of the late Mr. John Butt, of Sherborne. In early life he practised for some years as a special pleader, and in 1839, being then in his thirty-third year, he was called to the bar by the Hon. Society of the Inner Temple, and went on the Western Circuit, where he soon rose into reputation, and acquired an extensive practice. In 1845, during the Chancellorship of Lord Lyndhurst, Mr. Butt was made a Queen's Counsel, and shortly afterwards was elected a Bencher of the Inner Temple. At the general election in July, 1847, Mr. Butt offered his services to the electors of Weymouth, but was defeated, losing his election, however, by only three votes. In July, 1852, he again stood for Weymouth, and this time with more success, as he was returned at the head of the poll, the other candidates being Colonel W. L. Freestun and Mr. Oswald. Mr. Butt was a professed adherent of the Conservative party, but differed from that body in many important political points.

CABALLERO, Firmin Agosto, a Spanish journalist and statesman, was born in 1800 at Barajas de Melo. Having received a good education, he turned his attention to the study of geography,

and in a series of essays exposed the shortcomings of Minano's "Dictionary," which brought him at once into notice. In 1833 Caballero established the "Boletin de Comercio," and on its suppression he published the "Eco del Comercio," a paper which, mainly from the vigour of its original writing, speedily rose in popular favour. In 1843 Caballero became a member of the Cabinet, but did not long continue in office. His published works are mostly on geography, and one of the best of these is his "Manual Geographico Administrativo de la Monarquia Espanola."

CABET, Etienne, leader of the French Communists or Icariens, was born at Dijon on the 2nd of January, 1788. After completing his education he entered the bar as an advocate, and brought himself into public notice by his spirited defence of some conspirators in 1816. He then proceeded to Paris, but, owing to the violence of his political opinions, was prosecuted, and at length took refuge in England, where he remained for some years. On his return to France in 1839 he published a history of the Revolution of 1789, and became the advocate of Socialist opinions. In 1842 he brought out his "Voyage en Icarie," in which he sets forth the blessings of an imaginary State where all things were held in common for the public good, and whose government should simply exercise a paternal control over the masses. To put these ideas into practice he procured a grant of a tract of country in Texas, and a portion of his followers set out from France to found a social republic in the New World. Subsequently Cabet followed his disciples. In his journey through the United States he heard of the expulsion of the Mormons from Nauvoo, and in May, 1850, Cabet with his followers took possession of that city. He eventually returned to Paris, and pleaded his own cause against a sentence of imprisonment which had been passed against him. Besides the numerous statements he published for his defence, M. Cabet produced a declaration in his favour which had been given him at Nauvoo, entirely absolving him from many of the charges which had been brought against him. He fearlessly pleaded his own cause, and eventually gained an acquittal. After the *coup d'état* he found that all hopes of political advancement were lost, and he accordingly determined to return to Nauvoo. He eventually had to take severe steps with his followers, and becoming unpopular thereby, he fled to Saint Louis in Missouri.

CABRERA, DON RAMON, Count of Morella, a Carlist general, was born at Tortosa, in Catalonia, in August, 1810. His early life was spent in a very irregular manner, but taking advantage of an insurrection in 1833, he joined Don Carlos, under whom he soon distinguished himself by the boldness and ferocity of his disposition. The Carlists believed themselves, for a short time, masters of Spain, and Cabrera prepared to remove Isabella from the throne by a decisive stroke; but the defection of Maroto changed the face of affairs; and the Carlists, from being victors, were compelled to act on the defensive. On the fall of Don Carlos, being more attached to the cause than to the person of the Pretender, Cabrera made war on his own account, and established himself in a strong position amid the mountains of Catalonia and Arragon; but in 1840, his forces having been totally routed by Espartero, he was compelled to flee to France, where, not being looked upon in the light of a political refugee, he was confined in the fortress of Ham, whence he went to London in 1846. In 1848 he endeavoured to rekindle the civil war, and proceeded to Spain, where, however, he was defeated. On returning to England he gave up his warlike propensities, and married an English lady, with whom he afterwards went to Italy; but, having interfered in Italian affairs, he was expelled from Naples, and has since retired from public life.

CAILLIAUD, FRÉDÉRIC, a French traveller, was born at Nantes, on the 17th of March, 1787. Having completed his education at Paris, he travelled through the southern parts of Europe, and in 1815 proceeded from Constantinople to Egypt, remaining a number of years in the East, and rendering by his investigations, considerable service to its history. On his return to France in February, 1819, he brought with him a valuable collection of minerals and antiquities, and plans and copies of inscriptions, which were purchased of him by the French Minister of the Interior. He is the author of various works, the chief of which are, "Travels to Meroe, to the White Nile, beyond Fazoyl, to the south of Sennaar, to Syonah, and to five other Oases, between 1819 and 1822;" and "Researches in the Arts and Trades, the Usages of Civil and Domestic Life among the Ancient Races of Nubia and Ethiopia," followed by "Details on the Manners and Customs of the Modern Inhabitants of the same Countries."

CAIRD, JAMES, M.P., an eminent agricultural writer, was born at Stranraer, in Wigtonshire, in 1816, and received his education at Edinburgh. Mr. Caird, who is a proprietor in Wigtonshire, originally devoted himself to the practical pursuits of agriculture; and was first brought into public notice by contributing letters on the agriculture of England to the "Times," and by the publication of various works on farming. In 1853 he stood for the Wigton Burghs, and lost his seat by a majority of one vote against him; but at the general election of 1857 he stood for Dartmouth, was returned, and immediately became an authority in the House of Commons. He has lately travelled over a considerable portion of the United States and

Canada, noting carefully as he went, the modes of cultivation followed in the New World, and on his return publishing a little volume on "Prairie Farming." On agricultural questions his observations are always shrewd, intelligent, and practical. In 1859 Mr. Caird stood for the Stirling and Dunfermline Burghs in the Liberal interest, and was returned unopposed. His best known works are his "English Agriculture," a fifth edition of which was published in 1852; his "Plantation Scheme" (1850), of which several editions have been published; his "High Farming under Liberal Covenants the best Substitute for Protection;" and his "High Farming Vindicated."

CAIRD, REV. JOHN, D.D., a popular preacher of the Church of Scotland, was born at Greenock in 1823. After completing his studies at the University of Glasgow he was appointed minister of Newton-on-Ayr, and subsequently officiated in Lady Yester's church in Edinburgh. In 1850 he removed to Errol, and in 1858 from this country parish to Glasgow, where a magnificent church has been erected for him. Mr. Caird's pulpit appearances are marked by simplicity, earnestness, and fervour. A discourse preached before the Queen, in the parish church of Crathie, published by request of her Majesty, has attained an unprecedented popularity, and a collected volume of his sermons has recently won almost equal admiration.

CAIRNS, SIR HUGH M'CALMONT, ex-Solicitor-General for England, second son of the late William Cairns, Esq. of Calton, was born in 1819, near Belfast, in the county Down. He was educated at Trinity College, Dublin, where he was first-class in classics, and obtained other honours. He was called to the bar in 1844, and rose to considerable practice in the Court of Chancery, where he was soon considered a leading man. He was elected member for Belfast in 1852 by one of the largest majorities ever known in that borough; in 1856 he was made Queen's Counsel; and in 1858, under Lord Derby, Solicitor-General, with the honour of knighthood. He is considered one of the most effective orators on the Conservative benches, where he still represents his first constituency. His speech on the Paper Duties, and the Interpretation of the Commercial Treaty with France, delivered in the House of Commons in August, 1860, displays all the best characteristics of his eloquence.

CAMBRIDGE, H. R. H. GEORGE WILLIAM FREDERICK CHARLES, DUKE OF, is the son of Adolphus Frederick, first Duke, and is grandson of George III., and cousin to her Majesty. His Royal Highness was born at Hanover, on 29th March, 1819, and on the death of his father in 1850, succeeded to the dukedom. In 1837 he became Colonel in the army; in 1845, Major-General; in 1854, Lieutenant-General. He was appointed to command the Highlanders and Guards, which formed the first division of the army sent to the Crimea to support the interests of Turkey. At the battle of the Alma his Royal Highness displayed both ability and valour as a commander, leading his troops into action in a manner that gained the confidence of the men and the esteem of the officers. At Inkermann he had a horse shot under him, and displayed the same vigour and courage. On the retirement of Lord Hardinge, the Duke was appointed Commander-in-Chief of the British army, with whom he is as great a favourite as was his uncle the Duke of York. During his administration of this office he has introduced many valuable reforms, and has proved himself an untiring friend of the common soldier.

CAMPBELL, JOHN, LORD, Lord Chancellor of England, was born at Springfield, near Cupar, Fife, in 1779; his father being the parish minister.

He studied at the University of St. Andrews. On entering the legal profession he went to London, and kept his terms at Lincoln's Inn. Called to the bar in 1806, he became King's Counsel in 1827. In 1830 he entered the House of Commons for the borough of Stafford, as an ardent reformer. In 1832 he became Solicitor-General; in 1834 Attorney-General and member for Edinburgh, and in 1841 he was appointed Lord Chancellor of Ireland. The fall of the Melbourne Cabinet in that year left him at more leisure to prosecute literary pursuits, and he presented the world with the "Lives of the Lord Chancellors and Keepers of the Great Seal, from the earliest Times to the Reign of George IV.," and the "Lives of the Chief Justices of England, from the Norman Conquest to the death of Lord Mansfield." When Lord John Russell came into office, Lord Campbell was appointed Chancellor of the Duchy of Lancaster, and in 1850 became Lord Chief Justice of England, in which capacity he has presided at some very remarkable trials, displaying unabated vigour, power of attention, and sagacity. He remained Lord Chief Justice until the fall of the Derby Government in 1859, when Lord Palmerston removed him from the Queen's Bench to the Woolsack. He is now Lord Chancellor, and discharges the functions of his office with an ability scarcely to have been expected in a judge much more accustomed to common law than to equity procedure. As a constitutional lawyer Lord Campbell has no superior, and very few equals; as a judge his decisions have invariably been characterised by sound legal knowledge and acute discrimination. He married, in 1821, a daughter of Lord Abinger, who was created a peeress in her own right, with the title of Baroness Stratheden, and has seven children, of whom the eldest, William Frederick, born in 1824,

was for some time M.P. for Harwich, but since his mother's death, in 1860, has taken his seat in the House of Lords as Lord Stratheden. Lord Campbell's speeches at the bar and in the House of Commons were published in 1842.

CAMPBELL, Rev. John, D.D., a divine and journalist, was born in Forfarshire at the close of the last century. Between the years 1819 and 1823 he passed through a regular course of literary education at the Universities of St. Andrews and Glasgow, after which he studied theology in the Hall of the Independent denomination in Glasgow, under the presidency of the late Dr. Ralph Wardlaw and the Rev. Greville Ewing. He became pastor of the Independent church in Kilmarnock in 1827; and from the notice he soon attracted as a preacher, he was, in 1828, invited to the pastorate of the church assembling in the Tabernacle, Moorfields, London, erected by the celebrated Whitfield, one of the largest congregations in the metropolis. Here Dr. Campbell laboured with undiminished popularity for upwards of twenty years, till his health failed. Under these circumstances he was led to comply with the invitations of a body of Christian gentlemen to commence a popular religious newspaper, "The British Banner," which met with unexampled success. This journal he conducted for nine years, when he relinquished it, and on his own account established the "British Standard," to which two years afterwards he added the "British Ensign." In 1844, by the public vote of the Assembly of the Congregational Union of England and Wales, he was invited to undertake the editorship of a popular religious magazine, the "Christian Witness," which realized a monthly circulation of 30,000 copies. To this, two years afterwards, he added the "Christian Penny Magazine," which obtained a monthly issue of 100,000 copies. Dr.

Campbell is a voluminous author. Among his larger works may be mentioned his "Maritime Discovery and Christian Missions;" "Jethro," a hundred-guinea prize essay; the "Martyr of Erromanga;" the "Life of Nasmith, the Founder of City Missions;" "Popery and Puseyism;" and "John Angell James: a Review of his Character, Eloquence, and Writings." Dr. Campbell has entered largely into the ecclesiastical controversies of the day. In 1839 he issued a volume of Letters, reprinted from the "Patriot" newspaper, against the Bible printing monopoly, which contributed to a great reduction in the price of Bibles, and to greater accuracy in the correction of subsequent editions.

CANDLISH, THE REV. ROBERT, D.D., a Scottish clergyman, and leader of the Free Church. Dr. Candlish is distinguished by great subtlety and acuteness as a debater, and as an ecclesiastical leader has attained a distinguished position in Scotland. Excessive devotion to Free Church interests has left him little leisure to achieve that excellence as an author which his undoubted native powers might warrant us to anticipate. His works on "Genesis," on "Scripture Characters," on the "Atonement," on the "Resurrection," and on "Maurice's Theological Essays," all display great acuteness, although perhaps sometimes wanting in that fulness of information and carefulness of finish which greater leisure would bestow.

CANNING, CHARLES JOHN, VISCOUNT, Governor-General of India, was born in 1812, at Gloucester Lodge, Brompton. He is the son of the late Right Hon. George Canning, by a daughter of Major-General Scott of Balcomie, Fifeshire. He was educated at Christ Church, Oxford. In 1835 he married a daughter of Lord Stuart de Rothesay, a lady who, as Maid of Honour to Queen Adelaide, was in high favour at Court. In 1836 he was returned to the House of Commons as member for Warwickshire; but on his mother's death, in 1837, he succeeded to the title of Viscount, and took his seat in the House of Lords, where he acquired a reputation for good sense and intelligence as a speaker. For some time his political opinions were undecided, but eventually he adhered to the Conservative party. In 1841 he took office under Sir Robert Peel as Under-Secretary of State for Foreign Affairs, a post which he held until about the beginning of 1846, when a few months previous to the resignation of Sir Robert Peel he became Chief Commissioner of Woods and Forests. In 1853 he accepted office in the administration of Lord Aberdeen, and as Postmaster-General introduced great improvements into that institution, retaining the office under the ministry of Lord Palmerston. In 1855, on the resignation of the Marquis of Dalhousie, Lord Canning became Governor-General of India, a position which he has since held, through good and bad report, during a period the most critical in the history of our Indian empire. It is probable, that after the mists of prejudice have cleared away, and the heats of passion, together with the prepossessions of party, have subsided, it will be acknowledged by all parties that India never had a fairer or more honourable British chief. The severest trial Lord Canning had to undergo in his Indian government was when Lord Derby's Ministry was formed in 1858. Lord Ellenborough was appointed President of the Board of Control, and in that capacity forwarded a despatch to the Governor-General which conveyed heavy censure in not the most moderate language. Lord Canning's vindication of himself was triumphant, and Lord Ellenborough was obliged, by the voice of the country, and the demonstrations of Parliamentary hostility, to resign his seat in the ministry.

G

CANROBERT, François Certain, a French commander, was born in 1809. After receiving his military education at the school of St. Cyr, he in 1828 joined the army as a sub-lieutenant in the 47th Regiment of the Line; and in 1835, having been previously made lieutenant, he went to Africa. Having distinguished himself in 1842, he was made a chief of battalion, in 1846 lieutenant-colonel, and in 1847, colonel. In 1848 he was entrusted with the command of an expedition against the Arabs, in which he acquitted himself with great success and bravery. He then took command of the Zouaves, and marching against the Kabyles, was again victorious. Promoted to be general of brigade, in 1850 he led an expedition against Narah, one of the most powerful strongholds of the Arabs; but such was the ability of his attack, that after a few hours' determined fighting, the place was reduced. In 1852 Louis Napoleon made him one of his aides-de-camp, and in 1853 general of division. On the death of St. Arnaud he succeeded to the command of the French army in the Crimea, but, probably owing to the difficulties of his position, did not much distinguish himself in that capacity. It has been suggested that he permitted Napoleon, whose nominee he was, to dictate from Paris the tactics of the army, a procedure which Pélissier on his appointment at once repudiated. However, on his return from the East, the Emperor treated him with marked distinction, created him a Marshal of France, and despatched him on diplomatic service to the courts of Denmark and Sweden. In 1855 he received the Grand Cross of the Legion of Honour.

CANTERBURY, John Bird Sumner, D.D., Archbishop of, was born in 1780, at Kenilworth, in Warwickshire, of which his father was vicar. He was educated at Eton and King's College, gaining honours as Browne's Medallist, and Hulse's Prizeman. After publishing, in 1815, his principal work, entitled "Apostolical Preaching," he wrote his "Records of Creation," which gained the second Burnett Prize of £400 in the following year. In 1820 Dr. Sumner was a canon of Durham; in 1828 he was consecrated Bishop of Chester; and in 1848 translated to the Archbishopric of Canterbury. His patronage as Primate is large, and it is administered with discrimination, the intercourse of the Primate with subordinates being marked by uniform urbanity. He has been called on, by innovations introduced into the services of the Church of England, to express his decided hostility thereto, but he has always exhibited a conciliatory feeling, even in the rebukes he has administered. The Archbishop, who is a liberal in politics, is regarded as the head of the Low-Church party in the Church of England. Besides the works above mentioned, Dr. Sumner has published many others on theological subjects, together with several volumes of sermons.

CANTU, Cesar, an Italian historian, was born at Brescia in 1805. He was educated at Sondio, in the Valtelline, where, at eighteen years of age, he was appointed Professor of Literature in the college of that city. He afterwards resided at Como, Milan, and Piedmont. Owing to the expression of his political views in his "Reflections on the History of Lombardy in the 17th Century," Cantu was condemned to a year's imprisonment at the instance of the Austrian Government. Cantu's chief work is his "Storia Universale," a production which is considered as one of the most valuable contributions to the literature of Italy. His "Reformation in Europe" has been translated into English by F. Prandi. Besides the works alluded to, M. Cantu has produced many others, chiefly relating to historical subjects.

**CAPEFIGUE.** JEAN BAPTISTE HONORÉ RAYMOND, a French historian and periodical writer, was born at Marseilles in 1802. He received his early education in his native place, afterwards began the study of the law, and to complete his legal training went to Paris in 1821. In Paris he became connected with political affairs as editor of the "Quotidienne," and afterwards wrote articles for many of the Parisian journals. He was engaged preparing, in the meantime, his "Operations of the French Army in Spain." He obtained a post in the Foreign Office, which, however, he resigned in 1848, and subsequently devoted himself to historical studies, availing himself of the varied information which his official position placed at his disposal. The revolution, however, closed against him the archives of foreign affairs. He was one of the first who opposed the Republic in the National Assembly, and for two years his letters, dated from London, Vienna, and Berlin, guided the policy of the counter revolution. Among his principal works are the "Essai sur les Invasions," "Histoire de Philippe Auguste," the "Histoire de la Réforme, de la Ligue, et du Règne de Henri Quatre," "Richelieu, Mazarin, et la Fronde," "Louis XIV.," "L'Europe pendant le Consulat et l'Empire de Napoléon," "L'Europe depuis l'avénement de Louis Philippe," his latest work of note being "Avant 1789, Royauté, Droit, Liberté."

**CARDIGAN,** JAMES THOMAS BRUDENELL, EARL OF, was born in 1797. His father was sixth Earl of Cardigan. He entered the army on 8th May, 1824, and in December, 1830, attained the rank of lieutenant-colonel. Under the title of Lord Brudenell he sat in Parliament for Marlborough and Northampton. In 1837 he was called to the House of Lords, on the death of his father. The great fortune to which he became heir he employed in improving the condition of his regiment. He acquired a good deal of notoriety in connexion with the "black bottle" and other mess squabbles, terminating in a duel with Captain Tuckett, and his celebrated trial before the House of Lords, which broke down chiefly on technical grounds. After this period Lord Cardigan devoted himself to his military duties, and acquired great commendation for his services in this respect from the highest authorities in the army. In 1854 he was appointed Major-General, and took the command of the Light Cavalry in the Crimean War. His heroic charge at the battle of Balaklava will long be remembered as one of the most memorable incidents in the campaign. It invested his lordship for a time with well-merited popularity, which, however, was somewhat diminished, owing to the charges, well or ill-founded, brought against him by the Crimean Commissioners, although these in no respect affect his character as a gallant officer. In 1855 he was appointed Commander of the Bath, and in 1856 Commander of the Legion of Honour.

**CARDWELL,** RIGHT HON. EDWARD, a politician and member of Parliament, was born at Liverpool in 1813, and is the son of a merchant of that town. He studied at Oxford, and was called to the bar in 1838. Afterwards he entered on a political career, and was returned as member of Parliament for Clitheroe in 1842. He sat for Liverpool from 1847 till 1852, when he was defeated at the general election; and for Oxford from 1853 to 1857, when he was again defeated but afterwards returned, on adopting the views of the Peelite party. He was Secretary of the Treasury from February, 1845, to July, 1846, and President of the Board of Trade, under Lord John Russell, from 1852 to 1855, and is now Chief Secretary for Ireland. Since 1852 he has been a member of the Privy Council.

CAREY, HENRY C., an American political economist, was born in Philadelphia, the 15th December, 1793, where his father, Matthew Carey, a distinguished writer, had established a large publishing business. In 1821 Mr. Carey succeeded his father, and three years afterwards established the system of periodical trade-sales which are now the ordinary channels of exchange between American booksellers. He published an " Essay on the Rate of Wages, with an Examination of the Causes of the Difference in the Condition of the Labouring Population throughout the World," in 1835; and a work on the "Credit System of France, England, and the United States," in 1838. These treatises were reproduced and expanded into his " Principles of Political Economy" (1837-40). He has since published "Past, Present, and Future" (1848); "The Harmony of Interest, Agricultural, Manufacturing, and Commercial" (1850); and "The Slave Trade, Domestic and Foreign: why it exists, and how it may be extinguished" (1853). In 1858-9 he gave to the world the digested and methodized results of his studies and discoveries, under the title of "Principles of Social Science," in 3 vols., 8vo. His separate publications extend in the aggregate to something like four thousand pages, and his contributions to newspapers and periodicals to as many more. He has written various pamphlets, among which are "Answers to the Questions, What constitutes Currency? What are the Causes of its Unsteadiness? and What is the Remedy?" (1840); " Letters on International Copyright" (1853); "Letters to the President of the United States" (1858). In his essay upon the "Rate of Wages," Mr. Carey took his first step in opposition to the Ricardo-Malthusian system, affirming that profits and wages do not vary inversely, but that high wages are the index of prosperity to both capitalist and labourer. In the "Principles of Political Economy" he advanced to the position now universally known as his theory of *labour-value*, and generally accepted by economists as an exposition of *rent* and *value*, which places in the clearest light the errors of Ricardo and his school. In "The Past, Present, and Future," Mr. Carey overturned the assumptions of preceding economists in respect to the law which rules the occupation of the earth, and its capacity to support its ever-growing population. In his latest work, "The Principles of Social Science," all the doctrines of his completed system are arrayed in the form of a "Vindication of the provisions of Providence for man, in all his terrestrial surroundings." The author denies the alleged antagonism between Nature and human labour and capital, population, and subsistence. His principal works have been translated into Italian and Swedish; and within the current year his last and largest work will be published in French and German.

CARLEN, MADAME EMILIE, or SMITH, a Swedish novelist, was born at Stockholm in 1810. She is the wife of Mr. J. G. Carlen, a lawyer in Stockholm, who has acquired a reputation in Sweden by the publication of a hand-book of Swedish Jurisprudence, and various poems and tales. ‑Mrs. Carlen has written a great number of works, among which may be enumerated:—"Waldemar Klein" (1838); "The Representative" (1839); "Gustavus Lindorm" (1839); "The Foster Brothers" (1840); "The Church of Hammarby" (1840-41); "The Postboy" (1841); "The Rose of Tistelœn," and "Paul Vœrning" (1844); "The Hermit of John's Rock," and "One Year of Married Life" (1846); "A Night on Lake Pullar" (1847); "The Maiden's Tower" (1848); and "The Heroine of the Novel" (1849); "A Name," "The Tutor," "In Six Months," and numerous other romances. Madame Carlen is, after Miss Bremer, the most popular novelist of Sweden. She possesses remarkable fertility of invention, and great powers of description. She is a keen observer, and in her best works the interest is well sustained. Many of her works have been translated into English.

CARLETON, WILLIAM, a writer of fiction, was born at Clogher, Tyrone, in 1796. The son of a respectable and wealthy farmer, he was anxious to obtain a classical education; and as there was no proper school within twenty miles, he urged his friends to send him to Munster. This they did with a purse of twenty pounds in his pocket; but he never went farther than the town of Granard, from whence, overcome by his affection for his mother, he returned home the next day. Mr. Carleton's passion for adventure was produced by his perusal of Gil Blas, whereby he was tempted to seek the Irish metropolis, which he entered with only two and ninepence in his pocket, to begin a hard life, such as Savage and Chatterton had known in London. In Dublin he produced his first two volumes of the "Traits and Stories of the Irish Peasantry." Although published anonymously, they at once met with public favour, because of their pathos, humour, and truth. Thenceforward—1830—he lived by his writings, and could afford to publish them in small portions, and to bestow great pains on their preparation. Some of his works have been objected to, in consequence of their political bias; but his characters are always sharply defined, and his incidents have an amount of local colouring which never fails to give them a great charm. His Traits and Stories were translated into German so far back as 1825, and several of his subsequent productions into French and Italian. Mr. Carleton has been a voluminous writer, having published about forty-five volumes. Although in his sixty-fifth year, he is still fresh and vigorous, and will, doubtless, for years to come, be able to give to the public many other such works as those which have gained him such a high and universal popularity, and caused his fellow-countrymen to bestow upon him the honourable title of the "Father of Irish Literature." His latest production is "The Evil Eye; or, the Black Spectre."

CARLISLE, GEORGE WILLIAM FREDERICK HOWARD, EARL OF, K.G., long well known as Lord Morpeth, was born in April, 1802. As Viscount Morpeth he pursued his studies with great success at Oxford, and entered public life as Member for the Borough of Morpeth. In 1841, after being elected for Yorkshire, he became Chief Secretary for Ireland. Party feeling at that period ran immoderately high in the sister island, and Lord Morpeth was as much esteemed by one section of the people as he was condemned by another. He was, on the whole, a favourite of Mr. O'Connell, a fact indicative of his political bias. On the dissolution of Parliament which preceded the retirement of Lord Melbourne's administration in 1841, he stood again for the West Riding of Yorkshire, and was defeated. Afterwards he visited the United States, where unusual honours awaited him. On his return he was appointed Chief Commissioner of Woods and Forests, and subsequently Chancellor of the Duchy of Lancaster. As Lord-Lieutenant of Ireland under Lord Palmerston's administration, he was extremely popular. He was appointed to that high post in 1855, but when the ministry gave way he was removed, the Earl of Eglinton being his successor. In 1859 Lord Eglinton was recalled, and Lord Carlisle was once more placed at the head of the Irish Government, where he still continues. It may not be uninteresting to state that Lord Carlisle is as amiable and benevolent in private life as in public affairs he is just and impartial. The Earl has acquired a reputation altogether distinct from his political career as a public lecturer; his discourses, delivered at Mechanics' Institutes, on America, and the "Life and Writings of Pope," having merits of a high order as literary productions, and claims to notice altogether independent of the fact of their having been read by a lord to mechanics. Lord Carlisle is the author of "A Diary in Greek and Turkish Waters."

CARLYLE, THOMAS, an essayist and historian, was born on 5th December, 1795, at Ecclefechan, in Dumfriesshire. Educated at Annan, at the age of fourteen he removed to the University of Edinburgh, where he devoted himself chiefly to the study of mathematics and natural philosophy under Leslie and Playfair. His private studies were, however, at this period of more importance in his future career than the tasks of the classes. In the College library he read works in every department of literature, while he assiduously studied the modern languages of Europe, and especially German, which was then little cultivated in Scotland. He remained at the University for about seven years, with the view of entering the Church; but he changed his intention, and in 1820 became a teacher of mathematics at Kirkcaldy, in Fifeshire, where Edward Irving, who had been for some years his intimate friend, had settled in a similar capacity. After remaining two years in this situation, he resolved to enter on a new field of activity. He held the doctrine that the Press was the only true priesthood and governing power of the world, that literature was the best church, and that writers are the best preachers of modern times for all kinds of people and in all places. He steadily adhered to this principle on removing to Edinburgh, in 1822, where he enthusiastically devoted himself to authorship;

his first work being a translation of "Legendre's Geometry," to which he prefixed an "Essay on Proportion." In 1825 he published a translation of Goethe's "Wilhelm Meister," a work which directed his mind into a new current of thought. Once among the Germans, he went boldly to work on a "Life of Schiller," which was published from month to month in the "London Magazine." In 1825 Mr. Carlyle married Miss Veitch, a lady of cultivated tastes and much literary ability, and he shortly afterwards proceeded to Craigenputtock, a small farm in the moors of Dumfriesshire, where he kept up a correspondence with Goethe, and prosecuted the study of German literature. Here he wrote various articles for the Edinburgh Encyclopædia" and the "Edinburgh Review," to the former contributing the Lives of Montesquieu, Montaigne, Nelson, and the two Pitts, and to the latter his remarkable Essays on "Jean Paul," "German Literature," and "Burns." While living at this place he also wrote "Sartor Resartus," a history of the life and opinions of Herr Teufelsdröckh, an imaginary German professor, in which he set forth a whole philosophy of life and society. The mixture of subtle speculation, true poetry, and grotesque humour which characterised this work had their effect heightened by the use of a novel and peculiar phraseology, to some extent the imitation of a German literary slang, but to a greater extent still the product of Mr. Carlyle's invention. It enabled him to compress within a small compass a great variety of ideas, which could not have been expressed within the same space under the ordinary forms of pure, precise, and measured English prose; and it seems to have been found so serviceable and effective in this respect that it has been adhered to by the author in all his subsequent writings. In 1834 Mr. Carlyle removed to London, and has since resided in a house at Chelsea, exercising a strong personal influence on the most eminent literary men of the metropolis. During the first year of his residence in London "Sartor Resartus" was published in a separate form. It was not till 1837 that he published the "French Revolution," which placed him in the first rank of living writers. This work produced a profound impression on the public mind, abounding as it did in vividly graphic and picturesque description, and intensity of feeling. "Chartism" appeared in 1839. In 1840 Mr. Carlyle delivered a series of lectures on "Heroes and Hero Worship," which were published in 1841. "Past and Present" appeared in 1843, and in 1850 the "Latter Day Pamphlets," in which the author declaims vigorously against the revolutionary events of 1848: his "Life of John Sterling" (1851); and the "Letters and Speeches of Oliver Cromwell" (1847). The latter holds a high place as shedding new light on a character of the highest mark in British history. His latest work, "The Life of Frederick the Great," partakes at once of his failings and his genius, but is still as interesting as, and more instructive than, a romance. Few authors have been better abused, and more admiringly upheld, than Carlyle, but his influence over contemporary literature continues powerful. A uniform and handsome edition of his works, comprising sixteen volumes, has lately been published.

CARNOT, LAZARE HIPPOLITE, a French political writer and Minister of Public Instruction under the Republic of 1848, was born at St. Omer in 1801. He is a son of the celebrated republican general; and was originally intended for the Polytechnic School, but the events of 1815 compelled his family to seek an asylum in Germany, where he continued his studies, devoting his attention specially to philosophy and political economy. On his return to France he became a zealous adherent of the St.

Simonians, in the spirit of whose doctrines he conducted the "Revue Encyclopédique." On this becoming a religious sect, however, he withdrew from the body. As President of the Central Committee for the Paris Elections of 1839 he was chosen a deputy for the metropolis, and again in 1842 and 1846. He sat for nine years on the benches of the Opposition, taking an active part in the debates on foreign affairs, the reformation of prisons, colonial slavery, and juvenile labour in factories. Appointed Minister of Public Instruction after the Revolution of February, he exerted himself successfully in improving the condition of schoolmasters; proposed a law making elementary instruction gratuitous and obligatory on all; opened classes for the working people, evening lectures for those engaged during the day, houses of refuge, and a great school for administrative instruction, which was subsequently suppressed by M. de Falloux, one of Louis Napoleon's Ministers. He defended the Republic to the last, and when it was overthrown he left France of his own accord. However, the electors of the capital remained faithful to him, and re-elected him as a member of the legislative body. He returned, but refused to accept of the distinction conferred upon him, and, instead, explained in a published letter his reasons for declining to take an oath of allegiance to the Napoleonic Empire. In 1856 M. Carnot was elected for the seventh time, but he still persisted in his refusal, and has lived since in retirement at Paris, engaged in studious pursuits. He has written several books on politics, modern history, and German literature, and he is now on the eve of publishing "Memoirs of his Father's Life," which is certain to prove an important and attractive book.

CARPENTER, WILLIAM BENJAMIN, M.D., a physiologist, is the son of the late eminent Unitarian minister, Dr.

Lant Carpenter, of Bristol, and was born in 1813. Circumstances having induced him to devote his attention to medical science, he pursued the study of his profession for some years at home, afterwards in London, and finally in Edinburgh, where he graduated as M.D. in 1839. Whilst residing in Bristol he was appointed Lecturer on Medical Jurisprudence in the medical school of that city. Here it was that Dr. Carpenter wrote his "Principles of General and Comparative Physiology," and his "Principles of Human Physiology," which by competent critics is said to be the best work on the subject yet published. During the same period he commenced an elementary series of treatises on various departments of science, under the title of the "Popular Cyclopædia." Having determined to devote himself rather to the literary and scientific than to the practical department of his profession, and having been elected a Fellow of the Royal Society, Dr. Carpenter removed to London in 1844, on being appointed Fullerian Professor of Physiology in the Royal Institution. He soon afterwards undertook the editorship of the "British and Foreign Medico-Chirurgical Review," which he held for some years. Subsequently he became Professor of Medical Jurisprudence in University College, and Examiner in Physiology in the University of London. The latter of these appointments, however, he resigned on being appointed to the office of Registrar of the University; and in consequence of the recent increase of his duties in that capacity he has now withdrawn from every other public occupation. His larger treatises on "Physiology," as well as a smaller manual on that science, and a manual on the "Microscope," have gone through several editions. The latter is a most valuable work on microscopic science, being replete with instruction as to the construction and uses of microscopes of every kind. In 1849 Dr. Carpenter gained a prize of 100 guineas offered for the best Essay upon the Use and Abuse of Alcoholic Liquors, of which a people's edition, published by Bohn, has obtained great popularity. He has also been an occasional contributor to the leading reviews, as well as to the "Philosophical Transactions," and the "Cyclopædia of Anatomy and Physiology."

CARY, MISS ALICE, an American poetess, was born in Hamilton County, in the North American State of Ohio, in April, 1820. On her father's side she is of Huguenot descent. Up to 1850 Miss Cary resided at Clovernook, in her native county, where, although the ordinary means of a sound education were not within her reach, she seems to have acquired varied accomplishments by means of self-culture. When eighteen, she published her first volume of poems at Cincinnati, which met with a favourable reception from the public. She was warmly encouraged by many of the most eminent literary men in America. In 1850 she removed to New York, and since then she and her sister Phœbe have become regular contributors to the leading magazines and journals of America. In 1851 Miss Alice Cary wrote the first of her Clovernook Papers, a work which at once gave her a position as a prose writer. In 1852 she produced "Hagar, a Story of To-day;" and in 1853, a second series of Clovernook Papers, which, having been republished in this country, has met with great success. Her "Lyra, and other Poems," is a work placing her in the first rank among the American female writers of verse. In the following year she published the "Clovernook Children Papers," a little volume prepared especially for the young. A complete edition of Miss Cary's poems was issued in 1855, containing also a poem of a more elaborate, if not more ambitious, character than any that had preceded it, called

"The Maiden of Tlascala." It has been characterised as one of the best narrative poems yet produced in America. It is remarkable for purity of language, beauty of imagery, and energy and power in depicting passion. The last of the best known publications of Miss Cary was "Married not Mated," which was, in America, contrasted with some of Mr. Dickens's happiest efforts; and "Pictures of Country Life," published in 1859, and republished in the same year in London.

CASABIANCA, FRANÇOIS XAVIER, COUNT OF, a French senator, son of a Corsican general, and grandson of the Count of Casabianca, a Senator of the First Empire, was born at Nice, on 27th June, 1796, and studied at the Lycée Napoléon, where he took the prize in philosophy, and afterwards passed through the usual course of a legal education. He was called to the bar in 1818, but a considerable time elapsed before he obtained the success to which his talents entitled him. He was a liberal in politics, and at the same time an earnest supporter of the cause of the exiled Bonaparte family. After the Revolution of 1848 he was returned to the Constituent Assembly as representative of Corsica, and when, by the elections of December, Louis Napoleon became President of the Republic, M. Casabianca supported the policy of the Prince with energy and zeal. Towards the close of 1851 the President called him to his councils, first as Minister of Commerce and Agriculture, and next as Minister of Finance. When the *coup d'état* changed the aspect of public affairs in France, M. Casabianca was appointed to organize a new Ministry, which he did in January, 1852; but soon afterwards he gave up his various important offices to enter the Senate, where he still continues an able and sagacious adviser of the Emperor.

CASS, GENERAL LEWIS, LL.D., an American statesman of the democratic party, and of notorious pro-slavery predilections, was born at Exeter, New Hampshire, 9th October, 1782. He was called to the bar in 1802, and elected to the Ohio Legislature in 1806. Not being very successful in the legal profession, he entered the army of the United States, and was opposed to the English in 1812-14. He held the post of Governor of Michigan until 1831, when he became War Secretary under General Jackson's Presidency. He was appointed Minister to France in 1836, retaining that position till 1842. Two years afterwards he was a candidate for the chief magistracy of the Union, but was defeated; and in 1857 was appointed Secretary of State under Mr. Buchanan. He possesses considerable influence in the American Senate, of which he is a member. As a politician he seems to entertain an inveterate animosity towards Great Britain. Had affairs been at his disposal, he would have plunged America into a war with this country even while the Oregon dispute was in course of arrangement. He is the author of a work entitled "France: its King, Court, and Government." His life has been written by Mr. T. Young and W. L. G. Smith.

CATTERMOLE, GEORGE, a painter, was born at Dickleburgh, near Diss, in Norfolk, in 1800. When young he was an admirable architectural draughtsman. He contributed to the Annuals, but afterwards devoted himself to water-colour painting, and for more than twenty years his works adorned the Water-colour Exhibition. For the last five or six years, however, he has ceased to send his pictures there, and has devoted himself to oil-painting. He was one of the five English painters who received the first-class medal at the Paris Exhibition in 1855. In 1856 he was, by special diploma, elected a Member of the Royal Academy of Amsterdam, and also Honorary Member of the Belgian

Society of Painters in Water Colours. His pictures embrace a comprehensive range of subjects, historical and poetical. The Bible, Scott, and Shakspere have furnished him with ample materials on which to exercise his peculiar powers. His pictures invariably display great imaginative power, deep poetic feeling, delicate conception, and exquisite mastery of execution.

CAUSSIDIÈRE, MARC, a French politician, was born at Lyons in 1809, of a family of artisans. Up to 1834 he was little more than an obscure workman, employed in the manufactories of Lyons and St. Etienne. In the sanguinary revolutionary affrays of these cities, in 1834, he was at once a resolute leader and hardy combatant in the ranks of the insurrectionists. Condemned to imprisonment for his connexion with these proceedings, he was restored to liberty by the amnesty of 1837. His imprisonment appears only to have strengthened the ardour of his convictions, and soon after his release from incarceration he became recognised as one of the leaders of the advanced Reform party. At the Revolution of February, 1848, Caussidière, who was constantly found at the barricades up to the moment of the victory of his party, was installed Prefect of Police. Possessing a refined mind under a rough and unpolished exterior, he was a man of action in contact with the people, and surrounded by a militia ready for anything. During the brief reign of the Provisional Government, his energy contributed to restrain the imprudence of those Polish and Italian refugees with whom Paris swarmed, and who sought early to compromise the Republic by involving it in wars of aggression in the interest of foreign factions. His efforts to maintain order during several disturbances in Paris were of such a nature as to achieve this end, and at the same time render him popular with the people. He was elected to the Constituent Assembly for the department of the Seine; but being accused of supineness, he defended himself in the tribune, and resigned his office. In August the Assembly returned to the charge, and ultimately Caussidière felt flight essential to his safety, and he took refuge in London, where, giving up political life, he entered into business as a wine-merchant. Caussidière, in his exile, has published a memoir of the revolution, which has perhaps not received the attention its importance deserves.

CAVOUR, COUNT CAMILLE DE, an Italian orator and statesman, President of the Council of Ministers, and chief adviser of the King of Sardinia, was born at Turin in 1809. He is the second son of the late Marquis de Cavour, who belonged to one of the most ancient and distinguished families of Piedmont. When the reform movement began in 1847, he, with Count Balbo, founded the constitutional journal, " Il Risorgimento." After the fall of the democratic party he entered, in 1849, the Chamber of Deputies, and subsequently succeeded Santa Rosa as Minister of Commerce and Agriculture. In 1851 he was also entrusted with the Ministry of Finance, when he endeavoured to repair the injury caused by an unhappy war, and to restore the equilibrium of revenue and expenditure. In 1852, disagreeing with his colleagues, he retired for a brief space from the ministry, but was recalled in November of the same year, and succeeded M. d'Azeglio as President of the Council. During this period of his administration he introduced the principles of Free-trade into the commercial code of the kingdom of Sardinia, greatly reduced the tariffs, and by commercial treaties with several powers, among others with England, extended the commerce of Sardinia with foreign countries. In the beginning of 1855, through his exertions and advice, Piedmont joined the Anglo-French alliance, and despatched Sardinian troops to share in the Crimean expedition. At the peace he took an active part in the Congress of Paris, and there, for the first time, called the attention of the representatives of the great powers of Europe to the cause of Italy. He concluded the alliance, in 1859, between France and Sardinia for the deliverance of the Peninsula from the domination of Austria, resigning his office at the end of July, 1859, in consequence of the sudden termination of the campaign against Austria by the French Emperor. In January of the present year (1860) Count Cavour again assumed the Presidency of the Council, and was placed at the head of the department of Foreign Affairs, as well as of the Interior. He has since shown great political sagacity in the present crisis of Italian affairs, resulting from the successes of Garibaldi in Sicily and Naples, and at last has had the satisfaction of witnessing the annexation of both countries to the kingdom of Sardinia. Victor Emmanuel entered Naples on 7th November, 1860. Combining the highest qualities of a statesman and orator, Cavour is the firm friend of representative government. Under his administration Sardinia has taken a more conspicuous place in the European political system than she has ever formerly occupied; and the almost certain formation of a united Italy is destined to bring him more prominently under the notice of the English public, as a judicious and wise, yet liberal statesman, well able to guide his countrymen when they have attained that independence and influence to which they aspire.

CAYLEY, ARTHUR, a mathematician, was born on the 16th August, 1821, at Richmond, in Surrey. He entered at Trinity College, Cambridge, where he took his B.A. degree, and was in 1842 senior wrangler, and first Smith's prize-man, and a Fellow of the College. Afterwards he studied for the law; was called to the bar in 1849; and has since been in practice as a conveyancer. He was elected a Fellow of the Royal Society in 1852, and of the Royal Astronomical Society in 1857. Mr. Cayley is the author of various memoirs relating chiefly to pure mathematics, which have been published in the "Philosophical Transactions," the "Cambridge Philosophical Transactions," the "Memoirs of the Royal Astronomical Society," the "Cambridge, and Cambridge and Dublin, and the Quarterly Mathematical Journals," and the "Journals of Crelle and Liouville."

CÉLESTE, CÉLESTE ELLIOT, better known as Madame, an actress, and in the early part of her career a favourite *danseuse*, was born at Paris in August, 1815, of French parents, whose particular position in the world is not clearly known. She early received instruction in dancing at the Royal Academy of Music, and when fifteen accepted an engagement for the United States, where, at the early age of sixteen, she married a Mr. Elliot, who died some time afterwards. She then returned to this country, and devoted her attention to such pantomimic parts as that of "Fenella" in "Masaniello." After having appeared in all the principal cities and towns of the United Kingdom, she performed as a *danseuse* in London, and her unique style met with unbounded applause. In 1834 she returned to the United States. Wherever she went she met with an enthusiastic reception; and spent three years in a sort of daily ovation. In 1837 she reappeared on the boards of Drury Lane Theatre, no longer, however, in the capacity of a dancer, but as an actress; thence she proceeded to the Haymarket, afterwards accompanying Mr. Webster to the Adelphi, as directress of that theatre. Having remained in connexion with that establishment for several years, Madame Céleste dissolved the partnership, and at present manages the Lyceum on her own account.

CHADWICK, EDWIN, C.B., a legislative and administrative reformer and social economist, was born near Manchester, in 1800. Educated for the legal profession, he was called to the bar in 1830, and entered the public service in 1832. In 1828 he wrote an article in the "London Review," on the administration of public charity, which, with other papers on public questions, subsequently published, led to his being applied to and appointed first an Assistant-Commissioner, and afterwards one of the Commissioners of Inquiry into the means of improving the administration of the Poor-Laws. Mr. Chadwick's cardinal principle of administrative consolidation was in great part adopted, and the results were the Poor-law Unions in England and Ireland, and local Boards of Health, with their staff of paid officers. Lord John Russell stated that so far as Mr. Chadwick's measures had been applied they had saved the country from great social evils, if not absolutely from social revolution. In 1828 he contributed an article to the "Westminster Review," on "Life Assurance," which set forth some of the first principles of sanitary science. In 1829 he wrote a paper in the "London Review," on "Preventive Police," which induced a friendship with Jeremy Bentham, that only ceased with the death of that great thinker in 1832, when he bequeathed to Mr. Chadwick his library of Jurisprudence. In 1834, when the permanent Poor-law Commission was established, he was appointed Secretary to the Board. As one of the Commissioners of Inquiry into the labour of young persons in factories, he was charged with the preparation of the bill by which the short time system of labour, and the half-school time system of instruction, now in the course of extension, were introduced under Government inspection. While Secretary to the Poor-law Board, he was associated with Dr. Arnott, Dr. Southwood Smith, and Dr. Kay, in an inquiry as to how far the physical causes of fever in London might be removed by sanitary agencies. He was also selected to investigate the constitution of the Constabulary in England and Wales, his labours leading to the appointment of county police forces. His report on sanitary questions, completed in 1842, is a model of condensation and suggestive analysis. The water supply and drainage of towns did not escape his attention; he prepared separate reports on these questions, in which the measures he proposed are, for the most part, in course of adoption, under the superintendence of numerous local Boards of Health. Upon the report of a Committee of Inquiry, the constitution of the new Poor-law Board having been changed, he was appointed to the Sanitary Commission in 1847, and in that and the following years prepared reports which led to large alterations. The establishment of the General Board of Health led to the origination by Mr. Chadwick of many of those sanitary measures which have so materially altered the health of towns for the better; but the administration of the Public Health Act being placed in charge of a member of the House of Commons in 1854, he retired with a pension. He was one of the earliest advocates of the repeal of taxes on knowledge, on which he wrote an article in the "Westminster Review," in 1831. When the war with Russia ensued, he pointed out the disastrous effects certain to occur from want of proper sanitary arrangements in the army, and chiefly on his representation a commission was appointed to investigate the measures requisite for the protection of the army in India. His published papers and reports occupy many volumes. His measures have been alluded to in several royal speeches. Lord John Russell, Lord Brougham, and Lord Shaftesbury, have spoken highly of his labours; and continental statesmen have consulted him frequently on the subjects to which he has devoted his life.

CHAMBERS, MONTAGU, an English lawyer and politician, was born in 1800. He was at first intended for the army, and for some time studied at Sandhurst, obtaining a lieutenancy in the Grenadier Guards. He, however, resigned the profession of arms for that of the law, was called to the bar in 1828, and speedily became distinguished as an advocate. In 1845 he was made Queen's Counsel. He was elected Member for Greenwich in 1852, and as a politician has always advocated Liberal measures. As a pleader he has been engaged for many years past in some of the most remarkable cases on the Home Circuit.

CHAMBERS, WILLIAM and ROBERT, authors and publishers, were born in Peebles, William in 1800, Robert in 1802. Both brothers received a good education in their native town, Robert passing through a complete classical course, as preparatory to his adopting a learned profession. Through the misfortunes of their father, a cotton manufacturer on a scale of some extent, they at an early age were left dependent on their own exertions, by which their natural energy and self-reliance were called into play. The family having removed from Peebles to Edinburgh, William and Robert conducted separate establishments as booksellers until 1832, when they united in establishing their well-known "Journal." Since that time their course has been steadily upwards. Many anecdotes are told of their early struggles, their incessant labour, their ingenuity, and, above all, of their self-denial. At an early period of life Mr. Robert Chambers published his "Tra-

ditions of Edinburgh" (1824), and "Picture of Scotland." (1828), and contributed seven historical volumes to "Constable's Miscellany," including a very popular work, "The History of the Rebellion of 1745-6." Messrs. Chambers are, without doubt, the pioneers of cheap literature. The establishment of the "Journal," and its success, demonstrated that a respectable miscellany of original literature could be produced at a cost placing it within the reach of the masses. Now their printing and publishing house in High-street is one of the most remarkable and extensive in Scotland. Among the more important works they have published are their "Information for the People," the "Cyclopædia of English Literature," "Instructive and Entertaining Library and Tracts," "Educational Course," and "A Cyclopædia for the People." Mr. Robert Chambers has devoted great attention to literature and science. His chief works, besides those mentioned, are "Popular Rhymes of Scotland," the "Life and Works of Burns" (by far the best Life of Burns yet published), and the "Domestic Annals of Scotland." His "Ancient Sea Margins" is an important contribution to geological science. "The Book of Scotland," and "Things as they are in America," are Mr. William Chambers's chief works. In the early part of 1860 a splendid institution erected at Peebles, at the cost of Mr. William Chambers, was opened. It includes a museum and library, &c., and is a judicious application of the wealth which that gentleman has so worthily acquired during his past successful career.

CHAMBORD, HENRI CHARLES FERDINAND, DUC DE BORDEAUX, COUNT DE, head of the eldest branch of the House of Bourbon, was born at Paris, on the 29th September, 1820. The posthumous son of the Duc de Berri, assassinated in February of the same year, he was brought up in the principles of the ancient monarchy. At the Revolution of 1830 Charles X. made a futile effort to have him recognised as King, under the title of Henry V.; and the Count of Chambord, following the destinies of his family, went into exile. He resided by turns at Holyrood, Prague, and Goritz, and then travelled over most of Europe, in order to complete his education. In all the countries which he visited he was treated with the respect due to his misfortunes; and in many with the observances due to his pretensions. In 1846 he married Maria Theresa, daughter of the Duke of Modena. After the Revolution of 1848, and the flight of Louis Philippe, the Legitimists cherished hopes that the tide of events would establish the Count on the throne of France; but the revival of the Empire in 1852, if it did not dissipate every lingering remnant of expectation, adjourned its realization. The Duke of Bordeaux has no family by his wife, and it is assumed that the elder branch of the Bourbons will become extinct at his decease, and the family of Orleans be left in undisputed possession of all the privileges, real or imaginary, that may pertain to their legitimacy, and to the "divine right," which they will then be enabled to insist upon.

CHANGARNIER, NICOLAS AIMÉ THÉODULE, a French-African general, was born at Autun, in April, 1793. Leaving St. Cyr in 1815, with the rank of a sub-lieutenant, he entered, as a simple guardsman, one of the privileged companies of the Gardes-du-Corps of Louis XVIII., from which he passed as lieutenant to the Line. In Algeria he rose from the lowest position, as an officer in the French army, to his present rank. Throughout the whole of his career in Algiers, he was noted for his bravery and success. As chief of a battalion he distinguished himself by coolness in the campaign against Achmet Bey. For these services he was made lieutenant-colonel. At the termination of the Cheliff expedition he was made camp-marshal. In 1847 he received from the Duc d'Aumale the command of the Algerian division of the army. He was made Governor of Algiers in 1848, but, returning to Paris, he became connected with the events of June in that year, assuming the sole military command in that city. After being some time in the confidence of Louis Napoleon, who was then President, his command was taken from him. On the evening of the *coup d'état* he was arrested and conveyed to Mazas; since then he has been an exile. Lately permission to return to France was given him, in common with the other exiled generals, but was rejected, and he is now living in retirement in Belgium.

CHARLES XV. (LOUIS EUGÈNE), King of Sweden and Norway, and of the Goths and Vandals, was born on the 3rd of May, 1826. He is grandson of the celebrated General Bernadotte, who was the son of an innkeeper in France, and the only one of the soldiers of fortune elevated to royal dignity by the Emperor Napoleon I., who was able to preserve his throne after the fall of that conqueror. Charles XV. succeeded on the death of his father, Oscar I., on the 8th of July, 1859. He was married in 1850 to the Princess Wilhelmina, daughter of Prince Frederick of the Netherlands, by whom he has issue one daughter, the Princess Louisa Josephine Eugénie, born in 1851. The aged grandmother of his Majesty, the widow of Bernadotte, still survives (1860), in the 79th year of her age.

CHEEVER, GEORGE BURRITT, D.D., an American theological writer, was born at Hallowell, Maine, in 1807. He studied in the seminary of Andover, graduated at Bowdoin College in 1825, and was ordained pastor of Salem Church in 1832, and of Allen-street

Church, New York city, in 1839. In 1832 he visited Europe, and remained there two years and a half. In 1835 he published a vigorous temperance pamphlet, entitled "Inquire at Amos Giles's Distillery," which brought him into prominent notice, but which also contained such matter as gave rise to law proceedings, and a subsequent sentence of imprisonment. He has contributed extensively to religious periodicals in America, and is the author of "Lectures on the Pilgrim's Progress," "Wanderings of a Pilgrim in the Shadow of Mont Blanc," and other popular works.

CHELMSFORD, LORD, better known by the world as Sir Frederick Thesiger, and late Lord Chancellor of England, was born in London in 1794, and entered the navy in 1807. He subsequently left the navy, and entering the legal profession, was called to the bar at Gray's Inn in 1818. He almost at once succeeded, was for many years recognised as the leader of the Home Circuit, and in 1834 became a King's Counsel. He entered Parliament as member for Abingdon in 1844; was appointed Solicitor-General under the government of Sir Robert Peel, and in 1845 succeeded the late Sir William W. Follett as Attorney-General. When Sir Robert Peel retired, he also resigned office, but continued to sit for Abingdon until 1852, when Lord Derby's Ministry being formed, he was re-appointed Attorney-General, having a seat in Parliament for Stamford, which he continued to represent until his admission to the peerage. On the second accession of Lord Derby to power, in 1858, Sir Frederick Thesiger was created Lord Chelmsford, on his elevation to the woolsack. The resignation of Government deprived him of office. His chief characteristics as a pleader were dignity and energy, accuracy and acuteness, perfect self-possession and persuasive eloquence. An unprecedented incident occurred in his professional life. Pre-viously to his being raised to the Upper House he had been counsel in a cause which involved a large property; but considering the suit more one for extra-judicial settlement than litigation, he compromised it without directly consulting his client. Lord Chelmsford was but a few days Lord Chancellor when this client sued him for damages. The case has been heard and re-heard since; and judgment has been given in his lordship's favour. During the session of 1860 Lord Chelmsford has brought in several measures in the House of Lords.

CHESNEY, FRANCIS RAWDON, D.C.L., Major-General in the Royal Artillery, was born at Ballyrea, in the county of Down, Ireland, in 1789. He was educated at the Royal Military Academy at Woolwich. In 1804 he received his first commission in the Royal Artillery. In 1815 he obtained the rank of second captain; and in 1821 was ordered to Gibraltar. In 1829 he proceeded to Constantinople, expecting by means of Congreve rockets and steamers to give effectual assistance to Turkey in her struggle with Russia. The war having terminated soon after his arrival, he visited the contending armies and their various fortresses and positions, and prepared a report upon them for Sir R. Gordon, the British ambassador at Constantinople. His inquiries led to the consideration of an overland route to India. Proceeding to examine the mouths of the Nile, the shores of the Mediterranean, and the Isthmus of Suez, he sailed down the Red Sea, examined the lower course of the Nile, and arrived at the conviction that a voyage to India from Egypt by means of steam vessels could be performed in the course of about three weeks. He also urged the opening of a sea canal from Suez to the Mediterranean, through Lake Menzalch. From Egypt he proceeded to Syria, to explore the route between the Mediterranean and the Persian Gulf.

He crossed Northern Syria, caused a raft to be constructed on the Upper Euphrates, and surveyed the Great River down to the Persian Gulf. He returned through Persia and Asia Minor to the Upper Euphrates, explored other parts of Western Asia, and coming home to England in 1833, published an account of the relative advantages of both routes to India. He urged the further exploration of the Syrian route, and at last was enabled by a vote of the House of Commons to undertake an expedition to the rivers Euphrates and Tigris. Appointed Colonel on this service, he proceeded to the coast of Syria in 1835, with a staff of naval and scientific officers. He met with many difficulties in his progress, but finally put together and floated two steamers on the Euphrates. Four hundred miles of the survey had been completed when a fearful hurricane sent the Tigris steamer to the bottom with twenty of her crew. Colonel Chesney and eight others were saved, and with the remaining steamer he descended and surveyed 1,200 miles of river; thus solving the problem of the overland route through the Plains of Mesopotamia. The results of this expedition have an importance which can scarcely be exaggerated. Should the Euphrates route ever become frequented to an extent in any degree corresponding to that of the Suez line—and political events may any day have this effect,—it will bring Western civilization into intimate contact with the very heart of the Mahomedan east ; with regions which, previous to the dawn of European history, were peopled by vast and rich communities, which recovered their fertility and importance in the first ages of Arab civilization, and which may again, under the influence of European example and precept, be re-incorporated with the civilized world. He returned to England in 1837, and continued absent from military duties until 1842. In 1843 he went to China as Brigadier, commanding the Royal and East India Artillery, and remained there until 1847. He has been at the head of the Royal Artillery in the Cork district from that period until 1852. In 1851 he published his large work and maps on the Expedition to the Euphrates and Tigris, and in the same year received the degree of D.C.L. at Oxford. He has since published "Observations on the Past and Present State of Fire-arms," in which he discusses the effects of the new musket in warfare.

CHEVALIER, MICHEL, State Councillor of France, and Member of the Institute, was born at Limoges, on 13th January, 1806. He is the son of a small merchant, and was at the age of eighteen admitted to the Polytechnic School, from which he passed to the Mining School. Shortly before the Revolution of 1830 he was attached as engineer to the Department of the Nord. He then embraced Saint Simonian doctrines, and became director of the "Globe" newspaper, which supported the views of this sect. He exerted himself so strenuously in the advocacy of the "New Church," that he was prosecuted for outrages on public morals, and condemned to a year's imprisonment. After the expiration of his sentence, he did not hesitate to retract all he had written against Christianity ; and he afterwards obtained from M. Thiers a special mission to the United States, with the view of studying the American System of communication by water and railway. In 1836 he published his "Letters on North America," a brilliant work, which was highly praised by Humboldt. After visiting England in 1836, he published a work on "The Material Interests of France," a programme of industrial ameliorations which might be advantageously carried out by the State. He filled several high offices, and was appointed by Louis Napoleon to be *Ingénieur-en-chef* of France. He is a clever political economist, founding his deductions on the example of England, and he enjoys a high reputation as a writer on all subjects connected with industry and finance in his native country. He is at present engaged in working out the details of the Commercial Treaty between France and England.

CHEVREUL, MICHEL EUGÈNE, a French chemist, was born at Angers, on the 31st August, 1786. The son of a distinguished physician, he studied in the Central School of his native place. He went to Paris and became chemical assistant to Vauquelin, who soon recognised in his young pupil such aptitude and sagacity that he gave him the direction of his laboratory. He progressed rapidly. In 1826 he took, in the Chemical Section of the Academy of Sciences, the place which the death of Prévost had left vacant; and in 1829, succeeded his old master, Vauquelin, in the chemical chair appropriated to the Museum of Natural History. He has been Commander of the Legion of Honour since September, 1844, and was a member of the Juries in the Great Expositions of London and Paris. He has published a number of works, chiefly relating to Animal Chemistry, and to colours and their contrasts, which record many original researches. He has also contributed extensively to scientific periodicals.

CHILD, MRS. LYDIA MARIA, an eminent American educational writer, before marriage Miss Francis, was born in Medford, Massachusetts, on the 11th February, 1802. Her father was a baker, much respected for his integrity and native good sense, who made improvements in the manufacture of bread. She enjoyed merely the educational advantages common to all children in New England; but her early fondness for literature was much stimulated by the active mind and studious habits of a brother, somewhat older than herself, now Dr. Convers Francis, Professor in Harvard University. In 1828 she married David Lee Child, a lawyer and editor in Boston. She and her husband united with W. L. Garrison, at the very outset of his labours for the Anti-Slavery cause, in which their zeal remains unabated. This circumstance has rendered her books unpopular with the Pro-Slavery classes in America. While Miss Francis, she wrote "Hobomok," an Indian story, and "The Rebels: a Tale of the Revolution." After her marriage she edited "The Juvenile Miscellany" for eight years, and wrote "The Girl's Own Book" (1831), republished in England; "The Mother's Book" (1831), which was republished in England and Germany; "An Appeal in behalf of that Class of Americans called Africans" (1833); "The Oasis: an Anti-Slavery Annual" (1833); "History of Women" (1835); "Philothea: a Grecian Romance" (1836); "Letters from New York" (1843-4); "Fact and Fiction," a collection of stories (1845); "Flowers for Children" (from 1845 to 1856); "Progress of Religious Ideas" (1855); and "Autumnal Leaves," a collection of stories (1857); she edited "The Anti-Slavery Standard" during 1841 and 1842.

CHINA, EMPEROR OF. (See "HIEN FUNG.")

CHISHOLM, MRS. CAROLINE, eminent for her efforts to improve the condition of emigrants, was born at Northampton about the year 1810. She received from her mother an excellent education, which developed all her generous and charitable instincts. In her twentieth year she married Captain Archibald Chisholm, of the Madras army. She proceeded with her husband to Madras, and there commenced a work of benevolence by establishing an Industrial Home for the benefit of soldiers' daughters, who were thus removed from temptation, and instructed in different branches of useful knowledge. In 1838, owing to the failure of Captain Chisholm's health, they went to Sydney. Remaining there with her three children during her husband's return to India, she established "The Female Immigrants' Home," and its branches in neighbouring districts, whose objects were to provide for, and to protect friendless young women who were continually arriving from Europe. In 1846, Major Chisholm having rejoined his family, Mrs. Chisholm proceeded to England, taking with her a mass of addresses and facts concerning emigrants and their relations, collected laboriously in the interior of the colony, by going from farm to farm, in order to effect the reunion of families. Her first business on her arrival in this country was to send out shiploads of poor children who had been left behind by their parents when they themselves emigrated, for want of means to pay the charges demanded for children beyond a certain number. By her exertions the Emigration Commissioners were induced to ship them, as well as the wives and children of prisoners who were emancipated and well to do. In 1850 she instituted the Family Colonization Loan Society, in order to encourage a more general system of emigration, with the view of carrying out which Major Chisholm volunteered to proceed alone to Victoria in 1851, while his wife remained in England. He proceeded to South Australia and Victoria, and forming there committees of the most influential gentlemen in the colony to co-operate with the committee of the society in London, remitted in less than two years upwards of £10,000, paid into his office at Melbourne by relatives for the emigration of their kindred at home. Mrs. Chisholm joined her husband in Victoria with her six children in 1854, and immediately after her arrival proceeded to the "Diggings," where she discovered that much evil arose from the want of proper accommodation for travellers. At her solicitation the Colonial Government was induced to erect sheds, placed under the care of respectable couples, fifteen miles from each other, between Melbourne and the "Diggings," and by this means wives and children were enabled to rejoin their families by short stages, and at small expense. On account of serious and dangerous illness, Mrs. Chisholm went to Sydney in June, 1858, where she has since remained, unfortunately in rather indifferent health. Her untiring exertions in behalf of those who are compelled to leave their native homes for other lands, are universally held in high esteem.

CHRISTISON, ROBERT, a physician, and Professor of Materia Medica in the University of Edinburgh, son of the late Alexander Christison, Professor of Humanity in the same University, was born in the Scottish capital, 18th July, 1797. He became a student of Arts in the University in 1811, graduated in 1819, and afterwards studied in London and Paris. While in Paris in 1820-21 he was a pupil of Robiquet, and bent the powers of his intellect to the study of the department of science in which his name has become so eminent. After his return to Edinburgh in 1823, he was appointed Professor of Medical Jurisprudence, and nine years afterwards, in 1832, was elected to the chair of Materia Medica, his reputation both as a professor and physician ranking deservedly among the highest in the kingdom. His "Treatise on Poisons" (1829), has run through several editions, and is a standard work with the faculty.

CLARE, JOHN, the peasant poet of Northamptonshire, was born at Helpstone, 13th July, 1793. His father was an agricultural labourer, yet he managed to obtain some little knowledge of reading and writing from his scanty means. Obtaining a copy of Thomson's "Seasons," he was incited to attempt composing, and eventually produced a volume of poems, which met with success, and by the kind patronage of the Marquis of Exeter and Lord Milton, he was placed in comparatively easy circumstances. He was residing in Rutland, and married in 1820. His occupation being that of a farm-servant, doubtless affected the burden of his song, which was always descriptive of rural life and scenery. But when the wonder of a farm-servant being a poet had fallen away, his aristocratic friends took less interest in him. The anxieties of a family and the maintenance of his infirm father and mother preyed on his mind, and the result was that he dropped into a state of harmless lunacy. He entertains the hallucination that he is the author of the *chefs-d'œuvre* of Byron, Wordsworth, and Campbell, and affords a melancholy spectacle of a man of genius, whose mind is unequal to struggle with the realities of life.

CLARENDON, GEORGE WILLIAM FREDERICK VILLIERS, EARL OF, ex-Secretary of State for Foreign Affairs under Lord Palmerston's administration, was born 12th January, 1800. After studying at Cambridge, he entered the diplomatic service in 1820, as Attaché to the Embassy in Russia, and continued in that office for about three years, after which he was a Commissioner of Customs. In 1831 he negotiated a treaty of commerce with France; but his first prominent public appointment was that of Plenipotentiary to Madrid in 1833. On his accession to the earldom in 1838 he returned to England. In 1840 Lord Clarendon was appointed Lord Privy Seal. In 1846 he became President of the Board of Trade, under Lord John Russell, and in the subsequent year was nominated Lord-Lieutenant of Ireland. The circumstances under which Lord Clarendon commenced his duties were of the most perplexing nature. Disease

and famine were prevalent throughout Ireland, and political affairs were sources of disturbance in every part of the country. It was about this period that the Repeal Association was using its most active endeavours to produce universal discontent. The energy and prudence with which Lord Clarendon conducted himself during the crisis of 1848 added much to his reputation for sagacity by all classes of moderate liberals; and there is little doubt that he is destined to take a more conspicuous position than he has yet filled, in the political events of the future. Lord Clarendon held his office until the resignation of the Russell ministry in 1852. Under Lord Aberdeen he was appointed to the Foreign Office, a position which he likewise filled under the Government of Lord Palmerston. He had, during 1855, to take a leading position in the affairs relating to the Russian war, Lord Aberdeen having resigned, on account of the censure which had been cast on him by a vote of the House of Commons. Lord Clarendon also took part in the Congress at Paris, at which peace was concluded in 1856. When the ministry of his party was overthrown in 1858, Lord Clarendon, of course, changed to the opposition side of the House of Lords; but when a liberal Government was again formed in 1859, under Lord Palmerston, he was, at his own request, left out of the Cabinet. There is no statesman of the present day who is looked up to with higher respect than Lord Clarendon. He married in 1839 a sister of the present Earl of Verulam, by whom he has a family. He was created a G.C.B. in 1838, and in 1849 received the knighthood of the Garter.

CLARK, SIR JAMES, BART., M.D., Physician to the Queen, was born in 1788 at Cullen, in Banffshire. He went to school at Fordyce, took his degree of M.A. at Aberdeen, studied medicine in the University of Edinburgh, passed as physician there, and as surgeon in London, and afterwards travelled through several continental countries. He settled as a physician at Rome, remaining there for some years, also visiting the principal medical schools of Italy, France, and Germany. In 1820 Dr. Clark published a work entitled "Medical Notes on the Climate, Diseases, Hospitals, and Medical Schools in France, Italy, and Switzerland." He returned to England in 1826, settling in London, where he was appointed Physician to St. George's Infirmary. In 1829 he published his work "On the Sanative Influence of Climate;" the first accurate and philosophical book on the subject of which it treats. He was elected in 1832 a Fellow of the Royal Society, and in 1835 Physician to the Duchess of Kent and the Princess Victoria, becoming, on the accession of the latter to the throne, Physician in Ordinary. He published, in 1835, "A Treatise on Pulmonary Consumption and Scrofulous Diseases," which, propounding new views of these complaints, has had a remarkable effect in the mode of treating them, and has served to establish the reputation of the author as a medical adviser in affections of the chest. In 1838 Sir James Clark was created a Baronet, and since then he has received various other distinctions, been several times on the Council of the Royal Society, exerted himself in the cause of sanitary reform, and risen to the very highest distinction as a medical practitioner in the English metropolis.

CLARKE, Mrs. MARY COWDEN, authoress of the "Complete Concordance to Shakspeare," was born in June, 1809; she is the daughter of the eminent musician, Mr. Vincent Novello, and sister to the celebrated singer, Madame Clara Novello. She was married in 1828 to Mr. Charles Cowden Clarke. In 1829 she commenced to analyse the works of Shakspeare, possibly impelled to the task by the incomplete indices of Ayscough and Twiss. It apparently occurred to her that a "Concordance to Shakspeare" would be invaluable to the literary world; and towards accomplishing her grand purpose Mrs. Clarke devoted sixteen years of laborious toil. The work was brought out in 1846; it contains 2,578 columns, and about 309,000 lines, and so faithfully has it been prepared that the table of errata contains only thirteen lines, consisting exclusively of simple omissions, there not having been an "error," as yet, detected by the keenest critic. Mrs. Clarke has written other works, among which are "The Iron Cousin: a Novel;" "Kit Bam, the Modern Sinbad;" "The Girlhood of Shakspeare's Heroines;" "World-noted Women;" and "Many Happy Returns of the Day: a Birthday Book," lately published. She has also contributed to magazines; but her name is embalmed in the pages of the Concordance, which has conferred on her the distinguished honour of being the first female editor of Shakspeare.

CLAUSEN, HENRI NICOLAS, a Danish politician and theologian, was born at Maribo, in the Island of Laland, in April, 1793, and is the son of an eminent clergyman. He studied at Copenhagen, and from 1818 to 1820 visited Germany, Italy, and France. On his return he was named Professor of Theology at Copenhagen, though his tendencies were rationalistic. He published some works embodying his opinions; and though he met with numerous adversaries he gained the affections of the people and the esteem of the King. In 1836, when he had published "Popular Discourses on the Reformation," he became Rector of the University. Politically, he is an avowed partizan of Danish nationality, of civil liberty, of the liberty of the press, and a defender of all liberal and patriotic ideas. He has ceased to take an active part in public affairs, confining himself to his rectorial duties. His works, though not numerous, are highly esteemed in Denmark.

CLOSE, THE VERY REV. FRANCIS, D.D., late scholar of St. John's College, Cambridge, Dean of Carlisle, is an eminent preacher of the "Evangelical" school. He held for thirty years the Perpetual Curacy of Cheltenham, where he was extremely popular with the religious or evangelical section of the community. When Dr. Tait was elevated to the See of London, Mr. Close became Dean of Carlisle, and in the border city has displayed the same eloquence which characterised him at Cheltenham: retaining his popularity as a preacher, and affording in his sermons a faithful exposition of the doctrines of the Evangelical school in the Church of England. In 1826 he published "Discourses on Genesis;" in 1840 "Miscellaneous Sermons;" "Fifty-two Sketches of Sermons." He has since published a volume "On Church Architecture," which has become popular. His first work has gone through a great number of editions. Dr. Close has lately taken a very active part in advocating social reform, more especially in respect to the abolition of some customs, such as the use of tobacco, &c., and the evil tendency of various kinds of amusements. Both in the pulpit and by the pen, he has proved himself a formidable opponent to all who hold contrary opinions to those he maintains, and who have ventured into the lists against him.

CLYDE, COLIN CAMPBELL, LORD, Lieutenant-General, K.C.B., late Commander-in-Chief of the Indian Army, was born at Glasgow in 1792. In 1808 he joined the army as Ensign in the 9th Foot. In 1809 he was Lieutenant; in 1813 Captain; in 1825 Major; in 1832 Lieutenant-Colonel. He served in Portugal and Walcheren, and also under Sir John Moore in the Peninsula. He was wounded at San Sebastian, where he led the storming-party. He subsequently proceeded to the United States. In 1842 he was appointed colonel of the 98th regiment, and served in the expedition to China. In the Punjaub he was a General of Brigade, and as commander, he defeated the Sikhs at Ramnuggur, 22nd November, 1848; rendering also eminent service at the passage of the Chenab early in the following December. In 1851 and 1852 he commanded the Peshawur District, and in all his engagements was successful over the enemy. In 1854 Sir Colin was appointed to the Command of the Highland Brigade. At the Alma his coolness and intrepidity contributed in a singularly marked manner to the distinguished success of the British arms. At Balaklava he held the post of honour. The "thin red line" has become a thing of history. In 1854 he was promoted to the rank of Major-General, and subsequently he became Lieutenant-General, receiving at the same time the Grand Cross of the Bath, the Cross of the Legion of Honour, and the Sardinian Order of Maurice and St. Lazare, the freedom of the cities of London and Glasgow, and the honorary degree of D.C.L. at Oxford. He was, for some time after the Peace of Paris, Inspector-General of Infantry, and without being a martinet effected various improvements in the Line. So conspicuous had been Sir Colin's services in the Crimea, that when the revolt of the sepoys broke out, he was at once appointed to the command of the army in the East. "When will you be ready to start?" said Lord Palmerston. "To-morrow;" said the veteran; "all I want can be got in Calcutta as well as here." What Havelock and Outram so gloriously began, Campbell has no less gloriously terminated. These three share the honour of having crushed the Indian mutiny, and avenged our slaughtered ·

countrymen. His relief of Lucknow is, perhaps, one of the most brilliant examples of strategy any age or country has on record; and his after-military career in India has been one of continued victory, without a reverse — no check whatever, indeed, having caused a pause from the hour he entered the field. As a reward for these last services he has been raised to the peerage as Lord Clyde, and has taken his seat in the House of Lords. He has been heartily welcomed on his return home, and it is to be hoped that he may long live to enjoy his well-merited honours.

COBDEN, RICHARD, was born at Midhurst, Sussex, in 1804. His father, who was a small farmer, sent him from home, at an early age, to fill a situation in London, where he soon gained a thorough knowledge of business. He afterwards made a tour of the United States and a portion of Europe. He was energetic, and anxious to rise, and seeing a good prospect before him, he entered into business on his own account, in Lancashire, and soon became a prosperous man. A pamphlet from his hand, entitled "England, Ireland, and America," and another on "Russia," drew attention to his literary qualifications. He entered boldly on the question of Free Trade, and was one of the originators of the Anti-Corn-Law League—one of the most formidable political organizations ever known. Mr. Cobden was returned to the House of Commons in 1841, as member for Stockport. He "took" with the House, and Sir Robert Peel acknowledged that his measure of 1846, which practically admitted the justice of Mr. Cobden's principles, was elicited by the "unadorned eloquence" of the cotton printer. The Corn Laws repealed, Mr. Cobden was presented with a testimonial of £70,000 for his services to Free Trade. He was returned for the West Riding of York-shire in 1847, which he represented for some years, and then retired, under the impression that his re-election would not be secure. In 1857, after opposing Lord Palmerston's Chinese policy, and driving that ministry to a dissolution, he was started for Huddersfield and defeated—a surprise to himself and his friends, but he was immediately after elected for Rochdale. In 1859 he travelled over a large portion of the United States; and, during his absence, Lord Derby's ministry having been overthrown, Lord Palmerston proposed that he should accept office, but he refused. Mr. Cobden, we need scarcely add, is a Radical Reformer, and a member of the Peace Society. He is now in Paris, busily occupied as British Commissioner in arranging the details of the Commercial Treaty, which owes its origin in a great measure to himself. In this Mr. Cobden has been so far successful as to have acquired the esteem of the French manufacturers. The commerce between the two countries has much benefited by the fiscal changes which have already been effected, and it is not too much to expect that his exertions will tend to draw together the sympathies of the two nations, now engaged in the peaceful pursuits of commercial rivalry.

COCKERELL, CHARLES ROBERT, R.A., D.C.L., an architect, was born in London on the 27th day of April, 1788. His early life was spent among the architectural remains of classic lands, in a laborious study of the details of Greek and Roman architecture. He undertook many extensive excavations, and brought to this country several fragments of sculpture, now in the British Museum. An admirable draughtsman, in 1829 he was elected Associate of the Academy; in 1836 R.A.; and in 1840 Professor of Architecture in the Royal Academy, an appointment which he held during sixteen years. In 1848 he received the first Gold Medal of the

British Architectural Institute, of which he became President in 1860. He was elected in 1841 Foreign Member of the Institute of France; in 1843 a Member of Merit in the Academy of St. Luke, at Rome; in 1845 the honour of D.C.L. of Oxford was conferred on him; and in 1858 he became a member of the Dilettanti Society. He was appointed architect to the new Public Library at Cambridge, after a very long competition, and architect of the Taylor Buildings at Oxford, also after a competition; as well as standing architect to the Bank of England, and architect to the Cathedral of St. Paul's. He was the architect of the National Monument of Scotland, on the Calton Hill at Edinburgh, which has been only partly erected, and of various other buildings in England, Wales, and Ireland; amongst which are the "Sun" and "Westminster" Fire Offices, London, and the St. George's Hall, &c., in Liverpool. Mr. Cockerell is the author of a valuable work entitled the "Architectural Life of William of Wykeham." He has of late years devoted much attention to the study of Gothic architecture, and has published illustrations of the West Front of Wells Cathedral, and of the Sculptures of Lincoln Cathedral. His lectures, which he delivered regularly during his appointment as Professor of Architecture, contain much original and important information regarding the history and theory of architecture.

CODRINGTON, Sir William John, K.C.B., an English general, was born in 1800. He is the eldest surviving son of Admiral Sir Edward Codrington. In 1821 he entered the army; and in 1836 became Lieutenant-Colonel of the Coldstream Guards. In 1846 he attained the rank of Colonel, and in 1854 that of Major-General. He was always looked up to as a steady officer, attached to the ranks, and very accessible. When the British army went out to Turkey, Sir William accompanied it as a spectator. Being at Varna, immediately before the sailing of the expedition to the Crimea, Lord Raglan, requiring at the moment a Brigadier-General, and Codrington being at hand, he was appointed to the command of the first Brigade of the Light Division, vacant by the appointment of General Airey to the Adjutant-Generalship of the Army of the East. Sir William led this brigade with great steadiness and gallantry at the battle of the Alma. His bravery at Inkermann was highly spoken of by the Commander-in-Chief; and when Sir George Brown retired wounded to Malta, General Codrington was appointed to the command of the Light Division. On the death of Lord Raglan, and the resignation of General Simpson, he was appointed Commander-in-Chief of the British army in the Crimea. He has since been made a Knight Commander of the Bath, and on his return to England, after the peace, he was elected Member of Parliament for Greenwich. In 1859 he was appointed Governor of Gibraltar.

COLE, Henry, C.B., civil administrator, art critic, and editor of the "Journal of Design," was born at Bath in 1808. He entered the public service in 1822, and became an Assistant-Keeper of the Public Records. During this period he published "Henry the Eighth's Scheme of Bishopricks;" a volume of "Miscellaneous Records of the Exchequer;" and many pamphlets on record reform, which led to the establishment of a general record office, and the present system. He contributed to the Westminster and British and Foreign Reviews, and obtained one of the four prizes of £100 offered by the Treasury for suggestions for carrying out the penny-postage plan of Rowland Hill;— a measure which, as secretary of the mercantile committee on postage, he had helped to bring into public notice.

Under the *nom de plume* of Felix Summerley, he published several guide-books to the National Gallery, Hampton Court, &c., and several editions of children's books, illustrated by royal academicians and other eminent artists. He originated the series of "Art Manufactures," designed to associate the fine arts with the fabrication of objects of utility, and organized the exhibitions of the Society of Arts, which he proposed should culminate every fifth year in a national exhibition of arts and manufactures. The first of the series was intended to be held in 1851. The scheme adopted by Prince Albert was expanded by him into the great International Exhibition of that year, which was carried out so successfully. Mr Cole was one of the executive committee of management, and at the termination of his labours was made a Companion of the Bath. Subsequently he was invited to undertake the superintendence and reform of the Schools of Design, and his efforts led to the establishment of the Government Department of Science and Art, of which he was Senior Secretary and afterwards Inspector-General. He filled the office of British Commissioner for the Universal Exhibition at Paris in 1855, and accomplished the work effectively, whilst economizing £10,000 on the original parliamentary estimate. Since that time he has organized with unexpected success the South Kensington Museum, which is the first national institution lighted at night for exhibition. He is now Superintendent of this institution, as well as Secretary of the Science and Art Department under the Committee of Council on Education.

COLERIDGE, THE REV. DERWENT, youngest son of Samuel Taylor Coleridge, was born at Keswick, on 14th September, 1800. He was educated at Ambleside, and subsequently at St. John's College, Cambridge. His earliest contributions to literature were made to "Knight's Quarterly Magazine," under the signature of Davenant Cecil. His admirable memoir of his brother Hartley, whose "Poems" and "Biographies of Northern Worthies" he edited, is well known. Since the death of his sister Sarah, the Rev. Derwent Coleridge has edited his father's works. He is now Principal of St. Mark's College, Chelsea, and Prebendary of St. Paul's Cathedral.

COLLIER, JOHN PAYNE, a philologist and critic, was born in London, 11th January, 1789. His father was originally a Spanish merchant, but turned his mind to books early in life, and became editor of the "Monthly Register," and of the "Critical Review." About 1814 the subject of this notice entered the Inner Temple, as a law student, and was called to the bar, having previously been engaged in the arduous duties of parliamentary reporter for the "Morning Chronicle," a journal which at that period held the highest position in London. He had not been long on the "Morning Chronicle" when he became a law reporter to the "Times," occasionally lending his assistance in Parliament. In 1816 he married a lady who brought him a considerable fortune, and he subsequently devoted his leisure to the study of the earlier English poets, on whose works he has since written so many able criticisms and commentaries. His taste for the dramatic poets of the Elizabethan era was not a matter of a day's creation. It was manifested when he was a boy, and it strengthened with his years. Among his first works calculated to attract the notice of the judicious, was "The Poetical Decameron," consisting of dialogues on our early poets, and containing a fund of information unknown to general readers. As a supplement to a new edition of "Dodsley's Old Plays," he reprinted a number of dramas, all of them being of Shakspeare's day, and works, too, of great merit, though, of course, inferior to those of their wondrous prototype. Still studying in the same direction, he produced, in 1831, his "History of English Dramatic Poetry," which increased his reputation as an original writer, and as an accurate collector of forgotten but interesting facts. In every respect he was careful and conscientious. Many new sources of information were placed at his disposal; and it was in his varied researches in public and private libraries that he picked up the manuscripts or documents from which he wrote, in 1835, that delightful book, "New Facts regarding Shakspeare," a work which he supplemented by "New Particulars" and "Further Particulars,"—the latter in 1839. For many years he was engaged in preparing a Life of Shakspeare, which he published with the great poet's works in 1844, a task in which difficulties met him at every step of his progress, all, ultimately, being surmounted. A second edition of the whole undertaking has since been demanded. In 1850 he was appointed Vice-President of the Society of Antiquaries, in place of the late Mr. Hallam. He enjoys a pension of £100 a-year from the Crown, in acknowledgment of his services to literature. His "Book of Roxburgh Ballads," and "Memoirs of the Principal Actors in the Plays of Shakspeare," are or ought to be in every good English library; the latter was one of his contributions to the Shakspeare Society, of which for ten years he was a director. Mr. Collier, some years since, purchased an edition of Shakspeare in folio, published in 1632, with marginal notes, which has proved very useful in correcting spurious readings, and in supplying many new ones of indisputable value, all of which made their appearance in a volume published in 1852, entitled "Notes and Emendations to the Text of Shakspeare's Plays." With respect to the emendations, there can be no doubt that Mr.

Collier has acted with wisdom in claiming for many of them a place in every future reprint of Shakspeare's dramatic works, and that in point of fact they do, in the majority of cases, very much improve the old text.

COLLIN DE PLANCY, Jacques, otherwise Jacques Collin Danton, a French writer, was born at Plancy, near D'Arcis-sur-Aube, on the 28th of January, 1793. He is nephew of the famous Danton, and at the commencement of the Restoration changed the dangerous name of his relative to that he now bears. In 1812 he went to Paris, wrote for the booksellers, and became a bookseller and publisher. His commercial position being compromised in 1830, he took refuge in Belgium, where he cultivated the good will of the Belgians by advocating their nationality. He returned to France, after some years' absence, about 1837, and founded a sort of universal society, or *Société Phalanstérienne*, which has since, by a complete transformation, become the Society of Saint Victor. His writings are closely associated with the events of his life. From 1812 to 1815 the very titles of his publications were vehement against the pontificate; but since 1837 he has made the *amende honorable* to Rome. To the first period belong his "Infernal Dictionary," his "Memoirs of a Villain of the Fourteenth Century," "The Picturesque Biography of the Jesuits," and "The Devil Painted by Himself." To the second period belong his "Legends of the Holy Virgin," "Legends of the Seven Capital Crimes," and "The Christian Book of Songs" (Le Chansonnier du Chrétien), which contains much abuse of the philosophers put in rhyme.

COLLINS, Wilkie, an English biographer and novelist, was born in London in 1824. A son of the celebrated painter, the late William Collins, R.A., he was educated at a private school, and passed a considerable time in Italy. His biography of his father is remarkably interesting; not more as a life of the man than as a history of English art. "Antonina; or, the Fall of Rome," his first novel, became popular at once. His other works are, "Rambles beyond Railways," "Basil," "Mr. Wray's Cash-box," "Hide and Seek," "After Dark," and "The Dead Secret." Although roughly handled by many critics, those who have studied the works of Mr. Collins will bear testimony to their merits, as regards plot and variety of incident, and their clearness and simplicity of style. His earlier works were, no doubt, tinged with exaggeration; but with time came mellowness, and when he does write now, he writes well and vigorously. One of his dramatic productions is that of "The Frozen Deep," which was played before the Queen. His latest work of fiction is "The Woman in White," which appeared in weekly parts, in the columns of "All the Year Round," and has since been reprinted. He is also the author of a drama called "The Lighthouse," which has been played under the care of Mr. Dickens.

COMBERMERE, STAPLETON COTTON, VISCOUNT, G.C.B., an English field-marshal, was born in 1773. He is the eldest surviving son of the late Sir R. S. Cotton, M.P. for Cheshire. At eighteen years of age he entered the army, serving in the Flemish campaign of 1793-94. In 1796 he obtained the command of the 25th Light Dragoons. With them he proceeded to India, and took part in the war of 1798 and 1799 against Tippoo Sultan. After his return to Europe he accompanied Wellington to Spain, where he distinguished himself as a cavalry officer—and gained promotion after Talavera to the rank of Lieutenant-General. At the battle of Salamanca he was second in command. When the war was over, he was appointed, in 1817, Governor of Barbadoes and Commander of the forces in the British West Indies; in 1822 Commander of the forces in Ireland; and in 1825 Commander of the army in India, where he distinguished himself very much, more especially at the siege of Bhurtpore in 1825-6. For his Indian services he received the title of Viscount. After the Duke of Wellington's death he was appointed Constable of the Tower of London, and subsequently a Field-Marshal.

CONINGHAM, WILLIAM, member of Parliament for Brighton, was born at Penzance, Cornwall, in 1815. He is son of the Rev. Robert Coningham of Londonderry. After the usual course of study he entered the military service in 1834, as an officer in the 1st Royal Dragoons. He afterwards sold out, married in 1840, and in 1847 contested the representation of Brighton, but was defeated. At the general election of 1852 he stood for Westminster, but again without success. In 1857, however, he stood again for Brighton and was returned, and took his place among the liberals. He advocates the Ballot, a gradual extension of the suffrage, retrenchment, and Free-trade; and opposes the Maynooth endowment and church-rates. In a general sense, however, he supports the policy of Lord Palmerston. He is not a politician of extreme opinions, but his views, taken as a whole, are enlarged and liberal. He does not often address the House, but when he rises he is listened to with respect and attention.

CONSCIENCE, HENRI, a Flemish novelist, was born at Antwerp, in Belgium, on the 3rd of December, 1812. His father was a Frenchman, settled in Flanders as a ship-broker. In his boyhood, Conscience was passionately fond of books, and, as a means of gratifying his literary taste, became a teacher. In 1830 the Belgian Revolution broke off his studies, and he entered the military service as a volunteer. He soon became the poet of the army, and wrote songs full of ardour and point, which became very popular. Discharged in 1836, after having obtained the rank of Sergeant-Major, he was obliged, on account of bickerings with his step-mother, to break with his family, and, poor and lonely, to pick up as he best could the means of a precarious existence. By turns an assistant-gardener, an *employé* in a government office at Antwerp, and clerk to an academy of arts, he at last, in 1845, received the title of *Agrégé* from the University of Ghent. After obtaining this distinction he turned his attention to the revival of the Flemish national literature. His enthusiasm for the restoration of the Flemish idiom has led him to protest incessantly against the introduction of the French language. He is now a Commissaire d'Arrondissement, at Courtrai, but his official duties do not interfere with his literary pursuits, and every year he publishes two or three volumes illustrative of Flemish life. His first production was "The Year of Miracles," which is less a romance than a series of brilliant dramatic pictures of an interesting period in Flemish history. It was followed, in 1837, by "Phantasia," a collection of legends and Flemish poetry. In 1838 he published the "Lion of Flanders;" since that period, quitting the Middle Ages, he has produced very pleasant sketches of the manners of modern Flanders, "Hours of the Night," "The Executioner's Child," "The New Niobe," "The Conscript," and "The Poor Gentleman,"—one of his most touching works. In 1845 he published "The History of Belgium." He has since written "Quintin Matsys," "Pages from the Book of Nature," and "Jacques D'Artevelde." His most recent works are, "The Curse of the Village," "The War of the Peasants," "The Demon of Gold," and "Simon Turchi at Batavia." His works have

been translated into most modern tongues.

CONSTANTINE, NICHOLÆWITCH, second son of the late Emperor Nicholas, Grand Duke of Russia, brother of the present Czar, and Grand Admiral of the Imperial Fleet, was born in 1827. He was declared Admiral of the Fleet by his father in 1831, when he was four years old. His chief naval instructor was Admiral Lutke, celebrated by his voyage from Cronstadt to Kamtschatka and back in 1826-27. Constantine, in his boyish studies, displayed a marked predilection for everything Russian, His general reputation for talent earned him a wide popularity in Russia, more especially with the old Russian party. In 1847 he visited England, and went to all the public establishments, leaving a favourable impression upon all with whom he came in contact. In the late war he was entrusted with the control of the defensive operations in the Baltic. The high expectations entertained respecting his spirit and ability were scarcely realized during the contest. He again visited England (1859), inspecting the dockyards and forts of the country, and learning a due regard for that nation in peace, which his countrymen in the Crimea had learned to respect in war. The Grand Duke is a good English scholar, and is well acquainted with English literature, ancient as well as modern. He was married in 1848 to the Princess Alexandria Josefowna, daughter of Joseph Duke of Saxe Altenburg, by whom he has a family of four children.

COOK, ELIZA, a song writer, was born in 1817, at Southwark, where her father was a tradesman. When in her twentieth year, she gained considerable reputation as a poetical contributor to several of the London periodicals, and especially to the "New Monthly Magazine," and "Metropolitan and Literary Gazette." In 1840 a volume of her poems was published, numbers of them having been, and continuing to be, very popular. In 1849 "Eliza Cook's Journal" appeared; but it has since ceased to exist. Miss Cook's most popular poems are the "Old Arm Chair," "The Old Farm Gate," "Home in the Heart," "The Last Good-Bye," and "I Miss Thee, my Mother;" but she is the writer of many more of equal merit, and all characterised by great freedom, ease, and heartiness of sentiment and expression. "She makes you feel," says a distinguished writer, "that her whole heart is in all she writes; that she gives full utterance to the depths of her soul— a soul that is in sympathy with all that is pure and true." A complete collection of her poems has just been published.

COOKE, EDWARD WILLIAM, A.R.A., an English painter, was born in London in 1811. He seems to have acquired a taste for art from his father, who was an eminent engraver. His first productions were sketches of plants intended as illustrations for the "Botanic Cabinet," and "Loudon's Encylopædia." He subsequently engaged in marine sketching, and in 1832 commenced painting in oil. His artistic education was completed in Italy and France. In 1851 he was elected an Associate of the Royal Academy. The following of his productions are at present in the South Kensington Museum, —namely, "Lobster Pots," "Mending the Bait Nets," "Brighton Sands," "The Antiquary's Cell," "Mont St. Michel, Normandy," "A Mackerel," "Portsmouth Harbour," "The Hulks," "Hastings, from All Saints' Church," "Windmills, Blackheath," "Carp," "Portsmouth Harbour," "The Victory," "Dutch Boats in a Calm," and "The Boat House."

COOPER, THOMAS SIDNEY, A.R.A., a painter, was born at Canterbury on the 26th September, 1803. His parents were in trade, but not in opulent circumstances, and his father having, while the subject of this notice was a child, deserted his family, the boy was early thrown on his own resources. Having learned to draw, he succeeded in occasionally earning a few shillings by the sale of sketches of old buildings. He afterwards received instruction from Mr. Doyle, a scene painter, after whose death (which took place in the following year) he was employed in this capacity. In 1827 he went to Belgium, obtaining his living by the way through the exercise of his artistic skill. He at last reached Brussels, where he studied the works of the Old Flemish and Dutch Masters, without, however, copying their pictures, gained patrons, and ultimately settled and married. While resident in the Belgian capital, Mr. Cooper also mastered the methods of the living painters of Flanders and Holland, especially the style of the eminent animal painter, M. Verboeckhoven. In 1831 he returned to England—resolved to adopt animal painting as his particular department of art, and by the novelty of his manner at once caught attention and attracted purchasers. His first picture was exhibited at the Gallery of the Society of British Artists, and since that time his career has been one of continued prosperity. For some years he has painted cattle for the landscapes of Lee, and the harmony of the productions is unexceptionable, and the effect highly admired by the best judges of art. His "Farm Yard—Milking Time," a study from a farm near Canterbury, and "Cattle—Early Morn on the Cumberland Hills," are in the Vernon Collection at the South Kensington Museum.

COPE, CHARLES WEST, R.A., an historical and domestic painter, was born at Leeds in 1811; his father being an artist, highly esteemed in his own neighbourhood. Having studied under Mr. Sass, and at the Royal Academy, he painted a "Holy Family," which was purchased by the late Mr. Beckford.

His first picture for the Academy was exhibited in 1831, from which time he painted with great diligence and care, gradually adding laurels to his wreath, until 1843, when his cartoon, the "First Trial by Jury," obtained the £300 prize in the Westminster Hall competition. Thenceforward he met with great success, taking a high place among modern artists. In 1843 he was elected Associate of the Academy, and in 1848 elevated to the rank of Royal Academician. He has progressed surely, though not rapidly, still deservedly, for he has been a close student, and is a conscientious painter. Among his chief works are a "Pastorella," from Spenser; "L'Allegro" and "Il Penseroso," from Milton; the "Last Days of Cardinal Wolsey" (1848); "Lear and Cordelia" (1850); "Laurence Saunders, the Second Marian Martyr, in Prison" (1851); "Othello relating his Adventures" (1853); "The Children of Charles I. in Carisbrook Castle" (1855); and three frescoes for the New Houses of Parliament; namely, "Edward III. conferring the Order of the Garter on Edward the Black Prince," "Prince Henry's Submission to the Law," and "Griselda's First Trial," which are universally admitted to be among the most successful of recent attempts in this department of art. The following of Mr. Cope's productions are in the South Kensington Museum: "Palpitation," "The Young Mother," "The Hawthorn Bush," "Maiden Meditation," "Beneficence," "Almsgiving," "L'Allegro," "Il Penseroso," and "Mother and Child."

CORBAUX, Miss FANNY, a female artist, is daughter of a gentleman who was a well-known Fellow of the Royal Society. Miss Corbaux was born in 1812, and when quite a child exhibited decided talent in drawing. She practised at first for mere amusement, for she had no idea of ever turning her skill to other account. But misfortune overtook her father, who, reduced to poor circumstances, and old and feeble, was unable to help himself. Then came Miss Corbaux's trial. She was only fifteen, and her knowledge of art was but incipient. She scarcely knew the use of colours, and still less the art of mixing them; but the cares of the family urged her on, and she resolved on becoming the support of her father. The heroism of this young lady is not outdone in the history of the struggles of artists. She bore up under every trial, and at length had her reward. Even while she was drooping and toiling she received three high-art honours. Miss Corbaux was then sixteen. She gained first, the large silver medal of the Society of Arts, for a portrait in miniature; secondly, the silver Isis medal, for a copy of figures, in water-colours: and, thirdly, the silver palette, for a copy of an engraving. Next year, 1828, she again received the Isis medal, for a figure-composition, in water-colours; and in 1830 she obtained the gold medal, for a miniature portrait. She had studied with a diligence unknown to all but herself, in the National Gallery and the British Institution. In the same year that she received the gold medal she was admitted an honorary member of the Society of British Artists. Miss Corbaux has been chiefly occupied in portrait-painting, and in this department she has been highly and deservedly successful, her portraits being striking likenesses, her colour pure, and her manipulation firm. Miss Corbaux has not limited her thoughts to art—she permitted them to travel through the realms of sacred literature, and the result has been a series of investigations so acute and satisfactory that their conclusions have been adopted by numbers of the most learned of our time in Biblical history.

CORBOULD, EDWARD HENRY, an English water-colour painter, was born in London on 5th December, 1815.

His father and grandfather were well-known historic painters. He was educated at Dr. May's school, at Enfield, in a building which had been a palace of Queen Elizabeth. He left this place in 1832, and about a year afterwards he sent an original design, in water-colours, to the Society of Arts, "Phaeton drawing the Chariot of the Sun;" obtained the gold Isis medal, which he had again the following year for a model of "St. George contending with the Dragon," from Spenser's "Faërie Queene;" and afterwards he obtained the large gold medallion, for a model of a "Chariot Race," from Homer. In 1839 he produced "The Eglinton Tournament," "The Meeting of the Pilgrims at the Tabard Inn," from Chaucer; and "The Woman taken in Adultery." In 1843 he painted a cartoon, "The Plague of London," for which he received a prize of £100. His success in this instance induced him to devote his energies to fresco-painting, and work after work proceeded from his hand until 1847, when he seemed to have relinquished frescoes for water-colours exclusively. His subjects are chiefly historical, and treated in a dramatic manner. He has drawn his inspiration from the days of chivalry, with their pageantry and picturesque shows. In art he revived the form and semblance of mediæval times, as in literature Sir Walter Scott had given new life to the characters and sentiments of those who figured in the Middle Ages. His principal works, besides those already mentioned, are: "Fair Rosamond," "William of Eynesham reciting Valorous Deeds before a Chivalrous Court," "Destruction of the Idols at Bâle," and a "Scene from the Opera of the Prophète," painted by command of Her Majesty, and which is said to be one of his best productions. He is a brilliant colourist, and possesses extraordinary knowledge of ancient architecture and costume.

His whole manner and mode of thought, it is said, have been influenced by the picturesque old palace in which he was educated, and the pageantry of the Eglinton tournament, at which he was present, before the production of his first great picture, in which he has embalmed his impressions of that event.

CORMENIN, Louis Marie de la Haye, Vicomte de, a French political writer, was born at Paris, January 6, 1788. He is a member of a distinguished family, his grandfather being the Duc de Penthièvre. His early education was received at the school of M. Lepitre at Paris. He subsequently studied with great success in the legal schools, and was chosen an advocate in 1808. Meanwhile he had continued his literary studies under MM. Laya and Villemain in Paris. He at the same time exhibited a taste for poetry, and some of his early verses appeared in the "Mercure de France," and the "Almanach des Muses." At the early age of twenty-two he was appointed by Napoleon First Secretary of the Council of State, and while in that office was charged with drawing up some of its most elaborate reports. In 1828 Cormenin was elected Deputy, and continued to be re-elected during eighteen years. His intimate and comprehensive knowledge of jurisprudence, his logical method, whether of speaking or writing, gave him great power. In 1830 M. Cormenin protested strongly against the elevation of the Orleans dynasty to the throne of France. He resigned his position in the Council of State, and refused the highest offices. He also gave up his Deputyship. Repenting the latter step, he offered himself to the electors of Loiret, but was not elected. He was, however, sent to the Chamber by the Department of Ain in October, 1830, and sat on the extreme left. In 1831 he commenced his famous "Lettres sur la Liste Civile," during the discussion on the budget.

After the Revolution of 1848 he diligently set to work to remodel the Constitution, being President of the Commission named for that purpose. On the *coup d'état* taking place, he was appointed a member of the Council of State, reconstructed by Napoleon III. An advocate by profession, he has been the opponent of everything that displayed the semblance of abuses, never relaxing in his exertions to promote the cause of progress. M. de Cormenin is the author of a work on "The Parliamentary Orators of France," which was published under the name of "Timon." This book, containing a series of articles on Berryer, Guizot, Thiers, Dupin, Lamartine, Odilon Barrot, &c., &c., had an extraordinary success, and has been so highly appreciated by its numerous readers in France as to have passed through upwards of twenty editions. It has long been considered in France a model in the style to which it belongs, although the English translation has attracted no great attention in this country.

CORNELIUS, PETER VON, a German painter, was born at Dusseldorf on the 16th September, 1787. In his youth he had severe struggles. At the age of sixteen he lost his father, and was about to give up art for some other means of supporting the family, but his mother perceived his genius, and made many sacrifices for his advancement. At the age of nineteen he painted the cupola of the Old Church at Neuss, and in 1810 he executed designs for Goethe's "Faust," in which he did full justice to the ideas of the great German author. He proceeded to Rome in 1811, and in 1819 went to Munich. In 1825 he was appointed Director of the Academy in that city. Whilst at Munich he executed his most famous works, and the frescoes which decorate the Glyptothek. He also painted the walls of the Church of Saint Louis with frescoes, entitled "God the Father," "The Birth of Christ," "The Crucifixion," and "The Day of Judgment." He returned to Rome in 1833, and in 1841 visited Berlin. His designs, frescoes, and other works are very numerous, and exhibit the sterling qualities which denote genius.

COSTELLO, MISS LOUISA STUART, a popular writer of the day, was born in Ireland in 1815. In 1835 she published her "Specimens of the early Poetry of France," dedicated to Thomas Moore. In 1840 her "Summer amongst the Bocages and the Vines," a pleasant book descriptive of Normandy and Brittany, appeared. She continued to write with taste and discrimination of her continental wanderings, until in 1844 she produced "Memoirs of Celebrated Englishwomen." Thenceforward Miss Costello has been an indefatigable authoress and student of history; while her contributions to periodicals have been almost without a break. She is a poetess besides, although she rarely indulges in verse writing. Her brother, Dudley Costello, is a well-known contributor to periodical and light literature.

COUSIN, VICTOR, a French metaphysician, was born in November, 1792, at Paris, where his father was a watch and clockmaker. He gained various prizes at the Lycée Charlemagne; and showed a bias for metaphysical pursuits. A translation of "Plato" into French, published in 1812, first gave Cousin celebrity in the literary and philosophical world. In 1815 he delivered lectures on the history of philosophy in the University. He attached himself to the Royal cause, but after the fall of the Emperor, the freedom with which he uttered opinions against the restored monarchy caused the Government to insist on his ceasing to lecture. In 1828 he resumed his lectures, and was appointed Inspector-General of Education. In this capacity he visited Germany in 1831, and in 1832 published a report on the Prussian system of education, which has given popular instruction such an impulse over Europe. As a metaphysician, Cousin showed, in this early part of his career, a greater bias towards the Scottish philosophy than to any other. Sir William Hamilton's celebrated paper on the "Philosophy of the Unconditioned" was mainly directed against the principles of Cousin, and is accepted by many of the profoundest and most cautious thinkers as an effectual demolition of the theories of the brilliant Frenchman. He gave General Cavaignac, while in power, all the benefit of his experience and advice; but in 1849 he disappeared from public life. His works are very numerous, and are characterised by a style which places him among the first of living philosophical writers, and entitles him undoubtedly to the very first place among modern French philosophical authors. Mr. Cousin's chief works are, a "Translation of the Works of Plato," in 13 volumes (1825-40); an edition of "Descartes' Works," in 11 volumes; a "Course of Lectures on Moral Philosophy, delivered to the Faculté des Lettres, in 1818, on the Foundation Ideas of the Absolute, the True, the Beautiful, and the Good" (1836); "Lectures on the History of Modern Philosophy, delivered in 1816-17" (1841); "Lectures on the History of Moral Philosophy in the Eighteenth Century, delivered for the Faculté des Lettres, from 1816 to 1820," published in five volumes, Oct., 1840-41; "Lessons on the Philosophy of Kant" (1842); "A Dissertation on the Pensées de Pascal" (1842); and a series of studies on the distinguished women of the seventeenth century, including Madame de Longueville (1853), Madame de Salle (1854), Madame de Chevreuse and Madame de Hautefort (1856). M. Cousin, who has been a leading contributor to the "Revue des Deux Mondes," the "Memoirs of the Academy of Moral and Political Sciences," and the "Journal

des Savans," published in 1846-47 a collected edition of his works up to that period, in 22 volumes 18mo.

COUTTS, MISS ANGELA GEORGIANA BURDETT, was born in 1814, and is the youngest daughter of the celebrated Sir Francis Burdett who was imprisoned in the tower for his advocacy of reform in 1810. She is grand-daughter of the eminent banker whose name she bears, and to whose great wealth she has succeeded. Miss Burdett's enormous fortune came to her quite unexpectedly. Old Mr. Coutts had married the actress, Harriet Mellon, and when he died bequeathed to her all his vast fortune. Mrs. Coutts afterwards married the Duke of St. Albans, and before her death conveyed to Miss Angela Burdett everything she possessed, limited only by the condition that the heiress should adopt the name of Coutts. There are few of the wealthy classes whose names are more identified with public and private benevolence than is that of Miss Coutts. Her liberality is on the largest scale, and her means are expended in assisting every scheme which has for its object the moral or physical improvement of the masses. Amongst her numerous instances of benevolence, we may state that she has endowed a bishopric in Australia, and has built a handsome church in the west end of London.

COWLEY, HENRY RICHARD WELLESLEY, LORD, British Minister at Paris, was born in London, 1804. He entered the diplomatic service when only twenty, having become an attaché to the Embassy at Vienna in 1824, afterwards Secretary of Legation at Stuttgart in 1832, and Secretary of the Embassy at Constantinople in 1831. In 1848 he was Minister Plenipotentiary to Switzerland, when delicate negotiations called him to Frankfort. In 1851, during an anxious period for the German States, he was accredited to the Confederation, and in 1852 succeeded the Marquis of Normanby as Ambassador at the Court of the Tuileries. In conjunction with Lord Clarendon, he represented Great Britain at the Congress of Paris, when peace was proclaimed ; and so late as last year he proceeded on a brief mission to Vienna, the object of which was to lay before the Emperor of Austria England's views respecting the state of affairs in Italy.

CRAIK, GEORGE LILLIE, LL.D., a literary writer, was born in Fifeshire in 1798. He is the son of the Rev. William Craik. At the University of St. Andrew's he went through the usual course of a divinity student for the Church of Scotland, but never entered the ministry. Soon after the Society for the Diffusion of Useful Knowledge was formed, Mr. Craik wrote for it the "Pursuit of Knowledge under Difficulties," which was one of the works forming part of the "Library of Entertaining Knowledge." Though appearing anonymously, this work established its author's reputation as a writer of extensive and varied acquirements. To the "Penny Cyclopædia". Mr. Craik contributed some of the most valuable articles in history and biography. In 1839 he became editor of the "Pictorial History of England," writing himself all those parts of the work which relate to religion, laws, literature, and industry. His principal works, besides those referred to, are—"Sketches of the History of Literature and Learning in England from the Norman Conquest," "History of British Commerce from the Earliest Times," "Spenser and his Poetry," "Bacon : his Writings and his Philosophy," "Outlines of the History of the English Language," "The English of Shakspere," and the "Romance of the Peerage," the last being one of the most instructive and interesting books which have appeared during the present century. In all his writings Dr. Craik exhibits the same laborious research, accuracy, and capacity to explain in clear and graceful language subjects of a recondite character, and a most anxious desire to aid as far as he can in improving the education and habits of his countrymen. Dr. Craik is at present Professor of History and English Literature in the Queen's College, Belfast, and is engaged on an enlarged and corrected edition of his "History of English Literature."

CRANWORTH, ROBERT MONSEY ROLFE, BARON, late Lord Chancellor of England, was born in 1790. Educated at Winchester and Cambridge, he was called to the bar in 1816, and soon got into extensive practice. In 1834 he was appointed Solicitor-General, an office which he held, with a short interval, until 1839, when he was elevated to the Bench as a Baron of the Exchequer. He was appointed Vice-Chancellor in 1850, and in the same year raised to the peerage. He was one of the Lords Justices of Appeal in Chancery in 1851, and Lord Chancellor in 1852 ; continuing to hold this office during the Ministry of Lord Palmerston. He has since retired, taking no prominent part in the proceedings of the House of Lords, although he is firmly attached to the opinions of the Whig party.

CREASY, SIR EDWARD SHEPHERD, M.A., a lawyer and historian, and Chief Justice of Ceylon, was born in 1812, at Bexley, in Kent. He is the son of Edward Hill Creasy, of Brighton, who was at one time part proprietor of the "Brighton Gazette." The subject of this notice was educated at Eton, and at King's College, Cambridge, of which he became a Fellow in 1834. In 1837 he passed as barrister, and has since practised at the Common Law Bar, as a member of the Home Circuit. In 1850 he was appointed Professor of History in University College, London, and in the following year published "The Fifteen Decisive Battles of the World," a work now in its ninth edition. Professor

Creasy has also written the "Rise and Progress of the English Constitution," published in 1834, which is now in its fourth edition, having been reprinted in America, and translated into several foreign languages. "The History of the Ottoman Turks," published in 1856, the last work of the author, is about to be followed by a work on "International Law," which is now in the press. Mr. Creasy was knighted in 1860, on the occasion of his being appointed Chief Justice of Ceylon.

CREMIEUX, Isaac Adolphe, a French legislator, and ex-Minister of Justice under the provisional government of France in 1848, was born at Nismes, of Jewish parents, in 1796. After attending classes at the college of Louis-le-Grand, he studied law at Aix, and settled as an advocate at first at Nismes, and afterwards at Paris. His career was highly successful, until he received his first check by defending Guernon Ranville, one of Charles X.'s Ministers. In political pleadings in the courts, he was almost uniformly employed in defending the Radical party when attacked by the prosecution of their organs of the press. Cremieux was long a member of the Chamber of Deputies, entering the Assembly first in 1842, and being re-elected in 1846. He advocated Free Trade, and a law that no paid official should have a seat in the Chamber, with the exception of Ministers, always voting with the reform party against Guizot. When it was announced that the Government would put down the reform banquets, Cremieux exclaimed, "There is blood in this!" Meeting Louis-Philippe and his queen in the Place de la Concorde, on the Thursday of their departure, he urged the king to flee immediately, no hope for them being left. He subsequently urged in the Chamber of Deputies the formation of a Provisional Government. After the events of 1848, he, though a democrat, showed but little favour to Cavaignac, upholding the candidature of Louis Napoleon for the Presidency. However, after the election of December he became one of the most earnest orators of the Opposition. When the *coup d'état* took place, he was arrested and taken to Mazas. Since then he has confined himself to the bar, where his talents and the independence of his character have acquired for him universal esteem. He is an able lawyer, and is one of the authors of the "Code des Codes" (1835).

CRESWICK, Thomas, R.A., a landscape painter, was born at Sheffield, Yorkshire, in 1811. He was educated at Hazelwood, near Birmingham, thence proceeding to London to study art. Mr. Creswick became first known by pictures of Welsh streams, which, by their exquisite combinations of rock, foliage, and river, excited universal admiration. He was among the first oil painters to introduce the now common practice of painting in the open air direct from nature, and his pictures are often, even although this is not stated, faithfully transcribed from particular spots. In 1842 he was elected an Associate of the Royal Academy, and in 1851 a Royal Academician. After this period he produced his greatest works, among which may be ranked his "England," "The London Road a Hundred Years Ago," and the "Weald of Kent." In 1848 he produced his "Home by the Sands," and "A Squally Day;" and in 1850 his "Wind on Shore," and "Over the Sands." He has been extensively employed in furnishing designs for various publications, which have been highly appreciated.

CROLY, Rev. George, LL.D., a literary writer and divine, was born in Dublin, in 1780, and educated at Trinity College in that city, where he obtained a scholarship, took the degrees of B.A. and M.A., and was, some years after, presented voluntarily with his Doctor's degree. He was instituted in the year 1834 to the benefice of Broadleigh, in Devon, by Lord Brougham, then Chancellor; and in 1835 to the united benefices of St. Stephen's, Walbrook, and St. Benet's, by Lord Chancellor Lyndhurst. Dr. Croly has acquired great distinction as a pulpit orator, and has written various works in theology; among others, "The Three Cycles," (a Treatise on Divine Providence,) a new "Interpretation of the Apocalypse," a volume on Baptism, Sermons preached at St. Stephen's, and Sermons on Public Events. He is also the author of "A Political Life of the Right Hon. Edmund Burke," "A Political Life of George IV.," a volume of Historical Essays, a work on Luther, and various poetical works and works of fiction.

CROSLAND, MRS. CAMILLA, an authoress known in the literary world by the name of Miss Toulmin, was born in London on the 9th June, 1812. She was early distinguished for intellectual ability. When her father, and afterwards her brother, both solicitors, died, Miss Toulmin, having to depend on her own efforts, resolved to pursue literature, for which she was well qualified by her tastes and previous education. Her first effort was a poem, which appeared in the "Book of Beauty" of 1838; from that time forward she has written assiduously for "Chambers's Journal," "The People's Journal," and other periodicals; she edited for a time "The Ladies' Companion and Magazine." In 1848 she married Mr. Newton Crosland, a London merchant. Mrs. Crosland has published separately "Lays and Legends illustrative of English Life," "Partners for Life," "A Christmas Story," "Stratagems, a Tale for Young People," "Toil and Trial, a Tale of London Life," "Lydia, a Woman's Book," "Stray Leaves from Shady Places," "Memorable Women," "Hildred the Daughter," and a volume of poems. The principal aim in some of Mrs. Crosland's writings is, by showing the trials and temptations of the poorer and middle classes, to inculcate the advantages of political and social instruction. In executing what appears to be her main design Mrs. Crosland has been successful, so far as she has been instrumental in arousing all ranks from a state of apathy, and in giving an impulse to the consideration of questions which but for her might have continued unheeded by a large section of the community. Her talent for treating more abstract and imaginative themes has also been conspicuously evidenced. Mrs. Crosland is a granddaughter of the eminent physician, Dr. William Toulmin.

CROWE, MRS. CATHERINE STEVENS, an English authoress, was born at Borough-green, Kent, about 1803. Married in 1822 to Lieutenant-Colonel Crowe, she commenced her literary career in 1838 with "Aristodemus," a tragedy of merit, though not appreciated. A novel, "Manorial Rights," followed; but "Susan Hopley," shortly after, fixed her position among the female authors of the age. In 1847 "Lillie Dawson" appeared, followed by some translations from the German. In 1848 that curious work, "The Night Side of Nature," proceeded from her pen, and subsequently "Light and Darkness, or Mysteries of Life," with other books, among which is an agreeable little work for children, "Pippie's Warning." Mrs. Crowe's German reading seems to have drawn her fancy into mystic regions, but her works are yet forcibly written, and full of good sense and sagacity.

CRUIKSHANK, GEORGE, an eminent artist and caricaturist, was born in London on the 27th September, 1792, of Scottish parents, his father being from the Lowlands his mother, whose name was MacNaughton, from the Highlands. Isaac Cruikshank, his father, was an artist of considerable ability as a water-colour draughtsman and etcher of cari-catures, cotemporary with Gilray and Rowlandson. George had the advan-tage of seeing his father work, but be-yond this had little, or, indeed, no preparation for that profession which it was his fate, rather than his inclination, to follow. His aim was to be a sailor, but this desire, opposed strongly by his mother, was finally abandoned about the age of seventeen, upon the decease of his father. He then devoted his attention to drawing upon wood. His first etchings were frontispieces to cheap publications, such as song-books, dream-books, and jest-books, then political cari-catures, and, later in life, drawings on wood and etchings on copper and steel, as illustrations to works of much higher pretensions than those on which he had been at first engaged. To enumerate all his works would be almost impossible; but he is justly considered as the origi-nator of the now prevalent style of book illustration. Many works, where his name appears only as the artist, are, nevertheless, his original ideas and sug-gestions. He illustrated most of Hone's publications, "Life in London," "Oliver Twist," "Tower of London," "Comic Almanac." "The Bottle" and "The Drunkard's Children" are pictorial his-tories of the evils of intemperance, where almost every figure tells its tale of misery and degradation. Upon this subject he seems from early life to have felt strongly, and his attacks upon gin-shops, and his depictions of the evils of drunkenness, may be traced backwards in some of his earliest productions. All his life he has (we believe) had a strong desire to attain to the higher branches of his profcesion, but never had time or opportunity to study. The proverb, however, of "Never too late to learn," may be applied in this instance, for in spite of all difficulties and drawbacks he has for the last few years employed him-self principally in oil painting. His pictures at first betrayed the difficulty he felt in acquiring the use of the *brush*, after working for so many years with the *etching point;* but his later pictures show that he bids fair to take his place as an *oil painter* as well as an *etcher* among the most distinguished of our artists. A great critic, the late Samuel Phillips, has styled him the prince of living caricaturists; but his works have proved him something more than a cari-caturist, and we may add that a long life of integrity and honour has won for him the respect and regard of all classes who know him.

CULLEN, PAUL, D.D., the Roman Catholic Archbishop of Dublin, was born in Ireland, in 1805. He left his native country at an early age, to study in the seminaries of Italy, took holy orders, and eventually settled at Rome, where he obtained employment in the offices of the Vatican, and where for fifteen years he administered the ec-clesiastical affairs of Ireland. On the death of the Roman Catholic primate of that country in 1849, Dr. Cullen was chosen to fill his place, and was conse-crated in 1850. He subsequently be-came Archbishop of Dublin. He is a decided foe to any mixed system of education, denouncing alike the national schools and the Queen's Colleges, which are essentially secular, and he demands at the same time, a separate grant for such schools and colleges as may be established under Roman Catholic au-spices exclusively. In science he is be-hind the age, as he has attempted to demonstrate that the earth is immovable, that the sun and all the planets move round us as round a common orbit, and that none of the heavenly bodies are larger than they seem to the naked eye.

CUMMING, REV. JOHN, D.D., minister of the Scotch Church, Covent

Garden, London, and author of numerous devotional and controversial works, was born in Aberdeenshire, in November, 1810. Since 1833 Dr. Cumming has been a popular preacher in the metropolis, and may now be said to have taken the place of Edward Irving, as the great pulpit orator of London. He is distinguished as an indomitable adversary of the Papacy, having conducted on the Protestant side several discussions with followers of the Roman Catholic Church. The Apocalyptic mysteries form his other great topic. His principal works are — "Apocalyptic Sketches," scarcely noticed on its first appearance; "Daily Life," "Voices of the Night," "Voices of the Day," "Sabbath Readings" on the Old and New Testaments, and "God in History." Dr. Cumming preached before the Queen at Balmoral, and his sermon, entitled "Salvation," has been published. His latest work, "The Great Tribulation, or Things Coming on the Earth" (of which it is said 10,000 copies have been sold in less than three months), has been severely criticised.

CUNNINGHAM, PETER, an author and critic, was born at Pimlico, in London, on the 7th April, 1816. He is son of Allan Cunningham, the poet, and inherits no small portion of his father's intellectual vigour. The late Sir Robert Peel, as a token of respect for "Honest Allan's" memory, appointed the son in 1834 to a situation in the Audit Office, in which department of the public service he rose to be Chief Clerk. Mr. Cunningham is the author of the "Handbook of London," the "Life of Inigo Jones," the "Story of Nell Gwynne," the "Life of Drummond of Hawthornden," &c. Besides editing numerous standard works for Mr. Murray, Mr. Cunningham was for many years a regular contributor to "The Athenæum," and now writes weekly in "The Illustrated London News." The last work edited by him was the collected edition of "Horace Walpole's Letters" (1857). In 1842 Mr. Cunningham married the second daughter of John Martin, the distinguished painter of "Belshazzar's Feast," by whom he has three children. He retired from the Audit Office last year.

CUNNINGHAM, WILLIAM, D.D., a Scottish divine and Principal of the New College, Edinburgh, was born at Hamilton, in Lanarkshire, in October, 1805, and educated at the University of Edinburgh, where he greatly distinguished himself. Almost immediately after receiving licence to preach, he was ordained assistant and successor to the Rev. Dr. Scott, of Greenock. His acquirements as a theologian, and his powers as a preacher, induced the Town Council of Glasgow to invite him to become minister of one of the churches in that city, of which they were patrons. He declined the offer, but he was afterwards translated to Trinity College Church, Edinburgh. His principles were evangelical, and he contended strenuously against the intrusion of ministers on a congregation without their consent. When the struggle between the General Assembly and the civil powers took place, Dr. Cunningham was always found in the breach, maintaining his position and defending his cause with all the eloquence of conviction. But to sketch his life would be merely epitomizing a history of the ten years' conflict, with every passage in which he was closely associated. On the death of Dr. Chalmers, in 1847, Dr. Cunningham was appointed his successor, as Principal of the New College, which had been opened at Edinburgh in connexion with the Free Church.

CURTIS, BENJAMIN R., an eminent American lawyer, was born in 1809, in Watertown, Massachusetts. He graduated at Harvard University, in 1829, and studied law under Mr. Justice Story in the same institution. After practising in Boston he was appointed in 1851 Associate Judge of the Supreme Court of the United States, which office he resigned in 1857, when he returned to the bar. He is editor of "Reports of Cases in the Circuit Courts of the United States;" and of "Reports of Decisions in the Supreme Court of the United States, with notes and a digest."

CURTIS, GEORGE WILLIAM, an American author, was born at Providence, Rhode Island, in 1824. In his youth he was on intimate terms with Longfellow and Hawthorne. In 1846 he came to Europe, and after a journey to the East returned to the United States, where he published various works, among the most prominent of which are—"Nile Notes of a Howadji," "Lotus Eating," "The Howadji in Syria," and "The Potiphar Papers," "Prue and I," and a novel of American life, called "Trumps." For keen and elegant satire Mr. Curtis is viewed as a sort of modern Persius and Juvenal combined.

CUSHMAN, MISS CHARLOTTE, an American tragic actress, was born at Boston, about 1820. Of five children left fatherless she was the oldest. By her mother she was encouraged to cultivate her natural taste for music. After having sung in a concert with Miss Paton (Mrs. Wood), that lady induced her to make the lyrical stage her profession. Miss Cushman's family were strenuously opposed to her adoption of that mode of life; but she was determined to pursue it, and upon her *début* in New York, met with astonishing success, as the Countess in the "Marriage of Figaro." Her voice was an admirable contralto; but going to New Orleans after her triumph, the change of climate, and her efforts to strain her voice into a soprano, deprived her completely of her vocal powers. Resolute in will, she decided on becoming an actress, "pure and simple;" and, having studied zealously, she appeared in the difficult character of "Lady Macbeth." She succeeded, and returned to New York with laurels. In 1845, conscious of ability, she came to England, was engaged in London, and performed Romeo to her sister Susan's Juliet. Romeo was so unlike anything to be expected from a female performer, that it took the critics by storm; she was called "Macready womaned;" still she persisted, and in the end made her greatest impression in "Meg Merrilies," about as picturesque a representation as has ever been witnessed. She has played many and diverse parts, in none offending, and in many excellent. Miss Cushman seems to have left the stage, as of late years her name seldom or never appears before the public.

DAHLMANN, FREDERICK CHRISTOPHER, a German historian and publicist, was born at Wismar, in May, 1785, and studied with distinction at Halle. In 1813 he was nominated professor at Kiel, where he delivered lectures, in Latin, on the Plays of Aristophanes. A quarrel with the Danish Government obliged him to accept of the Chair of Political Economy at Göttingen, where he published an historical work, entitled "Original Documents relating to German History." In politics a moderate liberal, he offered his services to the Hanoverian Government in drawing up a charter then conceded to popular clamour. Two years afterwards he published a work, in which he opposed alike Democracy and Absolutism, entitled "The Science of Politics, based on facts," which has since gone through several editions. In 1837, when the constitution was put down, and M. Dahlmann was obliged with six of his fellow professors to leave Hanover, he retired to Leipsic, where he devoted himself to historical research. The result of his labours was "The History of Denmark," published in 1840-43, one of the most important historical works of the century. In 1842 he accepted the Professorship of History and Political Economy at Bonn, and published in the same year his "History of the English Revolution," and the "History of the French Revolution." He was elected a member of the National Assembly at Frankfort, and laid before it the project of Provisional Government, which was adopted by the majority. M. Dahlmann wished to confer the hereditary monarchy on the King of Prussia, but being zealously in favour of German unity he opposed the armistice of Malmoë, which had been entered into by Prussia without the authority of Parliament. After this reactionary policy set in, and the liberal cause being completely defeated, he returned to his professorship at Bonn, which had been kept open for him.

DALE, THE REV. THOMAS, M.A., Canon of Saint Paul's Cathedral, and Vicar of Saint Pancras, poet and popular author, was born at Pentonville, London, August, 1797. His mother died when he was but three years old, and his father having married again, went to the West Indies, to edit a public journal, where he also died, leaving his only son. A presentation to Christ's Hospital was eventually obtained for him, where, under the late Dr. Trollope, by whom he was most kindly treated, he received a superior classical education. In 1817 he entered the University of Cambridge, having previously published his "Widow of Nain," which was speedily followed by the "Outlaw of Taurus," and "Irad and Adah, a Tale of the Flood," his first work passing through six editions within a very short period. He was ordained in 1823 first curate of St. Michael's, Cornhill, London, and afterwards, in 1835, by the special favour of Sir Robert Peel, appointed to be Vicar of St. Bride's. In 1843, through the same influence, he became a Canon of St. Paul's; and, in 1846, Vicar of St. Pancras. He had previously held the Lectureship of St. Margaret, Lothbury, but resigned it in 1849. With the exception of his poems, of which a collected edition was published in 1836, his edition of Cowper, and his translation of Sophocles, his later writings are exclusively religious, consisting chiefly of Sermons—"The Domestic Liturgy and Family Chaplain," "The Sabbath Companion," &c. They display a fine tone of thought, solid erudition, and the purest taste.

DALHOUSIE, JAMES ANDREW BROWN RAMSAY, MARQUIS OF, is the tenth Earl of Dalhousie, born at Dalhousie Castle, near Edinburgh, in 1812. As Lord Ramsay, his title by courtesy, he was first educated at Harrow, and then took his degrees at Oxford in 1833. He contested without success the representation of Edinburgh, on Conservative principles, with Mr. Abercromby, subsequently Speaker of the House of Commons, and with Sir John Campbell, the present Lord Chancellor. By his frankness and manly straightforwardness, however, he won golden opinions, not less from his adversaries than from his partizans. In 1837 he was returned to the House of Commons for the county of Haddington, and on the death of his father, in 1838, he succeeded to the Earldom of Dalhousie. In 1843 he was appointed Vice-President of the Board of Trade, and in 1845 President, with a seat in the Cabinet, resigning with the Ministry in 1846. In 1847, on the return of Lord Hardinge from India, he was offered and accepted the Governor-Generalship, being the youngest man ever appointed to that important and responsible office. The Sikhs, shortly after his landing, broke out a second time into war. Under his management they were defeated everywhere. He then annexed the Punjaub, seemingly indifferent to public opinion as to that decisive step, but keenly alive to the interests of the country. Pegu, Bezar and Nagpore, and lastly Oude, came under the same system of political acquisition; but, while conquering and annexing, he did not forget to develop the internal resources of the country. Railways, canals, and telegraphs were established; he sought to reform the administration of the civil and legal departments, and extended education and public works. In 1849 he was elevated to the dignity of a Marquis, receiving at the same time the thanks of both Houses of Parliament. He is a K.T., and Lord Warden of the Cinque Ports. The marquis returned from his duties in the East in shattered health in 1856. Having no sons by his late wife, his cousin Lord Panmure is the heir of his Scottish titles.

DALLAS, GEORGE MIFFLIN, an American statesman, and at present representative of the United States at the court of St. James's, was born at Philadelphia, in July, 1792. His father, who was a lawyer, filled several important offices in the State. The son was destined for a similar career. Having taken first-class honours at Princeton College in 1810, he was afterwards called to the bar, but desirous of knowing the world, he obtained the post of private secretary to the Russian Special Embassy, of which Mr. Gallatin was the chief. After visiting various continental countries he returned to America, and in 1817 was named Deputy Attorney-General for the eastern district of Pennsylvania. Elected mayor of Philadelphia, he was in 1829 appointed district Attorney-General, and in 1831 was returned to the senate of the United States for Pennsylvania. In 1833 he retired from Congress, and resumed his profession with decided success until 1837, when President Van

Buren confided to his charge the American embassy at St. Petersburg, from which he was recalled in 1839 at his own request. A profound lawyer and dexterous pleader, he once more took his position at the bar, but was again induced to abandon the courts by his election to the Vice-Presidency of the Union, in 1844. This office he held until the elevation of General Taylor to the Presidency, in 1849, when he resigned and returned once more to the practice of the law. In 1856 he was named Ambassador to London, succeeding Mr. Buchanan. Mr. Dallas, whilst understood to be one of the democratic party, has invariably sought to maintain the most amicable relations between Great Britain and the United States, and his course as a diplomatist has been such as to procure him the confidence of his own countrymen, and to elicit the esteem of the British people.

DANA, JAMES DWIGHT, LL.D., Professor of Geology and Natural History in Yale College, Connecticut, was born in Utica, in the State of New York, on 12th February, 1813. He studied at Yale College, graduating B.A. in 1833, and shortly afterwards was appointed a Teacher of Mathematics to the youth of the American navy. In that capacity he sailed to the Mediterranean, returning in 1835, and acting afterwards for two years as Assistant Professor in the chair which he now fills. In 1836 he was appointed mineralogist and geologist to an exploring expedition to the Southern and Pacific Oceans, which sailed in 1838, and returned in 1842, after a voyage round the world. He was chosen Professor in Yale College in 1855, and he is now engaged in the discharge of the duties of that chair, to which he adds the editorship of the "American Journal of Science." He was elected in 1854 President of the American Association for the Advancement of Science. His principal publications are — "A

System of Mineralogy," "Manual of Mineralogy," "Report on Zoophytes," and "Report on Crustacea." He has contributed a number of papers to various learned societies in America. Professor Dana is a member of the Geological Society of London, and various other scientific bodies.

DANA, RICHARD HENRY, an American poet and essayist, was born in November, 1787. He is the son of Francis Dana, minister to Russia, member of Congress, and Chief Justice of Massachusetts. He originally adopted the profession of the law, but was obliged to abandon it in consequence of ill health. His leanings were literary; and he joined his relative, Edward T. Channing, in the editorship of the "North American Review," to which he contributed largely. In 1821 he commenced the publication of "The Idle Man," the "Review" having proved a failure. Dana's first poem, "The Dying Raven," published in the "New York Review" in 1825, was followed, in 1827, by "The Buccaneer." He published his writings in a collected form in 1833, adding some new compositions. Since then he has rarely appeared as an author. His works are characterised by a fertile imagination, and strength and delicacy of expression. His eldest son, Richard Henry Dana, is the author of "Two Years before the Mast," and "To Cuba and Back." The first-named of these works is marked by peculiar ability, its author having entered the merchant service from a love of maritime adventure.

DANBY, FRANCIS, A.R.A., a landscape painter, born near Wexford, Ireland, 1793. The third son of James Danby, Esq., of Common, he received his earliest lessons in design in the School of the Royal Dublin Society of Arts, and exhibited his first pictures in 1811, at the exhibition in that city, leaving Ireland for England in the same year. He meant to have made a mere tour, but on reaching Bristol he found that his funds had run short, and there accordingly he stopped to replenish. Under the circumstances he settled in Bristol, teaching drawing, and painting small pictures with such success as to become firmly established in that city. In 1817 he painted a large picture of "Criminals going to the Upas Tree," which was exhibited at the British Institution, London. "Disappointed Love," and "Sunset at Sea, after a Storm," were exhibited at the Royal Academy—the last picture being purchased by Sir Thomas Lawrence, at a price far above that put upon it by the artist. Sir Thomas Lawrence advised him to remove to London, which he did, and soon after produced the picture of "The Passage of the Israelites through the Red Sea." In 1825, after the exhibition of "The Embarkation of Cleopatra on the Cydnus," he was elected an Associate of the Academy. In 1829, owing to some domestic misfortunes, he left England, and remained till 1840 on the Continent. In that year he returned to England with his large picture, "The Deluge." Mr. Danby's landscapes blend great imaginative power with poetic refinement. In his own peculiar path, the historical landscape, Mr. Danby has long stood without a rival. Since 1845 he has resided at Exmouth. His sons having adopted the same profession, are rising to distinction in their career.

DANILO, PETROVITCH NIEGOSCH, reigning Prince of Montenegro, under the suzeraineté of the Porte, was born on the 25th May, 1826, the succession being collateral. In 1852 he was proclaimed Prince, after a struggle with his uncle, Thomas Petrovitch, in which the young prince was assisted by the Czar of Russia. He received the investiture at St. Petersburg, and returned to his native country with the idea of revolutionizing the institutions of Montenegro.

He separated the civil and ecclesiastical functions of the Prince, as Vladika, handing over the latter to one of his relatives, with the title of Archimandrite. He then undertook the construction of a great public road from his capital to Cattaro, and the preparation of a penal code, the chief object of which was to put an end to the vendetta in Montenegro. The war with the Sultan which followed put an end to these attempts at reform. It continued down to 1855, when it was terminated by the intervention of the Allied Powers. In 1855 Prince Danilo married the daughter of a banker of Trieste. With his wife he visited Vienna and Paris in 1857, in order to induce these powers to support his claims of exemption from the suzeraineté of the Porte, but without success. A conspiracy, supported by the old Russian party, compelled him to return. He has since, it is understood, made great preparations to join in any attempt to oppose the pretensions of the Turkish Government should they materially affect his independence.

DARGAN, WILLIAM, a capitalist and contractor, the projector of the Dublin Exhibition, was born in 1799, in the county of Carlow. The son of an extensive farmer, he received a good education. He was afterwards sent to a surveyor's office, whence he went as an engineer into the employment of Telford. Subsequently he became an engineer, or rather contractor, on his own account. His first work of importance he obtained in 1832, when he pulled down a market-house, cut open a street, and built a bridge, at Banbridge, in Ireland. He then became contractor for the first railway laid in Ireland, the Dublin and Kingstown, and since that time he has been connected with almost every public work in the sister country. He was the main stay of the Dublin Exhibition in 1853, his advances being over £60,000.

The Queen visited him at his country seat, near Dublin, at the opening of the Exhibition ; and he refused the honour of a baronetcy which it was proposed to confer upon him.

DARWIN, CHARLES, M.A. Cantab., F.R.S., an eminent naturalist and author. When a very young man he accompanied Captain Fitzroy in his voyage round the world, in H.M.S. "Beagle," during the years 1831—1836. His journal first appeared in 1839, as part of the general narrative of the voyage, and was subsequently re-published in a modified form under the title of "Journal of Researches into the Geology and Natural History of the various Countries visited by H.M.S. 'Beagle.'" In 1842, his work "On the Structure and Distribution of Coral Reefs" appeared, which was followed by his "Geological Observations on South America." Since this period he has contributed many papers to the Geological Transactions, and to other scientific periodicals. His chief contribution to Zoology is the "Monograph on the Family Cirripeda," in two large volumes, in which he points out many curious and interesting particulars in relation to the history and economy of the barnacles and sea-acorns, and furnishes a minute description of every known species of the family. He has recently (November, 1859) published a work entitled, "The Origin of Species by Means of Natural Selection ; or, The Preservation of Favoured Races in the Struggle for Life." This volume, as stated in the introduction, gives only in a condensed form the result of more than twenty years' study, and will hereafter be followed by a more detailed treatise on the same subject. Mr. Darwin's writings exhibit close observation and untiring industry in collecting and arranging facts. Mr. Darwin, although he has adopted conclusions contested by other naturalists, has always been very cautious in arriving at results without sufficient data. He is a clear and elegant writer; and his works, independently of their scientific value, are written in a style well calculated to render them highly attractive.

D'AUBIGNÉ, J. H. MERLE, D.D., a Swiss Church historian and theologian, was born at Geneva, 1794, and is the second son of Aimé Robert Merle d'Aubigné, a merchant in that city. He received his education in Geneva, and then proceeded to Berlin, to complete his theological studies. Here he formed a friendship with Neander. A visit to Wartburg Castle, where Luther was confined, and where D'Aubigné was present at the tercenary jubilee of the Reformation, stimulated him to write his "History of the Reformation of the Sixteenth Century." For some years pastor of the French Church at Hamburg, in 1823 he was appointed by the King of the Netherlands, minister of the Protestant Church at Brussels. In 1831 he returned to Geneva, where he was appointed Professor of Church History to the new Theological School founded by the "Evangelical Society." This chair he still retains, together with the Presidency. As a preacher, professor, and author, Dr. Merle D'Aubigné has achieved a wide-spread reputation throughout the Protestant world, but chiefly in England and Scotland. He has frequently visited this country, meeting with a warm welcome from the zealous members of the evangelical party in the various churches. In 1856 he received the freedom of the city of Edinburgh. Besides his great work, he is the author of "The Protector a Vindication" (1847), and "Germany, England, and Scotland: Recollections of a Swiss Minister" (1848).

DAVID, FELICIEN, a French musical composer, was born at Cadenet, in the department of Vaucluse, on the 8th of March, 1810. Left an orphan when a child, he early devoted himself to music, which he studied under the Chapel Master at Aix. Before he was twenty years of age, he was prevailed upon to proceed to Paris, to complete his musical education; but his relations forsook him, and his resources were limited. The St. Simonians, about the same time, sprang up; he joined them, and passed through various phases of fortune. In 1844, he produced his first great work, "The Desert," consisting of about 2000 pages of music, and written in a year! He has composed much, but his works are not generally known, or if known, not understood and appreciated at their full value. The following list contains his chief productions:—" Four Symphonies for a Grand Orchestra;" "The Desert," a symphony; "Moses on Sinai," an oratorio; "Christopher Columbus," a symphony; "Eden," an oratorio; "The Gate of the Desert," an opera in three acts; "Herculaneum," an opera in four acts; "The Captive," an opera in two acts; "Two Sonetti;" "Symphonies for Nine Musical Instruments;" "The Four Seasons," for twenty-four stringed instruments; "Two Trios, for the Piano, the Violin and Violoncello;" "Twelve Melodies for the Piano and Violoncello;" "The Brises d'Orient," for the piano; "Eight Symphonies," studies for the piano; "The Ruche" consists of thirty songs for the human voice, sixty romances and melodies, &c. A peculiarity of the compositions of David is the attempt to suggest by music, operations of nature, which are obvious only to the eye.

DAVIS, SIR JOHN FRANCIS, BART., K.C.B., was born in London, in 1795. He is the eldest son of S. Davis, Esq., formerly member of the Board of Revenue in India, and a Director of the East India Company. Mr. Davis was attached to Lord Amherst's embassy to Pekin in 1816, and was joint Commissioner with the late Lord Napier in China in 1834. On his return to England, two years afterwards, after a residence of more than twenty years in China, he published "The Chinese: a General Description of China and its Inhabitants," in two volumes, which was at once admitted to be the best work on China in the English language. In 1841 he published "Sketches in China," with observations on the war which was then going on. In 1841 Mr. Davis was appointed Governor and Commander-in-Chief of Hong-Kong, in which post he remained for the following six years. He was created a Baronet in 1845, and a Knight Grand Cross of the Bath in 1854. On his return to England, in 1847, he took up his abode in Gloucestershire, of which county he is a Deputy-Lieutenant. In addition to the works above mentioned, Sir John Davis is the author of a translation of "Chinese Moral Maxims," "Chinese Novels," "China during the War and since the Peace" (1852), and of various philological treatises, and literary papers on cognate subjects, some of which have been published in French and German translations.

DAWSON, GEORGE, M.A., a popular lecturer and preacher, was born in London in 1821. Educated at home, he thence proceeded to Glasgow, where he took the degree of Master of Arts. He came to the ministry of the Baptist nonconformists, and after remaining for some time unemployed, was chosen, in 1844, minister of Mount Zion Chapel, Birmingham; but not conforming in all particulars to the requirements of the trust-deed and views of a portion of his congregation, a separation took place, the majority, however, remaining with him. A new church, that of "The Saviour," was opened in 1847, in which he continues to preach, deviating more and more from the conventional style of preaching. He has attained his popularity more as a lecturer than as a preacher; and, indeed, in the former capacity he has met with pre-eminent success, in all parts of England and Scotland.

DECAZES, ELIE DUC, was born on the 28th September, 1780, at St. Martin de Laye, near Libourne, Gironde. He is descended from a Gascon family, ennobled by Henri Quatre in 1596. Commencing his studies in the military school of Vendôme in 1790, he was afterwards called to the provincial bar. He removed to Paris under the consulate, and married the daughter of the President of the Court of Cassation in 1805. In 1810 he was called to Holland by King Louis, as a confidential adviser, and after that sovereign abdicated the throne, he became attached to the service of the mother of Napoleon, as secretary and councillor. After Waterloo he acted as chief of police, and in the absence of the troops, maintained the peace of the city of Paris. He passed, in 1818, to the Ministry of the Interior, vacated by the Duke de Richelieu. In this office he did good service as a reformer in commerce, manufactures, science, agriculture, social progress, and prison amelioration. In 1830, M. Decazes was absent from Paris, but he publicly deplored the overthrow of the Royal Family. He has retired into private life for many years, but is still held in high esteem in France as a man and a patriotic citizen.

DE GREY, EARL. *See* RIPON, EARL OF.

DELACROIX, FERDINAND-VICTOR-EUGÈNE, French painter, was born at Charenton Saint Maurice, near Paris, on the 27th of April, 1798. There are but few incidents in his life to notice. He received a liberal education, his father having been a member of the Old Convention, a Minister under the Directory, and Prefect of Bordeaux at the time of his death. He had three miraculous escapes from death, and after the last went to college, where, notwithstanding his passion for art, he studied diligently. At the age of eighteen he entered the atélier of the classic painter Pierre Guérin, who had already for pupils, Géricault and Ary Scheffer. These pupils abandoned the traditions of their instructor, and became declared partizans of the romantic school. His principal pictures are "The Massacre of Scio," "Dante and Virgil in the Inferno," "Algerian Women," "The Jewish Wedding." Delacroix, though not likely to take rank in the high position his admirers claim for him, undoubtedly possesses superior power as an artist, and his influence upon contemporary French art has unquestionably been great. He is now admitted chief of the romantic school.

DELANE, JOHN T., chief editor of the *Times* newspaper, was born in 1802. He was educated at Magdalen Hall, Oxford, where he took his degree. He was afterwards called to the bar. His tact and talent as a writer were early appreciated, and he has been for many years acting editor of the *Times*, which has been conducted with an amount of skill and literary ability, with a discrimination and in a tone of right feeling and high morality which cannot be too strongly praised. To write a biographical notice of Mr. Delane would be nothing more or less than to trace the history of the *Times* since the death of Messrs. Walker, Barnes, and Bacon. Under Mr. Delane's admirable management the paper has continued to hold the first place among English newspapers, and exercises supreme influence on public opinion, both in England and abroad.

DELAROCHE, PAUL, a French historical painter, was born at Paris, on the 17th July, 1797. At an early age he turned his attention to the study of landscape painting; not wishing to appear as a rival to his brother, then an historical painter of some note. Two unsuccessful competitions for the prize awarded to landscapes by the School of Arts overcame his fraternal scruples;

and in 1816 he became a pupil of Baron Gros, under whose direction he made rapid progress. In 1819, when only twenty-two, he exhibited his first picture, "Nephthali dans le Désert." In 1836 the Government confided to his care the interior decoration of the Church of the Madeleine, and he proceeded to Italy to study carefully the works of the old masters. All was prepared for the work, when another artist was associated with him. Fearing that there would be a want of unity, he relinquished the undertaking, but as compensation was appointed to decorate the Palais des Beaux Arts. He travelled for about four years afterwards, and in 1841 completed his finest work, the paintings in the Hemicycle of the Palais des Beaux Arts. His productions are very numerous, and so excellent as to disarm criticism. Some of them have been exhibited in this country, and many have been engraved. Among his pictures may be enumerated the "Enfants d'Edouard," the best known of his pictures, which for many years has been in the gallery of the Luxembourg; "Cromwell contemplating the dead body of Charles I.," which, exhibited in 1833, was universally admired; "The Execution of Lady Jane Grey;" "The Youth of Galileo;" "The Assassination of the Duke of Guise in 'the Castle of Blois" (1835); and "The Death of Queen Elizabeth," also in the Gallery of the Luxembourg. M. Delaroche has also executed four great historical pictures for the galleries of Versailles, viz., "The Baptism of Clovis," "The Benediction of Pepin le Bref," "The Crossing of the Alps by Charlemagne," and the Coronation of the latter at Rome. The chief works of M. Delaroche have been engraved by the most eminent French artists.

DEMIDOV, or DEMIDOFF, ANATOL, a Russian patron of authors, is the most conspicuous member of a family of capitalists—the Rothschilds of Russia. He was born at Florence, about 1810, and is son of the Count Nicolas Demidov, celebrated for his taste in the arts, and for his prodigious fortune. The founder of the house of Demidov was a serf, who, in the days of Peter the Great, left his native village to escape enlistment in the army of the Czar. Niteita bound himself to a blacksmith at Tula, being paid for his work at the rate of about three halfpence a-week. Before the close of his career, on the birth of the prince Peter, he made the Empress a present of a hundred thousand roubles. Niteita was a special favourite of Peter the Great, and under his auspices he established the first iron foundry in Siberia. The gold and silver mines of the Ural mountains were discovered by his son and grandson. Prudently enough, however, they concealed this discovery, until they had ascertained that the Government would allow the proprietors of the land to work it to their own profit. In 1840, Anatol Demidoff was married at Florence to the Princess Matilda de Montfort, daughter of Prince Jerome Bonaparte, and of the Princess Catherine of Wurtemberg. The marriage produced no children, and after five years it was dissolved by mutual consent—the Princess Matilda receiving an allowance of 200,000 roubles a-year. He has founded an annual prize of 5000 roubles for the Academy of Sciences, at St. Petersburg. Demidoff resides chiefly in Italy.

DE MORGAN, AUGUSTUS, a distinguished mathematician, now Professor of Mathematics in University College, London, was born at Madura, in Southern India, in 1806. He was educated at Trinity College, Cambridge, but, from objection to the subscriptions, never took a higher degree than that of B.A. He studied some time for the bar, but relinquished that pursuit for the professorship already named, holding it from 1828 to 1831, when he resigned, returning to the chair again in 1836. He is one of the secretaries and a member of the council of the Royal Astronomical Society. His name was prominently brought forward by the controversy which he conducted in 1847 with Sir William Hamilton, relative to the title of the former to the discovery of a new principle in the theory of syllogism. He has acquired a very high and well-deserved distinction by his works, among which may be mentioned, "The Connexion of Number and Magnitude: an Attempt to explain the Fifth Book of Euclid" (1836); an "Essay on Probabilities, and on their Application to Life Contingencies and Insurance Offices" (1838); "First Notions on Logic, preparatory to the Study of Geometry" (1839); "Formal Logic; or the Calculus of Inference necessary and probable" (1847); and "The Book of Almanacs, with an Index of Reference, by which the Almanac may be found for every year up to A.D. 2000; with Means of finding the Day of any New or Full Moon from B.C. 2000 to A.D. 2000." He was an extensive contributor to the Penny Cyclopædia and the various publications of the Useful Knowledge Society, and has written largely in the "Athenæum," the "North British Review," and the various scientific Transactions.

DENMARK, KING OF. See CHARLES CHRISTIAN FREDERICK.

DERBY, EDWARD GEOFFREY STANLEY, EARL OF, was born in 1799, at Knowsley Park, Lancashire. He is the eldest son of the thirteenth Earl Derby, then only heir apparent to his father. After quitting Christ Church, he pursued, with eminence, his studies at Eton and Oxford, and entered the House of Commons in 1820, as member for Stockbridge. For four years he took but little part in the business of the House; but from the first time that he gave himself completely to politics, his surpassing power as a debater was universally acknowledged. From 1826 to 1830, he sat as member for Preston. Nominated, under the short-lived Goderich administration, Under-Secretary for the Colonies, Preston having elected Henry Hunt, then the idol of the English people, Windsor, at the same time a nomination borough, received the rejected of Preston, and for two years he kept his seat for that ancient town. In 1832 he was returned for North Lancashire, which he continued to represent until called to the House of Lords in 1845. In 1830 Mr. Stanley was appointed Chief-Secretary for Ireland, under the Grey administration, holding the office till 1833, when he became Secretary for the Colonies. In both capacities his energy and eloquence had been of signal service to the Whig government. But in 1834, in conjunction with Sir James Graham, the Duke of Richmond, and Lord Ripon, he separated from Earl Grey, upon the question of the reduction of the Irish ecclesiastical establishment and the secularization of a large portion of the revenues. In 1841 he took office in Sir Robert Peel's ministry, as Colonial Secretary, and continued till 1845, when he was raised to the House of Peers, under the title of Baron Stanley of Bickerstaffe, that the Government might then have the benefit of his great debating powers. Not long after this elevation, Sir Robert Peel having expressed his intention to repeal the Corn-laws, Lord Stanley resigned, and in the session of 1846 became leader of the Opposition, known as the Protectionist party. On the dissolution of the Whig cabinet in 1852, the Protectionist Conservatives were called to power. Of that ministry, Lord Stanley, now the Earl of Derby, was the chief. It lasted just ten months. In 1855 the noble Earl declined the task of constructing another ministry, and Lord Palmerston came into power as successor to Lord Aberdeen. On the fall of the Palmerston administration, he again became Premier, a position which he held from February 1858, to August 1859. In November of the latter year, he and his co-ministers were entertained at a banquet in Liverpool, where he expressed his principle of political action to be, not to needlessly thwart the administration for the time, but rather to assist the Government in any difficulty that might arise. In 1825 Lord Derby married Emma Caroline, daughter of the first Lord Skelmersdale, and has three children, of whom Lord Stanley, M.P., born in 1826, is heir apparent.

DESCHENES, PERCEVAL, ADMIRAL, was born in 1790. He early distinguished himself in his profession, and was present at the battle of Trafalgar. Commanding the French Baltic fleet, he gallantly seconded our navy in the attack on Bomarsund in 1854. The Emperor rewarded the gallant admiral's services, by conferring on him the Grand Cross of the Legion of Honour at the end of the war.

DEWEY, ORVILLE, D.D., a Unitarian divine, was born at Sheffield, Massachusetts, in 1794; he studied theology in the seminary at Andover, and was ordained a clergyman in 1823. He preached with great success, in the orthodox Congregational churches, for a year or so, but then joined the Unitarian body, filling Channing's pulpit when that theologian visited Europe. He also travelled in the Old World, and gave the results of his observations in a work entitled "The Old World 'and the New" (1835), which was succeeded by two or three volumes of sermons, one of them controversial. His reasoning is comprehensive, his illustrations are poetical, his style is easy and polished. A complete edition of his writings has been published in this country.

DICKENS, CHARLES, a novelist, was born in February, 1812, at Landport, Hants. His father, Mr. John Dickens, held a government situation, the duties connected with which compelled a frequent change of residence, and a portion of his son's education was thus received at Chatham. At the conclusion of the war, in 1815, the father, after his retirement from government service, became connected with the London press, in the capacity of a reporter. Intending his son for the legal profession, he placed him in an attorney's office. An early passion for literature, however, rendered him unwilling to remain in this career; and he became connected with the press. Obtaining an engagement first upon the "Mirror of Parliament," and subsequently upon the "Morning Chronicle," his abilities as a parliamentary reporter soon drew upon him conspicuous attention. It was in the "Morning Chronicle" that many of those "Sketches of Life and Character" appeared which were afterwards published as "Sketches by Boz." The success of this first effort was so decided, and showed the possession of so rich a vein of humorous and descriptive power, that the late Mr. Hall, of the firm of Chapman and Hall, proposed that he should write a story after the same manner. Thus originated the famous "Pickwick Papers." The success of these papers was so decided, that at the early age of twenty-five, Mr. Dickens had become the most popular of English novelists. Shortly after the publication of the first number of "Pickwick," Mr. Dickens married a daughter of Mr. George Hogarth, music writer and critic. When "Bentley's Miscellany" was started in 1836, he became its editor; and in that periodical originally appeared his novel of "Oliver Twist," afterwards republished in three volumes, which was rapidly followed by "The Life and Adventures of Nicholas Nickleby" and "Master Humphrey's Clock." Mr. Dickens now visited America. "American Notes for General Circulation" was the product of that tour. In 1843 he began his series of "Christmas Stories," which have proved so peculiarly attractive. In 1846 Mr. Dickens became editor of the "Daily News"—originated as a liberal morning paper, and in its columns appeared "Pictures from Italy." His connexion with the "Daily News" was soon found to be far other than a success. The paper made a very narrow escape from being ruined by the staff that had been gathered round it, among none of whom did it appear that the real editorial faculty was to be found. Political disquisition was not the forte of the novelist, and his connexion with the "Daily News" was abandoned. "Dealings with the Firm of Dombey and Son" was now commenced, followed by "The History of David Copperfield," "Hard Times," "Bleak House," and "Little Dorrit." In 1850 Mr. Dickens started "Household Words," a weekly periodical, which has been enriched by the contributions of some of the ablest and most popular writers of the day. This has been succeeded by "All the Year Round," which promises to be even more successful. The time has not yet come for an impartial estimate of the genius of this unquestionably most successful novelist of our own or of any age. Wherever the English language is known, Dickens is read, and not a few of his works have been translated into the various languages of Europe. Following the example of Thackeray and others, he for some time appeared to public audiences as the reader of his own works, and with marked success, in most of the principal towns of the kingdom.

DICKSON, SAMUEL HENRY, M.D., Professor of the Practice of Medicine in the Jefferson Medical College, Philadelphia, was born at Charleston, South Carolina, in 1798. He graduated as A. B. at Yale College in 1814, passed two years in the Medical University of Pennsylvania, received his diploma in 1819, and commenced practice in Charleston. After being the means of establishing a Medical College in that city, he was appointed Professor of the Theory and Practice of Medicine to the New York University, in 1847. After three years, upon special invitation from his former colleagues, he returned again to Charleston, where he remained until 1858, when he was appointed to the chair which he now holds, in the most flourishing and largest medical school in America. Dr. Dickson has produced a number of well-digested medical works, and is looked up to as being one of the most eminent American writers on medical science. He is, besides, a poet and an accomplished man of letters.

DILKE, CHARLES WENTWORTH, a journalist and critic, was born on the 8th of December, 1789. He began life in the Navy Pay Office. On a consolidation of offices in this department being effected, he retired, and purchased the "Athenæum," a journal which had previously been unsuccessful. Mr. Dilke took an active part in editing this paper until 1846; when he undertook the management of the "Daily News." In 1849 Mr. Dilke finally retired from active employment as a journalist, and now enjoys a life of learned leisure, contributing occasionally an article to the "Athenæum," but taking no share in the management of the paper.

DILKE, CHARLES WENTWORTH, JUNIOR, son of the above, was born in London, on the 18th of February, 1810. He was educated for the legal profession. He was one of the foremost promoters of the Great Exhibition of 1851, and was one of the active members of the managing committee. For his unwearied and successful services on this occasion, he was offered the honour of knighthood, but declined not only that, but all pecuniary reward.

DINDORF, WILHELM, an eminent German critic and scholar, was born at Leipsic, in 1802. He studied in the university of his native city; and, after an examination passed with *éclat*, became, in 1828, the Professor of Literary History. He resigned the chair in 1833, and for some years devoted himself exclusively to philological works, especially the new edition of Henry Stephens' "Thesaurus Greciæ Linguæ," published by Firmin Didot, of Paris. He has since edited for the University of Oxford, a series of the Greek classics, as well as several for Didot's "Library of Greek Classics," published at Paris. These works, in which the editor has given proof not only of erudition, but of a sagacity not always associated with it, have placed him in the first rank of living Greek scholars.

DISRAELI, BENJAMIN, a novelist, orator, and ex-Chancellor of the Exchequer, was born in London in 1805. He is the son of the amiable and learned author of "The Curiosities of Literature," who resided chiefly on his property, near Wycombe, in Buckinghamshire. Mr. Disraeli's education was carefully superintended by his father. When completed, he was articled to a solicitor, not with the view of following the profession, but with the purpose of acquiring the business habits and qualifications necessary to fill a situation in a public office, which had been secured for him by his father's influence. A short experience of the drudgery of a lawyer's office soon proved to young Disraeli, that the career traced for him by his father was hopelessly uncongenial to his tastes. Inheriting an independent fortune from his parents, he relinquished his chances in favour of his younger brother, who, entering the field thus opened to him, has ultimately risen to the important office he now holds, that of Registrar of the Court of Chancery. Subsequently to his short trial of business-life, Mr.

K

Disraeli visited the Continent, and wrote and published in 1827 his dashing novel of "Vivian Grey." He shortly afterwards went to the Continent a second time, and visited the classic regions and hallowed ground of Italy and Greece, whence he extended his tour to Turkey and Syria. Returning from travel at the moment the Reform Bill agitation had introduced a new era into British politics, he was anxious to obtain a seat in Parliament. Recommended by Mr. Hume and Mr. O'Connell, he was invited by the Tory corporation of Wycombe to stand for that borough, but was defeated. He never stood for Marylebone, as has often been erroneously stated. Resigning, for the present, all hope of parliamentary honours, he resumed his literary occupations, and devoted himself for about two years to purely literary avocations, during which time he published "Contarini Fleming," a psychological romance; the "Wondrous Tale of Alroy," a work so thoroughly Oriental in its style and diction that many have supposed it was originally written in poetry; "The Rise of Iskander;" "A Vindication of the British Constitution;" and "The Revolutionary Epic," which was, strictly speaking, an epic ridiculing revolutions. In 1835 he unsuccessfully contested the borough of Taunton, in the Conservative interest; or, as he has himself somewhere said, "on exactly the same principles as he had always professed." About this time he had a dispute which led to a hostile correspondence between him and the son of Mr. O'Connell. Subsequently the great agitator sought an interview with Mr. Disraeli in the House of Commons, to express his regret at what had occurred, having, as he said, "been misled and precipitate." In a letter written to O'Connell after the Taunton election, Mr. Disraeli thus alludes to his repeated failures :— "I

have a deep conviction the hour is at hand when I shall be more successful. I expect to be a representative of the people before the Repeal of the Union. We shall meet at Philippi." After his defeat at Taunton, Mr. Disraeli returned once more to his literary labours, and in 1836 appeared "Henrietta Temple," which the "Times" recently pronounced "the most perfect love story ever written." In 1837 he published "Venetia," which he intended as a philosophic view of the character of Lord Byron. His political ambition was now at length about to be gratified. At the age of thirty-two he was returned as one of the Conservative members for Maidstone, along with Mr. Wyndham Lewis. Unfortunately, however, the list of his failures had not yet closed; for his maiden speech was accompanied throughout by the laughter of the House, and at last he was compelled to resume his seat, uttering these words :— "I have begun many things several times, and have often succeeded at last. I shall sit down now, but the time will come when you will hear me." Within two years from this prediction of future success, arising from present failure, he began to gain the ear of the House. Within two years more he was recognised as the leader of the "Young England party." During the Peel ministry of 1841-46 he acquired the highest distinction as a master of sarcasm. During the whole period that Sir Robert Peel was developing his Free-trade policy, Disraeli's attacks on him were incessant, and his brilliant invective saved the Tory party from being broken up, and achieved for himself personal distinction and parliamentary position. On the fall of Sir Robert Peel's government, he was—with the exception of Lord George Bentinck, who died suddenly in 1848—the most conspicuous man in the Protectionist ranks. It is only justice to him to state, that after he had driven Peel from office, he never again made the slightest attack upon him, except on one occasion, when, shortly before his death, Peel made a rather severe onslaught on the Protectionist party. In 1846 Mr. Disraeli was returned for the county of Buckingham, and on the retirement of the Russell cabinet in 1852 he became Chancellor of the Exchequer, under Lord Derby, who was subsequently obliged to give way to Lord Aberdeen. On the breaking out of the Russian war in 1854, patriotism having for the time almost extinguished party feeling, faction was hushed, and a liberal support was accorded by Mr. Disraeli and his supporters—first to the Aberdeen, and subsequently to the Palmerston administration. On the break up of the Palmerston cabinet by the Conspiracy Bill, Mr. Disraeli again became Chancellor of the Exchequer, and resumed his position of leader of the House of Commons in the Derby administration of 1858 ; but in the following year, being again met by an adverse majority of the Lower House, Lord Derby and colleagues resigned. To the great annoyance of many of his own party, Mr. Disraeli frequently spoke, and always voted, in favour of the Jew Bill, except upon one occasion, when he was absent from the House for some time, from a severe illness. Mr. Disraeli is a warm advocate for government by party; and at the Liverpool banquet to Lord Derby in 1859, he declared himself "thoroughly convinced that with a Parliamentary Government, government by party was absolutely necessary." Mr. Disraeli still represents in Parliament the county of Bucks, and remains the undisputed leader of the Opposition in the Lower House. Should his life and health be spared, he will share all the honours and responsibility of his party, and, perhaps, rise to higher office than he has yet filled. Besides the early novels which appeared before he entered Parliament, Mr. Disraeli has written "Coningsby," "Sybil," and "Tancred," semi-political novels, known and admired in a far more judicious circle than that of the circulating libraries, and which will always entitle him to a high place among the most brilliant and distinguished of English novelists.

DIXON, WILLIAM HEPWORTH, of the Inner Temple, and editor of the "Athenæum," was born on the 30th of June, 1821, and is the son of Alexander Dixon, of Holmfirth, in the West Riding of Yorkshire, where his family had been settled from the time of the Roses. After spending some time in a merchant's office, and conducting for a short period a Cheltenham newspaper, Mr. Dixon repaired to London, where he entered as a student of the Inner Temple, and was in due time called to the bar. He wrote for the "Daily News" and the "Athenæum." His "Literature of the Lower Orders," originally published in the former journal, brought him into notice ; "London Prisons," another work from his strong and earnest mind, elevated him still higher in the world's opinion ; but the solid foundation of fame was laid in 1849, when he published "John Howard, a Memoir," written many years before, and one of his first finished works. He could not at first find a publisher for this work, although he offered to give away the copyright without any remuneration for authorship, on the simple condition of publication. At length, when it did come out, it ran through three editions in a year. He has followed up his Memoir of Howard with biographies of Penn and Blake, which have run through many editions, and have been largely reprinted abroad. In 1850 he was a Deputy Commissioner for organizing the Exhibition of 1851. In the following year he published an anonymous pamphlet, "The French in England ;" showing that if Napoleon I.

could not accomplish his purposes of invasion, to do so was beyond the power of Napoleon III. Mr. Dixon wrote two essays for the "Prize Magazine," and was the successful competitor. The proprietors of the "Athenæum" were struck with their ability, and engaged him on their staff. From about 1850 he was the working editor. In 1853 he was constituted sole and responsible editor of that journal; a position which he retains with honour to himself and advantage to literature. Mr. Dixon was one of the closest friends of the late Lady Morgan, and was selected by that brilliant wit and fascinating woman as her literary executor. He has travelled much of late years on the Continent. His object in these tours is known to be a careful examination of the scenery and geography of places connected with events in English history. He has been for thirteen years a constant reader of unpublished State papers; and two years ago, when the Tories were in office, he induced Lord Stanley and Sir E. B. Lytton to throw open these vast treasures to the free use of men of letters. The Master of the Rolls has often benefited by his advice in the conduct of the great national works now in progress of publication, viz. : "The Calendar of State Papers," and the "English Chronicle." Mr. Dixon for nine years past has published nothing with his name; reserving his strength for the "Athenæum," and an historical work on which he is engaged, the publication of which has often been announced in the journals as about to take place, and is anxiously expected.

DOBELL, SYDNEY, a poet, first known as "Sydney Yendys," was born in Kent, in 1824, and brought up in the neighbourhood of London. His father was a wine-merchant, who, when the poet was eleven years of age, removed his establishment to Cheltenham. In 1836 he entered the counting-house of his father as a clerk, and was actively engaged in business when he wrote his first work. In 1844 he married Emily, daughter of George Fordham, Esq., of Odsey House, in Cambridgeshire. He had received at home a liberal education, and did not find a close application to counting-house routine incompatible with poetry, for which he had early shown unusual powers. In 1850 he published "The Roman," and, in 1854, "Balder," both of which created a sensation, by their originality of conception and style. By one party of critics these works were pronounced to belong to the very highest order of poetry ; by another, they were severely condemned as unintelligible and spasmodic. In 1855 Mr. Dobell, in conjunction with Alexander Smith, the author of "A Life Drama," published a volume entitled "Sonnets on the War," and in 1856 appeared a book of lyrics, called "England in Time of War."

DOO, GEORGE THOMAS, R.A., line engraver, was born in January, 1800, in the parish of Christ Church, Surrey. Devoting his attention to line engraving when this art stood high in public favour, he was, in 1825, appointed engraver to his Royal Highness the Duke of York ; Historical Engraver in Ordinary to King William IV., in 1836; and in 1842 Historial Engraver in Ordinary to Queen Victoria. In 1852 he was elected Member of the Society of Arts, Amsterdam, and in the following year Member of the Academy of Fine Arts, Pennsylvania, U.S. In 1854 he became a Corresponding Member of the Imperial Academy of Parma, and in 1857 a Member of the Imperial Academy of St. Petersburg. In 1856 he was elected an Associate of the Royal Academy of Arts in London, and in 1857 Royal Academician. The works by which this distinguished artist is best known are his "Knox Preaching before the Lords of the Covenant," after Wilkie ; his admirable rendering of Etty's "Combat," and his elaborate version of Eastlake's picture of the "Italian Pilgrims coming in sight of Rome." Raffaelle's "Infant Christ bearing the Cross," and the "Ecce Homo" of Correggio, are also works possessing a rare order of merit. The very limited patronage which line engraving has of late years received, almost led Mr. Doo to abandon the profession, and for some time he painted in oil a number of highly characteristic portraits. He has now, however, returned to his own department of the profession, and several large engravings by him are now in progress.

DORAN, JOHN, Ph. D., F.S.A., an English writer, a member of an old Leinster family, was born in London in 1807. He was chiefly educated by his father, spending many years while a boy in France and Germany, afterwards becoming tutor in several noble English families. The first manifestation of his literary bent was the production of a melodrama, the "Wandering Jew," written when he was fifteen, and brought out at the Surrey Theatre. He has been an extensive contributor to periodical literature; but is best known by a series of racy works, the character of which may be inferred from their very titles, such as "Table Traits, and Something on them," "Habits and Men," "Knights and their Days," and "Monarchs retired from Business." The "History of Court Fools" is probably the best specimen of his quaint style and original method of thinking. "Anything," says the "Athenæum," "more quaint and surprising than Dr. Doran's tale of the origin of court fools is scarcely to be found in the pages of the greatest and most genial humorists." His last work, published in 1860, is a series of biographies of the heirs-apparent of England, under the title of "The Book of the Princes of Wales." Almost all his works have been reprinted in America.

DOUGLAS, GENERAL SIR HOWARD, BART., son of Admiral Sir Charles Douglas, who served under Rodney, was born at Gosport, in 1776. He entered the army when young; was at Walcheren and Corunna, and served in Spain and Portugal in 1808 and 1809, and again in Spain in 1811 and 1812. He published several treatises on matters connected with military science between 1816 and 1819, and was appointed Governor of New Brunswick in 1823, retaining that office till 1829. He was Lord High Commissioner of the Ionian Islands from 1835 to 1840, and in 1842 was elected member for Liverpool, holding the seat till 1847. In 1851 he obtained the rank of General, and became Colonel of the 15th Regiment of Foot. His principal publications are an "Essay on the Principles and Construction of Military Bridges, and the Passage of Rivers in Military Operations," "A Treatise on Naval Gunnery," "Observations on Carnot's Fortification," "Considerations on the Value and Importance of the British and North American Provinces," and "Naval Evolutions," a book which vindicated his father's claim to the origination of a brilliant manœuvre in 1782. He censured the conduct of the war in the Crimea in 1855, and showed, what afterwards turned out true, that Sevastopol could not be reduced without the plan of operations being changed. Several of his works have run through various editions, especially his "Treatise on Naval Gunnery," the recommendations of which were not acted upon by the Admiralty until 1830, thirteen years after its first publication.

DOYLE, RICHARD, an artist, was born in London in 1826. He is son of the author of the lithographic sketches which, with the signature of "HB" at the corner, created so much sensation some years ago, not more on account of their verisimilitude than because of the peculiarly quaint method in which an idea was conveyed in a sketch. He gave early indications of his particular talent as an art satirist, and the pages of "Punch" afforded him ample scope for the display of his power. He contributed for a number of years to this periodical, and his sketches have never been excelled for dry humour and sharp wit. He caught up the current follies of the day, and exposed them with a few touches of his pencil so cleverly that the very classes ridiculed—the ridicule always being good-natured—scarcely knew whether they should indulge in anger or mirth. Mr. Doyle eventually withdrew from "Punch," in consequence of the attacks on Roman Catholicism admitted into its columns, he having been brought up in the Roman Catholic faith. Since his separation from "Punch," he has been principally engaged in illustrating books, such as Leigh Hunt's "Jar of Honey," Ruskin's "King of the Golden River," and Montalba's "Fairy Tales from all Nations," and is the illustrator of "The Continental Tour of Brown, Jones, and Robinson."

DROUYN DE LHUYS, Edouard, a French statesman and diplomatist, was born at Paris, on the 19th of November, 1805. Having received an excellent education, at an early age he entered upon political life; but not before having spent some time in the study of the law. In 1830 he became *Attaché* to the French ambassador at Madrid, M. d'Harcourt, and subsequently to Count Rayneval, whose confidence he soon completely won. In 1833 he went to the Hague, as *Chargé d'Affaires*, and had there the chief share in conducting the diplomatic transactions arising out of the dissolution of the union between Belgium and Holland. The mode in which the diplomatist conducted himself in this critical juncture was highly gratifying to all

concerned. Prince Talleyrand, who had watched the progress of the conference, pointed him out to the French government as of the greatest promise. He was in Spain, as first Secretary and *Chargé d'Affaires* during the civil war, and was called to Paris by M. Thiers, in 1840, to fill the function of *Directeur* in the Foreign Office. In 1842 M. Drouyn De Lhuys, elected a member of the Chamber of Deputies, saw symptoms of the coming disaster which was to prostrate constitutional government in France, and remonstrated with Guizot upon the policy of the government, contending warmly for the reform movement. He represented the department of Seine-et-Marne in the Constituent and Legislative Assembly, and was made President of the Committee on Foreign Affairs. There he took a moderate stand, and always voted with the moderate party. On the election of Louis Napoleon to the Presidency, M. Drouyn De Lhuys was appointed Minister of Foreign Affairs. He was surrounded by difficulties; European politics presenting one mass of complications. He left the ministry in 1849, and, in the same year, was sent as ambassador to England. In 1852 Napoleon again entrusted him with the ministry of Foreign Affairs, and in that capacity he had to conduct the negociations relative to the recognition of the French empire by foreign powers. In 1855 he represented France in the conferences at Vienna, but for various reasons he was superseded by Count Walewski.

DUCHÂTEL, Charles Marie Tanneguy, Count, a French statesman, was born at Paris, on the 19th of February, 1803. His father, who was descended of an old Norman family, embraced the principles of 1789, was a deputy, and a peer of France, under the restoration. The subject of this notice studied law and came to the bar. Very soon, however, he manifested a predilection for politics. He joined the liberal party, and took an active part in founding and editing the "Globe." After the revolution of 1830, he employed all his powers and influence in favour of the Orleans' dynasty. He has held office as a Councillor of State, Royal Commissioner to the Chamber, Deputy in 1833, and in August, 1834, Minister of Commerce. In 1837 he declined to accept office under Count Molé. He re-entered the ministry under the presidency of Marshal Soult, as Minister of the Interior, an office in which he carried many very important and salutary measures, which were generally well received by all classes of politicians; and were in all cases consistent with the principles of sound and liberal parliamentary government. It was, invariably, to the influence and power of the Chamber, that Duchâtel looked for the support of the authority of the government; and he totally disregarded the clamour out of doors; which, however, was never specially directed against him. He was, during the long period of his parliamentary career, returned almost unanimously to the Chamber. The *coup d'état*, of course, put an end to the career of Duchâtel, and introduced an order of things under which the influence he retains with his countrymen could not be manifested.

DUDEVANT, MADAME AMANTINE AURORE DUPIN, by marriage—better known in England by her assumed name of "Georges Sand"—a French novelist, was born at Paris, in 1804. Owing to the death of her father, Mademoiselle Dupin was educated by her grandmother, the Comtesse de Horn. The Comtesse was an admirer of Rousseau, and her young charge was brought up in conformity with his views. When thirteen years of age, her grandmother was prevailed upon to send her to Paris, where she was placed in the Convent of the Augustines; with all the enthusiasm of her nature, she entered into the spirit of the place, and resolved to take the veil. Her family interfered to prevent this result, and at the age of seventeen she was married to M. Dudevant. The marriage was not a happy one, and in 1834 a separation was effected; Madame Dudevant, under a judgment of the court in her favour, retaining her fortune and children. When twenty-seven, she came to reside at Paris, and becoming acquainted with Jules Sandeau, the friends betook themselves to literature. "Rose et Blanche," a novel published in 1832, was the joint product of their labours. Madame Dudevant having been obliged to return to the place where she was educated, "Indiana" was produced by her labours; and to it, in commemoration of her friendship with the Parisian student, she affixed the name of "Georges Sand." The work at once conferred a celebrity upon her, which has been sustained and augmented by her subsequent writings. Madame Dudevant's prolonged familiarity with the leading thinkers among the philosophical democrats, and her own ardent genius, prepared her to hail with the impassioned rapture of her nature the triumph of democracy in 1848. She had then an interview with M. de Lamartine, whom she had long known; but, on this occasion, no discussion took place between them regarding political questions. She esteemed and admired this great man without participating in all his ideas. Since the accession of Louis Napoleon to power, Madame Dudevant has ceased to be a journalist. After 1848 she did not introduce political questions into her writings, the liberty of the press having disappeared from that period. Her more recent works are purely literary. Her autobiography appeared some time ago.

Several volumes of this work are filled with a narrative of the early life and military adventures of her father. To justify this elaborate introduction, "Georges Sand" asserts that every isolated life is a mystery; that thoughts, beliefs, instincts, are all an enigma, unless we can trace their origin in the past. Of her other works, the most remarkable are her novels, entitled "André," "Jacques," "Simon," "Mauprat," "La Dernière Adini," "La Petite Fadette," "Le Compagnon de la Tour de France," "La Mare au Diable," &c. She is the writer of various plays, which have met with great success, including "François le Champi," "Claudie," "Molière," &c.

DUFAURE, Jules Armand Stanislas, a lawyer and ex-minister of France, was born in 1798. He was educated at Paris for the bar, and for some time practised his profession at Bordeaux. He entered on political life in 1834, being elected Deputy for the arrondissement of Saintes, when he ranged himself among the constitutional liberals. In 1836, under the ministry of M. Thiers, he was nominated a Councillor of State. In the midst of the ministerial combinations brought about by Louis-Philippe, the last attempt at resistance by the republican party took place in 1839, when a cabinet was formed in which were included MM. Passy, Villemain, Duchâtel, and Teste, and in which M. Dufaure accepted the ministry of Public Works, for the first time set aside as a special department. In his capacity of minister, he conducted the discussions in the Chamber, on the question whether railways should be constructed by the State, or left to private companies. On the 1st of March, 1840, this ministry was replaced by that of M. Thiers, to which M. Dufaure offered no opposition. Under this ministry, and that of M. Guizot which followed, he acquired great influence by his active participation in the discussion of all great questions connected with finance and public works. A medal was struck in his honour, as a reward for the manner in which he had carried through the great *projet de loi* applicable to railways. After having been appointed Vice-President of the Chamber, under the patronage of the ministry, he was re-elected in 1845 by the votes of the Opposition. He was not connected with the agitation which preceded the expulsion of Louis-Philippe, and protested against the banquets as unconstitutional. After the revolution of February, he was elected representative of the Charente-Inférieure, and became one of the chiefs of the moderate democrats; voting, however, with the "left," for the banishment of the Orleans' family; but with the "right" against Socialism, and in favour of every measure calculated to restore and maintain order. Afterwards he became a constitutional minister under Louis Napoleon. When the President of the Republic resolved to usurp supreme power, Dufaure having always supported the cause of liberty, opposed the *coup d'état*, against which he protested, in common with all the eminent statesmen of France. He was obliged to retire, and has since withdrawn from the turmoil of French politics. Having been admitted to the Parisian bar in 1852, he soon rose to a high place in the profession. His political life had made his name familiar, and his acquaintance with practical business, and steady adherence to opinions in which the middle classes sympathised with him, soon secured for him a success which his forensic ability would have ultimately obtained for him. His powerful logic, and vigorous language, have now placed him in the very first rank among the legal practitioners before the law courts of Paris.

DUFF, Alexander, D.D., LL.D., an Indian Missionary, was born at Pitlochrie, in Perthshire, on the 25th of April, 1806. He studied at the University of St. Andrews, carrying off the highest honours in classics and philosophy, and graduated as M.A. in 1825. Thereafter, he pursued his theological studies at St. Andrews, and in 1829 was selected by the Church of Scotland as their first missionary to India. He was twice shipwrecked on the passage out. Immediately on his arrival, Dr. Duff laid the foundation of that great evangelistic system with which his name is so intimately connected; and, in particular, of that institution which, from small beginnings, soon became the largest and most influential for Christian and general objects in India—an institution in which, for nearly a quarter of a century, there have been upwards of one thousand *bonâ fide* pupils; and in which, in addition to a comprehensive elementary educational system, there is conducted a complete collegiate course in science, literature, philosophy, and Christian theology. In 1834 he was compelled, by severe illness, to quit the scene of his labours, and returned to Britain, where his efforts to diffuse a missionary spirit throughout the churches were unremitting. Shortly after his return he was created D.D. by the University of Aberdeen. In 1839 he again proceeded to India, and continued to labour incessantly for ten years, when, at the special invitation of the Free Church of Scotland, which he had joined in 1843, he once more returned to his native country. It was on this occasion that Dr. Duff organized a new system for the permanent support of the mission, which has been productive of the greatest good. In 1851 he was unanimously chosen Moderator of the General Assembly of the Free Church of Scotland, the highest honour the Church had it in her power to bestow. In compliance with the solicitation of the Protestant churches of America, Dr. Duff visited the United States and Canada in

1854. In 1855 he returned to Calcutta, *viâ* Bombay and Central India. For several years he was the sole editor of the "Calcutta Review;" and, on his return to India, after his last visit to Europe, he was at once nominated by Lord Canning a member of the committee appointed to prepare the scheme of the Calcutta University. Since that period, as Member of the Senate and Syndicate, and President of the Faculty of Arts, he has been unceasing in his exertions to promote its welfare. Dr. Duff has written largely on the subjects associated with his sphere of labour. His principal works are "India and Indian Missions," "Missions the Chief End of the Christian Church," "Lectures on the Church of Scotland," "Missionary Addresses," and "Letters on the Indian Rebellion." He has also been an extensive contributor to periodical literature.

DUFFERIN AND CLANDEBOYE, FREDERICK TEMPLE BLACKWOOD, BARON, was born at Florence in 1826. He studied with distinction at Oxford, and in 1849 was one of the Lords in Waiting to the Queen, but resigned in 1852 when the Conservatives came into power, resuming office in 1854. He sits as an hereditary peer by the title of Lord Clandeboye. There are few more accomplished noblemen than Lord Dufferin. He is an excellent scholar, a graceful lecturer, and a very lively and agreeable writer. He has taken as yet only a small part in public affairs; but there will be always interest attached to him as the inheritor of much of the genius of his great-grandfather, the celebrated Richard Brinsley Sheridan, his mother being a sister of the Duchess of Somerset and the Hon. Mrs. Norton. His claim to distinction as an author rests on his "Letters from High Latitudes, being some Account of a Yacht Voyage to Iceland, San Mayen, and Spitzbergen, in 1856," one of the liveliest, most readable, and pleasant books of the day.

Lord Dufferin has just been sent as British Commissioner to Syria.

DUFFY, CHARLES GAVAN, some years an Irish journalist of the anti-English school, at present a member of the Colonial Legislature of Australia, was born in the county of Monaghan in 1816. He was educated at Belfast, and went to Dublin about 1834, where he obtained employment on the Press. His first decided start in journalism was an appointment as editor of the "Vindicator," a newspaper established in Belfast to inculcate the principles of the party who clamoured for repeal of the Union and the dominancy of the Roman Catholic religion. He conducted that paper energetically, but in 1841 he left Belfast for Dublin, where he originated the "Nation," a journal once well known for its ultramontane and republican views. War to the knife was the doctrine of Mr. Duffy, whilst that of his leader, Mr. O'Connell, was moral force to accomplish a political change. Their parties separated, but not until Mr. Duffy had been imprisoned for sedition, in company with the most violent agitators of the day. Mr. Duffy's advanced opinions led him to assist in founding what was termed the "Young Ireland" party, which was only scattered by the arrest and transportation of Mr. Smith O'Brien. Mr. Duffy was tried for high treason, but the jury disagreeing, there was no verdict. In 1852 he was returned to Parliament for the borough of New Ross, and kept that seat until 1855, when he emigrated to Australia, and became so actively engaged in the politics of the new country that he was elected a member of the Colonial Legislature, and subsequently held office in the Colonial Government, from which, however, he has been removed.

DUMAS, ALEXANDRE, a French novelist, was born at Villers Cotterets, on the 24th of July, 1803. Young Dumas received an education which was very limited, in his native town, from the Abbé Grégaine. At the age of fifteen, having no resources independent of his own labour, he went to Paris and obtained a situation; but aspiring to literary pursuits, he resolved to try his fortune as a dramatist. "Henri III. et sa Cour" was the result, and was fairly successful. In 1820 Adolphe de Leuven, a young gentleman from Paris, who had begun to write for the theatre, proposed to him that they should unite their efforts. To write for the theatre, said Leuven, was a trade like any other, and only required practice. Thus commenced that career of romance and play-writing which has given Dumas so great a notoriety. He broke through the conventional laws of dramatic composition, and produced startling incidents, rapid changes, intricate plots, and villanous and virtuous characters in contrast. The fashion was new, and took with the giddy and volatile. His novels, first struck out in *feuilletons*, were perused and talked of, and what seemed a miraculous facility of composition induced people to wonder, and all the more to read. His famous lawsuit with the directors of the "Presse" and the "Constitutionnel," brought to light the fact that he was bound to furnish these journals annually with a larger number of volumes than the swiftest penman could copy, and that he had been assisted by a large staff of *collaborateurs*. The works of Dumas which have met with the greatest success are "Les Trois Mousquetaires," which at first appeared in the "Siècle" newspaper, in which it was continued under the title of "Vingt Ans Après," and "Le Vicomte de Bragélone;" "Le Comte de Monte Christo," which appeared in the "Constitutionnel;" and "La Reine Margot," published in the "Presse." These three works have done more to popularize the name of the author than any of his other productions. He has recently published a "Life of Garibaldi," which is a strange compound of fact and fiction.

DUMAS, ALEXANDRE, the younger, was born at Paris in July, 1824. He is the son of Alexandre Dumas, the novelist, and was educated at the Institution Goubaux and the Collège Bourbon. Among authors and artists his talents were early recognised, and he was admired by the society into which he was thrown, when very young, for his gaiety and brilliancy. He has produced a number of novels and dramas. In the former class of works the "Trois Hommes Forts" occupies the first place in point of talent ; in the latter, "La Dame aux Camélias" (1852), and the "Demi Monde" (1855), take precedence. These comedies have been successful in the highest degree ; but great fault has been found with their immorality, being considered even more pernicious in tendency than the worst productions of the elder Dumas.

DUMAS, JEAN BAPTISTE, a French chemist, was born at Alais, in the department of Gard, 1800. In 1814 he commenced his medical studies at his native place, and afterwards followed them up at Geneva, where his devotion to science attracted the attention of the professors. Having formed an acquaintance with Dr. Prévost of Geneva, Dumas and Prévost performed many experiments together, and published numerous papers on physiological subjects, and more particularly on blood and generation. The fame of these papers procured him an appointment in Paris, as Teacher of Chemistry at the École Polytechnique, and Professor of Chemistry at the Athénée. He was returned to the National Legislative Assembly as representative for the departement du Nord, 1849, and supported the President. He was appointed Minister of Agriculture and Commerce, then member of the "Commission Consultative." Afterwards he entered the Senate as Vice-

President of the Council of Public Instruction, and became President of the Municipal Council of Paris. At the Great Exhibition held in London in 1851 Dumas occupied a prominent position as chairman of one of the juries. Dumas' researches upon ether, the laws of isomerism, the law of substitution, and the atomic weights of elementary substances, stand out among the investigations that make the nineteenth century remarkable in the annals of science. As a professor he was noted for his fluency, eloquence of style, and the great ability of his demonstrations. His principal works, and those of the pupils of his school, have for their object organic chemistry. He has published "A Treatise on Chemistry applied to the Arts," in eight volumes ; "A Course of Chemical Philosophy," in one volume ; and "A Discourse on the Chemical Statics of Organized Beings."

DUNCOMBE, THOMAS SLINGSBY, M.P., an English politician, was born in 1796. He was returned to Parliament for Hereford in 1826, and ranged himself with the extreme Liberal party, and zealously supported the Reform Bill. In 1832 he was defeated by Lords Mahon and Ingestre, but early in 1834 was returned for Finsbury. He opposed the Irish Coercion Bill, and in 1842 presented the National petition, signed by above three millions of the industrious classes in favour of universal suffrage, vote by ballot, and a shorter duration of Parliament. Among other matters, he was virtually the means of establishing Jewish emancipation, by successfully carrying, in 1858, his motion for placing Baron Rothschild on a committee which was to hold a conference with the House of Lords ; since which, the doors of the House of Commons, which had been so long closed against the Jews, have been thrown open for their admission.

DUNDAS, VICE-ADMIRAL THE HON. RICHARD SAUNDERS, was born at Melville Castle, in the county of Edinburgh, on the 11th of April, 1802. He is a son of Lord Melville, who for many years was First Lord of the Admiralty; and entered the Navy in 1817. He served under different commanders as a midshipman, until June 1821, when he was appointed Lieutenant, and shortly after Commander, commissioned to the Sparrowhawk. Ordered from Halifax to the Mediterranean Station, he cruised until 1824, when he was promoted to the rank of Post Captain, subsequently taking command of the Volage and the Warspite, the latter a seventy-six gun-ship, and the first man-of-war that circumnavigated the globe. On his return to England in 1828 he was again appointed to the Mediterranean Station, where he remained some years, and in 1837 he was placed in charge of the Melville, seventy-two guns, and took a very distinguished part in the war with China. In 1845 Captain Dundas became private secretary to the Earl of Haddington, then First Lord of the Admiralty, but that post was relinquished in the following year on the resignation of Ministers. Meantime (1841) he had conferred on him the Military Companionship of the Bath. In 1851 he was appointed Superintendent of Deptford Dockyard, and in 1853 promoted to the rank of Rear-Admiral. In February, 1855, he was called on to command the British Fleet in the Baltic, superseding Sir Charles Napier. Some time after taking the chief command he bombarded Sweaborg, reducing the place to ashes, after a severe cannonade on the 9th of August. The war ended, Admiral Dundas was created a K. C. B., and received the honorary degree of D. C. L. from the University of Oxford, together with the French order of Grand Officer of the Legion of Honour. In 1858 he was advanced to the rank of Vice-Admiral of the Blue.

DUNDONALD, THOMAS COCHRANE,

EARL OF, was born on the 14th December, 1775. At an early age he joined the navy, but in consequence of the objections of his father he did not enter regularly into the service until 1793, when he joined the Hind corvette, of twenty-eight guns, under the command of his uncle, Sir Alexander Cochrane. He was not long in giving proofs of his daring character, distinguishing himself in May, 1795, as acting Lieutenant of the Thetis. After serving, in obedience to orders, from vessel to vessel, he joined Lord Keith's flag-ship, the Barfleur, in the Mediterranean. When, after cruising for some time in pursuit of the French fleet, Lord Keith shifted his flag to the Queen Charlotte, Lord Cochrane accompanied him. On the 21st of September, 1799, he executed a task which displayed at once his resolution and his judgment. The Lady Nelson cutter was hemmed in off Cabritta Point, Gibraltar Bay, by the French and Spanish vessels. He took with him the Queen Charlotte's boats, attacked the opposing force, and ultimately boarding some, rescued the beleaguered vessel. In March, 1800, in command of the war-sloop Speedy, he captured no fewer than 50 vessels, with 122 guns and 534 prisoners, his own ship mounting only 14 guns and carrying 54 men. He encountered the Gamo, 32 guns, 319 men, off Barcelona, on May 6th, 1801, and after a desperate struggle made her a prize. This action gained him his rank as Captain. But there is no sunshine without shadow. The Speedy was obliged, after a thirteen months' cruise, to surrender to a French squadron consisting of three ships of the line. Lord Cochrane became a prisoner of war, but was soon after exchanged. From that time, although very badly used by the Admiralty, he was scarcely ever out of service or out of danger, cruising in the Pallas and the Impérieuse, taking the enemy's ships here, and blowing up batteries there; when, in 1809, he was ordered, as the most intrepid commander at the time within reach, to destroy by means of fire-ships the French fleet, then in the Basque Roads. He undertook this mission of victory or death, went on board one of the ships, which contained a large quantity of gunpowder, and was successful. After being knighted, he became member for Honiton and then for Westminster. Lord Cochrane, while in Parliament, exposed the shortcomings and venality of the Admiralty, and was an inveterate opponent of ministers; the result of which was, that when, in the early part of 1814, a report was spread that Napoleon had fallen, and Lord Cochrane and his friends had taken advantage of this for their own interests, the ministry considering this a good opportunity to stifle his opposition, accused him of stock jobbing and fraud. He was found guilty of spreading a report that damaged thousands for his own gain, was fined, and deprived of all his rewards and decorations. In addition, he was to be imprisoned for a year. But before the term was concluded, his Westminster constituents considering that he was the victim of party feeling, re-elected him to the House of Commons, and escaping from jail, to the astonishment of the members made his bow to the Speaker. From a prison to foreign service was no unpleasant change. Lord Cochrane went to South America, and fought heroically for the independence of the Spanish colonies. He next gave the weight of his character and genius to Greece, after being a short time employed by the Brazilian government, and eventually, forty-four years after the war, was restored to his rank in the navy of Great Britain. He became Earl of Dundonald in 1831, Vice-Admiral of the Blue in 1841, and mounted once more the order of the Bath in 1847. In 1851 he was Vice-Admiral of the White, and in 1852 Rear-Admiral of the United Kingdom. It is much to be regretted that the Earl of Dundonald has not met with that cordial response throughout his life which his talents, energies, and patriotism have deserved. In former days he has had to contend with the jealousies of his inferiors in ability, although by the accidents of life they may have been his superiors in station. His various inventions, offered to different governments, prove him to be a man of genius; and although some of the improvements he has suggested in the mode of carrying on war may have appeared at first sight somewhat too highly coloured in their promised results, still the motives which induced him to present them to the judgment of the naval and ordnance boards, should at least have secured for them a careful examination. But he has outlived his enemies, and can now well afford to forget past circumstances. Calumnies have been disproved; the evil spirit that had haunted him is banished; and the maligned Lord Cochrane is more honoured than ever. Since his retirement from active service, he has turned his attention to the science of naval warfare, and has invented new projectiles and new methods of blowing up ships; but his plans have been always rejected by the powers that be. In his eighty-sixth year Lord Dundonald's activity is still on the ascendant, and he is occupied on the "Story of his Life," a memoir which will, in all time to come, stimulate the pluck and energy of English seamen.

DUNGLISON, ROBLEY, M.D., LL.D., a medical writer, was born at Keswick, in 1798. He commenced the practice of medicine in 1819 in London, but in 1824 went to America, having been chosen Professor of Medicine in the newly-established University of Virginia. In 1833, he was appointed Professor of Materia Medica in the University of Maryland; and, since 1836, of the Institutes of Medicine and Medical Jurisprudence in the Jefferson Medical

College of Philadelphia. Dr. Dunglinson's works are so many text-books, on which students and practitioners may place implicit reliance. He is one of the most popular medical authors of the day. So great has been the demand for his works, that of the "Medical Lexicon," "General Therapeutics and Materia Medica," "Human Physiology," "Human Health," "New Remedies," and the "Practice of Medicine," reprints of 100,000 volumes had been sold up to 1858.

DU PETIT THOUARS, ABEL AUBERT, a French navigator, was born in 1793. He entered the French Marine Service in 1804. He was promoted in 1819 to the rank of lieutenant; and in 1824 to that of captain of a frigate. In 1841, he was rear-admiral, when he proposed to Louis-Philippe to occupy the Society Islands. His proceedings there are well known; when he returned from the Pacific to France, they were disavowed. Under the Republic he sat in the National Assembly for the department of Marne-et-Loire, always voting with the majority. Latterly there has been nothing heard of him.

DUPIN, ANDRÉ-MARIE JEAN JACQUES, known as Dupin ainé, ex-President of the National Assembly, was born at Varzy, on the 1st February, 1783. He was called to the bar in February 1800; and in 1802, when the schools were re-opened, he was the first to pass as Doctor before the new faculty. He endeavoured to obtain a vacant professorship in the School of Law in Paris, but being refused, he commenced practice at the bar, where the piquant originality of his speech, the brilliancy of his wit, and the extent and accuracy of his knowledge, gained for him a great reputation. In 1811 he was recommended for the place of Advocate-General to the Court of Cassation, which he did not obtain, but he was almost immediately appointed to the Commission for Classi-

fying the Laws of the Empire, which immense undertaking was afterwards entrusted to his sole charge. His political life began in 1815, when he was returned to the Chamber of Representatives, and took part with the liberal opposition. He was, with M. Berryer, the defender of Marshal Ney, in 1815; he also defended the Englishmen, Wilson, Hutchinson, and Bruce, who had been so instrumental in the memorable escape of Lavalette; and as the steadfast enemy of the Jesuits, enjoyed an extended popularity under the Restoration. Dupin has directed great attention to the productive powers of France, and has written two works upon that subject. From 1815 to 1830 he was a member of the Representative Chamber. In 1830 he was a zealous supporter of Louis-Philippe, and in 1831 was named Procureur-Général. Towards the end of 1832 he became President and Speaker of the new parliament. His political career for a number of years presents few striking features. In 1842 he was named reporter of the project of law in favour of the Duke de Nemours being regent; and in 1848, he introduced the Count of Paris to the Chamber, recommending the members to recognise him as king and the Duchess of Orleans as regent. He made a show of moral opposition to the *coup d'état* when the Assembly was dispersed, but he has since seen it his interest to reconcile himself to the rule of Napoleon. In point of fact, Dupin is the solitary example of the seduction of any eminent statesman of the old *régime*, by the Emperor.

DUPIN, BARON FRANÇOIS PIERRE CHARLES, a French statistician and senator, brother of the preceding, was born at Varzy, in Nivernais, on 6th October, 1784. He studied in the Polytechnic School, and in 1808 was named engineer to the Marine Service, when he was employed in the preparation of the channel fleet and in forming the arsenal of Antwerp. He was four years at Corfu, whither he went after the Ionian Islands had been ceded to France. On his return to Paris, in 1812, he devoted his attention to the study of the construction of ships; in 1813 he founded the Maritime Museum, which has served as a model for the naval museum of the Louvre. A favourite pupil of Monge, and a friend of the republican Carnot, he witnessed the fall of the empire without regret. He asked permission of Fouché to defend Carnot. Entrusted with the superintendence of the dockyard at Dunkirk, he visited in 1816 the maritime establishments of England. Four years afterwards he began the publication of his "Voyages dans la Grand Bretagne entre 1816 et 1821," in which he pointed out the advantages of constitutional government. In 1815 he was admitted to the Institute. In 1824 Louis XVIII. conferred on him the title of Baron; but he continued true to liberal principles, and being returned Deputy for Tarn he made numerous speeches on public instruction, the navy and its organization, &c. He opposed Polignac, and was elected for Paris, July 1820. He filled various offices up to 1837, when he was created a peer of France; and since then he has maintained his principles without sacrificing his independence. Among his works may be enumerated a work entitled "Geometry and Mechanics, in their Application to Industry and the Fine Arts" (Paris, 1825 and 1826); "The British System of Administration" (1823); "Lectures on Industry, Commerce, Navigation, and the Sciences applied to the Arts;" "Opening Addresses to the Conservatory;" "The Eloge of Gaspard Monge," read on the 2nd of September, 1849, in the name of ,the Academy of Sciences; "Discourse pronounced at the Distribution of Prizes to the French Exhibitors on the 25th of November, 1851;" a pamphlet on the "Comparative Industry of Paris and London" (1852); and various other reports and éloges.

DUPONT DE L'EURE, JACQUES CHARLES, President of the Provisional Government of France in 1848, was born at Neubourg, Eure, on the 27th of February, 1767. In 1789 he was admitted as an advocate before the parliament of Normandy, and embraced the principles of the Revolution with ardour. He led a very active public life, filling many offices, his political creed being, liberty of the people and the press, equal civil and political rights, and a representative system. Through all the changes of dynasty that have occurred during his long life, M. Dupont De L'Eure has sustained the reputation of being a pure-minded citizen and an honest man.

DUPONT, PIERRE, a French poet and song writer, was born at Lyons in 1821. His parents were very poor, but, by one means and another, he received a fair education, and got to be employed in the office of a notary, and afterwards obtained a clerkship in a bank. In 1839 he went to Paris, and in time attracted notice. He published a volume of poetry, entitled "The Two Angels," in 1844; and its success, though moderate at first, evoked the spirit of poetry. He awoke one morning and found he had risen to fame by his song of "Les Bœufs." Thenceforward he devoted himself to the composition of songs, to most of which he composed music, without knowing anything of the science. After 1848 he was carried away by the Socialist notions of the day, and wrote a few songs which compromised him with the government. In December, 1851, he remained under concealment for six months; at the end of which he was discovered, and condemned to six months' banishment to Landessa, in Algeria. He, however, obtained a pardon, and since then he has not interfered in politics. The best known of his songs are, "Les Bœufs," "Le Braconnier," "Le Louis d'Or," "Le Chant des Nations," "Le Chant des Soldats," "Le Dahlia Bleu," "La Vigne," "La Chanson du Blé," "La Vache Blanche," "La Fin de la Pologne," &c. Various editions of his songs have been published, both with and without music. M. Dupont may be looked upon as the Burns of France.

DYCE, THE REV. ALEXANDER, an English author and critic, was born in Edinburgh, in June, 1798, and received his education at the High School of that city, and Exeter College, Oxford. Having completed his curriculum, he received episcopal ordination, and officiated for several years as a curate in Cornwall and Suffolk. On going to London he entered there upon a literary career, in which his general learning and critical sagacity have gained him merited distinction. After publishing "Select Translations from Quintus Smyrnæus," an edition of the poet Collins, and "Specimens of British Poetesses," he edited the works of Shakspeare, Beaumont and Fletcher, Peele, Greene, Webster, Shirley, Middleton, Marlowe, Bentley, and Skelton. Amongst his other publications are, "Specimens of British Sonnets;" "Remarks on Collier's and Knight's Editions of Shakspeare;" "A Few Notes on Shakspeare;" and "Strictures on Collier's new Edition of Shakspeare." The lives of Shakspeare, Pope, Akenside and Beattie, in the "Aldine Poets," were written by him; and he has edited various volumes for the Camden and Percy Societies. His "Recollections of the Table Talk of Samuel Rogers," has been several times reprinted. As a Shakspearian critic Mr. Dyce is perhaps most favourably known, and his text of the great dramatist has been pronounced by the "Quarterly," to be by far the best yet given to the world.

DYCE, WILLIAM, R.A., a painter of history, and writer on subjects connected chiefly with the Fine Arts and ecclesiastical antiquities, was born at Aberdeen, in 1806. He was educated at the University of Aberdeen, and took the degree of M.A. at the age of sixteen. He was intended for one of the learned professions, but subsequently devoted himself to art, and went to London in 1825 to be entered as a pupil of the Royal Academy. He was admitted; but his father having been advised to send him to study in Italy, Mr. Dyce set out for Rome in the same year. On his return, he produced a picture on a classical subject, which was exhibited at the Royal Academy in 1827. After a second visit to Italy, he finally returned to this country, and spent some years partly in London and partly in Aberdeen and Edinburgh. A pamphlet, which he wrote in 1836, "On the Application of Design to Manufactures," having been brought under the notice of the Board of Trade, he was summoned to London, and sent by the President—then Mr. Poulett Thomson—on a mission to the Continent, to report on the organization of Foreign Schools of Design, with a view to the formation of an establishment of that kind in London, which was then in contemplation. The report made by him was printed by the House of Commons, and he was appointed Director of the new establishment, with Mr. Herbert, R.A., as Head Master. He held this office for five years; and on his resignation in 1843, was appointed Inspector of the Provincial Schools, which had been established under his management, and a member of the Council. His occupations at the School of Design having become less engrossing, he again applied himself to art, and in 1844 exhibited his picture of "King Joash shooting the Arrow of Deliverance," the merits of which were so fully recognised that he was electe d

Associate of the Royal Academy. The same year he exhibited a specimen of fresco painting at the Westminster Hall Exhibition. He soon afterwards received a commission for a fresco for Buckingham Palace, and subsequently for Osborne. He was the first of the artists employed on the New Houses of Parliament, and so highly was his "Baptism of Ethelbert"—his grand fresco in the House of Lords—appreciated, that he has been for years engaged in adorning the New Palace. He was elected an Academician in 1848; but of late years, in consequence of his other commissions, he has exhibited few oil pictures. He published in 1843-44, in 2 vols. 4to, an edition of the Book of Common Prayer, with the ancient musical notation; accompanied by a Dissertation on Gregorian Music, and its adaptation to English words. He is also the author of a reply to a pamphlet of Mr. Ruskin on a theological subject; of a work on "The Management of the National Gallery;" and of numerous articles in periodicals to which his name is not attached. He is Professor of the Theory of the Fine Arts, in King's College, London.

EADIE, JOHN, D.D., LL.D., an eminent biblical critic, was born about the year 1814, in Alva, a small town in the county of Stirling. At a very early period Dr. Eadie began to manifest superior powers, and made rapid progress in all those branches of a liberal education, forming a necessary preparation for the ministry. Having completed his preparatory studies, Mr. Eadie entered the University of Glasgow; thence he passed with honour to the divinity hall of the United Presbyterian Church, then under the superintendence of Drs. Dick and Mitchell. Having completed his theological curriculum, Mr. Eadie became a preacher of the Gospel. His superior powers were soon appreciated, and at the early age of twenty-one he was, in 1835, ordained minister of the congregation of which he is still the pastor. On the death of the late accomplished Dr. Mitchell, Professor of Biblical Literature to the United Presbyterian Synod, such was the estimation of Dr. Eadie's scholarship and capacity, that he was unanimously appointed in 1843, by the Synod, to fill the chair of his quondam teacher. Dr. Eadie was in 1846-47 twice called to a pastoral charge in Edinburgh, but refused to go. While discharging with high acceptability the duties of this professorship, and continuing to minister to his large congregation, every seat in his chapel being let, Dr. Eadie has also devoted himself to the production of not a few works of great usefulness and ability. "Cruden's Concordance," which has since passed through twenty editions, was the first work with which his name was associated, and was undertaken in conjunction with the Rev. Dr. King. The "Biblical Cyclopædia," "Lectures on the Bible to the Young," "Early Oriental History," "Divine Love," "A Complete Analytical Concordance," "Paul the Preacher," and a "Life of Dr. Kitto," are all peculiarly popular and able works; while his Commentaries on Ephesians, Colossians, and Philippians are highly valuable contributions to the science of biblical interpretation. The second edition of the first of these is now in the press. Some of the most erudite and graceful papers in "The Journal of Sacred Literature," and also in "Kitto's Cyclopædia of Biblical Literature," were contributed by Dr. Eadie. The pages of the "North British Review" have likewise been enriched by his pen. His latest production is a touching and admirable estimate of that *facile princeps* of English Congregational theologians, the late Dr. Pye Smith. This essay has been appropriately prefixed to a new edition of the "Scripture Testimony to the Messiah," of that learned divine. Dr. Eadie is

L

now engaged in editing an Ecclesiastical Cyclopædia, as a companion to the "Biblical Cyclopædia." Dr. Eadie received the degree of LL.D. in 1844, from the University of Glasgow, and that of D.D. in 1850, from the University of St. Andrews.

EASTLAKE, SIR CHARLES LOCK, a painter, and President of the Royal Academy, was born at Plymouth, in 1793. Having passed through the usual course of education at the grammar schools of his native place, he adopted painting as a profession, and entered the Royal Academy, London, as a pupil of Fuseli, and afterwards visited Paris. He returned to England, and established himself as a portrait painter at Plymouth. When, after Waterloo, the ship of war which was to carry Napoleon to Saint Helena lay off Plymouth, Eastlake seized this opportunity for securing the last portrait of the ex-Emperor obtained in Europe. As the great man walked the deck of the "Bellerophon," the artist, while in a small boat, took sketches of him, and from them produced a full-length portrait, which gave quite a new idea of the personal appearance of Napoleon, the French portraits being in general highly idealized. After a tour to Italy, Sicily, and Greece, he, in 1823, forwarded to the Exhibition of the Royal Academy, views and sketches he had made. In 1828 he contributed his famous "Peasants on a Pilgrimage to Rome, first coming in sight of the Holy City." In 1830 Mr. Eastlake was elected R.A. His next great work, one of the most important of recent contributions to the English historical school of painting, was "Christ Weeping over Jerusalem." The deep sentiment of this great picture won its way to all hearts. It was followed by "Hagar and Ishmael." In 1841 Mr. Eastlake was appointed Secretary to the Royal Commission, formed for inquiring whether advantage might not be taken of the rebuilding of the Houses of Parliament, to promote the Fine Arts. In 1850 Mr. Eastlake was elected President of the Royal Academy, and in the same year he received the honour of knighthood. In 1855 he was appointed Director of the National Gallery, with a salary of £1,000 a year. Opinion is divided respecting the precise position of Sir Charles as an artist, although by many able judges he is esteemed not only the ablest, but also the most learned of English painters. He is the translator of "Goethe on Colours," "Notes to Kügler's Handbook of Painting," and "Contributions towards a History of Oil Painting."

EDWARDES, SIR HERBERT BENJAMIN, K.C.B., an Indian officer, was born at Frodesley, in Shropshire (where his father was rector), on 12th November, 1819. Educated at Richmond, Surrey, and at King's College, London, he received a cadetship in 1840. Having attracted notice by a series of letters on public affairs in the "Delhi Gazette," addressed by "Brahmince Bull to his cousin John Bull in England," he was appointed, in 1845, aide-de-camp on the staff of the Commander-in-Chief, Sir Hugh (now Lord) Gough. After taking part in the battles of Moodkee and Sobraon, and being wounded in the former engagement, he was entrusted, in 1846, with an important mission to the court of the king of Iummoo and Cashmere, in which he was completely successful. In the following year he was deputed by Sir Henry Lawrence to accompany, and control, a Sikh force, despatched to realize the arrears of tribute withheld from the Sikh government by the tribes of Burmoo, a hillbound country on the Afghan border of the Punjaub. The expedition was only partially successful; and, at Lieutenant Edwardes' advice, a second was despatched at the close of the year, permanently to reduce and occupy the valley. The complete success of the Lieutenant's plans is narrated in his "Year on the Punjaub Frontier in 1848-9." Scarcely had Burmoo been reduced than war broke out at Mooltan. Hearing of the murder of two English officers, Lieut. Edwardes, on his own authority, commenced military operations against Dewan Moolráj, the Sikh governor of that province; and his plans being approved of by Sir Frederick Currie (then officiating as President at Lahore during Sir Henry Lawrence's absence in England), he levied an irregular force from the border tribes, in aid of a force of Sikh Regulars, and obliged Moolráj to withdraw his army from the left bank of the Indus, and won a complete victory, taking eight guns from the enemy. This battle was fought on the 18th June, and is called "Kineyree," from the neighbouring ferry of the Chenab. The defeated rebels fled to Mooltan, were followed, and again defeated there, with Moolráj at their head, on July 1st, with a loss of two more guns. Moolráj then shut himself up in his fort, and was blockaded by the united forces of Lieut. Edwardes, General Cortlandt, and the Nawab of Bhawulpoor (commanded by another English subaltern, Lieut. Edward Lake, of the Bengal Engineers), till a regular British force under General Whish arrived to besiege the fortress. For these services Lieut. Edwardes was promoted to a Brevet-majority, was made an extra Companion of the Bath, and had a gold medal voted to him by the East India Company. During the operations he lost the use of his right hand by the accidental explosion of a pistol in his belt; in consideration of which the East India Company gave him a good service pension of £100 a year. On the assassination of the Commissioner of Peshâwur, in September 1853, he was selected to succeed him. His services in that post, though attracting less notice, are perhaps the most useful and solid which he has rendered; for

by a firm but kind administration, he gradually attached the frontier tribes, and induced government to retrace its former policy towards Afghanistan, and form a friendly alliance with Dost Mahommed, the Ameer of Cabul. The fruits of these labours were reaped in the memorable year 1857, when the native army of Bengal mutinied. Instead of fraternizing with the Sepoys, the tribes of the Peshâwur frontier sided with government, and furnished important levies for service in Hindostan, while Dost Mahommed maintained a friendly attitude throughout the war, instead of marching down to Peshâwur, and turning the scale against the English. In Indian politics Lieut.-Col. Edwardes is a decided advocate of an openly-avowed Christian policy, in opposition to the traditional policy of neutrality in religious matters, and advocates, in all government schools in India, the formation of a Bible class at which attendance may be voluntary. In 1850 he received the honorary degree of D.C.L. from Oxford, and on the 18th June, 1860, the honorary degree of LL.D. from Cambridge.

EGG, AUGUSTUS, a painter, was born in London, in 1816. Of his early life we have no record, but we find him exhibiting at the Academy in 1838, and elected an Associate in 1848. He is an admirable illustrator of Shakspeare and Le Sage, to some of whose lighter fancies he has given a charm beyond the reach of written description. Among his chief works are "Le Diable Boiteux," "The Victim," "Gil Blas exchanging Rings with Camilla," "Queen Elizabeth discovering that she is no longer Young," "Henrietta of England relieved by Cardinal De Retz," "Katharine and Petruchio," and "Buckingham rebuffed." A more important work is "Peter the Great seeing Catherine, his future Empress, for the first time;" a picture which, for conception and masterly handling, may stand comparison with any production of its class. It is excelled, however, by two other works of more recent date; one being "The Life and Death of Buckingham," exhibited in 1855, and the other a "trilogy" exhibited in 1858, which had no title, but was described in an extract from a Diary (termed by most of the papers a domestic tragedy). Mr. Egg was one of the artists selected to arrange the paintings at the Manchester Exhibition.

EGLINTON AND WINTON, ARCHIBALD WILLIAM MONTGOMERIE, fifteenth EARL OF, and K. T., late Lord Lieutenant of Ireland, was born at Palermo, in Sicily, in 1812. He succeeded to the peerage in 1819, and when he attained his majority took his seat in the House of Lords on the Conservative benches. Attached to field-sports, he encouraged racing and hunting; but though displaying what many were pleased to term eccentricities, he never neglected the culture of his intellect. At an early period in life, under the influence of ideas quite allowable in a young nobleman who represented the Sir Hugh Montgomery of Chevy Chace, he got up the famous tournament which was to evoke the spirit of the chivalrous age, and which indeed produced a lasting effect on the minds of many persons who witnessed it. The pageant was gorgeous. Lady Seymour, now Duchess of Somerset, was the Queen of Beauty, and the present Emperor of the French one of the spectators. In 1841 his lordship married the widow of the late Captain Cockerell, R.N., but who died in 1853, greatly regretted. Lord Eglinton took no very prominent part in political life; and when, in 1852, on Lord Derby's accession to power, he was appointed to the Lord Lieutenancy of Ireland, the Opposition sneered and the Ministerialists doubted; but both were discovered to have made a great mistake, when in the course of a few months he attained to a popularity never accorded to any of his predecessors. He displayed ability for which he had never got credit; he was accessible and genial; above all, for the first time in Ireland during a hundred years, he exhibited the novel spectacle of a nobleman resolved to govern the country without reference to party; and thus was turned the first leaf in the history of Ireland's social advancement. On the overthrow of Lord Derby's administration, in 1853, he was necessarily recalled; but on the reinstatement of the Conservatives, in 1858, he returned to Ireland as Lord Lieutenant; of course retiring when Lord Derby resigned in 1859. As a landlord, Lord Eglinton takes great interest in agricultural improvements. He is fond of out-door games, and there are few better curlers or bowlers in Scotland. He preserves his attachment to field-sports, but at the same time no one more highly appreciates intellectual cultivation, and he has endeavoured to the utmost to promote the diffusion of education through every class of the community. The Scottish rights question was warmly espoused by Lord Eglinton, on grounds which have been much misrepresented by the press. He was elected Lord Rector of Glasgow University in 1853; and he is Lord Lieutenant of the county of Ayr. He married, in November 1859, Lady Adela Capel, daughter of the Earl of Essex.

EHRENBERG, CHRISTIAN GOTTFREID, a German naturalist and microscopist, was born on the 19th of April, 1795, at Delitzch, in Prussian Saxony. He received his early education at Schulpforta, and there commenced the study of theology, which he afterwards abandoned for that of medicine, at Leipsic, in 1815. In 1817 the law of military service called him to Berlin, where he took the degree of Doctor of Medicine in 1818; and published in the

"Academia Leopoldina," his observations upon the germination of seeds. At this time he became acquainted with the celebrated Hemprich, with whom he was sent on a scientific expedition into Egypt. The two travellers visited the coasts of Lydia, Middle Egypt, Nubia, Dongola, and Syria, exploring the ruins of Baalbec and Mount Lebanon. After returning again to Cairo, they proceeded to Mount Sinai, the height of which was ascertained by Ehrenberg, and thence to the Red Sea, Arabia, and Abyssinia. On his return from his eastern journey, Ehrenberg was appointed one of the professors of the Faculty of Medicine, at Berlin. In 1829 he accompanied Humboldt to the Ural Mountains, directing his attention especially to microscopic investigations. Cuvier in the French Academy, and Humboldt in "Cosmos," have pointed out the immense scientific value of these inquiries. Ehrenberg's great work on "Infusoria," forming one part of his investigations, was published in 1838, and drew upon him the attention of scientific men all over Europe. In 1842 he was elected Perpetual Secretary of the Royal Academy of Berlin, having been a Fellow from the year 1827, and having contributed many memoirs to the Transactions, during the whole of the intervening period, among which may be enumerated one on "The Cynocephalus;" a second on "The Soil of the Desert;" a third on "The Corals of the Red Sea;" a fourth on "The Luminosity of the Sea." Since the publication of his "Infusoria," he has pursued his investigations of the fossil forms of microscopic organisms, the result of his inquiries being embodied in a work entitled "Micro-geologie," published in 1854. This work illustrates the microscopic life of the whole globe; more especially in its connexion with and influence upon rocks, the soil, the bed of the sea, and the atmosphere in which floats microscopic dust. From objects examined, and drawings made, during his travels in Africa, Syria, and Arabia, a great number of plates have been prepared and published at intervals, since 1828, the work not having yet been finished. Ehrenberg is a member of most of the learned societies of Europe, and enjoys a higher reputation with scientific men than with the general public, in consequence of the character of his researches, which have opened up new fields of scientific observation, in the cultivation of which he has throughout his whole career held the highest rank.

EICHWALD, EDWARD, a naturalist, was born in July, 1795, at Mittau, in Lithuania. He studied medicine, and the natural sciences, at Berlin. After travelling over a great part of Europe, he returned to Russia in 1821, where he delivered some popular lectures, and was appointed Professor of Zoology and Midwifery, at Casan. From 1825 to 1827 he explored the Caspian Sea, and the country of the Caucasus; and on reaching Europe once again, was appointed Assistant Professor in the University of Wilna. That institution having been suppressed, he was appointed, in 1838, Perpetual Secretary and Professor of Zoology and Mineralogy to the Medical and Surgical Academy of that place. Called then to St. Petersburg, he filled several scientific situations, and roamed through various countries, adding to his own knowledge, and the power of conveying it to others. In 1851 the learned Professor retired from the really active pursuits of his profession, and received the title of Councillor of State. He is a member of all the Academies of Russia, as well as of many foreign societies. Belonging to a German province of Russia, Eichwald has written his works in Latin, French, Russian, and German, but chiefly in German. Among the most important of his works, are his "Journey to the Caspian Sea and the Caucasus;" "The Ancient Geography of the Caspian, the Caucasus, and Southern Russia;" "A Treatise on the Silurian Deposit of Esthonia;" "Sketches, by a Naturalist, of Lithuania, Volhynia, and Podolia;" "Plantarum Novarum quas in itinere Caspio, Caucasico, observavit Fasciculi;" "Fauna Caspico-Caucasica;" "Researches on Russian Infusoria;" "The Palæontology of Russia," &c. &c.

ELGIN AND KINCARDINE, THE EARL OF, K.T., late Governor-General of Canada, and now British Ambassador Extraordinary to China, was born in 1811. Lord Elgin, the representative in the male line of the great Scottish house of Bruce, is the son of the distinguished nobleman who enriched the art treasures of this kingdom by his collection of sculpture, generally known as the "Elgin marbles." The present Lord Elgin was educated at his father's seat in Fifeshire, and afterwards at Oxford. He was returned to Parliament as member for Southampton, in 1841; and in 1842, on the death of his father, was called to the House of Peers. In the same year he was appointed Governor of Jamaica, where he continued to administer the affairs of the island with equal ability and success until 1846, when he was sent to Canada as Governor-General. His administration of the Canadian government was beyond all precedent successful. Recognising no party, he sought to develop the industrial and commercial resources of the colony, a difficult undertaking with a country which had long been distracted by intestine feuds. He encouraged agriculture and trade by every means at his command, and admitted no distinction between the citizens of the Upper and Lower Provinces. By his patience, forbearance, and a desire to accommodate himself to the habits of those with whom he had to deal, he conciliated all parties; and since that time, Canada has been one of the most, if not the most, prosperous of all the British colonies. In 1857, the serious disputes between the European and native population in China, which had broken into an open rupture, induced the British Government to look out for some able and resolute diplomatist to settle matters in that remote quarter of the world. His antecedents at once pointed out Lord Elgin as the fittest man to act in an intricate case with vigour and discretion. He accordingly proceeded to the East, arranged the difficulties, and procured a treaty which gave Britain freer access to China than she ever enjoyed before. His task was not only delicate, but dangerous; but he fulfilled it, so far as it lay in his power, with consummate address and skill. He regretted not having had the opportunity of overawing the Chinese Government in their capital before returning to Europe, which he seems to have considered absolutely necessary to bring them to a true sense of their position with regard to the European powers. After the return of the Earl of Elgin to England, and on the formation of the present ministry, he was appointed Postmaster-General. Owing to a breach of the Chinese treaty, he has again left this country for the East, where there can be little doubt that decisive measures will now be taken to curb the insolence of the "Celestials," and to protect both the European merchants and the native producers from the rapacity and stupidity of the ruling power.

ELLENBOROUGH, THE RIGHT HON. EDWARD LAW, EARL OF, was born on 8th of September, 1790. He is the son of the celebrated Chief Justice of the King's Bench, and was educated at Eton and Cambridge. He succeeded to his father's title and estates in 1818. In the Wellington ministry he held the office of Privy Seal, and in Sir

Robert Peel's government (1835) was President of the Board of Control. That administration existing but a few months, Lord Ellenborough had no post until 1841, when Sir Robert Peel placed him in his old situation. Lord Auckland having been recalled from the government of India, Lord Ellenborough succeeded him; arriving at Calcutta in 1842. He conquered Scinde, and reduced Gwalior ; but his opponents accused him of so many eccentricities, that the now defunct East India Company recalled him, though contrary to the wish of the ministry. In 1846 he was First Lord of the Admiralty, but went out with Sir Robert Peel. In 1858 he once again took charge, under Lord Derby, of Indian affairs, but an untoward despatch to Lord Canning, the Governor-General, having become public property, such a storm was raised as compelled him to resign office. Lord Ellenborough is an accomplished orator, though somewhat dogmatic in the expression of his opinions.

ELLIOTSON, JOHN, M.D. Cantab., F.R.S., was born in London about the close of last century. He studied in the Universities of Edinburgh and Cambridge, his earlier education having been received from private tutors. He attended the medical practice of St. Thomas's and Guy's Hospitals for about three years, and was elected one of the physicians to the former institution. In 1831 he was appointed Professor of the Practice of Medicine in the London University, where he became one of its most popular and effective of instructors. In 1834 he succeeded in establishing an hospital in University College, and then resigned his appointment at St. Thomas's. His lectures, published in the " Lancet " and " Medical Gazette," were universally attractive ; as was his translation of Blumenbach's " Physiology," with notes more voluminous than the text, a work which reached to five editions. He was the founder and President of the Phrenological Society ; President of the Royal Medical and Chirurgical Society of London, and is a Fellow of the Royal College of Physicians. In 1837 Dr. Elliotson became a convert to Mesmerism, as a curative and an anæsthetic agent. The council of University College not concurring with, but strongly opposing his views, he resigned his situation in 1838. He continued to follow his favourite pursuit, at great expense to himself, and established the "Zoist," a journal devoted to mesmerism and phrenology, and extending to fifty-two numbers. He is the author of many medical, mesmeric, and metaphysical writings ; the first chiefly published in the Transactions of the Royal Medical and Chirurgical Society, the two last in the "Zoist."

ELLIS, MRS. SARAH, formerly Miss Stickney, a writer on female education, was born about the beginning of the present century, and received her earlier schooling in a "friend's" seminary. Her first literary effort was a series of domestic stories, called "Pictures of Private Life." About the time of her marriage with the Rev. Wm. Ellis (1837), her mind was strongly directed to the position of women in modern society, and towards the best means for their moral and intellectual improvement. To aid in developing her ideas she wrote and published "The Women of England," which was followed by "The Daughters," "Wives," and "Mothers of England." The same tendency towards treating her favourite subject— the elevation of the female character— runs through all her works ; the "Sons of the Soil," "Family Secrets," "Prevention better than Cure," "The Education of Character," and "Social Distinction," being perhaps the happiest of her voluminous productions.

ELLIS, REV. WILLIAM, an English missionary. In 1814 Mr. Ellis became connected with the London Missionary Society. In November 1815 he married Miss Moor, a young lady devoted to missionary work, and in the following month embarked with his newly-married wife at Portsmouth for the scene of their future labours. From the period they landed in the South Seas, until 1824, Mr. and Mrs. Ellis were incessantly engaged in missionary work; and in his "Polynesian Researches" he has embodied the results of his acquaintance with the condition of the islands, and the character of the population. Having returned to England, Mr. Ellis acted as one of the secretaries of the London Missionary Society; and from information received from the missionaries, together with official documents, he prepared a "History of Madagascar." More recently he has published "Three Visits to Madagascar," a work which is highly esteemed, and very popular. He has also written a "History of the London Missionary Society," a "Vindication of the South Sea Missions," and "Village Lectures on Popery." Mrs. Ellis died in January, 1835, and in 1837 Mr. Ellis married Miss Sarah Stickney, a lady well known by her works on female education.

ELLIS, Sir HENRY, K.H., a writer, and principal librarian of the British Museum from 1827 to 1856, was born in 1777. Amongst his most valuable publications is "Original Letters illustrative of English History, from Autographs in the British Museum, the State Paper Office, and one or two other sources, with Notes and Illustrations." This work has brought to light new and important facts; and is a most interesting collection. Sir Henry Ellis has also been responsible editor of an enlarged edition of Dugdale's "Monasticon Anglicanum," a work of great research, and has edited, revised, and added to numerous publications on British antiquities, and history. The "General Introduction to Domesday Book" was also one of his successful labours.

EMERSON, RALPH WALDO, a distinguished American writer and speculatist, was born at Boston about the beginning of the present century. He belongs to the transcendental school of philosophers. Having graduated at the early age of eighteen, at Harvard University, Mr. Emerson accepted an invitation to become the pastor of a Unitarian church, in his native city, and during the next seven or eight years continued to discharge the duties of that office. Being afterwards severed from his church, he delivered lectures at Boston, devoted himself to study, and eventually published a work called "Nature," wherein he expressed some peculiar sentiments. "Man Thinking" was the next embodiment of his special opinions. Called in 1838 to deliver an address to the senior class in Divinity College, Cambridge, the "idealistic pantheism" of his philosophy was still more fully developed: subsequently he addressed the same views to literary societies of Dartmouth College, and produced a great effect by his orations. Mr. Emerson published the "Dial;" and in 1846 a volume of poems. In 1849 Emerson visited England, receiving a cordial reception from the literary society of London. His impressions of things as they are in England, the result of that visit, has since been published in a small volume, entitled "English Traits," not indeed wanting in mannerism, but singularly fair, and justly appreciative. A collected edition of Emerson's works has been published in England, but his influence upon the British mind has been comparatively limited. This circumstance is perhaps accounted for by the fact that he is more an interpreter of Coleridge and Carlyle, than an original thinker.

ENCKE, JOHANN F., an eminent

German astronomer, was born 23rd September, 1791, at Hamburg. In early life he was connected with military matters in the Prussian service, but having a taste for astronomy, he eventually devoted himself to the study of that sublime science. He is most known in connexion with his researches respecting the comet of Pons, now called after him, whose period of revolution he has fixed at 1,200 days; and also by his calculations of the distance of the earth from the sun. He also speculated on the existence of an ether as the cause of comets not re-appearing at their calculated time. These labours have secured for Mr. Encke a great reputation among German astronomers. He was appointed joint-director of the Observatory at Gotha, whence he was called to Berlin as Secretary of the Academy of Sciences and Director of the Observatory. He was also entrusted with the publication of the astronomical almanacs. He publishes regularly an account of the astronomical observations made at Berlin.

ENFANTIN, BARTHÉLÉMY PROSPER, a French politician and social reformer, was born at Paris, on the 8th February, 1796. He was admitted to the Polytechnic School in 1813, and was one of the pupils who, in March 1814, offered such a determined resistance, at the Barrière du Trône, to the allied armies. The school having been broken up he lost all chance of promotion in the army, and in 1821 entered a banking establishment. In 1825 he adopted the principles of the St. Simonians, and soon afterwards endeavoured to disseminate his opinions on social questions in the columns of the "Producteur," a journal which he and some of his friends set on foot. He and his fellow-labourers toiled zealously to place the doctrines of social reform, and the "religion of thought," on a firm basis. The conversion of the ladies was one of his especial objects. Neither he nor his friends desired any

profit from these exertions. Enfantin, indeed, lost his whole patrimony, and was ultimately prosecuted as an enemy to public morals, and condemned, in 1832, to a year's imprisonment. This sentence had the effect of dispersing the St. Simonians. After a confinement of a few months Enfantin was liberated, and proceeded with some of his followers to Egypt. There they remained for three years, studying carefully the Suez canal projects, and the embankments of the Nile. From 1839 to 1842 Enfantin was a Member of the Scientific Commission of Algeria. After his return to France, in 1845, abandoning his earlier social projects, he was appointed to carry through the amalgamation of the Paris and Lyons, Lyons and Avignon, and the Nord and Strasburg Railways. He is now acting manager of the Paris, Lyons and Mediterranean Railway, and Manager of the General Water Company at Paris.

EOTVOS, JOSEF, was born at Ofen, on the 3rd September, 1813. After enjoying the instructions of a private tutor, Eotvos was sent to a public school, and devoted himself to the study of his native language, of which he is the first living writer. Eotvos commenced his literary career by a translation of Goethe's "Goetz von Berlichingen," followed, in 1833, by two original comedies, and a tragedy, which were highly successful. After travelling in 1836 in Germany, Switzerland, France, and England, he returned to Hungary, and edited a work, the proceeds of which were given to the relief of the sufferers from an inundation at Pesth. "The Carthusian," a novel, was contributed to by him. Entering the Hungarian diet, the novelist soon distinguished himself in the arena of politics. In 1841, owing to family losses, Eotvos, from occupying one of the first positions in Hungarian society, was suddenly plunged into poverty. Eotvos, despite of temptation, remained faithful to the national cause, and rather than sacrifice his principles, preferred to seek a subsistence in the labours of his pen. In pursuance of this resolution, the "Village Notary" was produced. This work was followed by a romance entitled "Hungary in 1514." In 1848 Eotvos accepted the post of Minister of Public Instruction in the Batthyani administration, but the stormy course of events that shortly followed was ill suited to his feelings and character, and he retired to Bavaria, devoting himself to the preparation of a work on the "Influence of the Leading Ideas of the Nineteenth Century on the State."

ESPARTERO, DON BALDOMERO, DUKE OF VITTORIA, was born February 27, 1792, at Granatula, in the old province of La Mancha. Having received a good education, in 1806 he was sent to the University of Almagro, and entered the army as a volunteer to oppose the French invaders of Spain, in 1808. In a little more than a year from the time he had adopted the profession of arms, he entered a military school at Cadiz, acquiring a complete acquaintance with military science and tactics, and from 1811 to 1814 he continually advanced his position in the army. In the following year he proceeded to South America under General Morillo, to defend the Spanish provinces against General Bolivar and his companions in rebellion. After an adventurous ten years passed in South America, Espartero returned to Spain in November, 1825, enriched, and married the daughter of a wealthy Spanish proprietor. On the outbreak of the civil war, when the death of Ferdinand VII. left the Salic law to be a bone of contention (1833), Espartero quickly rose to the chief command of the Queen's troops. For his services against Don Carlos, he was created a Grandee of the First Class, with the title of Duke of Vittoria. On the usurpation of the regency by the Queen-mother, Espartero was appointed Regent of Spain. For two years after this appointment he continued to perform the duties of that office, and governed the country well and wisely; but the Queen-mother, incessantly engaged in attempts to grasp at power which she could only use for evil, had made a party which sought to restore her influence. Overthrown by this conspiracy against his authority, Espartero retired to London. He, the only true patriot Spain has had for a century, was decreed a traitor, and deprived of his dignities. For about six years he lived a quiet and retired life, but parties grew too numerous in Spain for the safety of the throne, and in the perplexity of the time the Queen and the Constitutionalists could fix upon but one man capable of extricating the nation from its troubles, and the Duke of Vittoria was the man. Having returned to Spain, Espartero was again placed at the head of the government in 1854, and continued to occupy that position for two years, when, through intrigues, his resignation was necessitated. The constitutional minister gave place to despotism and O'Donnell, one of those men whom the wicked fear, and the good dare not trust. From an humble position Espartero raised O'Donnell to a high position, made him a bosom friend and took him into his confidence. On the first opportunity O'Donnell intrigued to overthrow his patron. In most respects Espartero stands out as a noble exception to those who have lately been the advisers of the Spanish crown.

ESPINASSE, ESPRIT CHARLES MARIE, a French general, was born on the 2nd of April, 1815, at Saissac, in the department of the Aude. He entered the Military School of St. Cyr in 1833, and gained his first promotions in Algeria. As Chief of Battalion in 1845, he commanded the Zouaves; in July, 1851, was a Colonel; in 1852 General of

Brigade, and Aide-de-Camp to the Emperor. When war was declared against Russia, he commanded a brigade of the first division of the army of the East. He distinguished himself at the Tchernaya, and at the assault on the Malakoff, and in 1855 was advanced to the rank of General of Division. In 1858 he was called to be Minister of the Interior, a position which, however, he did not long retain.

EUGÉNIE, EMPRESS OF THE FRENCH, born at Granada, May 5, 1826, is the second daughter of the Count of Montijos, her mother being of Scottish descent. Having been educated partly in France and England, she visited Paris in 1851, and by her grace and beauty attracted great attention. Amongst her admirers was the Emperor, to whom she was eventually married on the 30th January, 1853, the ceremony being performed amidst the splendour which the rank of all parties demanded. Her Majesty has become the mother of a son, on whom the hopes of the imperial family are centred. She has accompanied the Emperor in most of his journeys, and with him visited Queen Victoria at London in 1855. She is highly esteemed for her kind and amiable disposition by all classes in France.

EVANS, LIEUTENANT-GENERAL SIR DE LACY, G.C.B., M.P., a native of Ireland, was born in 1787. In 1807 he became ensign in the 22nd Regiment of Foot, with which he served three years in India. In 1812 he joined the 3rd Light Dragoons, serving with them during the campaign of the Peninsula, and taking part in the chief actions of the war. In 1814 he served in the 5th West India Regiment as brevet lieutenant-colonel, and was present at the capture of Washington, the attack on Baltimore, and the operations before New Orleans. Returning to England early in 1815, he took part in the battles of Quatre Bras and Waterloo. In 1835 he became commander of the Spanish Legion, and again distinguished himself by his genius and bravery on the soil of the Peninsula. In 1831 General Evans was elected a member of the House of Commons. Having lost his seat for Rye, in 1833 he was chosen for Westminster. It was while in Parliament for this borough, that he was offered the command of the Spanish Legion already alluded to, which he accepted, with the sanction of his constituents. In this position his difficulties can scarcely be over-estimated; he and his legion were of great service to the Queen's cause, and, as usual in Spanish matters, were treated with ingratitude. He was promoted to the rank of Major-General in 1846. In 1854 he was appointed to the command of the second division of the army in the East, with the rank of Lieutenant-General. At Alma and Inkermann he behaved with great gallantry. On his return to England he received the thanks of the House of Commons, and was honoured with the Grand Cross of the Bath. Sir De Lacy Evans' military career has been as varied as it is extensive. India, the Peninsula, America, Waterloo, and the Crimea, are the witnesses of his genius and his valour. As a politician he has been a consistent Liberal.

EVERETT, EDWARD, D.C.L., was born in April, 1794, at Dorchester, near Boston, United States, and in 1811 graduated at Harvard University. After having studied law for some time, he abandoned it for theology. Succeeding the Rev. J. S. Buckminster, he fully sustained his already high reputation. His health failing, in 1815 he exchanged his pastoral office for that of Professor of Greek in Harvard University. Having received permission to visit Europe, Mr. Everett came to England, where he continued for a short time, when he proceeded to Göttingen, in order to study the German language and literature, and methods of instruction. Having visited

Paris, Rome, Greece, and Turkey, after an absence of five years he returned to America, and in 1820 became the editor of "The North American Review," which, by his exertions, obtained a high position in literature. The prominent part which Mr. Everett had taken in political affairs in the United States induced General Harrison, when he became President of the United States, to nominate him minister to the English Court, a post which he held for five years with the highest honour to himself and government. It was during this official residence in England, that Oxford bestowed upon him the degree of D.C.L. On returning home, Mr. Everett was elected President of Harvard University. Having resigned this office in 1849, from ill health, he remained without any specific appointment until 1853, when he was elected a member of the Senate of Massachusetts. Mr. Everett holds the highest position as a scholar and an orator. He has retired into private life, owing to the delicate state of his health.

EXETER, HENRY PHILLPOTTS, BISHOP OF, leader of the High Church party in the Church of England, was born in 1777. He studied at Oxford; was M.A. in 1798, and D.D. in 1821. He was first rector of Stanhope, and then chaplain to the Bishop of Durham. It was well understood, at the time, that he was appointed to the See of Exeter (1830), as a reward for the vigorous support he gave the Duke of Wellington's government on the question of Roman Catholic Emancipation, the year before. He was, at one time, a keen controversialist, and an indefatigable pamphleteer; whilst in the House of Lords he appeared in the light of an ecclesiastical Lord Brougham, for energy, fire, and independence. It may be remarked as a singular circumstance, that he was born in the same house as was Whitefield, the eminent dissenting minister.

FAED, THOMAS, a painter, was born, in 1826, at Burley Mill, near Gatehouse of Fleet, Kirkcudbrightshire. Shortly before his father's death, in 1843, he commenced his studies as an artist, under the careful eye of his eldest brother, then a miniature painter in Edinburgh, and now one of the leading artists in Scotland. He was for some time one of Sir William Allan's pupils, labouring with unremitting zeal, and gaining prizes at every competition in the School of Design. After being chosen an Associate of the Royal Scottish Academy (1849), and painting the often engraved and well-known picture, "Sir Walter Scott and his friends, at Abbotsford," Mr. Faed settled in London, in 1852, and rose rapidly in public estimation. In 1855 he painted the "Mitherless Bairn," which elicited the admiration of critics and connoisseurs. "Home and the Homeless," "Conquered but not Subdued," "First Break in the Family," "List'ners Hear nae Gude o' Themsels," and "Sunday in the Backwoods," are noble pictures, overflowing with genius, as well in composition as in treatment.

FAIRBAIRN, WILLIAM, a civil engineer and machinist, was born at Kelso, in 1789, and brought up as a mechanic in the vicinity of Newcastle-upon-Tyne. In 1817 he commenced business in Manchester in partnership with Mr. Lillie, and the firm soon rose into the very foremost position in the trade of that city; and when this partnership was dissolved, Mr. Fairbairn continued the business. About the year 1830 or 1831, he made various trials as to the shape of vessels, and employed a small iron vessel for that purpose. The success of the experiments emboldened the experimenter, and by 1836 he ventured on the construction of iron vessels of considerable tonnage. He was one of the earliest members of the British Association for the Advancement of

MICHAEL FARADAY  D C L  F R S

Science, to which he has contributed some valuable papers on engineering subjects. His practical knowledge has been employed in assisting some of the largest constructions, one of these being the bridge over the Menai Straits for the Chester and Holyhead Railway, and his experiments on the strength of iron are highly valued. Mr. Fairbairn has occasionally made his appearance in the lecture-room, discoursing upon engineering and other matters in a lucid manner. He is a Fellow of the Royal Society, and a corresponding member of the National Institute of France.

FARADAY, MICHAEL, an eminent chemist and electrician, was born in London in 1791, and from a comparatively obscure origin, has by his own unaided genius obtained a position as one of the most noted philosophers of Europe. Whilst working at a bookbinder's he was by accident introduced to a gentleman, who, perceiving his abilities, enabled him to attend some of Sir Humphrey Davy's lectures at the Royal Institution. To these young Faraday paid the deepest attention ; and by forwarding Sir Humphrey the notes he had taken, he thus became acquainted with that well-known chemist. This circumstance laid the foundation of his future fame. Young Faraday, disgusted with trade, which he considered as "vicious and selfish," already aspired to devote himself to science. Having communicated his longings to the great chemist, through his good offices he obtained, in March 1813, the post of assistant in the laboratory of the Royal Institution. Sir Humphrey, however, advised him not to give up the prospects he had before him, as "Science was a harsh mistress, and in a pecuniary point of view, but poorly rewarding those who devoted themselves to her service." In the autumn of the same year he went abroad with Sir Humphrey Davy ; and return-

ing in the spring of 1815, resumed his labours at the Institution, where he has ever since remained. Dr. Faraday's discoveries have raised him to a foremost place among that crowd of illustrious investigators of physical science that adorn our age. His distinguished merits have been long since acknowledged by nearly every learned body in Europe. In 1832 the University of Oxford named him D. C. L. His best known works are — (1) "Chemical Manipulation," the third edition of which was published in 1842 ; (2) "Experimental Researches in Electricity ;" (3) "Six Lectures on the Non-Metallic Elements," edited by Dr. Scoffern, 1853 ; and (4) "Six Lectures on the Various Forces of Matter," edited by William Crookes, F. C. S.

FAZY, JEAN JAMES, born at Geneva, in May 1796, is descended from a French Protestant family, exiled after the revocation of the Edict of Nantes. He studied in Paris, and early became a writer on political economy. His works, up to 1840, indicated that he preferred the material interests of society to speculative or theoretical politics. In July, 1830, he was appointed principal editor of "La Revolution ;" when he signed the protest of the journalists against the ordonnances of Charles X. He opposed, subsequently, the candidature of Louis-Philippe, and after that King's accession M. Fazy embraced the side of the Radical opposition. His views were of a character so violent that he was eventually obliged to relinquish the management of the "Revolution ;" and he then established the "Revue Républicaine." But the many miscarriages of the democratic party, the difficulties of the position he had taken, the discouragement of Lafitte and La Fayette, together with other causes, decided him to leave France, and change the field of his activity and his ambition. As a Genevan he was noted for his patriotism.

In 1833 he was marked as the head of the philosophical radicals, having long before rendered himself conspicuous. He then founded the "Revue de Genève," and in 1841, organizing a Radical committee, he initiated a revolutionary agitation. His labours were incessant; and he took part in almost all the political movements of the time. In the discussions of 1846, on the subject of the Jesuits, between the Protestant and the Roman Catholic Cantons, the State Council observed a neutrality that strengthened the hands of the Sonderbund—a policy which deeply irritated M. Fazy and the Radicals, and which led to such a demonstration of the popular will as constrained the Council to lay down its power. On the following day—October 9th—a Provisional Government was formed, M. Fazy being its chief. He exercised very considerable influence; and the Canton of Geneva was among those which, in 1848, adopted the new Federal Constitution. M. Fazy continued to maintain his republican opinions, advocating them through his journal, proclaiming his sympathy with all nations which then demanded liberty and independance. The reaction of 1849 modified his language, however, if not his ideas. He remained a member of the State Council of Geneva, and was elected its President, being at the same time a member of the Federal Assembly. He took an important part relative to the affairs of Neufchatel, zealously supporting Swiss nationality.

FERDINAND IV. (Salvator Marie Joseph Jean Baptiste Louis Gonzaga Raphael Renia Janvia), ex-Grand Duke of Tuscany, Imperial Prince and Archduke of Austria, and Prince of Hungary and Bohemia, was born on the 10th of June, 1835, and succeeded to a nominal throne, on the abdication of his father, on the 21st July, 1859, consequent upon the French invasion of Lombardy, and the war waged by the Emperor Napoleon III. for the "idea" of the enfranchisement of Italy. It is understood that the Grand Duke, whose subjects sternly refuse to recognise him, has taken refuge in the armies of his relative, friend, and patron, the Emperor of Austria.

FERGUSSON, James, an architect and archæologist, was born at Ayr, in the year 1808, and received his education at the High School of Edinburgh. From school he went into the counting-house, and thence to be partner in a large mercantile establishment, where prices current more engaged his attention than the Arts. After having devoted himself, during four years, to commercial pursuits in Holland and London, Mr. Fergusson proceeded to India in 1829, first as an indigo planter, and subsequently as partner of a firm in Calcutta. He afterwards returned to England, having realized a fortune, and has published the first volume of an "Historical Inquiry into the True Principles of Beauty in Art, more especially with reference to Architecture," and subsequently the "Illustrated Handbook of Architecture." Mr. Fergusson has since produced a work on Fortification, in which he recommends the employment of earthworks instead of masonry, and a larger development of artillery-fire for defence than had previously been thought of, and illustrated his proposals at the Exhibition of 1851 by a model. His theory, as a matter of course, was ridiculed by military martinets; but the prolonged defence of Sebastopol by earthworks has taught greater respect for his opinions. He is erudite, reflective, and suggestive, and all his works indicate minute and judicious research.

FIELDS, James T., an American poet, born at Portsmouth, New Hampshire, in 1820, is chiefly known in Europe from his being a partner in the celebrated publishing and bookselling house of Ticknor and Fields, Boston. Mr.

Fields is, however, regarded in his own country as an excellent critic, and he has edited numerous poetical works, besides writing poems himself, which are characterised by natural sentiment and refined expression. A volume of his poems was published at Boston, in 1849. He also printed, in 1858, a volume entitled "A Few Verses for a Few Friends." A collected edition of his compositions has been published.

FILLMORE, MILLARD, ex-President of the United States, was born on the 7th January, 1800, at Summer Hill, New York. His father was a small farmer, and the son's education was therefore limited. He was sent, at the age of fourteen, to Livingston County, to learn the trade of a tailor, and was then apprenticed to a wool-carder and cloth-dresser. His heart was fixed on supplying his educational defects, and with this view he for some time kept a school. Rising gradually, but slowly, he studied law, got into practice, in 1829 was elected member of the State Assembly, and in 1832 sent to Congress. He resumed his profession in 1835; but was again returned to Congress in 1837, where he continued till 1843. He soon took a distinguished position at the bar; in 1847 was elected Comptroller of the State of New York, and in 1848 Vice-President of the United States by the Whigs, General Taylor being President. The death of the General put Mr. Fillmore in possession of the presidental chair, July 9th, 1850. His constitutional term of office expired on the 3rd of March, 1853; and though he had many ardent friends, he took no steps towards a re-election. In 1854 he made the tour of the United States; and in 1855 and 1856 travelled through the continent of Europe, and while at Rome was nominated by the American party for the Presidency, but was not elected. He has now withdrawn from politics.

FOLEY, JOHN HENRY, R.A., a sculptor, was born in Dublin, in 1818. At an early age he studied modelling in the schools of the Royal Dublin Society of Art; went to London in 1834, and became a student of the Royal Academy, where he was distinguished for his talent and industry. The model of "Innocence," and the "Death of Abel," exhibited in 1839, were his first works of mark. His "Ino and Bacchus," a work of great beauty, brought his name prominently before the public in 1840. His next works of note were the "Houseless Wanderer," and "A Youth at a Stream." The latter, in conjunction with the group of "Ino and Bacchus," exhibited in competition at Westminster Hall, in 1844, obtained for him an appointment to execute works for the New Houses of Parliament; the results of this commission being the well-known statues of Hampden and Selden, erected in St. Stephen's Hall. In 1851 his group of "The Mother" was produced; and since that time, the statues of "Egeria" and "Caractacus," for the Egyptian Hall in the Mansion House. These works have helped to extend Mr. Foley's reputation in an eminent degree; but his greatest production is an equestrian statue of the late Viscount Hardinge, erected at Calcutta. This statue has been considered, by the most eminent artists of the day, to be "one of the finest works of sculpture of modern times," and they have united in signing and presenting to Mr. Foley a testimonial to that effect, at the same time recommending a duplicate of the work to be secured for erection on some public site in London.

FONBLANQUE, ALBANY, formerly editor of the "London Examiner," was born in 1797. This eminent journalist has of late years been withdrawn from the newspaper world, by his appointment as Statistical Secretary to the Board of Trade.

Mr. Fonblanque was originally intended for the bar; but directing his attention to the political questions of the day, he sent some articles to the "Examiner," which were so well received that he gave up law and took to the press. His style was brilliant, polished, and yet caustic—a mingling of Addison and Sheridan with Swift and Cobbett. Ultimately he became the editor of that journal, and his services to the liberal cause were such, that he was appointed to his present office at the Board of Trade. The only book that bears his name is "England under Seven Administrations," which is simply a reprint of leading articles published from time to time in the "Examiner."

FORBES, SIR JOHN, M.D., an English physician, was born in 1787, at Cuttlebrae, Banffshire. He studied, in the first instance, at the Marischal College, Aberdeen, and graduated at Edinburgh, as M.D., in the year 1817. He practised for some time in Penzance, Cornwall, then at Chichester, from which he removed to London. He was the first amongst English medical practitioners to recognise the importance and value of physical diagnosis as a means of detecting diseases of the heart and lungs. Dr. Forbes has drawn attention to the value of auscultation, and was one of the founders of the British Medical Association. As editor of the "British and Foreign Medico-Chirurgical Review," Sir John did much to elevate the tone of the literature of the profession; unfortunately, however, it was not successful in a pecuniary sense, although it greatly enhanced his reputation. He was appointed Physician in Ordinary to Her Majesty's household, and Physician Extraordinary to His Royal Highness Prince Albert, with the honour of knighthood, in 1853, and was elected a Fellow of the Royal Society, and created a D.C.L. by the University of Oxford. Sir John has taken a deep interest in the diffusion of knowledge, and in the improvement of education.

FORREST, EDWIN, a tragedian, was born in Philadelphia, on the 9th March, 1806. He was early trained to the stage; at twelve years of age he played one or two minor parts in his native city, and at thirteen appeared there as "Young Norval," two years afterwards entering upon his first regular engagement with Jones and Collins, managers of the Western Circuit. After several years of professional vicissitudes, he returned from the Backwoods to the Atlantic States, and in 1826, at Albany, he played second to Kean. In 1827 he first appeared in New York, in the character of "Othello," and was hailed as a powerful and true interpreter of Shakspeare. After performing several years in the principal cities of the United States, gaining new laurels everywhere, he visited Europe, in 1834. Preceded by a high reputation, he received offers to play in London, which he declined; his visit being one of study and observation. In 1836 he returned to his native country, and resumed his profession. The same year he received new proposals from London, which he accepted, and in November appeared at Drury Lane, as "Spartacus," and next as "Othello." His gigantic frame, deep sonorous voice, and a truly original conception of the Shakspearian parts he embodied, made him the lion of the season. Revisiting England in 1845, the applause which greeted his first appearance was revoked in some quarters, more from jealous feeling, it is said, than from any other cause. In 1837 he married, in London, a daughter of Mr. John Sinclair, the vocalist, from whom he separated in 1849. He has for some time, from ill health, been unable to resume his professional avocations.

FORSTER, JOHN, an English journalist and essay writer, was born at

Newcastle, in 1812. Having received an excellent preliminary education, Mr. Forster completed his studies at London University. He and his fellow-students commenced a work called the "London University Magazine." In 1834 Mr. Forster wrote for the "Examiner," of which he afterwards became the sole editor. As a journalist, Mr. Forster has long worked in a wide field of usefulness, and has never failed to exhibit a generous appreciation of merit. His "Lives of the Statesmen of the English Commonwealth" has been highly praised. Peculiarly exact in matters of fact, teeming with the best information respecting the men and the times of which it treats, remarkable for energy and grace of style, this work is at once one of the most useful and attractive memorials of that memorable epoch, when "the crown of England hung on a bush, and Cromwell sat on an ungarnished throne." Since this original publication Mr. Forster has given the literary world the most delightful and the most erudite "Life of Oliver Goldsmith" that has yet appeared. The publication of this work involved Mr. Forster in a controversy with another of Goldsmith's biographers, Mr. Prior, who sought to show that Forster had purloined his facts. In this controversy Prior forgot the old adage, "the tools are for those who can use them." The biographic genius of Forster had given a life and beauty to the sterile collection of dry-as-dust detail which Prior had brought together. It was impossible, after what had been done with respect to Goldsmith's memoirs, that different biographers should not traverse much ground in common. But though that was inevitable, Mr. Forster succeeded in showing that he needed not, in his intellectual opulence, to plunder the scanty treasury of Prior. The elaborate and valuable illustrative notes, with which the Life of Goldsmith abounds,

render the work at once most delightful and instructive. In addition to these independent contributions to literature and history, Mr. Forster has written some able articles in the Edinburgh and Quarterly Reviews. These articles have recently been collected and republished, with a new and elaborate paper on the Grand Remonstrance of 1641, in two volumes of Historical and Biographical Essays. Mr. Forster has also very recently published a volume upon the "Arrest of the Five Members by Charles the First." In 1856 he was appointed Secretary to the Lunacy Commission—an office for which he possesses every mental fitness and legal qualification. Few men enjoy in so large a degree the esteem and confidence of those who know them best, as does the author of the "Statesmen of the English Commonwealth." That chivalrous honour which he has so well described as animating the stern Republican of the seventeenth century, is his own guiding star; its brightest influence is shed over his character, and on every occasion where the weight of his name has been evoked, it has been to achieve some noble or beneficent purpose.

FORTUNE, ROBERT, a botanist and author, was born in the county of Berwick, in 1813. Being the son of a border farmer, his early education was confined to what he could glean in a parish school. His taste for horticulture was strongly manifested when he was a mere youth; and eventually he was engaged as an assistant in the Botanical Gardens at Edinburgh. He devoted his leisure to the study of Botany, attending the classes of the professor of that branch of science. His progress in his profession was rapid; and soon attracting notice, his services were sought for Chiswick Gardens. There he increased his knowledge of botany and his already extensive acquaintance with the species of plants. In 1842 the Botanical

M

Society of London appointed him collector of plants in North China, then for the first time opened to European explorations. Mr. Fortune fulfilled his mission with sagacity and zeal, wandering through many districts of the empire hitherto unknown to Europeans, and making himself well acquainted with Chinese life, without in any instance neglecting the main purpose of his travels and researches. After a three years' sojourn in the "flowery land," during which he collected and sent home a magnificent collection of botanical specimens, he returned to England, and in 1847 published a very interesting and valuable account of his travels, under the title of "Three Years' Wanderings in China." He was then appointed Curator of the Physic Garden at Chelsea, an office in which he gave the greatest satisfaction, and remained in the situation until the East India Company requested him to proceed once more to the East, to pursue investigations regarding the tea plant. He left England in 1848, and only returned in 1851, when he arranged the results of his observations, publishing in 1852 his "Two Visits to the Tea Countries of China." Soon after the issue of this work he left England for China for the third time, and he has since laid before the world the fruit of his investigations in a work entitled "A Residence among the Chinese: Inland, on the Coast, and at Sea."

FOULD, ACHILLE, a French statesman, was born at Paris, in October 1800. He is the son of a wealthy Jewish banker, who died in 1855. After leaving the Lycée Charlemagne, where he was educated, he travelled in Italy and the East. In 1842 he entered on political life, when he entered the Chamber as deputy for Turbes. Having early turned his attention to the study of economical questions, his opinions on taxation, finances, and general as well as special imposts, were always received with respect, frequently as authoritative, by the Chamber. He took an active part in the discussions of all questions relating to social and political economy, and to the improvement of the agriculture and commerce of the country. In 1844 he was nominated Reporter for the Commission appointed to inquire into the operation of the Stamp Duty on Newspapers; and in general he supported the foreign policy of M. Guizot. On the occurrence of the Revolution of 1848 M. Fould accepted the change as an accomplished fact, and his counsel and advice were placed at the service of the Provisional Government. At the elections of July he was returned to the Constituent Assembly, as representative for the Seine; and about that period he published two brochures on the assignats, expressing the danger likely to be incurred by adopting the monetary propositions of the parties then in power. His remarks in the Assembly on numerous points connected with the finances, gained him not only the esteem but the confidence of a large majority of that body; and he was, as a matter of necessity, nominated on the various commissions planned by government to regulate the internal affairs of the country. Under the presidency of Louis Napoleon he laboured to obtain and confirm the confidence of capitalists, and proposed several measures calculated to effect that end, subsequently preparing a considerable number of projects of law chiefly tending to modify the pressure of existing imposts. Finally, he projected the Bank of Algiers, and promoted the laws on civil pensions, the establishment of the penitentiary colony at Cayenne, and some important reforms in the commercial code, though he still adhered to the system of protective import duties. Though there occasionally arose differences between M. Fould and the President, these were not of such a character as to prevent him, in December 1851, from acting as Minister of Finance, but he resigned in January, 1852. On the 25th of the latter month he was created Senator, and shortly afterwards was recalled to power as a Minister of State. In this capacity he advanced various measures of importance, and was constituted a Commander of the Legion of Honour in December. He was one of the Directors of the Paris Exhibition in 1855, and from 1853 to 1857 much of his time, attention, and judgment were taken up with the completion of the new Louvre. M. Fould is warmly attached to the Fine Arts.

FOX, W. J., a politician and M.P. for Oldham, was born near Wrentham, in Suffolk, in 1786. Although of obscure origin, his talents procured him a good education at the College belonging to the Independents at Homerton, but he subsequently embraced Unitarian opinions, and officiated as pastor of the Unitarian Chapel, Finsbury. He became one of the most powerful platform advocates for the repeal of the Corn-laws. Guizot, in his Life of Peel, has honoured some of his speeches delivered during that struggle with selection as the most finished examples of oratory which the great conflict produced. In 1847 Mr. Fox was elected M.P. for Oldham. At the general election of 1852 he lost his seat, but in a few months afterwards was reinstated. He is understood to have been a contributor to the Westminster and Prospective Reviews, and to be now one of the contributors to the "Weekly Dispatch" London newspaper. Mr. Fox is the author of "Lectures to the Working Classes," and a philosophical dissertation on Religious Ideas.

FRANCIS JOSEPH I., EMPEROR OF AUSTRIA, KING OF BOHEMIA, HUNGARY, VENETIA, DALMATIA, CROATIA, ESCLAVONIA, GALLICIA, &c., eldest son of the Archduke Francis Charles Joseph, born August 18th, 1830, ascended the throne December 2nd, 1848, on the abdication— consequent upon the revolution of that year—of his uncle Ferdinand I., and the renunciation on the part of his father of all right to the crown. The difficulties of the Austrian empire were great, but the new monarch was too young to have added to them by any unpopular acts, and his accession was hailed as the salvation of the country. He promised his people a free constitution, equality of citizenship, and a representative constitution; but his ability to carry his words into effect was tested by unprecedented difficulty and danger, and found insufficient. Surrounded by evil counsellors, he was induced to dissolve the representative assembly, and to withdraw the charter from Hungary. The Hungarians, under the leadership of Kossuth, revolted, and after a noble struggle all but succeeded in acquiring their independence and their liberty; but with the aid of Russia he was enabled to crush them. The support of Russia was dearly bought—at the price of national humiliation. In 1851 the Emperor publicly declared himself an absolute monarch, after having re-conquered, by the vigorous and successful generalship of Radetzky, the revolted provinces of Lombardy and Venetia. The most pernicious act of his reign has been the Concordat with the Pope,—a humiliation even greater than his acceptance of Russian aid for the conquest of Hungary, and the evil effects of which have been visible alike in his foreign and in his domestic policy. In the conduct of the Italian war, forced upon Austria by the ambition of the King of Sardinia, and the still wider and more astutely schemed ambition of the Emperor of the French, the Emperor Francis Joseph has acted with more dignity than in other events of his reign; and though success did not attend his efforts to preserve Lombardy, or to repel the unjustifiable interference of a foreign power in a matter that in no wise concerned it, the governments of Europe, and such of the nations as look upon French military propagandism with alarm and distrust, have not been able to withhold their. sympathy from the Austrian Emperor in the arduous and yet unended struggle for the preservation of his hereditary dominions. His Imperial Majesty married, on the 24th of April, 1854, the Princess Elizabeth Amélie Eugénie of Bavaria, by whom he has two infant children,—the Archduchess Gisella Louisa Marie, born on the 12th of July, 1856; and the Archduke Rudolph, heir apparent to the throne, born on the 21st of August, 1858. In private life, the Emperor and his amiable Empress are models of the domestic virtues, and highly beloved and respected.

FRANCIS II., MARIE LÉOPOLD, KING OF NAPLES, OF THE TWO SICILIES, AND OF JERUSALEM, DUKE OF PARMA, PIACENZA, AND CASTRO, was born on the 16th of January, 1836, and succeeded his father, the late Ferdinand II. (the Bomba of an unhappy notoriety, and the most unpopular of European monarchs), on the 22nd of May, 1859. He was married on the 3rd of February, 1859, to the Princess Marie Sophie Amélie, daughter of Maximilian Joseph, Duke of Bavaria. His Majesty occupies a perilous throne, and is understood to have adopted in all essential points the retrograde and arbitrary policy of his unhappy father. He has already acquired among his people the too significant nickname of "Bombalino," or Little Bomba !

FRANCIS V., FERDINAND GEMINIEN, EX-DUKE OF MODENA, ARCHDUKE OF AUSTRIA, PRINCE OF BOHEMIA AND HUNGARY, DUKE OF REGGIO, MIRANDOLA, MASSA-CARRARA, AND GUASTALLA, was born on the 1st of June, 1819, and succeeded his father, Francis IV., on the 21st of January, 1846.

Like the Grand Duke of Tuscany, and every other Italian potentate connected by blood with the House of Hapsburg, and supported on his throne by Austrian bayonets, he was detested by his subjects ; and when the French marched into Italy, in 1859, the people rose in revolt and drove him from the throne, declaring their intention never again to submit to his rule, and voting the annexation of their state to the dominions of the Constitutional King of Sardinia. His Highness married, in 1842, the Duchess Adelgonde, daughter of Louis, ex-King of Bavaria, and sister of King Maximilian. The Duke and Duchess are both in exile.

FRANKLIN, LADY JANE, widow of the celebrated Arctic navigator, was born about the year 1802. She is the daughter of Mr. Griffin, of Bedfordplace, London, and became the wife of Sir John Franklin in 1826. When her husband was appointed Governor of Van Diemen's Land, in 1836, she accompanied him to that colony. On the 26th of May, 1845, the gallant and intrepid commander left England, on his third and, unhappily, his last expedition to the Northern Seas, in search of the impracticable North-west passage ; he, at the head of the expedition, hoisting his flag in the "Erebus," and Captain Francis Crosier, second in command, on board the "Terror." Two years passed without any intelligence being received of the progress of the expedition, and alarm began to be experienced throughout the country, regarding its probable fate. The anxiety grew into apprehension, and, for the first time, Lady Franklin came before the world prominently—offering, from her private means, rewards of two to three thousand pounds to those who should discover the missing ships, their officers, and their hands. Towards the same end Lady Franklin appealed to America : to her the cause was one of heart ;

to the world it was one of science; and the United States gave a noble response to her call, on both grounds. Government having sent out a searching expedition, in 1850, Lady Franklin gave additional assistance by fitting out the "Prince Albert," at an expense to herself of £2,500. This vessel returned, without bringing any tidings, in 1851. Six years had rolled away since Sir John Franklin had sailed for the North, and all hope was gone; but the great-hearted woman was resolved that though she could not save her husband, she would use every effort to ascertain his fate. Careless of personal sacrifices, she fitted out and dispatched the "Prince Albert," a second time; but with no more satisfactory result. Still Lady Franklin persevered. The lapse of time rendered the idea of Sir John Franklin surviving the rigour of the climate for so many years impossible. But this noble English lady left no stone unturned, corresponded with men of science in every quarter of the globe, incited the wavering, and strengthened the courage of the bold, rousing a genuine national spirit of sympathy with the living, and sorrow for the dead. Dr. Rae having found some relics of the lost expedition, she fitted out another, of which Captain M'Clintock was the commander. He sailed on his exploring enterprise with a full expectation of realizing one of two results: he would either discover the Franklin party or their remains, or recommend that all further Northern search should be abandoned. Captain M'Clintock's expedition was successful. He returned in his little vessel, the "Fox," bringing with him sad memorials of seamen who had not hesitated to endanger their lives for the glory of their country. But for Captain M'Clintock's search and its termination, we refer to his name in another place.

FRASER, ALEXANDER, a painter, was born in Scotland about 1796. He may be considered as one of the best delineators of the scenes and daily life of his native country. Amongst some of his best Scottish subjects are the "Laird's Dinner," the "Interior of a Highland Cottage," "Scene from the Prison of Edinburgh," &c. His "Robinson Crusoe," and the "Last Moments of Mary, Queen of Scotland," have gained him great praise, and are, perhaps, two of his best pictures. Nearly all of his productions are illustrative of homely and rural incidents, and he is extremely facile in executing them in a life-like manner.

FREDERICK VIII., CHARLES CHRISTIAN, KING OF DENMARK, was born 6th of October, 1808. He married, in 1828, the Princess Wilhelmina of Denmark, his cousin, which marriage was dissolved in 1837. He married a second time, in June 1841, the Princess Caroline, of Mecklenburg Strelitz, which marriage, proving as unhappy as the previous one, was dissolved in like manner, in 1846. The King, nothing daunted by these marital reverses, was married a third time in 1850, to Louisa Christine, Countess of Danner, a Lady of the Bedchamber to his previous Queen. This marriage, a private and morganatic one, and not giving the lady the rank of Queen, has rendered his Majesty exceedingly unpopular; and at one time in 1859, and again in 1860, threatened to lead to insurrection in the streets of the capital, and to the abdication of the King. His Majesty made a tour of the British isles soon after his accession to the throne, and inspected more particularly the great cotton and woollen manufactories in Lancashire and Yorkshire, as well as the Potteries and the mining districts.

FREDERICK WILLIAM IV., KING OF PRUSSIA, was born October 15th, 1795, and succeeded his father, Frederick William III., on the 7th of June, 1840. Having received his education under the most eminent professors in

Germany, he took part as a simple officer, in the campaigns of 1813 and 1814. For some years prior to the death of his father, the Crown Prince was looked upon as the hope of the absolutist party; but shortly before his accession to the throne, his feelings and principles are supposed to have undergone a change. It was seen with pleasure by the most enlightened men of Prussia that he inclined to the liberal side, and a policy was expected of him which would have the effect of bringing his administration into closer harmony with the national feeling, at least in so far as its foreign policy was concerned, which leaned too much to the side of Russia to please the patriotic and intensely German party; that desire to be German above all things, even more than it desired to be Prussian. When in the fulness of time he mounted the throne, these hopes seemed on the point of realization. He conceded several reforms which, though of a minor character, were hailed with delight as the precursors of a better system, and presented, in many respects, a marked and favourable contrast to his father, who had almost uniformly held and acted upon the doctrines of absolutism. The new reign was unmarked by any great event until the fatal year of 1848, when the revolutionary insanity of the period infected the people of Berlin, and led to collisions between the military and the citizens. The king took measures to calm the tempest of insurrection, placed himself at the head of the national party, and proposed to fuse all the German states into a great federal union, under a single monarch. His famous saying, "Prussia disappears and Germany is born," added fervour to the existing excitement throughout Germany. But the king's enthusiasm not only led him too far for the time, but very soon cooled. An unfortunate though accidental quarrel between the people of Berlin and the soldiers induced exasperation on both sides, and renewed bloodshed was the result. Prisoners were taken, but the king released them, following up his clemency by a general amnesty for political offences, and by forming a new administration from the ranks of men in the popular confidence. Restored tranquillity was the almost immediate consequence of his measures. Shortly afterwards, and still with German unity as his watchword, he undertook to protect Schleswig-Holstein in opposition to the claims of Denmark; but when the National Assembly at Frankfort passed over his pretensions, and elected the Archduke John Lieutenant-General of the German empire, Frederick William became convinced to all appearances that "German unity," such as is desired by the enthusiastic students of Germany, was a game too difficult for him to play; and that as a king he would better consult the interests of his kingdom, by giving more of his attention to Prussia, and less to Germany, than he had been in the habit of doing. At the same time, as if fearful of the fate of Louis XVI. and other weak though well-meaning monarchs, whose sad end is recorded in history, he thought it safer to act the part of a conservative than that of a revolutionary monarch, and entered upon a career of reaction, which exposed him to much ill-will, if not danger; but which never again eventuated in popular insurrection. At the outbreak of the Crimean war, it was confidently expected that the King of Prussia would have cast in his lot with Great Britain and France in support of the equilibrium of Europe, but with the vacillation which has marked every period of his career, his intentions were always in advance of his acts; and the reason for doing the right thing was balanced in his mind by some reason equally cogent for not doing it, or at all events for postponing it; and time wore on, and found him equally distrusted by Russia and by the powers opposed to her. In the year 1857 symptoms of mental aberration were observed by the physicians of his Majesty, and these symptoms continuing to grow stronger, it was at length deemed necessary to establish a regency; and on the 9th of October, 1858, the king's brother, Prince Frederick William Louis, the heir presumptive to the throne, was inducted into that office, and took the necessary oaths amid the general satisfaction of the people. The king was married on the 29th of November, 1823, to Elizabeth Louisa, daughter of the late Maximilian Joseph, King of Bavaria. There has been no issue by the marriage, so that after the actual regent, the heir presumptive to the throne of Prussia is the Prince Frederick William Nicholas Charles, married on the 25th of January, 1858, to the Princess Royal of England.

FREILIGRATH, FERDINAND, a German poet, was born June 17th, 1810, at Detmold, capital of the German principality of Lippe. Receiving his early education from his father, he was employed at a mercantile, and then in a banking establishment, and published some poems in 1838. Their success induced him to pursue literature as a profession. In 1841 Freiligrath married, and removed first to Darmstadt, and then to St. Goar on the Rhine, receiving a small pension from the Prussian government. This he afterwards gave up on his publishing some political poems which opposed the measures of the government. Owing to their great success, the author underwent a prosecution, and his work was suppressed. Compelled by the hostility of the government to expatriate himself, Freiligrath in 1844 passed from Belgium into Switzerland, and ultimately to that general rendezvous of the oppressed of Europe—London, where he became a banker's clerk.

He subsequently published translations into German of the poems of Victor Hugo, and of the more popular English poets, and in the spring of 1848 visited the United States, whence he soon returned to Germany. During the revolution he took an active part on the side of democracy, and composed a poem entitled "Die Todten an die Liebenden" ("The Dead to the Living"), for which he was prosecuted, but the jury would not convict him. The ill-will of his antagonists, however, finding fresh means to plague him, he, for a second time, emigrated in May 1851, since which time he has lived in London. His poetical works, originally published in 1838, have passed through eighteen editions, besides a large reprint of his complete works, issued at New York in 1858. The poetry is original in the highest sense, bearing almost no resemblance to the works of any former German poet. His translations from the English are numerous and excellent; the sense, spirit, and rhythm of the originals being most successfully rendered. He first introduced the songs of Robert Burns to the German public.

FREMONT, JOHN CHARLES, was born on the 21st of January, 1813, in Savannah. While he was but a boy, his father, who was of French extraction, died, leaving his mother in circumstances far from affluent, although she managed to give her son a good education. After studying in Charleston College he became a teacher of mathematics, and subsequently practised surveying. As second lieutenant in the corps of topographical engineers, he entered upon that series of explorations which opened to America the gates of her Pacific empire, and won for himself the title of "the Pathfinder of the Rocky Mountains," and his success at once made the name of Fremont famous. The report of the enterprise was published by the American government; the intrepid pathfinder was raised to the rank of brevet-captain, and the Victoria medal of the Royal Geographical Society of Great Britain was awarded to him. Captain Fremont now entered upon an exploring expedition, intended to give an uninterrupted view of the route from Missouri to the west coast of the American continent. This expedition was crowned with a success fully equal to his former enterprise. The task occupied many months, during which he completed a circuit of 12 degrees in diameter north and south, and 10 degrees east and west, having travelled some 3,500 miles. So soon as this second exploration was completed, Captain Fremont started on a third survey. The enterprise was one of peculiar difficulty, but at length every obstacle was surmounted, and he reached California, where he found the United States and Mexico were at war. Captain Fremont accordingly gave his country his energetic services. When these services were no longer needed, he became mixed up in a miserable quarrel between Stockton and Kearney, the military commanders, was tried by a court-martial, and deprived of his commission. Feeling keenly the injustice done him, he retired into private life. Having arranged to proceed to California, Fremont collected a strong party, and started in 1848 across the Rocky Mountains. So great were the difficulties of this last expedition, that even its stout-hearted commander began to quail. His mules were dead, his men began to droop: ten had perished amidst the deep snows of Sierra San Juan. Only after a series of unprecedented struggles, manifesting the most unconquerable energy and the sternest resolution, did the shattered remnant of his followers reach New Mexico; thence they proceeded to California. Fremont was afterwards sent as representative to Congress, and also received the Prussian gold medal as a reward for his eminent services to science. Mr. Fremont was a candidate for the presidency of the United States in opposition to Mr. Buchanan at the presidential election of 1857. His principal work is entitled "Colonel John Charles Fremont's Explorations" (1859), which contains an account of all his expeditions, with annotations and additions by several of the most eminent men of science. An account of his life and explorations by C. W. Upham (Boston, 1856), had a remarkable success, 50,000 copies having been sold as soon as it was issued.

FRERICHS, FREDERIC THEODORE, a German physician, was born at Aurich, in Hanover, on the 24th of March, 1819. He proceeded in due time to Göttingen, in order to study medicine, and the natural sciences. Being admitted a physician in the ordinary course, he successively visited Berlin, Prague, and Vienna, devoting his attention specially to the study of pathology and anatomy. He afterwards resided for a time in Holland, Belgium, and France, but eventually settled down at Göttingen. A Fellow of the School of Medicine, and attached to the Physiological Institute of Rodolph Wagner, he opened a course, which soon became one of the most popular of the University. In 1851 he was invited to Kiel, to direct the Polyclinical and Academic Hospital; but having taken a part, though it does not seem to have been an active one, in the dispute between Denmark and Schleswig-Holstein (1852), he found it necessary to return to Germany, and was almost immediately appointed Professor of Pathology and Therapeutics in the University of Breslau. In 1854 the King of Prussia conferred on him the order of the Red Eagle, and the King of Bavaria the order of St. Michael. He contributed actively and extensively to the "Physiological Dictionary" of Wagner; to Liebig's "Dictionary of

Chemistry," and to the "Supplement" of 1850-52, as well as to other publications of cognate character. In 1858-9 he went to Berlin, and succeeded to the chair of Clinical Medicine on the retirement of Schönlein; to whose large practice he has also in some measure succeeded. He is the author of a work on "Morbus Brightii," published at Brunswick, in 1851; and of another, on "Diseases of the Liver," published at Brunswick, in 1859, on which his reputation as a physician and pathologist is mainly formed. It is now being translated for the New Sydenham Society.

FRITH, WILLIAM POWELL, R.A., a painter, was born at Studley, Yorkshire, in 1819; and, like Lawrence, was the son of an inn-keeper. His picture of "Malvolio before the Countess Olivia," gave evidence of a future successful career being in store for him. This was succeeded by picture after picture, all of which rose in estimation and value. His composition is excellent, and his colour admirable. He throws into his works, occasionally, sly touches of humour, which produce a greater effect than he probably intends. Cervantes, Shakspeare, Goldsmith, Addison, and the British Classics, have been the wellsprings of his inspiration. "Coming of Age," and "Life at the Sea-side," are among his best known works. In 1853 Mr. Frith was elected a Royal Academician. In 1855 he sent to the Paris Exhibition his picture of "Le Bourgeois Gentilhomme," with several others, for which he received a gold medal. In 1858 was produced the "Derby Day," for which he received three thousand pounds.

FROST, WILLIAM EDWARD, was born at Wandsworth in 1810. He early studied as an artist, and soon distinguished himself by gaining prizes at the Royal Academy. His first remarkable picture was "Prometheus Bound," and in 1843 he gained a premium for his cartoon of "Una alarmed by Fawns and Satyrs," which was exhibited at Westminster Hall, and its success seems to have induced him to devote his efforts to the higher branches of art. Amongst his most noted productions are "Sabrina," "Nymphs Dancing," "Diana surprised by Actæon," a Bacchanalian Dance, "Chastity," "The Graces," &c. He has painted a great variety of pictures, mostly illustrative of classical subjects, and has been highly successful owing to the perfect execution and finish which he exhibits in all his productions. He was chosen Associate of the Royal Academy in 1846.

GARIBALDI, JOSEPH. This distinguished general, so well known by his efforts in the cause of Italian freedom, was born at Nice, on the 4th July, 1807. His father being a seafaring man, Joseph early followed the same calling, and soon became distinguished for his bravery and coolness in danger. Having read a history of Rome, and afterwards visiting that city, he felt a deep interest in the ancient glory of Italy, and these incidents seem to have laid the foundation of those attempts which he has lately made in rendering his country once more free. He first became mixed up with political matters about the year 1832, and fled his country from the fear that his name had been included in a list of parties suspected to have been engaged in a conspiracy against Charles Albert, then King of Sardinia. In 1834 he became connected with Mazzini, who made an unsuccessful descent on Savoy during the month of February. Garibaldi fled to France after this, and became captain of a French coasting vessel, but soon tiring of a comparatively inactive life he entered the service of the Bey of Tunis. Owing to the ill condition of the Barbary fleet, of which he then became an officer, he got disgusted with his employment, and in 1836 proceeded to South America, and again engaged in the coasting trade as a means of obtaining a bare subsistence. His restless spirit ill brooked this state of matters, and in 1837 we find him fighting for a Republican movement before Monte Video, where he was seriously wounded and cast into prison. After various fortunes he found a solace in his troubles in marrying a young lady named Annita, to whom he was devotedly attached, and who afterwards shared all his dangers and privations. After remaining some time in South America, and showing great energy in the popular cause, he embarked for Italy in the hope of engaging in the salvation of his country once more. He offered his services to Charles Albert, who, however, acted evasively, and eventually declined to employ Garibaldi, who thereupon went to Milan and was speedily engaged in hostility to the Austrians. He repaired to Rome after the Pope had fled to Gaeta, and thence he was ordered to defend a position endangered by the army of the King of Naples; but soon had to return to oppose the French army which was proceeding to invest the Roman territory. A battle succeeding, Garibaldi at last drove the French from the field, and gained a complete victory over them. He was equally successful against the Neapolitan army, but the French being reinforced again attacked Rome, which eventually fell into their hands, and Garibaldi and his brave volunteers took their departure by night, unknown to the besieging forces, and safely arrived at Tivoli on the ensuing day, July 3rd, 1849. After enduring great hardships, many of his followers surrendered to the Austrians, and Garibaldi with his wife barely escaped with their lives. His greatest misfortune had yet to come: chased by the Austrians, he and his wife were completely exhausted; and in a few days, from the fatigues she had undergone, she expired in a hut by the wayside. Worn out by adverse circumstances, Garibaldi now proceeded to the United States and South America, and after remaining there some years returned to Europe in 1854, and took the command of a small merchant steamer, plying between Nice and Marseilles. The opportunity which Garibaldi had long waited for was now approaching. Sardinia was menaced by the Austrians, and France hastening to her assistance, a general war in Central Italy commenced in the early part of 1859. Victor Emanuel, the King of Sardinia, hastened to avail himself of Garibaldi's services; and at the head of a choice band of volunteers, Garibaldi left Turin on the 20th of May, ready to meet his old and detested enemy. In the whole of the campaign, it is difficult to say which of the two characteristics showed by him are most to be admired, his courage or his stratagem. Never found *by* the Austrians, he was incessantly falling *on* them, and by a guerilla warfare harassed them in every possible direction. His band was constantly increasing; his name became a proverb of strength and success; he was, in fact, the terror of his enemies. On the hasty conclusion of the war, Garibaldi received high rank in the Sardinian army; but being dissatisfied with the slight results obtained towards the freedom of his country, determined to make war on his own account, and being assisted with money, muskets, and men from Sardinia, France, Great Britain, and America, he started from Genoa in the early part of the summer of 1860, and landing near Palermo, in Sicily, took that town with a mere handful of men. His volunteers soon increasing in number, and assistance flowing in on all sides, he next succeeded in taking Messina, which the Neapolitan troops evacuated, and crossing the straits he landed in Calabria, and is now progressing rapidly towards Naples. The Neapolitan army is continually losing by desertions to his ranks. The navy stands in a similar position, and the King of Naples is preparing to fight a kind of forlorn hope, or to take flight from the kingdom which he has so miserably and cruelly governed. In Garibaldi there are united all the qualities of a skilful general. He is bold yet cautious, rapid yet prudent, in all his plans ; his courage and energy are astonishing, and his successes almost without parallel in the history of any commander. Since the above was written, the following telegram has been received :—"*Naples, Sept. 9th.* Garibaldi has entered Naples. Great enthusiasm prevails."

GARNIER PAGÈS, LOUIS ANTOINE, a French journalist and statesman, a member of the Provisional Government and Executive Commission of 1848, was born at Marseilles, in 1803. Having settled as an accountant in Paris, M. Garnier Pagès took a part in the revolution of July, 1830, organizing the barricades in the quarter of St. Avoye. He was returned to the Chamber of Deputies by the arrondissement of Verneuil, and took up his seat at the extreme "left," where he devoted himself to finance and other political questions. In 1844 he induced the government to adopt the system of public loans by direct subscription. One of the promoters of the Reformatory agitation of 1847, M. Garnier Pagès made a conspicuous figure at the banquets. In 1848, appointed by acclamation mayor of Paris, he became, under the Provisional Government, Minister of Finance, and introduced reforms which obtained the general assent of all parties. He formed Comptoirs d'Escompte ; introduced into France the system of bonded warehouses and warrants ; saved the Bank of France, by declaring that its notes were not reimbursable ; amalgamated with it the banks of departments ; and resisted the creation of paper-money. He continued to hold various places in the government until he lost his seat in the Assembly, when he retired into private life, with an unsullied reputation. He is now actively engaged in preparing a "History of the Revolution of 1848."

GASKELL, MRS. L. E., a novelist, was born in 1822. At the age of twenty she married a Unitarian minister, in Manchester. She is the writer of several works which have attained to popularity; among which the most remarkable is "Mary Barton," a novel which aims not only at the delineation of the joys and sorrows, the loves and hatreds of our common humanity, but which also attempts to give a picture of the habits and feelings, opinions and character, and social condition of the working classes of our great manufacturing towns. It is a work of very great literary merit. She has also written the "Moorland Cottage," "North and South," "Ruth," "Cranford," and a "Life of Charlotte Brontë."

GAVARNI, otherwise Paul Chevalier, the most popular living French caricaturist, was born of an impoverished family at Paris in 1801, and became a machine maker. After his day's work was done, he attended the Free School of Design. He made rapid progress as an artist, but did not adopt the profession, and indeed derived no profit from his work until he was thirty-four years of age, when he got employment in drawing sketches for "The Fashions;" that is to say, for new styles of male and female attire. Succeeding in this occupation, he became manager of the journal entitled "Les Gens du Monde," to which he contributed an admirable series of lithographs. His best productions, however, were contributed to the "Charivari," which indeed owes its success, in a great measure, to his contributions. In 1849 M. Gavarni visited London, and contributed a number of characteristic drawings to the "Illustrated London News." He also published a series of sketches, illustrative of life in its lower phases in the English metropolis, under the title of "Gavarni in London." He has illustrated a great number of works, among which may be enumerated "Don Quixote," "Molière's Plays," "The Wandering Jew" of M. Eugène Sue, and the novels of Balzac. A collected edition of his productions was published at Paris, in four volumes, in 1845, with letter-press by Jules Janin, Théophile Gautier, and Balzac. M. Gavarni has been pre-occupied for many years with an attempt to construct an aërostat, or flying-machine, on which it is said that he has expended many efforts of mechanical ingenuity.

GAVAZZI, PADRE ALESSANDRO, an Italian priest, was born at Bologna, on 21st March, 1809. At an early age he distinguished himself by the vigour and liberality of his discourses, and was at all times the champion of the popular cause. During the Lombard revolution, Gavazzi, by his appeals to the patriotism of his hearers, assisted in forming a volunteer army, which fought against the Austrians. He fell, however, under the Pope's displeasure, but eventually, on the flight of the latter, held a prominent position in Rome, under the provisional government, which had then been formed. The failure of the patriotic cause compelled him to flee to England. His lectures, delivered in different parts of this country and America, have made him highly popular. The fervour of his language, and the eloquent expression of his sentiments, captivated his audiences, and drew from them that sympathy which has resulted so practically in the assistance lately given to Garibaldi, with whom Gavazzi has long been associated in attempting to obtain the freedom of Italy.

GEEFS, GUILLAUME, a Belgian sculptor, was born in 1806. After studying at Paris, he returned in 1830 to Belgium, and settled in Brussels. His productions, like those of his brother, are more remarkable for purity than power. While exhibiting national characteristics, they unite largeness of style with much grace and poetic feeling, and remind the critic, to some extent, of the school of Canova. He is first sculptor to the King of the Belgians, and member of the Royal Academy of Science, Letters, and the Fine Arts. The most remarkable of his casts at the Crystal Palace are a monument of Count Frédéric de Merode, at Brussels; a bust of King Leopold, a Francesca di Rimini, and a statue of Rubens, at Antwerp.

GEEFS, JOSEPH, brother of the preceding, born at Antwerp, in 1808, possesses no small reputation as a sculptor. Having gained the Academy's prize, he studied for some time at Rome. He is a member of the Royal Belgian Academy. Among his best productions may be enumerated his "Demon," "Adonis starting for the Chace," and "Science, Art, and Literature, paying Homage to Charles Van Hulthem."

GEORGE V., FREDERICK ALEXANDER CHARLES ERNEST AUGUSTUS, KING OF HANOVER, was born 27th of May, 1819. As Prince of the Blood Royal of Great Britain, Duke of Cumberland, Duke of Brunswick-Luneburg, he succeeded his father, Ernest Augustus (Duke of Cumberland in England), on the 18th of November, 1851. His majesty married on the 18th of February, 1843, the Princess Mary, daughter of Joseph, Duke of Saxe Altenburg, by whom he has a family of three children, two sons and one daughter. The eldest, heir to the throne, Prince Ernest Augustus William Adolphus George Frederick, was born on the 21st of September, 1845. The accession of his father to the throne of his ancestors, dissolved the connexion subsisting since the time of George I. between Britain and Hanover, and lessened to some extent the liability of this country to become involved in the complications and wars of the Continent. The king has suffered from his early boyhood the melancholy infliction of total blindness, which he has borne with such patient resignation as to have endeared himself to all who approach him, and which he has alleviated by the domestic affections, and by the cultivation of music and literature.

GERHARD, EDWARD, a German archæologist, was born at Posen, November, 1795, and educated at Breslau and Berlin. In 1816, he obtained a professorship in the Gymnasium, or High School of Posen, but in consequence of ill-health he was obliged to abandon the office. Proceeding to Italy, he fixed upon Rome as his residence, and remained in that city for fifteen years, devoting his mind to antiquarian study and research. Convinced that to advance the cause of archæological science, it was necessary to unite the scattered elements of knowledge which he knew to exist in Europe, he took great interest in the formation of an archæological society, called the "Institute of Archæological Correspondence," which by letters and other means was intended to systematize the results of antiquarian investigation. The project was conceived in 1828 by M. Gerhard, Baron Von Bunsen, the late M. Panofka, and the Duc de Luynes. The institution was placed under the protection of the King of Prussia, Frederic William IV., then hereditary Prince of Prussia, and still exists in the capital, with the aid of funds supplied by the Prussian Government. M. Gerhard directed the proceedings of the institution until 1837, when he returned to Prussia, and was appointed Archæologist to the Royal Museum, Professor in the University of Berlin, and the Royal Academy of Sciences. During his stay at Rome, he assisted in preparing a description of the city, embracing all its particular points of interest, ancient and modern. He has been a most voluminous author, so much so, that it would be impracticable to detail the titles of his works. As appears from what follows, nearly all of them are profusely illustrated, and they thus become of more than ordinary value to the antiquarian and student of history. His descriptions are graphic, his style clear, and his industry indefatigable. M. Gerhard has published detailed descriptions of the ancient monuments of the Vatican, of the Museum of Naples, and of that of Berlin. The principal works in which he has published inedited volumes are the Antike Bildwerke (Munich, 1827, sm. fcp. 140 pl. folio); A selection of Greek vases, found in Etruria (330 pl., in 4 vols., Berlin, 1840-4); A collection of Etruscan mirrors (240 plates, Berlin, 1840-4), and several publications descriptive of cups and vases in the Museum in Berlin (Berlin, 1840, folio). He has also published a Greek mythology at Berlin, in 1854, in 2 volumes, and a great variety of papers to the learned societies.

GERSTAECKER, FREDERIC, a German author, was born on the 10th of May, 1816, at Hamburg. The son of an actor, he was intended for a commercial career, and apprenticed accordingly; but, habituated from youth to a roving life, he emigrated to the United States, reaching New York about 1837. After several months passed in that city, he travelled on foot, first to Canada, and thence down to Texas, and back to the United States, where he was forced to accept any occupation that chance offered; being by turns stoker to a steam-boat, seaman, farmer, jeweller, wood-splitter, hunter, and innkeeper. In these varied employments he travelled over a great part of America; and returning to Germany, after six years' absence, he published the results of his transatlantic observations. In 1849, after writing his "Pirates of the Mississippi," he projected a new journey to the West; visited Rio Janeiro, Buenos Ayres, Valparaiso, California, the South Sea Islands, Australia, and Java, returning to Germany in 1852. He then produced the most successful of his books of travel. Several of his works have been translated into English, French, and Dutch, and are popular because of their vivid delineations of life. Mr. Gerstaecker is on the eve of starting on another voyage to North and South America.

GERVINUS, GEORGES GODEFROID, a German historian and philosopher, was born at Darmstadt, on the 20th of May, 1805. Having been for some time cashier and book-keeper in a large Darmstadt house, he felt that his tastes were incompatible with mercantile pursuits; he therefore abandoned them for the study of philosophy, and eventually he was appointed Professor of German Literature in the University of Göttingen. When the King of Hanover, by enforcing some arbitrary regulations, provoked a protest from Gervinus, which was signed by other professors, Dahlmann among the number, and which resulted in the subscribers being expelled from the University owing to political affairs, Gervinus went to Italy, and, returning to Germany in 1844, was named Professor in the University of Heidelberg, where he was received with the warmest enthusiasm. It was at that period he began to publish those great works which have contributed so largely to his reputation. His political opinions being liberal, he united himself to the constitutional party—a party which received an immense accession of influence by the discovery that, in 1834, the German potentates had entered into a treaty among themselves to the effect that none of them should be bound by their constitutions, but that they should assist each other with their armies against both parliaments and people. Gagern was an active leader of the constitutionalists, and Gervinus was a trusted counsellor of the party. For the free expression of his political opinions he was prosecuted before the tribunal of Baden; but the Government ultimately abandoned the proceedings. With the pen in his journal and his voice in the Chamber, he advocated constitutional doctrines, but at length retired definitely from the position he held as a Deputy. He has written no fewer than three works on the "Poetic Literature of Germany," which have reached several editions; his latest and most important publications being "Shakspeare" (1849), and a "History of German Poetry" (1853), in five volumes.

GHIKA, ALEXANDER, the ex-Hospodar of Wallachia, was elevated to the Principality in March, 1834, and adopted liberal views, founding schools, and using the best means at his command to promote the progress of the people. Under the influence of Russia two parties came into existence to thwart him, one composed of the liberals, and the other of the Boyards, whose personal enmity he had provoked. In 1837 he applied to Russia for assistance against the opposition in the Wallachian Assembly. It was only granted on concessions being made which virtually annulled the political and administrative independence of the country. In 1841 he incurred the resentment of Russia by taking measures against the persons connected with the insurrection in Ibraila, with which the Russian Consul at Galatz had been mixed up. The result was that he was exposed to persecutions on the part of Russia, and that Georges Bibesco, one of his bitterest foes among the Boyards, supplanted him as Hospodar, the Porte having been compelled to deprive him of his honours. He then went to Vienna, and remained there till 1853, when he returned to Wallachia, where there was a strong reaction in his favour. In July, 1856, after Prince Stirby had ceased to act as Hospodar, he was restored to his old functions. The Roumans expected that, under him, an effort would be made to reunite the two provinces, and that he would give strenuous support to the cause of Rouman nationality. But he did not display that energy of character necessary to give force to his convictions.

GIBSON, JOHN, an English sculptor settled at Rome, was born in 1790, in or near the town of Conway, North Wales. Gibson's parents, who were Welsh, speaking English imperfectly, when he was nine years old settled at Liverpool, where he was put to school. At 13 years of age he was anxious to become an artist, but the portrait painters demanded a premium which his father could not afford, and accordingly he was bound apprentice to Messrs. Southwell and Wilson, cabinet-makers. By the end of the first year Gibson became disgusted with his occupation. He induced his good masters to consent to draw out a new indenture, and was apprenticed to them as an ornamental wood carver for the remaining six years. By the end of the second year he, tired of his new occupation, refused to work; and when threatened with imprisonment, declared that he was determined to be a sculptor, and that he would rather serve his time in prison than continue at wood-carving. By this time he had begun modelling in clay. He was introduced to Messrs. Frances, the marble-cutters, and he was enchanted with some sculpture which he saw at their works. He showed these gentlemen his drawings and some models in clay, and they were so highly satisfied with his talents that they purchased his indenture for the sum of £70, he rebinding himself to them as an apprentice stone-cutter or sculptor. Gibson's new master presented him to Mr. Roscoe, the author of the Life of Lorenzo di Medici, who, appreciating his abilities, threw open to him his splendid library, his extensive collection of prints, and fine drawings by the old masters. He was invited to Allerton Hall once a week to pass the day, and dine with the distinguished persons who met there. When his engagement with Frances was drawing towards a close, Mr. Roscoe advised the young artist to go to Rome, which he said was the only place in Europe where sculpture could be studied with success. Notwithstanding the failure of Mr. Roscoe's bank, this gentleman collected among his friends a sum of £250 to enable Gibson to go to Italy. He left Liverpool for London with letters from Mr. Roscoe to Fuseli, R.A., to Flaxman, to a distinguished patroness of art, and to Mr. Christie, the auctioneer, a man of great taste and learning, who introduced him to George Watson Taylor, who became his generous patron. Mr. Flaxman urged Gibson to proceed to Rome. "Go, if possible," he said, "to that great university of art, and stay there as long as possible. The Marquis Canova," he added, "is most generous to young students of promise." Gibson left England on the 1st of October, 1817, with letters to the Marquis Canova from Lord Brougham, the late General d'Aguilar of Liverpool, and Fuseli. On his arrival at Rome, Canova looked over his drawings with great care. "If you have as much industry," said the great sculptor, "as you have talent, we may expect great results." He received the young sculptor as his pupil, and pressed upon him a handsome offer to pay all the expenses necessary to enable him to study upon a large scale. Mr. W. Taylor having removed all pecuniary difficulties, Mr. Gibson declined the generous offer of the Roman artist, whose invaluable instructions and advice he enjoyed up to the period of his death, five years afterwards. Gibson then placed himself under the tuition of Thorwaldsen. Canova introduced him to the English nobility who came to Rome, and thereby secured for him the patronage of the Duke of Devonshire, Sir George Beaumont, and other English patrons of art. From them he received numerous orders. For Sir George Beaumont he executed his group of "Psyche borne by the Zephyrs," of which he has since made copies for Prince Torlonia and the Emperor of Russia. The public works executed by Mr. Gibson at Rome and erected in London are, a colossal sitting statue of Her Majesty Queen Victoria, accompanied by "Justice and Clemency," placed in the Prince's Chamber in the new Houses of Parliament; a statue of Sir Robert Peel in Westminster Abbey; and a statue of Huskisson at Lloyd's, Royal Exchange. He executed two statues of Huskisson and one of George Stephenson at Liverpool, and another of Kirkman Finlay at Glasgow. Mr. Gibson was elected an Associate of the Royal Academy of London in 1833, and R.A. in 1836, and decorated with the Cross of the Legion of Honour for his works exhibited at the Paris Exhibition. He has been admitted a member of all the art academies of Europe. With the Chevalier Tenarani he now holds the highest place among the sculptors settled at Rome. Much of his technical skill he owes to Canova; but if he has not in excellency of this kind outstripped his master, he has far excelled him in the power of infusing sentiment and expression as well as beauty and grace into his figures.

GIBSON, The Right Hon. Thomas Milner, was born in 1807, at Trinidad. Having studied at Cambridge, he entered Parliament in 1837 as a Conservative for Ipswich; but having adopted the opposite class of political opinions, he resigned his seat in 1839, and was twice unsuccessful in attempting to re-enter Parliament. In 1841 he successfully contested Manchester on Free-trade principles, and in 1846 he took office as Vice-President of the Board of Trade under Lord John Russell, but relinquished the appointment in 1848, from a feeling that it fettered his independence. He was so strongly opposed to the war with Russia, and disapproved so heartily of the war with China, that at the general election of 1857 he was rejected by Manchester at the same time with Mr. Bright, who shared his then unpopular opinions. Subsequently he was returned for Ashton-under-Lyne. He framed the now famous amendment on the Conspiracy Bill, which shattered the administration of Lord Palmerston. When, in 1859, Lord Palmerston was again called to form an administration, Mr. Gibson was appointed President of the Board of Trade, an office he still holds.

GILBERT, John Graham, a painter, was born at Glasgow, in April, 1794. In independent circumstances, but loving art for its own sake, he became a pupil of the Royal Academy in 1818. In 1819 he obtained the first silver medal for a drawing after the antique, and the gold medal of the Academy in 1821 for an historical picture. After two years' study in Italy, during which he became distinguished for his knowledge of the Old Masters, he returned to Scotland, and rapidly rose to a high position as a portrait-painter. All Mr. Graham Gilbert's works, whether of portraiture or imagination, are characteristic. His drawing is accurate, the expression of his works true and graceful, his colour warm, and his handling spirited and refined. Few painters have done more to propagate a taste for the Fine Arts in Scotland than Mr. Graham Gilbert, and it is no small compliment to him to mention that many of his works are greatly appreciated on the Continent, where his style is much admired. He has painted fewer pictures than lovers of art could wish, but his circumstances are such that the productions of his hand became doubly valuable, inasmuch as none of them are painted for the market. He is a member of the Royal Academy of Scotland, and had he chosen might long since have been a Royal Academician.

GILFILLAN, THE REV. GEORGE, was born at Comrie, in 1813, and studied at the University of Glasgow, and at the United Secession Hall. He was licensed in 1835, and next year ordained minister of the School Wynd Congregation, Dundee, where he still remains. He became early attached to literature, and wrote a series of sketches of the principal literary characters of the day, which were published in 1845, and well received. In 1849 he published his second "Portrait Gallery," which was succeeded in 1854 by a third volume of the same series. In 1850 he published his "Bards of the Bible," now in its fifth edition; in 1851 the "Book of British Poetry;" in 1852 the "Martyrs, Heroes, and Bards of the Scottish Covenant," which has gone through six or seven editions; in 1853 the "Grand Discovery;" in 1856 the "History of a Man," supposed to be a sort of autobiography; and in 1857 "Christianity and our Era." He has also printed several of his pulpit discourses; and has issued forty volumes, forming part of a library edition of the "British Poets," with biographical and critical notes. He has just published a large work, entitled "Alpha and Omega; or, a Series of Scripture Studies."

GIRARDIN, EMILE DE, a French journalist, was born at Paris, on the 22nd of June, 1806. A false entry of his name was made in the register of births, in which he was described as Emile Delamothe, the son of an un-known father, and "of Demoiselle Lamothe, sempstress, daughter of one Sieur Delamothe, residing in Mans," all of these names being fictitious. We need scarcely say that he is an illegitimate child. For the first eight years of his life he was kindly treated by his father, Count Alexandre de Girardin, and his mother, Adelaide-Marie Fagnan, the daughter of M. Fagnan, financial secretary under Louis XVI. His father married; his mother also married. She became the wife of M. Dupuy, a member of the council of the Cour Royale of Paris. Then an attempt was made to bring him up in such a way that he should lose all trace of his origin, by boarding him with a horse-breaker at Pin, in Normandy. While living at this place, he attracted the notice of the Viscountess of Senonnes, who obtained, in 1824, a situation for him in the office of her husband, who was at the time a Cabinet minister. This gentleman, retiring soon afterwards, De Girardin was again thrown out of employment. He offered himself for enlistment in a regiment of hussars, but was rejected as too delicate. It was then that he took to authorship, and assumed the name of De Girardin, in defiance of his father and mother. In his first work "Emile," he describes his own condition. This work was very successful, and was criticised by Jules Janin as a *chef d'œuvre*. On April 5th, 1828, he started a weekly publication, consisting of articles judiciously selected from the journals, to which, with some audacity, he gave the name of "The Thief." In October, 1829, he set on foot a new publication called "La Mode," which was nearly as successful, and to which Balzac, Eugène Sue, and Georges Sand, contributed. In 1831, he commenced a third serial, under the name of the "Journal of Useful Knowledge," which immediately attained a circulation of

230,000 copies. It was not till the 1st July, 1836, that he published the first number of the "Presse," a daily newspaper, with which his name is now associated. It was issued at half the price of newspapers of the same class then in circulation, but the success of this new speculation fully justified the calculations on which he had proceeded. In 1831 M. de Girardin married Mademoiselle Delphine Gay; in 1836 he fought a duel with M. Armand Carrel, the editor of the "National," in which the latter lost his life, and in 1837 he defended himself successfully against the protest respecting his admission to the Chamber of Deputies, on the ground that he was a Swiss and not a Frenchman; satisfactory evidence having been obtained on the subject of his birth by a commission appointed to inquire into the facts. At eight o'clock on the morning of the memorable 24th February, 1848, he went to the Tuileries to advise Louis Philippe of what was going forward in Paris, and he then wrote the abdication of the king. After the accession of Louis-Napoleon, he had many quarrels with the government. On the 23rd of March, 1854, he received a fourth *avertissement*, in consequence of the appearance in the "Presse" of a letter from Manin, and on the 23rd of September he was officially warned not to continue a series of articles headed "The Track of Revolutions." In consequence he retired from the active editorship of the paper two years afterwards, selling his interest in it for £32,000. Madame de Girardin having died in June, 1855, he married towards the close of 1856, Mademoiselle Mina Brunold, Countess of Tieffenbach, the daughter of the widow of Prince Frederic of Nassau, uncle of the reigning Duke of Nassau. The limits of this work do not admit of any detailed account of the political opinions of M. Emile de Girardin. Suffice it to say that all his principal articles are based upon the thought: Let all come by civilization, nothing by revolution; all by immaterial force, nothing by material force. Let us have neither barriers nor barricades; let us not obey the people, but employ them. His principal articles have been collected and published under the title of "Questions of my Time," in 12 volumes 8vo, 1836 to 1856. A pamphlet which he published under the title of "La Guerre," in less than a fortnight ran through eight editions. His other chief works are "Le Droit," "La Liberté," "L'Empire non la Liberté," "Conquête et Nationalité," "La Civilisation et l'Algérie."

GLADSTONE, THE RIGHT HON. WILLIAM EWART, M.P., an English parliamentary orator and statesman, was born on the 29th December, 1809, and is son of the late Sir John Gladstone, Bart., an eminent Liverpool merchant. He received the usual education of the English youth of the wealthier classes, passing from Eton to Oxford, where he took what is technically termed a double-first,—that is, gained the highest excellence in classics and mathematics. On leaving the university he made the tour of the Continent, and on his return was elected member of Parliament for Newark. In 1834 he was appointed a Lord of the Treasury under Sir Robert Peel; and on the failure of the Hon. S. Wortley to obtain his seat when appointed Under-Secretary for the Colonies, Mr. Gladstone was transferred to the vacant office, which he held until the resignation of his chief in the spring of 1835. In 1841 he was appointed Vice-President of the Board of Trade, and Master of the Mint. In this situation he became the right hand of the government. His acquaintance with mercantile affairs enabled him to enter into the discussion of the most complicated commercial questions, and his literary ability and oratorical talent fitted him to unfold his views with a clearness and precision which a mere business man very rarely attains to. He held office as President of the Board of Trade for two years; as Colonial Secretary he supported Sir Robert Peel in 1846 in his Free-trade measures, and in 1847 became Member of Parliament for Oxford University. Having held the office of Chancellor of Exchequer under Lords Aberdeen and Palmerston, he resigned, owing to the latter consenting to the vote for a committee of inquiry into the state of the army during the Russian war. Mr. Gladstone's acceptance under Lord Derby of a mission to the Ionian Islands has been the topic of much comment, and some little censure. But whatever may be thought either of its policy or its success, the entire disinterestedness with which it was entered upon and executed is unquestionable. Lord Derby's Government, formed in 1858, giving way in the following year, Lord Palmerston was recalled to the helm of affairs, and in the constitution of his ministry appointed Mr. Gladstone once more Chancellor of the Exchequer. Mr. Gladstone married in 1839 the eldest daughter of the late Sir Stephen Richard Glynne, Bart. In the same year he published a work, "The State in its Relation to the Church," which Macaulay subjected to a trenchant criticism. This book was followed by another, "Church Principles Considered in their Results." Whatever difference of opinion might exist respecting the principles of these works, their publication stamped their author as one of the few original writers of the age. Mr. Gladstone's "Letters on the State of the Neapolitan Prisons," addressed to Lord Aberdeen, gave convincing evidence, that however much he might sympathise with what are called High Church principles, a wide gulf separated him from the creatures of sacerdotal tyranny. These letters produced a powerful sensation, and resulted in some little amelioration of the condition of the victims of the oppressor. Mr. Gladstone is one of the first orators in the House of Commons. His late speeches on the Budget and the repeal of the Paper Duties (1860) have placed him in the foremost position. Mr. Gladstone's latest work, "Homer and the Homeric Age," obviously the fruit of solid studies, is a noble contribution to the elucidation of the greatest monument of Greek literature.

GLEIG, THE REVEREND GEORGE ROBERT, a soldier, divine, and distinguished author, was born at Stirling, on the 20th April, 1796. He is the youngest son of the Right Reverend George Gleig, Scottish Episcopal Bishop of Brechin. At the age of thirteen he entered the University of Glasgow; whence, before he was fifteen, he was removed to Balliol College, Oxford. After keeping six terms, he evinced such a decided preference for the military profession, that a commission was procured for him; and having barely completed his seventeenth year, he joined the Duke of Wellington's army, then engaged in the sieges of St. Sebastian and Pampeluna, in the summer of 1813. At the close of the Peninsular war he proceeded to America, and was shot in the thigh while taking an American colour at the battle of Bladensburg. Returning to Europe too late for the battle of Waterloo, he soon began to grow tired of a soldier's life in peace; and though promoted to a company, on his father's suggestion he again proceeded to Oxford. He took his degree in 1818, and in 1819 was admitted into deacon's orders on the curacy of Westwill, in Kent. Mr. Gleig had early begun to write; while at Oxford he translated "Aristotle's Poetics." In 1820 he completed his first acknowledged work, "A Narrative of the Campaigns of the British Army at

Washington, in New Orleans." It obtained a fair, but not a large share of public favour. But when by and by, in 1826, the "Subaltern"—which appeared originally as a series of papers in "Blackwood"—came out, attention was drawn to the earlier volume, which passed within a few months through three editions. In 1822 Mr. Gleig was presented to the perpetual curacy of Ash next Sandwich; and in April, 1823, had the rectory of Ivy Church likewise given to him; both by Manners Sutton, Archbishop of Canterbury. Between 1822 and 1834 he produced, besides the two volumes already specified, "The Life of Sir Thomas Munro," in 3 vols.; "The History of the Bible," in 2 vols.; "The History of India" (in Murray's "Family Library"), in 4 vols.; "The Country Curate," begun like the "Subaltern" in "Blackwood;" "The Chelsea Pensioners," &c. The "Subaltern" had early obtained for him the friendship of the Duke of Wellington, who made him his frequent guest at Walmer Castle; and in 1834 Lord John Russell, attracted by the same work, made him the spontaneous offer of the chaplaincy of Chelsea Hospital, which had then become vacant. In 1846 he was promoted to be Chaplain-General of the Forces, being at the same time appointed Inspector-General of Military Schools; and in 1850 he was presented to a prebendal stall in St. Paul's. His latest work, published in 1858 and 1859, is "A Life of the Great Duke of Wellington," founded on the biography of Captain Brialmont, of the Belgian army; but much enhanced in value from private and public documents, necessarily inaccessible to a foreigner. Besides the books enumerated above, he has published, at various times, "The Life of Lord Clive," "The Story of the Battle of Waterloo," "The Leipzig Campaign," "Chelsea Hospital and its Traditions," two volumes of "Sermons," and "A

Guide to the Holy Sacrament." Two volumes of "Essays," collected chiefly from the "Edinburgh" and "Quarterly" Reviews, extending over a wide range of subjects, have been published separately, and have been well received. Mr. Gleig is an extempore preacher of acknowledged power and eloquence.

GLENCORSE, JOHN INGLIS, LORD, Lord-Justice-Clerk of Scotland, born about 1810, is the son of the late Rev. Dr. Inglis, long an eminent leader in the Scottish Church. After graduating at the Edinburgh University he entered the bar, to which he was called in 1835, and so unmistakeable were his general powers, that he could scarcely be said to have ever undergone the drudgery of a junior counsel. For a long series of years he stood at the head of the Scottish bar, and was so much esteemed by his brethren as to be elected Dean of Faculty. In 1852 he was appointed Lord Advocate of Scotland; and, with the view of being in Parliament, contested the borough of Lisburn, Ireland; where, though a perfect stranger, and opposed by powerful local influence, he was only defeated by a majority of fourteen votes. He had been previously defeated in a contest for Orkney, by a majority of but eleven votes. He held the office of Chief Law Adviser of the Crown in the northern part of the kingdom until the fall of the administration of Lord Derby, although unable to obtain a seat in Parliament. When the noble lord returned to power in 1858, Mr. Inglis was again appointed Lord-Advocate, a seat in Parliament being found for him at Stamford. After a brief but highly successful career in the House of Commons, on the death of the Hon. John Hope Mr. Inglis was raised to the bench as Lord-Justice-Clerk, and assumed the title of Lord Glencorse.

GODWIN, GEORGE, architect, editor of the "Builder," was born on 28th

January, 1815, at Brompton, Middlesex, and early embraced his father's profession. Possessing, however, a taste for literature and science, he contributed in 1835 to the "Literary Union," and afterwards received a medal from the Royal Institute of British Architects for his "Essay on Concrete." He is one of the founders of the London Art Union, of which he became honorary secretary in 1839, in which capacity he has continued to act up to the present time. He published his excellent and interesting work, "The Churches of London," in 1838, was elected a Fellow of the Society of Antiquaries in 1839, a Fellow of the Royal Society in 1840, and obtained a medal from the Société libre des Beaux Arts of Paris. His contributions to the "Art Journal," the "Civil Engineer and Architect's Journal," and generally to current art and literature, are so numerous, as to render a catalogue of them beyond our power of publication. In 1844 he became editor of the "Builder," and in 1853 published his "History in Ruins;" in 1854, his "London Shadows," an inquiry into the condition of the homes of the poor; and since, "Town Swamps and Social Bridges," "Memorials of Workers," &c. He has designed and erected a number of public edifices, and has been appointed Surveyor under the Metropolitan Building Act. Mr. Godwin was one of the jurors at the Great Exhibition of 1851, is a Vice-President (1860) of the Institute of British Architects, and a member of many learned societies. His services to the advancement of architecture, science, and social and sanitary improvement, have been as untiring as meritorious.

GOLDSCHMIDT, Madame (Jenny Lind), was born at Stockholm on the 6th October, 1821, and by her musical talents was at an early age taken notice of by an actress at the theatre of her native city, who became her best adviser and most valued friend. After receiving instruction from eminent masters, she eventually made her *debût* and achieved a complete success, and continued for some time at Stockholm. She afterwards proceeded to Paris, for the purpose of receiving lessons from Garcia, but from whom she received little encouragement. Her talents were, however, recognised by Meyerbeer, who offered her an engagement at Berlin. From this moment Mademoiselle Lind's fame became European. A constant series of engagements was offered to her, and her appearances at Berlin, Vienna, and at Her Majesty's Theatre, in London, were so many triumphs, in which the audiences were completely carried away in their enthusiastic reception of this gifted singer. To so great an extent did the *furore* exist in London, that the doors of the opera house were nightly crowded for hours before the commencement of the performances, and tickets were often re-sold at fabulous prices. Proceeding to America, where her reception was as enthusiastic and as profitable as she could possibly have desired, she was married to M. Otto Goldschmidt, in 1851. In the following year they returned to Europe. Since then, Madame Goldschmidt has rarely appeared in public, spending her time and fortune in assisting and founding various charitable institutions, and winning from all the highest praise for the benevolence of her disposition, as she had previously done by the exercise of her talents.

GOMM, General Sir William Maynard, G.C.B., was born in 1784. He received his commission as Ensign in the 9th Infantry on the 24th May, 1794. When but fourteen he served in Holland, with the rank of Lieutenant; was present at the battles of 19th September and 2nd October, 1799, and ever since, with the exception of some time passed in the Royal Military College, he has been actively employed. He has thus been sixty-six years under arms, and has seen as much actual service as perhaps any other British officer now living. In 1799 he served at the Helder under the Duke of York, and in 1801 served under Sir James Pulteney. In 1803 he was promoted to the rank of Captain, served in Hanover in 1805, and at Copenhagen and Stralsund in 1807. In 1809 he was distinguished in the Continental campaign of that year, in the Walcheren expedition, and at the siege of Flushing, and in 1810 he was ordered to the Peninsula, and took part in nearly all the great Peninsular engagements. He obtained his majority in October, 1811, and became Lieutenant-Colonel in July, 1812, being then thirty years of age. He was one of the victors at Waterloo, where he looked after Picton's celebrated division, the "Fighting Fifth," in the capacity of Quartermaster-General. In 1829 he became Colonel of the 13th Light Infantry, and has since received the Grand Cross of the Bath as an additional honour ; being one of those officers transferred from the Line to the Guards. A Colonel in 1829, and Major-General in 1837, in 1840 he was appointed to the command of the troops in Jamaica, and after returning to England was charged with the command of the army in the Northern District, from which he was removed in 1845, being nominated Civil Governor and Commander of the Forces in Mauritius. In 1846 he was elevated to the rank of Lieutenant-General, and on the resignation by Sir Charles Napier of the chief command in India in 1851, was appointed head of the Indian army, which he retained till the close of the year 1855.

GOODALL, EDWARD, an eminent engraver, was born at Leeds in 1795. At a very early age his mind was attracted to the study of the fine arts,

but specially devoting his attention to engraving. He has executed a vast number of engravings for illustrated works, among which connoisseurs rank those for Rogers's "Italy," and "Pleasures of Memory," as the best. The greatest of his works, however, are his large line engravings from Turner's "Cologne" and "Tivoli," and the various other engravings which he has executed from Turner's landscapes. Few engravers, either past or present, have more closely united vigour with refinement. For the last ten years (owing to the want of encouragement to landscape engraving) he has been almost exclusively engaged upon figure subjects, and principally from the pictures of his son, Mr. Frederick Goodall, among which may be mentioned "The Angel's Whisper," "The Soldier's Dream," "An Episode of the Happier Days of Charles I.," and "Cranmer at the Traitor's Gate." The last-named, remarkable for its vigorous execution, may be considered his finest historical plate.

GOODALL, FREDERICK, an historical painter, was born in London in 1822. He was instructed by his father in the elements of art, and at an early age obtained the Isis medal from the Society of Arts for a drawing of Lambeth Palace, and in the following year their large silver medal for his first work in oil, "Finding the Dead Body of a Miner by Torchlight." After travelling in Normandy in 1838, he sent to the Royal Academy's Exhibition (1839) his "French Soldiers drinking in a Cabaret," a most remarkable work, and one which manifested a peculiar talent for depicting popular subjects. Extending his travels, he soon obtained fresh subjects for his brush. Patrons, among whom was William Wells of Redleaf, freely assisted the young artist, by purchasing his productions ; the "Christening" obtained him a prize from the British Institution ; and in 1842 Mr. Vernon purchased the "Tired Soldier." At twenty, Goodall was thus a really great artist. In 1847 he produced his "Village Festival," which was immensely admired. "Hunt the Slipper," "Raising the Maypole," and "The Swing," are admirable for their touches of nature and character. "Cranmer at the Traitor's Gate," exhibited at Liverpool in 1858, gained the £100 prize. In 1852 he became an A.R.A., a position which he had fairly earned by his "Village Festival," painted some years previously.

GORDON, LADY LUCY DUFF, is well known by her able translations of the works of some continental authors. Of these the most valuable are, Ranke's "History of Prussia," Niebuhr's "Greek Legends," and Fuerbach's "Criminal Trials." In all her productions she is extremely studious to present to the English reader a faithful reproduction of the text of the original.

GORDON, SIR JOHN WATSON, P.R.S.A., R.A., was born in Edinburgh, towards the close of the last century. He is the eldest son of the late Captain James Watson, R.N., the name of Gordon having been subsequently assumed. His professional life has been spent in Edinburgh, where he is regarded as the not unworthy successor of Raeburn. During his long career, Sir John Watson Gordon has painted almost all the leading men in Scotland, and latterly many distinguished persons in England, and his portraits of his countrymen are thoroughly characteristic. In 1841 Gordon was elected an Associate of the London Royal Academy, in 1850 he became President of the Scottish Academy, was afterwards knighted, and appointed painter limner to the Queen in Scotland, and about the same time also elected a Royal Academician.

GORE, MRS. CATHERINE FRANCES, a well-known writer of fiction, was born in London in 1800. Her first produc-

tion, "Theresa Marchmont," was highly successful, and opened out a long and brilliant career for her as a clear, vivid, and imaginative writer. It would be impossible to enumerate in this slight sketch all the productions of Mrs. Gore's pen. She has succeeded most admirably in depicting scenes from daily life in her "Women as they are," "Mothers and Daughters," "Memoirs of a Peeress," and many similar works. In her "Hungarian Tales" she vividly portrays the habits and customs of Hungary. As a gentle satirist we may name her "Cecil, or the Adventures of a Coxcomb," "The Woman of the World," "The Popular Member," and "The Sketch-book of Fashion." As a moralist any of her works may be adduced as an illustration. There are few living writers who have been so successful in acquiring popularity, which perhaps may be owing to the life-like nature of all of Mrs. Gore's novels. In 1823 she was married to Captain Gore of the 1st Life Guards, and became a widow in 1846. She has been the mother of ten children, of whom two survive : Lady Edward Thynne, married to a son of the second Marquis of Bath ; and Augustus Wentworth Gore, A.D.C. to the Lord Lieutenant of Ireland, who served with distinction on the staff at Lucknow and in the Rohilcund campaign, and was repeatedly commended in despatches. Mrs. Gore has for some time past been deprived of sight.

GÖRGEI, ARTHUR, was born on the 5th Feb., 1818, at Toporcz, in Upper Hungary. In 1832 he was sent to the military school at Tuln, where he remained for five years, when he entered the royal Hungarian life guards at Vienna, and ultimately became lieutenant of Hussars. Subsequently he quitted the army, and devoted himself to the study of science, chiefly chemistry. At the call of the Hungarian committee of defence,

Görgei exchanged the laboratory for the camp, and became a captain of Honveds. From this comparatively humble rank Kossuth had so high an opinion of his talents that he raised him to the position of commander-in-chief of the Hungarian national army. General Moga being incapacitated for command, Windischgrätz was too able a general for Görgei, who was compelled to abandon Presburg, and only saved his army by a timely retreat. After being twice superseded, he resumed the chief command; meeting some reverses, and achieving some victories, he became Dictator *vice* Kossuth. Personal ambition and personal animosities paralysed his military genius, and, in a moment of adverse fortune, he surrendered at discretion to the representative of Russia. Since the fall of Hungary he has resided at Klagenfurth. In 1852 he published at Leipzig a vindication of his "treason," which has since appeared in England, under the title of "My Life and Acts in Hungary."

GORTCHAKOFF, PRINCE ALEX-ANDER, Russian diplomatist, cousin to Prince Michael, the General, born 1798, was a student at Zarskoe-Selo and made the friendship of the poet Pouschkin. In 1824 he was Secretary of embassy to London, and in 1830 was Chargé d'Affaires at Florence. In 1832 he was attached to the Russian embassy at Vienna, where the illness and subsequent death of his chief gave him great influence. In 1841 he was envoy to Stuttgard, with the title of Ambassador Extraordinary, and happily negotiated the marriage of the Prince Royal of Wurtemburg with the Russian Grand-duchess Olga, daughter of the Czar. For this service he received civil promotion corresponding to the rank of Lieutenant-General. In 1850 he proceeded to the Germanic Diet at Frankfort; and in 1854 succeeded Count Orloff at Vienna, to represent Russian interests at that court. He is one of the old Muscovite party, totally antagonistic to reform. As a statesman, he holds no status whatever, but as a diplomatist, he is looked to as little, if anything, inferior to Nesselrode.

GORTCHAKOFF, PRINCE MICHAEL DMITRIEVITCH, Commander-in-chief of the Russian army of the South, belonging to one of the great Russian houses descended of the stock of Rurik, the founder of the monarchy, was born in 1792. Entering the army in 1807, he served as an artillery officer in 1809 in Persia, and was afterwards at the battles of Borodino, Lutzen, Bautzen, Dresden, and Leipzig, taking part in the campaigns of the Allies against France. In 1828 he was general of brigade, charged to operate against the Turks on the Danube, where he exhibited great vigour and ability in conducting the passage of the river, and remarkable skill as an engineer in conducting the siege of Silistria. He served in the campaign against Poland, and was severely wounded on the memorable days of the 6th and 7th of September. In 1846 Prince Gortchakoff was named military Governor-general of Warsaw, and from this period he devoted much of his attention to the improvement of the Polish capital. He secured for it an ample supply of water before the period of the Russian war, and since then he has introduced gas and many improvements connected with the sanitary condition of the city. As a major-general, he in 1849 accompanied the Russian army which crippled the Hungarians in their struggle for nationality. In 1852 he attended the funeral of the Duke of Wellington as military representative of Russia; and in the succeeding year Gortchakoff commanded in the Principalities. He besieged Silistria, and maintained the land blockade for months, until at length orders were forwarded for the evacuation and raising the siege. The result of his generalship is a matter of contemporaneous history, which does not demand special exposition. "The passage of the Danube, in the month of March, 1854," says the "Nord" of 10th June, 1857, "the retrograde movement through the Principalities into Bessarabia, and the heroic defence of Sebastopol, are feats of arms and military combinations worthy of the greatest commanders; but if these services confer a title to the esteem and admiration of military men, the operations and movements which followed the evacuation of Sebastopol should secure for the Russian commander-in-chief the respect of every intelligent soldier and the gratitude of his countrymen." Politically, he has always entertained the opinions of an enlightened Russian. Prince Alexander Gortchakoff, the Minister of Foreign Affairs, is not brother, but cousin to Prince Michael Gortchakoff.

GOSSE, PHILIP HENRY, a writer on natural history, was born at Worcester, in 1810. His taste for his favourite study was early displayed. Proceeding in 1827 to Newfoundland, he there made an entomological collection. After some years he proceeded to Lower Canada, afterwards travelling through the United States. Two works, "The Canadian Naturalist," and "Letters from Alabama," resulted from these travels. He visited Jamaica, and as the result of his researches, on his return to England published works on the ornithology and general zoology of that island. He has since devoted much time to microscopic researches, chiefly in connexion with marine zoology and the aquarium, on which subjects he has published several volumes. His latest work (1860), and that on which his reputation will mainly rest, is "A History of the British Sea Anemones and Corals."

GOUGH, HUGH, LORD, a British soldier, was born in November, 1779, on his father's estate of Woodstown, in the county of Limerick. When fourteen he entered the army as Lieutenant in the 34th Foot, and in 1795 was engaged with his regiment at the capture of Cape Town, and of the Dutch fleet in Saldanha Bay. After taking part in the subsequent campaign in the West Indies, he became Major in the 87th, and went out to Spain in 1809, where he commanded his corps in the hard-fought fields of Talavera, Vittoria, Nivelle, Cadiz, and Tarifa. He was wounded in three of the actions, had a horse shot under him at Talavera, and was by the Duke of Wellington recommended to a commission as Lieutenant-Colonel as a reward for his gallantry. In 1837 he proceeded to India, but shortly afterwards was ordered to China, where he commanded the troops that attacked Canton. All the military operations against China then were under his direction; until the treaty of Nankin in 1842 concluded the war, and General Gough was raised to the Baronetcy, receiving at the same time the thanks of both Houses of Parliament. He was also made a G.C.B. He returned to India in 1843, as Commander-in-chief of the forces there, and led his troops against the Mahrattas, whom he signally defeated at Maharajpore. In 1845 and 1846, the Sikhs becoming inveterate in their animosity to British rule, Sir Hugh Gough commanded in person our army, and obtained the victories of Moodkee, Ferozeshah, and Sobraon, the latter one of the most arduously contested battles ever fought in the East. For his conduct, services, and generalship he was elevated to the Peerage, again receiving the thanks of the Houses of Lords and Commons. In 1848-49 the Sikhs once more attempted to overthrow British dominion, and once more Lord Gough was conqueror, and gained the triumph of Goojerat. For the third time he was thanked by Parliament, and the Crown, to mark his merit, created him Viscount Gough, receiving also a pension from the East India Company, and one from the nation. In 1854 he was promoted as Colonel of the 60th Rifles, as successor to the Duke of Wellington, and Colonel of the Royal Horse Guards, vacant by the death of the Marquis of Anglesea. In June, 1856, Lord Gough was deputed by her Majesty, as her representative, to present to the several officers of the English and French army in the Crimea the insignia of the Order of the Bath. In 1858 he was sworn one of her Majesty's Privy Council in England.

GOUGH, JOHN B., an eminent temperance lecturer, was born in 1817, at Sandgate, Kent. His father had been a soldier, and his mother was the village schoolmistress. At twelve years of age he left his parents and accompanied a family to America, for the purpose of learning a trade. Failing to attain his object after a residence of two years with this family, he, with his father's consent, removed to New York, for the purpose of learning a business there. In 1833 his mother and sister joined him in that city—his father, remaining in England, seeking to commute his pension. His mother died in 1834, and soon after Gough, yielding to temptation, sunk into very dissipated habits. In 1842 he made an energetic effort to reform, and after a hard struggle, in which he was foiled once, he obtained a victory, and since 1843 has been almost constantly engaged in advocating the principles of the temperance reformation, both in Great Britain and America. He has lately returned to America (1860), after lecturing in the leading towns in this country during the last few years.

GOULD, AUGUSTUS ADDISON, an American naturalist, was born on the 23rd April, 1805, at New Ipswich, New Hampshire, United States. Taking the degree of Bachelor of Arts, at the University of Cambridge, New England, in 1825, and of Doctor in Medicine in 1830, he has since that time practised his profession in Boston. His principal published works are—an "Abridgment and Translation of Lamarck's Genera of Shells;" "A Report on the Invertebrata of Massachusetts" (1841) ; "Mollusca and Shells of the United States' Exploring Expedition, under Captain Wilkes, 4to, Washington, 1852, with an Atlas of Plates, in alt. folio ;" "Shells of the North Pacific Expedition," under Capt. Ringgold and Rodgers (ready for the press); and numerous papers in medical and scientific periodicals. The "Principles of Zoology," which were written jointly with Agassiz, and published in 1848, were republished in Bohn's Scientific Library, 1851 ; and translated into German by Professor Brown, Stuttgard, 1851. The "Terrestrial Air-breathing Molluscs of the United States," by Amos Binney — a posthumous work edited, and to a considerable extent written by Mr. Gould—was published, with a biographical memoir, in 1851-55.

GOULD, BENJAMIN APTHORP, was born September 27th, 1824, in Boston, and graduated at Harvard College in 1844, and at Göttingen in 1848. In 1849 he established the "Astronomical Journal," which he edits with great ability. He has contributed to the "Reports of the Naval Astronomical Expedition" (1857), to the "Coast Survey Reports" (1852-57), and to various American scientific journals and periodicals, among others, to the "New York Quarterly," and the "American Journal of Science."

GOULD, JOHN, F.R.S., an English naturalist, was born at Lyme, in Dorsetshire, on the 14th September, 1804. At a very early age he manifested a decided inclination for the study of natural history. Mr. Gould published a description of one hundred Indian birds in his work called "A Century of Birds from the Himalaya Mountains," his accomplished wife being their pictorial illustrator.

This work was succeeded by the "Birds of Europe." In 1838 Mr. Gould proceeded to Australia, for the purpose of enabling him to publish his great works on the birds and mammals of that country. His other publications are—"The Birds of Asia," the "Birds and Mammals of Australia," "A Monograph of the Rhamphastidæ, or Family of Toucans," "A Monograph of the Trogonidæ, or Family of Trogons," "A Monograph of the Odontophorinæ, or Partridges of America," and "A Monograph of the Trochilidæ, or Humming Birds," the figures of which are taken from his unrivalled collection of these birds. All these works are in imperial folio, and it may be fairly said that it has never fallen to the lot of any individual to carry through with such complete success so fine a series of works on natural history.

GRAHAM, RIGHT HON. SIR JAMES ROBERT GEORGE, a distinguished English statesman, was born at Netherby, in Cumberland, in June, 1792. Educated at Westminster, and at Queen's College, Cambridge, he entered public life as Secretary to Lord Montgomerie, in Sicily, and subsequently acted under Lord William Bentinck. In 1818 he was chosen Member of Parliament for Hull, on principles which were quite opposite to those of his father, who accordingly declined to assist him in pecuniary matters. At this time Sir James was an eminent and prolific pamphlet writer, and maintained opinions of a very liberal character. He became Baronet on his father's death, and was elected for Carlisle in 1826, which city he represents at the present time (1860), and in 1830 became, under Earl Grey, First Lord of the Admiralty, where he introduced a system of rigid economy, and generally improved the administration of his department. In 1831 he was connected with the Reform Bill, and assisted greatly in procuring its passage through the House. In 1834, in conjunction with Lord Stanley, Sir James left the Grey cabinet, on what is known as the "Appropriation Clause," and for some years attached himself to no particular party. In 1841 he was Home Secretary under Sir Robert Peel. In 1844 he had the misfortune to become, for a time, the most unpopular of public men. The tragic fate of the brothers Bandiera induced Mazzini to suspect that his letters had been opened in the London post-office, and their secrets betrayed. By an adroit stratagem, suspicion was converted into conviction. The member for Finsbury, Mr. Duncombe, brought the subject before the House of Commons, commenting upon the espionage in a strain of the most withering invective, and assailing the Knight of Netherby with the bitterest personal taunts. When Sir Robert Peel inaugurated his Free-trade policy, Sir James was found by his side combating with all the vigour of his trenchant logic the fallacies of Protection. Sir James Graham retired from office on the defeat of the Irish Coercion Bill, the opposition to which was led by Lord George Bentinck and Mr. Disraeli as a matter of political revenge on Sir Robert Peel, for carrying the repeal of the Corn Laws. He did not again enter any government until he succeeded to his old position as First Lord of the Admiralty, under Lord Aberdeen. He resigned office under Lord Palmerston, from not sharing the opinions of his chief on the justice of the Russian war. In the House of Commons, Admiral Sir Charles Napier assailed Sir James Graham, with great heat, for his mode of fitting out the Baltic fleet, when the country "drifted into war." Sir James denied some of the Admiral's allegations, but the latter, returning to the charge, brought forward undoubted evidence to prove that Sir James was actually in fault; whether from an inordinate desire for economy, or from miscalculation, or from no special wish that the British Fleet should take decisive action against Russia, has never been clearly explained, for all three accusations were preferred against the First Lord of the Admiralty, and only evaded, not rebutted. In 1859, when Lord Derby's Reform Bill was discussed in the House of Commons, Sir James announced himself, in a speech of considerable ability, as holding opinions which verged upon advanced liberalism. He holds no office in the Government formed by Lord Palmerston in 1859, when Lord Derby resigned.

GRAHAM, THOMAS, F.R.S., D.C.L., M.A., Master of the Mint, was born at Glasgow in 1805. He was educated first at the Glasgow Grammar School, and afterwards at the University, where he took the degree of M.A. in 1826. After spending some time in Edinburgh he returned to Glasgow, and having lectured successfully to the Mechanics' Institution, he was elected Professor of Chemistry in the Andersonian University. In 1836 he was admitted a Fellow of the Royal Society, and in 1837 appointed Professor of Chemistry in the London University, having some three years before been awarded the Keith Prize of the Royal Society of Edinburgh for a work on the law of the diffusion of gases. In the meantime he had published several works connected with the science of which he was a professor, the principal of which is the "Elements of Chemistry," a book which has reached several editions in this country, and been translated into the French and German languages. In 1855 the University of Oxford conferred on him the degree of D.C.L., and the same year, when Sir John Herschel retired from the Mastership of the Mint, Dr. Graham was appointed to the office.

GRANT, FRANCIS, R.A. and Hon. Member R.S.A., an English portrait painter, was born in Perthshire, in 1810, and is the fourth son of Francis Grant, Esq., of Kilgraston. He was elected A.R.A. in 1842, and R.A. in 1851. In the commencement of his career he painted several hunting groups, such as the "Meet of His Majesty's Stag Hounds," the engraving of which is familiar to most of those who take an interest in art. This picture, which is now in the possession of the Earl of Chesterfield, was exhibited at the Paris Exhibition, and secured for the artist, with another picture sent at the same time, a first-class gold medal. Mr. Grant also painted the "Melton Hunt," a picture of the same class, which was purchased by the late Duke of Wellington, and is now at Apsley House. Subsequently this artist has especially devoted himself to portrait painting. Some years ago he might have been described as the painter of the *beau monde* in London, the most celebrated fashionable beauties of the day having sat to him. Of late years, however, he has been almost exclusively occupied in painting eminent statesmen, soldiers, lawyers, and divines, among whom may be enumerated several of the bishops, Lord Derby, Lord John Russell, Lord Hardinge, Lord Gough, Sir George Grey, Lord Truro, and Lord Campbell. The Queen and Prince Albert sat to him for an equestrian portrait, which is now in Christ's Hospital. He subsequently painted another equestrian portrait of Her Majesty for the Army and Navy Club. The style of Mr. Grant has been compared most injudiciously with that of Lawrence, whose meretricious and affected manners he has always avoided while aiming at truth and character combined with refinement. He always succeeds in touching his pictures with a certain aristocratic elegance, in arranging the various parts of his figures with grace, and in imparting a poetical character to them by the *pose* of the head.

GRANT, JAMES, a novelist, was born at Edinburgh, on the 1st of Au-

gust, 1822. He is the son of Captain John Grant, and at an early age went with his father and a detachment of soldiers to Newfoundland, where he continued several years. In 1839 he returned to the mother country, when Lord Hill made him an Ensign in the 62nd Regiment, the depôt of which he commanded for some time. Preferring literary to military pursuits, he has since published many works, among which may be enumerated the "Romance of War," "Jane Seton," "Philip Rollo," the "Adventures of an Aide-de-Camp," "Scottish Cavalier," "Bothwell," "Frank Hilton," "The Yellow Frigate," "Phantom Regiment," "The Black Dragoon," "Highlanders of Glenora," "Arthur Blane," "Hollywood Hall," and the "Legends of the Black Watch," which all bear the impress of his peculiar style. His "Philip Rollo" is well known in France as "Les Mousquetaires Écossais;" and his "Romance of War" is a favourite in Germany as the "Hochlander in Spanien." All his romances have been printed repeatedly at Leipzig. In addition to his novels, he has published several historical works —"Memoirs of Kirkaldy of Grange" (1849), "Memorials of the Castle of Edinburgh" (1850), "Life of Montrose" (1856), "Cavaliers of Fortune, or British Heroes in Foreign Wars" (1858), &c. He describes scenes, persons, and incidents, so as to make them stand out like pictures. Almost all his military works, so to call them, have been published in a cheap form, and have also been translated into the French, German, and Swedish languages. Mr. Grant married, in July 1854, the eldest daughter of James Browne, LL.D., Advocate, the well-known author of the "History of the Highlands and Highland Clans," &c. &c.

GRANVILLE, GEORGE LEVESON GOWER, EARL, was born May 11th, 1815. After studying at Eton and Oxford he proceeded to Paris as *attaché*, but returned to England in 1836, when he was elected Member of Parliament for Morpeth. He shortly afterwards made his maiden speech on the Spanish question, which was highly successful. In 1840 he married Maria, daughter of the Duc de Dalberg, who has recently died. He moved the address at the beginning of the next session, and then resigned in order to become Under Secretary of State for Foreign Affairs, and was re-elected in 1841. He succeeded to his father's title in 1846, became Master of her Majesty's Buckhounds, and afterwards Commissioner of Railways and Vice-President of the Board of Trade. As Chairman of the Royal Commission and Finance Committee of the Great Exhibition, Earl Granville contributed largely by his amiability and management to the general success of the enterprise. At the Paris Exhibition he highly pleased the noblesse and municipality by a speech spoken in the purest French and of the happiest allusion. At the close of the Exhibition he was called to the Cabinet, and succeeded the veteran diplomatist Lord Palmerston as Foreign Secretary. He has held office as President of the Council, and Chancellor of the Duchy of Lancaster. In 1856 he was chosen to assist at the coronation of the Czar, Alexander II., with the title of Ambassador Extraordinary. Lord Derby's resignation in 1859, leading to the formation of a new government by Lord Palmerston, Earl Granville was appointed President of the Council and leader of the House of Lords. In 1857 he was appointed Chancellor of the University of London and Knight of the Garter.

GRATTAN, THOMAS COLLEY, a popular novelist, was born in Dublin, 1796. Distantly connected with the celebrated Irish orator, Henry Grattan, he was set apart for the legal profession, but his love of books, not of the law, and his ardent temperament, led him to aspire to military glory. He got his commission, and was on the way to join his regiment, when he heard of the battle of Waterloo, and the conclusion of the war. He then offered himself to the South American army of Independence; but on board the vessel that was to convey him to Venezuela, he met with a lady passenger, to whom he became attached, was married to her, proceeded no further in search of fame at the cannon's mouth, but settled in the south of France, as an author. After great success he was sent to America as British Consul for one of the States. His principal works are— "Philibert," a poetical romance, published at Bordeaux, in 1819; "Highways and Bye Ways; or, Tales of the Roadside," 1823; "Traits of Travel," 1829; "The Heiress of Bruges," 1830; "The History of the Netherlands, to the Belgian Revolution," in 1830; "The History of Switzerland," and the "Legends of the Rhine." While British Consul at Boston, where he remained from 1839 to 1853, he wrote a pamphlet on the "North-Eastern Boundary Question, between Great Britain and the United States."

GRAY, ASA, M.D., an American botanist, was born at Paris, Oneida County, New York, in 1810. He took his degeee of M.D. from the University of the State of New York, in 1831, since which time he has entirely pursued botanical studies. Selected as Botanist to the U. S. South Pacific Exploring Expedition, in 1837, he resigned the appointment in 1838, when chosen almost simultaneously Professor of Botany in the University of Michigan, and Professor of Natural History in Harvard University, Massachusetts, which last situation he actually accepted. Both before and since his appointment to this chair, he has written many valuable books and papers on subjects connected with bo-

tanical science, among which may be enumerated his "Elements of Botany," his "Botanical Text-book," his "Flora of North America," and his "Manual of Botany for the Northern United States," and numerous contributions to the "New York Annals," "The Transactions of the American Philosophical Society," and the Smithsonian "Contributions to Knowledge."

GREELEY, HORACE, American journalist, was born at Amhurst, New Hampshire, February 3, 1811. At the age of fifteen he was indentured to a printer, in Vermont, who published a local journal. He continued there for a few years, but the paper being discontinued he returned to his father's farm, in 1830. He had experienced much in city and country, but nothing to exceed his self-education. As a journeyman, he got employment here and there, for somewhere about three years, when, in 1834, he commenced the "New Yorker," which continued to exist till 1841, when it became the "New York Tribune," a daily paper, the success of which was insured by the character of its predecessor, and of the "Log Cabin," another publication which Mr. Greeley had edited before changing the form of his journal. The "Tribune" was the organ of an opinion; it was bought largely and read; and the founder gained a seat in Congress. Visiting this country in 1851, he was chosen Chairman of one of the Juries at the Great Exhibition, and he wrote to the "Tribune" an account of Europe, and of his observations.

GREY, HENRY, EARL, a British statesman, eldest son of Charles, second Earl, born December 28, 1802, was educated at Cambridge, elected for Winchelsea in 1826, and in 1831 as member for Northumberland, and became Under Secretary of State for the Colonies. A difference of opinion on a plan advocated by Earl Grey, then Lord Howick, for complete Slave Emancipation, led to his resignation. In January, 1834, he was appointed Under Secretary of State for the Home Department, which he resigned in July following, on his father's retirement from the government. In 1835 he became Secretary-at-War under Lord Melbourne. At the general election in 1841, he was elected for Sunderland. In 1845 he entered the House of Peers, and in the following year was Colonial Secretary under Lord John Russell, a position in which he attained a large measure of unpopularity, which led to his resignation. Like his father, he seems to be a strange combination of liberal ideas and aristocratic prepossessions. As a statesman, Earl Grey holds an isolated position, which would seem to arise from the simple fact that he makes it a rule to think for himself. He is consequently termed "crotchety," but with no more cause than might have been attributed to his father, who, except in one or two instances, was one of the most consistent statesmen of his era. Unlike the great Earl of the name, however, he has few if any followers, and his temperament is described as by no means conciliatory. Lord Grey is the author of a work entitled "The Colonial Policy of Lord John Russell's Administration," published in 1853.

GREY, Right Hon. Sir George, Baronet, cousin of Earl Grey, was born at Gibraltar, in 1799, and graduated at Oriel College, Oxford, in 1821, where he highly distinguished himself. He joined the legal profession in 1826, and was elected for Devonport in 1832. His political views and talents have connected him with liberal measures, and he has held the offices of Colonial and Home Secretary under various administrations. He was Home Secretary under Lord Palmerston in 1855, but on that nobleman giving way to the Earl of Derby, Sir George necessarily resigned. When Lord Palmerston was again called upon to act in 1859, as Premier, he appointed Sir George Grey to the office of Chancellor of the Duchy of Lancaster. Sir George Grey is a G.C.B., and a Deputy Lieutenant for Northumberland.

GREY, Sir George, K.C.B., Governor of the Cape of Good Hope, son of Lieutenant-Colonel Grey, of the 30th Regiment, was born at Lisburn, Ireland, on the 14th April, 1812 ; his father having fallen at the siege of Badajoz, three days before his birth. He was educated for the army at the Royal Military College, Sandhurst, where he studied with the highest distinction. On attaining the rank of Captain, in 1836, he offered his services to the Colonial Secretary, to explore Australia, in conjunction with Lieutenant Lushington. The interior of Australia was then comparatively a *terra incognita*, and his offer being accepted by Lord Glenelg, he departed on his mission in 1837. He commenced his labours in November of the same year, and after experiencing many difficulties and dangers in the enterprise, returned to the Mauritius, in April, 1838. Resting a few months, he started in the September following to explore the Swan River district, returning in 1840 from that expedition. On his return to England, he commenced his "Journals of Two Expeditions of Discovery in North-Western and Western Australia," but had to lay them aside on being appointed Governor of South Australia, in which office he showed that administrative ability which has since characterised his career. Having acquired the native language, he was enabled to hold friendly personal intercourse with them. In 1846 he became Governor of New Zealand, and in that office his tact and moderation, added to the knowledge he acquired of the native language, served to calm down many asperities. His government, wise and conciliatory, became popular, and he maintained his position with advantage until

1854, when he was appointed Governor and Commander-in-Chief of the Cape of Good Hope, having previously, in 1848, been created a K.C.B. His government at the Cape displayed the same sagacity and calm energy which had rendered his measures so popular elsewhere. From turbulence he produced order, from discontent, peace and growing prosperity; but in 1858 the Home Government interfered with such utter want of discrimination, and clung to their unwise schemes with such pertinacity, that Sir George Grey perceived no other course open to him than resignation of his post. He returned to England, but so strong was the feeling at the Cape, that several leading colonists followed him to London, waited upon Ministers, urged the damage that would inevitably ensue from his removal, and in 1859 he was requested by the Colonial administration to resume his post. Without any question, he is the most popular Governor that ever set foot in our South African possessions. Besides his "Journals," already noticed, Sir George Grey has published "Polynesian Mythology: an Ancient Traditional History of the New Zealand Race."

GRIFFIN, JOHN JOSEPH, an English chemist and writer on science, was born in London, in 1802. He is the author of "Chemical Recreations," a work which has done more to popularize the study of chemistry in Britain than any other publication. Mr. Griffin is also author of a "Treatise on the Blowpipe," "The Radical Theory of Chemistry," and of a "System of Crystallography." To him the chemical manipulator is indebted for the invention of numerous cheap and handy articles of apparatus.

GRIMM, JACOB LUDWIG, a German writer, was born at Hanau on the 4th January, 1785. After studying for some time for the legal profession, he turned his attention to literary pursuits, and eventually became librarian at Wilhelmshohe in Westphalia. After receiving an appointment at Cassel, he went to Göttingen, where he was elected one of the professors of the university. Being expelled for political reasons from his professorship, he went to Berlin, in which city he still remains. He has contributed many valuable works relating to the history and archæology of Germany, such as his "German Mythology," "German Antiquities," with others relating to the characteristics of his countrymen, and devotes himself most energetically in bringing to light incidents and traditions of "Fatherland."

GRISI, GIULIA, an Italian singer and operatic performer, was born at Milan, in 1812. She is the daughter of an officer of engineers, who served in the army of the great Napoleon. Early remarked as possessing musical talent of no common description, her faculty was first developed by Marliani, the composer. Having received a good education, lessons from her sister, then a prima donna, and other teachers of ability, and encouragement from her friends, she made her first appearance in the theatre of Bologna, in Rossini's "Zelmira." She is said to have been then a beautiful girl,—only seventeen,— her voice a resonant contralto; her manner graceful and "winning. Rossini having predicted her future fame, she was engaged at La Scala, of Milan. There she met Bellini, who adapted, expressly with a view to her powers, the part of Adelgisa, in Norma, his greatest work. Pasta was the Norma on the first representation; and Bellini's music fell flat upon the ears of the audience, until Grisi's "Deh ! conte," roused them into enthusiasm. The opera was performed forty nights. Pasta's wondrous acting inspired Grisi with the ambition of being a great tragedienne: how she overcame obstacles, and tutored her voice into a superb soprano, is well known. She appeared first in England in 1834, in conjunction with Rubini, a magnificent tenor ; the musical world was enraptured. Her ambition was gratified, for she ultimately succeeded Pasta, though not until after the death of Malibran. In 1839 "Lucrezia Borgia" was produced, and since then her career has been unparalleled; and the recent announcement of her retirement from the stage has excited great regret. In her younger days she married M. de Melcy, a French gentleman ; but the marriage has been dissolved, and she is now the wife of Signor Mario, the great tenor.

GROTE, GEORGE, M.P., a politician and historian, was born in 1794, at Clayhill, Beckenham, Kent. He is descended from a German family, established in London during the early part of the last century. Receiving his education at the Charter-House school, he became connected with Messrs. Prescott, Grote, and Co.'s Bank in 1810. In 1832 he was returned as one of the members for the City of London, retaining his seat till 1841, when he retired. His political principles are of the advanced liberal school ; and for a number of years he was the zealous, though unsuccessful promoter of the Ballot Question in the House of Commons. It is, however, as a scholar and historical writer that Mr. Grote has earned distinction. Besides his great work "The History of Greece," he is the author of several talented pamphlets, and contributions to Reviews.

GUDIN, THÉODORE, a well-known French marine painter, was born at Paris, in 1804. After serving as an officer in the Royal Navy, he took part in the African campaign of 1830, when he received on the field of battle the Cross of an officer of the Legion of Honour. Having, in 1824, exhibited a picture at the Salon, he obtained the second-class medal. He was appointed first painter of the Royal Navy,

by Charles X. In the execution of this commission, which bore date 1838, Gudin worked assiduously for ten years, when the revolution of February, 1848, terminated his labours. During that decade his facile pencil had painted a large number of pictures for the royal galleries. Gudin having married the daughter of General Lord James Hay, has frequently resided in this country, and his pictures of Scottish scenery were produced during these visits. The Revolution of 1848 prevented twenty-seven of the series, painted for Versailles, from being placed beside the others ; the Emperor has, however, expressed a wish that the gallery should be completed by the addition of these pictures, which, indeed, are enumerated in the catalogues published in 1848. The last works of M. Gudin are destined to perpetuate two important events in the history of imperial policy, the one being "The Entrance of the Emperor to the Roads of Brest, on the occasion of his voyage to Brittany;" and the other, the "Arrival of the Queen of England at Cherbourg." These huge pictures, which are on the scale of panoramic views, like most of M. Gudin's productions, have met with high praise from the French art critics, and more particularly in "L'Europe Artistique" of 11th March last, where they are even said to be in advance of the previous works of the author.

GUIZOT, FRANÇOIS PIERRE-GUILLAUME, an historian, ex-minister of France under Louis-Philippe, was born October, 1787. His father, an advocate of Nismes, fell a victim to the French Revolution only three days after the triumph of Robespierre over Danton, Camille Desmoulins, and the men of the Committee of Public Safety. After this fatal catastrophe, Madame Guizot left Nismes to seek at Geneva consolation for her great sorrow in the bosom of her family, and in a solid education for her children. Guizot, placed at the Gymnasium of Geneva, devoted himself ardently to study. The child had no childhood, his playthings were books, and at the end of twelve years the young scholar was able to read, in their respective languages, the great masterpieces of the ancient and the modern world. Having completed his collegiate studies with brilliant success, M. Guizot proceeded to Paris in 1805, to prepare himself for the bar. The law schools had disappeared amidst the revolutionary whirlwind, and the young student, not caring for the imperfect knowledge private seminaries might supply, resolved to master it in solitude. The serious nature of the Genevese scholar found little that was genial in the dissolute society of the metropolis of France. The first year of his residence in Paris was one of sadness and isolation. In the following year he became attached, as tutor, to the household of M. Stapfer, minister for Switzerland at the French Court. This connexion introduced Guizot, not only to some of the most distinguished literary persons of the time, but to the society of the woman who was destined to exercise so noble and beneficial an influence over his whole life. Born of a distinguished family that had been ruined by the revolution, Mademoiselle Pauline de Meulan had found resources in an education as solid as it was varied, and, to support herself, had entered upon the career of a journalist. A serious malady, the result of excessive toil, obliged her to suspend her literary labours. Her situation threatened to become critical, hope had almost withered into despair, when she received an anonymous letter entreating her to be tranquil, and offering to discharge her duties on the "Publiciste" during the continuance of her illness. The letter was accompanied by an admirably written article modelled upon her own style. The article was accepted—published, and a similar contribution received every week until the editress was convalescent. Not until repeatedly solicited to disclose his incognito did the young student reveal himself. Five years after this romantic episode, Mademoiselle de Meulan became Madame Guizot. During these five years Guizot was busily occupied in those historical studies from which he has since reaped so large a harvest of fame. In 1809 he published his first work, a "Dictionnaire des Synonymes." In 1812 he became Assistant-Professor of History in the Faculty of Letters of the Sorbonne, and subsequently obtained complete possession of that chair. Here it was Guizot formed that attachment with the then Professor of the Philosophy of History, which has so often associated his name with that of M. Royer Collard. Guizot's career, hitherto purely literary, was now to become identified with the political fortunes of France. The post of Secretary-General to the Minister of the Interior, was his first step in the path of politics. In this position he took part in preparing those laws against the press which were, in 1814, presented to the Chambers by the Minister of the Interior, M. de Montesquieu. Placed amidst contending factions, more conservative than satisfied the instincts of the one, and more constitutional than suited the tastes of the other, Guizot in office was but ill at ease. Napoleon's return from Elba released him from the difficulties of his position, and he resumed his occupation as Professor of History. When the fall of the Emperor became evident, Guizot repaired to Ghent to plead the cause of the Charter before Louis XVIII., and was afterwards appointed Secretary-General to the Minister of Justice. In the violent storm which shook the Chamber of 1815, the constitutionalist did his utmost to moderate the partisans of absolute royalty, who censured him severely for his constitutional principles of action.

In 1818 he was made Councillor of State with an office specially formed for him. On the fall of the Ministry of Decazes, trampled upon as revolutionary by the counter revolution, Guizot accompanied the constitutional party into opposition, combating, with all the energy of his powerful pen, the administration of Villèle. Villèle avenged the antagonism of Guizot, by interdicting his lectures as professor. Renouncing the questions of the hour, Guizot now undertook that series of great historical works which have given him so distinguished a place in literature. At this time it was that the collection of "Memoirs Relative to the English Revolution." "The History of the English Revolution," "Memoirs Relative to the History of France," and "Essays on Shakspeare," were successively published. In 1827 death deprived him of the companion of his labours—that beloved wife whose serene and lofty intelligence had sustained him amid the agitations of his career. On the fall of the Villèle Ministry, in 1828, Guizot, reinstated in his professorial chair, began his lectures on the "History of Civilization in Europe." In 1828 he married his second wife—a niece of his first wife, who advised the union. On the formation of the Polignac Cabinet, he was elected for Lisieux, and voted for the address of the 221, adding to his vote these words: "Truth has already trouble enough in penetrating to the council of kings—let us not send it there pale and feeble." It was his wish that the throne should have one other chance, but the warning voice was unheeded. On the eve of the revolution, Guizot drew up the protest of the deputies against the ordinances of July; and, on the fall of monarchy, he read in the Chamber the proclamation which constituted the Duke of Orleans Lieutenant-General of France. Upon the accession of Louis-Philippe, in 1830, Guizot became Minister of the Interior, but only held office for a short time. In the Soult Cabinet, formed in 1832, he was Minister of Public Instruction, and in that capacity did much for the cause of education in France. He was a great favourite of the citizen King, and had the King only followed his stern counsel, the throne of the barricades had probably still stood erect—unmoved—unshaken. The two darkest spots on the fame of M. Guizot, as a statesman, are those which relate to the affairs of Tahiti, and the conduct of the Spanish marriages. It has been averred that the Minister acted only under the influence of the Crown in promoting the union of the Duc de Montpensier with the Infanta, but in the whole matter there was an amount of intrigue which Guizot should have resisted at any risk of the King's displeasure, and which ultimately assisted in the downfall of both.

GUTHRIE, THOMAS, D.D., a theologian, orator, and philanthropist, born at Brechin, in 1803. After studying in the University of Edinburgh, and entering the Scottish Church, he acquired a knowledge of medicine at Paris, with the view of adding to his usefulness as a clergyman. In 1830 he obtained a living in the county of Forfar. Subsequently he was appointed to the collegiate church of Old Greyfriars, Edinburgh; and in 1840 to a new church built for him. When the non-intrusion controversy arose, he was found by the side of Dr. Chalmers, combating with all the energy and all the earnestness of his nature for those principles of spiritual independence for which his party afterwards relinquished the emoluments and position of ministers of the National Church. No man exerted a wider influence upon the popular mind in connexion with that great struggle; but when the contest was over, scorning to sustain party antipathies, he betook himself to that career of active benevolence with which his name has long been so honourably associated. It is owing to his eloquence and energy that the Ragged Schools were first begun in Edinburgh, an institution which has effected much in the reformation of the young Arabs of our great manufacturing towns. Dr. Guthrie is an active promoter of the temperance movement, to which he has devoted a large amount of zealous effort. "The City : its Sins and Sorrows," is a memorial of his labours in that important walk of philanthropy. "The Gospel in Ezekiel," and "Christ the Inheritance of the Saints," embody good illustrations of his general pulpit efforts. In illustrative and pictorial power, Dr. Guthrie is without a rival among the pulpit orators of Britain.

HAGENBACH, Charles Rodolphe, a German Protestant theologian, was born at Basle, in 1801. The son of a distinguished naturalist and professor of anatomy and botany, he studied first at Bonn, then at Berlin, and afterwards at Basle, and was, in 1828, appointed Professor of Theology. With ample leisure to study and write, he has applied his powers with effect. Almost all his works relate to ecclesiastical history and theology; his book on the " Spirit and History of the Reformation" being perhaps his most satisfactory, as it seems to be the most earnest, of his writings. His " Guide to Christian Instruction" is an excellent work. His "Compendium of the History of Doctrines " has been translated into English by Carl and Buck. Edinburgh : 1846.

HAGHE, Louis, a water-colour painter, was born at Tournay, in Belgium in 1806, but has long resided in England. He started in his artistic career as a lithographer, his stone-drawings bringing him into great repute. He entered into partnership with Mr. Day, and produced some of the most important lithographic works published in Britain. He has a special aptitude for depicting the quaint old Flemish streets, and the richly decorated interiors of his native country ; his pictures are characterized by consummate skill in manipulation. He holds a prominent position in the New Society of Painters in Water Colours. Those who know his works may be surprised to learn that, full and detailed though his pictures are, they are executed with the left hand. For some years past he has devoted his time to painting in oil, which is now his chief study.

HAHN-HAHN, Countess Von, a German poetess, was born at Tressow, in 1805, and is daughter of Count Charles Von Hahn. She married her relation Count Frederic Von Hahn-Hahn, but the union was unfortunate, and it was dissolved by the Courts in 1829. Her poetic taste induced her to travel over most of Europe, and to visit the East. In 1850 the Countess abjured the Lutheran creed for the faith of the Roman Catholic Church. She now resides at the Convent of the Good Shepherd, near Mayence. She is the author of many works, both in prose and verse, the most remarkable of which are her novels : "The Countess Faustina," "Ulrich," " Sigismund Forster," and "Cecil;" and her books of travel, entitled "Beyond the Mountains," " Letters on Germany," "Reminiscences of France," "A Northern Tour," "Oriental Tales," and "From Babylon to Jerusalem."

HALEVY, Jacques-Elie Fromental, a French musical composer, was born at Paris, in 1799. His original name was Levy, his family being Jewish by race, as well as of the Jewish persuasion, to which he himself adheres. In 1809 he entered the Conservatoire and made such progress that when twelve years of age he carried off the prize for harmony against all competitors. Having studied composition under Cherubini, that great master, when he had occasion to visit London, left Halevy to conduct his class at the Conservatoire. In 1819, after obtaining the first prize for musical composition at the Institute, he visited Italy, and remained there some years, and it was not till 1827 that his opera, "L'Artisan," was brought out at the Opéra Comique, followed, in the same year, at the same theatre, by "Il Dilletante," and in 1829, at the Royal Italian Theatre, by "Clari," which he wrote for the celebrated Malibran. Other works appeared in rapid succession, until 1835, when he produced "La Juive," his *chef d'œuvre*. He afterwards brought out "L'Eclair," "Guido et Genevra," "La Reine de Chypre," and "Charles VI." In 1846 he wrote for the Comic Opera "Les Mousquetaires de la Reine," which had a great run, and in 1848, "Le Val d'Andorre," which was performed for 165 consecutive nights. He has since produced "La Tempestà," "Le Juif Errant," "La Magicienne," &c. He is admitted to be one of the first of living composers. He is a Professor at the Conservatoire, a Commander of the Legion of Honour, a Member of the Institute, and perpetual Secretary of the Academy of the Fine Arts, in which capacity he has written several interesting notices of artistic celebrities.

HALIBURTON, THE HONOURABLE MR. JUSTICE, M.P., was born in Nova Scotia, on 17th Dec., 1796, his father belonging to an ancient Scottish family. He graduated at King's College in that province, and became a Barrister-at-Law and member of the House of Assembly. In 1829 he was appointed Justice of Common Pleas, and in 1840 Judge of the Supreme Court. He resigned this appointment in 1850, and removed to England. Two years afterwards the honorary degree of D.C.L. was conferred upon him by the University of Oxford, and in 1859 he was returned to Parliament for the borough of Launceston. He has written the following works : "A General Description of Nova Scotia," "History of Nova Scotia," "Sam Slick, the Clockmaker" (1st, 2nd, and 3rd Series), "The Letter Bag of the Great Western," "Bubbles of Canada," "Rule and Misrule of the English in America," "Wise Saws and Modern Instances," "Nature and Human Nature," &c. The work by which he is most extensively known is "Sam Slick, the Clockmaker," which has been translated into several European languages, has passed through many editions in England, and has been republished in most of the principal towns of the United States, where it has been more extensively read than most works of the present century. A late reviewer remarks, that "Sam Slick" should become an immortal book from its wit, genuine humour, and profound knowledge of human nature.

HALL, MRS. ANNA MARIA FIELDING, a novelist and dramatic writer, born in Dublin, in 1802. She is descended, on the mother's side, from an ancient Huguenot family, who emigrated to England after the revocation of the Edict of Nantes ; and on the father's side, from a younger branch of the family of Fielding, to which the great English novelist belonged. She quitted Ireland at the early age of fifteen ; but her impressions were so vivid, and her recollections so permanent, that in her first works she could paint with the utmost freshness the scenes of her youth. In 1824 she married Mr. S. C. Hall ; and naturally desiring to co-operate with him in his literary labours, devoted the energies of her mind to literature. In 1826 she wrote her "Sketches of Irish Character." Her first novel, "The Buccaneer," was published in 1832. "The Outlaw," "Uncle Horace," "Marian," "The Whiteboy," and "A Woman's Story,"—novels—followed in succession. But, probably, the works on which her reputation mainly rests, are the "Tales of Woman's Trials," and "Pilgrimages to English Shrines." These were first printed, as was also her story of "Midsummer Eve," in the "Art Journal,"—a work conducted by her husband, and to which she has been a continual and valuable contributor. She is also the author of three successful dramas :—"The French Refugee," performed without intermission, seventy nights, at the St. James's Theatre, under Braham's management ; "The Groves of Blarney," in which Power sustained the three principal parts during a whole season, at the Adelphi ; and "Mabel's Curse," dramatized from one of her own stories. Another of her plays was lost with the lamented actor, when he perished in the "President." Mrs. Hall has also written many books for children; among others, "Uncle Sam's Money Box," which has obtained a very large circulation both at home and abroad. Mrs. Hall has enjoyed that kind of reputation of which a woman is ever most justly proud : a desire to extend the influence of religion, virtue, and loyalty, without any admixture of sectarian bias ; while in all her books on Ireland, she has laboured, and not unsuccessfully, to lessen or remove the prejudices which have long existed against our fellow-subjects of the sister isle.

HALL, SAMUEL CARTER, was born at Topsham, in 1801. He entered the Temple in 1824, and was afterwards called to the bar. Turning his attention to literature, he became editor of the "New Monthly Magazine" in 1830. He was at the same time employed as a political writer for newspapers, both in London and in the provinces. When the "Annuals" were at the height of their success, he edited one of the best, under the name of "The Amulet." He was also the editor of "The Book of Gems of British Poets and Painters," "The Book of British Ballads," "The Baro-

nial Halls of England," and other illustrated works, which obtained large popularity. The work to which he is mainly indebted for reputation, however, "Ireland : its Scenery and Character," was the joint production of Mr. and Mrs. S. C. Hall. The statistics, political inquiries, and the descriptive and heavy parts of the book were written by him, while the illustrative and characteristic sketches with which the work abounds, were supplied by the airy and fertile pen of Mrs. Hall. In 1839 Mr. Hall commenced the publication of "The Art-Union Journal," subsequently entitled "The Art Journal," and that work he has ever since conducted, having superintended the issue to twenty-one yearly volumes ; a rare circumstance in periodical literature. It is the only publication in Europe by which Art is adequately represented ; and it has exercised a great and very beneficial influence on the fine arts in this country, as well as on British industry. Mr. Hall is a Fellow of various learned bodies. Of late years he has delivered a number of public lectures, the most attractive of his series being that which he terms " Written Portraits of the Authors of the Age, from Personal Acquaintance ;" the list comprising nearly every name of note during the last forty years. Circumstances having brought Mr. Hall into relationship, more or less, with Scott, Southey, Hannah Moore, Thomas Moore, Mrs. Opie, Wordsworth, Coleridge, Montgomery, Miss Mitford, Miss Edgeworth, Mrs. Hemans, Theodore Hook, Thomas Campbell, Miss Landon, Lady Morgan, Thomas Hood, and many other "celebrities" of his time ; he is enabled to give personal sketches and reminiscences of a deeply interesting character.

HALLECK, FITZ-GREENE, an American poet, was born at Guilford, Connecticut, in August, 1795. He became connected with a bank in New York in 1813, and resided in that city for many years, as confidential agent for the American Rothschild, John Jacob Astor. Mr. Halleck commenced contributing to the journals of the day at an early age; and, when settled in New York, was known as an associate of the wits about town. In 1821 Mr. Halleck published his largest poem, "Fanny," a satire upon the literature and politics of the time, in the measure of "Don Juan." In 1822-23 he visited Europe; and the reflections suggested by his travels are embodied in his poems on Burns and on Alnwick castle, which, with some other pieces, were published in 1827. The "Burns" poem is one of the finest tributes to the memory of the bard the Muses have ever offered at his shrine.

HALLIWELL, JAMES ORCHARD, an author and editor, chiefly distinguished as a Shaksperian critic, was born in Sloane-street, Chelsea, in 1821. He commenced his literary career about 1838, and in the following year was elected a Fellow of the Royal Society, and afterwards of many other scientific and literary associations. His first work of much importance was a "Dictionary of Archaic and Provincial Words" (1847), a glossary of upwards of fifty thousand words of obsolete and provincial English, with numerous references and examples from recondite books. He has edited many of the works issued by the Camden, Percy, and Shaksperian Societies, between 1839 and 1850; amongst which may be noticed "Warkworth's Chronicle," "The Chronicle of William de Rishanger," "The First Sketch of Shakspeare's 'Merry Wives of Windsor,'" "Tarlton's Works," the "First Sketches of Henry the Sixth," and the "Thornton Romances." In 1848 appeared his "Life of Shakspeare," in the preparation of which he had the advantage of the unrestricted use of the records of Stratford-on-Avon. This biography, remodelled and partly re-written, has been introduced into his folio edition of Shakspeare, now in progress, nine volumes of which have appeared. This large work, commenced in 1853, aims at a greater elaboration of Shaksperian criticism, than has hitherto been attempted; a thick folio volume sufficing to include no more than two plays, with the editor's copious introductions and annotations. Amongst Mr. Halliwell's miscellaneous writings may be noticed, "An Introduction to the 'Midsummer Night's Dream,'" 8vo, 1841; "An Essay on the Character of Sir John Falstaff," 12mo, 1841; "Popular Rhymes and Nursery Tales," 8vo, 1849; and "An Introduction to the Evidences of Christianity," 8vo, 1859.

HAMILTON, THE REV. JAMES, D.D., minister of the English Presbyterian Church, Regent Square, London, was born in 1814, his father being the Rev. William Hamilton, minister of Strathblane. From a small parish in Perthshire, where he acted as assistant-minister he was called to a chapel-of-ease in Edinburgh, and in 1841 to the National Scotch Church, London, formerly presided over by the Rev. Edwd. Irving. He has published several works, among which the best known are "Life in Earnest," "The Mount of Olives," "The Happy Home," and the "Memoirs of Lady Colquhoun." He also edited "Excelsior," a periodical intended to promote the religious and intellectual progress of young men, and has published under the title of "Our Christian Classics," four volumes of "Readings from English Divines, with Biographical and Critical Sketches of the principal authors."

HAMPDEN, RENN DICKSON, D.D., bishop of Hereford, born in 1792, in Barbadoes, of an old English family. He entered Oriel College, Oxford, in 1810. Having been successively fellow and tutor; public examiner in classics; Bampton lecturer; professor of moral philosophy;

and regius professor of divinity, in 1847 Dr. Hampden was appointed bishop of Hereford. This appointment caused a fierce controversy in the English Church. Dr. Hampden's contributions to philosophical literature are numerous and valuable. His articles on Socrates, Plato, and Aristotle, in the "Encyclopædia Britannica," and the review of the scholastic philosophy in the "Encyclopædia Metropolitana," have elicited the commendation of all competent critics. With reference to his review of the philosophy of the schoolmen, Hallam has thus spoken :—"Dr. Hampden has the merit of having been the only Englishman, past or present, since the revival of letters, who has penetrated far into the wilderness of scholasticism." Sir William Hamilton, however, says of him :—"Dr. Whately's errors relative to Induction are, however, surpassed by those of another able writer, Mr. Hampden, in regard both to that process itself, and to the Aristotelian exposition of its nature. Southey condemned the appointment of Dr. Hampden as insulting to the University of Oxford, and not better than the conduct of James II. in obtruding a Romish president upon Magdalen, while the "Edinburgh Review" alleges that the Doctor was persecuted by blind consciences, corrupted by the habitual indulgence of evil passions. Among his principal works are "The Scholastic Philosophy considered in its relation to Christian Theology," preached in 1832 (Oxford, 1832); "Philosophical Evidences of Christianity;" "Lectures on Moral Philosophy;" "Parochial Sermons;" and four other Sermons (1836); "Sermons before the University of Oxford" (1848).

HANNAY, JAMES, an author and journalist, was born at Dumfries in February, 1827. Descended from a good Scotch family, he was educated in England, entered the Royal Navy in March, 1840, and served under various commanders until July, 1845. Then relinquishing the profession and devoting himself to literary pursuits, he became contributor to the leading journals and periodicals, his first sustained work being "Singleton Fontenoy," published in 1850, which immediately gave him a position among men of letters. He delivered, in 1853, a course of lectures on "Satire and Satirists," issued in a volume the year after, and published in 1855 the remarkably clever novel of "Eustace Conyers," which has been translated into German. In 1857 he was induced to stand for Dumfries, but though the mass of the people were in his favour, he was defeated—polling 185 votes. He is the author of a collection of fugitive naval pieces under the title of "Sketches in Ultramarine." Mr. Hannay has recently removed to Edinburgh to edit the "Courant" newspaper.

HANOVER, KING OF, See GEORGE V.

HARDWICKE, CHARLES PHILIP YORKE, EARL OF, an English statesman, late Privy Seal in the ministry of Lord Derby, and eldest son of the late Admiral Sir J. S. Yorke, was born on the 2nd of April, 1799. Educated at Harrow and the Royal Naval College, Portsmouth, he entered the navy early, and assisted at the bombardment of Algiers, when serving in the Queen Charlotte. He was returned member of Parliament for Reigate, in 1831, and in 1834, on the death of his uncle, was called to the House of Lords. He was a Lord in Waiting under Sir Robert Peel in 1841, Postmaster-General under Lord Derby in 1852, and Lord Privy Seal under the same premier in 1858. In 1854 he was promoted to be Rear-Admiral on the reserve list.

HARRIS, SIR WILLIAM SNOW, a distinguished English physicist, member of the Royal College of Surgeons, and Fellow of the Royal Society, was born at Plymouth in 1792. He has devoted himself through life to researches in physical science, especially in electricity, magnetism, and meteorology. In June, 1831, he was admitted a Fellow of the Royal Society ; in 1835 he received the Copley Medal, one of the highest honours this body can award ; in 1841 he received an acknowledgment from the Civil List for his scientific discoveries ; and in 1845 he received two honorary presents from the Emperor of Russia as a recognition of the practical value of his inventions. He was knighted by Her Majesty in 1847. The value of the researches of Sir William Snow Harris are, perhaps, not so widely known as they ought to be. He has the merit of having placed upon an intelligible and satisfactory basis the great question of the protection of ships and buildings by metallic conductors, a problem which for the best part of a century had divided the opinion of the eminent scientific men of Europe. The disputes as to whether metallic conductors attracted lightning, whether painted conductors were preferable or not to conductors terminating in rounded or spherical surfaces, whether a lightning conductor was liable to draw down upon a building more electricity than it could transmit, and so bring upon it that destruction it was intended to obviate, have been by Sir William Snow Harris completely set at rest, and that too by a course of laborious inductive observations and experiments. He has succeeded, by a general and comprehensive system of metallic conductors carried out on the hulls and masts of Her Majesty's ships, in placing the vessels of the royal navy beyond the reach of the destructive agency of lightning. During the great war Great Britain lost upwards of £10,000 a-year by damage done to the navy by thunder storms. Within five years forty sail of the line and thirty-five frigates and sloops were placed *hors de combat* from the same cause. Since the views of Sir W. Snow Harris have been acted upon not one vessel has been

damaged during a period of fully thirty years. His principles have been carried out in buildings on shore—such as the new Houses of Parliament, the Queen's palaces, the Government gunpowder magazines, the royal gunpowder works, &c. In this way Sir W. Snow Harris has given security to above ten millions of public property in storms of lightning. He is the inventor of various electrical instruments, and of a valuable new binnacle and steering compass. From what we have said the reader will understand the eulogium of Baron Charles Dupin when he said, in 1851, "Let governments, science, and humanity, proclaim the merits of Snow Harris." The scientific papers of Sir W. S. Harris, are very numerous, and will be found in "The Philosophical Transactions," "The Transactions of the Royal Society of Edinburgh," the "Nautical Magazine," and the "British Association Reports." He is, besides, the author of a work on "Thunderstorms," one volume, 8vo, Parker, London ; and an "Elementary Treatise on Electricity," published by Weale, and translated into French, by M. Garnault.

HART, SOLOMON ALEXANDER, R.A., a painter, was born at Plymouth, in April, 1806. After being some time at an engraver's in London, he studied in the Royal Academy, and turned his attention to miniature painting. He soon afterwards determined to pursue the higher branches of his profession, and accordingly undertook the illustration of historical subjects. His picture, "The Elevation of the Law," soon gained him considerable reputation, and in 1835 he became an Associate of the Royal Academy. Mr. Hart has been a most indefatigable painter, and amongst his numerous productions the following have been much admired—"Interior of a Jewish Synagogue at the time of the Reading of the Law," now in the South Kensington Museum, "Wolsey and Buckingham,"

"Milton Visiting Galileo in the time of the Inquisition, "The Parting of Sir Thomas More and his Daughter, "Reading for Honours," and "Reading for Pluck," &c. In 1840 Mr. Hart, in consequence of the exhibition of a large picture of "Lady Jane Grey at the Place of her Execution," was promoted to the rank of a Royal Academician, and he is now Professor of Painting in that Institution.

HARVEY, GEORGE, a Scottish painter, born at St. Ninian's, near Stirling, in 1806. He was apprenticed to a bookseller, but he devoted himself enthusiastically to his favourite study. At the age of eighteen, he entered the drawing school of the Trustees' Academy, Edinburgh, and soon attracted special attention by his superior powers. When, in 1826, the Scottish artists agreed to establish an academy, George Harvey joined the new institution, and since then he has zealously devoted himself to its interests. George Harvey is pre-eminently a Scottish painter; and among the small band of artists who have consecrated their genius to Scottish subjects, is unquestionably the most highly gifted. His best known works are "Covenanters Preaching," "The Covenanters' Baptism," "The Battle of Drumclog," "The Covenanters' Communion," "Curlers," "First Reading of the Bible in the Crypt of old St. Paul's," "A Highland Funeral," "Quitting the Manse." An intense sympathy with whatever is noble in Scottish story animates the painter, giving depth, power, and truthfulness to all his productions.

HAWTHORNE, NATHANIEL, an American writer, was born at Salem, Massachusetts, about 1807, and graduated at Bowdoin College, Maine, in 1825. His first literary production was a romance, published anonymously at Boston in 1832, and followed in 1837 by his "Twice-told Tales," of which he gave a second series in 1842. These had already appeared in "The Token," and in other periodicals. After publishing a collection entitled "Mosses from an Old Manse," he received a government appointment, and in his leisure hours conceived some of his most charming productions. In 1850 he published "The Scarlet Letter," a romance of deep interest, and written with great power. In the following year "The House with the Seven Gables" appeared, and in 1852 "The Blithedale Romance," wherein he expresses his experiences as a member of the Brook Farm Community. In the next year he was made American Consul at Liverpool. Mr. Hawthorne has published several works besides those already named, amongst which are his "Life of Henry Pierce, President of the United States," "The Wonder Book for Girls and Boys," "True Stories from History and Biography," and other minor productions. He ranks as one of the most popular of American writers, and his works have been extensively read and admired in this country.

HAYES, MRS. CATHERINE. Miss Hayes, one of the most celebrated vocalists of the age, was born in Limerick, in 1820. Her taste for music and talent for its acquirement were early displayed, and, taken under the patronage of the Bishop of the diocese, she was placed as a pupil with Signor Sapio, then an eminent teacher of music in Dublin. The progress of Miss Hayes was remarkable. She afterwards studied under Viardot Garcia at Paris, and Ronconi at Milan. Her first appearance was at Marseilles, in "I Puritani," in 1845, where her success was so great that no one knew her to be a *débutante*. She was afterwards engaged for La Scala, at Milan, where the beauty of her voice and the purity and simplicity of her style, at once commanded a success beyond even the expectations of her friends. In the following spring Miss Hayes visited Vienna, where she was equally successful. She then visited

Venice, returned to Vienna, and visited Rome, Florence, and Genoa, adding to her fame by each performance. In 1849 she entered into an engagement at the Italian Opera, Covent Garden. She came before the London public with a reputation scarcely inferior to that which heralded Jenny Lind. Her success in London was decided. At the close of the season she sang in the "Messiah," and with such success as to establish her reputation as one of the greatest living interpreters of sacred music. After visiting Ireland, where her reception was enthusiastic, she accepted an engagement in the United States in 1851. She travelled and performed in all the great cities of the United States, and then proceeded to California and South America. After performing in Australia and India, and Singapore and Batavia, she returned to London in 1855, when she appeared at Covent Garden with still greater favour than before. She returned to America in 1856, and subsequently was married to an American gentleman; since then her appearances have not been so frequent. Mrs. Catherine Hayes has not, and perhaps never has had, a rival in rendering with deep sensibility, mournful pathos, and heart-speaking expression, the ancient melodies of her native country.

HAYTER, SIR GEORGE, known as the "Court painter in ordinary," was born in London, 1792, and after having studied in the Royal Academy, passed some years in Italy. On his return, his works were so much admired for their delicacy of finish and poetical expression, that he was named first painter to the Queen, and teacher of drawing to the Royal Princesses. He was knighted in 1842. His finest picture, as a work of art, and the one that best develops the characteristics of his style, is "The Queen Taking the Coronation Oath." The details are elaborate, the colour harmonious, and the drawing unexceptionable. This picture is widely known by the engraving, but the plate affords little idea of the artist's treatment of the subject. His next best work is "The Marriage of Queen Victoria and Prince Albert," also well known by the prints, which, however, in this case, also, fail to convey the many beauties of the original.

HEAD, SIR FRANCIS BOND, BART., K.C.H., was born in 1793, near Rochester. He entered the army, and was a Captain of Engineers, in Edinburgh, in 1825, when he accepted a proposal from an association to work the gold and silver mines of Rio de la Plata. In the prosecution of his engagement he crossed the Pampas, from Buenos Ayres to Chili, in what may be termed flying journeys, during which he suffered many hardships. Returning to London, in 1826, he published his "Rough Notes of a Journey across the Pampas," which proved a successful work. In 1828 he was promoted to the rank of Major in the army, and in 1835 he was appointed Governor of Upper Canada, a post which, it is only fair to say, he accepted with much reluctance, and at the pressing instance of Lord Glenelg, then Minister for the Colonies. His measures while holding that responsible position, resulted in his being able to dismiss from Upper Canada the whole of the Queen's troops, and, supported only by the people, to suppress an insurrection. Sir Francis is one of the alarmists about a French invasion of Britain, and has consequently written copiously upon the defenceless state of the country. Many of his statements are perfectly true, and his suggestions are now being paid full attention to. Besides the work already mentioned, his chief works are "A Fagot of French Sticks," "A Visit to Ireland," and "Bubbles from the Brunnens of Nassau." In 1838 he was created a baronet, and receives a pension of £100 a year from Government.

HEADLEY, JOEL TYLER, an American author, was born at Walton, in the state of New York, on the 3rd of December, 1814. He graduated at Union College, in 1839, and studied theology at the Auburn Seminary. For upwards of two years he officiated as pastor of a church in Stockbridge, Massachusetts. Failing health compelled him to travel, and in 1842-43 he visited Europe. Returning to the United States, he gave to the world the result of his observations, in a work which was so favourably received as to lead him to embrace authorship as a profession. In 1854 he was elected a member of the New York legislature, and in the year following, Secretary of State for two years. He is the author of numerous biographies and works of travel.

HELPS, ARTHUR, an historian, was born in 1817. After studying at Cambridge, he entered the public service, in which he has risen to the high office of Secretary to the Privy Council. His leisure he has devoted to literature. The first publication from the pen of Mr. Helps was "Essays Written in the Intervals of Business" (1841), which has passed through numerous editions; two dramas, "Henry II." and "Catherine Douglas," followed; they appeared in 1843. The "Claims of Labour," a thoughtful and earnest book, treating of the reciprocal relations of employers and employed, came out in 1845; but the work which first established the position of Mr. Helps, was "Friends in Council," published in 1847. It is one of the most pleasant and readable books of the age, exhibiting great subtlety of thought and the utmost ability as an author. In 1851 appeared "Companions of my Solitude," a thoughtful book, full of wisdom, gentleness, and beauty. "The Conquerors of the New World, and their Bondsmen," &c., appeared in 1848-52; and "The Spanish Conquest of America," in 1855. He has written other volumes, but the above are the most interesting. As an author, the first modern critics have pronounced Mr. Helps equal to the task "of being of infinite use to his generation." A second series of "Friends in Council" appeared in 1859, which ably maintains the character of the first portion of the work.

HENGSTENBERG, ERNEST WILLIAM, a German theologian, was born at Frœndenberg, in October, 1802. He is the son of a Protestant minister, and was educated at the University of Bonn, where he devoted himself chiefly to the study of the Oriental languages, and the study of philosophy. In 1824 he published the first volume of a translation of "Aristotle's Metaphysics," having previously received honours from the Academy of Bonn, for his translation of an Arab work of the sixth century. In the same year he qualified himself as a private teacher in the Faculty of Philosophy in Berlin; and in the following year, as private teacher in the Faculty of Theology. He was appointed Joint Professor of Theology in 1826, and Ordinary Professor in 1829, obtaining at the same time the distinction of Doctor in Theology. The publication of the "Evangelische Kirchenzeitung," considered the ablest organ of the evangelical orthodox party in Prussia, was begun in 1827. His principal works are "Christologie des A.F., Commentar ueber die Psalmen;" and "Beitraege zur Einleitung ins A.F., Commentar ueber die Apocalypse." Professor Hengstenberg is employed at present in writing a "Commentary on the Gospel of St. John." The son of Professor Hengstenberg has also risen to distinction as a theological writer. He is the pastor at Interbag, and is perhaps best known by a series of articles which he published on the "Evangelical Alliance," after a long residence in Great Britain.

HENLEY, The Right Hon. Joseph Warner, M.P., late President of the Board of Trade, under Lord Derby, was born in 1793. Educated at Oxford, he graduated as a B.A. in 1816; twenty years afterwards took his degree as M.A.; and again, after an interval of another twenty years, received from his *alma mater* the honorary degree of D.C.L. At the general election of 1841, Mr. Henley was first returned to that seat in the House of Commons which he has ever since occupied—viz. as one of the three representatives of Oxfordshire. Chairman of the Sessions, since 1846, he has taken a great interest in local affairs. In 1852 he was selected by Lord Derby as President of the Board of Trade. The Reform Bill of the noble Lord not being satisfactory, he retired, in conjunction with Mr. Walpole, from his position in the cabinet.

HERAPATH, William, F.C.S., an English chemist, was born at Bristol, in May, 1796. His father was a maltster and brewer, and dying suddenly, young Herapath was called to conduct the business. His leisure hours were given up to the study of Natural Philosophy and Chemistry, and such became his proficiency and skill in these sciences, that he began to be consulted professionally. His reputation increasing, he abandoned malting and devoted himself exclusively to his favourite pursuits, taking up, among others, the subject of toxicology, in which he made discoveries of the utmost importance. He is one of the fourteen who originated the Chemical Society of London, and also was one of the originators of the Bristol Medical School, which was founded in 1828. He became its first teacher of chemistry, a position which he still holds as Lecturer on General and Practical Chemistry and Toxicology. He has received various municipal honours from his native city, of which he is now the senior magistrate.

HERBERT, John Rogers, R.A., was born in 1810, at Maldon, in Essex. He studied in the Royal Academy, and was for some time a portrait painter. His first attractive work, out of the portrait line, was "The Appointed Hour," which told a story of itself, and was very successful. He visited Italy, and painted numerous pictures, the subjects of which were chiefly drawn from Venetian history, not, however, confining himself to that class of works. Owing, it is said, to the influence of late Mr. Pugin, the architect, Mr. Herbert conformed to the Roman Catholic religion, a circumstance which has considerably influenced his choice of subjects, and has led him to adopt the church to which he adheres, as the stand-point from which he paints his illustrations of Scripture history. He was elected an Academician in 1846; and soon after he was called on to assist in decorating the New Palace at Westminster. His efforts were so successful, that he was appointed to execute nine frescoes for the robing-room of the House of Lords. Mr. Herbert, notwithstanding occasional eccentricities of manner, maintains a high place among the artists of the day.

HERBERT, Right Hon. Sidney, M.P., an English statesman, is the son of the eleventh Earl of Pembroke, and was born in 1810. He was educated at Harrow, and graduated at Oxford, in 1831, being elected member for South Wilts in the following year. Commencing public life as a strong Conservative, he gradually acquired more liberal views, and was among the earliest supporters of Sir Robert Peel on the latter changing his commercial policy in 1841. He held office in the Peel ministry, and also under Lord Aberdeen, as Secretary at War. He relinquished a subsequent connexion with the Palmerston administration, owing to a Committee being moved to inquire into the state of the army then at Sebastopol. Though he gave up from a sense of honour the position he held under Lord Palmerston, because of the censure he supposed implied in that appointment towards the government of Lord Aberdeen, no member of the House of Commons has given greater attention to army reform. Some of the ablest papers upon the question that have appeared in the reviews of the day, have proceeded from his pen. Mr. Herbert is not only an able statesman; he is also a singularly benevolent man. Much of his time and talent are devoted to the prosecution of schemes of social and general good. In 1846 Mr. Herbert married a daughter of General A'Court, a lady ever deserving honourable mention for her devoted exertions on behalf of the sick and wounded Crimean heroes. On the fall of Lord Derby's administration (his second unsuccessful effort), in 1859, Lord Palmerston appointed Mr. Sidney Herbert to the office of Secretary of State for War, which office he now holds. Mr. Herbert is heir presumptive to his brother the Earl of Pembroke.

HERRING, JOHN FREDERICK, an eminent painter of animal life, was born in Surrey, in 1795. His family was originally Dutch; but his father was born in America, whence he came to settle in London. Mr. Herring is essentially a self-taught artist. On the lookout for employment, he made his way to Doncaster, where he remained for eighteen years, principally employed as a coach-driver, but devoting his leisure to painting horses. His talent became known, and he was induced to exchange the reins for the palette. Mr. Herring progressed with astonishing rapidity in art. He "hit" the portraits of favourite horses and hounds with wonderful skill; and what is more surprising, he came to understand colour as though he had attended lectures at the Academy.

Once on the road, his idea was "forward." From horses, Mr. Herring turned his hand to the depiction of every other animal that came within familiar notice. His paintings appear to convey the idea of sympathy with the living beings he depicts, whether horses, cows, pigs, or dogs; while his close handling and minute attention to details, render his works extremely valuable as transcripts of things as they are. His "Members of the Temperance Society," "The Country Bait," "Feeding," "Straw Yard," "Roadside," and other well-known pictures, are unsurpassed in their special line. He has painted one or two ideal subjects, but in point of strength they have not matched his realities.

HERSCHEL, SIR JOHN FREDERICK WILLIAM, BART., K.H., was born at Slough, in 1792, and is the son of the great astronomer, Sir William Herschel. Proceeding to Cambridge, after graduating, he became senior wrangler, and Smith's prizeman, and subsequently devoted himself to the study of mathematical and physical science. His first work was a paper communicated to the Royal Society in 1812, and printed in the Transactions of that body for 1813, on a remarkable application of Cotes's Theorem. It was followed by several others on mathematical subjects in the years 1815, 16, 17, and 18, which will be found in the same collection, in the "Edinburgh Cyclopædia," and in the posthumous edition of "Spence's Mathematical Essays," edited by him in 1819. In 1820 was published at Cambridge his "Collection of Examples of the Application of the Calculus of Finite Differences," forming a supplement to a translation of "Lacroix's Treatise," executed by him in 1816, in conjunction with Messrs. Peacock and Babbage. His first contribution to physical science was his discovery of the hyposulphurous acid, and its salts (since become so useful in

SIR JOHN FREDERICK WILLIAM HERSCHEL, BART. F.R.

photography, and whose application to photographical purposes he was the first to point out). He wrote a series of papers in "Brewster's and Jamieson's Edinburgh Philosophical Journal," in 1819, followed in that and subsequent years by various memoirs, chiefly on optical, chemical, and electrical science, published in the "Transactions of the Royal Society" and other scientific collections. On the death of his father he devoted himself to the continuance of that great work of astronomical investigation around which his illustrious parent had shed so much renown. In 1825 he began an independent series of investigations of the sidereal heavens. He afterwards received the Royal Medal of 1833 for his researches on the orbits of double stars. As regards nebulæ and clusters of stars, a record of 2,306 observations was laid before the Royal Society, together with somewhere between three and four thousand observations upon double stars, and was again rewarded by that body with their Royal Medal for 1836. The Royal Astronomical Society voted him a gold medal for his eminent services to science. In 1830 he contributed a treatise on Sound to the "Encyclopædia Metropolitana;" and in the year following, a treatise on "Light" was furnished by him to the same work. Shortly subsequent to these contributions, his "Preliminary Discourse on the Study of Natural Philosophy" appeared. This last work exhibited its author as capable of sustaining a high reputation in scientific literature. In 1836 "A Treatise on Astronomy" added greatly to Herschel's popularity. He now resolved upon what has proved the greatest of his tasks as a practical astronomer, the survey of the southern hemisphere, hitherto all but utterly unknown to science. In the execution of this great design he sailed, with his family, for the Cape of Good Hope. The voyage proved quite propitious. On the 15th January, 1834, he arrived at the Cape, with all his instruments in admirable condition. After some search he selected a site for his improved observatory, about six miles from Table Bay, in a beautiful and shaded district of country. Here he set up his instruments. From March, 1834, until May, 1838, he continued his investigations; having, during these four years, swept the whole southern heavens. The scientific world in Europe and America waited with intense interest the results of the sublime labours of this solitary watcher. At distant intervals, this interest was gratified by glimpses of the progress that had been made. Complete results were published in regular form, in a work the cost of which was liberally defrayed by his Grace the Duke of Northumberland, and which the Royal Society distinguished by the grant of their Copley Medal for that year. Herschel suggested a plan of simultaneous meteorological observations, which he subsequently explained in a formal publication. It was carried out under military authority in 1844. On Herschel's return to England every honour was paid him, being made a baronet at the coronation of the Queen, and created a D.C.L. by the University of Oxford. In 1855 he was elected by the French Academy of Sciences one of the eight Foreign members of the Institute, of which, as well of most of the principal Scientific Academies of Europe, he had long been a corresponding Associate. Among his later publications may be mentioned a series of communications in the Transactions of the Royal Society on the Photographic and Calorific properties of the Prismatic rays of the Spectrum, which were rewarded with the Royal Medal of that body; several memoirs on mathematical subjects; a work entitled "Outlines of Astronomy," which has passed through five editions, and been recently translated into the Chinese language, and published in that empire; a volume of Essays on a variety of subjects, published in 1857, and a series of articles on Meteorology, Physical Geography, &c., in the Encyclopædia Britannica now in course of publication. In 1850 Sir John received the appointment of Master of the Mint, but failing health induced him to retire, when Professor Graham, the eminent chemist, was nominated. Sir John Herschel has ever taken the greatest interest in the diffusion of knowledge, occasionally lecturing to large mixed audiences. He married in 1829 Margaret Brodie, eldest daughter of the Rev. Blexandon Stewart, D.D., by whom he has a numerous family.

HERZEN (sometimes, but erroneously, spelled Hertzen), ALEXANDER, a Russian journalist and political writer, was born at Moscow on the 25th of March, 1812. Having terminated a brilliant university career, he was suddenly arrested on the ground of entertaining sentiments hostile to the government. After remaining in prison nearly a year, he was exiled to Perm and afterwards to Matra, for a period of five years. He was then set at large, but in 1840 he was again apprehended at Petersburg, and sent to Novogorod, being there detained during the years 1841 and 1842. On the surveillance being removed he left Russia for Paris, and opened bold warfare with the Muscovite despotism. While the government of Louis-Philippe still existed, he left France for Italy, where he collected materials for a series of letters subsequently published. After the Revolution of February he returned to Paris, and published various books in French and German, but his connexion with Proudhon and the "Voices of the People" resulted in his expulsion from the country in 1850. From Paris he went to Nice, and thence, in 1852, to London. Here a new career was opened to his activity. In the English metropolis he founded a Russian printing establishment, which has been in constant operation ever since. Up to the death of the Emperor Nicholas, Russian books were printed at this establishment without it being possible to sell a single copy in the empire of the Czar, but after his death a change took place. The following books were published in Russian by Herzen, at London:—1. "Letters on Italy and France;" 2. "On Despotism;" 3. "Stories Half Told." In 1855 he commenced the Review called the "Polar Star," and in 1856 a newspaper named "The Bull" (Kolokol), appearing once a fortnight. This journal has acquired great importance in Russia by exhibiting the evils of functionaryism.

HIEN FUNG, EMPEROR OF CHINA, of the Ta Tsing, or great Pun dynasty, was born about 1830. The fourth son of the Emperor Taou Kwang, he ascended the throne in 1851. He found the country at that time in a melancholy position, the result of the war with Great Britain on account of the opium traffic; and the successes of the British arms in various parts of the empire had compelled the signature of the Treaty of Nanking. Within the empire all was disorganization, and the state of the population was such as to presage a general dissolution of the established authority. Two parties were engaged in a hard struggle. One of these, which was to a certain extent progressive, seeking the overthrow of the Manchoo conquerors, but hitherto finding no support from the respectable classes of the Chinese, obtained influence with a small party of the friends of the Imperial family, and exhibited sounder views of the strength of western nations than those generally maintained in China, and had for a short time the ascendancy, but ultimately the reactionary party became successful, the standard of revolt was raised in many of the provinces, and an iusurrection broke out which spread from Kwang-si, having Hung Tsen Tseuen as its leader. The rapid progress of the civil war filled with consternation the court of Peking. It was said that an attempt was made to assassinate the Emperor in the palace gardens; disturbances multiplied; the finances of the Emperor became deranged; trouble succeeded trouble; but the Emperor probably kept in ignorance of the real state of affairs, was at the mercy of his ministers. A period of comparative tranquillity, however, at last came, but it was short-lived. The measures of Sir John Bowring for the protection of the British flag, burst on the quiet of Peking, and led to a war which terminated in a treaty signed by the Imperial Commissioners, authorizing the admission of a British plenipotentiary to the court of Peking. How it was violated is known to every reader. The Hon. W. Bruce, the British representative, relying on the treaty, was passing the mouth of the Tien Tien river, when the ships of war which formed his escort were assailed by masked batteries from forts on shore, and a heavy loss of life, as well as a loss of vessels, was the consequence. For this attack, Britain, supported by France, is now making reprisals. It rests with political philosophers to judge how far the Emperor of China, or those who make use of his name in our diplomatic intercourse with the empire, should be allowed to prohibit or restrain European intercourse with four hundred millions of the human race. The Emperor's family consists of four sons and a daughter: he has also two brothers living.

HILDRETH, RICHARD, an American author, was born at Deerfield, Massachusetts, on the 28th of June, 1807. His father was a Unitarian minister. He graduated at Harvard College, and was admitted to the bar in 1830. He became, in 1832, editor of the Boston "Atlas," a daily paper, and afterwards filled similar situations in various cities of the Union. He has published several educational works; but his name is best known by his works in opposition to slavery, and his "History of the United States of America." The latter work is a plain, unpretending, chronological narrative, useful for reference, but, perhaps, rather meagre and uninteresting in style—ample though not animated.

HILL, SIR ROWLAND, K.C.B., originator of the penny-postage system, and Secretary to the General Post Office, was born at Kidderminster, on the 3rd December, 1795. His father conducted a seminary near Birmingham, in the mathematical department of which the subject of this notice assisted, until in consequence of bad health he was obliged in 1833 to withdraw from that occupation. He subsequently received the appointment of Secretary to the South Australian Commission. For a considerable period his mind had been occupied with the consideration of the errors and abuses of the postal system, as it stood a quarter of a century since, and in 1837 he published a pamphlet on Post-office Reform, which aroused the feeling of the country in favour of his plans. In 1838 a committee of the House of Commons recommended the adoption of his proposals for reform; and, aided by the zeal and ability of Mr. Charles Knight, and the late Mr. Wallace, Member for Greenock, he persevered, until in 1840 he had the gratification of witnessing a practical recognition of his views, by the establishment of a uniform rate of postage, the charge for a short time being fourpence for a letter inland, to whatever distance conveyed. In 1842, much to the discredit of the Government of the day, he felt himself obliged to leave his post without having completed his changes; and in 1845 he became Chairman of the

P

Brighton Railway Company. In 1846 the country so warmly appreciated the merits of his system that he was presented with a money testimonial of £13,000. On a change of ministers in the same year, he received the appointment of permanent Secretary, and that of sole Secretary to the Post-office when Colonel Maberly retired in 1854. For his services in the cause of postal reform he was made a Knight Commander of the Bath in March, 1860. One of his brothers acts as assistant-secretary; a second is surveyor of stamps; and a third, the Recorder of Birmingham.

HIND, JOHN RUSSELL, an eminent astronomer, was born at Nottingham, on the 12th May, 1823. He is the son of the introducer of the Jacquard loom, now so much improved upon, and so extensively used. Mr. Hind was for some time assistant in the Greenwich Observatory. He is Foreign Secretary to the Royal Astronomical Society, and superintendent of the "Nautical Almanack." He is the discoverer of a large number of planets. The gold medal of the Astronomical Society was awarded to him in 1852 for his eminent services to science, and a pension of £200 a-year was granted him by Government for important astronomical discoveries. He is the author of several works on astronomical subjects, among which are—"The Solar System (1846)," "The Expected Return of the Great Comet of 1264 and 1556 (1848)," "An Astronomical Vocabulary (1852)," and "Comets: a Descriptive Treatise (1852)." Mr. Hind has been long engaged in Mr. Bishop's Observatory in Regent's Park.

HINDS, RIGHT REV. SAMUEL, ex-Bishop of Norwich, was born in 1794, in Barbadoes. He came to England when a boy, was educated at Oxford, and ordained in 1822. He was promoted to the see of Norwich in 1849, and was one of the few who, on the Episcopal benches of the House of Lords, attached themselves to the Liberal party. The revenue of the diocese is estimated at about £4,500 a year. This he resigned *in toto* in 1857. The learned prelate has published numerous writings on religious subjects, the principal of which is the "Rise and Progress of Christianity," which, since 1853, has passed through several editions.

HOLLAND, SIR HENRY, BART., a physician, was born 1788. Educated at the London Medical School, and at the University of Edinburgh, he graduated at the latter as M.D. in 1811, and after travelling three or four years in various parts of Europe, settled in London, where he rapidly grew into repute as a physician. Rising gradually to the highest eminence as a practitioner, he was appointed physician in ordinary to H.R.H. Prince Albert in 1840, and to Her Majesty in 1852. Early in life he published his travels in Albania, Thessaly, and Greece; but the work by which he is best known is his "Medical Notes and Reflexions." He was created a Baronet in 1853, and is a Fellow of the Royal Society, D.C.L. of Oxford, and a Fellow of the Royal College of Physicians in London. He married a daughter of the celebrated Rev. Sydney Smith, canon of St. Paul's, the brilliant and accomplished writer of her father's biography.

HOLMES, OLIVER WENDELL, M.D., an American physician and poet, was born at Cambridge, in Massachusetts, on the 29th August, 1809. He graduated at Harvard University in 1829, and devoted the next year to the study of law. In 1833 he visited Europe, and, having already exchanged Coke and Blackstone for Galen and Esculapius, attended the hospitals of Paris for some two or three years. In 1835 he returned to Boston, took his medical degree at Cambridge, United States, in 1836, was elected Professor of Anatomy and Physiology in Dartmouth College in 1838, and succeeded Dr. Warren, in Harvard University, in 1847. Two years after this appointment, Dr. Holmes relinquished general practice. The Doctor has been a frequent contributor to the medical literature of the United States, and is the author of a volume of excellent poetry, which has been republished in Britain. To the pages of the "Atlantic Monthly," Mr. Holmes has lately contributed a series of excellent papers, entitled "The Autocrat of the Breakfast Table." These have been reprinted in England as well as in America, and proved highly successful. Dr. Holmes is, according to the estimate of his countrymen, the most effective poet of the school of Pope that America has produced. His poem on the 'Burns Centenary' is incomparably the finest of the countless rhymes that celebration has called forth.

HOOK, THE VERY REV. WALTER FARQUHAR, D.D., Dean of Chichester and theological writer, is the son of the late Rev. Dr. James Hook, Dean of Worcester. He was born in London in 1798, and was educated at Winchester, and Christ Church, Oxford, where he graduated in 1821. He was appointed chaplain to George IV. in 1827, Vicar of Coventry in 1829, Vicar of Leeds in 1837, and Dean of Chichester in 1859. Untiring energy in the cause of church extension, and a zealous devotion to ecclesiastical literature, are the leading characteristics of this eminent divine. In 1856 Dr. Longley, Bishop of Durham, on taking leave of the clergy of the diocese of Ripon, mentioned that no fewer than twenty churches and thirty schools had been built in Leeds through the exertions of Dr. Hook. The dean belongs to the high-church party in the English Church, and is the author of "An Ecclesiastical Biography, containing the lives of the Ancient Fathers and Modern Divines;" "A

Church Dictionary;" "On the Means of rendering more effectual the Education of the People;" and "The Three Reformations." He has also published numerous sermons.

HOOKER, SIR WILLIAM JACKSON, K.H., D.C.L., a botanist, Director of the Royal Gardens at Kew, and formerly Professor of Botany in the University of Glasgow, was born at Exeter. Having terminated his university studies, and prompted by a strong predilection for the study of natural science, he joined a memorable expedition to Iceland, of which he, on his return, published an account under the title of "Journal of a Tour to Iceland" (Yarmouth, 1811). The flora of the island described in this volume, and a "Monograph of the British Jungermanniæ," published in 1813, having established his reputation as a botanist, he was offered the professorship of his favourite science at Glasgow, and which he accepted. Although in independent circumstances, he laboured most zealously in the discharge of his academical duties, publishing in 1818 the "Muscologia Britannica," the first complete treatise on British mosses, and also the "Musci Exotici," in 1821 "Flora Scotica," and in 1823 the "Exotic Flora," a work at the time much praised for the description it contained of new plants, susceptible of cultivation in this country, and for the care and finish with which it was got up. From 1830 to 1833, he published the "Botanical Miscellany," and from 1826 to 1837 the "Icones Filicum," which consisted of plates and relative descriptions of ferns. In the mean time he extended his "Flora Scotica" to the whole of the United Kingdom, and published in 1830 the extended work as the "British Flora." In 1836 he published a new edition of "Smith's Introduction to Physiological and Systematic Botany;" and in the same year received the honour of knighthood, as a reward for his scientific labours. From Glasgow, Sir William Hooker removed to Kew, to become Director of the Royal Gardens, a situation for which he was well qualified, having previously managed the Botanic Gardens at Glasgow. In 1847 he published a useful littl work, the "Guide to Kew Gardens," superintended the erection o the great conservatory and new museum, and obtained for the public facilities of admission which were not known before his time. Sir William Hooker, as editor of the "Journal of Botany and Kew Garden Miscellany," has, since the period of his appointment at Kew, described a very great number of plants, and fully sustained his high reputation as a systematic botanist.

HOOKER, JOSEPH DALTON, M.D., a botanist, son of Sir William Jackson Hooker, was born at Halesworth, in Suffolk, in 1817. He completed his medical studies and took the degree of M.D. at the University of Glasgow. He accompanied Sir James Ross on his expedition to the Antarctic regions in 1839, in the capacity of assistant-surgeon and naturalist. On his return, in 1843, he was directed by the Lords Commissioners of the Admiralty to publish the fruits of his researches, a work which has been completed in six quarto volumes, comprising the "Flora Antarctica," and those of New Zealand and Tasmania; to the two latter of which are essays appended, adding much to our knowledge of the laws which govern the distribution of plants over the earth. In 1847 Dr. Hooker proceeded on a botanical mission to the Eastern Himalaya, and other little known districts of India; whence he returned in 1851, having amassed a rich harvest of botanical observations, drawings, and living and dried plants, many from countries never before visited by a European, and where travelling was both difficult and dangerous. His adventures were recorded and published under the title of "Himalayan Journals," the botanical and scientific results being consigned to the "Flora Indica," a treatise on the Rhododendrons of the Sikkim Himalaya. In 1855 Dr. Hooker was appointed Assistant-Director of the Royal Gardens at Kew.

HOPE, GEORGE WILLIAM, M. P., was born at Blackheath, Kent, in 1808. He is the son of General the Hon. Sir Alexander Hope, who was fourth son of the Earl of Hopetoun. He was educated at Christ Church College, Oxford, and called to the bar at Lincoln's-inn, in June, 1831. Some time after, he entered Parliament, and held the office of Under-Secretary of State for the Colonies, in Sir Robert Peel's government, from September 1841, to December 1845. He at present represents the borough of Windsor, for which he was first elected in 1859. His political principles are Liberal-Conservative. He does not oppose rational changes, but resists any sweeping democratic measure which would render mere numbers predominant over property and intelligence.

HORNE, RICHARD HENRY, an author and dramatist, was born in 1807. After leaving the Military College of Sandhurst, he devoted himself to hard study at home in philosophy, poetry, and metaphysics. During this period he endeavoured to get a commission in the Polish Cavalry, but without success. He obtained about this time a medal from the Society of Arts for a pen-and-ink copy of an etching by Rembrandt. He then took a voyage to Vera Cruz, and on landing there was appointed interpreter and translator of the civil correspondence. On a second cruise he was mate of the gun deck, and assisted in taking a prize, was present at the bombardment of Vera Cruz and the taking of San Juan Ulloa, but caught the yellow fever, and proceeded, on his recovery, to New York, thence through different parts of Canada to England. He there devoted himself to literature, and produced a tragedy, which he never published, with other works, which were rejected by the publishers on account of the peculiarity of their subjects. His first published production was a series of articles on the Mexican Expedition, which appeared in the "London Journal." He afterwards brought out his "Exposition of the False Medium and the Barriers excluding Men of Genius from the Public." This was followed by the "Spirit of Peers and People," the "Death of Marlowe," which was very successful, and appeared in 1837, "Cosmo de' Medici," "Gregory VII.," and "Judas Iscariot." Mr. Horne also revised numerous works for the press, and contributed to the "Westminster Review," the "Monthly Chronicle," the "New Quarterly," "Fraser's Magazine," "Tait's," "Household Words," &c. Mr. Horne is chiefly known by his "Orion," of which it was his intention to give away the first three editions. An edition of this work has been published in Australia, and is to be sold, in the first instance, for a farthing per copy. Mr. Horne is at present in that country, and is occupied as a gold commissioner at Melbourne. He has lately taken great interest in the art of swimming, on which some years ago he wrote articles in the Penny Cyclopædia and Fraser's Magazine. He is also engaged in getting up a Wine-growing Company on the Goldburn River, in Victoria, which, he has hopes, will be very successful, and prove another source of wealth to that flourishing colony.

HORSLEY, JOHN CALLCOTT, a painter, was born in London, on the 29th January, 1817. He studied at the Royal Academy, and at the early age of eighteen exhibited his "Rent Day at Haddon Hall in the Sixteenth Century,"

His next great picture was "The Pride of the Village." At the Westminster Hall exhibition of 1843 he gained one of the three prizes of £200 for his cartoon of "St. Augustine Preaching." He followed up his success by painting the fine fresco of "Religion," which forms one of the decorations of the House of Lords. In 1847 he obtained a prize for his well-known work "Prince Henry, believing the King his father dead, assumes the Crown." These and several other works in the historical style were, however skilfully painted, out of Mr. Horsley's exact department, and he now confines himself to the treatment of more congenial subjects. His pictures "l'Allegro and Il Penseroso," painted for the Prince Consort, "The Madrigal," "Lady Jane Grey and Roger Ascham," and "A Scene from Don Quixote," indicate his peculiar powers. Several of his pictures have been engraved, and these display great variety of thought and aptitude to turn from grave to gay.

HOUDIN, ROBERT JEAN-EUGÈNE, a celebrated sleight-of-hand professor, was born at Blois, in 1805. The son of a watchmaker, he studied at the College of Orleans, and, at his father's instance, went into the office of a notary. He was not, however, destined to follow the profession of the law. Endowed with a talent for mechanical invention, in 1830 he produced a number of automata and deceptive instruments, which caught public attention at once. He became an itinerant lecturer or showman, and exhibited his curious and often inexplicable contrivances throughout Europe, for some years, with success. In 1856 he received a mission from government to go to Algeria, where he beat the Eastern magicians on their own ground, and so increased the prestige of the French. On his return he published (1859) a work containing his professional confessions, mingled with sketches of men and manners, which if not very instructive, is at least amusing.

HOUSSAYE, ARSÈNE, a French poet, was born at Bruyères, near Laon, in 1815, of an old family in that neighbourhood. His education was liberal, and he improved it by self-cultivation. He joined the French army in 1830, when a mere boy, but the martial spirit was kindled, and he could not resist its force. After the siege of Antwerp peace was proclaimed, and M. Houssaye returned to reside with his father, until 1832, when he made up his mind to remove to Paris, as the great central point from which fame and fortune radiated. His first literary appearance was in 1836, when he published two romances, "La Couronne de Bluets," and "La Pécheresse," neither of which then attained to much celebrity, though they have since been highly praised. Aided by the friendship of Théophile Gautier and Jules Sandeau, M. Houssaye published various works, besides contributing papers to the "Revue de Paris." He was accused of plagiarism, but without foundation, for he only drew his incidents or descriptions from sources common to all readers of books and students of the world and its ways. At the Revolution of 1848 he was an active politician of the democratic order, and in 1849 was appointed Director of the Théatre Français, which he brought into a condition of almost unprecedented prosperity, though when he accepted the control of that establishment its fortunes were at the lowest ebb. He resigned the appointment in 1856, on his nomination by the Emperor as Inspector-General of the Fine Arts. Among his works may be enumerated "Philosophers and Actresses," the "History of Dutch and Flemish Painting," and "Charlotte Cordaye," "Le Roi Voltaire," and "The Forty-first Chair of the Academy." As an art critic

M. Houssaye, now editor in chief of "L'Artiste," a newspaper specially devoted to the fine arts, has no superior in Paris

HOUSTON, SAMUEL, an American general, was born at Rockbridge, Virginia, in 1793. His early education was scanty, and after passing through various vicissitudes, he enlisted and served under General Jackson. His energy of character soon brought him into notice, and eventually turning his attention to political matters, he was elected a member of Congress. After being made Governor of Tennessee, he visited, in 1829, the Indians amongst whom he had spent his early days, and endeavoured to relieve them of burdens from which they had suffered, by proceeding to Washington. Having also assisted in the affairs of Texas, he undertook the command of an army in 1836, which had been raised to oppose the Mexicans, and was completely successful. He has been twice elected President of the Texican Republic, and since the annexation has represented Texas in the Senate of the United States.

HOWITT, MARY, a poet and novelist, wife of William Howitt, and the daughter of Mr. Botham, a member of the Society of Friends, was born at Uttoxeter, in 1804. She received an excellent education, and was at an early age well acquainted not only with the usual course of sciences taught in schools, but with ancient and modern literature. Her reflective character and love of nature are evidenced in "My Own Story." After her marriage, her literary career became in some degree blended with that of her husband, but her individual works are far the most numerous. Among these may be numbered, "The Seven Temptations," a dramatic poem, "Ballads and other Poems," "Wood Leighton," and "The Heir of Wast Wayland," two admirably told stories, not only developing country life and character, but pointing an excellent moral. Mrs. Howitt's works for the young, written originally for her own children, amount to upwards of twenty volumes, and are at once instructive and entertaining, and full of maternal love and wisdom. Amongst these may be mentioned "Strive and Thrive," "Hope on, Hope ever," "Alice Franklin," "Little Coin, much Care," "Work and Wages," "Stedfast Gabriel," "The Children's Year," "Sketches of Natural History," &c. &c. Mrs. Howitt has translated the whole of the works of Fredrika Bremer from the Swedish ; several of Hans Christian Andersen's and others, from the Danish ; besides translations from the German, both in prose and poetry. Apart from this great amount of literary labour, Mrs. Howitt has contributed largely to magazines and serials, and it is only justice to add, that her powers have ever been directed to the advocacy of the true, the useful, and the good—the alleviation of suffering, and the education of the youthful mind.

HOWITT, WILLIAM, an historian and novelist, was born in 1795, at Heanor, in Derbyshire, of an old Quaker family. Receiving his education in various schools connected with the society, he studied hard, and became well acquainted with science, without neglecting the languages. When twenty-eight years of age he married Miss Botham, of Uttoxeter, a lady of kindred taste. In 1823 their joint work appeared, "The Forest Minstrel," which, being highly approved of, made its way rapidly. Annuals— as they were called in those days—were growing into fashion, and to the earliest of the number the "Literary Souvenir," and the "Amulet," William Howitt was a contributor. In 1831 his "Book of the Seasons" was published ; in 1833 his "History of Priestcraft in all Ages;" in 1837, "Rural Life in England," and

"Visits to Remarkable Places." About this time he removed to Germany, where he resided for some time, writing there his "Student Life in Germany," and on his return publishing his "Homes and Haunts of the British Poets." The most unfortunate part of his career was his purchase of a share in the "People's Journal" in 1846, by which he was involved in much trouble and pecuniary loss. In 1847 he started "Howitt's Journal," but his capital being sunk, he found it impossible to proceed. In 1852, in conjunction with Mrs. Howitt, he published a "History of the Literature of Scandinavia," unquestionably the only complete account of that interesting literature in any language, no entire history of it yet existing in any of the Scandinavian dialects. In the same year, Mr. Howitt departed for Australia, to witness for himself the unparalleled progress of the colony. He returned in 1854, and published "Land, Labour, and Gold," an account of his experiences in the country. The works of Mr. Howitt have been so numerous, and are so well known, that a recapitulation of their titles is needless in a slight sketch of his life. His "Man of the People," a novel, published recently, is designed to show the amazing progress of England in the last forty years. Mr. Howitt is now engaged in writing "Cassell's Illustrated History of England," of which he has already completed four large 8vo volumes, there being still two in progress.

HUGO, VICTOR MARIE, VICOMTE, a French poet and writer, was born at Besançon, on 26th February, 1802. His early education was of the most desultory description. Before he was eight years old, he had been obliged to accompany his father through part of Italy, into Spain, to reside in Elba, and finally to journey from Madrid to Paris. Between 1813 and 1822 he produced a poem on the "Advantages of Study."

and a tragedy called "Irtamène," and was highly successful in his collegiate studies. In 1822 he established the "Conservateur Littéraire," and in 1823, the "Odes et Ballades" were published. Into the controversy raised between the classical and romantic schools, Victor Hugo plunged with all the impetuosity of his nature, and became the head of the romantic school, in France. Under this influence he produced a variety of works, among which was "Notre Dame de Paris," which still holds its place among the best novels which have been published in France. In 1841 Victor Hugo became a member of the French Academy, and was created a peer in 1845. In 1848 he was twice returned for the Assemblée Nationale as a democrat. In December, 1852, he was placed on the list for extradition, and being exiled from France, took up his residence in Jersey, and afterwards, in 1856, in Guernsey. From Jersey, he has, on more than one occasion, launched the lightning of his eloquence and scorn, both in prose and verse, against the present occupant of the French throne. The most telling of his productions being his "Napoleon the Little," which appears, from the date on the preface, to have been written prior to his leaving France. He also published the "Châtimens," a volume of poems composed in the same spirit which dictated "Napoleon the Little." He has been a prolific writer both of dramas and novels, the French critics placing him at the head of the romantic school. His "Last Days of a Condemned Criminal" is a very extraordinary effort of imagination, scarcely however consistent in doctrine with some of his other works. The permanent fame of Victor Hugo will rest upon his poetical works, which contain passages, perhaps, unsurpassed in the whole range of French literature for all the qualities which constitute true poetry.

**HULLAH, JOHN,** a composer and popular musical instructor, was born in 1812, at Worcester. His musical education was originally defective, and it was not until he was seventeen, when he became the pupil of the late Mr. Horsley, Bachelor of Music, that he received any regular instruction. In 1832 he entered the Royal Academy of Music, for the purpose of studying singing under Crevelli. He became first known as a composer by writing the music for Mr. Dickens's comic opera, "The Village Coquettes." He produced one or two other operas, when his attention was directed to the formation of popular singing classes, similar to those established in Paris. He commenced the foundation of such schools in London, in 1840; and was perfectly successful. His system is so widely ramified as to require no description; but it may be safely said that no man has done more, few so much, to extend and cultivate the musical genius of the country as Mr. Hullah. His system is recognised everywhere, and has always been found to succeed.

**HUNT, ROBERT,** F.R.S., a physicist, and writer on physics, was born 6th September, 1807, at Devonport. Mr. Hunt originally was apprenticed to a surgeon, but after a few years left this profession, and was brought up to the business of a druggist. His general attainments attracted the attention of the Cornwall Polytechnic Society, of which he was secretary for five years. Through Sir Henry De la Beche, who proved a steady friend, Mr. Hunt was appointed Keeper of Mining Records in the Museum of Practical Geology—which office he now fills—and in connexion with which he has organized and regularly published a system of "Mineral Statistics," the value of which is proved by the fact, that the mining interests have presented him with a handsome testimonial. In 1851 he assisted in the arrangement of the Great Exhibition, having written the "Synopsis and Hand-book" of the great gathering. He is an admirable lecturer, and a vigorous and lucid scientific writer. His best known works are "Researches on Light," the Poetry of Science," "Panthea; or, the Spirit of Nature," "Elementary Physics," and a "Manual of Photography." His labours and researches on light, heat, and actinism are very valuable. These inquiries secured him admission to the Royal Society.

HUNT, THORNTON, an English journalist, eldest son of Leigh Hunt, was born in September, 1810. After being educated as an artist, he spent a part of his early life in Italy, but the studio, ill suited to his peculiar temperament, was soon abandoned for the more congenial field of literature and politics. For a short time he was connected with a London morning paper, called the "Constitutional," afterwards becoming editor of the "Glasgow Argus." In 1840 he returned to London, publishing five years afterwards the "Foster Brothers," an historical romance, the scene of which is laid in Italy. Mr. Hunt, as a political writer, is liberal in the truest sense. Superior to party, he has ever devoted himself to the discussion of political questions in that broad and comprehensive spirit which alone befits the thinker. Mr. Hunt has been connected with some of the most important political organs, and at present is understood to be the conductor of the "Spectator."

HUNT, WILLIAM HOLMAN, an English painter, was born in London, 1827. He was a pupil in the Royal Academy, and exhibited his first picture in 1846. Between then and 1850 he displayed nothing striking in style or manner, and even his subjects were not taken from sources above the ordinary level; but in 1849-50, a peculiarity in art sprung up in Germany, and it caught the tastes of some young artists in Great Britain, as it promised to lead to a school of simplicity, beauty, and truth, which had been lost from before the days of Raphael. It was a dogma of those enthusiasts, that the refinement of Raphael, the power of Michael Angelo, the warmth of Titian, and the chiaroscuro of Correggio, were subversive of the depth and earnestness of Giotto, Perugino, and other previous masters. Thus some of the cleverest of this "Young England" school of painting banded themselves together as "Pre-Raphaelite Brethren." Mr. Hunt, if not exactly their leader, yet stood the most tenaciously of all by the principles on which the confederation was founded. How many soever the defections from the ranks, he maintained his allegiance, and painted in perfect accordance with the school's assertion of the rules of truth and nature. Too minute in detail to be other than a cause of confusion in a picture—too mediæval in conception and drawing to be perfectly harmonious as a whole—yet too exquisite in colour not to display the powers of the artists in a special direction, the Pre-Raphaelites divided opinion, and excited controversy. Mr. Hunt has clung by his own standard of artistic faith, and has produced pictures, that for accurate drawing and colour could not be surpassed; but he has fallen into a class of subjects—those of symbolism, which detract from his power and attractiveness. His latest picture, "Finding of the Saviour in the Temple," has excited profound attention and admiration.

INGEMANN, BERNARD SEVERIN, a Danish poet and writer, was born in May, 1789. He studied in the University of Copenhagen, and in 1812 obtained the first prize for an "Essay on Poetry and Eloquence." The year before he had appeared as a poet, and in 1813 he published a collection of lyric poems. These were followed by works in many departments of literature, including a number of good tragedies, which have been translated into various languages. After travelling over a great part of Europe, he returned to Copenhagen, and published in 1843 and 1845 his "Collected Works," in thirty-eight volumes, which have been enthusiastically received by the Danish public. They are divided into (1), Dramatic Poems, in six volumes; (2), Historical Poems and Romances, in twelve volumes, consisting chiefly of two Epic Poems, "Waldemar the Great," and "Queen Margaret," and of four Historical Romances, descriptive of the Middle Ages in Denmark; (3), Fairy Legends and Tales, in twelve volumes, the four last of which contain a novel entitled "The Children of the Village," the characters and descriptions in which belong to modern life; (4), Romantic Ballads, Traditions, and Fairy Legends in verse, in eight volumes, among which are the epic poem, "The Black Knights," and a volume of Psalms, and other religious poems; a "Gift for Catechumens" (1854), "Imaginary Letters from a Person Deceased" (1855), and the "Golden Apple," a fairy tale, in twelve cantos (1856), have been published since.

INGERSOLL, CHARLES JARED, an American author, was born at Philadelphia on 3rd October, 1782. He was elected a member of the National House of Representatives in 1812, and until within the last seven or eight years, has been actively engaged in public life in various capacities. His earliest literary work was a poem called "Chiomara," which was published in 1800, in the "Portfolio." In 1801 he produced a tragedy, entitled "Edwy and Elgiva," which was performed at the principal Philadelphia theatre. Afterwards, he wrote in succession "Rights and Wrongs, Power and Policy of the United States," the "Inchiquin, Letters of a Jesuit," which explain American literature and politics, "Julian," a tragic poem, and "History of the War of 1812-15, between Great Britain and the United States," together with numerous contributions to the democratic press, "Speeches Relating to the War with England," "Discourses and Orations," and a translation of a French work, "On the Freedom of Navigation, and the Commerce of Neutral Ships in Time of War." He has likewise published a large number of pamphlets; but his chief work is the "History of the War of 1812-15, between Great Britain and the United States.

INGRES, JEAN DOMINIQUE AUGUSTE, a French painter, born at Montauban, in 1781. His father being a musician, endeavoured to cast his son's tastes in a similar mould, but seeing that he would be a painter, sent him to Paris, where he became a pupil of David. In 1800 he obtained the second prize from the Académie des Beaux Arts, and subsequently he took the first prize. He then went to Italy, where he remained for many years. In 1808 he painted the picture of Napoleon, now in the Hôtel des Invalides, and in 1824 appeared his chief work, "The Vow of Louis XIV.;" during that year he returned to France. Appointed Director of the French Academy at Rome, he painted several portraits, but which were not equal in merit to his historical compositions. In 1834 he was made Chevalier of the Legion of Honour, and in 1845 Commander. His works are invariably chaste in outline, and graceful in expression, and he ranks as one of the first artists of France.

ISABEL II., MARIA ISABEL LUISA, Queen of Spain, eldest daughter of Ferdinand VII., by his fourth wife Maria Christina, now married to Muñoz, duke of Rianzares, was born on 10th October, 1830, in the city of Madrid, and succeeded to the Spanish throne on the death of her father in 1833. She was proclaimed Queen on the 2nd of October, 1833 ; and was placed under the guardianship of her mother during her minority. Although the Cortes met at Madrid, and took the oath of allegiance to the Infanta, the King's brother, Don Carlos refused to do so, asserting his claim to the throne, under the Salic law, by which a male heir had a right to the throne, and denying the power of the Cortes to annul or abrogate it. A civil war was the result of the assertion of this claim, and after varied fortune, Don Carlos was at last defeated, his party broken up, and himself compelled to flee the kingdom. In October, 1846, Isabel II. was married to her cousin, Don Francisco de Assis, and on the same day her sister, the Infanta, though only fourteen, was married to the Duke de Montpensier, youngest son of Louis-Philippe—unions which were offensive to the feelings of the European courts, but which the King of the French intended should secure to his family the succession to the Spanish throne. The rule of Isabel II. has shown marked signs of retrogression. Railways, the great instruments of civilization, have scarcely penetrated her dominions. The financial system is in a deranged state, and a nation, that seventy or eighty years ago ranked among the greatest in the world, has rapidly descended to that of a third-rate power. With a view to regain some portion of her vanishing prestige, Spain in 1859 declared war against Morocco, amid the general enthusiasm of the Spanish people, and which has terminated successfully. Isabel has two children, a princess, who was born in 1851, and the Prince of Asturias, born 1857, and heir to the throne.

ISABEY, EUGÈNE LOUIS GABRIEL, an historical painter, was born at Paris, on the 22nd July, 1804. His life presents few incidents. Son to the celebrated Jean Baptiste Isabey, he inherits his father's taste, and a portion of his genius. His first picture was exhibited in 1824, when he gained a medal. In 1855 he was awarded a medal of the first class for his picture " Le Départ de Chasse sous Louis XIII.," sent to the Paris Exhibition. His other works have been much admired, and he is held in much esteem as a painter.

ISTURITZ, DON XAVIER DE, a Spanish statesman, born at Cadiz, in 1790, and the son of a merchant residing in that town. He was elected to the Cortes in 1812. Proceeding to Madrid, he took a very active part in political matters, but to such an extent did he compromise himself with the government, as to compel him to take refuge in England, where he became connected with mercantile affairs. In 1834 he returned to Spain, and was appointed " Procurador," to the Cortes. Disagreeing with his colleagues, he was again forced to flee to England. Returning once more to Spain, he was elected by Cadiz to the Cortes in 1838, and became President in 1839. After many political changes he retired into private life, which was chiefly owing to an adverse vote of the Cortes.

JANIN, JULES GABRIEL, a French critic and feuilletonist, was born at St. Etienne, on the 11th December, 1804. His initiatory steps in learning were taken at a school in Lyons, from which he went to Paris, and entered the College of Louis le Grand, where he acquired a sound classical and general education. He finished his studies, and adopted the profession of a teacher, his principal occupation being the preparation of young men for the literary and scientific examinations of the University of France. Soon, however, he abandoned this professional mode of existence. He began to write for " Le Figaro," a theatrical paper, and his success in this line being almost immediate, he was soon installed as theatrical critic for the official news-

paper, the "Journal des Débats." M.
Janin has published few separate works,
his principal writings being scattered
throughout a long series of newspapers
and periodicals. He is the author of a
novel, "L'Ane mort et la Femme guillo-
tinée." Several collections of his tales,
essays, and sketches have been published.

JASMIN, JACQUES, a Gascon poet,
was born at Agen, in the department
of Lot-et-Garonne, on the 6th March,
1798. His kindred belonging to the
poorest peasantry of France, the education
he received was in consequence but scanty.
While a very young man he began business
as a hairdresser, which he yet follows.
His poetry, written in the Romance language, is admired over the whole of
Southern France. It would be tedious
to enumerate the presentations he has
received, and the popular demonstrations
made in his favour. Suffice it to say
that he had handed over not less than
£24,000 before the end of last year to
various charitable and religious societies,
from the proceeds of his séances, and
that more than thirty towns of Southern
France, from Bordeaux to Marseilles, have
conferred upon him the rights of citizenship. In 1852 the French Academy
crowned his three volumes of poetry in
the Romance dialect, and bestowed upon
him their great special prize of £200,
surnaming him at the same time, "Jasmin, the Moral and Popular Poet." His
countrymen, the representatives of an
almost extinct nationality, who are
proud of him, say that he is the last of
the Troubadours, and that no poet of the
day equals him in art, pathos, and delicacy. The poet has now a pension of
£72 a year, from the French department
of public instruction, as a national re-
compense. He draws no revenues from
his recitations, charging merely his coach
hire and railway fares, and other expenses, against those who get them up.

JELLACHICH, JOSEPH BARON VON,
Marshal in the Austrian service, and

Ban of Croatia, was born October 16,
1801. He was educated in the Military
Academy at Vienna; entered the Austrian army as Sub-Lieutenant in 1819,
and was promoted to be Lieutenant in
1825. In 1830 he held a temporary
command; in 1837 was a Major of
Infantry; and 1842 was Colonel of the
First Banat Regiment. The Hungarians had, temporarily, accomplished
their national independence in 1848;
and Austria, having induced the Croats,
&c., to make war on emancipated Hungary, the Emperor, at their request,
appointed Jellachich "Ban" or Commander-in-chief of the Croat forces. It
is now notorious, that the deputies who
waited on the Emperor at Vienna were
Jellachich's own purchased instruments.
Ban Jellachich collected his army, and
had 40,000 men, independent of a
considerable force from the Austrian
"regulars," besides arms and ammunition sufficient for every purpose. He
fought a battle near Siotok, and retreated; and during the night he withdrew his troops to fight again, in a most
treacherous manner. His courage, however, did not fail, and he continued to
take the field until Görgei's surrender
and the subjugation of Hungary, Hay-
nau being, part of the time, his commander-in-chief. The latest employment
of the Ban was in 1853, when a dispute
arising between Austria and Montenegro,
he was appointed commander of the corps
of observation on the Danube.

JERDAN, WILLIAM, a journalist, was
born at Kelso, on the 16th April,
1782, and became connected with the
press in 1806. After contributing to and
editing several newspapers, he established the "Literary Gazette" in 1817.
Continuing its editor for many years, he
did much to render both literature and
science accessible to the masses. He
retired from its management in 1850,
and in 1853 published his "Autobiography," which contains a great variety

of interesting reminiscences of his contemporaries.

JERROLD, WILLIAM BLANCHARD, an author and journalist, was born in London, in December, 1826. He is the son of the late Douglas Jerrold, and godson of the late Laman Blanchard. He was educated at the Grammar School at Brompton, and subsequently in France, where he spent several years. He contributed articles and illustrations to the "Illustrated News" in his seventeenth year. When about nineteen he was employed as a reporter on the "Daily News," afterwards, joining the staff of "Douglas Jerrold's Weekly Newspaper," as a regular contributor. His first attractive work was "The Disgrace to the Family," published in monthly numbers, commencing in 1847. He married, in 1849, Lavinia Blanchard, daughter of his godfather. In 1852 he published "Swedish Sketches," written from notes taken during a journey as Commissioner for the Crystal Palace Company, and in 1855, his "Imperial Paris" appeared, a book much and properly appreciated for its graphic delineations of Parisian life, from the palace to the haunts of the unwashed. He was appointed Commissioner for the "Daily News" to the Paris Exhibition of 1855; and editor of the Official English Catalogue of this exhibition. On his father's death in 1857, he was called to edit "Lloyd's Weekly Newspaper," where he continues. He wrote "Tutors of the Young Idea" (1857) in the "Dublin University Magazine." He has written "Cool as a Cucumber," a farce; "Beau Brummel," and the "Chatterbox," both two-act comedies; and also an excellent little vaudeville. His contributions to the "Athenæum" are characterized by genuine acumen; his political writing is true and manly, and his books are always entertaining. He has contributed interesting sketches to "Household Words" and "All the Year Round." In 1859 he published his "Life and Remains of Douglas Jerrold;" also a collection of Douglas Jerrold's "Witticisms." He is a member of the Reform Club, and one of the Council of the Ballot Society.

JEWSBURY, MISS GERALDINE ENDSOR, an English authoress, was born at Manchester in 1824. Her first work was "Zoë, or the History of Two Lives," published in 1845. "The Half Sisters" appeared in 1848, and obtained immediate and merited success. Changing her choice of subjects, Miss Jewsbury drew the materials for her next story, "Marian Withers," from the middle classes. "Constance Herbert," published in 1854, adds to Miss Jewsbury's reputation as an earnest thinker. The "Sorrows of Gentility," published in 1856, though not equal in merit to some of her works, is still worthy of a place among those books which, in their pages, narrate a story and convey a moral. The tendencies of Miss Jewsbury's works are of an elevating kind, and they are always written in a pleasing and easy style.

JOHNSTON, ALEXANDER KEITH, was born at Kirkhill, Scotland, December 28th, 1804, and entered the High School, Edinburgh, with the intention of following the medical profession. He, however, was apprenticed to Kirkwood, the engraver, and eventually devoted himself to the study of geography, and also, to extend his information, learned the German, French, and other continental languages. His first work, the "National Atlas," was published in 1843, and shortly afterwards he produced "The Physical Atlas." He is a Fellow of most of the European Geographical Societies, and was elected Fellow of the Royal Society of Edinburgh in 1850. He published the "Dictionary of Geography" in 1851, the last edition of which appeared in 1859. His present labours are devoted to the preparation of a series of six library maps of the great divisions of the globe, and on four sheets imperial, two of which, Europe and Australasia, have recently appeared; and the "Royal Atlas of General Geography," in folio, now (1860) in course of publication. His minor works comprise an atlas to the History of Europe, and educational atlases of general, physical, and classical geography, and astronomy.

JOMINI, HENRI, BARON, a French historian, born at Payerne, Canton de Vaud, March 1779, served in one of the Swiss regiments as a soldier of France, but the corps being disbanded, he turned his attention to mercantile pursuits. Some years after he became a colonel of militia, and Military Secretary in Switzerland. In 1804 he was a colonel in the French army, and served under Marshal Ney. In 1811 he was promoted to be General of Brigade. Napoleon, however, having taxed him with malversations, Jomini abandoned the French flag, and attached himself to the Russian service, was Aide-de-Camp to the Emperor Alexander I., and in 1822 was tutor to the late Emperor Nicholas. Since 1855 he has resided at Brussels. He has written various historical works, principally relating to the affairs of his own time, and concerning matters that came under his own observation.

JORDAN, SYLVESTER, a German politician, was born at Omer, near Inspruck, in December, 1792. Belonging to a hard-working family, with the assistance of his uncle, a popular poet and shoemaker, in the Tyrol, and the pastor of Axam, he, in 1806, proceeded to the College of Inspruck, then to Munich, and afterwards studied law at Landshut. Owing to the peculiarity of his opinions, he was obliged to leave the Tyrol, to which he had returned, and from 1815 to 1821 resided at Landshut, Heidelberg, Frankfort-on-the-Maine, and Munich. The merits of his works on Jurisprudence procured him the appointment, in 1821, of Assistant-Professor, and in 1822, Titular Professor, of Law in the University of Marburg, and of being called subsequently to represent the same institution in the States Assembly of Hesse-Cassel. His principles being too liberal for the Government of the day, in 1833 he was accused of affiliating with secret societies, and after being under surveillance for a long period, was at length, in 1843, formally arrested, tried, and condemned to five years' imprisonment. He appealed, but two years elapsed before the case was entirely disposed of; on which he was acquitted. He was sent, in 1848, by almost unanimous consent, to the Parliament of Frankfort, where he joined the moderate party, and in 1849 was re-appointed Professor in the Marburg University. His principal works are an "Essay on General Criminal Law," a "Manual of German Criminal Law," and a "Defence" of himself against the accusations of government. He has also contributed papers to various periodical publications.

JOSIKA, NICOLAS, BARON, an Hungarian novelist and author, was born at Torda, in Transylvania, on 28th September, 1796. His family was of ancient lineage and rich, and he was well educated. He entered the Austrian army, was a Lieutenant of Dragoons in 1813, and afterwards a Captain. Five years passed, and he threw up the profession of arms; made an unhappy marriage; learned several languages; and became an author. He has been styled the Walter Scott of his country. By the Hungarians, whether as regards style, manners, character, or observation, he is accepted as their greatest genius. His works are certainly remarkable for well-drawn character, and great descriptive powers. He married, the second time, in 1847, more happily than before. His works extend to about ninety volumes.

JUNGHUHN, FRANK WILHELM,

a German physician, naturalist and traveller, was born at Mansfeld, in Prussia, October 26th, 1812. He studied in the Universities of Halle and Berlin, and afterwards entered the Prussian army in a professional capacity. Engaging unhappily in a duel, he was condemned to twenty years' imprisonment, but after about eighteen months' incarceration, escaped to Paris. From Paris he proceeded to Algiers, where he joined the French army as an Officer of Health to the Foreign Legion. Obtaining the pardon of the Prussian King, he started from Holland for the Sunda Islands, in 1835, and after having remained a year in Batavia, he explored the Islands of Java and Sumatra. This expedition occupied him about six years, which he passed in ethnographical, statistical, and scientific study of the people and countries which he visited. Returning to Batavia in 1842, he continued his scientific excursions in Java, and in 1845, the Government of Holland named him a Member of the Scientific Commission. In 1849 he reached Holland in ill health, and published the observations he had collected during his travels. His most important work is "Java, from a Topographical, Geological, and Botanical Point of View:" a work pronounced by competent authorities to be the best existing in reference to the natural history of that island.

KANE, SIR ROBERT, M.D., was born in Dublin in 1810, and after receiving a medical education, entered the Meath Hospital, eventually becoming Professor of Chemistry at the Apothecaries' Hall, Dublin. He gained a prize for his work on "Typhus Fever," and in 1832 founded the "Dublin Journal of Medical Science." He is a member of the Royal Irish Academy, and was knighted in 1846. His measures for the formation of an Industrial Museum in Ireland, were adopted by Sir Robert Peel, and resulted in the establishment of that institution. He is the President of Queen's College, Cork, and has published many valuable works, amongst which may be specially named "The Elements of Chemistry," which was very favourably received by the scientific world, and generally adopted as a text book. He has taken an active part in the organization of the system of United Education in Ireland, and especially in its higher branches, and has sustained its defence against the partisans of "sectararian" instruction. His time and attention have consequently been of late years taken away from his earlier scientific pursuits.

KARR, JEAN BAPTISTE ALPHONSE, a French writer, was born in 1808, at Paris. He was educated at the Collége Bourbon, and became a teacher there, occasionally writing poetry. He wrote rapidly and incessantly, often turning his pen to romances, in more than one of which his own personal life is supposed to be portrayed. He contributed to all kinds of periodicals, and was once stabbed in the back by a lady who felt aggrieved by the freedom of his satire. Louis-Philippe created him a Chevalier of the Legion of Honour. His domestic tales are smartly told, and exhibit both originality and power.

KAULBACH, WILLIAM, a German painter and Director of the Academy of Arts, at Munich, was born at Arolsen, in the principality of Waldeck, October 15th, 1805. He went to Dusseldorf in his sixteenth year to study, and the experience gained in the Academy of Arts there was never forgotten. His progress, under his master Cornelius, was rapid; and in 1829 he painted the "Madhouse," which forthwith placed him on a level with the first German artists of the "positive" school, indeed of every or any school. Since then he has been an earnest artist. Hogarth seems to be his master or guide, and Goethe and Schiller his inspiration.

KAVANAGH, Miss Julia, an Irish authoress, is descended from an ancient Irish family, and was born at Thurles, county Tipperary, in 1824. Proceeding to the Continent in early life, she was educated at Paris, where she acquired that exact knowledge of French society and manners which she afterwards turned to such excellent account in her literary compositions. Returning to London in 1844, Miss Kavanagh contributed numerous papers to the periodicals for two or three years before trying her strength on any more decided effort. Her first book, "The Three Paths," was published in 1847, and in 1848 "Madeleine" appeared; both works being well received by the reading and thinking portion of the public. In 1850 Miss Kavanagh published her "Women in France of the Eighteenth Century," a most agreeable work of its class, illustrative of what may be termed the artificial life of that period of French history. Next year her "Nathalie," depicting the manners and mode of existence in the less known districts of France was given to the world, and no picture could be more faithfully or artistically drawn. She afterwards wrote " Women of Christianity," published in 1852, and in 1853, "Daisy Burn" issued from the press. After the latter publication Miss Kavanagh travelled through France, Switzerland, and Italy, and published "Grace Lee," and "Rachel Grey," two tales descriptive of the English life of the present day. Of Miss Kavanagh's writings it has been correctly said that they unite the accuracy of English observation to the grace of French vivacity.

KEAN, Charles, only surviving son of Edmund Kean, was born at Waterford, in January, 1811, and after being educated at Eton, where he greatly distinguished himself, entered on the theatrical profession, chiefly owing to domestic misfortunes. His earliest appearances on the stage were not successful, but by the exercise of patience and earnest attention he has obtained a high position, and in many instances, extraordinary success. He visited America in 1830, and also in 1839, and after returning to England married Miss Ellen Tree, in 1842. After playing at various places in Great Britain he again visited America, and altogether was comparatively successful. In 1850 he rented the Princess's Theatre, and for a long time had the utmost success as a reward of his spirited management. Since relinquishing the lesseeship of the Princess's, Mr. and Mrs. Kean have made tours through the provinces, and have been universally well received. He has for several years conducted the private theatricals at Windsor, and her Majesty has marked her sense of his exertions by many royal favours.

KEAN, Mrs., wife of the above, previously Miss Ellen Tree, has long been esteemed as one of the leading actresses in England, and during Mr. Kean's connexion with the Princess's, assisted very materially in promoting the success of the undertaking.

KEBLE, The Rev. John, M.A., vicar of Hursley, was born in 1800. He obtained high honours at Oxford, and was appointed Professor of Poetry. His various works, ":The Christian Year," " The Cathedral," " The Baptistery,". &c., have achieved a well-deserved popularity.

KELLY, Sir Fitzroy, an English lawyer, was born in London, in 1796. After being called to the bar, in 1824, he attended the Norfolk Circuit, where he soon acquired distinction in his profession. In 1835 he became king's counsel. He was afterwards elected Member for Ipswich, which borough he sat for till 1841, with the exception of a short time during which a petition was presented against him. Having lost Ipswich, he was elected as Member for Cambridge in 1843, and was made

Solicitor-General, under Sir Robert Peel, the honour of knighthood being conferred on him. He subsequently held office under Lord Derby in 1852, and was again Solicitor-General, having been elected Member for East Suffolk. He joined Lord Derby in 1858, and was Attorney-General during that noble lord's short administration of affairs. As a lawyer Sir Fitzroy Kelly has long stood foremost at the bar, and has been a consistent supporter of Conservative principles as a politician.

KEMBLE, MRS. FANNY, or more correctly Frances Anne, eldest daughter of the late Charles Kemble, tragedian and examiner of plays, was born in London, in 1811. Her first appearance was in the character of "Juliet," at Covent-garden Theatre, in October, 1829. Her father was the "Romeo," and her mother, the once celebrated and beautiful Miss de Camp played the "Nurse." For three or four years Miss Kemble took leading rôles in tragedy and comedy, her natural ability and anxious study placing her eventually among the first actresses of the time. In 1832 Mr. Kemble visited America professionally with his daughter, who there married Mr. Butler, of Philadelphia, a man of property, but owing to domestic differences a separation took place in 1849. Since then Mrs. Fanny Kemble, the name of Butler being dropped by her after the divorce, has not returned to the stage, but exercised her undoubted talents in giving public readings of Shakspeare, throughout this country, and in America. Mrs. Kemble is the author of "Francis the First," a tragedy, in which she acted the part of "Louise," at Covent-garden; of a "Journal" of her American experiences (1835); the "Star of Seville," a drama; "Poems" (1842); and "A Year of Consolation," the latter being her reminiscences of a visit paid to her sister, Mrs. Sartoris, in Italy. Mrs. Kemble is at present residing in Boston, Massachusetts.

KERN, J. CONRAD, a Swiss statesman, was born at Berlingen, near Arenenberg, in 1808. Diessenhofen and Zurich contributed to his earlier education, and after leaving the latter city he commenced a course of theology at Basle University, but turning to the legal profession he studied at Berlin, Heidelberg, and Paris. On returning to Switzerland, he chose his own path of public duty, and became, in 1837, President of the Supreme Tribunal for the Canton of Thurgovia, and of the Council of Public Instruction. In the capacity of Educational Minister, he displayed those qualities which render a statesman influential at once with his colleagues and the people. Distinguished as an orator, he was chosen to represent his canton before and after the settlement of the new Federal Constitution. In 1838, when the French Government demanded peremptorily that Louis Napoleon should be expelled from Switzerland, M. Kern, with an honest heart and the boldest eloquence, resisted the claims of Louis-Philippe, and the Council of Thurgovia, without a dissentient voice, adopted his views. In 1848 he went to Vienna, and afterwards, in concert with M. Druey, he was one of the most judicious of reformers, assisting to frame the new constitution, and afterwards identifying himself with the measures of the government. He has held other offices, and three years ago, when a contest arose between Prussia and Switzerland regarding the Canton of Neufchâtel, M. Kern was the senator specially chosen to uphold the liberties of his country, and the authority of the republic. M. Kern has since acted as Swiss Ambassador to the French court. His devotion to the interests of his country, whether in a political or social point of view, causes him to rank as one of the most eminent patriots in Switzerland.

Q

KINGLAKE, ALEXANDER WILLIAM, M.P., was born at Taunton, in 1809. He was educated at Taunton, Ottery St. Mary, and subsequently at Eton, and Trinity College, Cambridge. Having taken his degree he entered as a student in Lincoln's-inn, and was called to the bar in 1837. Soon after leaving the university, Mr. Kinglake went to the East. On his return, in 1844, he determined that he would put his impressions in print, but not being able to find any publisher who would undertake the risk, he agreed with Mr. Olivier, of Pall Mall, to publish the book, and guaranteed him against loss. The work proved highly successful, was translated into nearly all the languages of the Continent, and reprinted in America. This was "Eothen," a word meaning "From the East." Mr. Kinglake has never published any other book. Many years ago he wrote two articles in the "Quarterly Review," but with that exception he has never contributed to any periodicals. He accompanied the English army when it landed on the coast of the Crimea in 1854, and was present with Lord Raglan at the battle of the Alma, and during the flank march and the seizure of Balaklava. He remained at the British head-quarters during the first bombardment of Sebastopol, and being then attacked with fever, was obliged to return home. In 1856 he quitted the bar, and in 1857 was returned to the House of Commons as Member for Bridgewater, which seat he continues to hold. He is at present engaged upon a "History of the Crimean War."

KINGSLEY, THE REV. CHARLES, Rector of Eversley, Hants, Canon of Middleham, and Chaplain in Ordinary to the Queen, Professor of Modern History in the University of Cambridge, was born at Holne vicarage, near Dartmoor, Devonshire, in June, 1819. After a preliminary home education, at the age of twelve he became a pupil of the Rev. J. Knight, then, of the Rev. Derwent Coleridge, and subsequently, a student at King's College, London; he then entered Magdalene College, Cambridge, attaining distinguished honours, and holding a scholarship in that university. Mr. Kingsley at first contemplated the law, but he changed his mind and entered the church. His first cure was Eversley, a parish in Hampshire, and subsequently he was presented to the rectorship. In the literary world he is known as one of the boldest and ablest of the writers of our time. In conjunction with the Rev. F. D. Maurice, and some kindred spirits, he has largely interested himself in what Carlyle has called the condition-of-England question, especially on Social Science and Sanitary Reform. Mr. Kingsley's principal works are "The Saints' Tragedy," "Alton Locke," "Westward Ho!" "Hypatia," "Two Years Ago," "Glaucus," "Alexandria and her Schools," "Phaethon," and several volumes of sermons. In all his works, philosophical thought is, as it were, instinctively blended with imaginative and descriptive power; they exhibit a broad liberality of sentiment, and are pervaded by the one great idea—the intellectual and social omnipotence of the Christian religion. He is an admirable poet, many of the verses introduced through his various works being perfect gems. As an earnest and persevering philanthropist, he stands second to no man who with voice, pen, and means, assists in ameliorating the condition of suffering humanity. In 1860 Mr. Kingsley was appointed Professor of Modern History in the University of Cambridge.

KINKEL, GOTTFRIED, a German poet and art critic, was born in 1815, at Obercassel, on the Rhine. He was educated by his father, a Protestant minister, and afterwards entered the Gymnasium, and then the University of Bonn, where he greatly distinguished himself. In 1837 he travelled through Italy as a student, and on his return became a lecturer on divinity, especially on ecclesiastical history, for nine years. He urged with more boldness than was agreeable to the Prussian Government, a separation of church and state, and in consequence M. Eichhorn openly expressed his hostility to Kinkel. The young professor, seeing his career thus checked, surrendered theology and devoted his talents to literature, modern civilization, and the fine arts. He was at length, in 1846, regularly appointed as Professor in the University, receiving at the same time the degree of Doctor in Philosophy. He lived quietly, until the revolution of 1848 drew him from retirement into the bustle of public life, when, as a democrat, he gave great offence to the court party in Prussia, especially in 1849, by his opposition to the Manteuffel Ministry, in his capacity of Member of the Lower House of Legislature of Prussia. In June, 1849, he entered a volunteer corps for the defence of the Frankfort constitution, was wounded in the field, taken prisoner by the Prussian troops in the Grand Duchy of Baden, and condemned by court-martial to imprisonment for life; he was confined in a house of correction, and treated in the most cruel and inhuman manner. In 1850 he made his escape from the fortress of Spandau, proceeded to Edinburgh, ultimately removing to London, where he now lives as a Professor of the German language and literature, and a Lecturer on the History of the Fine Arts.

KINNAIRD, GEORGE WILLIAM FOX, LORD, born in 1807, is the ninth baron of the title. He succeeded to his father's honours in 1826, and was elevated to the rank of a British peer, under the title of Baron Rossie, by

Lord Grey in 1831. He filled the office of Master of the Buckhounds in 1840-41, and is a member of the Privy Council. His politics are of the liberal order; but his name is most associated with an act of parliament repressive of the spirit trade in Scotland, generally recognized as "Forbes Mackenzie's Act." Though Lord Kinnaird and Mr. Mackenzie differed on many party questions, they agreed on the wisdom of adopting measures to arrest the spread of intemperance among the people of Scotland. They abandoned their distinctions as whig and conservative, and lent themselves to carry the restrictive enactment as it now stands. Lord Kinnaird has lately been created a Baron of the United Kingdom.

KISS, AUGUSTUS, a Prussian sculptor, was born at Pless in Upper Silesia, in 1802. He was educated in the School of Gleiwitz, and afterwards proceeded to Berlin, where he placed himself under Rauch and Tieck, and produced various works for a fountain at Charlottenhof, near Potsdam. He afterwards finished "The Mounted Amazon attacked by a Tiger," which was much admired and eventually cast in bronze. That production placed Kiss on his proper platform, and since then his reputation has steadily increased. He executed three colossal equestrian statues of Frederick the Great, and two of Frederick William III., which were cast in bronze; and the statues of four heroes of the Seven Years' War—viz. the Prince of Anhalt-Dessau, the Generals Schwerin, Winterfeld, and Seydlitz, also cast in bronze, destined for the square called Wilhelms-Platz, at Berlin.

KISSELEFF, PAUL DMITREVITCH, a Russian general and diplomatist, was born at Moscow, 1788. He entered the army at an early age, and having obtained various grades, became a trusted aide-de-camp to the Emperor Alexander I., whom he accompanied to the Congress of Vienna, and afterwards to the second entry of the Allies into Paris. His success in various missions secured him the favour of Alexander, and of his successor the Emperor Nicholas. In 1828 he distinguished himself in the war against the Turks, and was created Lieutenant-General. He turned his attention to diplomacy in the Principalities, and exercised art and influence to render Moldavia and Wallachia subservient to Russia. On his recall to St. Petersburg he was highly fêted, and at length was made first officer under the crown. He was appointed Russian minister at Paris after the Crimean war.

KLAPKA, GENERAL GEORGE, was born at Temesvar in Hungary, on the 7th April, 1820. After receiving a military education he was appointed to the 1st Royal Hungarian Life Guards. On the revolution breaking out he joined the patriotic party, and by his energy and skill obtained rapid promotion. Having gained an advantage over the Austrians, he was preparing to push his results still further, but was prevented by the disastrous events which occurred to Georgëi and Kossuth. After surrendering the fortress of Komorn he proceeded to England, and subsequently published a work entitled "Memoirs of the War of Independence in Hungary." He now resides in Geneva, where he has been naturalized.

KMETY, GENERAL GEORGE, a Hungarian soldier, was born at Pokoragy, Hungary, in 1813. He entered the 19th Regiment of Hungarian Infantry in 1833, and in 1840 was promoted to the rank of sub-Lieutenant and Regiment-Adjutant. In 1848 he was named to the command of a company in a battalion of his regiment which was serving against the Croats and Servians. Soon afterwards, on the breaking out of hostilities between Austria and Hungary, he received the command of a Honved battalion, and devoted himself to the service of his native country. During the battle of Isaszegh he found himself in the same position as Gerard under Grouchy during the battle of Waterloo, unable to induce his commander Gaspar to overlook the strict letter of his orders and fall upon the rear and flank of the army of Windischgrätz, which would have decided that campaign. At the taking of Bude on the 21st May, he, at the head of his division, stormed the entrenchments near the bridge, and was wounded. Named General and appointed to the command of a detached division, he beat the Austrians signally at Csorna, 13th June, where their commander General Wiess was killed. On the 27th June he had a combat at Thaszi, after which he was sent with his division to the Lower Danube, where, on the 16th July, he forced the Austrians to raise the siege of Peterwardein. In the unfortunate battle of Temesvar, 9th August, he commanded the extreme left wing, and alone retired in good order, so that on the 15th August, that is to say two days after the surrender of Görgei, he fought on the heights of Lugos, the last battle of the Hungarian war, which secured the retreat of the refugees into Turkey. The remaining forces of the general being reduced to the utmost distress he disbanded them, and made his way into Turkey, and was "internè" at Aleppo till the end of the year 1851. Having fled to England he published a refutation of the misstatements of Görgei, which appeared in his memoirs. At the beginning of the Russian war, in 1853, he returned to Turkey, offered his services, and was sent to the army of Anatolia. During the blockade of Kars, he commanded a Turkish division under the name of "Madjar Ismail Pasha." In the great battle of the 29th September, 1855, he saved Kars for the moment by defeating a Russian army of 30,000 men, which attacked the heights of Takmass. In front of this position the enemy left 6,000 dead bodies, which fact shows this to have been one of the most bloody battles of modern times. At the surrender of Kars, General Kmety, not wishing to fall into the hands of the Russians, received permission to leave the army, and accompanied by a small escort of Kurds, cut his way through the enemy's lines. Those who knew Kmety, at Kars invariably speak of him as "Dear old Kmety," for he possessed an intuitive power of winning affection. In the ill-organized army which defended the fort, there was scarcely a man that would not have died to preserve the general. There is hardly an example on record of one man making so much good out of such bad materials. His men were badly provisioned, worse clad, were in arrear of pay, and even short of ammunition; yet he kept them together, and held out until the arrival of General Williams.

KNIGHT, CHARLES, an English author and publisher, was born at Windsor, in 1791. His father was a bookseller, printer, and publisher in the town, into whose business the subject of this memoir was introduced at the age of sixteen. In 1812 he went to London to acquire skill in reporting, and experience in the general management of a newspaper. On his return he started the "Windsor Express," a paper which still exists, although Mr. Knight's connexion with it ceased in 1826. From 1820 to 1822, in conjunction with Mr. C. H. Locker, he edited "The Plain Englishman," which was perhaps the first of the cheap miscellanies destined to drive out of the market the foolish and mischievous tracts which then formed the cheap literature of the people. In 1820 he also began the publication of the "Etonian," the success of which led to the establish-

ment, in 1823, of "Knight's Quarterly Magazine," and his removal to London. There, as a member of the Society for the Diffusion of Useful Knowledge, he projected and submitted to the society the plan of the "British Almanack," and the "Companion to the Almanack." The plan being approved, its execution and the responsibility were left to Mr. Knight. These works proved a great success, and had the effect of expurgating much of the astronomical trash which previously had disgraced this class of books. In the same way, and under the same responsibility, he edited the "Penny Magazine." The same may be said of the "Library of Entertaining Knowledge," of which the volume on "The Elephant" was written by Mr. Knight. "The Penny Cyclopædia," says the "Companion to the Almanack" for 1858, p. 15, "was projected by the same publisher to form a moderate-sized book of eight volumes. The plan was perhaps unavoidably departed from. The committee had the honour of the work in its extended form, but without incurring any of the risk, or contributing one shilling to the cost, the literary expenditure alone having reached nearly £40,000. Upon the completion of the Cyclopædia the balance upon the outlay above the receipts was £30,788." In a second great undertaking of the society, "The Biographical Dictionary," it took upon itself the financial responsibility, and broke down after completing the letter A. In 1830, during a time of mischievous agitation against the use of machinery, Mr. Knight wrote and published "The Results of Machinery," which had an almost unprecedented sale, and must have produced most beneficial effects. His chief publications since then have been, in 1831, "The Rights of Industry, Capital, and Labour;" in 1839, "The Pictorial Shakspeare;" in 1843, "William Shakspeare," a biography; in 1841, and following years, "London;" in

1843, and following years, "The Shilling Weekly Volumes, extending to 126 numbers, for which he wrote the "Life of Caxton;" in 1856, "The Popular History of England," of which six volumes have been published. Mr. Knight is now editing the English Cyclopædia based upon the Penny Cyclopædia, but enlarged and separated into divisions, of which the Geographical, Natural History, and Biographical Sections have already appeared.

KNOWLES, JAMES SHERIDAN, a dramatist and author, was born at Cork, in 1784. About the year 1792 his father removed to London, taking with him his son James, then about eight years of age. Four years later his passion for the drama had displayed itself, and at that early age he wrote a play for a company of juvenile actors, of which he was himself the chief. At the age of fourteen he wrote the ballad of the "Welsh Harper;" he was soon after introduced to Mr. Hazlitt, whom he always mentioned with pleasure for his continuous kindness to him, and through Charles Lamb he made the acquaintance of the leading literary celebrities of the metropolis. After residing in London for some years he exchanged the English for the Irish metropolis as his residence; and in Dublin it was that his *début* as an actor was made. The success of the effort was not very promising, and for a time the stage was abandoned; though afterwards resumed at Waterford, where he was an actor and singer in the same company as Edmund Kean, for whom he wrote a tragedy entitled "Leo, or the Gipsy," but which has not been preserved. Some years afterwards, having repaired to Belfast, in the theatre of which his first tragedy, Caius Gracchus, was produced, he was induced to open an academy as a teacher of elocution and grammar. Subsequently he settled for some years in Glasgow, where his

first standard drama, "Virginius," was produced and played with great success. In 1820 this fine play was brought out at Covent-garden, with Macready as "Virginius," and, in the great centre of criticism, established Knowles' reputation as the first of living dramatists. He afterwards wrote the "Hunchback," the "Wife," the "Love Chase," "Women's Wit," "Love," &c. &c., all ranking among the highest efforts of dramatic genius. Mr. Knowles acted for years in his own plays, both in London and the provinces, and some of his personations, such as "Master Walter," in the "Hunchback," could not be excelled for their development of character. About ten years ago a pension of £200 was conferred upon him. In 1858 his health giving way he proceeded to the Continent, remaining there for six months, and returning in 1859 with renewed strength. Mr. Knowles has written one or two theological works, which display a far more extensive acquaintance with doctrine and the laws of controversy than could have been expected from his early training.

KOBELL, FRANZ VON, a German poet and man of science, was born at Munich, in July 1803. He studied in his native city, and at the age of twenty-three became one of the professors of mineralogy. He has written numerous works on this branch of natural history. For his services to the cause of science he has been decorated with a number of orders, is member of the Bavarian Academy of Sciences, and has the principal charge of the mineralogical collection at Munich, besides holding other situations of profit and honour. He is also the author of several poetical works, chiefly popular in Bavaria, as they are written in the dialect or patois of that part of Germany.

KOCK, CHARLES HENRI EMMANUEL, a German naturalist and traveller, born in 1809, at Weimar, and educated at Würtzbourg. In 1836 he undertook a scientific expedition through a portion of Russia, publishing his observations in 1842, which were chiefly relating to the Caucasus. In 1843 he departed from Germany to the East, proceeding through most part of Turkey, Armenia, and along the shores of the Caspian Sea. This journey supplied him with materials for his " Travels in the East," a work of considerable merit, published in 1846. His works are very voluminous, principally relating to the scientific and social aspects of the various countries which he has visited.

KOCK, CHARLES PAUL DE, a French novelist, born at Passy, 1794, received an imperfect education, and was intended for a commercial life, but his attachment to literature was such that he dismissed every other thought and embraced the profession of letters. At an early age he finished his first novel " L'Enfant de ma Femme." The effort was not successful, and he turned his attention to writing for the theatres, labouring diligently in that department of literature until 1820, when he re-sumed novel writing. " Les Enfants de Maître Pierre " (1825), and " Le Camp du Drap d'Or " (1828), placed him in the first rank, and he has since main-tained his reputation. In a moral sense some of his productions are very excep-tionable, but his inventive genius and skill in the depiction of character are unquestionable. He is one of the most voluminous writers of the age.

KOSSUTH, LAJOS DE KOSSUTH FALVA, ex-Governor of Hungary, was born in September 1802, at Monok, in the county of Zemplin, in Hungary, of an ancient though not wealthy family. He was educated at the Protestant College of Saros Patak, and afterward studying law, took high honours on ob-taining his diploma as an Advocate in 1822. For the following eight years he practised at the bar, and became an in-fluential member of the liberal party in his native country. He particularly distinguished himself at the time of the cholera riots in 1831, by the cool deter-mination with which he faced the rioters. In December 1832 he went to Presburg to the Diet, and, for the first time in Hungary, reported correctly the proceedings of both Houses in a M.S. Journal. The Government threw difficulties in his way, prevented him from using a lithographic press, and restricted the circulation of his news-letters, which, however, soon acquired important political influence. In 1836 Kossuth, who had removed to Pesth, and edited these M.S. news-letters reporting the proceedings of the county meetings all over the country, took an active part in the defence of prisoners prosecuted at the time for political offences, and roused the majority of the counties to a protest against the illegalities of the Royal Court of Justice. He was arrested in 1837, and sentenced in 1838 to three years' imprisonment. Forbidden to communicate with his friends, to write letters or even to read any papers or political books, the prisoner was allowed to have an English Grammar, Walker's Pronouncing Dictionary, and Shaks-peare's works in his solitary cell, and it was during this confinement that he acquired that mastery of the English language, which, at a later period, enabled him in England to denounce the tyranny of the House of Hapsburg-Lorraine. In May 1840, several liberal measures passed, and Kossuth was liberated by a general amnesty. In 1841 he obtained permission to edit a political newspaper, the "Pesth Hirlap," under the control of a mitigated censor-ship. The influence of this publication was enormous, the Government became alarmed, when even the opposition of Court Szechenyi, who represented the Liberal Conservatives could not prevail against Kossuth's prestige. In the autumn of 1847 Kossuth was returned to the Diet by the county of Pesth, in spite of the bribery and intimidation resorted to by the administration. Kossuth's masterly eloquence, the comprehensive grasp of his mind, and his immense popularity in the country, gave him at once the complete command of the opposition, over the head of the former parliamentary leaders, whose jealousy led to several unsuccessful cabals against him. The French revolution of February 1848, and the electric shock which pervaded all Europe, silenced those petty intrigues, and on the 3rd March Kossuth delivered his celebrated speech, in which he demanded Constitutional Government for the hereditary provinces of the Austrian Empire, as the only real guarantee for the Constitution of Hungary against the despotic tendencies of the Court. The effect of this speech upon the German population of the empire surpassed every expectation. On the 13th Prince Metternich resigned, and the Emperor promised a Constitution. The deputation of the Hungarian Diet, petitioning now for a responsible ministry, arrived on the 15th at Vienna, was graciously received, and at the request of the court, Kossuth quieted the threatening agitation of the inhabitants. Count Louis Bathyany then formed his Ministry, which carried the abolition of serfdom, the equality of taxation, and the extension of the franchise. Kossuth was appointed Minister of Finance, an invidious post, since he had to extend taxation to the lands of the nobles, which, up to that time, had enjoyed a complete immunity. As soon as the court functionaries had recovered from their first alarm, they made attempts to stir up a civil war among the different races of Hungary. Bands of armed marauders, enlisted and equipped by the Austrian consul at Belgrade, crossed the Danube from the

principality of Servia, and raised the standard of revolt, whilst Baron Jellachich, appointed in March 1848, Ban of Croatia, not only dissolved the union between the two countries, but made active preparations against Hungary, and refused to come to any arrangement with the Provisional Government. In September the invasion of the Croat army took place. Bathyany, resigning his office to Archduke Stephen, Palatine of Hungary, and Commander-in-chief of the army, took to flight, and but for the indomitable energy of Kossuth, and the boldness with which he, under desperate circumstances, seized the reins of government, even the enthusiasm of the nation would scarcely have prevented Jellachich's success. All the efforts of the country being now concentrated by Kossuth in one direction, the Croat army was defeated, Jellachich expelled from Hungary, and the progress of the Austrian intrigue checked. The revolt of the Viennese on the 6th of October allowed Kossuth a few weeks more to organize the resources of Hungary, and to prepare for an unavoidable struggle with Austria. The attempt to relieve the besieged Viennese failed however, owing to the want of energy on the part of General Moya, and the pusillanimity of the Viennese themselves. The battle of Schwehat at which Kossuth took part in person, was lost on the 29th October. Kossuth raised Colonel Görgei on the battle field to the rank of General, and gave him the command in chief. In December 1848 Hungary was invaded on every side by Austrian armies, while a Russian army entered Transylvania. As Prince Windischgrätz advanced upon Pesth, Kossuth and the Diet retreated to Debreczin, and during the unusually severe winter, at a time when all Europe gave up Hungary as lost, he raised, organized, clad, and armed those troops of Honveds (defenders of the country), who, in a short but sanguinary campaign of three months, defeated the armies of Prince Windisch-grätz, of Count Schlick, of Ban Jella-chich, and of General Puchner, the insurgents, and the Russian garrisons of Southern Transylvania. The country was free, the Austrians expelled, but the defeated and demoralized court pre-ferred Russian intervention to an ho-nourable arrangement with the Hunga-rians, and the Hungarian Constitution was formally abolished in March by the Em-peror Francis Joseph, who refused to be crowned in Hungary. Accordingly, the Diet proclaimed on the 14th of April, the independence of the country, the de-position of the house of Hapsburg-Lor-raine, and elected Kossuth Governor. Görgei, raised to the command of one of the victorious armies, now jealous of the fame and influence of the civilian Kossuth, tried to organize a military party against him in the army and in the Diet, with the object of seizing the supreme power, and opening negocia-tions with the Austrians. Trusting, however, exclusively to Russian assist-ance, the Viennese Government did not respond to Görgei's overtures. But the slow progress of the Austro-Russian ar-mies, and the defeat of Jellachich by General Vettel, induced at last the Rus-sian General Rüdiger to enter into com-munications with Görgei, who marched his army to Arad, insisted upon and forced Kossuth's abdication, and on the 14th of August, 1849, surrendered un-conditionally the army and government at Vilagos, to the Russians, receiving as a reward for his treachery, an Austrian pension, on which he has lived since, at Klagenfurt. Kossuth fled to Turkey, where he was advised to embrace Is-lamism as the only means of preventing his extradition to Austria; he refused to save his life at such a price. The Sultan, however, soon declared, that even at the risk of a war, he would not comply with the Austro-Russian de-mands, and upon the advice of the English Government, he had Kossuth removed to Kutahia, in Asia Minor, where the illustrious exile was treated with the respect due to the distinguished position he had held, though he was kept under restraint as to his movements be-yond the town. At the intercession of the Government of Washington, he was released on the 1st of September, 1851, and embarked on the steam frigate "Mississipi," sent by the American President, expressly for this purpose, to Turkish waters. Before crossing the Atlantic, Kossuth first visited England, where he arrived in October, 1851, and was greeted with boundless enthusiasm at Southampton, the city of London, Manchester, and Birmingham. In No-vember he sailed to the United States, whither he had been invited by the Pre-sident and Congress, and where he was treated as the guest of the nation. He returned to England in July, 1852, and since that time has often lectured on fo-reign affairs in their connexion with Hungary, receiving on all occasions par-ticularly in Scotland, an enthusiastic reception. In 1859, when France and Sardinia resolved to make war against Austria, Kossuth was invited by the Emperor Napoleon first to France, and then to the head-quarters of the army in Italy. After several interviews with the French monarch, a legion was raised from the Hungarian deserters and prisoners of war, and active preparations made for an expedition to Hungary, but the peace of Villafranca put a sud-den stop to the arrangements. Kossuth returned to England, after having suc-ceeded, through the Emperor Napoleon, in securing not only the free return, but likewise the final discharge from Aus-trian military service, of all those who had taken service in the Hungarian legion. Like Victor Emmanuel and Count Cavour, he was disappointed by the results of Villafranca, but he has publicly declared that neither he, nor the cause of Hungary, was betrayed by Napoleon.

KUGLER, FRANZ THEODORE, a German author, was born on the 19th January, 1808, at Stettin, in Pomerania. He studied in several universities, devoting a large portion of his time to the early history of painting and architecture, entering besides on the study of poetry and music. He visited Italy, and wrote voluminously; his greatest work being the "Handbook of the History of Painting, from the Age of Constantine to the present Time" (1837). The immense research and profound thought requisite to produce such a work, though it had been a mere skeleton, were speedily appreciated, and the book was at once caught up by art students, and translated into most of the European languages. In 1850 a second edition was issued, considerably enlarged, and containing a large amount of new material. Sir Charles Eastlake published an English edition of the "Handbook," which was enriched by numerous illustrations of the old masters, and copious notes. He has lectured in the University of Frederick William and the Royal Academy of Berlin, for many years past. Dr. Kügler's works are one and all of a high order; most of them indispensable to the art student, and of interest to the artist.

LABORDE, LÉON EMMANUEL SIMON JOSEPH, COUNT DE, archæologist and traveller, born at Paris, June, 1807, proceeded to Egypt when twenty years old, and explored Arabia Petrea in company with M. Linant, filling his sketch-book by the way. Returning to Europe in 1830, he published an account of his travels, which experienced so favourable a reception as to induce him to venture on a similar work, called "Voyage en Orient." The arts, for which he had always a taste, now occupied a more prominent place in his mind, and, in 1839, he began his "Histoire de la Gravure," with other works of a kindred nature. His father dying in 1840, he succeeded him in the Academy of Belles Lettres, publishing, previously to his election, a "Commentaire Géographique sur L'Exode et les Nombres" (1842), in which he incorporated his investigations in the East. Being returned as a member of the Chamber of Deputies, he almost invariably supported the existing minister, without reference to his general politics. In 1847 he was appointed by Louis-Philippe "Conservateur" of the Museum of Antiquities in the Louvre, a post which he resigned at the revolution of 1848. Being restored to his office, he devoted himself to the study of art, and has written on the subject well and learnedly. In 1851 he was a Commissioner of the Great London Exhibition, and in 1855 he filled a similar position in Paris. For various reasons he has retired from his appointment of "Conservateur."

LACORDAIRE, JEAN BAPTISTE HENRI, a French ecclesiastic, born May 18th, 1802, at Recey-sur-Ource (Côte-d'Or). He studied first at Dijon, and was chiefly remarked for the determination with which he defended Voltarian opinions, as well as for his otherwise enlarged intelligence. He left Dijon College in 1819, and assisted to found a literary society of young men, among whom he became conspicuous for his sceptical views, and his attacks on Roman Catholicism. Turning his attention to the bar, he proceeded to Paris, and became acquainted with Berryer and other eminent persons. Suddenly, however, in 1824, his views on religious matters were entirely changed; he proceeded to St. Sulpice, and emerged three years after in the capacity of an ordained priest. He was chaplain to the College of Henry IV., at the revolution of July, 1830, He became connected with a journal called "L'Avenir," which took for its double motto "God and Liberty—the Pope and the People;" but the vehemence and audacity of his language were such as, in 1831, to bring him before the law courts. He pleaded his own cause, and was acquitted. Other troubles awaited him; and he eventually dissolved his connexion with the paper. Resigning secular occupation, he now preached with uncommon eloquence and fire; his manner was new; and he excited both curiosity and interest. For a short time he sat in the National Assembly but resigned his seat and has now the direction of the College of Sorrez.

LA MARMORA, ALPHONSE MARQUIS DE, a Piedmontese general, and late Minister of War, was born in November, 1804. In 1816 he entered the Military Academy of Turin, and became a Lieutenant of Artillery in 1823, Captain in 1831, and Major in 1845. In 1848 he was named Chef d'Etat Major of the division commanded by the Duke of Genoa, which took so active a part, particularly at the battle of Custoza. At Milan, on the 5th of August, when the King, Charles Albert, was surrounded in the Palais Grippi, La Marmora found means to leave the palace, and returning with a battalion delivered the King who was in imminent danger. In October of the same year he was promoted as General of Brigade and Minister of War. In February, 1849, he had the command of a division which was sent from La Spezzia to Parma, and immediately after the disaster of Novara, was despatched to Genoa, which city was in complete revolution on the 4th of April. At the head of the "Avant Garde" he took some detached forts and scaled the walls of the fortresses, and the next day, after a combat which lasted many hours, he became master of the town. He was named at the same time Lieutenant-General and Royal Commissioner, and took the command of a corps d'armée concentrated at Genoa. In October of the same year he was called to the Ministry of War, where he remained till April 1855, when he sailed for the Crimea, as Commander-in-Chief of a corps d'armée of 17,000 men, and although late in arriving, he rendered essential services to the allies, particularly at the Tchernaya. After the resignation of the Ministry of Count Cavour, and the truce of Villafranca, he was again named Minister of War and Marine, and President of the Council of Ministers, where he remained until the 20th January, 1860.

LAMARTINE, ALPHONSE DE, was born in Macon, about the year 1790, and receiving his early education at Milly, where his family retired during the revolution, and afterwards entered the College of the Pères de la Foi, at Belly. After travelling through Italy he proceeded to Paris, and on the restoration of the Bourbon family, espoused their cause. Experiencing various changes in his course of life, he suddenly appeared as a poet, by the publication of his "Méditations Poétiques," which instantly achieved a great success for him. His public life now commenced, and coming under the notice of Louis XVIII. he obtained his first political position, as an Attaché to the embassy at Florence, and afterwards that of Secretary to the French Minister in London. In England he was fortunate in meeting with a lady of property and education, to whom he was subsequently married. On returning to France he was sent as Minister to Greece, but resigned this position on the accession of Louis-Philippe to the throne, and having failed to obtain a seat in the senate, determined on making an Oriental tour. Having been elected to the Chamber during his absence, he returned to his native country, and speedily gained great renown for the brilliancy of his intellect, and the liberality of his political views. In 1848 he boldly espoused the cause of the revolution which drove Louis-Philippe from France, and became a member of the Provisional Government which was then formed. It was to his prudence and eloquence that France was indebted for the prevention of the scenes of Robespierre's government being repeated, and for the formation of a temporary republic. After the *coup d'état* Lamartine retired into comparatively private life, and devoted himself to literary pursuits. Among his various productions, perhaps the most successful is his "History of the Girondins," in which he gives full expression to his political views. He has also published the "Death of Socrates," "Last Canto of Childe Harold," "Impressions of a Voyage to the East," with others of a varied character. It is almost impossible to offer a review of Lamartine's public life which would do him justice. It may be remarked, however, that his views were, at all times perhaps, of too Utopian a character, although his patriotism cannot be called into question. It is much to be regretted that owing to the sacrifices he made, during the revolution of 1848, he has been plunged into almost inextricable pecuniary difficulties, from which it was hoped, but in vain, that the general feeling in his favour in France would have relieved him. He is about to publish a collected edition of his works, which may possibly assist him out of his misfortunes.

LAMORICIERE, CHRISTOPHE JU-CAULT DE, a French general, late minister and representative, born at Nantes, February, 1806, was a pupil in the Polytechnic School till 1826, and in 1830 was made a Lieutenant, on joining the French Army of Algiers. He advanced with striking rapidity, and being noted for intelligence and courage, was made Captain of the Zouaves. In 1839 he, then a Colonel, was recalled to Paris; and on his return to Africa, he so distinguished himself, that in 1843 he was General of Division, in 1844 Commander of the Legion of Honour, and interim Governor of Algiers in 1845. He assisted in the capture of Abd-el-Kader, and in 1846 he was returned to the Chamber of Deputies, for the College of St. Calais. In 1848 he took an active part in the revolution, and became Minister of War, under the Provisional Government. He was faithful to the policy of Cavaignac, but was arrested and thrown into prison when Louis Napoleon made his notorious *coup d'état*, in 1851. After being released, permission was accorded him to return to and reside in France, but he refused to accept the amnesty, preferring voluntary exile. He has lately entered into the service of the Pope (1860), of whose armies he became Commander-in-Chief. He endeavoured to bring the soldiers into discipline, but has since been defeated by Cialdini, the Sardinian general, and the whole of his army completely disbanded. He fled to Ancona, and on its surrender was made a prisoner of war and conducted to Turin.

LANCE, GEORGE, a painter of fruit, was born at Little Easton, Essex, in 1802, and was for some time a pupil of Hayon. His early taste was soon shown by a successful painting of fruit, and he has ever since devoted himself chiefly to this class of subjects in his various pictures. He has attained to a similar position in illustrating vegetable life to that occupied by Sir Edwin Landseer in animal illustrations. His productions are life-like pictures, and impress the idea on the mind of the admirers that they are beholding the real instead of the imaginative, owing to the finished execution displayed. Some of Mr. Lance's paintings are now in the South Kensington Museum, forming part of the collection which the late

Mr. Vernon has bequeathed to the nation.

LANDOR, WALTER SAVAGE, was born at Ipsley, in Warwickshire, in January, 1775. Receiving his early training at Rugby School, he then proceeded to Oxford. His circumstances in early life being somewhat affluent, he was left to the bent of an impetuous disposition, and joined the insurrection in Spain, in 1808, assisting the patriotic cause by all the means in his power, but he gave up all his offices on the return of Ferdinand to the throne. He subsequently returned to England, and married, removing afterwards to Florence, where he purchased an estate, on which he resided for many years. Devoting himself to literary pursuits from that time, he has published a great variety of poetic and imaginative productions, amongst which may be named his "Idyllia Heroica," "Imaginary Conversations," "Popery, British and Foreign," "Letters of an American," with several others of a similar class. He returned to England, and until lately resided at Bath, but owing to circumstances induced by the naturally strong and impassioned temperament which he unfortunately possesses, he has been compelled to retire from England, and to return to Italy once more.

LANDSEER, SIR EDWIN, an English painter, was born in London, in 1803, and from his earliest days showed a strong taste for painting and the fine arts. Owing to the judicious early training of his father, he soon became an accurate sketcher from nature, which, doubtless, laid the foundation of his future fame. His picture of "Dogs Fighting" first brought him into public notice, and since its exhibition his career has been one of unbroken and almost unequalled success. The whole of his paintings are characterized by accuracy of detail, and he has succeeded in reproducing to perfection the minute traits of his subjects in such a manner as to direct attention to all the peculiarities of breed, and other such incidents in the animals which he represents on canvas. As a landscape painter, Sir Edwin equally demands our admiration, and his Highland scenery, forming the background of many of his pictures, conveys to the mind a vivid idea of the solitude and grandeur of many of the wilds, lochs, and mountain passes of Scotland. It is, of course, beyond our power to catalogue the whole of his productions, most of which are familiar to the eye of all classes in Great Britain. As instances of animal painting, we may refer to his "Laying down the Law," "A Distinguished Member of the Humane Society," "The Stag at Bay," "The Dog Watching his Master's Corpse," "There's Life in the Old Dog yet," &c. Amongst his descriptive pictures are "Bolton Abbey in the Olden Time," "A Scene from the Midsummer Night's Dream," "Peace," and "War," "A Highland Breakfast," "The Drover's Departure," "A Jack in Office," &c. He has introduced some fine landscape scenery in "Night," and "Morning," "An Early Evening Scene in the Highlands," "The Tethered Rams," &c. Most of his works have been engraved, and he has been fortunate in securing the patronage of royalty, and the delight of every critic of the fine arts. He is also one of the most popular artists living with those, who while ignorant of the rules of art, yet delight in gazing on the painter's representations of nature. Sir Edwin has been a Member of the Royal Academy since 1831, was knighted by her Majesty in 1850, and many of his pictures now adorn the walls of the National Collection in the South Kensington Museum. His last painting is "The Illumination."

LANGENBECK, MAXIMILIAN, a German physician, is son of a surgeon, who was extensively known by his anatomical works, and who died in 1851. He studied medicine chiefly under the direction of his father, and became eventually Professor in the University of Göttingen. Among other works, he has written "Klinische Beitraege aus dem Gebiete der Chirurgie und der Opthalmologie," and "Über die Wirkamskeit der Medicinischen Polizei." He has lately visited England (1860), and was received at the Chatham garrison by the Medical Officers with the distinction due to his abilities.

LANKESTER, EDWIN, M.D., was born at Melton, Suffolk, in 1814. After receiving his early education at Woodbridge and University College, London, he entered the medical profession. He is a well-known lecturer and writer on subjects connected with Natural History, and has contributed papers to the "Penny Cyclopædia" and the "English Cyclopædia of Natural History." He is a Fellow of many of the learned societies, President of the Microscopical Society, and has lately been engaged in the Department of Manufactured Products, &c., in the South Kensington Museum, where he has delivered some highly interesting and popular lectures.

LANSDOWNE, HENRY PETTY FITZMAURICE, MARQUIS OF, K.G., an eminent English statesman, was born 2nd July, 1780, and received his early education at Westminster, Edinburgh, and afterwards took his degree of M.A. at Cambridge. From his earliest years he has identified himself with liberal principles, and after spending some time in the study of continental politics, he entered the House of Commons as member for Calne, in the Whig interest. As might be expected, he often spoke in opposition to William Pitt's measures, and through his talents as a debater, and his political consistency, he was chosen to succeed Pitt, as Chancellor of the Exchequer, in the year 1806. Shortly after the resignation of Lord Granville, under whom he held office, Lord Lansdowne was called to the House of Peers, having succeeded to the family title, and for many years was chiefly known by his energetic support of liberal measures, under various administrations, without, however, holding any official position until he became Secretary of State under Lord Canning in 1828. Since that period, the only office he has held, has been that of President of the Council. In his place in the House of Lords he has acquired from all parties the highest character for prudence, foresight, and political ability. In social and literary circles, Lord Lansdowne is justly esteemed, not more on account of his acquirements, than for the affability and condescension of his demeanour.

LATHAM, ROBERT GORDON, a physician, was born at Billingborough, Lincolnshire, in 1812. He studied at Eton, graduated at Cambridge, and after a tour in the north of Europe devoted himself to the study of medicine. Having become Licentiate, he was soon afterwards appointed Physician to the St. James's and St. George's Dispensary, from which he was promoted to be Assistant-Physician of the Middlesex Hospital, where he lectured on Forensic Medicine and Materia Medica. He is a Fellow of the Royal College of Physicians, of the Royal Society, ex-Vice-President of the Ethnological Society, and member of various other learned bodies. Dr. Latham is best known, however, by his ethnological researches, and as one of the earliest members of the Ethnological Society he has contributed a large amount of information, characterized by deep research, on every branch of that interesting study. Amongst his leading works may be named, the "Varieties of Mankind," "The Ethnology of Europe," and his "History of the English Language," in all of which, and in others not here specified, he has added many interesting facts as to the origin and connexion of the various languages spoken in different parts of the world.

LAUDER, Robert Scott, R.S.A., a painter, was born at Silver Mills, near Edinburgh, in 1803. At an early age he displayed considerable aptitude for drawing, and advice and encouragement were given to the young aspirant by David Roberts. When fifteen he resolved, after a visit to an exhibition of pictures, to become a painter. But it is to the late Rev. John Thomson, of Duddingstone, that he is chiefly indebted for his first introduction to the great principles of art, as exemplified in the schools of Italy. Sir Walter Scott's influence obtained him entrance as a student in the Edinburgh School of Design, where he remained for some years, and afterwards studied in the British Museum. In 1826 he returned to Edinburgh, where he discharged for two years the tutorial duties of Sir William Allan. In 1833 he visited Italy, and in the study of the old masters of the different schools, the great truths inculcated by Mr. Thomson were perceived and appreciated. In 1838, returning home, he resided chiefly in London for about fourteen years, when being invited to take the directorship of the Government School of Design, he again returned to Edinburgh. He has exhibited many excellent pictures, his works being appreciated both for their colour and finished execution. He has taken many subjects from Scott's romances, but he has achieved a more worthy position by his scriptural subjects, such as "Christ Teaching Humility," and "Christ Walking on the Water," which are noble works of their class.

LAWRENCE, Sir John, late governor of the Punjaub, is a member of a family which has been long identified with Indian affairs. Little notice was taken of his early services in India though he distinguished himself from the first. It was only when troublous times commenced that the energy of his character and his great talents became known. For nearly twenty-seven years Sir John has laboured in India. The first ten years were spent at Delhi and the surrounding district. This was his training school, and well did he take advantage of it. Separated from all Europeans, and associating only with the natives, he learned "to know the races it was his lot to rule." After a short visit home he again returned to India and resumed his duties in the Delhi district. It was about this time that the war on the north-west frontier broke out, when the Sikhs crossed the Sutlej with a large force, and were not repelled without great loss to the British army. A judicious, firm-minded man had to be chosen to govern this restless frontier, and Sir John Lawrence was selected as Commissioner of the ceded territory. When the Punjaub was annexed to India, in 1849, Lord Dalhousie formed a Board of Administration for the government of the new province, and two of its members were Sir Henry and Sir John Lawrence. Subsequently Sir Henry withdrew, and Sir John Lawrence was appointed sole Governor of the Punjaub. During that disastrous period, which is so fresh in the memory of all, when regiment after regiment mutinied—when treachery appeared on all sides, and the blood of hundreds of our countrymen was sacrificed to native ferocity—when we almost feared that our Indian possessions were to be torn from us—then did Sir John Lawrence, under Providence, prove himself the "saviour of India." So wise, so firm had been his rule, so well organized his policy, that not only did the Punjaub remain faithful, but its troops were spared to stem the tide of rebellion, and to re-capture the capital of Delhi. Through his long and bright career as a ruler in India, Sir John Lawrence has proved his efficiency for every emergency, distinguishing himself by his untiring perseverance and zeal, and his enlightened Christian views of Indian administration. It may not be known that the father of Sir John was an officer of distinction, and served in the Mysore campaign under the Marquis Cornwallis. Three of his brothers are high in the Indian service. On his departure from India in April, 1859, on account of his health, an address was presented to him by the officers, civil and military, and others residing in the Punjaub, expressing their admiration of his public career in the country. Again, on Sir John's return to England, a congratulatory address was presented to him from the most distinguished noblemen of the country, clergy of all denominations, and every merchant who had any knowledge or interest in Indian affairs, acknowledging gratefully his great services, both civil and military, more especially his firmness in endeavouring to promote the cause of Christianity in India. Nor has the Government overlooked his services, for it has conferred on him the honour of a Baronetcy, and a seat in the new Indian Council, where, doubtless, his past experience of Indian affairs will render him a most valuable member of that Council. The freedom of the city of Glasgow has lately been conferred on Sir John Lawrence (September, 1860).

LAYARD, AUSTEN HENRY, a celebrated English traveller, was born in Paris 1817. After coming to England, where at first he proposed to enter the legal profession, in 1839 he proceeded to the East, intending to take an overland journey to India, and having remained some time in Constantinople went on to Persia, where he visited Susa, the "Shushan" of the Book of Esther, and the tomb of Daniel. He was subsequently induced, by the interesting nature of the incidents he met with, to attempt the exploration of Nimroud, and by the assistance of the British minister in Turkey, Mr. Layard has succeeded in bringing to England some most interesting relics, which will ever associate his name with the study of Assyrian antiquities. He subsequently published a work entitled "Nineveh and its Remains," and in that and other productions of his pen, he has opened out a field of the deepest interest to all students of Archæology and Ancient History. Mr. Layard was elected member for Aylesbury in 1852, and has since held office under Government. The honour of D. C. L. was conferred on him by the University of Oxford. He has not taken much interest in political affairs since the conclusion of the Russian war, but went to India shortly after the breaking out of the late revolt in that country. He is Chairman of the Ottoman Bank, which was established shortly after the conclusion of the Russian war.

LEDRU, ROLLIN, a French politician, was born at Paris in 1808. After passing through a course of legal studies, he became an advocate, and speedily rose to distinction at the bar, where he was generally employed in defending persons charged with offences against the government. He became a member of the Chamber of Deputies in 1841, and soon evinced the most decided opposition to the ministry under Guizot. In the revolution of 1848, Ledru Rollin, together with Lamartine, occupied the foremost position in the formation of a provisional government, and he afterwards became a candidate for the presidentship, but was defeated by the present Emperor. Shortly afterwards Ledru Rollin left France for England, where he has ever since remained. He has published several works, all of which are characterized by extreme views in reference to political matters, and attacking with great violence all those who do not agree with him.

LEE, FREDERICK RICHARD, R. A., a

landscape painter, well known for his representations of English and Scottish scenery, was born at Barnstaple, in Devonshire, in 1799. He entered the army when young, and served in the campaigns in Holland and Belgium in the year 1814. In consequence of severe illness, contracted in the service, he was placed on the half-pay list, and afterwards cultivated his natural talent for art. It is not too much to say that the English school would have been without one of its most accomplished masters, had Mr. Lee remained in the army. His landscapes are remarkable for their freshness and natural tone; they seem as though painted in the open air, they are so true, and no painter that ever lived excels him in aerial perspective. His first success was at the British Institution, where he received a £50 prize. In 1824 he exhibited at the Royal Academy; in 1834 was elected an Associate of that institution, and in 1838 received the distinction of a Royal Academician. The greater number of his more important paintings have been purchased for the collections of the Marquis of Lansdowne, the Earl of Ellesmere, Earl Spencer, the Marquis of Breadalbane, and other noblemen of kindred tastes, while some are to be found in the galleries of Sir John Warrender, Sir Thomas Baring, and Mr. Salomons. At a late period in life he associated himself, in the production of pictures, with Thomas Sidney Cooper, A.R.A., and his "Near Redleaf," "Gathering Sea Weed," and a "Distant View of Windsor," are now in the collection at the South Kensington Museum.

LEE, Rev. Robert, D.D., was born at Tweedmouth, Durham, in 1804. On leaving the Grammar School of Berwick-on-Tweed, he went to St. Andrew's University. His first charge was at Arbroath, and having been minister at Campsie, he eventually became pastor of the Grey Friars' Church in Edinburgh, with which he is still connected. Dr. Lee is also a chaplain to the Queen, and was chosen Professor of Biblical Criticism in the University of Edinburgh in 1846. He has taken a prominent part in the proceedings of the General Assembly and other church courts, always on the liberal side, and often maintaining opinions and defending measures which greatly scandalize his brethren. In 1859 Dr. Lee was engaged in a keen controversy with the majority of his presbytery on account of his having introduced the practice of reading prayers. The General Assembly, however, pronounced a judgment which was favourable to his views and proceedings. He has published numerous sermons and lectures, a controversial treatise on Infallibility, two books of prayers; and a reference Bible—an unostentatious but very laborious work.

LEE, Mrs. A. Bowdich, an English authoress, was born about 1800. She accompanied her first husband, Mr. Bowdich, to Africa, he being despatched on a pacific mission to the Caffres, then threatening to root out the settlements in the vicinity of their grounds. During the stay of the lady at the Cape of Good Hope, and her journey through the colony, she gathered the materials which were afterwards woven into her interesting book, "Stories of Strange Lands," published in 1825. This was followed by "The African Wanderer," a work which from its spirited recital of adventure, and its evident fidelity of depiction, became immediately popular, and ran through various editions. The current of Mrs. Lee's mind runs towards natural science, and when she fixed her residence in Paris she wrote several works on natural history and its varieties, among the principal of which are "Familiar Natural History," and the "History of Fresh-water Fishes," which were illustrated by herself.

LEECH, John, the well-known caricaturist, was born in London, in 1816, and received his early education at the Charter-House. There is, perhaps, no artist living who is so popular as Mr. Leech. His weekly contributions to "Punch" are admirable and so effective, that the inquiry, "What is in 'Punch' this week?" has become a household word throughout Great Britain. He succeeds in completely hitting the most salient points of the incidents he illustrates, and his likenesses are so well sketched, as at once to suggest the unfortunate subject of his pencil in all possible peculiarities. It is, of course, impossible to select where all are good, but Mr. Leech has saved that trouble, by publishing, in a collected form, some hundreds of his sketches, entitled "Pictures of Life and Character;" an inspection of which is sure to produce mirth and hearty laughter from even the most serious of its readers.

LEMON, MARK, a journalist and dramatist, was born in November, 1809. Although well known by his dramatic and other effusions, it is in connexion with "Punch" that Mr. Lemon has been most successful, and of which he has been the editor nearly ever since its commencement. Owing to its excellent illustrations, and the admirable hits at the current events of the day, this work has become the most popular of productions of the comic kind, and has outlived a number of competitors which have been brought out in vain to share public favour with it. Like all kinds of "punch," the periodical owes much of its piquancy to the addition of a "Lemon." Mr. Lemon has published several farces, which have been frequently performed in public, and he is a leading contributor to the "Illustrated London News," and many serials.

LENNEP, JACOB VAN, a Dutch novelist, was born at Amsterdam, on the 25th of March, 1802. He received, under his father's direction, an excellent education, embraced the profession of the law, rose into repute, and was appointed King's Advocate in 1825. While devoting himself to the duties of his office, he made his début as an author, by publishing his "Academic Idyls." He then composed romances, on the plan of introducing historical events and characters, as their principal groundwork. His first work of this class was the "National Legends," based on the traditions and heroic annals of his country; but the production which stamped him as an author of celebrity, was "Our Forefathers;" a book in which Van Lennep passed in review the ancient and mediæval history of Holland. He has written a complete history of the Netherlands, and a number of novels; many of which have been rendered into different languages. Well versed in English literature, he has translated into Dutch several poems of Byron, Moore, Tennyson, and others, as well as Shakspeare's "Othello," and "Romeo and Juliet." He is also the author of several original dramas, which are popular in Holland. Mr. Van Lennep has been from 1853-1856 a member of the States-General. He is President of the Dutch Royal Academy of the Fine Arts, member of the Royal Academy of Sciences, and of several scientific associations.

LEOPOLD, GEORGE CHRISTIAN FREDERICK, KING OF THE BELGIANS, DUKE OF SAXONY, and PRINCE OF SAXE COBURG GOTHA, son of Duke Francis of Saxe-Coburg, Saalfeld, was born at Coburg, December 16, 1790. Having received an education which gained him the reputation of being one of the best instructed princes in Europe, he, on the marriage of his sister to the late Grand Duke Constantine of Russia, determined to enter the Russian service. As a General of Cavalry he displayed both courage and talent in several campaigns; and for his valour in the field, he received the orders of St. George and Marie Thérèse. After the entry of the allies into Paris, he accompanied the Emperor Alexander to England, when he had the good fortune to make an impression on the heart of the Princess Charlotte, only child of the Prince Regent, and heiress-apparent to the throne of Great Britain. He spent a short time at Vienna, and was then called to military duties, by the escape of Napoleon from Elba. After the battle of Waterloo, and the pacification of Europe, he revisited England; was naturalized a British subject, in March, 1816, and espoused the Princess Charlotte, amid the general approbation and cordial good wishes of all classes of the people, in May of the same year. From this union the country entertained ardent hopes of a direct succession to the crown, but these were dissipated by the untimely death, in child-bed, of the Princess Charlotte, on November 5th, 1817. Prince Leopold retired to the palace of Claremont, bearing with him, in his solitude, the sympathies of the whole nation. Until 1827 he passed his life in comparative seclusion, but when Great Britain, France, and Russia, had combined against Turkey, in support of the independence of Greece, and the battle of Navarino, which destroyed the Turkish navy, had been fought and won, the throne of Greece was offered to him by the Greeks, with the acquiescence of the powers that had established it. Prince Leopold rejected the offer, unless upon conditions which were not ultimately ratified. In the year 1830, the Belgians, excited to discontent and turbulence by the obstinate perversity and misgovernment of the King of the Netherlands, and his attempts to force the Dutch language upon them, to the exclusion of French; and animated at the critical moment by the example of the Parisians, in the expulsion of the elder Bourbons, succeeded, after an ar-

duous and noble struggle, in achieving their independence as a separate nation. A temporary chief having been elected in the person of M. Surlet de Chokier, the crown of constitutional Belgium was offered to Prince Leopold by the National Congress, on the 4th June, 1831, and accepted conditionally on the 26th of June, and definitively—the conditions having been acceded to—on the 12th of July. The King made his entry into Brussels on the 21st of July, and took the oath of the constitution. In 1832 he married the Princess Louise, daughter of Louis-Philippe, King of the French. Since that period, the Belgians have greatly prospered under the wise and equitable rule of the monarch of their choice; who, amid difficulties and dissensions, that always exist in constitutional countries, and aggravated in the case of Belgium, by the pretensions of the Ultramontane party, has been able alike to preserve the popular rights and the royal prerogative, and to consolidate the nascent liberty of the country. By Queen Louise, who died in October, 1850, his Majesty has four children,—Leopold Louis-Philippe Marie Victor, Prince Royal, Duke of Brabant, and heir to the throne; Prince Leopold Ferdinand; Prince Philippe Eugène; and the Princess Charlotte.

LEPSIUS, CARL RICHARD, an archæologist and historian, was born at Naumberg, on 23rd of December, 1810. After attending the Royal School of Pforta, near Naumberg, he studied successively at Leipzig, Göttingen, and Berlin, and from the latter university received the degree of Doctor in 1833. His philological productions brought him into notice, and in 1842 he was appointed by Frederick William IV. as head of a commission, which proceeded to Egypt for the purpose of commencing researches into the antiquities of that country. In these labours he was highly successful, and at the end of four years had collected a large number of relics, &c., which were taken to Berlin, and added a vast collection of interesting facts relating to the early history of Egypt. He has written several works on Egyptian Antiquities, and his opinions have been held in high esteem by those capable of forming an accurate judgment on the subjects he takes up. He is at present Professor in the University, Director of the Egyptian Museum, and Member of the Royal Academy of Sciences, Berlin.

LESSEPS, FERDINAND DE, a French diplomatist, was born at Versailles, in 1805. He commenced his diplomatic life by attaching himself to the Consulate-General of Lisbon, and passed through a variety of consular offices, until at last he became, in 1842, Consul at Barcelona, where the honourable and independent spirit he exhibited, obtained for him several marks of distinction. He was in Rome during the revolution, and exerted all his influence to control the passions of the people on the one hand, and the pressure of the government on the other. It is principally as the originator of the Suez Canal scheme that its active promoter has become generally known. In surveying, in obtaining powers, in developing the probabilities of success of this great undertaking, he has spared neither time nor funds. He believes the work capable of accomplishment, and towards it he has spent a life of profound study and activity. He is now in Egypt superintending its construction, being assisted by the Pasha, who has staked a large sum in shares in the undertaking, and also finds a large proportion of labourers.

LEVER, CHARLES, a distinguished writer of fiction, was born at Dublin in 1809, educated at Dublin, and also at Göttingen. For some time he practised as a physician, but relinquished the profession for that of literature, in which he has been eminently successful. His first work, "Harry Lorrequer," brought him into great celebrity as a novel writer, and he has since published a large number of works of a similar style. As a writer Mr. Lever excels in brilliancy and life of expression, and he infuses a rich comicality in his descriptions of the manners and peculiarities of his countrymen. He was for some time Editor of the "Dublin University Magazine." His "Tom Burke," "Charles O'Malley," "St. Patrick's Eve," and "The Commissioner," have been much admired, and it may not be an exaggeration to say that few of the novelists of the present day have been more successful than has Mr. Lever, in acquiring extended popularity. Some years ago he left England, and is residing at the present time at Florence.

LEVERRIER, URBAN JEAN JOSEPH, a French astronomer, was born at St. Lo, in the Department of La Manche, on 11th March, 1811. After leaving the school of his native place, he entered the Polytechnic School of Paris, where he soon showed great partiality for mathematical science and chemistry, but eventually devoted his leisure time to the study of astronomy. After making some interesting investigations into the higher branches of astronomical science, he directed his attention to the perturbations of the planet Uranus, and eventually came to the conclusion, that another, and as yet unseen agent, was the disturbing cause of the motion of Uranus. He was enabled to predict the place at which the supposed planet might be seen. The suggestion turned out correct, and Dr. Galle, a German astronomer, was one of the first to verify the prediction by observing Neptune, on 23rd September, 1846. Mr. Adams, at Cambridge, was at the same time engaged in similar researches (see Adams). The success of his calculations soon caused M. Leverrier to be overwhelmed with honours, and most of the learned

societies in Europe enrolled his name amongst their members. He has also some political reputation, being a Senator of France, and in this capacity has done great service to the cause of education, in promoting the pursuit of science in that country.

LEWES, GEORGE, was born in London, on the 18th April, 1817. He was educated at Dr. Burney's school, at Greenwich; entered a Russia merchant's office, and quitted it to become a student of medicine. He eventually turned to literary pursuits, and taking up his residence in London, has been a most active contributor to all the leading serials. The more remarkable of his independent works are a "Biographical History of Philosophy," written in a most attractive style, and exhibiting a profound and varied acquaintance with the history of human thought. The "Life of Maximilian Robespierre," and his "Life of Goethe," exhibit an admirable mastery of the craft of the biographer, with a deep insight into character. The equal ease with which the politician and the poet are dealt with, indicates the surpassing versatility and power of the biographer. Mr. Lewes is the Macaulay of scientific writers, with a range of speculative power to which the popular historian did not aspire. Mr. Lewes is also known as a dramatic author, by the tragedy of "The Noble Heart," and other works; and as a novelist, by "Ranthorpe," and "Rose, Blanche, and Violet." Of late years his labours have been almost exclusively scientific, embracing papers read at the Meetings of the British Association for the Advancement of Science, and two popular works, "Sea-side Studies," and the "Physiology of Common Life," both of which have been translated into German.

LEWIS, JOHN FREDERICK, a water-colour painter, was born in London in July, 1806, and his education was superintended by his father. His pictures of Spanish scenes, exhibited from 1833 to 1837, were of great excellence. A fancy for the picturesque induced him to visit the East, where he remained for ten years, losing no time, but making sketches which he turned to the best account. When he returned to England, in 1850, he produced his "Hhareem," a water-colour painting, the subject being new, and treated in an original style; it had hosts of admirers. Abandoning water-colours for oil, he produced pictures which are of a high class, as shown by the "Armenian Lady," exhibited in 1855. In 1858 Mr. Lewis resigned the Presidency of the Society of Painters in Water Colours, and in the following year he was elected into the Royal Academy. Mr. Lewis is honoured by the profession, and the esteem in which he is held, as an artist and a man, has not been unworthily won.

LEWIS, SIR GEORGE CORNEWALL, BART., an English statesman, was born in 1806, and having studied at Eton, he graduated and took honours at Oxford in 1828. In 1831 he was called to the bar, in 1839 was Poor Law Commissioner, and in 1847, having been elected member for Herefordshire, he was made Secretary of the Board of Control. He became Secretary to the Treasury in 1850, and resigned in March, 1852, with Lord John Russell's Government. He was an unsuccessful candidate for Herefordshire in that year, and remained out of Parliament till 1855, when he became member for the Radnor Burghs, and was Chancellor of the Exchequer under Lord Palmerston. In 1859, on the resignation of the Earl of Derby, he was appointed by Lord Palmerston Secretary for the Home Department, an office he now holds (1860). Sir G. C. Lewis is well known as a thorough classical scholar, and has published several works relating to history and cognate subjects. He acted for a short time as editor of the "Edinburgh Review," but relinquished that onerous duty, owing to the pressure of his political engagements. He has been at all times a strong supporter and leading member of the liberal cause.

LIDDELL, THE VERY REVEREND HENRY GEORGE, D.D., an English divine, nephew to the late Lord Ravensworth, was educated at the Charter-House, and Christ Church, Oxford, and afterwards became Head Master of the Westminster School. He subsequently acted as Tutor at Christ Church, and was appointed Chaplain to the Prince Consort. He has written a "History of Rome," and partly edited a Greek Lexicon, of which the fifth edition is in the press. In 1855 he was appointed Dean of Christ Church, Oxford.

LIEBER, FRANCIS, LL.D., Professor of History and Political Science in Columbia College, New York, was born at Berlin, on the 18th of March, 1800. In 1815 he joined the army and took part in the battle of Waterloo. Four years afterwards he was accused of propagating revolutionary doctrines, and imprisoned, but was soon after released, and proceeded to Jena to complete his education. He took part in the first Greek war of Independence, and, on the conclusion of that struggle, made his way to Rome where he was befriended by the historian Niebuhr. In 1823 he published his "Journal in Greece," and afterwards returning to Prussia was imprisoned the second time, but eventually discharged through the influence of Niebuhr. Learning, on his release, that a further arrest was impending in the event of his publishing a volume of poems he had written during his confinement, he took flight to England. In 1827 he proceeded to Boston and commenced the publication of the "Encyclopædia Americana," a work consisting of thirteen 8vo volumes, which occupied him for nearly five years. He also published several translations into English, which were very successful.

From Boston he repaired to New York, where he translated the work of De Beaumont and De Tocqueville on the Penitentiary System, adding notes to the translation; and likewise wrote a plan of education and instruction for Girard College. He afterwards removed to Philadelphia, still continuing his literary pursuits, when in 1835 he was invited to a professorship in South Carolina College, an office which he filled for upwards of twenty years with distinguished ability. In 1844 he revisited Europe, and in 1857 returned to New York, a new chair in Columbia College having been expressly created to secure his services. He has been a very voluminous writer, but the works by which he is best known are his "Manual of Political Ethics," "Legal and Political Hermeneutics," and "Civil Liberty and Self-Government." Most of his publications have been translated into other languages, and nearly all have passed through several editions.

LIEBIG, JUSTUS, BARON, a German chemist, was born at Darmstadt in 1803. Having studied in his native town, at Bonn, and Erlangen, he proceeded to Paris in 1822, where he became the first and only pupil of that eminent chemist Gay Lussac. Having been introduced to the celebrated Humboldt he was appointed Extraordinary Professor of Chemistry at Giessen. He there established the first school of analytical chemistry, and by the invention of a new apparatus for organic analysis, gave the first impulse to the study of organic chemistry. Liebig is now Professor of Chemistry in the University of Munich, President of the Royal Academy of Sciences, and Conservator-General of the Royal Scientific Collections. It is no exaggeration to state that the science of chemistry has never had a more indefatigable, and successful investigator, than Professor Liebig. By the extent and accuracy of his researches, he has

D.  JUSTUS LIEBIG.

opened out an entirely new field in the chemistry of organic bodies; and, in fact, the study of this branch of science may almost be dated from his first researches. Giessen laboratory has become a kind of nucleus from which some of our most eminent chemists have proceeded, and expanding on the views of Liebig, they have introduced into the arts, manufactures, and agricultural processes of Europe, an entirely new and beneficial operation. Liebig was one of the first to call urgent attention to the use of chemistry in connexion with farming, and the proper employment of manures; and, by the researches which he instituted, he has been a benefactor to the human race, so far as the production of cereal and other crops are concerned. His work on the "Principles of Agriculture" is highly valued, as is also another entitled "Researches on the Chemistry of Food," whilst the elegance and simplicity of style found in his "Letters on Chemistry" have called forth the admiration of the general reader. He has published other works which have been translated into English, in all of which he displays accuracy of research and high generalizing power. Most of the learned societies of Europe have enrolled him as a member, and he has contributed valuable papers to the British Association on more than one occasion.

LINDLEY, JOHN, M.D., Ph.D., an English botanist, was born at Catton, near Norwich, in February, 1799. His father being an extensive nursery-gardener, enthusiastic in the study of botany, he devoted himself at an early age to this science. In 1819 he published his translation of the "Analyse du Fruit" of Richard. In 1820 he was elected a Fellow of the Linnean Society; and about the same time appeared his "Monographia Rosarum." In 1821 he published a folio volume entitled "Monographia Digitalium," and commenced his "Col-

lectanea Botanica." In the year 1822 he took charge of the Horticultural Society's great experimental garden at Chiswick. In 1828 he was elected a Fellow of the Royal Society, and appointed Professor of Botany in University College, London, an office which he continued to hold till the present year, when he resigned it upon being appointed one of the Examiners in Botany in the University of London. He had previously become associated with the late Mr. Loudon in preparing the "Encyclopædia of Plants," a work published in 1829. In the following year he produced his "Introduction to the Natural System of Botany," in 1832 the "Introduction to Systematic and Physiological Botany," and a "Synopsis of the British Flora," in 1833 the "Nixus Plantarum," in 1836 "A Natural System of Botany," which was afterwards incorporated with his great work—"The Vegetable Kingdom;" and during the time he was engaged on these works he laid the foundation of a number of others illustrative of the science to which he specially devoted himself, besides furnishing papers to the "Penny Cyclopædia," and acting as editor of "The Botanical Register." "Botany," in the "Library of Useful Knowledge," was one of his best works; it laid open the pathway to the student and had an important influence on the botanical studies of the period when it was published. In 1832, upon the death of Sir James Edward Smith, he was appointed by the trustees of Dr. Sibthorp to complete that botanist's magnificent "Flora Græca," of which three and a half volumes, folio, remained unpublished. At a later period (1838) he brought out a folio volume called "The Sertum Orchidaceum," illustrating the extraordinary family of Orchids, of which he possesses by far the most complete collection ever made. In 1841 he undertook the editorship of the "Gardeners' Chronicle." Recognized as one of the first botanists of the day, he had been in 1831 appointed Lecturer on Botany at the Royal Institution, and in 1835 Lecturer at the Botanic Gardens, Chelsea. His latest works are "The Elements of Botany," "School Botany and Descriptive Botany," prepared for the use of botanical students, and his "Folia Orchidacea," which appearing in parts, at intervals, displays the extraordinary richness of his noble herbarium. His other publications are far too numerous to detail. In the year 1858 he received the Royal Medal from the Royal Society, in recognition of the services he had rendered to science.

LINDSAY, ALEXANDER WILLIAM CRAWFORD, LORD, eldest son of the Earl of Crawford and Balcarres, Premier Earl of Scotland, was born 1812. He was educated at Trinity College, Cambridge, and his studies being terminated he travelled in Europe and the East. In 1838 he published "Letters on Egypt, Edom, and the Holy Land;" in 1841 "Letter to a Friend on the Evidence and Theory of Christianity," and "Sketches of the History of Christian Art" in 1847. Lord Lindsay's recent productions have been confined to family biography, the chief being the "Lives of the Lindsays."

LINDSAY, WILLIAM SCHAW, M.P., was born in Ayrshire, in 1816. Early left an orphan he went to sea in 1831, determined to work his way in the world. Obliged to submit to privations that would have driven to desperation a less courageous nature, he struggled on, and, at last, in 1834, had won the rank of second-mate in the "Isabella" West-Indiaman—a ship in which he had served as cabin-boy. In 1835 he became chief-mate, and in 1836 was Commander of the "Olive Branch," a situation which he held until 1840, when he left the service. Careful, cautious, and prudent, he had accumulated some little wealth, and attached to literature he

had studied books as he had observed men. His early hardships left their impression on his mind, so that at twenty-four he looked about him with a prudence and wisdom far beyond his years, and as among the most industrious of business men he never neglected the culture of his mind, he gradually advanced until he rose to be one of the largest shipowners and shipbrokers in the kingdom. Tynemouth returned him to Parliament in 1854, after a severe struggle, and again in 1857. In 1859 he was returned one of the members for Sunderland by a large majority. His attention to the shipping interest and the laws that affect navigation has been incessant, but his views are not universally popular. In the earlier part of his political career he advocated the principle of reciprocity, and finally he supported the abolition of all restrictions on free-trade in maritime affairs, contingent on the removal of those burdens which press heavily on the mercantile marine of the kingdom. In 1858 he was a member of the Royal Commission appointed to investigate the subject of Harbours of Refuge on the British and Irish coasts, and also a member in the same year of the Royal Commission appointed to inquire into the manning of the navy. He has just gone to America (September, 1860), partly for the purpose of improving the state of the shipping interest between Great Britain and the United States, a mission which, although private, has several opponents amongst the British shipowners.

LINNELL, JOHN, an English painter, was born at London, in June, 1792. He learned to draw by copying prints and pictures, and to paint in oil by seeing Mr. Hunt, who was a pupil of George Morland, paint. He copied many of the pictures of this artist, but made more rapid progress after drawing from casts. He received in 1805 instructions weekly from Benjamin West, and about the same time studied at the Royal Academy. In 1806 he was under Mr. John Varly, the water-colour painter, but he copied none of his works. In 1807 he obtained a silver medal for a drawing from the life, and in the same year exhibited it at the Royal Academy. In 1808 he exhibited at the Royal Academy, at the end of the same year obtaining a premium of £50 against John Chalon, who was afterwards R.A. He continued to paint landscapes and figure subjects, as well as portraits, till 1847, when he relinquished the latter. He has since left London for Redhill, where he now resides. Mr. Linnell not having kept his name upon the lists of the Royal Academy, has not even been elected an Associate. "The Windmill," "The Heath Scene," "Crossing the Brook," "The Timber Waggon," and "The Village Spring," all testify to his power of delineating English landscape in its homely and genial loveliness. The "Eve of the Deluge," on the other hand, is remarkable for the sublimity of its imaginative conception, and the facility and strength of its execution. His pictures, "The Wild Flower Gatherer," and "Milking Time," are in the National Collection at the South Kensington Museum.

LISZT, FRANZ, a pianist, was born at Rœding, October 22nd, 1809. At an early age he evinced a decided taste for music, and soon became a proficient in the art. After receiving lessons at Vienna, where he made his début, and was highly successful, he went to Paris, and in 1825 produced an opera. His fame had now largely extended, and although yet a youth, he was known as one of the first pianists of the day, both in London and at Paris. His execution is very rapid, and although often taking liberties with the text of composers, his brilliancy enchants his hearers, and covers faults which arise from his neglect of strict artistic rule. He has been singularly fortunate in receiving decorations and rewards from many royal personages, and has performed in most of the leading cities in Europe with great success.

LIVINGSTON, THE REV. DAVID, LL.D., D.C.L., an eminent African missionary and traveller, was born in 1817, in the village of Blantyre, Scotland. His father a small tea-dealer, by his kindness of manner and winning ways, made the heart-strings of his children twine around him as firmly as if he could have bestowed upon them every worldly advantage. He died in 1856, while his son was on his homeward journey, anticipating no greater pleasure than telling beneath the paternal roof-tree the story of his adventures. Dr. Livingston's recollections of his mother recall a picture often seen among the Scottish poor—that of the anxious housewife striving to make both ends meet. At the age of ten, young Livingston entered Blantyre factory as a "piecer." With part of his first week's wages he purchased Ruddiman's "Rudiments of Latin." The labour of the factory extended from six in the morning until eight at night; the Latin was learned at an evening school, and by dint of energy and perseverance the piecer lad had fully mastered the classical authors before he reached his sixteenth year. In addition to the classics, books of travel and scientific works were his special delight. On an exploratory tour in the vicinity of his native district, he entered a quarry to collect the shells found in the carboniferous limestone which crops out in High Blantyre and Cambuslang. Addressing this query to a quarryman, "However did these shells come into these rocks?" "When God made the rocks he made the shells in them," was the damping reply. At the age of nineteen Livingston became a cotton-spinner. He had now resolved to devote himself to the work of a medical missionary. Having passed through the classical, medical, and theological curricula, Mr. Livingston was admitted a Licentiate of the Faculty of Physicians and Surgeons, Glasgow, and was accepted by the London Missionary Society as one of its agents. China had been his contemplated sphere of labour, but the opium war closed that field of benevolent enterprise. Mr. Moffat was then in England urging the claims of Africa, and in 1840 Dr. Livingston embarked for that continent, reaching Cape Town after a voyage of three months. During sixteen years he laboured there with surpassing zeal and devotion. The story of these years is told with unadorned eloquence in that now well-known work, his "Missionary Travels." For eight years he lived far in the interior with a Bechuana tribe, guiding them in the paths of industry, virtue, and Christianity. He discovered the magnificent lake Ngami, traced the course of the great river Zambesi, in Eastern Africa, and penetrated the interior of that continent to the 8th degree of southern latitude, 26 degrees north of the Cape of Good Hope. Having superintended the publication of his "Travels," and received the most satisfactory and substantial testimonials of the esteem of his countrymen of all classes, from his old comrades in Blantyre mills, to the most accomplished *savants* of Britain, the intrepid traveller, provided by government with the necessary outfit, has gone forth on a fresh voyage of discovery. Since Dr. Livingston returned to Africa with this exploring expedition, he has found many obstacles to surmount, on which he had not previously calculated. He continues to write home, however, in a hopeful and cheerful spirit. It cannot be expected, however, that a year or two, even with the best appliances, ill show the same results that seventeen years of toil were scarcely sufficient to obtain. Dr. Livingston is married to a daughter of Mr. Moffat.

Their elder children have been left behind them to receive a British education.

LLANOVER, BENJAMIN HALL, LORD, an English statesman, was born in 1802. He was educated at Westminster School, and Christ Church, Oxford. In 1831 he was returned to Parliament for Monmouth, and was elected for Marylebone in 1837, which he continued to represent until his elevation to the peerage. In 1838 Sir Benjamin Hall was created a Baronet. He is the advocate of education, extension of the suffrage, and of the abolition of church-rates. In 1855 he succeeded Sir William Molesworth as First Commissioner of Public Works. On the fall of the cabinet of Lord Palmerston, the Right Hon. Baronet retired from office. On the formation of Lord Palmerston's government in 1859, he declined the offer made to him of office without a seat in the cabinet; whereupon, in acknowledgment of the services already rendered by him to the state, he was in June, 1859, elevated to the peerage with the title of Baron Llanover, of Llanover and Abercorn, in the county of Monmouth.

LONDON, THE RIGHT REVEREND ARCHIBALD CAMPBELL TAIT, D.C.L., BISHOP OF, was born at Edinburgh, in 1811. After passing through his early studies in his native city, and Glasgow, he proceeded to Oxford, and graduating in 1836, had conferred on him the title of D.C.L., in 1842. He was long highly esteemed at Rugby, of which he held the honourable office of Head Master. In 1856 Dr. Tait was chosen the successor to Dr. Blomfield, as Bishop of London, and has, by his subsequent administration of the duties of that high position, shown himself the enemy of innovation, and a strong supporter of the evangelical doctrines of the Church of England. Within the last few years he has been called by circumstances to exercise firmness with discretion, and his success in this delicate duty, has acquired for him the esteem of all parties, and, generally speaking, the respectful submission of those whom he has had to check. As a member of the House of Lords, Dr. Tait is at all times respected for the clearness and force of his expressed opinions.

LONGFELLOW, HENRY WADSWORTH, an American poet, was born at Portland, Maine, February, 1807, and graduated with distinguished honours at Bowdoin College in 1825. Contemplating law as his future profession, he entered his father's office; but after spending some time acquiring the mysteries of the legal craft, he accepted the professorship of modern languages in Bowdoin College. Longfellow visited Europe, travelling in France, Italy, Spain, Germany, Holland, and England. His European tour left a deep impression upon his mind, and has coloured the whole of his subsequent career. To its influence may be traced that eclectic rather than national character stamped upon his writings. Returning to America in 1829, he entered upon the duties of his professorship, and while discharging them also became a frequent contributor to the "North American Review." Mr. Ticknor, the historian of the literature of Spain, having resigned the professorship of the modern languages and belles lettres in Harvard University, Mr. Longfellow was called upon to succeed him, but before entering upon his new duties, he again visited Europe, acquiring a knowledge of the Scandinavian languages and literature. From 1836 Mr. Longfellow has held his professorship in Harvard University. The following is a list of his works, and the dates of their publication:—
"Coplas de Maurique" (1833), "Outre-Mer" (1835), "Hyperion" (1839), "Voices of the Night" (1839), "Ballads and other Poems" (1841), "Poems on Slavery" (1842), "The Spanish Stu-

dent" (1843), "The Belfry of Bruges" (1846), "Evangeline" (1847), "Kavanagh" (1849), "The Seaside and the Fireside" (1850), "The Golden Legend" (1851), "The Song of Hiawatha" (1855), and "The Courtship of Miles Standish" (1858).

LOUGH, JOHN GRAHAM, a sculptor, was born at Greenhead, Northumberland. Owing to the limited resources of his family, he is another of those instances of genius breaking through all difficulties, and at last rising to fame. He accidentally met with a kind patron, and eventually proceeding to London, succeeded in producing a statue of "Milo," which soon brought him into notice, and out of the poverty from which he had suffered. He found a kind friend in Haydon, and many noblemen at once gave him commissions after the exhibition of his "Milo" at the Royal Academy. Amongst many productions of the chisel, Mr. Lough has excelled in his "Roman Fruit Girl," "Samson," "Hebe Banished," and "The Mourners." He executed the statue of the Queen at the Royal Exchange. His "Satan Subdued by the Archangel" was, with many others, exhibited at the London Exhibition of 1851.

LOVER, SAMUEL, an Irish novelist and poet, is the son of a bullion broker at Dublin, and was born about the year 1800. Destined to succeed his father, he had for some time to attend to pursuits with which he had no sympathy, but by a brilliant sally at a banquet given to Moore, the Irish poet, Mr. Lover at once succeeded in throwing off the shackles of commerce, and in devoting himself to the muses and fine arts. In his early attempts at painting he had great success, and he exhibited at the Royal Academy in 1833. Mr. Lover is, however, better known by his literary and musical productions, and had he never written more than his "Molly Bawn," "Rory O'More," and

"The Angel's Whisper," these alone would have sufficed to have rendered him universally popular. He has great power in illustrating the humour of his countrymen, and he has been a liberal contributor to many magazines. His novels of "Rory O'More," "Handy Andy," and "Treasure Trove," are among the most popular of the day. He has visited America, where his humorous illustrations were a complete success. He is now in comparative retirement, and in receipt of a pension from the Treasury, which he has well earned by his numerous literary and artistic productions.

LOWELL, JAMES RUSSELL, an American poet, was born in Boston in 1819. Having studied at Harvard College, he entered the legal profession, but speedily changed it for that of literature. He has published several poems, in which he incorporates his political and social opinions, as may be found in his "Anti-Texas," "The Fugitive Slaves," &c. He is well known in the United States through his connexion with the Anti-Slavery cause, to the success of which he has contributed greatly with his pen.

LUCAS, HIPPOLYTE JULIEN JOSEPH, a versatile and prolific French author, was born in December, 1807, at Rennes, where his father practised as an attorney. He studied in the college of his native city, and then proceeded to Paris, with a view of embracing the legal profession. Appointed Advocate he returned to Rennes, but devoted himself to the composition of poetry in preference to solving the intricacies of law. On the pretext that he was to become a Doctor of Laws, he went back to Paris in 1829, and had full scope for the indulgence of his literary tastes, being almost immediately appointed translator of articles in the "Edinburgh Review," and of the reports of the debates in the British Parliament for the "Globe"

Newspaper. About the same time he wrote a drama founded on Lord Byron's "Corsair," which was accepted at the Odéon. The revolution of July saw him once more at Rennes, but without renouncing his love of letters. He assisted to found the "Revue de Bretagne," and wrote his first separate work, "Le Cœur et le Monde," which was published in 1834, and met with marked success. He afterwards contributed successively to the "Cabinet de Lecture," "Le Voleur," "Revue du Théatre," "Bon Sens," "L'Artiste," "Charivari," the "National," and the "Siècle," and was one of the founders of the Society of Men of Letters. In 1847 he received a decoration from Holland, and was dignified with the title of Chevalier of the Legion of Honour. His writings have been uncommonly numerous, and deal with every department of literature, romance, poetry, history, biography, and the drama; but it is to the latter that he has given his best attention. "Les Nuées," "Alceste," and "Médée," are constructed on the Greek model; some others are after the Spanish; and he has composed the *libretti* of several operas, "Linda di Chamouni" and "L'Étoile de Séville" being among the number. Of his prose works the most prominent are a "Philosophical and Literary History of the French Theatres." "Dramatic and Literary Curiosities," and the "Portfolio of a Journalist."

LUDERS, GENERAL ALEXANDER NICOLAIEWITCH, of the Russian army, was born in 1790, of a German family which had been long established in Russia. He entered the military service in 1807, and took part in the campaigns against Napoleon; his bravery and coolness, displayed in many dangerous encounters, recommended him for promotion. In 1831 he commanded a brigade in Poland, and was a chief instrument in the conquest of Varsovia.

In 1843 he commanded a division in the Caucasus, and measured swords with Schamyl, though without gaining a victory over the patriarch of the mountain tribes. Sent in July, 1848, to the Danubian Principalities, he succeeded by menace in rendering the country tranquil, and in 1849 he went to Transylvania as Commander of one branch of an army destined by the Czar to assist Austria in crushing Hungary. Opposed to Bem, he succeeded twice in defeating that general; and, afterwards, by a series of strategical manœuvres, compelled the surrender of Görgei. That event finished the Hungarian revolutionary war; and the Emperor Nicholas was so well satisfied with the ability displayed by General Lüders that he despatched him to Bessarabia as second in command to Prince Gortschakoff. He took part in the Eastern war in 1855, was elevated in rank by the new Czar, Alexander II., and was prepared to contest every inch of ground with the Allies at the Crimea, when peace was declared in March, 1856, and he retired from active service, spending a considerable time subsequently in visiting Germany, Italy, and France.

LYELL, SIR CHARLES, an eminent geologist, was born at Kinnordy, the seat of his family, in Forfarshire, on the 14th November, 1797. From Midhurst he afterwards went to Exeter College, Oxford, and became A.M. in 1821. Intended for the legal profession he was called to the bar and practised for some time, but he eventually withdrew from the courts to follow a more congenial pursuit, and in 1832 was appointed Professor of Geology, at King's College, London. This situation he afterwards relinquished, without however abandoning scientific investigation. He was one of the earliest members of the Geological Society, and has been a large contributor to its "Transactions," his papers invariably indicating acute ob-servation and power of comparison. He first became widely known, however, by his work entitled "The Principles of Geology," which he commenced in 1830, and completed by 1833. It has since, in a complete form, reached the tenth edition. A part of it was subsequently separated and published under the title of "Elements of Geology," in 1838; and as a "Manual of Elementary Geology," of which several editions have appeared. He twice visited the United States of America, with the object of examining the geology of that continent, publishing the result of his observations in various forms, principally in papers communicated to the "Proceedings" and "Transactions" of scientific societies. His "Travels in North America" appeared in 1841, and contained his impressions of the United States, Canada, and Nova Scotia, mingled with personal incident and the institutions of the country. His geological dissertations have been much read. His work "A Second Visit to the United States," was issued in 1845, and records his views of the Southern States as well socially as geologically. He has also travelled over the greater part of Europe, investigating various geological features which came under his notice. In 1831 he was appointed a deputy-lieutenant of Forfarshire. He has been an active member of the British Association, and in 1836 was elected President of the Geological Society. In 1848 received the honour of knighthood, and in 1855 the honorary degree of D.C.L. was conferred on him by the University of Oxford. Sir Charles Lyell is one of the most fascinating writers on geology, and he invests with an almost poetic interest, that which would otherwise be to ordinary readers a very dry subject.

LYNDHURST, JOHN SINGLETON COPLEY, LORD, an English orator and statesman, and ex-Lord Chancellor, was born at Boston, in the United States, in

1772. When an infant he was brought to England, and after preliminary studies went to Cambridge, at which university he highly distinguished himself, obtaining high honours, and eventually proceeding to America. He joined the bar on his return to England, and for some time travelled the Midland Circuit without any special success, but at last came into notice through some political trials, and entered Parliament in 1818. As Solicitor-General he was engaged in the trial of Queen Caroline, was subsequently Attorney-General, and in 1827 became Lord Chancellor during the administration of Lord Canning. He was about this time opposed to the emancipation of the Roman Catholics, but at last yielded to external pressure and assisted in passing the bill. On the retirement of his party from government he was chosen Chief Baron of the Exchequer by its successors. He again became Lord Chancellor under Sir Robert Peel, but since the break-up of his administration in 1846, Lord Lyndhurst has not held office. At the present time he is found as a supporter of the conservative cause, and his opinions are always received in the House of Lords with the highest respect. As a Chancery Judge, Lord Lyndhurst has been highly spoken of by all parties. As an orator he has few to equal him amongst the peers. His last appearance of any note in public (1860) was on the occasion of the Bill for the Repeal of the Paper Duties being introduced into the Upper House. It had been contended, that as it was a money bill, the Lords could not constitutionally alter it; but Lord Lyndhurst, although on that day eighty-eight years of age, spoke with such clearness and force of argument, adducing precedent after precedent in support of his views, that eventually the House was induced to withhold its sanction from the measure, and it was accordingly lost.

LYTTON, THE RIGHT HONOURABLE SIR EDWARD GEORGE EARLE LYTTON BULWER, BART., a novelist, poet, and statesman, was born in 1805. He is son of the late General Bulwer, of Heydon Hall, Norfolk, and of Elizabeth Lytton, of the ancient house of Lytton, of Knebworth, Herts. After receiving education from tutors until he was of the proper age to enter himself at one of the Universities, he proceeded to Cambridge, where he gained the Chancellor's Prize Medal for an English Poem on "Sculpture," and took the degree of M.A. His first attempt at prose fiction, in which his greatest laurels were to be won, was published in 1827, under the title of "Falkland." At first, it excited no particular attention; but when in 1828 he published the brilliant novel of "Pelham, or the Adventures of a Gentleman," it was at once admitted by readers of all degrees of intelligence, whose opinion was entitled to respect, that a writer of original genius had entered among the *athletæ* of letters destined to achieve still more brilliant triumphs, and to enrich still further the already overflowing treasures of English fiction and romance. The promise was not disappointed, and there followed in rapid succession from his pen, "The Disowned," "Devereux," "Paul Clifford," "Eugene Aram," "Godolphin," "The Pilgrims of the Rhine," "The Last Days of Pompeii," "Rienzi," "Ernest Maltravers," "Alice, or the Mysteries," "Leila, or the Siege of Grenada," "Night and Morning," "Zanoni," "The Last of the Barons," "Lucretia, or the Children of Night," "Harold," "The Caxtons," "My Novel," and "What will he do with it?" These stories exhibit various degrees of excellence and power, they are widely different in form, substance, and treatment, and they show immense and well-trained powers of observation and description; are full either of wit, wisdom, or poetry, or of a combination of these qualities; and if they are sometimes to be found fault with on a point of moral philosophy, they are never to be justly criticised for inferiority as works either of art, or of genius, to any novels in the language. Sir Bulwer Lytton was, in 1833, the editor of the "New Monthly Magazine," and published in its pages a series of papers, under the title of "The Student." Among his other prose works, are "England and the English," and "Athens," an historical fragment. But it is not only as a prose writer that he has challenged and gained the public attention, but as a poet and a dramatist, in both of which walks of literature he has achieved successes that might of themselves satisfy any ordinary ambition. In 1830 appeared a satirical poem, under the title of the "Siamese Twins," and at considerable intervals, "The New Timon," "King Arthur," and "St. Stephens," which proved his remarkable industry, versatility, and perfect command over the resources of language. As a dramatist he has been more successful in pleasing the public than as a poet, and has produced five plays: "The Lady of Lyons," "Richelieu," "Money," "The Duchess de la Vallière," the "Sea Captain," and the comedy of "Not so Bad as we Seem;" the first-named being perhaps the most popular and effective play produced in recent times. In 1831, while still Mr. Lytton Bulwer, and before he took the additional name of Lytton, in conformity with his mother's will, he represented the borough of St. Ives upon liberal principles; and in that year he introduced and carried the "Dramatic Author's Copyright Bill," a measure which has been of essential service to the devotees of this branch of literature. In the Parliament of 1832, he was returned for the city of Lincoln, which he represented during ten consecutive years. He introduced in 1835 a measure for the abolition of the News-paper Stamp Duty, which was afterwards reduced from four pence to one penny, mainly through his exertions, and has since been repealed altogether. In this year he published a pamphlet called "The Crisis," in opposition to Sir Robert Peel's short-lived government, which rapidly ran through no less than twenty editions, and had considerable political effect. In 1842 he was unsuccessful in contesting the city of Lincoln, and retired for nearly ten years from political life. In the meantime her Majesty, on the occasion of her coronation, conferred upon him the title of a Baronet. In 1852, not having followed the party with which he had generally acted, in its conversion to the principles of Free Trade, he contested the county of Herts, in support of Lord Derby's government. In this contest he was successful, and still continuing to represent that important county in 1858, when Lord Derby's second adminstration was formed on the overthrow of that of Lord Palmerston, he accepted the office of Secretary of State for the Colonies. In this new field of usefulness he proved himself an able administrator, and a thorough man of business, and won the respect and good will of every colonial functionary who had to transact affairs with his department. During his tenure of the seals of the colonial office, the new colony of British Columbia (to which it was at one time proposed by the colonists to give the name of Lyttonia) was founded and organized; and the subjects of differences and disputes between the Canadians and other colonists of British North America, and the Hudson's Bay Company, were earnestly considered, and put into such a state, as to promise both a steady and a satisfactory settlement. Sir Bulwer Lytton married, in 1827, the daughter of Francis Wheeler, Esq., of Limerick, by whom he had issue a son and daughter, of whom the son alone survives, the heir to the baronetcy, and who, under the *nom de plume* of "Owen Meredith," is a writer and poet of no mean promise.

M'CULLOCH, HORATIO, a landscape painter, was born in Glasgow, in 1806. His first work of any importance was produced at the Edinburgh Exhibition of 1833, when it attracted the notice of Professor Wilson, and the Rev. John Thomson of Duddingstone. Their encouragement at the time, and their subsequent friendship, tended materially to ensure to Mr. M'Culloch the popularity which he has enjoyed all over Scotland ever since. Amongst various pictures may be named those of "A View on the Clyde," "A Highland Loch," &c. Mr. M'Culloch is a member of the Royal Scottish Academy.

M'CULLOCH, J. R., a political economist, was born in Wigtownshire in 1789. He was for many years a contributor to the "Scotsman" newspaper. In 1828 he left Edinburgh, and was appointed Professor of Political Economy in the new University of London. He held that chair until 1832, when he gave in his resignation. Since 1838 he has been Comptroller in the Government Stationery Office, and enjoys a pension of £200 a-year for literary services, granted to him by Sir Robert Peel. His " Dictionary of Commerce and Commercial Navigation " is one of the most valuable works in the language. His "Statistical Account of the British Empire," and his "Dictionary of Geography," have been repeatedly republished, and are invaluable for reference. His writings on political economy have been numerous, and are held as standard publications by cultivators of the science. He is one of the foreign Associates of the Institute of France.

MACDOWELL, PATRICK, R. A., a sculptor, was born at Belfast in 1799. When eight years old he was placed under Mr. Gordon, a schoolmaster in his native town, by whom he was taught drawing. He remained with him until his mother came to England, and then went to board with a clergyman, in Hants. When fourteen years of age he was apprenticed to a coach-builder. Eventually he became acquainted with a French sculptor, and thus had his natural genius directed into its proper channel. His first work of consequence was a successful model intended for a monument to Major Cartwright. He thus entered into considerable notoriety, and meeting with that eminent patron of art Sir James Emerson Tennent, he soon became highly successful in his profession. To enumerate all Mr. Macdowell's productions would far exceed the limits of this necessarily imperfect sketch. Amongst the most prominent are his "Cupid," "Psyche," "A Girl Reading," "Early Sorrow," "A Girl going to Bathe." Mr. Macdowell was chosen to execute two statues for the Houses of Parliament, namely, "The Earl of Chatham," and "William Pitt."

M'HALE, THE RIGHT REV. JOHN, D.D., Roman Catholic Archbishop of Tuam, was born in 1792, at Tubbermacrine, a hamlet in the county Mayo. He received his elementary education at Castlebar, entered Maynooth College in 1807, in 1814 was ordained a priest, and was afterwards appointed Professor of Theology. The law of the kingdom being such that no Roman Catholic dignitary could rule a diocese, Dr. M'Hale, and all Roman Catholic bishops, were obliged to adopt foreign titles, though that legal prescription was frequently violated. In 1825 he was consecrated Bishop of Maronia *in partibus*, and coadjutor of Killalo, succeeding to the see (nominal) in 1834, the same year being removed to Tuam. Dr. M'Hale is a keen and resolute controversialist. He opposed the Ecclesiastical Tithes Act with much vehemence, denounced every Government that did not recognise the Church of Rome as the Church of the country, pronounced the Queen's Colleges of Ireland "godless," while Sir Robert Peel was endowing Maynooth as "a message of peace" to Ireland, and always lays claim to the title, though he cannot lawfully to the income, of Archbishop of Tuam. To a mixed educational system he is an untiring enemy, seizing every opportunity that occasion affords for its condemnation. At one period his influence with the Roman Catholics of Ireland was only second, if second, to that of O'Connell; but of late years, probably on account of advanced age, he appears to have withdrawn from public life.

MACKAY, CHARLES, a poet and journalist, was born at Perth, in 1814. He is a descendant of an honourable Highland family, the Mackays of Strathnever. Having received the rudiments of his education in London, he was in 1827 sent to a school at Brussels, and he remained in Belgium and Germany for some years. On his return to this country he abandoned his intention of entering the East India service, for which he had been originally intended by his uncle General Mackay, and devoted himself to literature. In 1835, after the publication of a small volume of poems which attracted the notice of Mr. John Black, he became connected with the "Morning Chronicle." While employed in his arduous duties as subeditor of a daily paper, Mr. Mackay published two poetical works, "The Hope of the World" and "The Salamandrine," a third edition of which, illustrated by Gilbert, appeared in 1850; within the same period he published three works in prose, viz. : "The Thames and its Tributaries," "Popular Delusions," and "Longbeard, Lord of London, a Romance." In 1844 he removed from London to Glasgow, to succeed the late Mr. Weir as editor of

the "Argus," then a leading liberal journal in the West of Scotland. During his residence in Scotland, he produced "The Legends of the Isles, and other Poems," "A Series of Twelve Letters to Lord Morpeth on the Education of the People," and a volume entitled "The Scenery and Poetry of the English Lakes : a Summer Ramble." He also published "Voices from the Crowd," which contained the spirit-stirring song, "The Good Time Coming." It was while Mr. Mackay remained in Scotland that he received from the University of Glasgow the honorary degree of LL. D. In 1847 he returned to the metropolis, where he succeeded to the political editorship of the "Illustrated London News." He published in 1848 his "Town Lyrics;" in 1850 "Egeria, or the Spirit of Nature ; and other Poems," to which was prefixed "An Inquiry into the alleged Anti-Poetical Tendencies of the Present Age." In 1851 he edited for the Percy Society, with Notes and an Introduction, an important antiquarian work, entitled "A Collection of Songs and Ballads relative to the London 'Prentices and Trades ; and to the Affairs of London generally, during the Fourteenth, Fifteenth, and Sixteenth Centuries." He also edited "A Book of English Songs," and "A Book of Scottish Songs, with Notes and Observations." In 1856 Dr. Mackay published the "Lump of Gold," and in the following year "Under Green Leaves," two poetical works abounding with verses of the utmost melody, rich with the choicest English epithets and phrases. After the publication of these works, Dr. Mackay made a tour to America, where he delivered lectures upon "Poetry and Song," receiving everywhere a cordial and enthusiastic reception; his poetry and songs, owing perhaps to the higher standard of education in the Northern States, being well known and appreciated among our Transatlantic cousins. After his return to this country he published his "Life and Liberty in America," which is characterised in "The Athenæum" as a bright, fresh, and hopeful book, worthy of an author whose songs are oftenest heard on the Atlantic. He also edited a Christmas book, entitled "The Home Affections as portrayed by the Poets." Dr. Mackay lately published a narrative poem, entitled "A Man's Heart," and has just edited "A Collection of the Jacobite Ballads of Scotland." He is still actively engaged in journalism, having recently founded the "London Review." Like all the great song writers, Dr. Mackay is a musician, and the composer of the melodies published with many of his songs. He possesses in a high degree the rare faculty of a true lyric poet, that of working his words and music up into harmony and unison with the feelings they express.

MACLAREN, CHARLES, a journalist, was born in 1783. He is a man of humble birth, but well educated, and has been distinguished through life for energy, ability, and modesty of character. In conjunction with the late Mr. William Ritchie, he commenced the "Scotsman" newspaper. Under Mr. Maclaren's management, the "Scotsman" rose to the highest position in journalism; though, perhaps, as Lord Cockburn remarks, "just a little heavy occasionally." Mr. Maclaren is not only an able editor, but is also a geologist and geographer. "The Topography of Troy," and "The Geology of Fife and the Lothians," with his various communications to the "Encyclopædia Britannica" and "Edinburgh Philosophical Journal," bear testimony to his scientific attainments. He is a member of the Royal Society of Edinburgh and of the Geological Societies of London and Paris. Under the initials "C. M." he still occasionally contributes papers, chiefly scientific, to the "Scotsman."

MACLEOD, REV. NORMAN, D.D., an eminent Scottish divine, was born at Campbeltown, Argyleshire, on the 3rd June, 1812. He is the son of the Rev. Norman Macleod, D.D., Minister of St. Columba's (Gaelic) church in Glasgow, who is also one of the Deans of the Chapel Royal, and has been a Moderator of the General Assembly of the Church of Scotland. He studied at Glasgow and Edinburgh, and in Germany, and was appointed to the ministerial charge of Loudoun, in Ayrshire, in 1838, and of Dalkeith in 1843. In 1851 he was called to the Barony parish, Glasgow, the largest, and one of the most important, in Scotland; and he has continued to discharge the duties of his onerous office since then with zeal and ability. Dr. Macleod's works are of a practical character, the two most extensively read being "The Earnest Student," and "Home Education." He at present edits a literary and religious periodical, entitled "Good Words," which has obtained the widest circulation of any publication of its class hitherto known in Scotland. The constant claims of large and populous parishes have, however, rendered it almost impossible for Dr. Macleod to devote any but occasional time to literary pursuits. His principles are evangelical; his oratory is free and graceful, and he is an ardent friend to the working classes. He received the degree of D.D. in 1858. He has lately commenced special services for the labouring classes in his church, and is connected with several associations for their benefit in Glasgow.

M'CLINTOCK, SIR FRANCIS LEOPOLD, a celebrated Arctic navigator, was born at Dundalk, Ireland, in 1819. When quite a boy, in 1831, he entered the navy as midshipman, and in 1845 obtained his lieutenancy, on account of his distinguished services under Sir Charles

Hotham when H. M. ship "Gorgon" was stranded at Monte Video. Having chosen his profession, he resolved to master it, as well in theory as in detail; and to that end studied with unremitting zeal, when opportunity afforded, at the Royal Naval College, Portsmouth, where he was warmly commended for his proficiency in science. When the Enterprise and Investigator were despatched by Government, in 1848, to search for Sir John Franklin, under the command of Sir James Clark Ross, M'Clintock was appointed Lieutenant on board the Enterprise. In all the three expeditions sent out in search of Franklin, he was actively employed, distinguishing himself by the extraordinary journeys he made overland on foot, and the great additions he made to geographical knowledge. In 1849, he and Sir James Ross were absent from the ship forty days, during which time they traversed 500 miles of coast; and again, in 1851, when attached to Captain Austin's expedition, he made a pedestrian journey of 900 miles, which occupied about 80 days. In 1853 he commanded the Intrepid, one of the four ships forming Sir Edward Belcher's searching expedition. He had given much attention to the subject of sledge-travelling, as a most important means of exploring the country; and he is accordingly found improving on the systems previously adopted, achieving his purpose so well that it has been stated that every part of the sledge scheme carried out by Sir Edward Belcher was grounded entirely on M'Clintock's original ideas. The advantages of his system are now thoroughly recognised; but the best proof of its value rests on the fact that in his sledge journey of 1853 he accomplished on foot the extraordinary distance of 1,400 miles in 105 days, thus not only surpassing himself, but every other competitor. As such a journey was never performed before, the proba-bility is that it will never be equalled. It is, however, by the recent voyage of the "Fox," its successful issue, and the unerring skill joined to the indomitable perseverance of its commander, that Captain M'Clintock's name will ever rank among the first and greatest of our Arctic heroes. All previous efforts at penetrating the mystery of the fate of the Franklin expedition had proved abortive, though aided by the resources of the two most powerful maritime nations of the world. It was reserved for Captain M'Clintock, with a steam-yacht of but one hundred and seventy-seven tons burden, and only twenty-four of a crew, to solve the problem. For eight months his little craft was helplessly beset in the pack of ice in Baffin's Bay. Many commanders would have abandoned the undertaking then, but he was not to be deterred from the prosecution of his object by any impediment short of destruction. He persisted; the ice gave way; the "Fox" was liberated; and the termination of his toils and dangers was success. Into the particulars of this eventful voyage it is not necessary to enter; but it may be observed that, while Captain M'Clintock never lost sight of his primary purpose, he left no opportunity of advancing the cause of science unimproved. He has seen more Arctic service than, perhaps, any other officer in the Royal Navy, having spent six winters within the Arctic circle, and travelled on foot, on his exploring journeys, not less than 5,500 miles, without his health suffering. He has brought home many interesting relics of the lost expedition, and amongst other things, the original despatch stating the date and circumstances of Sir J. Franklin's death.

MACLISE, DANIEL, an English painter, was born at Cork, in 1811. His father had served in the Elgin Fencibles, and his grandfather in the 42nd regiment of the line. He was early intended for commercial pursuits, and spent some time in a banking establishment in his native town; but preferring the pursuit of the Fine Arts, he speedily gave vent to his earnest desire by producing sketches, &c., which brought him into some little notoriety. He at last proceeded to London and entered the Royal Academy, and here soon obtained leading prizes for his drawings from life, and for the best copy of a picture. He sketched for "Fraser's," and other periodicals, and then devoted his talents to oil painting, in which he has since met with extraordinary success. He was elected a member of the Royal Academy in 1840. His productions have been very numerous, and some of the following are specially admired :—" The Vow of the Ladies, and the Peacock," "Henry the Eighth's Interview with Anne Boleyn," "Gil Blas and the Parasite," "The Sleeping Beauty," "Hunt the Slipper," "The Sacrifice of Noah," "Caxton in his Printing Office," "Merry Christmas and the Baron's Hall," "Shakspeare's Seven Ages," &c. &c. He has also made many designs for illustrated works, is a first-rate draughtsman, and has painted several frescoes in the New Houses of Parliament. Two of his best pictures are in the national collection at the Kensington Museum, namely, his "Play Scene in Hamlet," and "Malvolio and the Countess."

MACLURE, Sir Robert Le Mesurier, an Arctic discoverer and traveller, was born at Wexford, in January, 1807. Having been kindly provided for by an intimate friend of his father during his early years, he was sent to Eton, and afterwards to Sandhurst. Being disgusted, however, with the prospect of a military life, he secretly left the College, and was, through the influence of his old friend, placed as midshipman on board the "Victory." He passed some years in the navy, and having become lieutenant, entered into that line of service which has since rendered him so much known and esteemed. His first Arctic voyage was under Sir George Back, and in 1836 he went with him to the northern seas, but was nearly shipwrecked on his return. In 1848 he proceeded in search of Franklin, who had been absent for three years, and of whom no account had been received since he re-victualled at Greenland, shortly after his departure from England. This voyage, however, was unsuccessful, and the whole party returned to England towards the end of 1849. Another expedition was fitted out in the ensuing year, in which Captain Maclure commanded one of the vessels, the "Enterprise;" and in this voyage he obtained a result which had been long sought, namely, the discovery of the North-West passage. The description of Arctic voyages always includes accounts of severe hardship and privation, but in this case the crews seem to have been in the greatest danger, not only from the ice, but also from their provisions falling short. Instead of proceeding northwards to Greenland, which is the usual course, Captain Maclure sailed round to Behring's Straits, and then pursued an eastern course. He travelled by sledge and on foot from the Pacific to the Atlantic ; and although perceiving no traces of the Franklin expedition, he succeeded in that which had hitherto baffled every other navigator. On his return home, after overcoming all difficulties by great perseverance, and receiving also assistance from Captain Kellet, who had been sent out to relieve him, Captain Maclure was heartily welcomed to his native shores, was knighted by her Majesty, and received a portion of the reward which had been many years previously offered for the discovery of a passage to India by proceeding in a north-westerly direction, instead of the usual route by the Cape of Good Hope. He at present commands a vessel in the Chinese seas, and will most probably be called on to exercise, in warlike matters, those talents which have already rendered him famous in his past career.

MACMAHON, MARIE EDMÉ PATRICE MAURICE DE, Marshal of France, and Senator, is descended from an ancient Irish family who attached themselves to the cause of the Stuarts, and left their native country after the defeat of King James II. at the Boyne. Marie Edmé was born in 1807, at Autun, Saone-et-Loire, and after being educated at the School of St.˙ Cyr, joined the army. As captain in 1833, he signalized himself in Africa at various serious engagements. After leaving Africa he joined the French army before Sebastopol, and there acquired great renown by his bravery and success. He led his division against the Malakoff, and although this was stoutly defended by the Russians, he effected a lodgment. For four hours he was assailed by the Russian forces, who fought desperately, but with Macmahon the position was one of death or glory, and he held it against every effort of the enemy, who eventually retreated only to witness the French masters of the position. Dignities, chiefly titular but ennobling, were showered on him, not the least of which were the British Order of the Bath, and the rank and emolument of a Senator of the Empire. On the war of 1859 breaking out with Austria, General Macmahon was again selected for the field; and, having been triumphant in the sanguinary contest of Magenta, promptly received the bâton of a Marshal. A testimonial has just been presented to him by his "countrymen," the Irish, in the shape of a sword. In the inscription reference is made to "the oppressed Ireland," and many of the subscribers do not hesitate to express the hope that he may one day be called upon to rescue "their country" from the hand of the Saxon, and, as a descendant of its ancient kings, occupy the throne of his ancestors.

M'NEILE, THE REV. HUGH, D.D., a clergyman, and Canon of Chester, was born in 1795, at Ballycastle, near Belfast, in the county of Antrim, Ireland. He graduated at Trinity College, Dublin. He was for some years Rector of Albury in Surrey, and then frequently preached in London, where his eloquent and energetic style of pulpit oratory attracted great attention, and filled the churches where he officiated. He was invited to the incumbency of St. Jude's, Liverpool, which he held for many years, but removed to that of St. Paul's, Prince's Park, near Liverpool. He has published several theological works, together with separate sermons and controversial pamphlets, and his writings have acquired great popularity, some having reached as many as seven editions.

M'NEILL, SIR JOHN, G.C.B., Knight of the Lion and Sun of Persia, a diplomatist, was born in 1795, at Colonsay, Argyleshire. He was educated in St. Andrew's University, and subsequently joined the Bombay army. In 1821 he was sent to Persia as assistant to the Chargé d'Affaires; in 1831 he became Assistant Secretary; in 1834 was British Minister, and remained in that position till 1844. For his services in Persia he was created G.C.B. in 1839. Sir John availed himself of the opportunity thus afforded him of observing the peculiarities of Oriental customs and government. He was chosen a President of the Scottish Poor-Law Board, on his return to his native country. He was also engaged in the inquiry into the state of the army before Sebastopol, for which service he was specially fitted on account of his previous acquaintance with the resources of the neighbouring countries. He was nominated a member of the Privy Council in 1857, as a.

recognition of the services he had rendered to the nation.

M'NEILL, Sir John, LL. D., F.R.S., C.E., was born at Mount Pleasant, near Dundalk, county Louth, Ireland. He was educated as a military engineer, but adopted instead the civil branch of the profession, and was in 1842 appointed Professor of Practical Engineering in Trinity College, Dublin. He was chief engineer for the Dublin and Drogheda Railway, and on the opening of the line in 1844, received the honour of knighthood from the Lord Lieutenant. He has constructed most of the principal railways in Ireland, as well as the celebrated bridge over the Boyne, and the large viaducts on the Great Southern and Western Railway, and the Dublin and Belfast Railway.

MACREADY, William Charles, a tragedian, was born in London, in 1793. His early education was received at Rugby, but owing to his father's misfortunes he was compelled to abandon the hope of other prospects, and assumed the theatrical profession, of which his parent was a member. He made his *début* at Birmingham in 1810; and after performing in many of the leading provincial theatres, appeared before a London audience, in Covent Garden, in 1816, as "Orestes," in the "Distressed Mother." His reception on this occasion was most enthusiastic, and had the effect of encouraging him to persevere in the study of some of Shakspeare's principal characters, in which however he did not appear, owing to professional jealousies, till his success, and a *furore* to see him in "Richard III.," in November 1819, placed him indisputably at the head of Covent Garden Theatre. He subsequently represented "Coriolanus," and other leading characters of Shakspeare, in the same season; and at its termination acted in Knowles's tragedy of "Virginius," which confirmed his position and reputation. He afterwards made a tour in the United States, and

also appeared in the French capital. In 1837 he became lessee of Covent Garden Theatre; but after two years' trial gave it up, on the grounds of injustice and rapacity—according to his own statement—on the part of the proprietors. He afterwards performed at the Haymarket, and in the provinces. Assuming the management of Drury Lane, he endeavoured to elevate the taste of the *habitués* of the theatres; but, like all public benefactors, did not meet with an adequate pecuniary return for his exertions. He performed in America in 1849; but through the malice of an actor was in danger of losing his life during a riot which took place in the theatre where he was performing. He returned home, and after appearing in many of his favourite representations in different parts of the kingdom, he retired from the stage in 1851. He now resides in Dorsetshire, where he applies his past experience and eminent talents to the improvement of the social and mental condition of his neighbours.

MADDEN, Sir Frederick, K.H., F.R.S., M.R.I.A., an antiquarian writer, was born at Portsmouth, in 1801. His first literary occupation was that of assisting Mr. Roscoe in 1825, in making a catalogue of manuscripts belonging to the Earl of Leicester. In the course of a year afterwards he became an Assistant in the British Museum, and in 1837 was appointed Keeper of the Manuscript department. Sir Frederick has been a most valuable contributor to English history, and has edited many works relating thereto. Amongst the most important of these may be named "The Holy Bible in the earliest English Version, by Wycliffe;" his "Privy Purse Expenses of the Princess Mary, afterwards Queen Mary, with a Memoir of the Princess, and Notes;" "Havelock, the Dane;" "Layamon's Brut, or Chronicle of Britain;" "Sir Gawayne," &c. He is at present engaged in preparing for the press, under the sanction of the Master of the Rolls, "The Minor Chronicle of Matthew Paris, the Historian of St. Alban's Abbey, of the Thirteenth Century." He was nominated companion of the Guelphic order in 1832, knighted by King William IV. in 1833, and in 1834 was appointed one of the Gentlemen of the King's Privy Chamber.

MADOZ, PASCAL, a Spanish statesman and author, was born at Pampeluna, in May 1806. He pursued his legal studies at the University of Saragossa, but becoming mixed up with political matters, he was cast into prison, where he remained for many months. He graduated after his release, but was expelled from the university on account of his theological opinions. He commenced to practise in the legal profession in 1835, and was soon after made Judge of the First Instance, at Barcelona. He became deputy to the Cortes, and in 1854 was elected President of that assembly. As Minister of Finance, he proposed the sequestration of the Church and other property, in the following year, and as such incurred the odium of the Church party ; taking part with the popular cause, he was compelled through its want of success to quit Madrid, in 1856. He has published some valuable works, the two most important being his "Collection of Celebrated Law Cases," and "A Geographical and Statistical Dictionary of Spain," the latter of which he printed himself. He is of decided liberal opinions, and has at times had considerable influence in Spanish affairs.

MAGNAN, PIERRE BERNARD, a French Marshal, was born in Paris, on 7th December, 1791. He originally intended to follow the profession of the law, but when eighteen years old voluntarily entered the 66th Regiment of the Line, and remained in it during the campaign in Spain and Portugal.

His services procured him the distinction of admission to the Imperial Guard, and with the rank of Captain he served in the campaign of 1814, after which he was created an officer of the Legion of Honour. In 1827 he obtained the command of the 49th Regiment of the Line, and took part in the Algerian expedition of 1830. Here again he distinguished himself by his conduct at the battle of Staouëli, and for his services was rewarded by obtaining the rank of Commander. In 1831 he received an order to march upon Lyons, which was then in a state of insurrection, and he succeeded in putting down the insurgents; but his conduct not being approved of by the Government, the command of the regiment was taken from him. He was then sent on a mission to Belgium. Appointed a General of Brigade by the King of the Belgians, he set himself assiduously to effect the re-organization of the Belgian army, of which he commanded the vanguard at the time when war was imminent between Belgium and Holland. Peace having been concluded, he asked and obtained permission to return to France, where he had been named a General of Brigade in 1839. He was appointed to the command of the Department of the Nord, which he retained for seven years. When the revolution of 1848 broke out, having no command, he placed himself at the disposal of the Minister of War, and was the only general officer who accompanied the Duchess of Orleans and her children to the Chamber of Deputies. Under the Provisional Government he soon obtained the command of the 3rd division of the Army of the Alps. Appointed in the month of July, 1851, to the chief command of the Army of Paris, and devoted to the schemes of Prince Louis Napoleon, he was one of the small number of persons who prepared for the *coup d'état*. He aided by his able and energetic advice the projects of the President during the eventful days of the 2nd, 3rd, and 4th of December, and was rewarded by the dignity of Marshal of France. He remained in command of the Army of Paris during the Crimean and Italian campaigns, the confidence of the Emperor retaining him in that important position.

MALMESBURY, THE RIGHT HON. JAMES HOWARD HARRIS, third Earl of, Secretary of Foreign Affairs in the ministry of Lord Derby, was born 25th March, 1807. He was educated at Eton, and Oriel College, Oxford. Shortly after quitting the university, he married Lady Emma Bennet. In 1841, as Viscount Fitz-Harris, he was returned to the House of Commons as member for Wilton. Scarcely, however, had he taken his seat among the people's representatives, when the unexpected death of his father called him to the Upper House. His conduct there was singularly unobtrusive; and not until 1852 was public attention drawn towards him. His selection by Lord Derby as Minister for Foreign Affairs, during his short-lived administration, first drew the noble lord from the obscurity he had hitherto courted. The friends of the noble earl claim for him the merit of having preserved inviolate the national honour at that critical juncture, when Lord Palmerston, expelled from office, was succeeded by Lord Derby; but an impartial observer might be apt to deny to the minister more merit in that crisis than simply belongs to the registrar of the national will. On Lord Derby's restoration to power in 1858, Lord Malmesbury again became Foreign Secretary, and it spoke well for the administration of that department, that, on Lord Derby's retirement in 1859, the succeeding government stated their intention, so far as regarded foreign policy, of following in the track of their predecessors.

MANTEUFEL, BARON OTHO THEO-DORE, Prussian Minister of Foreign Affairs, was born at Lubben, Brandenburg, Feb. 1805, and after taking the ordinary collegiate course, studied law and political science at the University of Halle. In 1827 he went to Berlin, where he was appointed to a small office, which he left, and was afterwards named successively to various posts of trust in Brandenburg, for which province he became Deputy to the Provincial Diet in 1837. From 1841 to 1843 he directed the internal affairs of the government of Königsberg; in 1843 he obtained the Vice-Presidency of the government of Stettin. The year following found him Special Counsellor to the Prince of Prussia, and member of the Council of State; in 1845 he was Under-Secretary to the Minister of the Interior; in 1847 he defended the Prussian Constitution with all his power; and in 1848 was appointed Minister of the Interior, under Count Brandenburg. The kingdom was somewhat unsettled at the time, and as Manteufel exhibited an amount of administrative ability and moderation in his course of proceeding not expected from him, he gained popularity and influence. In 1850, when a serious disagreement between Prussia and Austria was at its height, he was appointed Minister for Foreign Affairs. In 1852 he was constituted President of the Council of Ministers, and in 1856 he was a party to the Peace Congress of Paris, when he represented the Prussian government. Different ideas of his policy are entertained. A large section in France express themselves by designating him gloomy and austere; but the general Prussian opinion is probably the correct one, that he is emphatically a Prussian politician, endeavouring, with the best of his ability, to hold the balance equal between conflicting interests, whether at home or abroad.

MANZONI, COUNT ALESSANDRO, an Italian poet and novelist, was born at Milan, in 1784. Having studied in his native city, he completed his education at Pavia, and afterwards proceeded to Paris. His most popular novel is "I Promessi Sposi," which has appeared in English as "The Betrothed Lovers." He has also produced tragedies and poems, on which, however, his reputation does not depend. Amongst his other works are "A Vindication of Catholic Morality;" "Storia della Colonna Infame," an historical essay treating on some supposed means of secretly propagating the plague which in 1630 ravaged Milan; and several odes, composed as illustrative of different events connected with history.

MARIO, JOSEPH, an Italian singer, was born at Turin, in 1810, and received a first-rate musical education. He entered the Sardinian army as an officer in 1830, but for some cause quitted the service and went to Paris, where his fine tenor voice soon obtained him an engagement at the Opera, with a handsome salary. It was here that he assumed the name of Mario, in place of his proper title—the Marquis of Candia. In December, 1838, he made his *début* in "Robert le Diable," and in the following year appeared in the Italian Theatre, where he was the rival of Rubini. He subsequently travelled in Russia, where he remained for some years. Since then he has repeatedly appeared in London and Paris at the Italian Opera houses, has achieved successes in every engagement, and acquired a European reputation for the taste and excellence of his vocalism.

MAROCHETTI, BARON CHARLES, a sculptor, was born at Turin, in 1805. After studying at the Lycée Napoléon, he entered the ateliers of Bosio and Gros. He subsequently spent some time in Italy, and returning to France in 1827, exhibited in that year his "Young Girl Playing with a Dog," which was greatly admired for its combination of

vigour and grace. In 1831 he produced his "Fallen Angel," and some time afterwards executed the equestrian statue of Emanuel Philibert, which is erected at Turin. The statue of the Duke of Wellington, erected in front of the Royal Exchange in Glasgow, was produced by him in 1844. Since his removal to London, in 1848, he has executed numerous well-known statues, which have been greatly admired. His "Richard Cœur de Lion" was exhibited at Hyde Park in 1851. The statue of her Majesty, erected in Buchanan-street, Glasgow, was produced in 1854. He has also executed busts of the Queen and Prince Albert, and of many well-known public individuals. He stands high in popular favour, owing to the force and felicity of all his numerous productions.

MARSH, MRS. ANNE CALDWELL, an English authoress, was born in Staffordshire, about the end of the last century. Having received an excellent education at home, she proceeded, after marrying Mr. Marsh, to London, and published her first literary effort, "Two Old Men's Tales," which at once secured her success as a writer. After producing in 1836 her "Tales of the Woods and the Fields," and the "Triumphs of Time," she again received the praise of her readers for her work entitled "Mount Sorel," which appeared in 1843. Since then Mrs. Marsh has been a most indefatigable writer; and in all her works her depth of feeling and high descriptive powers are eminently apparent. Her "Emilia Wyndham" has had extraordinary success as a popular novel. Amongst many others, the following may be named as the best of her publications:—"Father Darcy," "Time the Avenger," "Aubrey," "The Protestant Reformation in France," "Angela," and "The Heiress of Haughton." Mrs. Marsh's style is exceedingly attractive; and she infuses much of truth and high-toned morality in all her charming works of fiction.

MARSHALL, WILLIAM CALDER, R.A., a sculptor, was born at Edinburgh, in 1813. He studied in the Royal Academy of London, and became the pupil of Chantrey and Bailey. After visiting Rome he settled in London, and commenced those labours in sculpture for which he has since become so well known, and wherein he has been a successful competitor against men of the highest rank in the profession. Perhaps one of the best of his works is the colossal statue of Sir Robert Peel, which has been erected at Manchester. He received the prize for a model of the national monument to the Duke of Wellington, the bas-relievos of which he is at present executing, and which will be placed in St. Paul's Cathedral. The public statues he has executed in London are those of Dr. Jenner, Thomas Campbell, and Captain Coram. He is an Associate of the Scottish Academy, and a Royal Academician. The following are some of Mr. Marshall's choice productions :— "Una and the Lion," "Cupid and Psyche," "Caractacus," "Paul and Virginia," "Hebe Rejected," "Godiva," "Imogene Asleep," "Dancing Girl Reposing," "The Grecian Maid," "Sabrina," and his "Clarendon" and "Somers," in the New Houses of Parliament.

MARSTON, JOHN WESTLAND, a dramatic author, was born at Boston, in Lincolnshire, on the 7th of January, 1820. He entered the office of his uncle with the view of adopting the legal profession ; but on the completion of his articles he abandoned the profession, and now writes principally for the theatres. His "Patrician's Daughter," "Strathmore," and "Ann Blake," are well known as among the most sterling of modern dramatic works. All his plays have been successful, and he is one of our few writers for the stage who disdain to borrow the material of their works from foreign sources. Besides the above-named plays, and others in blank verse, Mr. Marston has written two or three prose dramas, of which the one entitled "A Hard Struggle," has excited the most attention.

MARTINEAU, MISS HARRIET, an English authoress, was born at Norwich, on 12th June, 1802. She is descended from one of the old French families who sought a refuge in England on the revocation of the Edict of Nantes. At the cost of much self-denial, the parents of Miss Martineau secured for their children a superior education, the best masters at home being provided for them without stint. Miss Martineau's specialty was music, singing, and the pianoforte. A sound classical education, combined with steady, regular, mental discipline, and an innate love of literature, rendered composition a pleasure and a profit. Some years after the death of her father, who was a manufacturer, his successor in business failed ; and as the family had left their money in the concern, Miss Martineau and her mother and sisters lost their all. With a noble spirit she resolved to maintain herself; it was a great struggle, but she saw its end. In 1823 she published a volume of "Devotional Exercises for Young Persons ;" in 1824, "Christmas Day ;" in 1826, "Principle and Practice," and "The Rioters," succeeded by "The Turn Out," "Mary Campbell," and "My Servant Rachel,"—a series of tracts on subjects relating to the working classes, of whose interests she has invariably been an ardent advocate. In 1831 her "Traditions of Palestine" appeared, and was successful. The Committee of the British and Foreign Unitarian Association having offered prizes for three tracts on the introduction and promotion of Unitarianism among the Roman Catholics, the Jews, and the Mahomedans,

Miss Martineau sent in three essays for competition, and she was awarded the first prize for each. Shortly afterwards she projected the publication of a monthly series of tales, illustrative of political economy, and offered one of them to the Society for the Diffusion of Useful Knowledge; but being rejected by that body, they were brought out independently, and became extremely popular. The "Illustrations of Political Economy" were followed by "Illustrations of Taxation," a series of six tales; and these were succeeded by others on "Poor Law and Paupers." In 1834 Miss Martineau visited the United States; and on her return published a work entitled "Society in America," and a "Retrospect of Western Travel." In 1838 she wrote "Deerbrook," the most widely circulated of any of her works, except the series on political economy. For some years her health was impaired, but she did not abandon literature altogether. In the course of this protracted period of suffering she wrote "The Playfellow," "The Hour and the Man," and "Life in the Sick Room." Recovering her health in 1844, she resumed authorship, and produced "Forest and Game Law Tales." After publishing "The Billow and the Rock," a charming story, in 1846, she visited Egypt, Arabia, and the Holy Land, the result of her observations being given to the world in a work entitled "Eastern Life, Present and Past," published on her return. Miss Martineau, afterwards, at the instance of Mr. Charles Knight, brought to a conclusion the "History of the Thirty Years' Peace," which that gentleman had commenced, but for various reasons had not completed. This is generally considered her greatest work. She has since given to the English public a translation of Comte's "Positive Philosophy." Miss Martineau for some years has been closely confined to her residence at Ambleside, labouring under heart-disease, from which she suffers greatly.

MARTINEZ DE LA ROSA, Francisco, a Spanish poet, historian, orator, and statesman, was born at Granada, in 1789. He studied for the legal profession, and before completing his twentieth year was appointed a professor and lecturer on Ethics at the College of San Miguel. In 1811 his first literary productions were given to the world. Up to 1813 he wrote and published dramas and poems; and in the latter year was elected Deputy to the Cortes by the city of Granada. After having been imprisoned, for political reasons, for nearly six years, the insurrection (of 1820) introduced the second constitutional rule in Spain, and Martinez was liberated. When the French overthrew the constitutional government once more, Martinez left Spain. In the meantime he was composing some of his best dramas; but the French revolution of 1830 alarmed Ferdinand of Spain, and Martinez obtained permission to return to Granada. On the death of Ferdinand, Martinez was recalled to power, became head of the ministry, and established a new constitutional system, founded on that of Great Britain. From various causes his influence declined, until, in 1836, he resigned office. In 1840, when Espartero assumed the Regency, Martinez left Spain, but returning to Madrid, he was made Spanish Ambassador to Paris in 1847, and was first Secretary of State in October, 1857. He has been a voluminous writer, particularly of dramas; and as a politician, it is agreed that his integrity and patriotism are unquestionable.

MARTIUS, CARL FREDERICH PHILLIP VON, a German botanist, was born at Erlangen, on 17th April, 1794. His earliest predilections were for the science of botany. He studied for medicine at the University, and after graduating, he proceeded to the Brazils with the zoologist Spix. He there had every opportunity of practically pursuing his favourite study, and in the course of four years returned to Germany with a splendid herbarium, and subsequently published the results of his observations in a work called "Travels in Brazil." His reputation was thus so far enhanced as to procure him the appointment of Professor of Botany at Munich, and Director of the Botanic Garden. He has also been elected a member of most of the European scientific societies. Amongst his numerous botanical works are the following:—"Nova Genera et Species Plantarum," "Icones Plantarum Cryptogamicarum," "Flora Brasiliensis," and his "Genera et Species Palmarum," which is at once attractive and highly instructive. Besides these, he has published numerous papers on medical botany, physiology, and the geographical distribution of plants, which have gained for him a high reputation for accuracy as a man of science.

MASSEY, GERALD, an English poet, was born May 1828, near Tring, in Herts. His parents were so steeped in poverty that the children received scarcely any education. When only eight years old, Gerald was sent to work in a neighbouring silk mill; but the mill being burned down, the boy took to straw-plaiting. He had learned to read at a penny school; and when fifteen went up to London as an errand boy, and spent all his spare time in reading and writing. When out of a situation, he has gone without a meal to purchase a book. His first appearance in print was in a provincial paper; he published a small collection of his verses in his native town, and during the political excitement of 1848, edited a cheap paper called the "Spirit of Freedom." His writing was so bold and vigorous, that his political manifestations cost him five situations in eleven months. He was a warm advocate of the co-operative system, and thus was introduced to the Rev. Charles Kingsley and others who were promoting that movement. Still continuing to write, his name began to be known; and in 1853 "Christabel" took the public completely by surprise. Five editions of the work were published in two years; his pecuniary circumstances improved in proportion to his fame as a poet; and in 1855 he removed to Edinburgh, where in 1856 he issued "Craigcrook Castle," in his own estimation his best work. A collected edition of his poems has just been published.

MASSON, DAVID, Professor of the English Language and Literature at University College, London, was born 2nd December, 1822, at Aberdeen. After studying at Marischal College, Aberdeen, he entered the University of Edinburgh, and for some time subsequently was editor of a Scottish newspaper. After removing to London he returned to Edinburgh, and for some time was a contributor to various reviews and magazines. Taking up his residence in London again, he was chosen Professor of English Literature at the London University. A volume of "Critical and Biographical Essays" (1856), "Life and Times of Milton" (vol. i, 1859), and "British Novelists and their Styles" (1859), are his chief independent contributions to literature. The remainder of Mr. Masson's productions have been read with delight by all who love vigorous, poetic, and original expression. Mr. Masson has become the editor of "Macmillan's Magazine," which he conducts with the greatest ability.

MAURICE, REV. FREDERICK DENISON, M.A., Chaplain of Lincoln's Inn, Minister of Vere Street Chapel, Marylebone, and formerly Professor of Theology at King's College, London. Mr. Maurice was in early life educated as a Unitarian, his father being a minister of that denomination; but being desirous of a University education, he, at the age of eighteen, proceeded to Cambridge and was entered of Trinity Hall, his father, although not approving of the step, generously providing the means; but not being a member of the Church, he left Cambridge without a degree. Having changed his views respecting the Church, Mr. Maurice went to Exeter College, Oxford, and took the degree of B.A. in 1831, was ordained Deacon in 1834, and Priest in 1835, in which year he also received his M.A. degree. The first work which made any sensation was anonymous—"Subscription no Bondage." In 1830 he edited the "Athenæum," receiving some assistance from his friends the late Archdeacon Hare and John Sterling. "Eustace Conway," a three volume novel, was disposed of in 1831 to Mr. Bentley (then in partnership with Mr. Colburn), but was not published till 1834, after the author had taken orders. "The Kingdom of Christ," a work which had much influence upon members of the Society of Friends, appeared in 1841. During the time Mr. Maurice held the appointment of Chaplain of Guy's Hospital he published a volume of sermons; and in 1846, the year in which he was appointed Professor of Theology at King's College, he published an expository work on "The Epistle to the Hebrews." Although not unfrequently classed amongst that section of the Church of England known as the "broad," Mr. Maurice is too honest and out-spoken to be tied down by the formularies of any party, and consequently he has been both misunderstood and misrepresented. While at King's College, some of his views respecting the eternity of future punishment raised such a storm of disapprobation that he was obliged to resign the professorship in 1853. He "denounced the popular teaching respecting eternal punishment, believing it to be at variance with the scriptural revelation of God in

Christ; that eternity in Scripture and in our creeds has an altogether different meaning to that which is given it by popular preachers, who, in their attempts to make their notion tell upon the terrors of their congregations, set at nought the Gospel, as well as all the real terrors which should deter them from sin." No question was raised by the authorities at King's College respecting the soundness of Mr. Maurice's views respecting the Atonement; they knew that he had always preached the doctrine "that God was in Christ, reconciling the world to Himself," and "that Christ's death was a full, perfect, and sufficient sacrifice, oblation, and satisfaction for the sins of the whole world." In 1849 Mr. Maurice exerted himself successfully in establishing the Queen's College for Ladies, and more lately in founding the College for Working Men, in Red Lion Square, and there are few social questions in which he does not feel a warm interest. Mr. Maurice believes that the Church of England ought to grapple intellectually with the most advanced forms of scepticism and error, in order to exhibit the supremacy of religion: "That the Church is sent into the world to proclaim Christ as the Head of all human society, and that she fails in her mission when she substitutes a mere æsthetical religion for the teaching that men are brothers of each and all others, and that God is their Father in heaven." Mr. Maurice was married to Miss Hare, sister to the late Archdeacon of Lewes, who also married a sister of Mr. Maurice. Mr. Maurice is the author of numerous other controversial and theological works; but his most important contribution to literature, is the article on Moral and Metaphysical Philosophy, in the "Encyclopædia Metropolitana," and which has been republished in a greatly enlarged form. Mr. Maurice has recently been appointed to the ministry of Vere Street Chapel, London.

MAURY, MATTHEW F., an American hydrographer, son of Richard Maury, was born in Spottsylvania County, Virginia, on the 14th January, 1806. After receiving an ordinary education, Maury applied for and obtained a midshipman's appointment, and made several voyages, in which he highly distinguished himself. He then commenced his celebrated Wind and Current Charts, and gradually came into notice as a scientific man. In 1853 he visited Europe for the purpose of inducing the maritime nations to agree upon, and carry out, some general plan of observation at sea. For this purpose he called a conference, for August of that year, at Brussels. He was there met by representatives from England, France, Holland, and the other principal maritime powers. The plan of observation then adopted is now carried on under all flags. In acknowledgment of the services rendered by Lieutenant Maury in the advancement of science and improvement of navigation, the Emperors of France, Russia, and Austria, the Kings of Denmark, Sweden and Norway, of Prussia, Holland, Belgium, Portugal, and Sardinia, have either awarded him medals, conferred orders of knighthood, or offered ribbons. Humboldt ascribed to him the credit of founding a new department of science, called the "Physical Geography of the Sea," and, in token of his estimation of its value, requested his king to bestow the great Cosmos medal upon the American lieutenant. His principal work is the "Physical Geography of the Sea," of which several editions have been published both in this country and America.

MAXIMILIAN II. (JOSEPH), KING OF BAVARIA, COUNT PALATINE OF THE RHINE, DUKE OF BAVARIA, FRANCONIA, AND SWABIA, was born on the 28th of November, 1811, and assumed the reins of government on the abdication of his father, King Louis, on the 21st of March, 1848. This abdication was the direct consequence of the French Revolution of February, but was expedited and prepared, not only by the deep offence which the ex-king had given to the Jesuits in his dominions, but by the displeasure excited in the minds of his subjects by the influence exercised over him—in his senility—by the young and fascinating and too notorious Lola Montez, whom he had made Countess of Landsfelt, and laden with wealth and favour. The present king has reigned without exciting any attention beyond the boundaries of his own kingdom, or taking any conspicuous part in European politics. He was married in 1842 to the Princess Frederica, daughter of William, Prince of Prussia, the uncle of the king, by whom he has two sons —Louis Otho Frederick William, born 25th August, 1845; and Otho William Leopold Adalbert Waldernaz, born 27th April, 1848.

MAYHEW, HENRY, author of "London Labour and the London Poor," was born in London, on November 25th, 1812. He was sent for his education to Westminster School, but rebelling against the discipline enforced, he ran away. He was then placed as midshipman in the East India Company's service, but soon left the sea. Returning to London from a stay in Wales, he, in partnership with the late Gilbert A'Beckett, became manager of the Queen's Theatre, where his farce of the "Wandering Minstrel" was produced, but the speculation was a failure. In 1841 he projected and obtained the co-operation of the principal writers in "Punch," which he edited for some years, when he had a difference with the proprietors and vacated his office. He was editor of "The Comic Almanac," after leaving "Punch," and contributed to numerous magazines and other periodicals. In 1842 he published a small work entitled "What to Teach, and How to Teach it," in which he contended stoutly against task-work, flogging, and prizes in schools. From 1846 to 1850 several works of a lively and comic character appeared, George Cruikshank being the illustrator. His chief work is "London Labour and the London Poor," showing the condition and earnings of those who will work— those who cannot work—and those who will not work. In 1856 Mr. Mayhew struck out the idea of an association for the reformation of criminals, and towards promoting this object he called meetings of the thieves of London, of whom several narrated their experience of the world and its ways. The association seems to have proceeded little farther than the prospectus. Mr. Mayhew's latest publication is the "Great World of London," a work which, owing to the sudden death of Mr. Bogue, remains incomplete. Mr. Mayhew is also the author of several works for young people, of which the most recent is "Young Benjamin Franklin."

MAZZINI, JOSEPH, an Italian politician and revolutionist, was born at Genoa, in 1809. Having had the advantage of home training, he entered the legal profession, but soon turned aside to political pursuits. The circumstances of Italy were at that time most unfortunate. Discontent, tyranny, and oppression were dominant throughout the land; and Mazzini, touched with a strong patriotic feeling, determined to devote himself to the liberation of his oppressed country by any and every means of which he could avail himself. He soon brought himself into notice by the productions of his pen, and conceived the idea of forming a universal society, whose objects were the spread of revolutionary ideas through every class of society by secret means. Mazzini thus fell under the displeasure of the Piedmontese government, and after being imprisoned for some time was expelled Italy, and settled at Mar-

seilles in 1831. Here his pen was again called into use, and he urged a general insurrection as the only means of freeing Italy. By correspondence with refugees and others, he succeeded in organizing, in 1833, an extensive conspiracy, which however came to nothing, but compelled Mazzini to take refuge in Switzerland. Again engaged in revolutionary attempts, he had to leave Switzerland, and went to London, where for some time he wrote for various journals and engaged in literary pursuits as a means of gaining a subsistence. In 1848 Mazzini took advantage of the continental revolutions, and proceeding to Rome was there elected Triumvir of the Republic, and became the soul of the defence of the Eternal City against the arms of France. Again was he doomed to disappointment, and fled to England on the occupation of Rome by the French army. Till lately he has resided in London; but since the astonishing progress of Garibaldi in Sicily and Naples, Mazzini has once more returned to Italy, and at the present time (September, 1860), it is greatly feared that his peculiar republican views will come into collision with those of Garibaldi and Victor Emmanuel, and that scenes of bloodshed and anarchy will, through the disunion of her sons, render Italy, one of the fairest spots on the earth, a disgrace and blot to civilization.

MEISSONIER, JEAN LOUIS ERNEST, a French painter, was born at Lyons, in 1815. In 1836 he exhibited two pictures at the Salon, which were greatly admired, and were followed by "Le Liseur," in 1840; "La Partie d'Échecs," in 1841; and in 1843 he produced his "Le Peintre dans son Atelier," for each of which he obtained a medal. In these and his other productions M. Meissonier generally chooses familiar subjects for illustration, and he is distinguished by the care and complete execution which he always bestows on them. He was made a Chevalier of the Legion of Honour in 1846, and officer of the same in 1856, after having obtained one of the ten large medals offered to painters at the Exhibition in Paris, held during the previous year.

MELVILL, THE REV. HENRY, B.D., President of Haileybury College, Herts. Mr. Melvill is a preacher of singular eloquence, and was educated at Cambridge, and became a Fellow of St. Peter's College. He was then appointed minister of Camden Chapel, Camberwell, London. Having received the degree of B.D., he was appointed by the late Duke of Wellington Chaplain to the Tower of London; by the East India Company he was made President of Haileybury College. He held for seven years the Tuesday morning lectureship at St. Margaret's, Lothbury, and is one of her Majesty's Chaplains in Ordinary. In 1856 he was appointed by the Queen a Canon of St. Paul's Cathedral. He has published a considerable number of volumes, all on religious topics, most of them being sermons.

MELVILLE, HERMAN, an American author, was born in New York, August 1st, 1819. At an early age, being seized with a passion for the sea, he embarked as a common sailor, and visited many parts of the globe. His first work, "Typee," giving an account of his adventures in the Marquesas, had a great success, and was followed by "Omoo," "Mardi," and a number of others.

MENCHIKOFF, PRINCE ALEXANDER SERGIUS, a Russian general, was born in 1789. He entered the diplomatic service in 1805, and was for some time attached to the Embassy at Vienna. The Emperor Nicholas sent him on an Extraordinary Mission to the Shah of Persia, Abbas Mirza, in 1826, which was not successful; he was detained, and at last escaped with considerable trouble. In 1828 he had the command of a division, possessed himself of Ana-

pu, then passed into Europe as General-in-Chief, and undertook the siege of Varna, where he was so badly wounded that he was obliged to retire from the campaign. In 1831 he received the command of Finland after having been created Vice-Admiral and Chief State Major of the Russian Marine. His government was characterised by great rigour and severity. In 1853 the Emperor confided to him the Embassy to Constantinople. His insults to the Sultan, his ultimatum, and abrupt departure from Constantinople, which was equivalent to a declaration of war; the massacre at Sinope, and his persistent, though unsuccessful, defence of the Crimea, are fresh in the memory of every one. Shortly after the death of the Czar he fell ill and was replaced, and afterwards charged with the defence of Cronstadt. He is the recognised chief of the old Russian party, and the declared adversary of all reform.

MENZEL, WOLFGANG, an eminent German critic, littérateur, and historian, was born at Waldenbourg, in Silesia, in 1798. He studied at Breslau, Jena, and Bonn, where, seized by the enthusiasm of the times, he became the head of the patriot students' corps, and a zealous liberal. In consequence of the decrees of the Congress of Carlsbad, in 1819, he left Prussia, where politics had become reactionary, and for some years lived as a professor at Aarau, in Switzerland. Since 1825 he has resided at Stuttgart, in the kingdom of Wurtemberg, and was elected deputy to the Estates, after the revolution of July, and during the revolutions of 1848 and 1849. He has published a "Journal of Literature," founded in 1826, and continued, with an interruption of only two years, namely, 1848 and 1849, to this day; a "History of the Germans," which has, since 1824, gone through five editions, and been translated into English; a "History of the last Forty Years," published in 1855; a work on "German Literature" (1828), twice translated into English; and a "History of German Poetry" (1858). He published in 1840 a pamphlet against Russia, which was translated into English; in 1854, "Christian Symbolics," and in 1856, a "History of Nature in a Christian point of View."

MÉRIMÉE, PROSPER, a French littérateur and senator, born at Paris, September 1803, is son of Mérimée, the artist. He studied law, and became an advocate, but he rarely if ever pleaded, literature being more consonant to his tastes than the bar. After the revolution of 1830, he became successively Secretary to the Count d'Argout, Secretary both to the Minister of Commerce and Minister of Marine. In 1831 he was appointed Inspector of the Historical and Antiquarian Monuments of France. In connexion with this office he travelled extensively, extending his journeys into Spain, where he became acquainted with the family of the Empress Eugénie. He was chosen by the Provisional Government, in 1848, one of the Commissioners to decide upon the extent and value of the property of the House of Orleans; and some time after, when his friend M. Libri was condemned by the tribunals for contumacy, M. Mérimée inserted two letters in the "Revue des Deux Mondes," impugning the judgment, for which act he was sentenced to fifteen days' imprisonment. In 1853 he was elevated to the rank of senator. M. Mérimée has published various archæological works, based on his French and Corsican travels; and has also entered frequently into the regions of history and romance. Of his histories, perhaps the "Chronique du Règne de Charles IX.," though it is tinged with romance, and the "Histoire de Don Pèdre I., Roi de Castille," are the best specimens of his style. His works, "La Vénus d'Ille," "La Peste de Tolédo," "La Partie de Trictrac," "La Double Méprise," and, above all, "Colomba," are charming novels, full of life and character. Originally printed in the "Revue de Paris," and the "Revue des Deux Mondes," they were afterwards republished in a separate form. Whether to mislead or puzzle critics, his first two literary efforts were published under the *nom de plume* of "Hyacinthe Maglanowich." The "Théâtre de Clara Gazul" (1825), and "La Guzla" (1827), certainly did mystify many persons, as they professed to be mere translations of which the originals were unknown, and in the search for which ingenuity was baffled.

MÉRY, JOSEPH, a French poet, was born in January, 1798, and after receiving instruction at home he completed his studies at Marseilles. Witnessing some of the strange scenes which were coeval with the restoration of the Bourbons, he was drawn into the ranks of the Bonapartists. After being in prison for a sharp satire in verse, in 1820 he took his first journey to Paris, where he eventually obtained a place on the journal called the "Nain Jaune," where he subsequently became the leading man. Becoming intimate with Victor Hugo and Barthélemy, he published satires and wrote politics until 1826. When M. de Martignue was Minister, he ceased penning satires; but the advent of M. Polignac to power was his signal to recommence the use of his formidable weapon, and so keenly was it employed, that he contributed greatly to the revolution of July, 1830. M. Méry took up arms during the "three days," and celebrated the victory over Charles X. in a hymn entitled "La Tricolore," and a poem called "L'Insurrection." The hopes M. Méry entertained from the revolution were so disappointed, that he resolved to retire to Marseilles, and abandon politics; but M. Barthélemy having announced a new journal, M. Méry was induced to participate in it as

T

editor. He wrote with great vigour, but the journal ceased to appear in 1832, and M. Méry departed for Italy. Not previously much known as a prose writer, he turned his mind, after some time, to that department of composition, and produced with considerable rapidity a number of lively romances and *feuilletons*, together with a few successful dramas. Among his works may be mentioned "Scènes de la Vie Italienne," "Un Amour dans l'Avenir," "Van Dyck au Palais Brignola," "Les Adeptes de l'Immortalité,' "La Comtesse Hortensia," and several others, published between 1837 and 1843, among which may be noticed "Les Nuits de Londres," written after visiting England in 1840. The specialties of M. Méry's genius consist in his extraordinary faculty for creating the incidents of a romance or a drama at will; and for the vivacity of his descriptions and elimination of character.

METZ, FREDERICK AUGUSTE DE, founder of the Reformatory of Mettray, was born in May 1796, studied the law in Paris, and when twenty-five was named Assistant Judge to the Tribunal, and successively became Examining Magistrate, Vice-President of the Chambre de Police Correctionnelle, and, lastly, Counsellor to the Court. While a judge his attention had been drawn to the best means of effecting the reformation of juvenile criminals. A society had been established for that purpose in Paris, which De Metz joined. After examining various schools in the Netherlands and other places, De Metz returned to France in 1839, and founded the establishment at Mettray, near Tours, for the reception of young offenders. Twenty-three youths, respectably connected, were trained as teachers; in 1840 twelve young criminals were admitted, and the number gradually increased. The exertions of De Metz are incessant; he considers the young criminals in the light of an adopted family, and he brings to bear upon them the law of kindness, and the light of religion. His success gave the first real impulse to the establishment of Reformatory Schools in Great Britain, as well as to the exertions of individuals who have given their mind to the rescue of young offenders from the evil associations of prison life. M. de Metz has published a few works which fully explain the details of his favourite schemes.

MEYERBEER, GIACOMO, a German composer, was born at Berlin in 1794, and belongs to a family of Hebrew descent. Having been some time under a music master of some repute, Meyerbeer proceeded to Darmstadt, and placed himself under the care of Volger; the great Weber, composer of "Der Freischutz," being one of his fellow-pupils. His first dramatic piece, entitled "Jephtha's Daughter," was not very successful on its first performance. He then proceeded to Vienna, where he remained for some time, and produced "The Two Caliphs," which was scarcely more successful than "Jephtha's Daughter." Meyerbeer now discovered that he was working upon a mistaken principle, and repaired to Italy to study melody. His first successful work, "Romilda e Constanza," was performed at Padua in 1818. Since that time his reputation has been steadily increasing, until now he occupies the highest position among the living masters of his art. In 1832 he visited London for the first time to superintend the bringing out of "Robert le Diable," and a second time on the occasion of producing his "Étoile du Nord." "Les Huguenots," "Le Prophète," "L'Étoile du Nord," "Le Pardon de Ploermel," or "Dinorah," and "Robert le Diable," are the operas by which Meyerbeer is best known. Meyerbeer enjoys various honours; he is Musical Director to the King of Prussia, Commander of the Legion of Honour, Associate of the Academy of Fine Arts in Paris, besides being decorated with numerous orders.

MIALL, EDWARD, editor of the "Nonconformist" newspaper, and late M. P. for Rochdale, was born at Portsmouth, in 1809. After being educated at a Dissenters' college in Herts, he was successively the pastor of Independent congregations at Ware and Leicester. He then proceeded to London in order to edit a newspaper, intended as the organ of the Dissenting interest. Mr. Miall entered Parliament as member for Rochdale in 1852, and distinguished himself by an energetic opposition to Church-rates, and endowments of every kind. His political views are extremely liberal, but since 1857 he has not been again returned, although he has contested two boroughs with that object.

MICHAUD, LOUIS GABRIEL, a French author and publisher, was born at Bourg-en-Bresse, in 1772. He founded a printing and publishing establishment in Paris in 1801, his first publication of consequence being a "Biographie Moderne, ou des Hommes Vivants," which was issued in 1802, attracted notice, and called forth many strictures. In 1811 he commenced a new series of a similar publication, under the title of a "Biographie Universelle," afterwards changed to the "Biographie Michaud," which was continued from 1811 to 1837, and is at once a voluminous and carefully edited compilation. Another work, with the same object, and conducted much like his own, having appeared, M. Michaud gained a legal decision as to his exclusive property in the editorship, and the title of the "Biographie Universelle." M. Michaud's talents have not been confined to mere publishing. He has written a History of the Crusades, some excellent articles for his own works of reference, and edited numerous publications on various subjects.

MICHELET, JULES, a French historian, was born at Paris, in 1798. From an early period he has been engaged in teaching history and philosophy, and is distinguished by his earnest advocacy of opposition to the Jesuits. In England he is best known by his works "Priests, Women, and Families," and the "People," which, while they created a great sensation here, had the effect of putting an end to Michelet's public prelections in Paris. The majority of his writings are highly popular, but his histories of Rome and of France have obtained him the highest praise from literary critics. Amongst his later works are "L'Oiseau," "L'Insecte," "L'Amour," and "La Femme," which have been widely read throughout France. M. Michelet's productions are vivid, energetic, and their descriptive parts so true as to fascinate and rivet the attention of the most cursory reader.

MIGNET, FRANÇOIS AUGUSTE ALEXIS, a French historian, was born at Aix, in 1796. After leaving the university he turned his attention to legal pursuits, and was the successful competitor, shortly afterwards, for a prize offered by the Academy of Nîmes. He first appeared as an author by the publication of two works, one on "Feudalism," and the other, the "History of the Revolution." After having contributed to various journals, he assisted M. Thiers in bringing out the "National" newspaper. Under Louis-Philippe he became Director of the Archives, Councillor of State, and, in 1837, Secretary to the Academy, of Moral and Political Science. He was appointed a Commander of the Legion of Honour in 1840. M. Mignet has published several historical works, among which may be named his "History of Mary Stuart," "Life of Franklin," and a collection of his lectures delivered before the Academy on historical subjects.

MILL, JOHN STUART, a political writer,

was born in 1806, and received his early education under the care of his father, the historian of British India. He was gradually promoted in the East India service, until in 1856 he became Examiner of Indian Correspondence. Mr. Mill is the author of several papers contributed to the Edinburgh and Westminster Reviews, the principal of which have been reprinted under the title of "Dissertations and Discussions." His "System of Logic, Ratiocinative and Inductive," and "Essays upon some Unsettled Questions of Political Economy," appeared in 1843 and 1844. In 1848 he published his popular work, "The Principles of Political Economy, with some of their Applications to Social Philosophy." Mr. Mill has always been identified with liberal political views, and for some time edited the "Westminster Review." His latest work, an "Essay on Liberty," is a valuable contribution, on account of its cautious and legitimate views on a very delicate subject, and was extremely apposite to the events which preceded its publication.

MILLAIS, JOHN EVERETT, A.R.A., a painter, was born at Southampton, in 1829. He belongs to a Jersey family, his childhood having been passed in that island and in France. Exhibiting a remarkable talent for art, he was sent at an early age to Sass's art school, in London, to prepare for the Royal Academy, which he entered in his eleventh year; his progress was remarkable, and in 1847 he achieved a high position by gaining the gold medal for his picture, "The Tribe of Benjamin seizing the Daughters of Shiloh." In 1849, Mr. Millais and Mr. Hunt exhibited respectively "Isabella" and "Rienzi," which were looked upon as invasions of the conventionalities of the schools. Mr. Millais' conceptions are almost invariably poetical, but many of his works are marred by their excessive minuteness of detail.

It seems, however, from his more recent productions, as if he were gradually taking leave of his old and working out a new style, though he has not entirely abandoned some of his early peculiarities. One of the most attractive of his works is the "Order of Release,"—a picture superbly coloured, and finely conceived. It is scarcely necessary to add, that Mr. Millais was one of the founders of "The Pre-Raphaelites," a school which is fast losing its influence. He is an Associate of the Royal Academy.

MILLER, THOMAS, a poet and novelist, was born in 1809, at Gainsborough, in Lincolnshire. He was almost entirely self-taught. He was at first a farmer's boy, and afterwards adopted the humble trade of a basket-maker. He neglected no opportunity of reading; but though those opportunities were few, the poetic spirit was within him; and some of his verses having caught the attention of Moore, Campbell, Rogers, and others, he was encouraged and assisted forward. He has been no idle author, having written altogether forty volumes of history, poetry, biography, and novels; his most attractive publications being those which relate to country life,—such as "A Day in the Woods," "Beauties of the Country," "Rural Sketches," "Country Scenes," "Our Old Town," &c.

MILMAN, THE VERY REV. HENRY HART, DEAN OF ST. PAUL'S, an author and divine, was born in London, in 1791. He is son of Sir Francis Milman, who was physician to George III. After being educated at Greenwich and Eton, he entered Brasenose College, Oxford, where he graduated, and became a Fellow. In 1812 he carried the Newdegate prize for an English poem; and in 1815 published his noble tragedy of "Fazio." He took orders in 1817, and afterwards became Vicar of St. Mary's, Reading. In 1818 he published an heroic poem, entitled "Samor, Lord of the Bright City;" and in 1820 his dramatic poem, "The Fall of Jerusalem," one of the greatest works of its class. He was appointed in 1821 Professor of Poetry, at Oxford, and produced sóme dramatic poems, of which the "Martyr of Antioch" is the chief. In 1840 he published the "History of Christianity, from the Birth of Christ to the Abolition of Paganism in the Roman Empire," which evidences talent of the highest order. In 1849 he was made Dean of St. Paul's, being already Rector of St. Margaret's, and a Canon of Westminster. He has published an edition of "Horace, with a Life of the Poet and Critical Remarks," much valued for its elegance of style and critical acumen; and also an edition of Gibbon's "Decline and Fall," and "The History of Latin Christianity, including that of the Popes to the Pontificate of Nicholas V.," 6 vols. 8vo, of which the first edition appeared in 1855-6, the second in 1857.

MILNES, RICHARD MONCKTON, M.P., a poet and statesman, born in 1809, is the only son of Robert Pemberton Milnes, of Fryston Hall, and Bawtry, Yorkshire. Educated at Cambridge, he graduated in 1831. In 1837 he was elected member for Pontefract, and is generally a supporter of liberal measures. He is a philanthropist, and earnestly advocates public education, religious equality, and various reforms in the state of our criminal population. He brought into Parliament, in 1846, the great Act for establishing Reformatories, most of the provisions of which are now the law of the land. Whether in the world of literature or politics, he has secured an honourable position. Mr. Milnes is the author of "Memorials of a Tour in Greece," "Poems of Many Years," "Palm Leaves," "Poems, Historical and Legendary," "Life, Letters, and Literary Remains of John Keats,"

and has contributed many political and literary articles to the Westminster, Edinburgh, and Quarterly Reviews; but his literary acquirements are principally recognised in his poetical works. He is Hon. D.C.L. of the University of Oxford, Deputy Lieutenant of the West Riding of Yorkshire, and Captain of the Second West York Regiment of Militia. He married the daughter of John, second Baron Crewe.

MINIÉ, CLAUDE, inventor of the rifle which bears his name, was born in Paris about 1810, and entered the French army at an early age, taking part in some of the campaigns of Algiers. He was captain in a battalion of Chasseurs, when he turned his attention to the improvement of fire-arms, and under the patronage of the Duke de Montpensier several of his alterations were adopted. Having a practical knowledge of gun-making, he succeeded in effecting still further improvements; and his name got so far abroad as Russia, from which he received tempting offers to superintend a royal manufactory of fire-arms at St. Petersburg, but which he declined. He continues to work in his *atelier*, at Vincennes, still experimenting with his leather apron before him, and the decoration of the Legion of Honour on his breast. M. Minié's improvements consist chiefly in using an elongated instead of a spherical ball, which thereby insures a revolution on an axis parallel to the line of flight, instead of at right angles to it, as is the case of the common bullet. By a peculiarity of construction, the ball expands during its passage through the barrel, and so prevents the loss of speed by windage. The Minié rifle is now known all over the world, and has been the model on which many recent improvements have been effected.

MITSCHERLICH, EILHARD, a German chemist, was born in the Grand Duchy of Oldenburg, in January 1794, and had as his primary teacher the historian Schlosser. In 1811 he proceeded to Heidelberg, where he studied philology and history, removing thence to Paris, to facilitate his study of the Oriental languages. In 1814 he returned to Germany and commenced the composition of an historical work, of which only a fragment has been published, and which still remains incomplete. His studies now took another direction, geology and chemistry supplanting history and the languages. During his investigations he discovered a new law, namely, that bodies of different component parts can assume similar crystallized forms. The celebrated Swedish chemist, Berzelius, visiting Berlin in 1819, was at once struck with the discovery. It has received the title of "Isomorphism," or "equal-formed." Mitscherlich afterwards proceeded to Sweden, and remained there for two years, returning to Berlin in 1821, when he was named a Member of the Academy of Sciences, and appointed Professor of Chemistry in the University. He contributed numerous papers to the "Annals" of the Academy of Sciences, at Berlin; but the production by which he is best known is "A Manual of Chemistry," the preparation of which occupied his leisure for four years, and which has run through numerous editions, and become a standard work. He treats his various subjects in an attractive style. Among the chemists of Germany he is considered to have no superior.

MOCQUARD, CONSTANT, a French politician, author, and private Secretary to the Emperor Napoleon III., was born at Bordeaux, in November 1791. He studied at Paris with considerable distinction, obtaining honours. In 1812 he was sent to Wurtzburg with General Montholon, as Secretary of Legation, and in 1813 was appointed Chargé d'Affaires. Towards the close of that year he was recalled to Paris, when he completed his legal studies, and was called to the bar. He became closely connected with the liberal party on the restoration of the Bourbons. In 1817 he pleaded with power and eloquence for those who were accused of conspiracy; but his health failing, he was constrained to leave the bar in 1826. The revolution of 1830 drew him from retirement, and he was appointed Sous-Préfét of Bagnères-de-Bigorre, but resigned in 1839. Cultivating friendly relations with the Bonaparte family, Louis Napoleon became warmly attached to him. After paying the Prince a visit in 1840, in London, he returned to Paris, and acted as editor of the "Commerce," a journal devoted to Napoleonic ideas. He zealously defended the cause of the Prince, when the issue of the Boulogne affair rendered Louis Napoleon a captive at Ham, and also in 1848 he was his active partisan. When Louis Napoleon was elected President of the Republic, M. Mocquard was named Chief of the Cabinet. Having initiated some of the primary steps of the *coup d'état*, he assisted in carrying them out, and since that event has continued to act as private Secretary to the Emperor, with the title of Chief of the Cabinet. He has published several works, among which are a "Biographical Notice of Queen Hortense," a book entitled "Nouvelles Causes Célèbres," and several dramas.

MOFFAT, ROBERT, a missionary agent of the London Missionary Society in South Africa, is a native of Inverkeithing, Scotland. In 1816 he was appointed, in conjunction with the martyr of Erromanga (John Williams), to the work of that association. Mr. Moffat's labours were commenced in Namaqua Land. Subsequently he removed to the Bechuana country. In 1840 Mr. Moffat visited England, after an absence of nearly a quarter of a century; he published a volume entitled

"Missionary Labours and Scenes in Southern Africa;" and produced a translation of the New Testament, and the Psalms, in the Bechuana language. His daughter is married to the Rev. David Livingston, LL. D., another world-wide known missionary, and explorer in the same country. They are both now engaged in penetrating into the interior of the country north of the Cape of Good Hope. To facilitate these explorations, the British government has just despatched a steam-vessel, which will proceed to the Zambesi River. (September, 1860.)

MONTALEMBERT, CHARLES FORBES, COMTE DE, a French politician, was born in April 1810, and after remaining some time in Sweden, entered the University of Paris. When scarcely twenty-one, he joined the Abbé Lacordaire in opening a free school for Roman Catholic children in Paris; in order to assert by this means the freedom of public education, which had been promised by the charter of 1830. The school having been closed by the police, the matter was carried before the Chamber of Peers, and Montalembert having just entered the Chamber, vindicated the cause of free education in a speech of remarkable ability. This speech created a great effect; but the defendants were condemned to a trifling fine. From that period till 1848 he distinguished himself by his zeal for the defence of Poland, of Belgium, and particularly of the interests of the Catholic Church, which he has always attempted to combine with the progress and maintenance of political liberty. In literary matters he was also highly successful by the publication of a "Life of St. Elizabeth," &c. In January 1848, the opinions he expressed on Switzerland attracted great notice, and his views were subsequently verified by events. He was elected a member of the National Assembly. He then became one of the leaders of the Conservative majority; and, together with M. Thiers and M. de Falloux, took a prominent part in the debate which led to the restoration of Pius IX. by the French army, and to the settlement of the long-vexed question of public education. He subsequently took part with Louis Napoleon, as President of the Republic, against the different parties of the National Assembly. After the *coup d'état*, and the confiscation of the Orleans' property, he refused a seat in the new Senate, and became a decided antagonist of the Empire. His "Catholic Interests in the Nineteenth Century," and "The Political Future of England," are the works in which his opposition to the Imperial policy and institutions have been most conspicuously displayed. In October 1858, in an article contributed to the "Correspondant," on the "Indian Debate," he, under cover of a eulogy of England, assailed the despotism of Napoleon in a strain of the most eloquent invective. For this article the Count was put upon his trial, and being convicted, was fined and imprisoned. Pardoned by the Emperor, he resented the injustice of the prosecution, and appealed to a higher tribunal. The appeal was only partially successful. Louis Napoleon discovered he had committed mistake, and again gladly tendered the Count a remission of the mitigated sentence of the Supreme Court. In October, 1859, he published another pamphlet, entitled "Pie IX. et la France, en 1849 et 1859," protesting against the Emperor's policy towards Rome; and giving the signal of the numerous *brochures*, to the amount of two or three hundred, which that question has called out. This pamphlet was seized throughout France, and another prosecution begun; but the Count having been called up before the Court, and having there maintained his usual ground, the proceedings were suddenly quashed.

MONTEAGLE, LORD, THOMAS SPRING RICE, an English statesman, was born at Limerick, in February, 1790. His father being a gentleman of considerable landed property in the counties of Limerick and Kerry, he was sent to study at Trinity College, Cambridge, where he graduated M.A. After becoming a bencher of Lincoln's-inn, he stood for Limerick in 1818, and in 1820; and was elected member. He retained the seat for twelve years; afterwards representing Cambridge, and supporting liberal measures on all occasions. Having filled the office of Under-Secretary for the Home Department, in 1827, he was appointed Secretary to the Treasury in 1830, which post he held until 1834, when he became a member of Lord Grey's cabinet, as Colonial Secretary of State. In 1836 he was named Chancellor of the Exchequer, in Lord Melbourne's administration; and in 1839 was appointed Comptroller of the Exchequer, and raised to the peerage as Lord Monteagle, of Brandon. Of late years Lord Monteagle has taken but little part in public affairs, with the exception of having given his most strenuous opposition to the Repeal of the Paper Duties during the late session (1860).

MONTI, RAFFAELLE, a sculptor, was born at Milan, in 1818. Having completed his education in his native city, and gained a prize medal, he proceeded to Vienna, in 1838. He had already produced two fine works; namely, "Alexander Taming Bucephalus," and "Ajax Defending the Body of Patroclus." He made a visit to England in 1847, and then produced his "Veiled Vestal," which was greatly admired. On his subsequent return to Milan, he became involved in political affairs, and was compelled to revisit London, where he has since settled. His works exhibited in Hyde Park, in 1851, brought him into popular favour; and

of these, his "Circassian Slave," and "The Boy Catching a Grasshopper," were, perhaps, the most admired, next to his veiled figure, which was also there.

MORNY, CHARLES AUGUSTE LOUIS JOSEPH, COMTE DE, a French diplomatist and politician, was born at Paris on the 23rd of October, 1811, and received his early education under the Comtesse de Souza. After passing some time in the military school, he left it as a Sub-Lieutenant, and eventually served in Africa, where he exhibited considerable daring and gallantry. Quitting military affairs, we next find him engaged in industrial matters in 1838, his attention being specially devoted to the production of sugar from beet-root. In 1849 he entered into the political questions of the day, and being, it is said, related to the present Emperor of the French, he heartily espoused his cause, and as his confidant, participated in the successes which followed the *coup d'état* of December, 1851. Despatched to Moscow on the coronation of the present Emperor of Russia, Count Morny married a most accomplished and handsome lady, and subsequently returned to France. He has for many years past held a prominent position in commercial and industrial circles, and the possession of a taste of a refined character is evidenced in his splendid gallery of paintings.

MORSE, SAMUEL FINLEY BREESE, an American artist, and one of the inventors of the Electric Telegraph, was born in Charlestown, Massachusetts, in 1791. He was educated at Yale College, and took his Bachelor's degree in 1810. Having a great taste for art, he decided on becoming a painter, and, with a view to the prosecution of his profession, in 1811 he proceeded to London, to study in the Royal Academy, under Benjamin West. In 1813 he received the gold medal for his first effort in sculpture, "The Dying Hercules." On his return to America he followed his profession with moderate pecuniary results, but he succeeded in laying the foundation of the National Academy of Design, in organizing the schools and exhibitions connected with it, and in associating the artists of the United States into a harmonious brotherhood. He was annually elected President of the Academy for nearly twenty years. In 1829 he again visited Europe, for further study in the schools of the Continent, and resided in Rome, Florence, Venice, and Paris for three years. On his voyage home, in 1832, he conceived and made drawings of the Recording Telegraph, which bears his name. A portion of the apparatus was constructed before the expiration of the year 1832, but his professional avocations caused so many interruptions, that it was not until the year 1835 that he completed his first rude instrument. In 1837 it was improved upon, and publicly exhibited at work upon a circuit of upwards of ten miles. By the aid of the American Government he had, in 1844, the satisfaction of establishing the first telegraphic line on his plan between Washington and Baltimore, a distance of forty miles. His patents in America have been the means of a handsome competency. In 1848 the degree of Doctor of Laws was conferred upon him by his Alma Mater, Yale College, and in the same year he received from the Sultan of Turkey the decoration in diamonds of the Nishan Ifftichar. The gold medals of scientific merit of their respective states were awarded him by the Kings of Prussia and of Wurtemburg, and by the Emperor of Austria. More recently he has received the decoration of Chevalier of the Order of the Legion of Honour from the Emperor Napoleon ; of Knight of the Danebroge, from the King of Denmark ; and of Knight Commander of the Royal Order of Isabella the Catholic, from the Queen of Spain. He is also member of numerous learned societies in Europe and America. The most distinguished mark of public gratitude, however, for his invention, has been conferred upon him by a Congress of Representatives of ten of the Governments of Europe, specially convened for the purpose in Paris in 1858, at the suggestion of the Emperor Napoleon, when it was unanimously decided that the sum of 400,000 francs should be presented to him. Mr. Morse's telegraph differs from that we use in Great Britain, inasmuch as his, by means of dots and strokes on paper or cloth, *prints* the message. Those generally employed in this country *indicate* the message by the alternate divergence of one or two magnetic needles acted on by electric currents passing over them in different directions.

MÜLLER, JOHANNES, a German physiologist, was born of humble parents at Coblentz, on the Rhine, in July 1801. The earlier stages of his education were passed in the Gymnasium of Coblentz, and in 1819 he entered the University of Bonn. Four years afterwards he took his degree in medicine ; and in 1824, having obtained a prize for an essay, he repaired to Berlin, where he succeeded Professor Charles Rudolphi in 1833. Professor Müller may be said, by his works, his experiments, and his lectures, to have reversed many of the ancient speculative physiological doctrines and hypotheses, and to have substituted acute observation and rigid deduction, bringing physiology within the range of a positive science. Some time after the publication of the "Physiology of Man," Professor Müller commenced a journal devoted to his favourite study, and has continued it up to the present time, often contributing extensively to its pages. He has not, however, limited his investigations to physiology, but turning his mind to the structure and classification of animals, he has rendered many important services to science. His writings are so numerous that it would be impossible to detail them. His separate publications are carefully illustrated, the plates adding, if possible, to the literary and scientific value of the works.

MULOCH, Miss DINAH MARIA, an authoress, was born at Stoke-upon-Trent, Staffordshire, in 1826. It was not, however, until 1849 that she became known to the literary world. In that year she published her charming work, "The Ogilvies," which immediately attracted the attention of the public. "The Ogilvies," though a fiction, exhibited a genial quality of heart, a philosophy of enlarged benevolence, and a keenness in the perception and delineation of character, which rendered the work, to all appearance, more one of reality than of imagination. It is at once deep in thought and pathetic in sentiment, while there runs through it here and there an occasional vein of humour. In 1850 she published "Olive," which fully sustained her reputation, and perhaps advanced it, as the latter work displayed a riper style, and a closer penetration into minute phases of character. In 1851 appeared "The Head of the Family," one of the most admirable stories of Scottish life that has been written since the time when Galt was in his zenith. A fairy tale, entitled "Alice Learmont," a composition which seems to have given her thoughts a new direction, was published in the same year. Miss Muloch's other works are "Agatha's Husband," "John Halifax, Gentleman," one of the most popular works in English fiction, "A Life for a Life," "Romantic Tales," "Bread upon the Waters," "Nothing New," "A Woman's Thoughts about Women," and "Poems," and "Dramatic Tales." She has also written various books for young people, among which we may cite "Cola Monti," "A Hero," "The Little Lychetts," "Our Year," and others, which are of an exceedingly instructive and interesting nature.

MULREADY, WILLIAM, R.A., a painter, was born at Ennis, in Ireland, in 1786. In his fifteenth year he entered the Royal Academy as a student. His pictures at first were small, and it was not until 1815, when he exhibited his "Idle Boys," that his position was assured, its merits being recognised by his election as an associate of the Academy. In 1816 his "Fight Interrupted" insured his elevation to the rank of R.A. He never relapsed in his efforts, or in his studies, even when a perfect master of his art, always considering there was something to learn. His works are exceedingly numerous, but latterly he has appeared only on rare occasions before the public. The following of Mr. Mulready's works are now to be seen in the National Collection at the South Kensington Museum: "Near the Mall," "Blackheath Park," "The Seven Ages," "The Fight Interrupted," "Giving a Bite," "First Love," "The Sailing Match," "Choosing the Wedding Gown," "The Toyseller," "Hampstead Heath," and several others.

MUNCH, PETER ANDREAS, a Norwegian historian, geographer, and philologist, was born at Christiania, on the 15th December, 1810. After being educated at Skien, he entered the University of Christiania in 1828, and passed his examination for the law in 1834; but history and language having been his favourite studies, even in his school-days, he soon devoted himself entirely to them, and since 1837, when he obtained the Chair of History in the University of Christiania, his labours have been essentially literary. In 1859 he paid a visit to the Orkneys, in order to trace the vestiges of the ancient Norsemen. His works are very numerous, and to the class of readers and students to whom they are specially addressed, are of no ordinary importance. His chief work is "The History of the Norwegian People" ("'Det Norske Folks Historie'"), from the earliest times, in six volumes. He has constructed and published several maps of Norway, among which those of Southern Norway (Christiania, 1845), and of Northern Norway (Christiania, 1852), are the largest and most accurate which have hitherto appeared. At present he is living at Rome, whither he has been sent by the Norwegian Government, in order to search for documents illustrating the history of Norway, in the Vatican and other archives; and in this work it is said he has succeeded far beyond his expectations.

MURCHISON, SIR RODERICK IMPEY, D. C. L., a geologist, was born at Tarradale, in Ross-shire, in 1792. He received his education at the Durham Grammar School, and afterwards at the Military College of Marlow. From 1807 to 1815 inclusive, he acted as an officer, first in the 36th Foot in Spain and Portugal, afterwards on the staff of his uncle, General Sir Alexander Mackenzie, in Sicily; and latterly, as a captain in the 6th Dragoons. He carried the colours of his first regiment, the 36th, at Vimiera, under Wellesley; advanced with the army to Madrid, and under Moore shared in the dangers of the retreat to Corunna. At the peace of 1815 he married the only daughter of General Hugonin, and left the army. After some years of foreign travel and occupation in field sports, he was led, by the persuasion of his wife and the advice of Sir Humphry Davy, to devote himself to science. In 1825 he was elected a Fellow of the Geological, and in 1826, of the Royal Society. He chose Geology in the field for his special line, and his early military habits peculiarly qualified him for its pursuit. Mr. Murchison then undertook extensive geological tours, which comprised the greater portion of Europe. These have lasted for thirty-five years, and have resulted in the greatest advantage to the science of Geology. His first great work, completed after seven years of close and hard labour in England and Wales, was the "Silurian System," by which the older rocks containing organic remains (till then a chaotic assemblage) were reduced to a clear order. The next comprehensive effort was to parallel the geological formations of Russia into those of his own country, as published in 1845 (in conjunction with his colleagues De Verneuil and Von Keyserling) in the large quarto volumes entitled "Russia and the Ural Mountains." From the experience so obtained, he was the first to predict the existence of gold in Australia. His ardour in promoting the cultivation of geographical science is well known. He was not only one of the founders of the Royal Geographical Society, but has always been on its council; he has presided over it for seven years, and has had the satisfaction of seeing it rise under his auspices, to a high state of prosperity. In 1845 Mr. Murchison having completed his survey of Russia, the Emperor Nicholas presented him with the Grand Cross of the Order of St. Stanislaus and the commandership of St. Anne in diamonds, and upon his return to England he obtained the royal permission to wear these Imperial orders, and received the honour of knighthood. Sir Roderick Murchison, to great scientific eminence, unites the most generous regard for, and manifests the most prompt recognition of obscure worth. Many men of genius, explorers of distant lands, have been indebted to him for the frankness with which, when yet all unknown to fame, he proclaimed their merits. In 1855 Sir Roderick became Director-General of the Geological Survey of Britain, including the Direction of the Government School of Mines. He has received the honorary degrees of M.A. from the Universities of Cambridge and Durham, and is D.C.L. of Oxford; he is also a Trustee of the British Museum, of the British Association for the Advancement of Science, of the Hunterian Museum, and a member of most of the scientific academies in Europe and America. Besides the works above mentioned, Sir Roderick has published numerous memoirs in the Transactions of scientific societies—in all upwards of one hundred—the most striking of which are probably his "Alps, Apennines, and Carpathians," and his recent classification of the rocks of his native Highlands, for which the first Brisbane Gold Medal of the Royal Society of Edinburgh was presented to him at the Aberdeen Meeting of the British Association. The Copley Medal, or first honour of the Royal Society of London, was awarded to him in 1847, for his "Silurian System." The condensed views of all his labours in clearing away the obscurities in which the order and relations of the oldest rocks were involved, is given in the last edition (1859) of his work "Siluria."

MUSSET, PAUL EDMÉ DE, brother of the late Alfred de Musset, was born at Paris on the 7th of November, 1804. He is best known by his novels, which are written in a style at once calm and chaste. He resided for some time at Venice, where he translated the eccentric memoirs of Gozzi, publishing them in the "National," in 1846. In 1848 he became editor of the dramatic department of that journal, and was esteemed for his conscientious criticisms. He has written a few dramas, represented at the Odéon, but his principal works are the romances "La Table de Nuit," "La Tête et le Cœur," "Lauzun," "Anne de Boleyn," Les Femmes de la Régence," "Le Bracelet," "Mignard et Rigaud," "Orginaux du XVII. Siècle," "Madame de la Guette," "Jean le Trouveur," "Voyage en Italie," and "Nouvelles Italiennes." He has contributed a number of articles to the "Revue des Deux Mondes."

NAPIER, ROBERT, a shipbuilder and mechanical engineer, was born at Dumbarton in 1791, where his father, though but a blacksmith by trade, gave his son a liberal education. From an early age, Mr. Napier had a great taste for mechanical pursuits, and despite his father's desire that he should proceed to college, he preferred being a skilled craftsman, and was therefore apprenticed to his parent. At the end of his time he went to Edinburgh in 1811; and afterwards, in 1815, commenced business on his own account in Glasgow, with very moderate means. In 1823 he completed his first marine engine for a Clyde boat, and from that date his career has been one of continued prosperity. In 1840 he built and engined four steamers for the Cunard Line, and these were followed by others for a similar service. In 1856 he launched the Persia from his yard near Glasgow, which is the largest steamer afloat, with the exception of the Great Eastern, and belongs to the Cunard Company. Mr. Napier has held numerous government contracts, amongst which is one for an enormous steam-ram, which is now in course of construction (September 1860). His extraordinary success has entirely depended on the excellent workmanship with which all his vessels are constructed, and a consequent freedom from failure. His firm employs several thousand hands, and is the most extensive concern on the Clyde.

NAPIER, VICE-ADMIRAL SIR CHARLES, K.C.B., M.P., late commander of the Baltic fleet, born 1786, is the eldest son of the late Hon. Charles Napier of Merchiston Hall, and grandson of the sixth Lord Napier. Sixty years ago Sir Charles entered the navy as a first-class volunteer, and during this long period of service he has always distinguished himself as a brave and dashing tar. He

served before Martinique, and was the first to scale its walls, for which service he obtained promotion. He was engaged on the coast of Sicily in 1811, served in North America in 1813, and in 1829 was sent on special service to the coast of Portugal. In 1833 he was appointed to the command of the Portuguese fleet, engaged with the fleet of Don Miguel, and gained a decisive victory for Don Pedro. In 1839 he was appointed second in command to Sir Robert Stopford in the Mediterranean, and after distinguishing himself in several actions he assisted at the taking of Acre. For his Syrian and Egyptian services he received the thanks of Parliment, the dignity of K.C.B., and the decorations of almost all the military and naval orders in Europe. He afterwards held for some time the command of the Channel fleet. Such was the prestige of his name that, although no special favourite of government, when the Russian war was about to be proclaimed, he was appointed to the command of the Baltic fleet. In that command, however, he was doomed to be an example of the signal folly into which the hero falls, who, when putting on his armour, boasts as one who is putting it off. The Baltic fleet was to take Cronstadt, but beyond the blockade and the affair of Bomarsund, nothing was done. Sir Charles blamed the Admiralty for not having furnished him with the fitting fighting tools; and there was no doubt that much of the cause of the resultless character of the expedition was due to official bungling. But although no very brilliant deed was done in the Baltic by Sir Charles in the late war, his previous services confer sufficient renown. Egypt, Syria, Spain, have, each in turn, owned his prowess. But not alone as a naval commander is Sir Charles known; his pen is ever quite as vigorous as his sword. The innumerable caustic epistles he has issued from time to time, have rendered him a thorn in the side of nearly

every administration during the last twenty years. Sir Charles Napier was elected member for Southwark in 1855, and at the dissolutions in 1857 and 1859, was again returned to the House of Commons. He has lately distinguished himself in the House by his continued onslaught on the Board of Admiralty respecting the state of the navy, and has brought forward several motions, which, however, have produced no effect.

NAPOLEON III., CHARLES LOUIS NAPOLEON, Emperor of the French, born at Paris, in the Palace of the Tuileries, April 20th, 1808, is the third son of Louis Bonaparte, formerly King of Holland, by Hortense Beauharnois, daughter of the Empress Josephine. Louis Napoleon was baptized November, 1810, by Cardinal Fesch, his great uncle; the Emperor and his new Empress, Maria Louisa, standing sponsors. After the final overthrow of the fortunes of the first Napoleon, at Waterloo, all the kings and queens of his race or favour, with the sole exception of Bernadotte, King of Sweden, who had proved false to him, were removed from their thrones. The Queen of Holland took refuge in Geneva, from whence she removed to Aix, in Savoy, to Augsburg, and lastly to Thurgovia, on the Swiss shores of the Lake of Constance. Here Louis Napoleon passed the quiet years of his early youth and manhood. His first preceptor was the Abbé Bertrand, by whom he was instructed in the rudiments of knowledge. He subsequently studied classics under M. Lebas, since professor at the Paris Athenæum. While at Augsburg the Prince acquired a high reputation at the Gymnasium, and exhibited considerable aptitude for the sciences, as well as for the study of the dead and living languages. He also devoted some attention to chemistry, in which he received instruction from M. Gaspard, at that period the principal manager of a chemical manufactory in

Switzerland. The military education of the Prince was not neglected, for he became a good fencer and rifleman, and an admirable horseman. At the garrison of Constance he received his first lessons in practical drill; and having joined the camp at Thurr, canton of Berne, he became proficient in artillery practice, under General Dufour, a veteran of the Empire. At this period of his youth, when freed from study, it was his pleasure to take pedestrian journeys over the mountains and through the passes. During one of these trips the news of the revolution of July, 1830, reached him. The Bonapartes at once imagined that their opportunity had come to return to France. When it was known that Louis-Philippe, Duke of Orleans, had been "elected" king, Louis Napoleon and his family petitioned for liberty to return to their native soil. The request was refused. Louis Napoleon subsequently asked to be allowed to serve as a common soldier in the French army, but the only answer he received, or had a right to expect, was a renewal of his banishment. He was at Rome, with his mother and his elder brother, when the revolution swept over Italy, and he took so active a part in the struggle of the Romans for civil freedom, that he was obliged to abscond from Rome. He met his brother at Florence, and both together fought against the Papal troops until hope was gone. His brother died at Forli, and he himself fell ill of fever at Ancona. Hunted at every turn, he contrived, amid many dangers, to make his way to England—the harbour of safety for all political refugees. He continued in London for a few months, and then removed to Arenenberg in Switzerland. From 1832 to 1835 he wrote and published "Political Reveries," "Political and Military Thoughts on Switzerland," and a "Manual of Artillery." The Duke of Reichstadt being still alive, the hopes of the Bona-

partist and Republican party in France turned towards him, during the early years of the reign of Louis-Philippe, and before the power of that monarch had been consolidated. In 1832, the death of the son of the great Napoleon left Louis Napoleon heir to the fortunes and the traditions of the Empire. In 1836 he planned an attack on Strasbourg, calculating that, if successful, he could march upon Paris, rouse the provinces, and convert to his cause the garrisons of Alsace and Lothringen. He gained over a number of adherents to this daring and reckless plan, everything seemed favourable, but an unlucky accident, a division in his followers, one part marching in one direction, and the other part another, caused the scheme to miscarry, and the Prince was made prisoner. His punishment was slight,—exile to the United States. Returning to Europe, he bent his steps once more to Switzerland. The government of Louis-Philippe, repentant when too late of their former clemency, fearing the outbreak of some new conspiracy, demanded that the exile should be expelled from Switzerland; but as he had been enrolled as a Swiss citizen, the Cantons decided upon resisting the demand, as contrary to their rights as a free people. The French Government pressed their demand by threat, and Louis Napoleon acting with a wise discretion, which he did not always exhibit, at that time sought shelter in more powerful England, where he arrived in 1838. In 1840, impelled by that self-reliance, if not fatalism, which marks his character, he undertook to make another desperate struggle for the Crown of France. He chartered a steamer in London, and with Count Montholon, and some fifty others, made a descent upon Boulogne-sur-Mer, 6th August. He in vain tried to induce the soldiers of the garrison, one of whom he shot dead, to join his standard, and after a futile attempt to retreat on board the "City of Edinburgh" he was captured. Again the French government was lenient. The Prince was tried, with his followers, in the following October, and condemned to imprisonment for life in the citadel of Ham. Here, in solitude and in suffering, for upwards of six years, he had leisure to meditate upon the failure of his last schemes, and to devise greater ones for the future, all the while schooling his mind by the noble teachings of adversity. Suddenly, he astonished France, and all Europe, by making his escape in the dress of a common workman. Again hospitable England was open to him, and he reappeared in London, no one suspecting the greatness of his destiny, or looking upon him as other than a desperate and rash adventurer. But his long-formed design was seldom absent from his mind, and it is related that when Louis-Philippe was foolish enough to attempt to fan up the embers of his own fast fading popularity by obtaining the consent of the British government for the removal of the remains of the great Napoleon from St. Helena to the Invalides at Paris, the Prince called upon an ambassador in London, with whom he was personally acquainted, and rubbing his hands joyously together exclaimed—"*Comme il est bête, ce Louis-Philippe, il fait mon jeu.*" ("What a fool Louis-Philippe is; he is playing my game!") The result verified the prediction, and when the corruption of that monarch's system of government at home, and his intrigues abroad, more especially in Spain, had so exasperated the French people as to lead to the memorable outbreak of February 1848, and his expulsion from France, one of the first measures of the new Government, upon the motion of M. Louis Blanc, was the nullification of the decree of exile passed upon all the members of the Bonaparte family. Prince Louis Napoleon did not immediately return to France, but ten weeks after the abdication of Louis-Philippe served as a special constable in the streets of London, in defence of law and order, when both were imperilled by the great Chartist demonstration of the 10th of April. Elected a member of the National Assembly by several places, he made choice of Paris, and took his seat in that body, which it afterwards became his "destiny" to overthrow. A candidate for the Presidency of the Republic, in opposition to General Cavaignac, who had rendered himself unpopular with the ultra-democracy by the rigour, if not cruelty, with which he had crushed an insurrection of the people, he was elected by 5,534,520 votes, while his opponent had less than two millions. His oath, on assuming the Presidency, may be quoted here:— "In the presence of God, and before the French people, I swear to remain faithful to the Democratic Republic, and to fulfil all the duties imposed on me by the Constitution." But the ultra-Democrats and Socialists, aided by the impracticable National Assembly, and its duly appointed general, Changarnier, brought affairs to a dead lock; and there would have been an end of the Bonapartes, or at all events of the President, had he not acted in self-defence. Having previously prepared all his measures, the President and his chosen friends began to work. On the morning of December 2nd, every influential man known in Paris to be opposed to the Bonapartist system, was seized, imprisoned, or escorted to the frontiers. The Assembly was 'dissolved, and the President proclaimed Dictator. So daring an act was not effected without bloodshed. The troops shot down in the streets all who appeared in favour of the Constitution; and thus having completely subdued all opposition, and baptized the new *régime* in blood and fire, he offered himself to the nation as

President for ten years. Opposition was in vain, for the army was staunch in support of the nephew and representative of the great Napoleon, and he was triumphantly elected. This condition of affairs continued for about a year, when in 1852 he resolved to make a tour of the departments, and test the popularity of his name, and the opinion of the country. Wherever he went he was received with shouts of acclamation and cries of *Vive l'Empereur*. It cannot be denied that these manifestations were genuine and spontaneous, and he accepted them as the will of the nation that the "Empire" should be restored. All having been pre-arranged prior to his tour, and the country being really, though unwisely, alarmed at the projects of Socialists and Red Republicans, and knowing moreover that change of title could add nothing to the already supreme authority of the President, he was elected Emperor. He was accordingly proclaimed in December 1852, exactly one year from the date of the *coup d'état*. He assumed the title of Napoleon III., and was at once recognised by Great Britain as a sovereign elected by the people, and more tardily by the other great powers. The new Emperor declared that his empire was "peace," but the promise has not been realized. Having put forth pretensions connected with the custody of the Holy Places in Palestine, projects deeply laid, and with ulterior views on the great question of the Papacy, the Emperor of Russia became alarmed for the stability of his influence in the East; and sent a mission to Constantinople, under Prince Menschikoff, the complications arising out of which produced the alliance between Great Britain and France, intended to curb the ambition and the pretensions of the Czar. The war in the Crimea was the speedy result, a war humiliating to Russia, and in its progress not altogether satisfac-

tory to the high spirited people of England. Its cost, however, was too great for the resources of France, and the war was not so popular among his people as the Emperor wished. Sebastopol, after a long siege, having been captured, with the lion's share of the glory to the arms of France, the Emperor suddenly declared himself satisfied, and would go no further. Great Britain reluctantly acquiesced : an unsatisfactory peace was made ; and the popularity gained for the Emperor in this country grew less and less fervent, and threatened to be entirely extinguished, if not replaced by animosity or jealousy. This growing ill-feeling was strengthened in 1857-8, by the injudicious demand made upon the British Government, by that of the French Emperor, to alter the laws affecting political and other exiles in England, to meet the case of the persons supposed to be implicated in the cowardly attempt at assassination, with which the name of Orsini is so infamously associated. This attempt to dictate to a friendly nation, so jealous and so susceptible of its dignity as Great Britain, and the manner in which the British Government appeared disposed to yield to it, led to the downfall of the Palmerston administration, and increased the pre-existing coolness for the person and policy of the Emperor. The large military, but more especially the naval armaments of France, and the fortifications of Cherbourg, within five hours' sail of our coast, and which seemed to have no possible object or necessity but an invasion of England, created, if not a panic, a wide-spread alarm, that we were not sufficiently prepared to confront such a peril ; and the press, the people, and the parliament, being of one mind upon the subject, the Government was compelled to take the necessary measures for securing our naval supremacy against the attacks of all comers—whether France alone, or France in combination with any power or powers on the earth. In the midst of these preparations, Europe was startled on the 1st of January, 1859, by a declaration of the Emperor of the French to the Austrian ambassador, at Paris, expressive of his regret that the relations between the two countries were no longer satisfactory. The price of the public funds went down rapidly in every capital of the civilized world; and it was calculated that within three weeks after the ominous words had been spoken, public securities in the various capitals of Europe had been depreciated by them to the extent of, at least, sixty millions sterling. In due time, Austria having been placed in such a position that she must either fight or lose her Italian provinces and her rank in Europe, the Emperor, Francis Joseph, played the game of the Emperor of the French, by declaring war against the King of Sardinia, and his French ally. The Emperor Napoleon placed himself at the head of his army, appointed the Empress to act as Regent during his absence, and in the course of a few weeks proved to foes as well as to friends, that he was both a theoretical and a practical soldier, and that he had all the qualifications of a great general. He marched from victory to victory; gained laurels at the hard-fought field of Magenta, and finally defeated the whole Austrian army at the great and decisive battle of Solferino. The famous quadrilateral of fortresses, supposed to be impregnable, lay before him, where Austria might have accepted the prolongation of hostilities, with something like a well-founded anticipation that Solferino would be the last victory of the year, and that the tide of battle might be turned against the invader. But no one suspected peace. Yet peace was imminent and pre-arranged. The Emperor of the French thus proved himself as great in war as in domestic administration : he had wrested Lombardy,

with its beautiful capital of Milan, from the grasp of Austria, and done enough for his future fame, as well as for his present purpose. An armistice was concluded between the two Emperors; who, on the following day, had a private interview at a little road-side house in the small town of Villafranca, and, to the surprise of the whole world, agreed to the terms of a peace ; by which Lombardy was ceded to France, and by France to Sardinia ; and Venetia, with the quadrilateral, left in the possession of Austria. The Emperor of the French agreed, at the same time, to the restoration of the sovereigns of Parma, Modena, and Tuscany, who had been expelled by their subjects, when the French army entered Italy ; but the attitude assumed by the Tuscans and Modenese, and the support they received from the public opinion of all Italy, as well as of England, whose government declared itself against the right of any power to force back their sovereigns upon the people against their clearly expressed wishes, placed him in a dilemma. To escape from it, so as not to incur any reproach from Austria, for breach of faith with regard to the treaty of Villafranca, he proposed a Congress of the European powers, to assemble in Paris, to discuss the whole subject of Italy. But the project fell through, and Italy remains armed and expectant, determined to be mistress of her own destinies. The quarrel with Austria, and the general results of the Italian campaign, not having been of a nature to regain for the Emperor the lost sympathies of the British people, whose alliance he seems earnestly to court as one of the surest bulwarks of his throne and dynasty—he made, early in 1860, a new and more sagacious move than he had hitherto attempted. Though the French people, with the sole exception of the wine growers of Bordeaux, Burgundy, and the Rhone, are universally Protectionists, the Emperor—fond of surprises—declared himself a convert to the principles of Free-trade, and notified an approaching relaxation of the suicidal stringencies of the French tariff. Aided by the experience and advice of Mr. Cobden, who was charged with a confidential mission to that effect from the British Government, a treaty of commerce between France and Great Britain was drawn up, of which the principle was triumphantly affirmed in the British House of Commons; and the Emperor regained that popularity in England which he enjoyed in the early stages of the Crimean war. This is, perhaps, the most important act, both to France and England, of his remarkable and eventful career; and pregnant with untold and unimagined blessings to both nations. Though it cannot be said that the Emperor has given the French the freedom which they covet, it cannot be denied that he is in other respects a great, an illustrious, and a magnificent sovereign. He has done what previous sovereigns longed, but did not dare, to attempt. He has completed the Louvre and the Rue de Rivoli, and made Paris—beautiful even before his time—the most eminently beautiful city in the world. Improvement has followed his footsteps wherever he has gone; and if Napoleon I. was the Julius Cæsar of France, Napoleon III. is justly entitled to be called her Augustus. The Emperor having failed to ally himself with some of the royal houses of Europe, married, on the 29th January, 1853, Eugénie Marie de Guzman, Countess de Teba, born 5th May, 1826, by whom he has one son, Napoléon Eugène Louis Jean Joseph, Prince Imperial, born March 16th, 1856.

NARVAEZ, DON RAMON, DUKE OF VALENCIA, was born in Andalusia, in 1800. He entered the military service at an early age as a cadet, and soon became distinguished by his gallantry. In 1822 he ranged himself on the liberal side, and most courageously contributed in quelling an attack made by the royal party against the revolutionists in July of that year. Having, however, been wounded, during the next year he retired from active life to his native place for nearly ten years. In 1836 he took command under Espartero; but about four years afterwards, he entirely changed his political views, and leaving the cause of the Constitution, became a Royalist. In 1844 he became President of the Council, and was created Duke of Valencia, but sustained a reverse of royal favour within three years afterwards. The revolutionary events of 1854 to 1856 again served to raise Narvaez to power in place of O'Donnell. He was again made President of the Council, and used energetic efforts in restoring the regal authority. However, in a country like Spain, where intrigue is the rule, and consistency the exception, it is no matter of surprise that the year 1859 found O'Donnell at once Prime Minister, Commander of the forces, destined to chastise Morocco in the war which has just been concluded, and thus at the same time the supplanter of Narvaez.

NASH, JOSEPH, water-colour painter, was born in 1813, and is eminent for his illustrations of architectural interiors. His career has been one of unbroken success, as, from the moment his drawings from the architecture of the Middle Ages became known, his works have been in demand. His "Mansions of England in the Olden Time," published in lithography, over a space of ten years, forms a splendid gallery of architectural portraiture as it was some century or two since. He has illustrated Shakspere and Sir Walter Scott with great felicity. All Mr. Nash's works are remarkable for their exceeding care and conscientious handling: however trifling the object may be, it receives its proper treatment. He has three water-colour paintings in the South Kensington Museum, viz., "The West End of Rouen Cathedral," "Rochester," and "The Hall at Speke."

NASMYTH, JAMES, a practical engineer, was born at Edinburgh, on the 19th August, 1808. At an early age he showed a taste for mechanical pursuits, and was accustomed by his father to the use of tools and the employment of a pencil. After studying at the University, where he was much esteemed, he set out for London in 1829, and entered the engineering establishment of Messrs. Maudslay and Field. Returning thence to his native city in 1832, he remained two years arranging tools for his intended entry into commercial life on his own account. In the spring of 1834 he settled in Manchester, and commenced on a small scale those now extensive works with which his name is associated. He had there many difficulties to overcome, the chief of which was, the repeated attempts of Trades Unionists among the men in his employ to subject his establishment to the dictation of their society's rules; but the successful resistance he offered resulted in the perfect emancipation of the manufactory from all such interference. He erected workshops at Patricroft, and there brought out in a short period his pile-driving machine, steam hammer, and other contrivances for facilitating the production of machinery, which have made his name known wherever the value of modern mechanism is understood. He retired from the concern at the close of 1856, with an ample reward for the exertions of mind and body which he had made during his previous successful career.

NEES VON ESENBECK, CHRISTIAN GODFREY, a German botanist, was born at Reichenberg, in the Odenwald, February 1776, and studied medicine at the University of Jena. He practised for several years, and was appointed suc-

cessively Botanical Professor in the Universities of Erlangen, Bonn, and Breslau. At Breslau he held the chair from 1831 to 1851, when he was removed on account of his assumed connexion with the revolutionary movements of 1848. He is an able botanist, a skilful classifier, and gives to the science a philosophic tone which is now becoming prevalent in Germany. His botanical works are very numerous, and he has written, besides, several volumes on philosophy and the politics of the day. His first treatise, "Die Algen des Süssen Wassers, &c.," was published in 1814; and his last, "A Series of Researches and Observations on Animal Magnetism," in 1853.

NESSELRODE, CHARLES ROBERT, COMTE DE, a Russian diplomatist and politician, was born at Lisbon, in 1780. His early career was in connexion with military affairs, but he soon showed the bent of his disposition by entering into the diplomatic service, in which he has acted successfully in Russian matters for more than half a century. His first occupation was that of "attaché" to the Prussian court. In 1807 he was connected with the embassy to Paris, and subsequently took part in the various events which transpired till the fall of Napoleon in 1814, suiting his policy to the various changes, as expediency rather than principle induced him. From that period till very lately, the administration of foreign affairs has been mostly in his hands. He was somewhat compromised in Russia with the patriotic party, owing to his supposed want of integrity during the late Crimean war, and has not lately taken an active part in public matters, although he still retains high office in Russia.

NEWCASTLE, HENRY PELHAM CLINTON, DUKE OF, was born 22nd May, 1811. After being educated at Eton, he studied at Christ Church, Oxford, and first entered Parliament in 1832, as member for South Nottinghamshire. As Lord Lincoln he held several offices under different administrations from 1834 till 1846, when he was for a short time the chief Secretary for Ireland. When Sir Robert Peel commenced his Free-trade measures, Lord Lincoln became a supporter of that statesman, and was member for the Falkirk Burghs till 1851, when he succeeded to the dukedom on the death of his father. He was also a member of Lord Aberdeen's Coalition Ministry, which, although including "all the talents," had the misfortune not to include that of success. The general feeling of the country being, that the war in the Crimea was not vigorously and judiciously managed, the Duke, who was Secretary at War, although feeling that he was not to blame, made himself the victim of popular clamour, and resigned in 1855. He shortly afterwards visited the seat of war, for the purpose of investigating the condition of matters there. On the return of Lord Palmerston to power in 1859, the Duke was made Secretary for the Colonies. He has lately (1860) accompanied the Prince of Wales to Canada, and by his judicious and affable demeanour has acquired the esteem of all parties with whom he has had to deal.

NEWMAN, REV. JOHN HENRY, D.D., brother of F. W. Newman, was born in London, in 1801. After being some time at a school at Ealing, he proceeded to Trinity College, Oxford, where he made a rapid and successful progress. In 1818 he gained a scholarship, in 1822 was made Fellow of Oriel, in 1824 was ordained deacon, in 1825 priest, and in the same year was chosen Vice-Principal of one of the Halls, and subsequently Vicar of St. Mary's. Dr. Newman is best known as the author of a celebrated tract, "No. 90," published in 1841, which produced an astonishing sensation throughout theological circles, and which was in reality an attempt to fuse the doctrines of the English establishment with those of the Roman Catholic Church. Dr. Newman, like many of his followers, thought it his duty to secede from the Church of England, and in 1845 he joined the Catholics, becoming Principal of the Roman Catholic University of Dublin, in 1851. He has subsequently resigned this office, and has lately appeared on the Continent as a preacher in some of the leading Catholic cathedrals, where he has most earnestly held forth in favour of the dogmas of the Romish Church. He has published several pamphlets relating to the controversies of which he has been the *pars magna;* and is the author of the article on Miracles in the "Encyclopædia Metropolitana," and of many volumes of sermons. Dr. Newman is understood to be engaged on the new translation of the Scriptures which the English Roman Catholics have at present in preparation.

NEWMAN, FRANCIS WILLIAM, a theological and literary author, was born in London, in 1805. His early education was conducted at Ealing. In 1822 he went to Worcester College, and was Fellow of Balliol College in 1826. Mr. Newman, like his brother, seceded from the Church of England, but on entirely different principles, and has been distinguished for an energetic defence of opinions, which by some have been thought to be verging towards scepticism. He is the author of several works on religious subjects, the best known of which are—"The Soul, her Sorrows and Aspirations," "The Phases of Faith," and a "History of the Hebrew Monarchy." His other writings are a translation of the "Odes of Horace," "Regal Rome," "Lectures on Logic," "Lectures on Political Economy," and a "Grammar of the Berber Language." He contributed articles for many years to the Eclectic and Prospective Reviews, and he now writes on political subjects for the "Westminster Review." To give some idea of the range of his acquirements, it may be added that he is the author of papers on Elliptic Integrals, &c., which imply extensive reading in the higher mathematics.

NICHOLS, JOHN GOUGH, F.S.A., an antiquarian, was born in London, in 1807. He was educated at Merchant Taylors' School, and embarked in literary pursuits before he had attained to manhood. After materially assisting his grandfather in the completion of the "Progress, &c. of King James I.," he completed that work, when left unfinished at his grandfather's death. For thirty-two years, from 1824 to 1856, he compiled the obituary for the "Gentleman's Magazine;" and from January 1852 to June 1856, he was the sole editor of that time-honoured periodical. The "Collectanea Topographica et Genealogica," set on foot by Sir Thomas Phillipps, Sir Frederick Madden, and the Rev. Dr. Bandinal, in 1834, was chiefly conducted by him, and completed in 8 vols. 8vo, 1843. He also edited its sequel, the "Topographer and Genealogist," in 3 vols. His distinct works are "Autographs of Royal, Noble, Learned, and Remarkable Persons conspicuous in English History;" "London Pageants;" "Description of Fresco Paintings discovered in the Guild Chapel of Stratford-upon-Avon, and of the Corporation Records of the same Town;" "Description of the Monuments of the Earls of Warwick, &c., in the Beauchamp Chapel;" "The Pilgrimage of Canterbury and Walsingham," translated from Erasmus; "The Armorial Windows of Woodhouse Chapel." After having acted as treasurer of the Sarley Society from its formation in 1834, a position which he still retains, Mr. Nichols, in 1838, set on foot the Camden Society, which has, up to the present time, issued more than eighty works, besides suggesting the establishment of many book-printing societies on the like popular plan as the Shakspere, the Percy, the Parker, and the Sydenham Societies.

NIEPCE, DE SAINT VICTOR, CLAUDE MARIE FRANÇOIS, a French chemist and photographer, was born at St. Cyr, on 26th July, 1805. Having studied at Saumer he entered the army, and after passing through various grades became a *chef d'escadron* in 1854. M. Niepce had meanwhile devoted himself to scientific pursuits, and it is chiefly from his discoveries in photography that he became so well known. To his uncle and M. Daguerre are due the merit of the first successful attempts to obtain likenesses by the action of light on salts of silver. M. Daguerre used for this purpose silver plates, whose surfaces were rendered sensitive to the action of light by exposing them for a short time to the vapour of iodine, &c. M. Niepce improved on this troublesome and uncertain process, by showing that the surface of glass properly prepared with albumen, &c., might be employed with advantage; and the present mode of photographing on glass where collodion is used, is simply an expansion of the ideas first suggested by him. M. Niepce next showed that, by certain agents, light might not only be employed to give the effect of an ordinary picture, but also be used to engrave the result on plates of metal. This process has since been extended, and at the present time excellent engraved copper plates are produced, entirely by the action of light and electricity, and without the least skill or work on the part of the operator beyond that of applying the chemical agents. M. Niepce has published several works on his favourite pursuit, among which are his "Photography on Glass," "The Production of Coloured Images by the Action of Light," and "Sun Engravings on Steel and Glass." His principal productions are collected in one work of eight volumes, entitled

"Photographic Researches." M. Niepce is a member of many of the learned societies of Europe, and is a Chevalier of the Legion of Honour.

NIGHTINGALE, MISS FLORENCE, an English philanthropist, was born at Florence, in 1820. She was principally educated at home, and there acquired a knowledge of several modern languages. Very early, even in childhood, she manifested sympathy with affliction in every form that presented itself. This gentle and true spirit was sustained in her by her friends, who gave her ample encouragement. She visited schools and hospitals within reach of Lea Hurst, where she was brought up, her appearance being always welcome to the poor, the sick, and the needy. But the field of Lea Hurst was too narrow for her expansive benevolence. She wished to understand suffering in all its phases, and to administer to its alleviation. She went to London and examined workhouses, reformatories, and hospitals; observing, as she proceeded, the modes of nursing invalids, and then visited many hospitals in the country towns with a similar feeling and sentiment. Miss Nightingale came to the conclusion that a staff of educated nurses is essential, and that a school for training them to their duties was much required. She learned that such an establishment existed in Germany, that it was successful, and she resolved to enter it as a voluntary nurse. She there spent upwards of six months, and saw many ladies attending the sick without dread of catching disease. It was thus that she acquired all absence of fear, and fully felt the grandeur of her earthly mission. Leaving Germany in 1851, she visited the hospitals and asylums for the poor in France and Italy. After returning to England, she was for some time in ill health; but, notwithstanding, pursued her career of self-training. The war in the Crimea breaking out, the Secretary-at-War found the wounded of the French soldiery carefully tended by French Sisters of Charity, and urged Miss Nightingale to take the superintendence of a staff of nurses attached to the British camp. She acceded to this request, and leaving her family and friends, proceeded to the Crimea, to enter on her mission of mercy. Sickness spread to an alarming extent through the British forces in the East; at one time, ten thousand men were ill in the various hospitals. Miss Nightingale was everywhere, and by her cheerful demeanour and thoughtful consideration smoothed many a rough pillow. She returned to England in 1856, weak in health, but honoured by her country—from the Queen down to the lowest subject. A subscription was raised for a testimonial to her, but she requested that it might be applied to founding an institution for training nurses. Since her return, although a complete invalid, she has been the prime mover in the wise and successful measures initiated by Mr. Sidney Herbert and his colleagues to reduce the high rate of mortality in the British army, and has taken a most lively interest in the establishment of the Army Medical College at Chatham. Miss Nightingale has lately published a work entitled "Notes on Nursing," which, from its eminently practical nature, is calculated to do much good.

NOEL, THE HON. AND REV. BAPTIST WRIOTHSLEY, M.A., born in 1799, is the third son of Sir Gerard Noel Noel, Bart., and brother to the Earl of Gainsborough. He was educated, and took his degree of M.A., at Trinity College, Cambridge. Mr. Noel was for many years an eminent member of the Church of England, and one of her most faithful ministers; and as a popular preacher exerted himself strenuously in the cause of missions, but taking views of baptism different from those inculcated by the Church of England, he, though apparently with reluctance, severed his connexion with that Church, and became a Baptist minister. He produced a great effect by his pamphlet on the Corn-laws, which was published many years ago, and in which he nobly pleaded the cause of the poor. Previous to leaving the Church of England, he was one of her Majesty's Chaplains. He has published several popular devotional works, and has long been esteemed for his eminently philanthropic spirit.

NORMANBY, CONSTANTINE HENRY PHIPPS, MARQUIS OF, an English diplomatist, was born in May, 1797. He was educated at Harrow and Cambridge, and returned to Parliament on the Whig interest for Scarborough, in 1818. He was in favour of Roman Catholic Emancipation, and of Parliamentary Reform. His father finding fault with him for advocating these principles, he resigned his seat and went to Italy, but after being absent about two years he returned and sat for Higham Ferrers. He succeeded to the peerage as Lord Mulgrave in 1831, and shortly afterwards was appointed Governor of Jamaica, and during his term of office the emancipation of the slaves was effected. In 1833 he returned to England, and in 1834 was Lord Privy Seal. In 1835 he accepted the then difficult office of Lord Lieutenant of Ireland, which position he held for four years. He was made a marquis in 1838 ; and in 1839 became Secretary for the Colonies, but after holding that office a few months he was appointed Home Secretary. In 1846 he was Ambassador to Paris, and in that capacity recognised the Provisional Government in 1848, approving the measure of Cavaignac to suppress further insurrectionary manifestations. He remained in Paris until after the *coup d'état,* and the election of Louis Napoleon as Emperor. In 1854 his diplomatic services were transferred to the court of

Tuscany, a change generally considered indicative of his ultimate removal from diplomatic employment. He was relieved of the Tuscan embassy in 1858, and has since resided in England, taking frequent part in the debates of the Upper House on questions of continental policy. Lord Normanby has written some four or five novels, which were popular, but are now almost forgotten. His latest literary production is "A Year of Revolution," being his Parisian experience of 1848-9. This work has been severely criticised.

NORTON, THE HONOURABLE CAROLINE ELIZABETH SARAH, granddaughter of the celebrated Richard Brinsley Sheridan, was born in 1808. Her father died when she was very young, and she and her two sisters, the present Duchess of Somerset and the Dowager Lady Dufferin, were educated by their mother. Mrs. Norton wrote verses at an early age, but it was not until after her marriage with the Honourable G. C. Norton, one of the police magistrates of London, that she became known to the literary world. Her first work was "The Sorrows of Rosalie," published anonymously in 1829, which was followed in 1830 by "The Undying One." This volume established Mrs. Norton's place among the most eminent of living poetesses. A number of other works, chiefly poetical, succeeded, but none so popular as "The Undying One." She contributed to the Annuals for several years, and has written one novel, "Stuart of Dunleath."

NOVELLO, MADAME CLARA, Countess Gigliucci, an English vocalist, is daughter of Mr. Vincent Novello, a musician of considerable repute, and was born in London, June 1818. In 1827, when quite a child, she commenced her musical studies at York, and was afterwards entered a pupil of the Conservatoire de Musique Sacré at Paris. Young though she was, Miss Novello, by devoting her whole heart to the subject, became distinguished in the Academy for her intelligent manner of rendering Church music. In 1833 she returned to England, and made her first appearance at a concert given at Windsor, and was afterwards engaged to sing at the Ancient Concerts. Mendelssohn invited her to Leipsic, and she charmed the public of that city. Russia, Prussia, Austria, and Germany were visited by her, and on account of the beauties of her style she was highly successful. Possibly her first great appearance was made at the Manchester Festival, in 1836, when she fairly divided the palm with Malibran in oratorio music. She afterwards studied for the lyric stage, and took for her first part "Semiramide," at Padua, Rossini recommending that special line of art. It was one of the most difficult *rôles* that a young *cantatrice* could undertake, but Miss Novello carried the piece through brilliantly, and thenceforward she was eagerly sought for to appear on the stage, in the concert-room, and at oratorios. She married in 1848, but returned to the stage in 1850. At the Glasgow Musical Festival, in January 1860, she gained golden opinions. She then returned to Italy to fulfil an engagement at the Scala of Milan. But her career may now be regarded as closed. The two great performances of sacred music, at the Crystal Palace, October 1860, were her *adieux* to the public of the metropolis. At length, the brighter days which have begun to shine on Italy, and other circumstances, now allow her to cease from her self-imposed toils—no longer Madame Clara Novello, but the Countess Gigliucci,—to retire with her husband to the enjoyment of her proper social position in her adopted country.

O'BRIEN, WILLIAM SMITH, an Irish politician of the independent school, is descended from the ancient kings of Munster, and was born at Dromoland, in 1803. He was educated at Harrow and Cambridge, and having inherited a considerable fortune from his mother, he was returned to Parliament for the borough of Ennis in 1830, afterwards in 1835 for Limerick. Though closely connected with various aristocratic families, he joined O'Connell in demanding a repeal of the Union, as the only remedy for Irish grievances. But the great agitator and Mr. O'Brien differed on one essential point; the former believed in the efficacy of moral force, while the latter contended that nothing could be extorted from the British Government, except by demonstrations of physical power. The Young Ireland party, of which Mr. O'Brien was the leader, was gaining ground but slowly, when the French Revolution of 1848 broke out, and seemed the Irish opportunity. Mr. O'Brien proceeded to Paris; was received with sympathy by the Provisional Government, and returned fully impressed with the conviction that he would be supported by France in separating Ireland from England. The Earl of Clarendon, then Lord Lieutenant, saw the approaching danger, and prepared for it, by suspending the Habeas Corpus Act, and placing the disaffected districts under martial law. Mr. O'Brien held on his way, reviewed assemblages of peasantry, and pronounced insurrection inevitable. As a commencement he attacked a police station at Ballingarry, July 29, 1848, but his followers fled and he escaped. In the following September he was arrested on a charge of high treason—his disciples took care of themselves—he was tried for the imputed State crime, found guilty and condemned to death, on the 9th October, but the punishment was commuted to transportation for life, and even that penalty was mitigated by the Crown in 1856. In the latter year Mr. O'Brien once more found himself free on his native soil. During the seven years of his involuntary exile, political excitement had died a natural death in Ireland; the country was fast improving; agitation was at a discount; and without abandoning his cherished opinions, Mr. O'Brien has since taken no active steps towards their promulgation.

O'DONNELL, LEOPOLD, DUKE OF TETUAN, marshal and minister of Spain, was born in 1808, and is descended from an old Irish family. He entered the army when young, and in the civil war in Spain, incited by Don Carlos, on the faith of his claim to the Crown, O'Donnell took part with the Queen, and in 1838 was chief of the staff, and subsequently became Commander. Espartero was his patron and friend; but forgetful of all he owed to the patriot Regent, O'Donnell eventually adopted the cause of the Queen-mother, and was obliged to throw up his command and fly to France for safety. In 1841 he returned to Spain, but no sooner had he set his foot within the Escurial than he commenced to plot for the overthrow of Espartero, who at last fell through his intrigues. He afterwards was Governor of Cuba, where he became very rich by the slave trade. He returned to Spain, and was appointed Director-General of Infantry. Narvaez soon after gave way to Sartorius; O'Donnell raised an insurrection in Andalusia, but was defeated at all points, and his property confiscated. He was, however, again restored to office, and made Secretary-at-War, and again betrayed Espartero, who had twice saved him from destruction. O'Donnell was nominated President of the Council, in place of Espartero; but the change was unpopular, and he signalized his elevation by means similar to those adopted by Louis Napoleon on the 2nd December, 1851. The streets of Madrid were gorged with the blood of citizens, and the minister was triumphant, but only for a season, for Narvaez plotted and O'Donnell was forced to retire. He returned to power again, however, in 1858, and in 1859 held the double position of Prime Minister and Commander-in-Chief of the forces despatched to wage war against Morocco. His campaign has been highly successful. The Moors have been obliged to capitulate, pay a heavy sum towards the expenses of the war, and submit to a loss of territory. O'Donnell, on his return to Spain, has been received with high honours, and created by the Queen Duke of Tetuan.

OLIPHANT, LAWRENCE, an English author and traveller, was born in 1832. His father belonged to an old family in Perthshire, and was Sir Anthony Oliphant, C.B., Chief Justice of Ceylon. Educated in England, Mr. Oliphant, before completing his professional studies as a lawyer, went out to India, and while in Ceylon received an invitation from Jung-Bahadoor to accompany him to Nepaul. This invitation he accepted. He visited the native court of that country, and after enjoying unrivalled opportunities of attaining information as regards the manners and feelings of the inhabitants, he, on his return, wrote an account of his tour, which he published under the title of "A Journey to Katmandu." That this work was the production of a mere youth does not appear to have been detected by the critics. It displayed some of the best qualities which characterise Mr. Oliphant's subsequent efforts. It received high praise for its graphic power, and the sagacity of its observations. The author having returned to this country from India, studied law at the University of Edinburgh, and was called to the Scotch bar, and subsequently to the English bar, at Lincoln's Inn. In the autumn of 1852 he made a tour to Russia, in the course of which he descended the Volga, and visited the Steppes of the Don Cossacks, and the Crimea.

This journey furnished the materials for another work, entitled "The Russian Shores of the Black Sea," which, making its appearance in 1853, at a period when the Crimean war was on the eve of breaking out, and furnishing the most recent information regarding the countries to which our armaments were proceeding, became at once popular, and in the course of a few months passed through four editions. A well-written and lively book, displaying everywhere good sense and careful observation, it secured for its author the reputation of being one of the best writers of modern books of travel. Shortly after his return to England from this autumnal tour, Mr. Oliphant became private secretary to the Earl of Elgin, then Governor-General of Canada. In this capacity he went to America, where he held a responsible situation in connexion with Canadian and Indian affairs. He travelled to most parts of the continent of North America at this period, visiting the latest settlements in the backwoods of Canada and the United States, as well as the countries of Central America, where the English and Spanish race have come into collision. The materials collected in the course of his rambles through the Northern States were embodied in " Minnesota,"—a work in which narration of adventure, pleasant glimpses of American scenery, and with descriptions of the latest European settlements in the far West, were mingled with broad views of political events. This work entitled Mr. Oliphant to be considered something better than a mere writer of Impressions, or Voyages. Pursuing the same spirit of generalization, he wrote at this period an anonymous pamphlet, entitled "The Coming Campaign," in which he advocated views as to the mode of conducting the struggle with Russia, at variance with those adopted by Government. This work was republished in 1855,

under the title of "The Trans-Caucasian Provinces, the Proper Field of Operations for a Christian Army." In the meantime Mr. Oliphant returned to the countries referred to in this work, and accompanied Omer Pacha in his most dangerous expeditions, participating in all the hardships and dangers of the campaign, as a correspondent of the press. "The Caucasian Campaign of Omer Pacha; a Personal Narrative," was the result of this expedition, in the course of which districts were visited which had hitherto been all but unknown to Europeans. Not long after the conclusion of the Russian war, Lord Elgin, who had in the interval returned from Canada, was appointed Special High Commissioner to China; Mr. Oliphant again became his private secretary. He accompanied the expedition, of which he was the historiographer. His daring journey to Sou-Chou with M. de Cintades, through the midst of a hostile population, was one of the most memorable episodes in the expedition, throughout which, however, he distinguished himself by his pluck and readiness to face danger where there was any chance of obtaining information. The voyage made by Lord Elgin up the Yang-tse-Kiang, past the great city of Nankin, and far into the interior of vast regions never before explored by Europeans, gave the undertaking an importance altogether independent of its political object, and made it highly desirable that its details should be recorded by a competent pen. Mr. Oliphant was well fitted for this task. His account of it, entitled a "Narrative of the Earl of Elgin's Mission to China and Japan, in the Years 1857-58-59," published at the end of last year, is unquestionably the best official history we have of any diplomatic expedition of the kind. It is a well-arranged and well-written book, giving all the information that could be desired on the subject to which it refers, in a shape attractive to general readers. Mr. Oliphant is a contributor to "Blackwood's Magazine," the "Cornhill Magazine," and various other periodicals. His latest work, published within the last few months, is entitled "Patriots and Filibusters, or Incidents of Political and Explorating Travel."

OLMSTED, DENISON, was born at East Hartford, Connecticut, in 1791; educated at Yale College; and has filled in turn the chairs of chemistry, mathematics, and astronomy, in the university of North Carolina. He is the author of numerous scientific papers that have appeared in the American journals, but his speciality is more as a popularizer of science than a philosopher. .

OMER PACHA, whose real name is Michel Lattas, late Commander-in-Chief of the Turkish forces in Europe, was born at Vlaski, a village of Austrian Croatia. His relations adhered to the Greek Church. His education was primarily at the military school of his native village, and afterwards at the School of Mathematics in Thurm, Transylvania, from which he passed as cadet into the Austrian army. He wrote a superior hand, was a good mathematician, and had served but a short time when he was appointed Assistant Surveyor of roads and bridges. An unfortunate circumstance obliged him, when about twenty-eight, to leave the Austrian service. He repaired to Bosnia, became tutor in the family of a Mohammedan merchant, and embraced the faith of the Moslem, assuming the name of Omer. Having proceeded with his pupils to Constantinople, he married a wealthy heiress; in 1833 he became chief of a battalion, was introduced to the late Sultan, gave lessons in writing to the present Sultan, and advanced in favour. His first actual military service was in 1839, when he took part in the contest with Ibrahim Pacha. In 1842 he received

the title of Bey, and was afterwards sent to suppress an Albanian insurrection, in which he was so successful that he received the title by which he is at present known. In 1848 he was appointed to command the army of occupation in Wallachia, when the Russian army entered that territory to check the Hungarians. His conduct on that occasion met with general approbation. Having put down one or two insurrections, he was next despatched to quell the disturbances in Montenegro in 1852, but Austrian interposition at Constantinople caused him to withdraw his troops when on the verge of completing the subjection of Montenegro. His successes in war and politics raised him now to the highest position. The war with Russia was declared in September 1853, and Omer Pacha took command of the army of the Danube. The events of that struggle are too recent to call for recapitulation. He gained victory after victory, until he was ordered to the relief of Kars. In this expedition he was unsuccessful, the general belief being that his delay was premeditated. Subsequent inquiry, however, has shown that his failure arose from obedience to higher authority, which marked out a route for his forces impossible of accomplishment within the necessary time. The conclusion of the war withdrew him from the public eye, but he has received various honours from the Sultan, and is decorated with the Grand Cross of the Legion of Honour.

ORBIGNY, CHARLES D', a French naturalist, was born at Coueron, in the Department of the Loire-Inférieure, in December, 1806. He was educated at Rochelle, where his father was a medical practitioner, and in 1827 went to Paris for the purpose of studying medicine. His views changed, however, and in 1832 he directed his attention almost exclusively to the natural sciences.

In 1835 he was appointed Assistant Naturalist to the Museum of Natural History, where he still continues. M. d'Orbigny is held in much repute on the Continent as a man of extensive scientific acquirements. He has published various works, the most important being the "Dictionnaire Universel d' Histoire Naturelle," in thirteen octavo volumes. His latest publication, issued in 1855, is a treatise on Palæontology.

ORLOFF, ALEXIS, PRINCE, a Russian soldier, diplomatist, and statesman, was born in 1787. He entered the army, and took a distinguished part in all the Russian campaigns against Napoleon I., receiving several wounds at the battle of Borodino, in 1812. After having been attached to the person of the Grand Duke Constantine, he was appointed Aide-de-camp to the Emperor Alexander I., and afterwards promoted by the same sovereign to the dignity of principal Aide-de-camp in 1819. During the great insurrection of 1825, and on the famous day of the 14th of December, he commanded the regiment of horse-guards, by means of which he powerfully contributed to crush the rebels and secure the victory to the Imperial government. After this period he became the most intimate and faithful friend of the Emperor Nicholas throughout the whole of his reign. In 1833 he was appointed Ambassador and Commander-in-Chief of the forces sent by his sovereign to the assistance of the Sultan against the Viceroy of Egypt, and he negotiated the famous treaty of Unkiar Skelessi, the most advantageous arrangement for Russia which has been entered into with the Porte. He was Ambassador of Russia at the coronation of the Emperor Ferdinand of Austria, and repaired to Vienna to ensure the neutrality of the Emperor Francis Joseph during the Eastern war in 1853-4. In 1856 he sat in the quality of first Russian Plenipotentiary to the Congress of Paris, and negotiated the treaty of the 18th March, after the signature of which he was raised by the Emperor Alexander II. to the highest dignity in the state, as President of the Council of the Empire and Ministry, functions with which he is still invested.

O'SHAUGHNESSY, SIR WILLIAM BROOKE, K.C.B., was born at Limerick in 1809. After studying at the University of Edinburgh, he entered the East India service, and became Professor of Chemistry at Calcutta College. He was the first to introduce the electric telegraph into India, and through his exertions that vast empire has now become covered by a network of telegraphic wires, reaching over about five thousand miles in length. An attempt has been lately made to extend the telegraph from Suez to Kurrachee, and when completed, India will be, telegraphically speaking, within a few hours' reach of London. About four years ago Sir William visited England, when he was made K.C.B., and on returning to India took with him several young gentlemen who had been carefully trained in electric science, as assistants in future telegraphic extensions. The British and Indian Governments derived the greatest advantage from Sir William's arrangements during the late war; and to the completeness of the telegraphic apparatus then used many of the successes of the armies under Lord Clyde and others were due.

OTHO I., KING OF GREECE, second son of Louis I., ex-King of Bavaria, and brother of Maximilian II., was born on the 1st of June, 1815. When the Greeks, after a long, arduous, and romantic struggle against the Turks, (in which they were supported by the active sympathy, no less than by the pecuniary aid of all the ardent minds of Europe, who were imbued with the classic recollections of that illustrious land,) had involved the great powers in their quarrel, the question of the establishment of their independence became the question of the day. After the battle of Navarino Turkey had no alternative but to submit to a dismemberment; and by the preliminary Convention held at London on the 6th of July, 1827, Greece was declared an independent state, and taken under the protection of the contracting powers, Great Britain, France, and Russia. Count Capo d'Istria was elected Provisional President or Governor of the new state, and destined to fill the office until 1832, when the Greeks, having in vain offered their crown to Prince Leopold of Saxe-Coburg, now King of the Belgians, made choice of the young Prince Otho of Bavaria, then in his seventeenth year. By a treaty concluded at London, on the 7th of May, 1832, and ratified by the King of Bavaria on the 27th of the same month, the powers of Europe supported the proposition of the Greeks. The Prince accepted the offer in October of the same year, and arrived in Greece in the January following (1833), when he was proclaimed King, but submitted to the control of a Regency until he should have attained his twentieth year. He finally took the reins of government into his own hands in June, 1835; and in the following year was married to the Princess Mary Frederica Amelia, daughter of the Grand Duke Augustus of Oldenburg. The reign of King Otho over the Greeks has not been peaceful or successful. He has laboured under the great disadvantage of being a foreigner, and committed the great imprudence of endeavouring to support his authority against an often unwilling and discontented people by the aid of German and other foreign and mercenary troops. The Queen has made herself the ruling spirit in Greece; her influence is entirely pro-Russian, and under her actual agency, and the sleepy acquiescence of the King, Greece has become independent only in name, and a virtual appanage of the Russian empire. Convulsion has succeeded convulsion at Athens, till violent revolution has often appeared the only remedy for the deep-rooted evils of the state. Hitherto this unlucky specimen of a constitutional monarchy has been of little use to the world, or to itself, except as an example to prove that free constitutions are not sufficient of themselves to make a free and happy people; and that knowledge, patience, and self-control on the part of the citizens, are at least as necessary to procure and maintain good government as are charters of liberty, or constitutions on the British or any other model. There being no issue by the king's marriage, the crown of Greece will descend (revolution not intervening) to Prince Adalbert of Bavaria, his majesty's younger brother.

OUDINOT, NICHOLAS CHARLES VICTOR, DUC DE REGGIO, son of the famous marshal of that name, was born November 3rd, 1791, at Bar-le-Duc, Meuse. In 1805 he was one of the Emperor Napoleon's pages; in 1809 he became, by brevet, lieutenant of the 5th Hussars; and notwithstanding his youth, he was appointed Aide-de-camp to Massena, and had his share in the vicissitudes of the Portuguese campaign. He returned to France in 1811, and afterwards signalized himself by his undaunted courage at Leipsic, Hanau, Montmirail, and Craonne—at the latter conflict being seriously wounded. In 1814 he was named *chef d'escadron*. Napoleon after his abdication had promoted him to the rank of colonel; but the Count d'Artois, though he might have cancelled the commission, confirmed Oudinot in his grade, and charged him with the organization of a regiment of Hussars. During the "Hundred Days," Oudinot was faithful to the Bourbons, and he was appointed to the command of the Hussars du Nord, which he exchanged, in 1822, for the First Horse Grenadiers of the Royal Guard. In 1824 he acted as field-marshal, of which he had the rank, and was charged with the re-organization of the School of Cavalry at Saumur, on a broader basis than before. He retained that position until .the revolution of 1830. True to his sentiments he resigned office, and was not again called to active life until after the death of his brother in 1835. He was despatched to Africa, and distinguished himself; but being injured by an explosion, he returned to France. In the same year he was promoted as Lieutenant-General, and became one of the Inspectors-General of Cavalry. From that period until the revolution of 1848, he took as a deputy but a moderate part in public affairs; but the Republic proclaimed, he adhered to the change, and was elected representative for Maine-et-Loire. In March, 1848, he was placed at the head of the Army of Observation assembled at the foot of. the Alps.: Marshal Bugeaud succeeded him in command in January, 1849, and he was re-elected by the department of Maine-et-Loire to the Legislative Assembly shortly afterwards. Selected to command in chief the expedition sent against the revolutionists of Rome, he debarked at Civita Vecchia on the 25th April. The city of Rome was not taken till July 3rd. Handing over his command to M. de Rostolan, he returned to France, and took his place in the Legislature. He was one of those who protested against the *coup d'état* on December 2, 1851; and by a unanimous vote of the Assembly was chosen to command the troops of the first military division, and the National Guard; he was arrested and detained some days at Mont Valérien. On obtaining his liberty he passed into private life, as a retired general-in-chief. General Oudinot is the author of a few military works, which profes-sional readers say possess considerable merit.

OUTRAM, GENERAL SIR JAMES, a British military commander, who has signalized himself in India, was born at Butterley Hall, Derbyshire, in 1805. His father, who was an eminent engineer, sent him to study at Aberdeen, and afterwards, in 1819, procured him a cadetship. He left for India, and after some time was appointed Adjutant to the 23rd Regiment of Native Infantry, and disciplined the corps. Subsequently he was Political Agent at Goojerat, Commissioner at Upper Scinde, and Resident at Hyderabad, Sattara, and Lucknow; in all which offices he exhibited administrative ability combined with military skill. When he left Scinde, he wrote a severe animadversion on Sir Charles Napier's conquest of that country; a publication which seemed to have had no small effect in retarding his promotion. He afterwards bore an active share in the extinction of the Thugs, and was one of the Marquis of Dalhousie's most judicious coadjutors in the project for the annexation of Oude. He was created Knight of the Bath in 1856, and sent to Persia in command of the British expedition, with full diplomatic powers and the rank of lieutenant-general. The short war that ensued was marked by the judicious conduct of Sir James Outram. Bushire fell, and he signed an armistice, all points demanded by General Outram being conceded by the Shah, and he returned with his army to Bombay. When the Indian insurrection broke out he was nominated to a difficult command, being sent against Dinapore and Cawnpore, but he was equal to the emergency; and recent events have demonstrated that his skill as a general is equal to his wisdom as a cabinet councillor. For his gallantry in India he has received the Grand Cross of the Bath.

OVERBECK, FRIEDRICH, a German

R.d. Owen

painter, was born at Lubeck, July 1789. His love of art and his natural talents were displayed at an early age. He went to Vienna in 1806, where he studied diligently for four years. Proceeding to Rome in 1810, he became there an enthusiastic student of the old Italian masters. It fell to the lot of Overbeck, in conjunction with a few other artists who participated in his views, to effect a complete revolution not only in the choice of subjects, but in the method of treating them; and though the young painters were at first laughed at, they persevered until their efforts commanded the admiration of Germany and the applause of Europe. In 1811 Overbeck's "Madonna" gave occasion for both hostile and friendly criticism; but the pictures that followed stamped his position as the leader and genius of the New School. His picture of "Christ entering Jerusalem," finished in 1816, is certainly one of the grandest works from Scripture subjects produced for centuries. Amongst his leading pictures are "Christ bearing His Cross," "Hagar in the Desert," "St. John Preaching in the Wilderness," "Christ Raising the Daughter of Jairus," and numerous others, chiefly on religious subjects. He has for a long time resided at Rome, a city whose associations harmonize with his temper and disposition.

OVERSTONE, LORD, SAMUEL JONES LOYD, was born in 1796, and educated at Eton and Cambridge. He was at one time a partner in the firm of Jones, Loyd, and Co., bankers, but retired on his elevation to the peerage in 1850. He has long been eminent as a financier, and it was stated at the time Sir Robert Peel brought forward his Bank Charter Act, that the minister was indebted to Lord Overstone for suggesting the most valuable portions of the bill. He has published several pamphlets on banking and commercial matters, and in many circles is considered an authority on such subjects. He sat for Hythe, in the House of Commons, in 1819, and has been frequently proposed by the liberal party of London as a member for the City, but he refused to stand, although at all times he lent his influence to secure the election of liberal men. A collection of his papers has been recently printed, in two volumes, for private circulation.

OWEN, RICHARD, F.R.S., a physiologist and comparative anatomist, was born at Lancaster, in 1804. He received his first education at the grammar-school of that town, and afterwards at the University of Edinburgh. Besides attending the lectures of the ordinary professors, he studied anatomy under the learned Dr. Barclay, who was a private and successful teacher in the city. Through this gentleman's influence and example Mr. Owen acquired a taste for the study of comparative anatomy. In 1825 Mr. Owen went to London, and commenced studying at St. Bartholomew's Hospital, where from his decided talent he became an anatomical assistant to the celebrated Abernethy, who in 1836 obtained for him an appointment in connexion with the Hunterian Museum. Here he prepared the "Catalogue of Collections of Physiology and Comparative Anatomy," which had been purchased by Parliament in the preceding century, of the executors of John Hunter. To this circumstance Mr. Owen is much indebted for his subsequent fame, and he made so good use of it as to have raised himself to the highest position amongst living naturalists. He succeeded Sir Charles Bell at the College of Surgeons as Hunterian Professor in 1836, and after retaining this position for many years, became the Superintendent of the Natural History Department in the British Museum in 1856. On the revival of the Lectureship on Philosophy, on the foundation of Sir Robert Read, in the University of Cambridge, he was appointed Professor, and received the honorary degree of Doctor of Laws at the termination of the course. He is also Fullerian Professor of Physiology in the Royal Institution of Great Britain. He filled the office of President of the British Association for the Advancement of Science at their meeting at Leeds in 1858, in which office he was succeeded at Aberdeen by H. R. H. the Prince Consort, in 1859. Professor Owen was an active member of the Sanitary Commissions for the Health of Towns in 1844-5, and for the metropolis in 1846-7. He took part in the organization of the Great Exhibition in 1851, was President of one of the juries, and served in the same capacity on an international jury of the Exposition Universelle at Paris, in 1855. On this occasion he received the decoration of the order of the Legion of Honour from the Emperor of the French. He was elected in 1859, on the decease of the great botanist, Robert Brown, one of the eight Foreign Associates of the Academy of Sciences in the Institute of France; and his name is enrolled as member of most of the learned societies in Europe and America. Professor Owen has, by his indefatigable industry and sagacity, effected for natural history a larger amount of scientific research and induction than perhaps any other person. He has brought to its study astonishing powers of observation, combined with accurate and severe reasoning; and the additions he has made to the general stock of information in every department of the science have been so varied and extensive, as to make it a matter of surprise that one man could ever have produced such results. In reference to the principles inductively established in Professor Owen's chief work on "The Archetype of the Animal Framework," it has been concisely remarked, that "he is the Newton of Natural History."

OXENFORD, JOHN, an author and dramatic writer, was born at Camberwell, London, in 1812. He was ori-

ginally intended for, and pursued, the legal profession, but relinquished that for the more congenial pursuit of literature. As a dramatist he is well known to London audiences, many of his productions in this line being highly popular. As a German scholar he has translated "Eckermann's Conversations," "The Autobiography of Goethe," Tische's "Bacon," &c.; and has also produced translations of French songs. Mr. Oxenford is understood to be the theatrical critic for the "Times" newspaper. His last dramatic production is a libretto for "Robin Hood," now being performed in Her Majesty's Theatre.

OXFORD, THE RIGHT REV. SAMUEL WILBERFORCE, BISHOP OF, was born in 1805, and is the third son of the late William Wilberforce, M.P. He was educated at Oriel College, Oxford, and after having obtained several ecclesiastical preferments, was consecrated Bishop of Oxford, in 1845. He has published a few works, all of a religious character. As a spiritual peer the Bishop of Oxford takes a prominent part in the debates in the House of Lords, but is often complained of for his want of decision in dealing with a public question. Nevertheless, he is an eloquent and graceful orator. The Bishop of Oxford is popularly recognised as one of the "High Church" party.

PAKINGTON, THE RIGHT HON. SIR JOHN SOMERSET, an English statesman, was born in 1799. His surname was Russell, which he changed to that of his uncle on his mother's side in 1831. Having been educated at Eton and Oxford, he entered Parliament in 1837, representing the borough of Droitwich. Throughout his political career he has held Conservative principles, and of late years has been a conspicuous member of that party. He held the office of Colonial Secretary under the Earl of Derby in 1852, and was First Lord of the Admiralty in 1858, when Lord Derby again took the reins of office. In 1859 he was made a G.C.B. Sir John has most fortunately disappointed the opinions of his opponents by the able manner in which he has filled his official appointments. Till within the last few years he was comparatively unknown; but on retiring in 1859 he had the gratification of receiving one of the highest possible political compliments, in finding that his successor in office considered it best to follow the plans he had laid out for the improvement and extension of the British navy.

PALGRAVE, SIR FRANCIS, K.H., F.R.S., an antiquarian, was born in London in 1788, and entered the Inner Temple in 1827. He has chiefly devoted himself to researches into and the publication of facts relating to British history. In 1831 he published his "History of England during the Anglo-Saxon Period," which is replete with useful and interesting information. The next year he produced his "Rise and Progress of the English Commonwealth," in which he dilates on the customs, laws, policy, and other questions relative to the history of our Saxon ancestors. In 1833 he was made one of a commission to inquire into the state of municipal corporations, but dissented from the report issued by his brother commissioners, and afterwards published the reasons which induced him to take that course. He was then appointed Deputy-Keeper of the Public Records, in which capacity he annually presents a report to Parliament. Sir Francis has published a great variety of contributions to the history of our country, the success of which must be ascribed to the exercise of his natural taste, and the facilities which his position affords him in their composition. Of these are his "Rotuli Curiæ Regis," "Ancient Calendars and Inventories of the Treasury of the Exchequer," "History of Normandy and England," &c. He still holds the office of Deputy-Keeper of the Public Records under the Master of the Rolls.

PALMERSTON, HENRY JOHN TEMPLE, VISCOUNT, an English statesman and diplomatist, was born at Broadlands, Hampshire, on 20th October, 1784. His title belongs to the Irish peerage, although he is of Saxon descent. After being some time at Harrow, he studied at Edinburgh, and subsequently graduated in 1806 at Cambridge. He contested Cambridge unsuccessfully with the present Lord Lansdowne, and entered Parliament as member for Bletchingley. After sitting for Newport, Isle of Wight, he became member for the University of Cambridge. The talents of Lord Palmerston attracted general attention in the House at this time, and in 1807 he was called to fill an official position as a Junior Lord of the Admiralty, and subsequently as Secretary-at-War in 1809, an office he retained for nearly twenty years. During this period his political views seem to have undergone considerable modification, and eventually assumed so liberal a form as to permit him to join a Whig Cabinet. Accordingly in 1830 he became Foreign Secretary, and in this position attained a diplomatic status in Europe which has acquired for him either the fear or esteem of continental states. Retiring in 1834, he resumed his office in 1835, became member for the borough of Tiverton, which he has ever since represented, and continued in office under Lord Melbourne till 1841, when Sir Robert Peel came into power. In 1846 Lord Palmerston became Minister for Foreign Affairs under Lord John Russell; but differences with that statesman in 1851, in reference to the policy of this country in connexion with the then passing events in France, led to his resignation. In 1852 he took office under Lord Aberdeen, as Secretary for Home Affairs, which he filled till 1855.

Owing to the strong feeling existing in the country at that period, in reference to the conduct of the war against Russia, Lord Aberdeen was compelled to resign. This circumstance made way for the elevation of Lord Palmerston, and he was next called to exercise his eminent talents as Prime Minister, in the early part of 1855. Having, however, shown a leaning to French policy, by introducing into the House the celebrated "Conspiracy Bill," shortly after the attempt by Orsini on the life of the Emperor of the French, a storm of indignation compelled him to retire. He was succeeded by Lord Derby, who, in turn, had to resign in 1859. Lord Palmerston then returned to power as Premier, an office he still holds (1860). Having confined this sketch to the mere historical statement of the offices held by Lord Palmerston, it may be further remarked, that as a diplomatist he has been identified with the foreign policy of this country in some of the most important events of the last fifty years. The affairs of Italy, Spain, Portugal, France, and their various revolutions, have called on him during that period for the exercise of the highest qualities which a politician can possess. His evident partiality for the policy pursued by the Emperor of France, has given umbrage in some quarters. As an administrator of home matters he has shown himself liberal; and in the distribution of church patronage has gained the respect of the best friends of the Church of England. During the past session, attempts were made to pass a Reform Bill, which was introduced by Lord John Russell, and strenuous efforts were made by the Opposition to remove Lord Palmerston from power; but in this, as in most other affairs, his sagacity and discretion have proved a match for his opponents. Although between seventy and eighty years of age, his personal appearance, activity, and industry would do credit to a much junior man; and in the present state of political parties, it is a question if any man amongst our statesmen could be found who would more ably, or in so popular a manner, conduct public affairs.

PANIZZI, Antonio, the Librarian of the British Museum, was born in the Duchy of Modena, in 1797. He studied classics at Reggio, and law at Parma, where he took his doctor's degree. In the Italian troubles of 1821 he was seriously compromised, but eventually succeeded in reaching England, where, through the influence of Mr. Roscoe and Lord Brougham, he was appointed to the Chair of Italian Literature in the University of London. Subsequently, in 1831, he became Assistant Librarian at the British Museum. He was in 1856 nominated Principal Librarian of that institution, and has rendered great service to the public by his improvements in its management. He has published a few excellent works on Italian Literature, among which the most attractive is his edition of "Orlando Furioso."

PANMURE, The Right Honourable Fox Maule, K.T., G.C.B., a British statesman and peer, was born at Brechin, in 1801. His early education was received at the Charterhouse, from which he entered the army as ensign, and for some time served in Canada. On returning to England, he entered Parliament as member for Perthshire in 1835, and subsequently was Under-Secretary for Home Affairs. Having lost his seat, he afterwards represented the Elgin Burghs, but soon again became member for his old constituency. He held office in the Board of Trade, the Board of Control, and was Secretary at War for some time. On the death of his father in 1852, he removed to the House of Lords, and in 1855 became Secretary at War under Lord Palmertson. The management of Crimean affairs now devolved on him, and his administration in this department of his duties was attended with the happiest results to the army. He effected many reforms in most of the military branches of the service, and continued to hold office till the fall of Lord Palmerston in 1858. Since then he has not taken any prominent part in political affairs. As a private nobleman, Lord Panmure is highly esteemed, and he extends a liberal hand in attempts to improve the moral and mental condition of the tenants and others on his estates in Scotland.

PARDOE, Miss Julia, an English authoress, was born at Beverley, in 1812. Her taste for literature was early evinced, and after proceeding to Portugal for the benefit of her health, she produced a highly successful work, called "Traits and Traditions of Portugal," and which laid the basis of her future fame. After her return to England she went to Turkey, and there acquired a mass of interesting facts relating to Turkish life and customs, which she gave to the world in a most fascinating work, the "City of the Sultan." The peculiarly facile style which Miss Pardoe exhibits in all her productions, has secured her great popularity. Her "Romance of the Harem," "The Confessions of a Pretty Woman," "Flies in Amber," "The City of the Magyar," &c., have been extensively read. The latter was written during a sojourn of nine months in Hungary. Amongst her historical works the most conspicuous are her Lives of Louis XIV., Francis I., and Marie de Medici.

PARIS, Count of, Louis Philippe Albert, Duke of Orleans, head of the younger branch of the house of Bourbon, and heir of Louis Philippe I., King of the French, was born in August, 1838, and is the son of Ferdinand Philippe, Duke of Orleans. His father was accidentally killed by a fall from his horse, while riding in the Champs Elysées on the 13th of July, 1842, to the great grief of the king and of the French nation. The mother of the Count de Paris, the Duchess Hélène of Mecklenburg-Schwerin, after the melancholy catastrophe that deprived her of a husband, devoted herself with all the tenderness and energy possible to the education of her sons. On the abdication of Louis-Philippe, after the fatal days of February 1848, in favour of the Count de Paris, the Duchess attended in the Chamber of Deputies, leading her son, then in his tenth year, by the hand, to hear the abdication read, and to claim the vacant crown for his young head. The Chamber, touched by the scene, appeared on the point of yielding, when a loud voice, from some unknown and never discovered spectator in the gallery, suddenly called out the fatal words, "Too late." The ominous expression was but too truly expressive of the real state of the case, and of the popular feeling out of doors. It immediately changed the aspect and intention of the Chamber, which accepted the abdication of the old king; but not the succession of the new one; and proclaimed "The Republic" one and indivisible. Since that time the young prince has lived in exile, mostly with his mother, until the death of that estimable lady in May, 1858, and sometimes in England with the other members of the Orleans family. A party in France, though at present neither large nor influential, regards this prince as the future constitutional monarch of the country, in whom in the course of nature the claims of the two families of the house of Bourbon will finally merge. The surviving uncles of the Count de Paris are the Duke de Nemours, the Prince Joinville, the Duke d'Aumale, and the Duke de Montpensier.

PARTON, Mrs. Sara P., née Willis, known to the reading public as "Fanny Fern," an American authoress, was born at Portland, in the State of Maine, on the 9th July, 1811. She is a sister of the well-known American author, N. P. Willis, and was educated at a seminary in Hartford, conducted by Miss Catherine Beecher, sister of Mrs. Harriet Beecher Stowe, the authoress of "Uncle Tom's Cabin." She was married in 1839 to Mr. Charles Eldredge, cashier of the Merchants' Bank in Boston ; but being left a widow in narrow circumstances, she resorted to her pen as a means of earning a livelihood for herself and her children. Her success was immediate, as she threw off in rapid succession a series of brief and racy sketches, which gave celebrity, first to the newspaper in which they appeared, and afterwards to herself. A volume of her collected articles, under the title of "Fern Leaves," reached the extraordinary sale of 70,000 copies. She has since published seven or eight volumes of tales and sketches, which have all been reprinted in England. During the last five years she has been a leading contributor to the "New York Ledger," a weekly literary journal, which has a circulation of 450,000, a success never before attained in the United States. The writings of this lady are pithy, bold, and original, and are pervaded at the same time by a humane and religious spirit ; their tendency being to quicken the intellect and improve the heart. She has exhibited a singular aptitude for engaging the attention of children, and few of her works have been more approved of than those designed for young folks, such as "Little Ferns," and the "Play-day Book."

PATMORE, COVENTRY, an English poet, was born at Woodford, in Essex, on 23rd July, 1823. His father was in his day a well-known literary celebrity, and in 1846 Mr. Coventry Patmore became an Assistant Librarian to the British Museum, which office he continues to hold. He has published three volumes, of which the second, the "Angel in the House," is a poem of undoubted merit ;

but the third, "Faithful for ever," has been severely criticised. He is understood to be a contributor to the "Edinburgh Review."

PATON, JOSEPH NOEL, R.S.A., an historical painter, was born at Dunfermline, in Fifeshire, in 1823. The son of Mr. J. F. Paton senior—an able artist and pattern designer, still living—he never studied at any public school of art, though in 1843 admitted a student of the Royal Academy of London. He first became known to the public as the author of "Outline Illustrations to Shakspere and Shelley ;" productions whose fanciful grace scarcely compensates for their want of simplicity and nature. His first serious effort was a cartoon of "The Spirit of Religion," produced in 1845. To the competition of 1847 he sent two oil-pictures of striking dissimilarity in character : "Christ Bearing the Cross," and "The Reconciliation of Oberon and Titania," the latter of which received the second class prize of £300, having been previously purchased for the Gallery of the Royal Scottish Academy. In 1849 he painted "The Quarrel of Oberon and Titania," now in the Scottish National Gallery, which, exhibited with other productions of modern English artists, at the Paris Exhibition of 1855, received "honourable mention" from the jurors. His pictures of "Dante," and "The Dead Lady," prepared the public for the more serious tone of succeeding works, and more especially for his large and elaborate allegorical picture, "The Pursuit of Pleasure," which confirmed the high reputation of the artist. "Home," representing the return of a Crimean soldier, exhibited at the Royal Academy in 1856, enjoyed a wide popularity, was esteemed as one of the artist's most perfect works, and copied for the Royal Exhibition by command of her Majesty. "In Memoriam," a work of high aim and minute truthfulness of execution, was one of the leading pictures in the Royal Academy's exhibition of 1858. The earlier works of this painter are characterised by overflowing fancy and elaborate detail; those which he has produced of later years have obviously a higher and more serious purpose, and, though not less minute in execution, are much more true to nature. The prices which this artist has received for his recent works, show the high estimation in which he is held. His "Pursuit of Pleasure," sold to Mr. A. Hill, a printseller of Edinburgh, was again sold by him for two thousand guineas, while "In Memoriam" fetched twelve hundred pounds.

PAXTON, SIR JOSEPH, an architect and horticulturist, was born at Milton Bryant, in 1802, and was educated in the Free School of Woburn, Bedfordshire. His abilities as a gardener were the means of introducing him to the Duke of Devonshire; and after remaining some time at Chiswick, he went to Chatsworth, and by the taste and skill which he evinced in the gardens of that beautiful domain, soon became well known in his profession. In the erection of extensive glass conservatories, Sir Joseph obtained the germ of the idea which was afterwards expanded in the Crystal Palace of 1851, and of which he was the designer and architect. For his exertions and success in this novel and noble undertaking he received the honour of knighthood. Since then, Sir Joseph has been connected with many public works. He superintended the construction of the Palace, and designed the plan of the grounds, at Sydenham. The beautiful park at the west end of Glasgow was laid out on plans furnished by him. Sir Joseph sits in the House of Commons as Member for Coventry, which city he has represented since 1854. He is a member of many of the learned societies in Europe, and has published works on horticulture and botany, which are highly popular.

PAYEN, ANSELME, a French chemist, and member of the Institute, was born at Paris, in January, 1795. Son of a gentleman of property, who was thrown into industrial enterprises by the Revolution, M. Payen studied chemistry under Vauquelin and others, and was admitted to the Polytechnic School. He embraced the new career of his father with ardour, and directed at Vaugirard an important manufactory of sugar from beet-root. He continued at the head of this establishment for a number of years, extending his attention to various other articles, and introducing new applications of science, which materially contributed to reduce the cost of a number of articles of food in ordinary use. M. Payen has filled various municipal situations at Vaugirard and Grenelle, and was one of the reporters on French Industry, from 1827 to 1844. In 1836 he became member of the council and a professor of the School of Arts and Manufactures. He has since undertaken a similar charge at the Conservatoire des Arts et Métiers, and is a member of numerous scientific societies. In 1847 he was created an officer of the Legion of Honour. M. Payen has written a considerable number of works, the principal of which are devoted to agricultural and industrial chemistry; he has also contributed to periodicals many papers of value.

PEDRO V., KING OF PORTUGAL, PEDRO D' ALCANTARA MARIA FERNANDO MIGUEL RAPHAEL GABRIEL GONZAGA XAVIER JOÃO ANTONIO LEOPOLDO VICTOR FRANCISCO D'ASSIS JULIO ANEOLIO, names enough for all the sovereigns of Europe, born September 1837, is son of Donna Maria II. di Gloria and Fernando of Saxe-Coburg-Gotha, King Consort. He succeeded his mother under his father's regency; visited England in 1853, and the Great Exhibition of Paris in 1855, also making.

a tour of Italy, Switzerland, and Belgium. He attained his majority in 1855. In 1857 he married the Princess Stephanie Frederica Wilhelmina Antoine, of Hohenzollern-Sigmaringen ; but in less than two years her Majesty died, leaving no family to aid in the consolation of the bereaved husband. The relations of Portugal with the British Court are intimate and cordial ; and do not threaten to be impaired under the present popular and enlightened monarch.

PEEL, FREDERICK, son of the late Sir Robert Peel, was born in London, in 1823, and educated at Harrow and Cambridge. Called to the bar in 1849, he was, in the same year, elected member for Leominster, and in 1852 returned for Bury, taking his place among the liberal-conservative party. He was appointed Under-Secretary for the Colonies in 1851, resigning on Lord Derby's accession in March, 1852. In the Coalition and subsequent administrations, he held the same office from December, 1852, till February, 1855. From the last date till 1857, he was Under-Secretary at War ; in 1857 he failed to obtain a seat in Parliament ; but at the general election of 1859, he was again elected for Bury.

PEEL, THE RIGHT HONOURABLE JONATHAN, Secretary at War in the late Derby administration, and Lieutenant-General in the British army, is the fifth son of the first Sir Robert Peel, and was born on the 12th of October, 1799. He entered the army in 1815, just before the great European conflicts of forty years were about to close ; and has risen, in the ordinary course of promotion, to his present rank as a general. In 1826 he was returned by Norwich as its representative in the House of Commons, and continued to sit for that town during the five following years. In 1831 he was returned for Huntingdon, which he has represented ever since the passing of the Reform Bill. From 1841 to 1846 he held office under his brother, the late Sir Robert Peel, as Surveyor-General of Ordnance. From 1846 until 1858 he remained out of office. Upon the formation, in the February of that year, of the government of Lord Derby, he accepted the appointment of principal Secretary at War, resigning with the ministry in 1859.

PEEL, SIR ROBERT, BART., eldest son of the late statesman of the same name, born in London in 1822, was educated at Harrow and Cambridge, and entered on a diplomatic career in 1844 as an Attaché to the embassy at Madrid, passing to Switzerland in 1846, as Secretary of Legation, and after some months in that capacity, remaining till 1850 as Chargé d'Affaires. At the latter date he succeeded his father, and was elected member for Tamworth ; and his views being of a liberal cast, Lord Palmerston appointed him one of the Lords of the Admiralty in 1855. He afterwards accompanied Lord Granville on the special embassy to the coronation of the Czar ; but on his return to England resigned his connexion with the ministry. Since then he has taken but little part in public affairs, except on continental questions, speaking strongly against the aggressive designs of Louis Napoleon.

PÉLISSIER, AMABLE JEAN JACQUES, DUC DE MALAKOF, Marshal in the French army, was born at Maromme, on the 6th November, 1794. After completing his general and military education at St. Cyr, he entered the French military service, and obtaining promotion, went to Spain in 1823, where he highly distinguished himself. From his return home till 1829 he was occupied in various services, and in that year proceeded to Greece, where his talents and bravery again became conspicuous, and were duly rewarded. His next campaign was undertaken in Africa, serving in Algiers, till from the failure of his health he was obliged to return to France. In 1840 he was again sent to Africa, and had to contend with the wild tribes of the desert for some years. It is to be regretted that the name of so great a man should ever have been tarnished ; but from his having, as a *dernier ressort*, destroyed some six hundred human beings, in a cavern into which they had retreated, by burning fagots at its mouth, Pélissier drew on himself the indignation of all civilized countries. However, in a few years afterwards, his bold and gallant behaviour in the Crimea effaced these evil reminiscences. He joined the French army before Sebastopol in 1855, and succeeding Canrobert in the chief command, was highly successful, and for his gallantry was created Duke of Malakof, Marshal of France, and G.C.B. of Great Britain. He succeeded M. Persigny as Ambassador to London in 1858, from which office, however, he retired a short time since.

PELOUZE, Théophile Jules, a French chemist, was born at Valognes, in February, 1807. After studying pharmacy, he proceeded to Paris in 1827, where he was engaged as an assistant in a laboratory, with Gay-Lussac and Lassaigne. He remained in that position for two years, and assisted in maturing various discoveries. The municipality of Lille having founded a Chair of Chemistry, M. Pelouze was appointed Professor in 1830. In this position, one of his earliest investigations was into the nature, the composition, and the qualities of beet-root sugar. He pursued this and other inquiries, until he was invited to Paris to supply the place of his old teacher, Gay-Lussac, at the Polytechnic School. In 1836 he visited Germany, where he cultivated the friendship ,of M. Liebig, subsequently making various useful scientific discoveries. He was admitted to the Academy of Sciences in 1837, and filled various chairs in the College of France and the Polytechnic School. Since 1849 he has been a member of the Municipal Council of Paris, without abandoning the practice of instructing pupils. He resigned his last professorship in 1851, shortly afterwards being created Commander of the Legion of Honour. His scientific writings have been very numerous, chiefly in the form of papers and lectures, which have appeared in the " Annales de Chimie et de Physique ; " and it is universally conceded that his essays elevate him to a level with the highest cotemporary chemists. He is at present President of the Imperial Mint at Paris.

PENNEFATHER, Lieutenant-General Sir John Lysaght, was born in the county of Tipperary, in 1800, and entered the army in 1818. He greatly distinguished himself in India in 1843, during the war in Scinde, and for his gallantry received the thanks of the British Parliament. He was present in the Crimea during the Russian war, and at the Alma performed prodigies of valour, and likewise in the battle of Inkermann. He is a Knight Commander of the Bath, and the Emperor of the French conferred on him the order of the Legion of Honour.

PENNETHORNE, James, an architect and surveyor, was born in Worcester in 1801. He went to London in 1820, remained with Pugin two years, and then travelled through Italy and Sicily. In 1828 he became principal assistant to Nash, and planned a great number of works both public and private. He was appointed to a situation in connexion with the Woods and Forests, which he still retains. Some of the leading improvements in the formation of new streets in London have been effected under his superintendence, and he is held in high esteem by his brethren in the profession.

PEPE, Florestan, an Italian general,

was born in Calabria, in 1780. He entered the army when young, and was a Lieutenant when the French entered Naples in 1799. He served in Spain as Brigade Major in 1806, and rose gradually until, in 1811, he held the rank of General of Brigade. In 1812, during the Russian campaign he led his Italian corps to Dantzic, and during the retreat he covered with his cavalry the French rear-guard. Ill and severely wounded, he fell into the hands of the enemy, after having performed extraordinary feats of valour. Liberated, he returned to Italy, and in 1815, for the gallant stand he made against the Austrians in Upper Italy, Murat gave him the grade of Lieutenant-General. To quell the insurrectionary movements of 1820 he was sent to Sicily with 5,000 men, but the terms of the capitulation of Palermo not being satisfactory to those in power, he was dismissed and went abroad, afterwards residing in Naples as a private individual. In 1848 he resigned his honours, together with his position as a general on active service. Since then his name has rarely come before the public.

PEPE, GABRIEL, brother of Florestan, was born at Bojano, in 1781. He studied law, but forsook it for the army in 1799. His first prominent appearance as a soldier was in 1806, when he took service under Joseph Bonaparte, and passed through the Spanish campaigns. He was a Colonel under Murat, yet after the restoration of King Ferdinand he commanded a regiment, and held the garrison of Syracuse. At the revolution of 1820 he was named a member of the National Parliament at Naples, and voted for the removal of his brother; but when the Bourbon dynasty was again restored, he was arrested and cast into prison at Olmutz, where he was confined strictly for two years. After his release he retired to Florence, and instead of embroiling himself with politics he turned

his mind to the pursuits of science. Removing from Florence, he fixed his abode at Nice, where he has resided for a number of years.

PEPOLI, CHARLES, an Italian littérateur, was born at Bologna, of a noble family, in 1801. His education was received at various academies, but chiefly in that of his native city, where he devoted himself to the study of the Fine Arts. When but a young man he was introduced to public life; and at the insurrection of Central Italy in 1831, he was one of the members of the Provisional Government of Bologna. The revolution stifled, Signor Pepoli and a large number of his compatriots embarked for Corfu, but the ship was captured by the Austrians, and all the passengers, ninety-six in number, were brought to Venice as prisoners of war. M. Pepoli suffered much for some months of his captivity, and, eventually exiled, he landed in France. From Paris he repaired to Geneva, but returned to the former city at the request of Bellini the composer, for whom he wrote the libretto of "I Puritani," afterwards producing libretti for two operas, one by Costa, the other by Vaccai. In 1837 he settled in London, and after two years of literary difficulties he was appointed Professor of Italian Literature in the London University. Taking a lively interest in Italian affairs, he was called to Rome as a deputy in 1848, and elected Vice-President of the Assembly. When the Italian cause broke down he returned to London, but owing to infirm health he was compelled to suspend his literary labours, though, after his country, they formed the dearest attachment of his life. He retained his professorship for nine years, and is a facile and eloquent writer.

PERSIGNY, JEAN-GILBERT-VICTOR FIALIN, a French politician and diplomatist, was born in January, 1808. His father having lost his patrimony by bad speculations, entered the army, and was killed at the battle of Salamanca, in 1812. Victor Persigny commenced his studies at Limoges, removing to Saumur, and afterwards serving as Quartermaster to a regiment of Hussars (1828). At this period his opinions were Royalist; but owing to certain influences they became greatly modified, and in 1830 he took an active part in the military movements of Pontivy, which favoured the revolution of July. He went to Paris in 1833, in search of employment, and became for a short period attached to the "Temps" journal. He some time afterwards undertook a journey to Baden, and through Bavaria and Wurtemberg, and on his return published an account of his observations. Though an active supporter of the Bourbons, he appears in 1834 to have been converted to the cause of the Bonapartes, and in a paper which he founded, he advocated the cause of the "Napoleon ideas" with great vigour. He attached himself to Louis Napoleon, and was the principal instigator of the Strasbourg attempt. He clung to the fortunes of the Prince, whether for good or evil, followed him in his dangers, and prompted his measures. He was tried, imprisoned, and released when health failed him. In 1848, he fulfilled his part, in adopting with great zeal the Bonapartist cause, and aiding everywhere the election of Louis Napoleon, as President of the Republic. He was not unrewarded. The President elevated him in position, and it was he who afterwards carried out, if he did not plan, the *coup d'état.* In 1852 he was appointed Minister of the Interior, but in 1854 he resigned on account of his health; was afterwards appointed Minister at the British Court (1855), and retained that post till 1858, when he was succeeded by Marshal Pélissier. He married a Russian lady in 1852, and received with her a large marriage portion, and a

gift and the title of Count from the Emperor. He afterwards returned to London, as ambassador, where he still remains.

PETERMANN, August Heinrich, a German geographer, now Director of the celebrated establishment of Justus Perthes, in Gotha, was born at Bleicherode, in Prussia. He showed an early predilection for geographical studies, and was sent to Potsdam as special pupil of the *savant* Berghaus, in 1839. He remained at Potsdam, and there acquired the friendship of Humboldt, who entrusted him in 1841 with the execution of his "Map of Central Asia." In 1845 he assisted Mr. A. K. Johnston, of Edinburgh, in preparing the "Physical Atlas," and, two years after, proceeded to London, where he published his "Atlas of Physical Geography." He was a zealous promoter of the expeditions of Barth to Africa. In 1855 the University of Göttingen conferred on him the degree of Doctor of Philosophy. He founded in the same year his "Geographical Journal," the best work of the kind in existence, which has attained a large circulation, five thousand copies being published every month, with a running collection of excellent maps of the most important new discoveries and geographical investigations. Sir Roderick Murchison said of this work, in his "President's Address to the Royal Geographical Society," in 1857—that "it is exercising a powerful and salutary influence on the progress of geographical science." "The American Journal for Science and Art" makes the remark, in the following year, that "Mr. Petermann, by his wide correspondence and relations with various scientific men in England, Germany, and America, is better able than any other man of science to give early and reliable intelligence in respect to all important explorations."

PETO, Sir Samuel Morton, Bart., M.P., a contractor for large engineering works, was born at Woking, in Surrey, in 1809. He was placed for seven years with his uncle, Henry Peto, a contractor and builder, under whom he obtained a thorough and practical insight into the various branches of the business to which, on his uncle's death in 1830, he succeeded, in conjunction with his cousin, Mr. Thomas Grissell, of Norbury Park. After the dissolution of partnership with that gentleman in 1845, Mr. Peto devoted his attention chiefly to railway works, both alone, and jointly with Mr. Brassey and Mr. Betts, and constructed various important undertakings, amongst which may be mentioned, the Western Railway of France; the Grand Trunk Railway of Canada, including the Tubular Bridge, two miles long, over the St. Lawrence, near Montreal, lately opened by H.R.H. the Prince of Wales (September, 1860), confessedly the largest work of its kind in the world; the Royal Danish Railway, and many others, both on the Continent and in England. During the Russian war in 1854, Mr. Peto constructed for the Government a line of railway from Balaklava to the English camp before Sebastopol, and that in the most disinterested manner to himself, and at the cost of his seat in the House of Commons, for Norwich, which city he had represented for several years. In recognition of this patriotic service, the honour of a baronetcy was in the following year conferred upon him by her Majesty. In 1859 Sir Morton was invited to become a candidate for Finsbury, and was returned by a larger number of votes than had ever previously been polled in that important metropolitan borough. Sir Morton Peto was one of the Royal Commissioners for the Great Exhibition. He is a Director of many railway and other companies, and a Deputy-lieutenant for Suffolk. Sir Morton Peto makes good use of his great wealth, in building and

endowing chapels and schools, and his purse and influence are ever open for the furtherance of any scheme calculated to promote the happiness and welfare of his fellow-creatures.

PHELPS, Samuel, an English tragedian, was born at Devonport, in 1806. He was not intended for any particular profession, and should have gone to Cambridge, where his brother, the present Master of Sidney College (the Rev. Dr. Phelps), is still; but his attachment to the dramatic art overcame all other aspirations, and in 1827 he made his first appearance at the York Theatre. His early career, like that of all performers, was chequered with reverses; but he was an earnest and persevering student of his art; and his versatility was without limit, his tragedy and his comedy being true to nature. His talents were not long overlooked by London managers, and accordingly he was engaged at the Theatre Royal, Haymarket; appearing first as "Shylock," and afterwards as "Hamlet." When Mr. Macready undertook the management of Covent Garden, Mr. Phelps was at once secured as a leading man among a brilliant band of actors; and many critics pronounced him the only performer on whom the mantle of Macready was worthy to descend:-which opinion Mr. Macready also expressed in his speech at the dinner given him on his retirement from the stage in 1851. The legitimate drama was at the lowest point, when Mr. Phelps resolved to attempt its revival in what was deemed an uncongenial region. In 1844 he opened Sadlers' Wells Theatre, and in that unclassic locality his experiment was completely successful. His skill in management, his own unrivalled acting, and his judicious selection of performers, carried all before them. He created a new era in the drama, and the "Wells" became famous as a theatre where the plays of Shakspeare were enacted. He has continued to manage that theatre until the present time without a failure, maintaining his place as an artist, who unites the force of the old histrionic masters with the more subtle discrimination of the modern school. He has edited an excellent edition of Shakspeare, a work for which he was eminently qualified by learning and experience.

PHILLIPS, JOHN, M.A., LL.D., F.R.S., Professor of Geology in the University of Oxford, and Assistant-general Secretary of the British Association, was born on December 25th, 1800. Few living geologists possess a more intimate or wider acquaintance with the geology of England. With his uncle, William Smith, the father of English geology, he early acquired that intimate and practical knowledge of his favourite science which has rendered him so acceptable and valuable a teacher. In addition to his independent works, Mr. Phillips, in his capacity of Secretary to the British Association, has arranged and edited twenty-seven volumes of reports of proceedings and transactions. Mr. Phillips succeeded Dr. Buckland in the chair of geology at Oxford, having previously occupied similar positions in King's College, London, and Trinity College, Dublin. He was elected President of the Geological Society in 1858 and 1859.

PICCOLOMINI, MARIA, was born at Sienna in 1835. When only a child she gave the highest promise of the eminence she has since attained. Her parents, desirous of encouraging her favourite passion, confided her musical education to Romani, one of the leading professional teachers in Italy. Under his instructions she made her *début* in Florence, in 1852, in "Lucrezia Borgia." For twenty successive nights, and always with immense success, did she appear in this part. On the last night of her engagement at the theatre, a band of young men, enthusiastic in their admira-

tion of the *artiste*, sought to usurp the place of the horses in her carriage. Piccolomini sternly rebuked their levity, and ironically called upon them to keep their strength for their country. After this successful *début* in the capital of Tuscany, she spent four years in a tour through Italy, remaining a season at each place of importance. Wherever she appeared, she immediately became a favourite. This Italian triumph at once attracted the attention of the directors of the operas of London and Paris; and, in 1856, Mademoiselle Piccolomini appeared, for the first time, before an English audience. Her success in England and America has been equal to that she attained in Italy, but she was severely censured by the critics for choosing to appear as the heroine in "Traviata," one of Verdi's most finished productions. The lady's success has sprung more from her youth, her *naïveté*, and her dramatic power, which is unquestionably great, than from her vocalism.

PICKERSGILL, FRED. RICHARD, R.A., a painter, was born in London in 1820, and studied at the Royal Academy. His first oil picture, "The Combat between Hercules and Achelous," was produced in 1840. At the Exhibiton in Westminster Hall in 1843, Mr. Pickersgill received a prize for his cartoon of the "Death of King Lear," and in 1847 one of the first-class prizes for the "Burial of Harold." This picture was of great advantage to him in his career. His powers had before been doubted, but the drawing and execution of this work were excellent, and the picture was at once purchased for the New Houses of Parliament. In that year he was elected A.R.A., and in 1857 became a Royal Academican. Since then he has been a regular exhibitor.

PIUS IX., GIOVANNI MARIA MASTAÏ FERRETTI, was born in Sinigaglia, on the 13th of May, 1792. At the age of sixteen he went to Rome with the intention of completing his ecclesiastical studies, his desires having always tended to the priesthood. But in consequence of the sad events which shortly afterwards ensued, he retired in 1810 to Sinigaglia. Two years after this he was summoned to join the guard of honour in Milan, but an exemption was granted him on account of, epileptic fits, to which he was then subject. He continued to reside in his native city until the return of Pius VII. to the States of the Church, after which he hastened once more to Rome. He was ordained priest in 1819, and sent in 1823 upon a special mission to South America. In 1827 he became Archbishop of Spoleto, and afterwards of Imola. During his episcopate he was remarkable for the assiduity with which he discharged his duties. He was elected Pope on the 16th of June, 1846, and crowned on the 21st of the same month. Seated in the chair of St. Peter, he gave himself to the task of granting liberal reforms to his people, but his intentions were frustrated by the violence of the extreme revolutionary party, and he was ultimately forced in 1848 to leave his capital, and to take refuge at Gaeta. He was restored to Rome by the arms of France, in 1850. The war of 1859 in Italy occasioned fresh disturbances in the Legations, and Napoleon III., by an autograph letter of December of the same year, counselled the Pope to give up the disturbed provinces; but in an encyclical letter of the 19th of January, 1860, Pius IX. declared that he could never consent to any dismemberment of his states. In August of this year, when the progress of Garibaldi in Italy threatened the entire destruction of the Papal power, the Pope placed his forces under the command of Lamoricière, who endeavoured by enlisting Germans, Swiss, and Irish, to form an army which might enable him to resist the progress of the enemy. But Sardinia having sent a large army, under the command of Cialdini, into the States, many of the provinces near Rome broke out into insurrection. The result has been that Lamoricière was routed, the Roman forces entirely disbanded, and the Pope has now no support of any kind but that of the French garrison in Rome.

**PLANCHE, JAMES. ROBINSON,** a dramatist and historian, was born in London, in February, 1796. Receiving his early instruction from his mother, a lady of literary habits, his inclination for the drama was early manifested; and a burlesque of his having been produced in 1818, at Drury-lane Theatre, with complete success, he determined to pursue dramatic authorship as his profession. He devoted his attention especially to matters of costume, and furnished Mr. Charles Kemble with numerous designs for the costume proper to the representation of Shakspeare's plays. In 1826 and 1827 he travelled on the Continent, afterwards publishing his "Lays and Legends of the Rhine," and the "Descent of the Danube." In 1828 his dramatic work, and perhaps his best, "Charles XII.," was brought out at Drury-lane. His "History of British Costume" was published in 1834, the "Regal Records" in 1838, and the "Pursuivant of Arms" in 1852. In 1855 he published the "Countess d'Aulnoy's Fairy Tales," which for excellence admits of no comparison. Mr. Planché has, at one time and another, written a great number of dramatic pieces, not one of which has failed. He is a Rouge Croix Pursuivant at Arms.

**PLAYFAIR, LYON, C.B.,** an English chemist, was born in Bengal, in 1819. He received his early education at St. Andrew's University, Fifeshire; and from his decided taste for chemical pursuits was sent to Glasgow to study under Mr. Graham. After returning

Lyon Playfair

from India, whither he had gone on account of ill health, he placed himself as an assistant to his old master, who had then become Professor of Chemistry in University College, London. In 1839 he was induced to proceed to Giessen, whose laboratory was under the management of Liebig; and, like many other eminent British chemists, he studied organic chemistry under that celebrated professor, engaged in original investigations, and became Doctor of Philosophy of Giessen University. After holding the Professorship of Chemistry at the Royal Institution, Manchester, Dr. Playfair removed to London, where he was much employed in royal commissions and Government inquiries, and took an active part in the Exhibition of 1851. He was also appointed Inspector-General of Schools and Museums of Science, to the Government. In 1858 he was elected to the Chemical Chair in the University of Edinburgh, vacant by the death of another of Liebig's pupils, Dr. Gregory.

POERIO, CARLO, was born at Naples, in 1803. He is the second son of the celebrated lawyer, Joseph Poerio, Baron of Balustro. At twelve years of age Carlo followed his father into exile, who had been counsellor of state and attorney-general in the High Court of Justice at Naples. Carlo was educated at Florence, with his only brother Alexander, and his cousin the Duke of Diano, by some of the most distinguished professors in Tuscany. He afterwards returned to Naples with his father, but followed him again into exile in 1821, when the constitution fell, and with it the Chamber, of which he had been member. On this occasion, for State reasons, his father was banished to Austria, together with Generals Colleta (the historian), Arcovite, and Padrinelli, and the deputies Borelli (the philosopher) and Pepe. In 1824 the Poerio family went to Tuscany, and Carlo remained in Florence with them until 1828, when he accompanied his mother to Naples, where he applied himself to his studies, and to the profession of an advocate, and became distinguished as the leading gratuitous defender of prisoners at the High Court of Justice. Living in the closest intimacy with the leading men of the country, and professing openly the principles of representative government, his politics were distasteful to the ruling powers, and he was three times subjected to prosecution for political offences. In 1848, when a free and representative government was introduced into Naples, Carlo Poerio was chosen by the King as Director, and Under-Secretary for Home Affairs, and, as such, he had charge of the general police regulations of the kingdom; and after filling these posts for a month, he was advanced to a seat in the cabinet as Minister of Public Instruction. The Duke of Sorracapriola, the Chevalier Beralli, Prince Cariata, Baron Savarese, Prince Torella, General Degli Uberti, Counsellor Saliceti, Baron Bonani, and Prince Dentice, were his colleagues. In his ministerial position he took part in the council which was held, at the instance of Lord Minto, for the settlement of the Sicilian question. Carlo resigned office on the 3rd April, 1848, and he was returned to parliament at the general election, as deputy for the city of Naples, and province of Terra-di-lavora. On the sad 15th May, when the lazzaroni were set on by the King's myrmidons to pillage the city of Naples, he was sent upon a deputation to the ministry, with his colleagues Capitelli, Pica, and Imbriata, and struggled hard to avert that fratricidal conflict. Having been re-elected to the Chamber, after the *coup d'état*, for Naples and Gaeta, he sat on the opposition, and strenuously defended the constitution, to which the King had sworn, against the inroads of a reactionary policy. When the Chamber was dissolved, and the dreadful system of persecution, which continued for the last ten years, commenced, Poerio resorted to every lawful means in combating the deceitful spirit of re-action. The government then offered passports to Poerio ; but he, having re-fused to leave the country, was impri-soned provisionally, as a matter of pre-caution, with some of the most distin-guished men of his country, until the celebrated prosecution of the "Unita Italiana" was laboriously concerted for his destruction. After the revelations disclosed by Mr. Gladstone, of that judi-cial assassination, derived from honest and impartial witnesses, it would be superfluous to dwell on them particu-larly. He bore the terrible consequences without flinching, with a firm and serene mind, and without addressing a single word of remonstrance to the govern-ment during the entire ten years of his suffering. Released from his dungeon by the late King of Naples in 1859, he, with Settembrini and a number of others, was placed on board a vessel bound for the United States. The crew of the ship was not so numerous as were the exiles. The Italians took no practical advantage of their strength, but, waiting on the captain, informed him of their determination to put into the nearest British harbour. Remon-strance was useless, and the exiles were landed at Cork, Poerio proceeding direct to London ; his companions, headed by Settembrini, making their way to Bristol, thence to the metropolis. Po-erio's gentleness, and abstinence from all demonstrations of ill-feeling, have gained for him the friendship of men of all political parties.

POGGENDORF, John Christian, a German physicist and chemist, was born at Hamburg, on the 29th December, 1796. He studied in his native city, and afterwards proceeded to Berlin, where he became in 1834 Professor of Physics in the University, and in 1839 Member of the Academy of Sciences. His earliest appearance as a writer on subjects of science was in 1821, when he published a paper "On the Magnetism of the Voltaic Pile." In 1824 he un-dertook the editorship of the "Annals of Physics and Chemistry," which, under his management, became one of the first scientific journals of Germany ; and he subsequently joined Wöhler and Liebig in the publication of a "Dictionary of Chemistry," which is also received as a standard work. He has published several papers on the exact sciences, but his researches seem to have been more especially directed to electricity and magnetism, the department of physics in which the greatest progress has been made in our time. He invented in 1827 the magnetometer, afterwards used by Arago and others in their researches in terrestrial magnetism. His valuable writings are written in a clear style, and replete with suggestive observations.

POLLOCK, Right Hon. Sir Frede-rick, an English judge, was born in London in 1783. Having received an excellent preliminary education at St. Paul's School, he entered Trinity College, Cambridge. Having chosen the law as a profession, he afterwards entered the Middle Temple, and was called to the bar in 1807. Becoming King's Counsel in 1827, he was elected member for Huntingdon in 1831, and assumed office as Attorney-General in 1834 ; again occupying that position, after various changes in the administration, in 1841. He was subsequently appointed, in 1844, Lord Chief Baron of the Exchequer, an office he retains at the present time. Sir Frederick received the honour of knighthood in 1834.

POOLE, Paul Falconer, A.R.A., an English painter, was born at Bristol, in 1810. His first work was "The Well, a Scene at Naples." His "Solo-mon Eagle exhorting the People to

Repentance," the subject being drawn from the history of the Plague in London; "The Beleaguered Moors;" and "The Visitation of Zion Monastery," exhibited in 1846, were triumphs of art, the latter work being specially admired for its free treatment and romantic conception, though not properly belonging to the romantic school. In 1847 he competed at Westminster Hall, gaining a second-class prize of £300. Since then he has produced a great number of works, attractive from their sentiment, true colouring, and dignity of manner. "Job, and his Friends receiving the Tidings of his Calamities," is Mr. Poole's most striking production, for he has travelled out of the beaten path of routine, and given free and full scope to his power of dealing with a massive subject in a massive style.

PORTUGAL, KING OF. (*See* PEDRO V.)

POTTER, CIPRIANI, a pianoforte player and composer, was born in London, in 1792. His father was a Professor of Music. Cipriani Potter had excellent instructors for the pianoforte and in the science of music, having also studied under the celebrated Woelfl. During a twelvemonth's sojourn in Vienna he renewed his study of counterpoint with Förster, and of composition with Beethoven. He spent two years on the Continent, adding to his stores of musical knowledge, and on returning to England was engaged in various musical avocations. On the death of Dr. Crotch, Mr. Potter succeeded him as Principal of the Royal Academy of Music in London, where he had been for years before one of the most distinguished professors. He is an active member of the London Philharmonic Society, and has done more than any other man in the profession to preserve and elevate the classical school of music. He has written numerous orchestral compositions, quartetts, &c.

POTTER, LOUIS JOSEPH ANTOINE DE, a Belgian statesman, was born at Bruges, April 1786, of a noble family, who were exiled at the Brabant Revolution, being suspected of Austrian partisanship, but it would appear without reason. M. Potter received his early education in Brussels, and from 1809 to 1811 he resided in France, whence he removed to Italy, where he remained for thirteen years. He returned to Brussels in 1824, and renounced his title of nobility, his father having died some time before. His first efforts were directed to uniting all parties in Belgium, Catholics and Liberals, against the common enemy of liberty of conscience and of toleration, and he published his opinions in the "Courrier des Pays Bas." Arraigned for this offence before the Court of Assize, in December 1828, although he had retained two eminent advocates, he fully stated himself his political creed, and demanded, in the name of justice, the abolition of the Censure, Ministerial responsibility, the restitution of trial by jury, the adoption of the French language in all matters official—in short, an entire change in the mode in which Holland had ruled Belgium. The sentence of the judges was an imprisonment of eighteen months, and the payment of a fine of 2,140 francs. The national party became all the more compact because of their champion's conviction; and M. Potter continued to write. The law of imprisonment for such escapades had been abrogated, yet still he was detained illegally. A new article from his hand, published in the journals, called down on him the rigour of the Executive, and he was sentenced to eight years' exile, and eight years' surveillance. This extreme condemnation took place in April 1830. Out of prison, Prussia and France refused him protection; but as time went onward, changes occurred for which he probably was not prepared. Belgium was separated from Holland, and M. Potter re-entered Belgium in triumph. During the brief period of the revolutionary conflicts of opinion, he was a member of the Provisional Government, and with all his energies advocated the establishment of a pure Republic. His views, however, were most strenuously opposed; and when the Provisional Government fell, he was obliged to take refuge in France. Since that period he has taken no active personal part in politics, but his writings have invariably tended to promote the principles which he so earnestly supported, alike during his difficulties and his comparative prosperity.

POUILLET, CLAUDE SERVAIS MATHIAS, a French physicist, and author of a number of philosophical and meteorological treatises, was born at Cuzance, February 1791. In 1811 he entered the Normal School, first as assistant-professor, afterwards becoming principal lecturer. He filled various important offices until 1829, when he was appointed sub-director of the Conservatoire des Arts et des Métiers and Professor of Physics in that institution. In 1831 he was chosen to succeed Dulong in the Chair of the Polytechnic School, but his health giving way he was constrained to resign his post. Some time afterwards he was named Director of the Conservatoire, and Professor in the Faculty of Sciences of Paris. He shone brilliantly at the Sorbonne; his manner was lively and animated; his elocution was graceful; his diction was pure and classic; and, above all, he possessed the art of interesting his audience. Attached to the Orleans' dynasty, M. Pouillet was returned to the Chamber as Deputy for Jura, and in that capacity supported the Ministers of the king. After the revolution of 1848, he retired from political life, and devoted himself to the work of public instruction in science. An *émeute* having broken out in the Conservatoire, in June 1849, M. Pouillet was accused of not having used sufficient energy for its repression, and, in consequence of the accusation, his appointment as Director was revoked. He justified his conduct with great ability, but without effect. After the *coup d'état* of 1851, he turned his entire attention to the correction and revisal of his formerly published works, and to the preparation of new treatises; not, however, neglecting the Academy, but in the meantime continuing one of its most active members. M. Pouillet is one of the most eloquent writers on science which France possesses.

POWERS, HIRAM, an American sculptor, was born at Woodstock, Vermont, 29th July, 1805. He is the son of a small farmer, whose untimely death left his family unprovided for. He commenced life as a waiter at an hotel in Cincinnati, but the bent of his genius soon showed itself; and being taken by the hand by a Prussian sculptor, he made rapid advances in designing and modelling. He then removed to Washington, where he succeeded so well that he was enabled to visit Italy. His powerful work, "The Greek Slave," is considered one of the finest pieces of sculpture of modern times.

PROCTER, BRYAN W., an English poet, who writes under the name of Barry Cornwall, was born in 1787. He was educated at Harrow, and being intended for the legal profession, was for two or three years in a solicitor's office in Wiltshire, before being called to the bar. For a number of years he has been a Commissioner in Lunacy. In addition to his poetical works, Mr. Procter has published essays and tales in prose, and is the author of "A Sicilian Story," "Marcian Colonna," "The Flood of Thessaly," and a series of "English Songs," a "Life of Edmund Kean," an "Essay on the Genius of Shakspeare," &c.

PROUDHON. PIERRE JOSEPH, an

eminent French political writer, was born at Besançon, July 1809. He was the eldest of five children of a poor cooper, and was destined to follow the trade of his father. Some benevolent persons noticed the boy's parts, and charitably paid for his education. He went, after some time, to be an apprentice to a printer; and was distinguished for his habits of order and the excellence of his work; while he led a life of privation, saving every sou to assist his parents. He refused, in 1830, to be connected with the management of a journal of the "prefecture," preferring to a ministerial sinecure the independence of an honest artisan, however obscure. As he laboured, he improved his mind; and from putting in type the writings of others, he began to be a writer himself. He proceeded to Paris, and after contributing to several periodical publications, he wrote on his own account, propounding the monstrous dogma, "La Propriété, c'est le Vol," meaning that those who own property, however acquired, are thieves, and robbers of those who possess nothing. He started several journals, in which he advocated this levelling doctrine; eventually he founded a bank, which did no business; was imprisoned for his escapades, married after his release, and retired from public life. Proudhon is a philosophic socialist. His views, as expounded by himself, are utterly subversive of the present order of political and general society.

PRUSSIA, KING OF. (See FREDERICK WILLIAM.)

PULSZKY, FERENCZ AUREL, DE LNBO'ER AND CSELFALVA, an Hungarian politician, and a writer in the German, Hungarian, and English languages, was born on the 17th of September, 1814, at Eperies, in the county of Saros. He was educated at the Protestant College of his native town, which had long been under the patronage of his family. He studied law, as is customary in Hungary with all those who prepare themselves for a parliamentary career, and took high honours in passing as an advocate in 1835. Having been one of the founders of the Debating Society in Hungary, which was prosecuted in 1836 by the Austrian government, he escaped arrest only by leaving on a tour to this country, and through continental Europe. After his return he published "Observations on England," in German, and "On Germany," in Hungarian. In 1839 he was elected to the Hungarian Diet, just when his essays on the "History of Hungary," "On Currency," and on "The Navigation of the Danube," had attracted the attention of the public. He assisted in drawing up a Code of Commercial and Bankruptcy Law, which received the royal sanction in 1840. He was afterwards elected member of the Parliamentary Committee for the codification of the Criminal Law, and a Fellow of the Hungarian Academy. Engaged for three years upon the Criminal Code, Pulszky did not stand for re-election in 1843. He revisited Italy and Germany about that time. In 1845 he married, and retired to his country seat, devoting his time to local politics, political essays in Kossuth's paper, and to the management of his extensive estates. In 1846, at the first intelligence of the revolution at Vienna, he hastened to Pesth, where the old boards of government had abdicated, and the new ministry was not yet confirmed. He was appointed by the Palatine, Archduke Stephen, one of the three commissioners for the maintenance of public order. At the final formation of the Batthyany cabinet he became Under-Secretary of State for Foreign Affairs under Prince Esterhazy, who, having lent his name to the national movement, and unwilling to incur any serious risk, left the management of the relations between the Hungarian cabinet and the Austrian Ministers in Pulszky's hands. At the

Y

desire of Jellachich he was dismissed. The Hungarian Diet sent him back to his post at Vienna, then about to undergo a siege. He soon left again, and succeeded in evading the vigilance of the besiegers, went to the Hungarian army, where he met his friend Kossuth, and, together with his chief, took part in the battle of Schmechat. His extradition was insisted upon by Prince Windischgrätz in the capitulation of Vienna, but not being found in the captured town, a sentence of death was recorded against him. At the end of the year he was appointed to proceed to England, in order to prevent the intervention of the Russians, who had already garrisoned the frontier towns of Transylvania. After many dangers, he managed to escape from the Austrian dominions, but his mission to England remained unsuccessful, since the English ministers believed at that time that the integrity of the Austrian empire was necessary for the balance of power. After the fall of Hungary, Pulszky's estates were confiscated, and he himself hung in effigy. In 1851 he accompanied his friend, the ex-Governor Kossuth, to America. On his return to Europe in 1852, he took up his abode in London, and followed literary, political, antiquarian, and philological pursuits. He has published in English, a novel, "The Jacobite in Hungary;" and, assisted by his wife, a racy account of their tour in America, under the title of "White, Red, Black." He is a frequent contributor to English and American reviews and newspapers.

PULSZKY, MADAME FERENCZ, an Hungarian authoress, was born in 1819, at Berlin, and married in 1845 to the Hungarian Ferencz Pulszky. Whilst her husband was in England in 1849, the Austrian government gave orders for arresting her and her infant children. Prince Windischgrätz occupied and confiscated her estates, as well as those of M. Pulszky. She had to fly for her life ;

and after several unsuccessful attempts, at last succeeded in eluding the Austrian authorities, who were bent upon imprisoning her. She joined her husband in July 1849, but it was several months later that her children were brought in disguise through Austria to England by a faithful friend. She has displayed remarkable command in the English language, which has been acknowledged by the press, in her "Memoirs of an Hungarian Lady," "Tales and Traditions of Hungary," and "Three Christmas Plays for Children."

PUSEY, EDWARD BOUVERIE, D.D., a theologian and founder of the party called Puseyites, was born in 1800. Having studied at Eton, he proceeded to Oxford, where he graduated and became Fellow of Oriel. He subsequently was appointed to the Regius Professorship of Hebrew, and Canon of Christ Church. Dr. Pusey is chiefly known in connexion with the tracts, published in 1833, called "Tracts for the Times;" which, on their appearance, raised a tremendous storm in the Church of England. Their tendency was to introduce Romish practices into the English Church, and their authors did not hesitate to support the dogmas of transubstantiation and auricular confession. Their effect has been to cause the secession of many of the younger members of the Church of England, who have gone over to Rome. It is to be regretted that many such retain their benefices at the present moment, although their views are entirely opposed to the taught doctrines of the Church of which they are ministers. The popular opposition to their opinions has lately occasioned serious riots in the east of London, and in other places.

PYAT, FELIX, a French writer and son of a devoted royalist advocate, was born at Vierzon, in October 1810. His early education was carefully conducted with a view to his adopting the profession of his father; and towards that end he studied law in Paris; but in 1829 his sentiments and principles became strongly defined, for he toasted the National Convention, and proposed to substitute the bust of La Fayette for that of Charles X. In 1831 he was admitted an advocate. He might have succeeded in this profession, but despite all remonstrance, opposing the urgent entreaties and earnest prayers of his friends and relatives, he determined to pursue the most fickle of literary careers, that of a journalist. He commenced with "Figaro" and the "Charivari," and wrote incessantly, until he worked his way up to the "Siècle" and the "National." It is principally, however, by his dramatic compositions that M. Pyat is known and recognised as a clear and pungent writer. His style is melodramatic, and he often indulges in political allusions which are far from gratifying to a French administration. On the proclamation of the Republic he abandoned literature and adopted politics, joining the ranks of the democratic Socialists. He was elected one of the Commissioners-General for Cher, and voted constantly with the "Mountain." In 1849 he became the intimate associate of Ledru Rollin, thinking and acting with him, until both were compelled to resort to involuntary exile; M. Pyat taking refuge in Switzerland, and then removing to Belgium, where he has since resided.

PYNE, JAMES B., an artist, was born at Bristol, in 1800. He was educated for the law, but abandoned that profession to study art, and removed to London in 1835. His landscapes, from their characteristic style, began to make way with the public. In 1846 he took his first trip to Italy, and made a longer tour upon the Continent in 1851. His style is original and free, and remarkable for the skill bestowed on atmospherical phenomena. He struggled hard for years for the title of Royal Academician, and exhibited regularly at the Academy, but eventually he joined the Society of British Artists, of which he is one of the leading members, having been Vice-President from the commencement of his membership up to the present time. He exhibited in the Paris Exposition, in 1855, his "Derwent Lake," "A View of Heidelberg," and "Eton College."

QUINET, EDGAR, a French author and statesman, born at Bourg, Ain, in 1803, is son of a commissary of war. He obtained a liberal education, and went to Germany, where his talents and special tone of thought attracted the notice of the professors at Heidelberg. He was appointed Professor of Foreign Literature to the Faculty of Letters, at Lyons, in 1839, and repeatedly elected to the Chamber; but in 1852, he was expelled from France, and took up his residence in Brussels. He has been rather a prolific author, and at one time was a co-labourer with Michelet. The politics of M. Quinet are remarkably liberal, and some of his works on ecclesiastical matters tend to latitudinarianism.

RAFFLES, THE REV. THOMAS, D.D., LL.D., an Independent minister, was born in London, May 17th, 1788. After studying at the Theological College of Homerton, he was appointed Minister of the Congregational Church, Hammersmith, where he became so popular by the eloquence of his discourses as to be called to undertake the pastoral duties of an important congregation at Liverpool. For nearly fifty years Dr. Raffles has filled the ministerial office at Great George-street Chapel, in that town; and has, by the energy and activity of his pulpit addresses, become one of the most popular of living divines. He has published several works, including a volume of poems, "Letters during a Tour in France, Switzerland," &c., a "Life of the Rev. Thomas Spencer," and "Lectures on Religion—Doctrinal and Practical," in two volumes.

RAMSAY, WILLIAM, M.A., a classical scholar and Professor of Humanity in the University of Glasgow, was born in Edinburgh, on the 6th of February, 1806, and is the youngest son of Sir William Ramsay, Bart., of Banff. He was educated at the High School and at the Universities of Edinburgh and Glasgow. At the latter seminary he studied for three years, and carried off first prizes in the Latin, Greek, and mathematical classes. He then proceeded to Trinity College, Cambridge, and at the College examination at the close of his third term was placed (June, 1826) in the first class, and declared the first man of his year. In 1829, while still an undergraduate, he was invited to undertake the duties of the mathematical chair in the University of Glasgow, the professor having fallen into bad health. This invitation Mr. Ramsay accepted, and was thus precluded from becoming a candidate for honours at Cambridge, although he took his degree of B.A. at a bye term in 1830. He acted as Professor of Mathematics for two winters at Glasgow, and in the second of these undertook the charge of the Senior Humanity Class also. In August, 1831, Mr. Walker, the Professor of Humanity, died, and Mr. Ramsay was unanimously chosen as his successor. He took the degree of M.A. at Cambridge, in 1833. He is author of "A Treatise on Latin Prosody," "Elegiac Extracts from the Latin Poets, with copious Notes," "A Manual of Roman Antiquities," "An Elementary Treatise on Latin Prosody," "An Elementary Manual of Roman Antiquities," "The Speech of Cicero for Cluentius, with Prolegomena and Notes;" all of which have passed through several editions. Mr. Ramsay was one of the principal contributors to the "Dictionary of Greek and Roman Anti-

quities," and to the "Dictionary of Greek and Roman Biography," edited by Dr. William Smith, and has written articles in various literary journals.

RANKE, LEOPOLD, a German historian, was born at Wiche, in Thuringia, on the 21st of December, 1795. His taste for history was manifested at an early age, and he acquired considerable reputation in that branch of study by publishing in 1824, his "History of the Roman and German People." After holding a professorship at Berlin, he made a tour through the Austrian and Italian States, and embodied his extensive observations in two works published in 1827-31. The work by which Ranke is chiefly known is that of his "History of the Popes," which was succeeded by his "German History in the Times of the Reformation," and a "History of England." As an historian, Professor Ranke holds the highest reputation; and from the originality, minuteness, and philosophical nature of his productions, the student of history may always reap advantage.

RANKINE, WILLIAM JOHN MACQUORN, civil engineer, received his university education at Edinburgh, and studied engineering first under his father, Lieutenant David Rankine, and afterwards under Sir John M'Neill. He has held the Professorship of Civil Engineering and Mechanics in the University of Glasgow since the session of 1855-56. He is a Fellow of the Royal Societies of London and Edinburgh, and a member or honorary member of various other scientific bodies. He was President of the Institution of Engineers in Scotland for the first two years following its foundation, and has been President of the Mechanical Section of the British Association. He received the honorary degree of LL.D. from the University of Dublin, on the occasion of the meeting of the British Association there in 1857. In 1849 he commenced the publication of a series of original researches on the mechanical action of heat, for which, in 1852, the Keith Medal of the Royal Society of Edinburgh was awarded to him. Those researches have been continued to the present time (1860). He is the author of various papers on engineering, scientific, and philosophical subjects, which have appeared from time to time since 1842, and of a series of works of which there have appeared, entitled respectively, "A Manual of Applied Mechanics" (1858), "A Manual of the Steam Engine and other Prime Movers" (1859), and "A Manual of Civil Engineering." The most important and original of his writings are those which relate to heat, elasticity, and the laws of physical energy in general, to which he has given the name of "Energetics." In 1859 he took a leading part in raising and organizing the 2nd Lanarkshire, or Glasgow University Corps of the Rifle Volunteers, to the command of which he was in consequence appointed.

RASPAIL, FRANÇOIS VINCENT, a French chemist and politician, was born in Jan., 1794. He was originally destined for the Church, but after receiving a philosophical and theological training, he refused to take orders, contenting himself with a modest position in the college of his native village, and devoting himself to science. The first fruits of his scientific labours was an essay on "Classification," written in 1824. From this period to 1830, he continued to prosecute his researches in botany, zoology, and palæontology, with great success. In 1830 political passions drew the savant from the laboratory to the barricade. Raspail appeared among the combatants in the revolution of the three days, in the party of the republic. Condemned under the government of Louis Philippe, he continued throughout the reign of the citizen king completely estranged from his régime. Politics did not, however, seduce Raspail from his favourite studies; these he continued to prosecute with unflagging devotion and continuous success, until the Revolution of 1848 once more brought him prominently upon the stormy arena of political life. In his journal, "Ami du Peuple," and in his club, he preached a refined communism—the communism of sentiment rather than of subversion—being, in point of fact, what has been not unaptly called a rose-water revolutionist. On the establishment of the government of Louis Napoleon, Raspail was again imprisoned. Since his liberation he has lived chiefly in Belgium, prosecuting scientific studies. He has published a work on "Organic Chemistry," which has been translated into English; and also several works on botanical and physiological subjects.

RAUCH, CHRISTIAN, a German sculptor, was born at Arolsen, in Waldeck, on 2nd of January, 1777. Having early evinced a taste for art, his education was made to foster his inclinations. He obtained an appointment in Berlin in 1797, which gave him sufficient leisure to pursue sculpture, and he eventually received instruction from Canova and Thorwaldsen. He afterwards produced several works, and was commissioned by the King of Prussia to execute his bust, and that of the Queen. Proceeding to Rome, he produced several busts and statues during his stay in that city. His statues of Blucher, Goethe, and Frederick the Great, are masterpieces of art, the latter being Rauch's *chef d'œuvre*. Besides the works already named, he has produced a vast variety of statues and busts of eminent men, which, from their finished execution, have raised him to the highest position in his profession.

RAUMER, FREDERICK LOUIS GEORGE VON, an eminent German historian, was born at Wörlitz, on 14th of May, 1781. Having studied at Berlin, Halle, and

Göttingen, he entered on his judicial career in 1801, and in 1810 took his place as Councillor in the Cabinet of the Chancellor of State for Hardenberg. Previous to this appointment he had published several works which elevated his reputation, and in 1811 he obtained a professor's chair in the University of Breslau. From 1815 to 1817 he travelled through Italy, Germany, Switzerland, and other countries, and gave the result of his observations in two new works, which were considered so important that he was called to occupy the chair of political economy and history in the University of Berlin. From that time forward he filled various public situations, among the most prominent of which was that of Secretary to the Berlin Academy of Sciences; but an eulogium which he passed on Frederick II. was so unfavourably received by the members, that he resigned his office. The citizens of Berlin, not being of the same mind as the Academy, elected him first to the Municipal Council, and secondly to the Parliament of Frankfort, where he took his place among the moderate party; afterwards being sent to Paris in the capacity of ambassador. On his return to Berlin, M. Raumer was elected member of the First Chamber of Prussia; and in 1859, seeking repose after a long and arduous life, he obtained the title and emoluments of Professor in the Berlin University. His works are very numerous, and are popular with all classes of readers in Germany; whilst in this country and France they are well known through translations.

RAWLINSON, SIR HENRY CRESWICKE, belongs to the old Lancashire family of Rawlinson, settled in Furness since the time of Henry V., and was born at Chaddington, Oxfordshire, in 1810. He was educated at Ealing, and entered the East India Company's service in 1827. Serving with the Bombay army till 1833, he was appointed to Persia to assist in organizing the Shah's army. In 1835 he commenced the study of the cuneiform inscriptions of Persia, being then stationed at Kermanshah. In 1836 he visited Baghdad, travelled in Luristan and Susiana, returned to Teheran, and accompanied the Persian army to the Junernan frontier; whence he was sent back on duty to Ispahan, and ultimately to Kermanshah. In 1837-38, being again stationed at Teheran, he announced to the Royal Asiatic Society of London, his cuneiform discoveries; and also published, in the "Geographical Society's Journal," his Susiana travels. In 1839, being stationed at Baghdad, in consequence of the interruption of relations with Persia, he wrote his paper on "Ecbatana," for the "Geographical Society's Journal," which obtained him the society's gold medal at the next anniversary meeting. He also, during the same year, forwarded to the Royal Asiatic Society, an abstract translation of the greater portion of the "Bekistun Inscription," in order to secure priority of discovery. Recalled to India in 1840, he travelled through Scinde to Candahar, and thence proceeded to Cabool to be associated with Captain Arthur Conolly, in the mission to Khiva, Bokhara, and Tokand. His services, however, being required in Afghanistan, he was sent back from Cabool to Candahar, where he remained as political agent until our final evacuation of the country at the end of 1842. He was present in all General Nott's actions with the enemy at this period, and finally accompanied the Candahar column as political agent, on the advance to Ghuzni and Cabool, and subsequent retirement to India. In 1843 he was appointed political agent in Turkish Arabia, and proceeded from Calcutta to Baghdad; where, with the exception of occasional excursions to the Persian mountains, and a visit to England for two years in 1850 and 1851, he resided uninterruptedly until 1855, when he returned home. During this period he was throughout diligently occupied with the study of the cuneiform inscriptions—Persian, Median, Assyrian, and Babylonian; and published numerous papers on the subject in the "Royal Asiatic Society's Journal," the main results of which have been embodied in the translation of "Herodotus," recently published by his brother, the Rev. G. Rawlinson, of Oxford. He received a commission as Major, in Persia, in 1836, and as Lieut.-Colonel, in Turkey, in 1850; was made a C.B., in 1854, for military services in Afghanistan, and received the first class of the Persian order of the Lion and Sun, and the third class of the order of the Doorauee Empire. He was further granted the commission of Consul at Baghdad in 1844, and of Consul-General in 1851. His literary honours also have been numerous. He was admitted into the Institute of France, as Corresponding Member, as early as 1837; was made a F.R.S. of London, and D.C.L. of Oxford, in 1850; and received the Order of Merit from the King of Prussia, in 1852. He has also been honoured with diplomas from almost all the historical, geographical, and antiquarian societies, both of England and of the Continent, and even from the American universities. In 1856 he retired as Lieut.-Colonel from the East India Company's service, and was immediately afterwards appointed a Crown Director of the East India Company, having been previously made a Civil K.C.B. In January, 1858, he was elected member for Reigate; and on the extinction of the East India Company, in the same year, was appointed a member of the Council of India, being obliged thereby to vacate his seat in Parliament. In April, 1859, he appointed her Majesty's Envoy Extraordinary and Minister Plenipotentiary

to the Court of the Shah, and was granted the rank of Major-General in Persia. He is now residing at Teheran.

READE, CHARLES, a novelist, was educated at Oxford. His first work, "Peg Woffington," at once brought him into notice. Mr. Reade still further increased his literary success by producing his "Never Too Late to Mend" in 1856. He has since published several works of fiction, which are highly popular and have been extensively read. His papers contributed to different serials are at once amusing and captivating in their style, and possess a lively and continuous interest. His last work is "The Eighth Commandment."

REBOUL, JEAN, a French poet, was born at Nismes, on 23rd of January, 1796. His early education was received in a school of his native place, and although of a very moderate kind, he soon improved on it by his own assiduity. For some time he followed the trade of a baker, but his natural genius for poetry soon became evident, in the production of songs and satires composed for a circle of private friends. In 1828 his "Angel and Child" appeared in the "Quotidienne." In 1836 he published a collection of poems, which speedily ran through five editions. Proceeding to Paris in 1839, he was received with great enthusiasm in literary circles. He has composed some tragedies, and his last production is a volume of poems published in 1857, under the title of "Les Traditionnelles."

REDDING, CYRUS, a journalist and author, was born at Penrhyn, Cornwall, in 1785. He commenced his literary career in 1806, by contributing to the "Pilot," which was then edited by Sir Herbert Compton, late Chief Justice of Bombay. He then passed to the "Plymouth Chronicle," which, after editing, he purchased, and parting with it, in 1814, returned to London. In 1811 he published "Letters to Lord Holland, on the Question of Libel," and also "Mount Edgecumbe," a poem. He edited, about the same time, the "Dramatic Review;" contributed to the "Morning Chronicle," and published "Specimens of Kœrner and Goethe," afterwards proceeding to France. In 1820 he was connected with the "New Monthly;" but subsequently, with Campbell, the poet, started the "Metropolitan Magazine." After a variety of literary engagements he produced, in 1833, a work by which he is well known; namely, his "History of British Wines." After editing the "Bath Guardian," he went to Lichfield, and took the management of the "Staffordshire Examiner," in 1836. Since then Mr. Redding has been connected with the London "Examiner," and has also published various works connected with general and political literature, distinguishing himself by the liberality and uncompromising nature of his opinions.

REDGRAVE, RICHARD, R.A., an English painter, was born in London, on the 30th April, 1804. His father's business, in which he had been engaged, falling off, Mr. Redgrave followed the bent of his inclination, became a student of art, and in 1826 entered the schools of the Royal Academy. His first really successful picture, though he had previously exhibited a number of others, was "Gulliver on the Farmer's Table," exhibited at the British Institution in 1837, which was at once purchased. Thenceforward his course was steady and unimpeded. He aimed at drawing attention by his works, to the struggles of those who had seen better days, and in most instances achieved his purpose. He was elected an Associate of the Royal Academy in 1840; and, since then, has been a constant exhibitor. Six of his works having been secured for the Sheepshanks' collection, and one for the Vernon Gallery, his position was established as one of the greatest artists of the day. He was elected an Academician in 1851. For some years he was Head-Master of the School of Design; and on that institution being incorporated with the Department of Science and Art, he was appointed Art-Superintendent, and subsequently Inspector-General of Art Schools, which office he still retains, together with that of Surveyor of Crown Pictures, conferred on him by her Majesty on the death of Mr. Uwins, R.A. in 1857. His pictures in the South Kensington Museum, at the present time, are "Cinderella about to try on the Glass Slipper," "The School Teacher," "Gulliver exhibited to the Brobdignag Farmer," "Throwing off her Weeds," "Ophelia weaving her Garland," "Bolton Abbey," and "Country Cousins."

REED, THE REV. ANDREW, D.D., philanthropist, divine, and author, was born in London on the 27th November, 1788. Early in life he was designed for business, but having evinced a great passion for study, and remarkable skill in the mastery of languages, he relinquished business and went to college. In 1812 he was chosen the minister of one of the most important congregations among the Dissenters, where he remains to the present day, having for forty-nine years discharged all the duties there without assistance. In 1818 a work entitled "No Fiction," issued anonymously from the press, and the fact that it ran rapidly through many editions, the present being the twenty-fourth, shows that it is a popular favourite. This work was subsequently acknowledged by Dr. Reed. It has been reprinted in America, Germany, and Holland. The great feature in Dr. Reed's life has been his devotion to the noble works of benevolence with which, as founder, his name has become familiarly associated. He has seized on the work as soon as he has seen it, and besides giving his whole time gratuitously to the building up of these institutions, he has been foremost as a munificent contributor to their support. In 1820 he felt the want of a provision for orphan children, and commencing it in his own house, he founded the London Orphan Asylum at Clapton, where thousands of respectable men and women of the present day have received their education. The same need was perceived for infants, and he founded the Infant Orphan Asylum at Wanstead. In addition to this, he established, in 1847, the Asylum of Fatherless Children at Reedham, near Croydon, for children of any age, till old enough for apprenticeship. Travelling abroad, Dr. Reed's attention was drawn to the state of the poor idiot, and when he returned home he investigated the condition of this class of suffering humanity in this country. From this has risen the Asylum at Colchester, and the noble Earlswood Asylum at Croydon, exhibiting a treatment of a most remedial character. The Hospital for Incurables is the last of the institutions owning Dr. Reed as founder. It occurred to him that something should be done for the poor objects who were discharged from our great hospitals as incurable, and having no provision of support, were forced to seek a place to die in the workhouse. This hospital is now full, and a building is to be erected at Coulsden. In 1834 Dr. Reed was chosen by the United Body of Congregationalists to visit the churches of America, and he travelled through the States and Canada during ten months, publishing, on his return, a narrative of his visit, two vols. 8vo. Some other works on revivals of religion, and many sermons, are also from his pen. Descended from an ancestry personally attached to the cause of the Commonwealth, Dr. Reed early espoused advanced liberal principles, but through life he has ex-

hibited a singular catholicity of spirit in co-operation with others differing from him in opinion on public questions, and his administrative power and talent for organizing have gained for his many philanthropic projects the help of all classes of society at home and abroad.

REGNAULT, HENRI VICTOR, a French chemist, born at Aix-la-Chapelle, in July 1810, was a pupil of the Polytechnic School in 1830, and afterwards became Chief Mining Engineer, Director of the Imperial Manufactory of Sèvres Porcelain, Professor of Physics in the College of France, and of Chemistry at the Polytechnic School. He has been a member of the Academy of Sciences since 1840, and is corresponding member of the Academies of Berlin, St. Petersburg, &c. In 1850 he was created Officer of the Legion of Honour. Though a most distinguished chemist, and a profound scientific scholar, it is, nevertheless, as a physician that he holds a first place in the ranks of the learned men of his day. He is considered in France to be one of the most precise and definite practitioners in the empire; leaving nothing to chance, but submitting the diagnosis of every disease to philosophical and experienced investigation. He has not been a voluminous writer, but the works he has published are universally held as authorities on the subjects of which he treats.

REICHENBACH, CHARLES, BARON DE, a German naturalist, was born at Stuttgard, February 1788. His education completed, he conceived, at the age of sixteen, the peculiar idea of founding a new German State in the South Sea Islands. He followed up this project with ardour for about three years, but owing to French interference it was broken up. He then turned his attention towards science and manufactures; and after having visited the principal works in France and Germany, he founded similar establishments at Villingen and Hausach. He embarked in undertakings of the same description in Moravia and Germany Proper; and having acquired a large fortune, the King of Wurtemberg raised him to the dignity of a Baron. Though chiefly known as a manufacturer, he is held in considerable estimation as a man of science, and has written works on geology, electricity, animal magnetism, the laws of heat, and physiology. He resides principally at Reisenberg, where he has a magnificent museum. His chief works are "Researches in Electricity and its Relation to the Vital Force," and others relating to sensation and nervous action with respect to magnetism.

REID, CAPTAIN MAYNE, a novelist, was born in Ireland, in 1818, and is the son of the Rev. Mayne Reid, for many years senior clerk to the General Assembly of the Irish Presbyterian Church. He was educated for the ministry, but soon gave way to a desire of seeing the world, and before he was twenty years old he left his native country for Mexico. Proceeding up the Red River, he became acquainted with the Indians, his observations here no doubt affording materials for his future works. He subsequently visited the United States, in 1845 joined the American army in the war against Mexico, and in a battle fought during the campaign, was wounded. Having a special taste for military affairs, he next turned his attention to Hungarian matters; but through the sudden fall of the popular cause, his hopes of service were disappointed. He then resolved to pursue literature, and has been exceedingly happy in rendering the scenes of his early days interesting to the general reader, by publishing them embodied in novels. His chief productions of this class are "The Rifle Rangers," "The Scalp Hunters," "The Quadroon," and "Occola." He has published many other works intended for juvenile readers.

REMILLY, OVIDE, a French politi-

cian, was born at Versailles, Nov. 18, 1800, of an old and wealthy commercial family. He chose the law for his profession, and was in due time admitted advocate, though he subsequently turned his attention to politics. His energy, public spirit, and generous disposition, brought him into prominent notice, and he was elected Mayor of Versailles in 1837; a position which he retained for many years, with credit to himself and advantage to the community. From 1839 to 1848 he had a seat in the Chamber of Deputies, but though ordinarily voting with the majority he never sacrificed his independence. After the revolution of February, he was elected to the Constituent Assembly, and exerted every effort to preserve order, placing himself in the ranks of the moderate republicans, and restraining as far as in his power the wild schemes of the extreme democrats. He opposed the repressive laws bearing on societies, clubs, and the press; although, when he perceived that a special line of policy was essential to the public safety, he supported Louis Napoleon. From 1849 to 1851 he was a member of the Legislative Assembly, occupying the best part of his time in reforming and extending the system of public instruction, but still adhering to the necessity of a parliament to secure good and free government for the people. After the *coup d'état* he refused to enter the Corps Legislatif, and the people of his native city, to testify their high estimation of his worth and esteem for his public rectitude, had a gold medal struck in his honour. His moderation, candour, and upright principle have commanded the favour of all the governments under which he has lived and held office for nearly sixty years.

RESCHID, PASHA, a Turkish statesman, was born in Constantinople in 1802. He was educated by a relative, entered the army, and was also engaged in various political matters during the earlier years of his life. In 1834 he was sent on a mission to London and Paris, where he was first struck with new ideas of Western civilization; and, setting himself to study the customs and laws of the countries to which he was accredited, he returned to Turkey, after an absence of two years, carrying with him an influence previously unknown. He had been in England during the passing of the Reform Bill; saw to his astonishment that a great constitutional change had been effected without bloodshed; and being observant, he became deeply impressed with the desire of reforming the Turkish government. This object he steadily pursued, though surrounded by discontent and hostility. It is highly probable, that had his views been adopted, many of the difficulties in which the Sultan now finds himself involved, might have been avoided. Though holding the highest situation in the power of the Sultan to bestow, Reschid Pasha has been the victim of intrigue. He was accused of mismanagement of the public funds in 1859, and obliged to resign; afterwards being called again to power, and resigning once more.

RICHARDSON, CHARLES, LL.D., an English lexicographer, was born in July, 1775. He was intended for the profession of the law, and educated with that object; but a predilection for literary rather than legal studies, induced him to abandon law and devote himself to literature. In 1805 his first work, "Illustrations of English Philology," appeared. Subsequently he became a contributor to the "Encyclopædia Metropolitana;" and in 1835 his "Dictionary," as a separate work, began to be issued by Mr. Pickering. In addition to this great work, Dr. Richardson has published an essay on the "Study of Language," besides contributing some interesting papers on his favourite study to the reviews of the day. The philological principles that lie at the basis of Dr. Richardson's investigations are substantially the same as those Horne Tooke enunciated in his "Diversions of Purley."

RICHARDSON, SIR JOHN, K.C.B., a naturalist and Arctic explorer, was born in 1787, at Dumfries, in Scotland. After completing his early education at the grammar-school of his native town, he entered the University of Edinburgh, in 1801, prosecuted his studies in medicine, and then served in the Navy as medical officer for some years. He took his degree of M.D. in 1816. In 1819 he sailed with Franklin, as surgeon and naturalist, and in 1825 joined the same intrepid navigator on a second exploratory voyage. Dr. Richardson, in 1829, began the publication of the zoology of these northern regions, a work which established his reputation as a naturalist. In 1838 he was appointed Physician to the Fleet; in 1840 an Inspector of Hospitals; in 1846 a Knight Bachelor; and in 1850 was made a Companion of the Bath. In 1848 he once more set out for the Arctic regions, this time in search of his former companion, Sir John Franklin. An account of this "Arctic Searching Expedition" was published by Sir John in 1851. His works are numerous and valuable. He is a Fellow of the Royal Society of London, an Honorary Fellow of the Royal Society of Edinburgh, and a member and associate of many foreign and scientific bodies. He has retired from active service for some years.

RIPON AND DE GREY, GEORGE FREDERICK SAMUEL ROBINSON, EARL OF, was born on the 24th of October, 1827. The son and heir of the first Earl of Ripon, who succeeded Mr. Canning for a short time as First Lord of the Treasury, the subject of this notice was known for many years under the courtesy title of Lord Goderich. After leaving the university he entered Parliament, and represented successively Hull, Huddersfield, and the West Riding of Yorkshire. Adopting advanced liberal opinions, he advocated the introduction of competitive examinations in the Civil services, and other measures of a similar kind, which have lately been partially adopted in our administrative system. For some time he held office as Under-Secretary of State for the War Department. On his father's death, in January 1859, he succeeded to the title of Earl of Ripon, and took his seat in the Upper House. In November of the same year he, on the death of his uncle, acquired the title of De Grey, and is now known as Earl De Grey and Ripon.

RIPON, Right Rev. Robert Bickersteth, D.D., Bishop of, was born in Suffolk, in 1816. He was at first intended for the medical profession, but eventually proceeded to Cambridge, where he gained a scholarship and graduated in honours. After holding the curacy of Sapcote, in Leicestershire, of which his father was rector, Dr. Bickersteth became Incumbent of St. John's, Clapham; and by the eloquence and force of his discourses, was soon known as one of the most popular ministers in the metropolis. He was subsequently Rector of St. Giles's, London, and Canon of Salisbury. In 1856 Dr. Bickersteth became Bishop of Ripon, and since then has been distinguished by the judicious performance of those duties which his high position devolves on him. A Charge to the clergy of his diocess, lately delivered, has attracted the attention and approval of many of the best friends of the Church of England.

RISTORI, Adelaide, an Italian actress, was born in 1821. Her father was an obscure comedian, and she appeared early on the stage. Her life, like the lives of all who engage in the profession, was for years an uphill struggle with difficulties, and presents few features of interest, unless the plays in which she appeared, and the various degrees of success she achieved, were to be minutely noted. Her first great triumph as an actress was in 1855, when the *prestige* of Rachel was in the ascendant, and when she appeared in Paris before a somewhat prejudiced audience. The power of her genius surmounted all antagonism; she carried the house with her; and her fame has not since been clouded by a reverse. She lately visited England, and created a wonderful impression by the truthfulness and brilliancy of her representations.

RITCHIE, Leitch, a journalist and popular writer, was born at Greenock, of a respectable family, in the beginning of the present century. After being in various mercantile situations, he settled in the metropolis as an author by profession, and in a short period his name became familiar to the public. He furnished the letter-press of some of Charles Heath's splendid annual volumes, travelling in most of the countries of Europe to pick up the light materials requisite for this work. He contributed to the miscellaneous annuals, editing one of them for several years; and wrote innumerable papers in reviews and magazines, on all questions of passing interest, from the Irish Poor-law to the fiscal reforms of Indian trade. After editing the "Indian News" for some time, he became proprietor of that journal, which he afterwards sold on removing from London to Edinburgh. He then edited "Chambers's Journal," till the close of 1858, when he returned to London, where a small selection from his Edinburgh papers was published in two volumes, with the title of "Winter Evenings." Of the works of fiction by which this versatile writer is best known to the public, the "Magician" and "Schinderhannes" have been several times reprinted; but "Wearyfoot Common," his last production of the kind, gives, perhaps, the best idea of his manner and spirit.

ROBERTS, DAVID, R.A., an artist, was born at Stockbridge, a suburb of Edinburgh, on the 24th October, 1796. After being with a house painter in that city, he studied at the Trustees' Academy, and in 1821 went to London and became a scene painter. From distemper he took to oil-painting, and soon exhibited some of his productions. His sketches and pictures, painted after a visit to Spain, gained him great and deserved credit. He was elected A.R.A. in 1839, and a Royal Academician in 1841. He has recently presented to the Royal Scottish Academy one of his finest works, for which he received not only the thanks of that body, but of the citizens of Edinburgh at large. The "interiors" of Mr. Roberts are held by connoisseurs to be the finest works of their class ever painted. His "Sketches in the Holy Land, Syria, Idumea, Arabia, Egypt, and Nubia," engraved by Haghe, with descriptions by Dr. Croly, are well known, and have contributed perhaps beyond all other productions to his popularity as an artist. The following pictures painted by Mr. Roberts are now in the collection at South Kensington Museum:—"Entrance to the Crypt, Roslyn Castle," "Old Buildings on the Darro, Granada," "The Gate of Cairo," and "Interior of the Cathedral at Burgos."

ROBSON, FREDERICK, a comedian, was born at Margate, in Kent, in 1821. Having received a general education, he was apprenticed to a copperplate engraver in London ; but the occupation not being suitable to his tastes, he eventually abandoned it, and entered that profession in which he has since become so eminent. His *début* was made in an amateur performance, in Catherine-street, where he acted the part of Simon Mealbag, in "Grace Huntley." He was, however, by no means successful,

and his friends endeavoured to dissuade him from again appearing on the stage, but his perseverance enabled him to overcome all difficulties. Having appeared at Whitstable and Uxbridge, he returned to London, and accepted an engagement at the Grecian Saloon, which lasted from 1844 till 1849. He next appeared at the Queen's Theatre, Dublin, where he soon became an established favourite. His great success during this engagement, obtained him an offer from the lessee of the Olympic, London, where he appeared in 1853, and has ever since been a most popular actor. Mr. Robson's style is perfectly unique.

ROEBUCK, JOHN ARTHUR, of the Inner Temple, Q.C., a politician and M.P., was born at Madras in December 1802. In 1815 Mr. Roebuck visited Canada, and returned to England in 1824. In 1832 he was called to the bar of the Inner Temple, and in the same year was elected one of the members for Bath against the brother of Sir J. Cam Hobhouse (now Lord Broughton), a circumstance alleged by his friends to have been the main cause of the opposition he has invariably met with from the Whigs from that day to the present. As an orator Mr. Roebuck stands high in the House. The startling way in which he brings forward facts which he has got hold of, often causes opposition to his opinions from persons who afterwards, when better informed, entirely agree with him. In 1837 Mr. Roebuck lost his seat for Bath, but in 1841 was re-elected. In 1843 he was appointed Queen's Counsel, and called to the bench of the Inner Temple. In 1847 the Whigs at Bath canvassed for "the two Lords" Duncan and Shaftesbury, and Mr. Roebuck in consequence was unsuccessful ; but in May 1849 he was elected for Sheffield, for which borough he now sits. In 1855, after a period of severe illness, Mr. Roebuck resumed active life in

Parliament, and moved for the famous inquiry into the state of the army before Sebastopol. The Government was averse to this step, but the motion being carried against them, the Aberdeen Ministry resigned. Mr. Roebuck, after every means had been tried to prevent his being Chairman of the Committee, was appointed to that post. Many improvements in the army have resulted from the investigations then made. Mr. Roebuck some years ago contributed to the Westminster and the Edinburgh Reviews. He is the author of "A History of the Whig Party," and of a work entitled "The Colonies of England," which exposes and meets the difficulties of colonial legislation. These are distinguished by great ability and fairness to political opponents. Mr. Roebuck has been in the directorate of various commercial undertakings during the last few years. As a politician he maintains a severe independence in the House of Commons, allying himself to no party, and occasionally attacking both friends and foes.

ROGER, GUSTAVE HIPPOLYTE, a French vocalist, born at Paris, August 1815, is the son of a notary, who intended him to follow the same business, but the taste for the stage was too decided, and he entered the Conservatoire in 1837. Having obtained the first prize for singing and elocution, he made his *début* at the Opéra Comique in 1838, and was received with unusual favour. He remained in that establishment for several years, taking part in rendering effective the works of Auber and Halévy. He afterwards quitted the Opéra Comique and came to England, and on his return to France reappeared with increased power. Subsequently, visiting Germany, he sang with Mademoiselle Wagner and Jenny Lind; at Frankfort he was fêted; at Hamburg and Berlin he was applauded to the height of his ambition; and at Paris he continues one of the chief favourites of the lyric stage. His voice is a pure tenor, and he manages it with consummate skill. Owing to an accident, he was some time since obliged to submit to the amputation of an arm, but recovered in health, and with a mechanical substitute, which can scarcely be distinguished from a living limb, he is performing and singing as perfectly as ever.

ROGERS, HENRY, a critic, was born at St. Alban's, Herts, in 1806. He was originally destined for the medical profession, and passed through the usual preliminary course; but subsequently studied in one of the colleges of the Independents, with a view to the ministry, though a very feeble voice gave him but moderate prospects of success as a pulpit orator. Convinced, for this and other reasons, after a brief trial, that the pulpit was not his sphere, he devoted his attention to the duties of a college tutor, and to literature. In 1836 he was appointed Professor of the English Language and Literature, University College, London, a chair which he vacated in 1839 for that of Philosophical Tutor in the newly founded Independent College, at Spring Hill, Birmingham. There he remained nearly twenty years, when he accepted the principalship of the Lancashire Independent College, Manchester. His first literary efforts of any considerable extent were critical essays on the genius and writings of Jonathan Edwards, Edmund Burke, and Jeremy Taylor, prefixed respectively to editions of the works of those authors. His contributions to the "Edinburgh Review" have been published in a collected form, and, with his "Eclipse of Faith" and a "Life of John Howe," are his principal literary productions.

ROGERS, HENRY DARWIN, Professor of Natural History in the University of Glasgow, was born in Philadelphia, United States. Both his parents were of Scotch-Irish extraction. Like the

Gregories and Thomsons, he belongs to a family in which the passion for science seems hereditary. His father long held the important appointment of Professor of Physics and Chemistry in nearly the most ancient seat of learning in America, the old College of William and Mary; and, trained in the laboratory of their father, three brothers of the professor have held scientific appointments in the United States. At the age of twenty-one, Professor Rogers was appointed to the Chair of Chemistry and Natural Philosophy in Dickinson College, Pennsylvania. After holding this appointment for two or three years, he repaired to Europe, partly to increase his scientific knowledge, partly for the benefit of his health; and devoted himself assiduously to the cultivation of analytical chemistry and practical and theoretical geology. Returning, after two more years, with renovated strength, he was entrusted with the geological surveys of New Jersey and Pennsylvania. From the limited extent of territory, the New Jersey survey was but a minor task, and early completed. Pennsylvania, a state as large as half the area of Great Britain, and a region of complicated geological structure, was a more gigantic work, occupying some twenty-two years. The results of the survey have lately been published in three volumes, illustrated by numerous engravings and elaborate geological maps of Pennsylvania and its coal-fields. This work is the most complete survey that has yet been made of any of the coal-fields of the world. Professor Rogers is a Fellow of the Royal and Geological Societies of London, and of the Royal Society of Edinburgh, as well as of the chief scientific societies of the United States; and recently the University of Dublin conferred upon him the degree of LL.D. In 1857 he was appointed Regius Professor of Natural History in the University of Glasgow.

ROGET, Peter Mark, M.D., F.R.S., an English physician, the nephew of the late Sir Samuel Romilly, was born in London in 1779. He was educated for the medical profession in Edinburgh, and graduated there in 1798. He held for some years the appointment of physician to the Manchester Infirmary, Lunatic Asylum, and Fever Hospital, and afterwards settled in London, where his knowledge of science being appreciated, he was elected a Fellow of the Royal Society, and for a period of one-and-twenty years discharged the duties of Secretary to that learned body. He is a Fellow of the Royal College of Physicians, and of the Astronomical, Geological, Zoological, and Entomological Societies. He is also a member of the Senate of the University of London, where he was, for some years, one of the Examiners in Physiology. His publications embrace a wide range of subjects. His "Animal and Vegetable Physiology" forms one of the Bridgewater Treatises, published in 1834, and is perhaps his greatest work, though his treatises on "Electricity," "Magnetism," "Physiology," and "Phrenology," are held in high esteem. He has published a mass of other papers on subjects that came within the scope of his investigations, and has contributed extensively to periodicals connected with his profession. His more recent publication, entitled "A Thesaurus of English Words and Phrases, classified and arranged so as to facilitate the Expression of Ideas, and assist in Literary Composition," which has reached its ninth edition, is a work of extensive utility to all classes of English writers.

ROKITANSKY, Charles, a physician, was born in Bohemia on the 19th of February, 1804. He studied medicine at Prague and Vienna, and receiving his degree as Doctor in 1828, was attached to the Institution of Pathological Anatomy in the latter city, afterwards acting as Clinical Surgeon to the School of Medicine. The post-mortem examinations and dissections which he has conducted or superintended, amount to many thousands. He was named in 1848 Honorary Director of the University of Prague, and member of the Academy of Sciences at Vienna. In 1849 he became Dean of the professors of the School of Medicine, and in 1850 Rector of the University of Vienna. His principal work is a "Manual of Pathological Anatomy." Rich in facts and observations, and precise as well as new in its conclusions, this work has been warmly received by the profession, and has been translated into various modern languages.

RONGE, JOHANNES, an educational and religious reformer, was born at Bischofswalde, Silesia, in 1813. Owing to the humble circumstances of his parents, he received but a scanty education. However, after attending the College of Neisse, he proceeded to Breslau, where he studied theology. He was afterwards appointed Chaplain at Breslau; but owing to the jealousies which his zeal excited, and the decided stand he made against the conduct of his ecclesiastical superiors, he was soon deprived of his charge. This seems to have laid the foundation of that violent opposition to the Catholic authorities which he afterwards evinced; and he took the opportunity which the fame of the "holy coat" of Treves afforded him of writing a letter, which, exposing the worship of relics, aided in producing a schism in the Romish Church. Ronge soon found himself at the head of numerous followers throughout Germany, and forming them into societies, their number increased to an astonishing extent. His next difficulty arose with the government, which, viewing these associations as a source of political danger, decided on their speedy suppression. Ronge soon after fled to England, where he has since resided, and engaged himself in originating schools for the education of young people on plans peculiar to his views.

ROSAS, DON JUAN MANUEL DE, was born at Buenos Ayres in 1793, and is descended from an ancient family of the Asturias. In 1831 Rosas was chosen Captain-General of Buenos Ayres. After subduing the Indians, against whom he had been sent, he took measures to unite the whole States in the Argentine Confederation (1835); but his sole object being to advance the condition of Buenos Ayres, he took such extreme steps as led to a war with Brazil. He was defeated, but resisted notwithstanding, for five years. He became too absolute in his mode of government. A revolt ensued; and in February, 1851, Rosas and his forces were put to flight at Moron, he only escaping by disguising himself. Urquiza then took charge of affairs in Buenos Ayres, and Rosas sought the hospitable shelter of England, arriving in the early part of 1852.

ROSE, GUSTAVE, a German chemist and Professor of Mineralogy in the University of Berlin, was born on the 18th of March, 1798. His father, Valentine Rose, was a chemist of some distinction, who died, however, when the subject of this notice was only eight years of age. In 1815 he and three of his brothers took part in the war of liberation, but he withdrew at the end of the year from military service, with the view of studying mining. In 1816 he went to Königshütte, near Tarnourtz, in Upper Silesia, to learn the practical department of the business, returning in autumn to Berlin to prosecute the scientific studies connected with it. His success as a student in mineralogy, geology, and chemistry, was such that he abandoned all intention of entering upon a practical career. After defending publicly a thesis which was afterwards published in "Leonhard's Mineralogical Manual" (in 1822), he obtained the degree of Doctor of Philosophy. In 1821, having obtained permission to work in the laboratory of Berghaus, he joined his brother Heinrich Rose, and Mitscherlich at Stockholm, who had been there for nearly a year previously. In the autumn of the same year he visited the most important districts in Sweden and Norway, returning to Berlin in November, where he continued his chemical studies in the laboratory of Mitscherlich. At the same time he compiled his "Treatise on the Feldspars," in which he promulgated views which have become the basis of the new science of Petrography. In the autumn of 1822 he was appointed assistant to Professor Weiss, of the Mineralogical Museum of the University. He qualified himself as a private lecturer, and opened his first course on mineralogy in the early session of 1823. His lectures were interrupted for a year, while he made a tour in France and England, staying for six months in Paris, where he was much in the society of Alexander Humboldt. In 1826 he was appointed an adjunct Professor in the University of Berlin. Two years afterwards he accompanied his friend Ehrenberg and Alexander Von Humboldt in their journey of exploration into Central Asia. He afterwards published, in a narrative form, an account of the mineralogical observations made during this memorable expedition. In 1834 he was elected a member of the Academy of Sciences at Berlin, and in 1839 Professor in the University. After the publication of his travels he took part in the geological survey of Russia, his share in the work lying in Silesia. The first two maps have just appeared, the remainder being in preparation. Up till 1856 he was almost constantly employed in this work. In 1850, however, he spent his autumn holidays in visiting the Hyères group of islands, and in 1852 made an excursion to the extinct volcanoes of central France. On the death of Weiss, in 1846, he was appointed Director of the Mineralogical Museum at Berlin. He is a member of most of the scientific societies of Europe. Besides the travels to which we have referred, Gustave Rose is the author of "A Treatise on the Elements of Crystallography," of which an edition, which has been completely recast, is in preparation ; and of a "Crystallo-Chemical System of Mineralogy." His numerous mineralogical and chemical papers have been published in "Poggendorff's Annals," the Transactions of the Academy of Science of Berlin, the Geological Society of Germany, and extend over a period of from 1836 to 1859.

ROSE, HEINRICH, a German chemist, was born at Berlin in 1795. He studied and graduated at Berlin, and in 1835 became Professor of Chemistry in the University of that city. He is well known for his ability as an analyst; and his work entitled "A Manual of Chemical Analysis," has been extensively read, and is often used as a text-book in this country. He has chiefly restricted his researches to inorganic bodies, and has thus rendered a service in that department of science similar to what Liebig has done in organic chemistry.

ROSETTI, CONSTANTINE, a revolutionary writer, was born at Bucharest, about 1816; entered the militia in 1833, and left the service in 1836 to pursue literature. His first efforts were translations of Byron, Voltaire, and Lamartine ; and after obtaining some popularity, he was appointed to a command in the police, but resigned that post in 1845. He then went to Paris, married, and returned to his native city, where, to the astonishment of the Boyards, he opened a bookseller's shop. In 1846 he was a member of the Revolutionary Committee, and in June of that year was arrested, but liberated by the people, and afterwards filled several offices under the Provisional Government, besides founding the "Pruncul Rumân," a democratic journal. In September, having protested against the re-establishment of what were termed the Organic Regulations, he was again arrested, with several of his companions, and exiled to Orsowa, but escaped and took refuge in Paris. In the French capital he founded one or two journals specially devoted to the advocacy of his political principles, and published a work justifying the revolution. For some time past Rosetti has rarely appeared before the public, either as an author or a politician.

ROSS, REAR-ADMIRAL SIR JAMES CLARK, KNIGHT, an Arctic explorer, was born in London, on the 15th of April, 1800. He entered the navy in 1812, under his uncle Sir John Ross. In 1822 he was promoted to be Lieutenant, and in 1827, for his services under Sir E. Parry in an attempt to reach the North Pole, during which the lat. of 82¾° N. was attained by travelling over the sea in sledge-boats, he was made Commander by the Duke of Clarence, then Lord High Admiral. He embarked with his uncle in 1829 on the remarkable voyage of the "Victory" steamer, equipped by Sir Felix Booth to seek the North-west Passage. After an absence of four and a half years, and when all expectation of their return had been abandoned, they arrived in England in October, 1833. For the determination of the exact position of the North Magnetic Pole and eminent scientific and geographical discoveries, he received the rank of Post-Captain in October, 1834. He was next employed in 1836, in Sound Cove, having volunteered in the depth of winter to cross the Atlantic to carry provisions to the whale ships in Baffin's Bay, an arduous and hazardous service. On his return to his country he spent the two following years in making a magnetic survey of Great Britain and Ireland by order of the Admiralty. In April 1839 he was appointed, with Captain Crozier under his orders, to command the "Erebus" and "Terror," and to proceed on a voyage of discovery to the Antarctic Ocean; and the expedition left in September of that year, and was absent about four years. In the Southern regions he discovered a tract of ice-bound land, and acquired valuable information respecting the natural history of those inhospitable regions. On the 31st January, 1848, he was appointed to command the first expedition sent in search of Sir John Franklin. He returned to England in November of the following year, receiving for his services the thanks of the Admiralty, and on the first vacancy that occurred, the good service pension, which he enjoyed until his promotion to the rank of Rear-Admiral in December, 1856. Sir J. C. Ross was elected a Fellow of the Linnæan Society in 1823; of the Royal Astronomical Society in 1825; and of the Royal Society in 1828. He is also a member of the Royal Society of Antiquaries of Copenhagen, and corresponding member of the Institute and Geographical Society of Paris. He received in 1833, the thanks of the city of London, and a handsome piece of plate from the subscribers to the Land Arctic Expedition. He obtained in 1841, the Founder's Gold Medal from the Geographical Society of London; in 1842 the Gold Medal of the Geographical Society of Paris; was knighted in 1844, and received the honorary degree of D.C.L. from the University of Oxford in the same year. He married on the 18th of October, 1843, Anne, eldest daughter of Thomas Coutman, Esq., of Whitgift Hall, Goole, by whom he has four children. Lady Ross died on the 25th of January, 1857.

ROSSE, EARL OF, WILLIAM PARSONS, an astronomer, was born at York in 1800. He was educated at Oxford, where he gained great distinction as a student of mathematics. He represented, under his title by courtesy of Lord Oxmantown, King's County for many years, and in 1845 entered the House of Lords as one of the Irish representative peers. Lord Rosse has acquired a European reputation on account of his extraordinary devotion to practical astronomy. His gigantic telescope, erected at his residence, Parsonstown in Ireland, is the largest ever constructed. The speculum is about six feet in diameter, weighs over three tons, and its tube is about fifty-six feet in length. This instrument, which cost an immense expenditure of time and money, has been of the highest value in resolving nebulæ, which inferior telescopes had failed to divide, and has shown the falsity of theories of the nebulous system which had previously received great countenance from men of science. Lord Rosse was President of the Royal Society for some time, and his name is enrolled amongst the members of the leading scientific associations of Europe.

ROSSINI, JOACCHINO, an Italian musician and composer, was born at Pesaro, in 1792. His parents followed the musical profession, and young Rossini speedily gave evidence that he possessed extraordinary talents in that line. He studied at Bologna, and having discovered the channel in which his musical genius would have free course, he abandoned the practice of music for that of its composition, and resolved to devote himself to the production of operas. After severe study of the best masters, he produced "Tancredi," at Venice in 1813, which soon brought him into high repute. Its success encouraged him, and he afterwards produced others, which, however, did not meet with so good a reception. Having become Musical Director at Naples in 1816, he brought out two operas, one of these being the well-known "Il Bar-

biére di Siviglia." These were followed, in 1817, by "La Cenerentola" and "La Gazza Ladra," "Mosé in Egitto," "La Donna del Lago," "Zelmira," and "Semiramide." He visited Paris and London in 1824, and in both cities his talents obtained for him an enthusiastic reception. His "Guillaume Tell" was produced in 1829, since which he composed his "Stabat Mater," one of the last effusions of his genius. He has for some years retired into private life, and takes but little interest in subjects to which he had devoted his earlier days.

ROTHSCHILD, LIONEL NATHAN, M.P., BARON DE, a capitalist, and one of the firm of the Rothschilds, was born in London in 1808, and is the son of Baron Nathan, who, after leaving Manchester in 1800, became resident in London. He succeeded to his father's connexions and title in 1836. Baron Rothschild was the first member of the Jewish persuasion who ever attempted to enter the House of Commons. In 1847 he was proposed and elected together with Lord John Russell and others as one of the four members for the city of London. Declining, however, to take the necessary oaths, "on the true faith of a Christian," he was precluded from taking a seat in the House till the session of 1858, when Mr. T. S. Duncombe succeeded in placing him on a committee which the rules of the House did not provide against. Eventually a resolution was passed by means of which he was enabled to sit as a member. The city of London had returned him at every election during the interval, and had thus asserted its rights as to the choice of its representatives. Baron Rothschild is liberal in his politics, but has never taken any prominent position in the House of Commons.

RUDERSDORFF, MADAME, a vocalist, is a native of Russia, having been born at Ivanofsky, in the Ukrane. Coming to England with her father while a child, she sung in Hull when only twelve years of age. Under the distinguished masters Bordogni, Rubini, and Lablache, she afterwards studied at Paris, and, at the age of fourteen, sung Mendelssohn's Hymn of Praise with great success in Leipsig, at the celebration in honour of the centenary of printing. Subsequently the youthful *artiste* went to Italy, to complete her musical training under the Cavalier Michcroux, the celebrated master of Pasta. Having accomplished that object, she returned to Germany, and sung there at all the principal Courts. Persuaded by the Grand Duchess of Baden to go on the stage, Madame Rudersdorff made her first appearance in that new sphere at Frankfort, with remarkable success. Subsequently she appeared at Berlin, Vienna, Dresden, Hamburg, and London, with equal acceptability, exciting peculiar admiration from the remarkable diversity of her style.

RUHMKORFF, N., a French instrument maker, was born in Germany in the early part of the present century. He is chiefly known in scientific circles as the inventor of a coil machine, which produces astonishing effects by electromagnetic induction. By carefully considering the construction of the old form of coil machine, M. Ruhmkorff was led to the construction of an instrument which has been of the highest value to electricians, inasmuch as it has completed the link which was long wanting between the sciences of frictional and voltaic electricity. A modification of his coil was some time employed in working the Atlantic telegraph, for which it seemed suitable, on account of the great intensity of the current it produces. M. Ruhmkorff's coils have been improved upon by Messrs. Bentley and Hearder, of this country. In 1855 he received a medal and decoration of the first class at the Exposition Uni-

verselle of Paris, for his various applications of electricity.

RUSKIN, JOHN, an art critic, was born in London in February, 1819. His education was completed at Oxford, where, in 1839, he carried off the Newdegate prize for an English poem, and graduated double fourth class in 1842. Art was his favourite study, and conceiving an extraordinary admiration for Turner, and deeming that artist entitled to a higher place in public estimation than that conceded to him, he commenced a letter, in reply to some of Turner's censors, which ultimately expanded into a treatise, with the title of " Modern Painters : their Superiority in the Art of Landscape Painting to all the Ancient Masters, by a Graduate of Oxford." This work at once secured for its author a high position as a man of genius. He took very bold ground, not scrupling to condemn, with all his force, the great old masters in landscape, such as Claude, Poussin, Salvator, Ruysdael, and numerous others, as compared with such men as Turner. He did not even stop there, for he dealt his blows on all sides at the modern painters of the French and German schools. The work startled every one; it was thoroughly iconoclastic in its tone, knocking down, without remorse, the art idols of centuries. After an interval of ten years, the subsequent portions of this work were published. " Modern Painters " was followed by " The Seven Lamps of Architecture," and " The Stones of Venice," a work of sound criticism. Lectures on " Architecture and Painting;" Elementary Treatises on Drawing and Perspective; Notes on the " Construction of Sheepfolds;" a pamphlet on " Pre-Raphaelitism," and notes on the " Exhibitions of the Royal Academy," are his chief recent productions. Mr. Ruskin is reported on good authority to have abandoned all other studies, in order to

devote his future labours exclusively to the works of Turner and the Venetians.

RUSSEL, ALEXANDER, a journalist, was born at Edinburgh, in 1814. Having no desire to follow the legal profession, of which his father was a member, he turned his attention to literature, and commenced writing papers for various magazines. He was successively editor of the "Berwick Advertiser," the "Fife Herald," and eventually of the "Scotsman," with the latter of which he has been connected for many years, and edits at the present time. His consistent and able defence of liberal principles, and the steady devotion to objects of social improvement which Mr. Russel always exhibits, have lately been acknowledged by a testimonial of nearly two thousand pounds, which has been presented to him by his readers and admirers throughout Scotland.

RUSSELL, JOHN SCOTT, F.R.S., an engineer, was born in the Vale of Clyde, in 1808. He received his education at the Universities of Edinburgh, St. Andrews, and Glasgow, and graduated at the latter place in 1824. He was from childhood fond of mechanical pursuits, and his bias being encouraged by his friends, he studied mathematical and physical science at Edinburgh, besides acquiring considerable practical expertness in mechanics. After being for some time at the head of a ship-building establishment in Greenock, and afterwards of an engineering concern in Edinburgh, he removed to London in 1844; though not until he had tried the experiment of running steam coaches on common roads. His mind was eminently inventive. The construction of iron ships and boats directed his attention to the forms of vessels. He experimented largely on the question of the oscillations produced in canals by vessels, and embodied the result of his investigations in a paper read before the British Association in 1835. The subject ex-

cited great interest; and for some years, with every description of model, on the ocean, on lakes, canals, rivers, and estuaries, he continued his experiments, which amounted to the almost incredible number of 20,000. He at length conceived the idea of constructing a ship's hull of such a form as to receive the least possible resistance from water in its progress through that liquid. The first vessel constructed on his "wave principle" was the "Wave," in 1835, which was followed by the "Scott Russell" in 1836, and the "Flambeau" and "Fire King" in 1839. These ships were all successful. This principle was adopted by Mr. Brunel in designing the "Great Britain," and it has steadily made its way both in Britain and America. The greatest triumph of Mr. Scott Russell's genius is the "Great Eastern," which is a wonder of skill and science. The difficulties of its construction were very great, owing to its enormous size. It has, however, satisfactorily proved that Mr. Russell's theory is well grounded; and the perfection of its construction, and its realization of the speed which had been predicted, stand out as high testimonies to the intelligence and ability of its builder. During its late trip to America, a speed of sixteen statute miles was frequently attained for hours together, and its passengers enjoyed an almost entire immunity from the distressing effects of seasickness. In 1837 he was awarded the gold medal of the Royal Society of Edinburgh; and, in 1849, was elected a Fellow of the Royal Society of London.

RUSSELL, THE RIGHT HONOURABLE LORD JOHN, M.P., was born in London, 18th of August, 1792. He was educated at Westminster School, and Edinburgh University. His political life commenced in 1813, when he entered the House of Commons as member for the Whig borough of Tavistock, and joined the opposition against Lords Liverpool and

Castlereagh. His repeated motions on Parliamentary Reform, combined with the progress of popular opinion, prepared the country for the bill of 1832. In 1826 so small was the majority existing against the measure, that the question appeared virtually settled. In 1827 Canning was created Premier. The junction of Lord Lansdowne and Mr. Tierney with Mr. Canning, who was pledged against reform, delayed the question for some time, and it was not until 1828 that Lord John was left free to pursue his reform policy. From the beginning of 1828 until 1830, no one of the reform leaders in the House of Commons exhibited greater activity, or greater tenacity of purpose in the advocacy of all those liberal measures which it is now deemed the glory of our Parliament to have adopted. In 1830 Lord John Russell entered office under Earl Grey, as Paymaster of the Forces. The Grey cabinet was pledged to carry Parliamentary Reform, and the most onerous part of the labour of the ministry, in connexion with the question, was performed by Lord John Russell. In conjunction with Sir James Graham, Lord Durham, and Lord Duncannon, he was appointed to prepare the bill that was to be submitted to the House. On the 1st March, 1831, after having submitted the results of their joint labours to their colleagues in the ministry, Lord John Russell introduced the Reform Bill in the House of Commons, which, after strong discussion, passed by a majority of one, and Parliament was dissolved. In the new Parliament the bill was again introduced, and passed through all its stages in the new House. The bill was, however, thrown out in the Lords. The ministry were ready to resign ; but a vote of confidence passed in the Commons prevented them, and Parliament was prorogued. On re-assembling, the bill, somewhat modified, was again introduced in the Lords, but

was again rejected. The ministry resigned ; the Duke of Wellington came into power. The responsibility of office disclosed to the duke the fact that Toryism, such as his, had then become an impossibility. He gave way to necessity, and on the 7th of June the Reform Bill became law, Earl Grey being Premier. Through all this crisis the conduct of Lord John Russell was of that intrepid character which adds intensely to popularity. After Lord Grey's retirement in 1834, and the accession of Lord Melbourne to the premiership, he gave the government his strenuous support ; and when that ministry fell, towards the close of the same year, he went into opposition with a stainless reputation as a consistent and energetic Whig. On the resignation of Sir Robert Peel in April, 1835, a ministry was formed under Lord Melbourne, and Lord John became Home Secretary, and leader of the House of Commons. The post of Home was subsequently exchanged for that of Colonial Secretary. Lord John, now member for Stroud, having been defeated in his family county of Devon, gave the world a series of letters addressed to his constituents, on the principles of the Reform Act. Public confidence, however, not returning to the Whig party, and the results of the general election of 1841 being decidedly unfavourable,—in August, 1841, the ministry resigned. During the ministry of Sir Robert Peel the anti-Corn-law league became a "great fact," and Lord John Russell was elected for the first time member for the city of London in 1841, on Free-trade principles, for which city he has sat ever since. If he did not exactly think with Lord Melbourne, that the repeal of the Corn-laws was the maddest thing he ever heard of, he was at least averse to so extensive a proposal, his pet scheme being a fixed duty. In the autumn of 1845, however, he became a convert to immediate repeal. On the fall of the ministry of Sir Robert Peel, Lord John became Premier; but in March, 1852, the country with indifference beheld him making way for Lord Derby and Mr. Disraeli. On the fall of the Derby administration Lord John Russell became Foreign Secretary in the Coalition cabinet of Lord Aberdeen until 1853, when he resigned in favour of Lord Clarendon. In June, 1854, he became Lord President of the Council, and brought forward his new Reform Bill. The Russian war, however, prevented it from receiving consideration. Disapproving of the conduct of the war by the Aberdeen cabinet, Lord John Russell resigned. When Lord Palmerston became Premier, Lord John became Colonial Secretary. Subsequently he accepted the appointment of British plenipotentiary at the Vienna conferences, but the results of his negotiations were unsatisfactory; and in June, 1855, he resigned. He is at the present time (October, 1860) Secretary of State for Foreign Affairs. During the late session a new Reform Bill was introduced under his care in the House of Commons; but owing to a general apathy on the question, it was eventually shelved, with a promise of being introduced during 1861 in a modified form. Lord John has at all times taken deep interest in educational questions, and in societies intended to promote such objects. In addition to his labours as a statesman, Lord John Russell is not unknown to the world of letters. In 1819 he published a Life of his ancestor, Lord William Russell; in 1821 an essay on the " History of the English Government and Constitution, from the Reign of Henry VII. to the Present Time;" in 1822, "Don Carlos," a tragedy, appeared. This effort in verse was followed by a memoir of the "Affairs of Europe, from the Peace of Utrecht." Memoirs of Moore, of Fox, of the Fourth Duke of Bedford, &c., have also issued from his pen.

RUSSELL, WILLIAM HOWARD, LL.D., a journalist and special correspondent of "The Times," was born at Lily Vale, in the county Dublin, in September, 1821. Educated at a school in Dublin, he entered Trinity College in 1838. During the second and final Repeal agitation Mr. Russell contributed a series of articles and correspondence to "The Times," in reference to the movements inaugurated and fostered by Mr. O'Connell, which led to a closer connexion with that journal, and ultimately to a relationship with it which has existed almost uninterruptedly up to the present time. In 1843 he proceeded to London, and a few years afterwards entered the Middle Temple. He was called to the bar in 1850, but his literary engagements and his position as a journalist attached to a London daily paper did not permit him to go circuit, and he was obliged to restrict his efforts to obtain legal distinction to the Courts in Westminster. On various occasions he was selected by "The Times," to proceed as correspondent to Denmark, France, and elsewhere on the Continent. In 1854 the active position taken by England in opposition to the demands of Russia on the Ottoman Porte led to the despatch of an English force to the East, which he accompanied, at the request of the proprietors of "The Times," as their Special Correspondent. In that capacity he was present, and was under fire, at all the actions of the Crimean campaign; and the details which he wrote of the war, and of the progress of the siege of Sebastopol, as well as the accounts of the sufferings of our troops, commanded public attention, and were looked for with intense interest throughout Europe. He returned to England in 1856, on the evacuation of the Crimea, and was but a few days at home when he started for Moscow, to attend the coronation of the Emperor, after which he travelled south and revisited the Crimea, and reached London in the beginning of 1857, after a tour overland from Moscow to Paris, by Sebastopol, Odessa, Belgrade, and Czernovich. In the same year he received the degree of LL.D. from his "Alma Mater," and at the close of 1857 he departed for India, and arrived in time to accompany Lord Clyde to the attack and capture of Lucknow, and to witness the operations which led to the subjugation of Oude and Rohilcund, and the suppression of the rebellion. His communications respecting these operations and the state of the country, civil and military, excited attention in England, and were approved of by statesmen in India. On his return to England from India in 1859, with health impaired by a severe sunstroke at the battle of Bareilly, and an injury to a limb from a kick by a horse, he published a work called "My Diary in India," which has met with great success. Dr. Russell is now engaged in editing a weekly journal, which he established in the beginning of 1860, devoted to the interests of the services, and called "The Army and Navy Gazette," but still retains his connexion with "The Times." His "Letters from the Crimea" have been published in a collected form, and have passed through many editions.

RUSSIA, EMPEROR OF. (See ALEXANDER II.)

SABINE, MAJOR-GENERAL EDWARD, an English philosopher, descended from an ancient Italian family, was born about 1790. He joined the British army as an officer of artillery, and first became known by having taken part in the Northern Exploring Expedition of 1819 and 1820, under Ross and Parry. His magnetic observations during the course of that voyage gave the first great impulse to the systematic study of the phenomena of terrestrial magnetism, while his papers inserted in the "Philosophical Transactions" of the Royal Society demonstrated previously unascertained facts relative to the variations of the magnetic needle. His mind was drawn into a particular channel of observation in physics; and to extend his knowledge, and confirm, by minute investigation, the truth of his theories, he commenced in 1821 a series of voyages, which ranged from the Equator to the Arctic circle. The results were published in 1825, under the title of "Pendulum, and other Experiments." In 1827, having obtained leave of absence from his regiment, he was chosen Secretary of the Royal Society, which office he held until ordered in 1830 to military duty in Ireland. While employed on the general staff of the army in that country, he occupied his leisure time in pursuing his favourite researches, the fruits of his investigations being almost invariably laid before the British Association for the Advancement of Science. In 1836, and the two following years, he made reports to the Association, and to him it is we owe a vast system of magnetic observatories, which have altogether changed the aspect of that branch of science. The colonial observatories are under his superintendence, and he has directed them with the greatest care and the most profound skill. His papers contributed to various learned bodies are voluminous, and full of research. He has been twenty-three years a member of the British Association, twenty-one years one of its Secretaries, and eight years General Secretary, filling the office of President in 1853. He is a Fellow of the Royal Society, and since 1850 has been Treasurer of that body, and Vice-President. He is the author of thirty-four memoirs, published in the "Philosophical Transactions."

SAINTE-CLAIRE DEVILLE, HENRY, a French chemist, was born in 1818, at St. Thomas, in the Antilles. Receiving his early education in France, he devoted himself ardently to the study of chemistry, and achieved great success, although entirely unaided by any of the usual instructions in science, being, in fact, entirely dependent on his own abilities. In 1845 he became Professor at the Faculty of Science in Besançon, and afterwards succeeded M. Balard in the chemical chair of the Normal School. He distinguished himself by various original researches in chemical science, but owes his reputation to the discovery of a means of producing in quantities the metal aluminum, one of the constituents of common clay. Although Sir Humphrey Davy had imagined and M. Woehler had proved that clay or alumina was the oxide of a metal, neither had been able to produce sufficient of the metal itself to be of any value in the arts or commerce. Thanks to the scientific tastes of the Emperor of the French, M. Sainte-Claire Deville was enabled to carry on his experiments till they ended in a successful result. The new metal, which is not heavier than the same bulk of glass, has all the excellent qualities of silver, which it much resembles in appearance. On its first production in 1855, it was eagerly purchased at a higher price than gold, but at the present time it is sold in the form of spectacles, brooches, and even helmets, medals, &c. have been made from it; and its cost is less than that of the same weight of silver. The discovery has, strange to say, had an effect on the Greenland shipping trade, as the Cryolite from which the metal is produced is obtained from that country.

SAINT LEONARDS, EDWARD BUR-TENSHAW SUGDEN, BARON, (ex-Lord Chancellor), was born in 1781, and entered the bar at Lincoln's Inn in 1807. His great abilities and numerous legal works brought him great employment as a conveyancer; but in 1817 he came to the conclusion to change his branch of practice. The fact becoming known, it at once obtained for him an extensive practice at the Chancery bar. He was elected for Weymouth in 1828, and in 1829 was made Solicitor-General. In 1835 he was made Lord Chancellor of Ireland, under Peel. Resigning this position on Peel going out of office, he resumed it in 1841, when Sir Robert again became Premier. Retiring with his party in 1846, when Lord Derby succeeded to power in 1852 he became Lord Chancellor, being raised to the peerage with the title of Baron St. Leonards. His lordship is distinguished by his zeal as a law reformer, and several important legal works of a popular character, written by him, have attained a great and deserved fame. In Parliament he was not distinguished as a debater, but his knowledge of the law rendered him a most valuable adherent to the party whose cause he espoused.

SALA, GEORGE AUGUSTUS, an English essayist and tale-writer, was born in London in 1827. His father is understood to have been an Italian, and his mother a native of the West Indies. Educated as an artist, he abandoned his first profession for literature. To the earliest numbers of "Household Words" Mr. Sala was a contributor, and he afterwards wrote some of the best of the many good articles which appeared in that popular publication. Among these may be enumerated— "The Key of the Street," "The Secrets of Gas," "Tattyboy's Rents," "The Musical World," "The Compassionate Broker," "Jack Alive in London," "Getting up a Pantomime," "Little Blue Mantle," "A Dead Secret," "Phases of Public Life," and "Acon Verlaz and the Little Blind Girl." In 1856 Mr. Sala published in verse a Grand, National, Historical, and Chivalric Pantomime, "Ye Belle Alliance; or, Harlequin Good Humour and ye Fielde of ye Cloth of Gold." Two years afterwards he reprinted in a separate form a series of his articles which had appeared in "Household Words," under the title of "A Journey due North : being Notes of a Residence in Russia in the Summer of 1856." This work has gone through a second edition. He has since republished two other works from the popular serials in which the first made their appearance. One of these is "Twice Round the Clock ; or, the Hours of the Day and Night in London ;" originally contributed to the "Welcome Guest," and the other "The Baddington Peerage; Who bore it and Who wore it : a Story of the Best and Worst Society." In all his writings, Mr. Sala exhibits great descriptive powers, and he enjoys a very high reputation as an author with a numerous class of readers, and as rivalling Dickens and Thackeray in their peculiar styles. He is one of the most prolific writers of the day.

SALDANHA, OLIVIERA E. DAUN JOAO CARLOS, DUKE OF, a Portuguese marshal and politician, was born at Lisbon, on the 17th of November, 1790. He held already the rank of Captain when General Beresford took the command of the Portuguese army in 1808, and at the end of the Peninsular war he commanded a brigade. In 1814 he first visited England. In 1816 he commanded two of the three divisions forming the Portuguese army in the war against Artigas. Refusing all the inducements offered him to remain in Brazil by the Emperor Don Pedro, he returned to England in 1823. On his return the Portuguese government wished to appoint him Viceroy of Brazil, and place him at the head of an army and navy for the recovery of the country; but he refused to accept the command. In 1826 he was appointed Minister at War. In 1827, for the second time, Saldanha came to England, but was recalled to Portugal by Don Pedro, and took the command of the constitutional army. In March, 1833,

he kept his ground, in spite of the overwhelming numbers of the enemy, and gained numerous victories. In 1836 he returned to Lisbon, where he has taken a prominent place in all the movements and counter-movements which have since occurred. Besides being an able soldier, Saldanha is a leading speaker in the Portuguese Chambers. He is also an author, having published works on various subjects. Perhaps the most remarkable are those entitled "The Concordance of the Natural Sciences," and "Geology with Genesis." The latter work made a great impression in Roman Catholic countries. On its publication the Pope sent Saldanha the Grand Cross of Saint Gregory. He is also the author of a work entitled "The State of Medicine in 1848." He is Vice-President of the Academy of Sciences at Lisbon, of which the sovereign is always the President, and member of most of the scientific academies of the Continent, and has been decorated with medals and crosses by nearly all the sovereigns in Europe.

SALOMONS, DAVID, M.P., was born in London, in 1801. Being of the Jewish persuasion, he is well known as having succeeded in occupying leading positions in the affairs of the city of London, and, like Rothschild, at last entering the House of Commons, despite the lengthened opposition which was shown to the admission of their co-religionists to offices of responsibility in the state. Thrice was he elected alderman, and each time repelled from the court on account of his religious persuasion ; he, however, succeeded in his attempt in 1847. He was elected member for Greenwich in 1851, but did not take his seat until 1858, owing to his objecting to the form of oath, which had to be taken "on the true faith of a Christian." In 1855 he was elected Lord Mayor of London, being the first Hebrew who ever held that position. Mr. Salomons is held in high esteem amongst his brethren, on account of his charitable and generous disposition.

SANTA ANNA, Don Antonio Lopez de, a Mexican statesman and soldier, was born in the city of Talapa, on the 21st of February, 1798. He entered the Spanish army in June, 1810, and was raised to the rank of Lieutenant-Colonel in 1821. While he was engaged in a survey near Vera Cruz, Iturbide issued a proclamation, to which Santa Anna gave his adhesion. Placing himself at the head of the Mexican troops, in seven months he defeated more than 10,000 of the Spaniards, and completely reduced under his power the province of Vera Cruz. On the 2nd December, 1822, he proclaimed the Mexican Republic, the sovereignty assumed by "Emperor Iturbide" having by that time terminated its brief existence; and in 1829, he defeated the Spanish division which invaded Mexico by way of Tampico, with the intention of reconquest. At different times, and with varied success, he fought in Texas against the Filibusteros of North America, in defence of the integrity of the Mexican territory, and on the 6th of October, 1838, repulsed a body of French troops which had made an attack upon Vera Cruz, driving them into the sea at the point of the bayonet. In this action he had the misfortune to lose one of his legs by a gunshot wound. In 1847 and 1848 he commanded the Mexican troops against the army of the United States, under General Taylor and General Scott. With the former he fought in Angostura, while with the latter he had encounters, with various success, and dreading the policy of the Mexican people, who were intent on having peace at any price, and not accepting the democratic principles which some political parties have sought to establish in Mexico, he thought it wise to abdicate power and to take up his abode beyond the Mexican frontiers. He feels keenly the miserable situation in which the country has been placed since his departure, and which he strenuously sought to avert during his tenure of office. He has received the Spanish decoration of the Grand Cross of Charles III., and the Prussian Grand Cross of the Red Eagle. During the civil war in Mexico he was always victorious, and he has been generally recognised as the ablest of the Mexican generals. He is still at the head of a powerful party of his countrymen.

SANTINI, Giovanni, an Italian astronomer, was born in Tuscany in June, 1786. He was educated principally in the University of Pisa, science occupying much of his studies, until 1814, when he replaced Cheminello as Professor at the Observatory of Padua. In 1825 he became Principal of the University. He holds at present the double office of Professor of Astronomy and Director of the Mathematical Classes. Santini's works embrace both mathematics and astronomy, and are considered very lucid expositions of the subjects he undertakes to illustrate and explain.

SARDINIA, King of. (See Victor Emmanuel.)

SARTORIUS, Ernest William Christian, a German Protestant theologian, and one of the most earnest orthodox controversialists of his age and country, was born at Darmstadt, in May, 1797. He studied at Göttingen, and becoming devoted to divinity, was, at the early age of twenty-six, appointed Professor of Theology in the University of Marbourg. In 1824 he was nominated to a similar office at Dorpat, in Russia. He returned to Germany in 1835, and accepted the Direction of the Consistory at Königsberg. In politics as in religion he takes his place under the standard of fixity. What is should not admit of change—such is his view. Being, however, one of the Evangelical school of divines, his principles are tolerant, and possibly there are few theologians in Germany who elicit such universal respect. His first work of consequence was the "Drei Abhandlungen, &c., or Three Dissertations," which was published in 1820, treating of important matters in exegetical and systematic theology. In 1822 he published a treatise on the Protestant doctrine, as regards temporal authority, and thenceforward he continued to issue works in defence of the evangelical faith, most of which have passed through several editions, and been translated into other languages. Though his orthodoxy is severe, his style of writing is graceful, and quite divested of pedantry.

SAULCY, LOUIS FÉLICIEN JOSEPH CAIGNART DE, a French antiquarian, was born at Lille, in March, 1807. In 1826 he was admitted to the Polytechnic School, and entered the army as an artillery officer. He employed his leisure hours in the study of numismatics and archæology. Promoted by degrees, to the rank of captain, and stationed as Professor to the Military School of Metz, he became the most noted antiquarian of the province. His publications were attractive; and in March, 1839, he was elected a Corresponding Member of the Academy of Inscriptions and Belles Lettres, having previously obtained the prize awarded by the Institute for an "Essay on the Classification of Byzantine Coins." His tastes led him to Paris, and being installed as Conservator of the Musée d'Artillerie of the capital, he was elected in 1842 to succeed Mionnet, as Numismatist in the Académie des Inscriptions. Faithful to his predilections, M. de Saulcy turned his attention to the deciphering of the cuneiform and other Eastern inscriptions, and with the view of studying the subject, left France for Palestine in 1850. On his return he announced a number of discoveries he had made in the East, and published his "Voyage autour de la Mer Morte et dans les Terres Bibliques," which was illustrated by maps and engravings. M. Saulcy is one of the most happily and variously gifted antiquarians of France. He retired from the artillery with the rank of Chef d'Escadron, and was raised to the dignity of a senator in 1859. He has made several journeys to the East, and has besides travelled in Iceland and Greenland, and in all parts of Europe.

SAY, HORACE ÉMILE, a French political economist and member of the Institute, was born at Paris in March, 1794, and educated at Geneva. The son of the great economist, Jean Baptiste Say, he commenced his career in the commercial establishment of a relation, proceeding in 1813 to the United States, as a supercargo; and two years afterwards he went to Brazil, where he remained for a lengthened period. Up to 1831 he devoted his energies to commercial enterprise; but in that year he was chosen Judge of the Tribunal of Commerce of the Seine, and in 1834 became a member of the Chamber. He was elected member of the Municipal Council, and the Council-General for the Department of the Seine, in 1837 and 1846, retaining his position under the Republic and the Empire. The National Assembly in 1849 appointed him one of the Council of State, but he retired from that body on the memorable 2nd of December, 1851. The works of M. Say are not numerous, but they indicate high ability and express liberal views of commercial policy. His chief work is a "History of the Commercial Intercourse between France and Brazil." He has edited with discriminating care the great work of his father, "The Complete Practical Course of Political Economy." He is also the author of a "Report on the Inquiry undertaken by the Chamber of Commerce of the Seine," which gained the prize of the Academy of Sciences in 1853. M. Say is the founder of the "Journal of Political Economy," to which he contributed numerous articles, the chief of which have been collected and published separately.

SCARLETT, GENERAL, THE HON. SIR JAMES YORKE, an English general, was born in 1799, and is son of the late Lord Abinger. His early education was received at Eton, whence he proceeded to the University of Cambridge. After entering the army, he spent some time in military study at Sandhurst, and subsequently rose in his profession, until he became Colonel in 1852. On the breaking out of the war with Russia in 1854, he entered into active service, and as commander of the heavy cavalry, highly distinguished himself in a splendid charge on the Russians, who had attacked Balaclava on 25th October, 1854. As an acknowledgment of his services, he was made Major-General towards the close of the year, and shortly afterwards succeeded Lord Lucan as Commander of the Cavalry. He is a Knight Commander of the Bath.

SCHAMYL, a Caucasian warrior, was born in 1797, in the north of the Caucasian district of Daghestan. He belongs to the "Sufi" party, the reformers of Islamism. He commenced his career in 1824, and entered with his whole heart on what was to him a holy war against the Russians. In 1831 the Circassians gained some decided advantages; Schamyl was left for dead in one instance; another was chosen for chief, and Schamyl acted under him, on his recovery, without a murmur. He has been the reputed leader of the Circassians since 1836, and has performed some wonderful military exploits while contending with superior bodies of Russians. So few reliable accounts are to be obtained of a struggle which lasted upwards of thirty years, that much remains for conjecture; but, at all events, it is certain that while Schamyl achieved many victories, he was anxious to obtain Western assistance during the war in the Crimea. He has been termed the Abd-el-Kader of the Caucasus; and, like the Arab chief, has fallen into the hands of his enemy. Deserted by numbers on whom he had placed dependence, Schamyl and his son became in 1859 captives, and Russia at length took possession of the long-coveted territory.

SCHNORR, JULES, a German painter, was born at Leipsic, on 26th March, 1794. His education was chiefly received in the Academy at Vienna, where, with the assistance of some friends, he founded a society for the encouragement of rising artists. In 1817 he went to Rome, where he remained for some years, and returning to Germany, he obtained a chair at the Academy of Fine Arts at Munich, in 1827. His works are chiefly on Scriptural subjects, amongst which may be mentioned his "Marriage at Cana," "Jacob and Rachel," "The Flight into Egypt," and "The Annunciation of the Virgin." He undertook, in conjunction with M. Neurenther, the preparation of a series of wood-cuts, illustrative of Bible scenes.

SCHŒLCHER, VICTOR, a French democratic politician and author, was born in July, 1804. His education was received at the College of Louis-le-Grand, and almost immediately on leaving that seminary, he attached himself to the ultra party, which opposed the restoration, and became connected with the "Friends of Truth," then with the "Aide Toi" society, and thirdly, with the Society of "The Rights of Man." Decided in his advocacy of republicanism, he opposed the monarchy of July, 1830, and contributed both money and able advice to the journals in the republican interest. Having, however, visited the United States, Mexico, and Cuba, he imbibed so strong a detestation of slavery, that its abolition became with him the special question. In order to obtain a fuller and more accurate knowledge of the system, he travelled to almost all the countries where it exists, and from time to time published the fruits of his investigations, incessantly pleading the cause of the coloured races. In 1847 he made a journey to Africa, and on his return was engaged in preparing a work on the condition of the black population, when the revolution of February, 1848, took place. He arrived in Paris on March 3rd, 1848, and was on that day nominated to the Ministry of Marine, and the office of Under-Secretary of State. On the 4th, he appointed a commission to draw up a project of law on the subject of emancipation. In the same month he issued a decree abolishing the lash in the maritime service, and in April he decreed the abolition of slavery in the French colonies. Returned to the Legislative Assembly, he defended his measures and principles alike from the tribune and through the press, while as Vice-President of the Montagne party, he invariably voted with the extreme left. The *coup d'état* of December, 1851, brought about his expulsion from France, and he retired to England, where he still remains.

SCHOMBURGK, SIR ROBERT HERMANN, a traveller and naturalist, was born in Thuringia, in 1804. Having devoted himself to Natural Science, he undertook an exploratory voyage to Guiana in 1835, under the auspices of the Royal Geographical Society of London, and his botanical researches were rewarded by the discovery of that remarkable plant, the Victoria Regia water-lily. His success in this exploratory mission was acknowledged by the honour of knighthood being conferred on him, and the award of the gold medal of the Royal Geographical Society. Sir R. H. Schomburgk has published a "Survey of British Guiana," "Views in the Interior of Guiana," and a "History of Barbadoes." As British Consul at St. Domingo he pursues his favourite studies, and sends papers to the Geographical and other Societies. He is a Knight of the Russian Order of the Red Eagle ; of the Saxon Order of Merit ; a Chevalier of the Legion of Honour, and a Doctor of Philosophy of the University of Königsberg.

SCHÖNLEIN, JOHANN LUK, a German physician of eminence, was born at Bamberg, in Bavaria, November 30th, 1793, and was educated at the Gymnasium of that place, and the Universities of Landshut and Würzburg. Having completed a still further course of study at Göttingen and Jena, he was appointed joint professor, and in 1824, Titular Professor of Clinical Medicine, Würzburg Charged with the direction of the Hospital of Würzburg, he achieved in a brief period the double reputation of being an able practitioner and a learned lecturer. In 1833 he became Professor of Clinical Medicine at Zurich, and held that position until 1839, when he was invited to Berlin, where he has since remained, exercising the functions of Professor of Pathology in the University, Professor at the Medical and Surgical Military Academy, Counsellor of the Minister for Medical Affairs, and Physician to the King of Prussia. Professor Schönlein is distinguished throughout Germany by his reported lectures, which are held in the highest estimation by the profession, and by the cases published by his pupils, both of which have, in most instances, been translated into other languages. He has published nothing whatever himself, but his opinions can be gleaned with tolerable accuracy from some of his pupils' publications, among which the more prominent are "Allgemeine und Specielle Pathologie und Therapie," "Krankenfamilie der Typhen," and "Klinische Vorträge im Charité Krankenhause zu Berlin."

SCOTT, GEORGE GILBERT, A.R.A.,

an English architect, was born in the year 1811, at Gawcott, near Buckingham. Having evinced a taste for architecture, he was articled to an architect in London in 1827, and commenced practice in 1835. He was, for some years, in partnership with a fellow pupil, Mr. Moffatt, during which time he undertook a great number of important works. Those more immediately of the style in which he has since excelled are the Martyrs' Memorial at Oxford, St. Giles' Church, Camberwell, and the restoration of St. Margaret's, Stafford. The partnership was dissolved in 1845 or 1846, about which time he had been selected as the architect to the new church of St. Nicholas, at Hamburg, said to be one of the finest works of its class in Germany, and which is equal in size to some of the largest cathedrals. In competition with the most eminent architects of Europe he again bore away the first prize for erecting the Hôtel de Ville of Hamburg, in 1855. Among Mr. Scott's principal works, besides those already mentioned, may be enumerated the complete portion of the cathedral of St. John's, Newfoundland; the restoration of the choir of Ely Cathedral; the new church of St. George, Doncaster, of All Souls', Halifax; the new chapel, library, and other buildings at Exeter College, Oxford, Kelham Hall, Nottinghamshire, Walter House, Warwickshire, Pipbrook House, Surrey; the restorations of Newark Church, Hereford Cathedral, and St. Michael's Church, Cornhill. Mr. Scott was elected architect to Westminster Abbey in 1849. He has, for some years past, been an Associate of the Royal Academy, and, since the virtual retirement of Professor Cockerell, has undertaken the Architectural Lectures at the Academy, in conjunction with Mr. Sydney Smirke. He received the Royal Gold Medal from the Institute of British Architects in 1859, a few months previously having been appointed architect to the new Foreign Office, and joint architect with Mr. Digby Wyatt to the new India Office. Mr. Scott has published several works on architecture, and is one of the founders of the London Architectural Museum.

SCRIBE, Eugène, a French dramatic writer, was born on the 25th December, 1791, at Paris. At an early age he began a career as an author which has been eminently successful. Having a taste for the drama, his friends recommended him to abandon the bar, which he had followed, for the stage. He is a most voluminous writer, and one of the most ingenious inventors of a plot. He writes chiefly for the stage, and perhaps no country is more indebted to him in that respect than England, which is incessantly receiving free translations of his works. He has written the libretto to more than one popular opera, and always displays the faculty of suiting his words to the composer's music. Among his best known pieces are "La Muette de Portici," "Fra Diavolo," "Les Diamants de la Couronne," &c.

SEDGWICK, Amy, (Mrs. Parkes,) an English actress, was born at Bristol, in 1835. In early life she exhibited a decided taste for the profession in which she has since so highly distinguished herself. In 1852 she occasionally performed in amateur theatricals, and made her début at Richmond in 1853, as 'Julia' in the "Hunchback," achieving considerable success. She afterwards returned to Bristol, and subsequently appeared at Cardiff, as 'Pauline,' in the "Lady of Lyons." After performing in many of the principal towns in the kingdom, she, in 1857, made her appearance before a London audience at the Haymarket, as 'Pauline,' in which, and as 'Constance' in the "Love Chase," she was most enthusiastically received. Miss Sedgwick, however, did not long continue in what was evidently promising to be, for her, a most successful career, as since her marriage she only occasionally appears on the stage.

SEDGWICK, MISS CATHERINE MARIA, a popular American writer, was born in 1790, at Stockbridge, in the State of Massachusetts, and is the daughter of an American judge and Speaker of the House of Representatives. Her first work was published in 1822, under the name of the "New England Tale." It was followed by "Redwood," a novel, republished in England, and translated into French and Italian. In 1827 appeared her most popular book, "Hope Leslie ; or, Early Times in America," and in 1835 "The Linwoods." "Letters from Abroad to Kindred at Home" were published in 1840, various other works having since, at intervals, appeared from her pen.

SEDGWICK, THE REV. ADAM, M.A., F.R.S., F.G.S., Corresponding Member of the Imperial Institute of France, Woodwardian Professor of Geology in the University of Cambridge, was born in 1785, at the parsonage of Dent, in Yorkshire. After passing through the usual preliminary training, he entered Cambridge University, and pursued his studies there with distinguished success, graduating in 1808, and in 1810 obtaining a fellowship in Trinity College. In 1818 he succeeded Professor Hailstone in the chair he now occupies, and in the same year was elected a Fellow of the Royal Society. He became a Fellow of the Geological Society of London, and was its president in 1829. He has given great attention to the study of palæozoic and crystalline rocks in England and Wales, and in making out the true relations of the stratified rocks of Devonshire and Cornwall, labours which employed ten or twelve summers. A "Discourse on the Studies of the University of Cambridge," and a "Synopsis of the Classification of the British Palæozoic Rocks," form the chief independent works of the learned professor. His chief geological essays are found in the early volumes of the Transactions of the Cambridge Philosophical Society, in the Transactions, Proceedings, and Quarterly Journal of the Geological Society, and in the Annals of Philosophy. He has also, during his long-continued residence in Cambridge, published several tracts and pamphlets in defence of the University, when it was attacked unjustly, and in vindication of his opinions on certain questions of academical reform. Most of the latter have been brought to a conclusion by the Royal Commission, of which he was a zealous member.

SENIOR, NASSAU WILLIAM, an English political economist, was born at Uffington, Berkshire, in September, 1790. Educated at Eton, he was called to the bar in 1817. In 1826 he was named Professor of Political Economy in the University of Oxford, and, having vacated the chair for some time, he resumed it in 1847. Possessing both practical ability and theoretical knowledge of administrative questions, he was placed upon various Government Commissions, and distinguished himself by his suggestions in relation to the laws which regulate poor relief and the condition of the pauper inmates of workhouses. His publications on Political Economy, particularly his article on that subject in the "Encyclopædia Metropolitana," and on the Poor Laws, are very valuable, and most of his suggestions have been adopted by the executive government. He was for many years Master in Chancery, but ceased to hold this office in 1853. His last work is a "Journal kept in Turkey and Greece in 1857 and 1858."

SEYMOUR, RIGHT HON. SIR GEORGE HAMILTON, G.C.B. and G.C.H., an English diplomatist, was born towards the close of the last century. He was educated at Eton and Oxford, and commenced public life in 1817, and was afterwards in the Foreign Office in 1819. From

1822 till 1846 he occupied official positions in Frankfort, Berlin, Constantinople, Tuscany, and Belgium, being British Minister at Lisbon in 1846. Five years afterwards, Sir Hamilton was removed to St. Petersburg, where he remained to within a few weeks of the late war being declared. He was subsequently appointed Ambassador at Vienna, after which he retired in 1858 from the public service. In all his diplomatic engagements he has been distinguished by extreme penetration into the designs of the courts at which he resided; and equally so for the patriotic manner in which he conducted the affairs of Great Britain, whose interests he represented.

SHAFTESBURY, ANTHONY ASHLEY COOPER, LORD ASHLEY, EARL OF, was born on 28th April, 1801, and was educated at Harrow and Oxford. As Lord Ashley he successively represented Woodstock in 1826, Dorset in 1831, Bath in 1847, and in 1851 succeeded to the peerage, on the death of his father. During the whole of his parliamentary career, he was earnest in his support of all measures tending to relieve the working classes, and to his energetic exertions they are indebted for the passing of the Ten Hours Bill. It would be impossible to name the various philanthropic societies with which Lord Shaftesbury is connected officially; to do so would require us to mention almost every scheme on foot in Great Britain, having for its object the moral, religious, and physical improvement of society. As a member of the Church of England, Lord Shaftesbury is distinguished for his liberal principles; in the House of Lords he is regarded with the highest respect, and in the country at large his moral influence has never been equalled since the days of Wilberforce. To Lord Shaftesbury's assistance we are indebted for that valuable institution, the Ragged School, and lately he has taken the deepest interest in the reformatory and sanitary questions, and is one of the leading members of the recently-founded Social Science Association.

SHUTTLEWORTH, SIR JAMES PHILLIPS KAY, was born July 20, 1804. Having completed his education, he became Secretary of the Privy Council Committee on Education. The value of his educational zeal has been the theme of conflicting opinions,—a certain section of the community viewing it favourably, and another deeming its tendency likely to strengthen the bureaucratic element that has for some time been gradually creeping into the administration of the state. The controversy upon the views of Sir James continued for several years, but at length he had the satisfaction of seeing his opinions adopted in the highest quarters. In 1850 Dr. Kay relinquished his connexion with the educational committee of the Privy Council, and was made a baronet. He still evinces great interest in the cause of education.

SIMPSON, GENERAL SIR JAMES, G.C.B., was born at Edinburgh in 1792, and studied in the University of his native city. In 1811, when nineteen years of age, he obtained his first commission, that of an ensign in the Guards, served in the Spanish campaign of 1812, and afterwards went in command of the 29th Regiment to the Mauritius. Recognised as an able officer, he was in 1845 ordered to India, and thence to Scinde, as second in command to Sir Charles Napier, whom he would have succeeded had the latter been placed, by any cause, *hors de combat.* He returned to England in 1846, and took the command at Chatham. He went out to the Crimea originally as chief of the staff, and on the death of Lord Raglan was appointed his successor. Considering his advanced age, he displayed wonderful vigour and activity. On the 12th of November, 1855, he resigned his command, having

A A

been, for his distinguished services, honoured with the Grand Cross of the Bath, and made General. He has since lived in comparative retirement, being in infirm health.

SIMPSON, JAMES YOUNG, M.D., was born at Bathgate, in 1811. He was educated for the medical profession, and took his diploma of M.D. in Edinburgh University, becoming assistant to the late Dr. Thomson, and afterwards Professor of Midwifery in Edinburgh, in 1840. His lectures are remarkably popular; and he has introduced measures of alleviation in his more immediate professional department, the obstetric, that had been previously never thought of, though now they are generally recognised. When the anæsthetic properties of ether were first discovered, or at least made known in America, Dr. Simpson immediately saw their value; but he was not satisfied with the effects produced in every case, and he brought his habits of investigation to bear on the discovery of some more efficient agent. The result was chloroform, the nearest approach, though not a perfect agent, to the desired end. The medical skill of Dr. Simpson, his general and large scientific acquirements, are, strange to say, even more admired in France than at home. He has filled some of the highest positions attainable in his profession in Scotland, and foreign Governments have acknowledged his great merits by conferring on him decorations and orders.

SINCLAIR, MISS CATHERINE, an English authoress, was born at Edinburgh on the 17th April, 1800. She is the sixth daughter of the late Sir John Sinclair, who sat in Parliament for thirty years, and was celebrated for the impulse he gave to agricultural improvement in the north of Scotland. At a very early age, Miss Sinclair became her father's secretary, being, from education and taste, well qualified for the labour.

Two children's books, "Charlie Seymour" and the "Lives of the Cæsars," were written in the intervals snatched from Sir John's demands on her time. In 1835 she published "Modern Accomplishments, or the March of Intellect," and in the year following "Modern Society." These volumes were followed by "Hill and Valley" and "Scotland and the Scotch," the one consisting of sketches in Wales, and the other of mental photographs of Scotland. Both were interesting, and executed with much graphic power. In 1839 she published "Holiday House," a sort of autobiography of her youth, which was followed by "The Journey of Life" and the "Business of Life," compositions which strongly inculcate the principles of religious cultivation. Several novels founded on fashionable life, subsequently appeared, namely, the "Mysterious Marriage," a continuation of "Holiday House," "Modern Flirtations," "Lord and Lady Harcourt," &c. "Torchester Abbey" and "Anecdotes and Aphorisms," published in 1855, are her latest works. Since then Miss Sinclair has been largely occupied in attending to charitable institutions, but she is now preparing a new edition of all her works, which is to appear in twelve volumes, to be issued monthly.

SKODA, JOSEPH, a German physician, was born at Pilson, in Bohemia, on the 10th December, 1805. He studied medicine at the University of Vienna. Receiving his diploma as doctor in 1831, he practised in Bohemia while the cholera raged in that country, and in 1833 was appointed second physician to the General Hospital of Vienna. Initiated by Heine and Gutbrod into the special scientific uses of the stethoscope, he resolved, influenced by his connexion with Kolletschka and Rokitansky, to devote his attention to the study of Pathological Anatomy. His course of practice in this department of medical science was attended with such advantages to the public that he became, in 1840, physician to that division of the Hospital of Vienna which is set apart for consumptive patients, in 1841 Principal Physician of the hospital, in 1846 Clinical Professor, and 1848 Member of the Academy of Sciences. By some, his system of treatment is said to be peculiar, but even by his opponents he is admitted to be an excellent pathological anatomist.

SLADE, SIR ADOLPHUS, a captain in the British navy and vice-admiral in the Turkish service, where he is known as Mushaver Pacha, was born in 1803, and is the fifth son of the late Sir John Slade, Baronet, of Maunsel Grange, Somersetshire. Educated at the Royal Naval College, he entered the service at the usual age, and as midshipman and lieutenant was engaged for twelve years on the Pacific, Brazilian, West Indian, and Mediterranean stations. In 1829, during the war between Turkey and Russia, which led to the Peace of Adrianople, he served as a volunteer in the Turkish fleet in the Black Sea. From 1834 to 1837 he was placed under the command of the late Admiral Sir L. Rowley, and employed by that distinguished officer on various missions in Turkey and the south of Russia. After returning to England, and spending some time in mathematical and professional studies, he took the command, in 1846 and 1847, of the experimental iron vessel the Recruit, and threw light, by a series of experiments, on the subject of induced magnetism. After sharing in the operations for quelling the insurrection in Portugal, Madeira, and the Azores, in 1849, he was appointed additional captain to the flag-ship in the Mediterranean, for special service in connexion with the Turkish fleet. In September, 1850, on the invitation of the Sublime Porte, and with the consent of the Admiralty, he joined the Turkish service, with the rank of rear-admiral. During the late war between Turkey and Russia, serving in the Black Sea with the Turkish fleet, he co-operated in conveying the allied armies from Varna to the Crimea, and was present at the bombardment of Sebastopol. For his services during the war, he received promotion from the Turkish Government to the rank of vice-admiral. He was appointed Admiral of the Port of Constantinople, with jurisdiction over other ports of the empire, and President of the Supreme Admiralty Court. From the English Government he received the honour of Knighthood of the Bath. He is the author of "Records of Travels in Turkey," "Turkey, Greece, and Malta," and a work on "Maritime States and Military Navies."

SMIRKE, SIR ROBERT, an architect and Royal Academician, son of the late Robert Smirke, R.A., was born in 1780. In the early part of his life he was for a short time in the office of the late Sir John Soane, who does not, however, appear to have exercised any perceptible influence over the architectural tastes of his pupil. Before the subject of this notice entered into the active practice of his profession he visited many of the principal cities of Europe, and remained some years abroad, especially in Italy, Sicily, and Greece, where he doubtless contracted that marked partiality for the simple forms and severe features of the early Greek and Roman architecture, which he has constantly displayed in his works. Amongst his most successful efforts may be enumerated the late Theatre at Covent Garden, the General Post Office, London, and the British Museum. Sir Robert Smirke has been always admitted by competent judges thoroughly to understand the constructive principles of his art. The general use of concrete foundations in marshy or insecure sites, has also been justly ascribed to him. But perhaps the merit of this eminent architect which has been most universally conceded to him, at least by his employers, is the great fidelity with which he succeeded in bringing the ultimate costs of his various works within the limits of those estimates on the faith of which they were undertaken. Sir Robert Smirke became an academician in the year 1811, was for many years one of the architects of the Board of Works, and when that Board was finally remodelled under the administration of Lord Melbourne, he received the honour of Knighthood, in testimony of his services. He has recently deserved well of the profession by resigning his academical station and honours, when he found that failing health and advancing years had (in his own opinion, at least) disqualified him for the useful performance of his professional duties.

SMITH, ALEXANDER, a poet, was born on 31st of December, 1830, at Kilmarnock, Ayrshire. His early intention was to qualify himself for the ministry, but circumstances of various kinds prevented him from entering on the preparatory studies. While following the business of a lace-pattern designer, in Glasgow, he began to write verses, and sent some extracts from his first sustained poem to the Rev. George Gilfillan, of Dundee, then understood to be one of the writers for the "Critic," who inserted them in that journal. His "Life Drama" was afterwards published, and although severely criticised, was admitted on all hands to contain lines of the highest poetical merit. In 1854 Mr. Smith was elected to the secretaryship of the Edinburgh University. His "Life Drama," and "City Poems," are his principal works.

SMITH, SIR HENRY GEORGE WAKELYN, BARONET, an English general, was born at Whittlesea, in Cambridgeshire, where he was educated under the Rev. George Burgess. In 1805 he entered the army as second lieutenant in the Rifle Brigade, served in the storm and capture of Monte Video, in the attack on Buenos Ayres, and in the Peninsula. In 1814 he married Donna J. Maria de los Dolores de Leon. In the same year he was adjutant-general of the forces which captured Washington and New Orleans. He was an assistant quartermaster-general of the sixth division at Waterloo. In 1835-6 he commanded on the frontier in the Kaffir war, and was warmly commended for his services. From the Cape General Smith went to India. He distinguished himself greatly in the battles of Moodkee and Ferozeshah. He conducted the manœuvres which terminated in the decisive battle of Aliwal on the Sutlej, in 1846, when seventy-six guns of the enemy were captured. He fought and was present at the battle of Sobraon. In 1847 he was appointed Governor of the Cape of Good Hope, whence he returned in 1852, after having conducted the Kaffir war of 1851-2. He was appointed lieutenant-general in 1854, and commanded the northern and midland districts of England from 1854 to 1859. He is one of the strongest and most influential advocates of the Rifle movement. Sir George has twice received the thanks of Parliament, and had the honour of a baronetcy conferred on him in 1846.

SMITH, THOMAS SOUTHWOOD, M.D., an English physician and sanitary reformer, was born about 1790. He graduated at the University of Edinburgh in 1816, and went to London in 1820. He was one of the founders of, and earliest writers in, the "Westminster Review." About 1825 he was appointed Physician to the London Fever Hospital, and somewhat earlier to the Eastern Dispensary. Here it was that he learnt the true sources of epidemics, which he expounded in his "Treatise on Fever," published in 1830. The revelations he made as to the condition of the localities and dwellings of the poor, in his "Reports on the Physical Causes of Sickness and Mortality which are capable of Removal by Sanitary Regulations," aroused the attention of the public and the Legislature, and gave rise to Sanitary Reform. To the knowledge obtained by extensive experience, he thus gave a practical direction. He was an arm of strength to Lord Shaftesbury in obtaining the Factory Ten Hours Act; and more persevering and self-denying efforts have not been made in the history of the country than those of Dr. Southwood Smith, to improve the sanitary condition of the people. The Public Health Act, and the various methods adopted for drainage, sewerage, and the prevention of malaria, are chiefly to be ascribed to his zeal and labours.

SMITH, WILLIAM, LL.D., a classical scholar, author, and Examiner in the London University, was born in London in 1814. He was educated at the London University, and was intended for the bar; but his taste for the classics was so great that he devoted himself entirely to their study, and became Professor of Greek and Latin literature at the Colleges of Highbury and Homerton, afterwards amalgamated into the "New College, London." In 1853 he was appointed Classical Examiner in the University of London. He has published numerous classical works, among which may be mentioned the "Dictionary of Greek and Roman Biography and Mythology," the "Dictionary of Greek and Roman Antiquities," a "Dictionary of Greek and Roman Geography," a "Latin and English Dictionary, based on the works of Forcellini and Freund." Dr. Smith has also edited an edition of "Gibbon's Decline and Fall of the Roman Empire," which is certainly the best extant.

SOMMERVILLE, MRS. MARY, was born at Burntisland, in Fifeshire, in 1790. Until after her first marriage she displayed no special aptitude for the study of the exact sciences, though by her father, who was an officer in the Royal Marines, she was instructed in Greek and Latin, and led to cultivate music and painting. The first positive public appearance made by this lady was in the publication of her "Mechanism of the Heavens," but she became known in scientific circles by her interesting experiments on the magnetical influence of the solar rays. She is the author of the "Connexion of the Physical Sciences," and "Physical Geography," and honorary member of the Royal Astronomical Society. Mrs. Sommerville enjoys a pension of £300 a year for her services to literature.

SOULOUQUE, FAUSTIN, the ex-Emperor of Hayti, was born in Saint Domingo, 1789. Brought into the world a slave, he received his freedom when but twelve months old, and therefore never personally experienced the degradation of being a bondsman. At fourteen he entered the army, and took part in the expulsion of the French from Hayti; he was captain in 1820, and gradually rose until he obtained the rank of colonel, then general of brigade, and in 1846 general of division. Having obtained a high reputation for sagacity and prudence, the Republic of Hayti, having been on the point of dissolution by the contests of antagonistic factions, Soulouque, in imitation of the Emperor of the French, destroyed the republic, and declared himself Emperor, under the title of Faustin I. Unlike his model, he was moderate in his demands on the pecuniary resources of his people, for he merely required for his civil list the annual stipend of £4,000, while his chief ministers of state were paid at the yearly rate of £120 each. Early in 1859 his imperial career came to an end, which might have been expected, from his violence and tyranny. The Haytians rose against him as one man, and he was expelled, with all his family, from the island, all his personal property being confiscated by the victors. First seeking an asylum in Jamaica, he proceeded to Europe, and it is understood that, retired from the world and all its vanities, he leads a quiet life in one of the southern provinces of France.

SOUTH, SIR JAMES, F.R.S., M.R.I.A., F.L.S, F.R.A.S., an astronomer, was born towards the close of the last century. He was educated for the medical profession, and practised for some time, but he became absorbed in astronomical science, and acquired distinction as an observer. In 1820 he helped to form the Royal Astronomical Society, and in 1821 became Fellow of the Royal Society. In pursuit of his cherished science he was most ardent, and made extensive additions to our knowledge of the stellar heavens. For his discoveries he was presented with the Copley medal, by the Royal Society, in 1826. At this period he removed to the Kensington Observatory, where he has ever since pursued his astronomical observations. He was knighted in 1830, and a sum of £300 a year was granted him for the promotion of astronomy.

SPAIN, QUEEN OF. (See ISABEL II.)

SPARKS, JARED, an American biographer, was born of poor parents, at Wellington, in Connecticut, towards the close of last century. Placed under the care of a Unitarian clergyman, he was educated for the ministry, and ordained in 1819. His attention, however, was next given to historical studies, and he retired from the ministry, and was in 1839 elected Professor of History in Harvard University. Three years later he was chosen Principal of that University; but, in 1852, was obliged to retire, on account of the state of his health. Since then he has lived at Cambridge, United States. His best known work is the "Life and Writings George Washington," and he is now engaged on a great work on the History of the American Revolution.

SPURGEON, THE REV. CHARLES HADDON, was born on 19th June, 1834, at Kelvedon, Essex. His father was minister of an Independent church; but his son considering the baptism of believers by immersion to be a scriptural ordinance, was immersed before he was sixteen. Shortly after, he commenced his career as a preacher; and when nineteen he made his first appearance before a London audience. In a short time New Park Street Chapel was crowded, Exeter Hall was also filled, and subsequently in the Surrey Music Hall he attracted a congregation which filled it, spacious as it is. He was preaching there, to an immense congregation, when the false alarm of fire, on a preconcerted signal by disturbers, caused a rush, by which a number of persons were killed, in October, 1856. A new tabernacle is nearly finished for the reception of his congregation, which, from the grandeur of its proportions, will contain from 5,000 to 6,000 persons. Like all class orators, whether in the pulpit or on the platform, his mode of preaching has been denounced by one party and lauded by another. Probably the middle method of characterising it would be nearest the truth; but it has never been questioned that he is a most original preacher. In doctrinal points Mr. Spurgeon is a High Calvinist, and in all his discourses gives prominence to those opinions.

STANFIELD, CLARKSON, R.A., an English marine painter, was born at Sunderland about 1798. He early showed a predilection for the sea, and whilst serving on board a vessel, gave the first indication of his love of art, by painting scenes for an amateur performance by the officers. Leaving the sea, he became scene painter to one of the theatres in London. His style was bold and easy. He was afterwards employed as scene painter at Drury Lane, and produced pictures such as never had graced its stage before. He then turned his attention to oil-painting, and rose so rapidly in public estimation, that in 1832 his merits were recognised by his being elected an A.R.A., and in 1835 he became R.A. It is impossible to convey any impression of the beauty of his works, or of the facility with which he paints. But many of them are well known, and the following characteristic specimens may be seen in the South Kensington Museum :—" Entrance to the Zuyder Zee," "The Battle of Trafalgar," " The Lake of Como," " The Canal of the Giudecca, Venice," " Near Cologne," "A Market Boat on the Scheldt," and " Sands near Boulogne."

STANHOPE, PHILLIP HENRY, EARL OF, better known as Lord Mahon, F.R.S., an English historian, was born at Walmer, Kent, in 1805, and was educated at Oxford. He entered Parliament for Wootton-Bassett in 1832, and was returned for Hertford in 1835, retaining that seat for seventeen years. In the latter part of 1834, and the early months of 1835, when King William IV. dismissed the Melbourne ministry and called Sir Robert Peel to the Treasury, Lord Mahon held office as Under Secretary of State for Foreign Affairs, going out with Ministers in the latter year. He was appointed Secretary to the Board of Control in 1845, and held that office for a year, when he again retired with Government. His tone as a politician was taken in a great degree from Sir Robert Peel, to whom he was warmly attached ; and his exertions secured the passing of the Copyright Act of 1843. In 1855 he succeeded to the peerage, on the death of his father. His principal works are a "History of the War of Succession in Spain," a " History of England from the Peace of Utrecht to the Peace of Versailles," in seven volumes, a "History of Spain under Charles the Second," a " Life of Belisarius," a "Life of Joan of Arc," a series of "Historical Essays," a " Life of Louis, Prince of Condé," and the "Memoirs of Sir Robert Peel." Lord Stanhope has edited several publications, and the manner in which he has performed the duty of selecting, arranging, and revising, may be pointed to as a model for all who aspire to follow this walk of literature. As an historian, his facts are always carefully weighed, he extenuates nothing, but is rigidly impartial, his reflections being just, whilst his style is always polished, and often rises to eloquence. Lord Stanhope was, some years ago, President of the Society of Antiquaries, and in 1834 had the honour of D.C.L. conferred on him at Oxford.

STANLEY, REV. ARTHUR PENRHYN, was born in December, 1815. After having been at Rugby school in 1833, he graduated at Oxford in 1838, became a scholar of Balliol College in 1839, and a Fellow and Tutor of University College, Oxford, in 1841. He was appointed one of the Canons of Canterbury in 1851, and Regius Professor of Ecclesiastical History in the University of Oxford in 1856. He is the author of the "Life and Correspondence of Dr. Arnold," the " Memoir of Bishop Stanley," " Sermons and Essays on the Apostolical Age," " A Commentary on St. Paul's Epistles to the Corinthians," " Sinai and Palestine in connexion with their History," " Historical Memorials of Canterbury," " Sermons preached in Canterbury Cathedral on the Unity of Apostolical and Evangelical Teaching," "Three Introductory Lectures on the Study of Ecclesiastical History," and numerous other works.

STANLEY, THE RIGHT HON. EDWARD HENRY SMITH, M.P., an English statesman, was born at Knowsley, the seat of his father, the Earl of Derby, on the 21st of July, 1826. He received his early education at Rugby, where he was a pupil of the late Dr. Arnold. He afterwards entered Trinity College, Cambridge, where he closed a distinguished university career by graduating in the spring of 1848, as a first-class in the classical tripos, gaining also mathematical honours. Very shortly after leaving the university he unsuccessfully contested the borough of Lancaster, and so not finding his way into the House of Commons, he went abroad to add a knowledge of mankind to his knowledge of books. On this tour he visited Canada, the United States of North America, and the West Indies. Whilst travelling he was elected member of Parliament for King's Lynn, vacant by the death of Lord George Bentinck, and on receiving intimation of this, he returned to England, and took his seat in the House of Commons. Lord Stanley afterwards visited India, not troubling himself so much with scenes of Oriental magnificence as desirous to whet his intellect and extend his knowledge by intercourse with the representatives of British wisdom and British valour; and in his absence was appointed Under Secretary of State for Foreign Affairs, in the first administration of his father, in March, 1852. The news of this unexpected appointment hastened his journey homewards, and cut short his opportunity of acquiring that complete knowledge of the position and prospects of our Oriental empire which a more lengthened residence would undoubtedly have conferred. The policy recommended by the noble lord in 1853 on Indian reform, was a foreshadowing of that which, in 1858, was adopted to preserve our disorganized empire in Hindostan. Shortly after this, in a pamphlet entitled "The Church - Rate Question Considered," he exhibited that antagonism to church rates which has made his lordship so great a favourite with the Noncon-

formists of England. In 1853 Oxford created him a D.C.L. On the death of Sir William Molesworth in 1855, Lord Palmerston offered Lord Stanley the Seals of the Colonial Office; the appointment was, however, declined. On the formation of Lord Derby's second Cabinet in February, 1858, the same post was offered and accepted. The sudden resignation of Lord Ellenborough left Lord Derby's Cabinet without a President of the Board of Control. In this crisis Sir Edward Bulwer Lytton became Secretary for the Colonies, and Lord Stanley took Lord Ellenborough's position at the Board of Control. Under his Presidency the "Double Government" fell; and the President of the Board of Control became a creature of the past, Lord Stanley having held his office under the style and title of Secretary of State for India. On the overthrow of Lord Derby's ministry in 1859, Lord Stanley necessarily went out of office; but his assiduous attention to the affairs of India while presiding over the council, was the theme of unqualified approbation with all who had an interest in our Eastern Empire. During the session of 1860 he has taken little share in politics.

STEELL, JOHN, R.S.A., a Scottish sculptor, was born in Edinburgh, in 1804, his father being a carver and gilder in that city. He studied at Edinburgh, and afterwards at Rome. His principal productions are—the statue of Sir Walter Scott, under the arch of the Scott monument; the Queen, above the Royal Institution; the Duke of Wellington, an equestrian statue, placed before the Register House, Edinburgh; Admiral Lord de Saumarez, in Greenwich Hospital, London; and the Marquis of Dalhousie, at Calcutta.

STIRLING, WILLIAM, M.P., a biographical writer and art critic, was born at Kenmuir, near Glasgow, in 1818. He is the representative of an ancient and wealthy Scottish house, the Stirlings of Keir. He graduated at Trinity College, Cambridge, in 1843, and afterwards repaired to the Continent, where he devoted himself assiduously to the study of Spanish literature in the libraries of France and Spain. In 1852 he stood for the representation of Perthshire, and since then has sat in Parliament for that county. He is the author of "The Annals of the Artists of Spain," "The Cloister Life of Charles the Fifth," and "The Life of Velasquez."

STOWE, HARRIET ELIZABETH BEECHER, an American authoress, was born in 1814, at Lichfield, Connecticut, where her father, the Rev. Dr. Lyman Beecher, was minister. For a time, Harriet assisted her sister, Catherine Esther Beecher, in teaching a school; but in 1832, circumstances having called her father to Cincinnati to superintend a theological seminary, Harriet accompanied the family, and there married the Rev. Professor Calvin E. Stowe. Mrs. Stowe was an occasional contributor of tales and sketches to the newspapers and periodicals of the day, and a collection of these was published in New York in 1844, under the title of "The Mayflower," which obtained considerable popularity. Mrs. Stowe's attention was called in 1850, by certain circumstances, to the more atrocious features of "the peculiar institution," which resulted in the production of "Uncle Tom's Cabin," a work which has had a greater popularity than perhaps was ever before known, and it would be difficult to find any civilized part of the world where this thrilling narrative has not been read. Some criticism to which the work was subjected in the United States, induced Mrs. Stowe to publish, in 1853, as a "Key to Uncle Tom's Cabin," the documents and facts on which it was based. In that same year she visited England, Scotland, and the Continent. Returning to America, she published,

under the title of "Sunny Memories," her impressions of her journey. This work was followed by "Dred; a Tale of the Dismal Swamp," published in 1856. In 1856 Mrs. Stowe visited Europe; and again in 1859, when she completed a work on the social condition of the new world, entitled "The Minister's Wooing."

STRATFORD DE REDCLIFFE, STRATFORD CANNING, FIRST VISCOUNT, a British diplomatist, was born in London, January 6th, 1788, and received his early education at Eton. In 1806 he entered Cambridge University, but left in the following year on receiving a junior appointment in the Foreign Office. Having in the interim filled satisfactorily various subordinate positions in the diplomatic service, in 1812 he returned to Cambridge, and took the degree of M.A. In 1814 he was sent as Envoy to Switzerland. In 1820 he acted as British Plenipotentiary to the United States. After a three years' sojourn at Washington, he was appointed on a special mission to St. Petersburg, and subsequently to Vienna. He was next sent to Constantinople as Ambassador Extraordinary in 1825. At that time Mr. Canning's good offices were energetically exerted with the Sultan on behalf of the Greeks. In 1827 Mr. Canning returned to England, and entered the House of Commons as member for Old Sarum. In 1829 he was decorated with the order of K.G.C.B., and then represented the now extinguished borough of Stockbridge. In 1831 he went to Turkey with reference to the fixing of the boundaries of the kingdom of Greece. Having settled the treaty, on the basis of which Otho ascended the Greek throne, Sir Stratford Canning was then appointed a special envoy to the courts of Lisbon and Madrid. In December, 1834, he was elected for King's Lynn, Norfolk, which he continued to represent until—having twice previously refused the Governor-

Generalship of Canada—he was sent out to Constantinople in 1841. In 1852 he became a peer, under the title of Viscount Stratford de Redcliffe. After a long, and often anxious servitude, Lord Stratford retired in 1858 from the Turkish embassy, and has since his return, spoken frequently and with effect, in the Upper House, on questions of Eastern as well as foreign policy generally. His influence in Turkey has been invariably exerted in behalf of civilization and Christianity, and science and Protestantism have ever found in him a warm friend.

STRAUSS, DAVID FRIEDRICH, a German theological writer, was born at Ludwigsbourg, in Wurtemberg, on the 27th January, 1808, and educated in his native town, and subsequently at Blaubeuren and Tübingen. In 1831 he was an Assistant Professor in Maulbronn; in 1832, a teacher in the Theological Institute of Tübingen. He was dismissed from his situation on account of the startling doctrines he promulgated, and became a private tutor at Stuttgardt. In 1839 he was appointed to be Professor of Divinity and Church History in the University of Zurich. Public meetings were held, and the popular discontent was so warmly expressed that the Council of Education was obliged to relieve him of his duties. He returned to authorship, and published several works, when in 1848 he was sent to the Wurtemberg Diet, as representative for his native place. His mode of proceeding in the Diet was such as to highly exasperate his constituents, and he felt compelled to resign his seat. He again returned to literary pursuits. His most noted work is his "Life of Jesus," which is considered highly heterodox, and he has published others, also of a theological nature.

STRICKLAND, MISS AGNES, an English authoress, was born in 1806. She had the best opportunities of culti-vating her genius, on account of her father's literary acquirements. Her first published work was a metrical romance in four cantos, entitled "Worcester Field; or, The Cavalier," followed by a poem in heroic verse, entitled "Demetrius: a Tale of Modern Greece." After the death of her father she made her first visit to the metropolis, and while staying with a relative obtained a ticket of admission to the British Museum; and becoming a daily student of its treasures, she commenced to collect materials for her "Royal Female Biographies," a task in which she was assisted by her eldest sister. She published in 1840 the first volumes of "Lives of the Queens of England; from the Norman Conquest to the Death of Queen Anne:" the series was concluded in the year 1848, when it was reprinted as a whole, and subsequently stereotyped. "The Lives of the Queens of Scotland, and English Princesses, connected with the Regal Succession of Great Britain" followed, as a necessary companion and adjunct to the first series of Royal Female Biographies. This second series contains the most complete and really authentic life of Mary, Queen of Scots, that has been published; because, embodying a great amount of recent discoveries, gathered from the State Paper Offices of Great Britain, France, and various foreign libraries, and many sources of private information, in the correspondence of the times, preserved among the archives of noble families, both in England and Scotland, which have never been introduced into any other of the numerous, but necessarily imperfect, lives of Mary Stuart. In these royal biographies Miss Agnes Strickland has originated an entirely new school of history, which has since been very extensively, but not always successfully, imitated by some of her contemporaries. Her last published work is of a lighter character, being a series of scenes and sketches, illustrative of life in the Eastern Counties, where she has had peculiar opportunities of studying the manners and dialects of the people : it is entitled "Old Friends and New Acquaintances." She has recently published a volume of poems, entitled "Historic Scenes."

SWAIN, CHARLES, an English poet, was born at Manchester, in 1803. His father died when he was but six years of age, and his mother's brother, a French gentleman, named Tavaré, settled as a dyer in Manchester, generously provided for the widow and orphan, gave the right direction to the boy's education, and encouraged his taste for literature. In the year 1818, he received him into his works as a clerk, and in this establishment he remained for fourteen years; but the pursuit was uncongenial, and he abandoned it to become an engraver. On commencing verse-writing his earlier pieces were published in the "Literary Gazette" and some of the annuals, but the first marked impression Mr. Swain made on the public mind was in 1827, when he published his "Metrical Essays," a delightful volume of thought and fancy. In 1831 he gave to the world "The Mind, and other Poems," which obtained instant popularity, passed through several editions, and established the author's position. In 1832 he wrote a poem on the death of Sir Walter Scott, which he named "Dryburgh Abbey," and which, for the union of imagination, feeling, eloquence of diction, and descriptive power, is up to this moment without a rival in its class. In 1847 he published "Dramatic Chapters, and other Poems;" in 1849, "English Melodies;" and in 1853, "The Letters of Laura D'Auverne, and other Poems," books which many years hence are likely to be perused with pleasure, as records of unaffected sentiment.

SWEDEN AND NORWAY, KING OF. (See CHARLES XV.)

SYME, JAMES, a physician, was born in Fifeshire, in 1799. His education was received at Edinburgh University, where he early manifested a taste for scientific pursuits. He studied anatomy under Liston. Having passed his examination as a Surgeon, in London, he returned to Edinburgh, and soon became eminent as an anatomist and lecturer. He published in 1831 his "Treatise on the Excision of Diseased Joints," and in 1833 became Professor of Clinical Surgery in the Edinburgh University, and subsequently Surgeon to the Royal Infirmary. He was chosen Professor of Surgery at University College, London, but after being a short time there, he returned to Edinburgh, and resumed his professorship. He is considered by the profession as one of the most finished of living operators. Amongst various works and memoirs, the following have gained him great reputation, namely,—his "Treatise on Diseases of the Rectum," "Contributions to Pathology," "The Practice of Surgery," and other treatises referring to practical surgery.

TAGLIONI, MARIE, a Swedish danseuse, was born at Stockholm, in 1804, of a family the members of which had long followed the profession of ballet-dancers. Her father being ballet-master in several of the continental opera houses, she received lessons at Vienna, Stuttgardt, and Munich, from 1822 to 1826, making her first appearance at the French Opera in 1827, when her reception was of the most flattering description, and her success undoubted. She subsequently appeared on the stage of every principal city in Europe ; married Count Gilbert de Voisons in 1832 ; and took leave of the profession in 1847, retiring to Italy, where she has two splendid residences, one at Venice, and the other on the Lake of Como. By her exertions, Mademoiselle Taglioni acquired a large fortune, being enabled, after her first season in Paris, to command her own terms. It has been stated, that during the height of her career she has been paid by the management of Her Majesty's Theatre, in the Haymarket, the enormous sum of £120 per night ; and adding to her pecuniary engagement the presents she received from the court of St. Petersburg, her Russian remuneration exceeded £200 per night !

TAUNTON, THE RIGHT HONOURABLE HENRY LABOUCHERE, LORD, a British statesman, is son of the late Mr. P. C. Labouchere, of Rylands, Essex, and was born in London, in 1798. He was educated at Christchurch, Oxford, where he took a first class in classics in 1820, and graduated Master of Arts eight years afterwards. He was first returned to Parliament by the electors of St. Michael's, and held the seat until 1830, when he exchanged it for Taunton, representing the latter borough until he was elevated to the peerage in 1859. Lord Taunton's political experience thus embraces a period of upwards of thirty years, and during that time he has taken part in almost every public movement. A liberal from the first, he has rendered valuable service to the party with which he associated himself, and the recognition of his services has not been more marked than merited. From 1832 till 1834 he was a Lord of the Admiralty ; from 1835 till 1839 he filled the two offices of Vice-President of the Board of Trade, and Master of the Mint ; in the early part of the latter year exchanging his post for that of Under Secretary for the Colonies, a position which he held but a few months, when he was appointed President of the Board of Trade. He continued in the last-named office until 1841, when Sir Robert Peel's accession to power caused his retirement. On the resignation of the Peel government in 1846, he was appointed Chief Secretary for Ireland. He administered Irish affairs for about a year, when he was recalled, and placed again at the head of the Board of Trade, holding that office till March, 1852, when he retired with ministers. In November, 1855, he became Secretary of State for the Colonies, and continued to direct that department until Lord Derby was called to power in March, 1858. On the dissolution of the Derby government, and the re-accession of Lord Palmerston, Mr. Labouchere was raised to the peerage.

TAYLOR, ALFRED SWAINE, an English physician, was born at Northfleet, Kent, on 11th December, 1806. In October, 1823, he became a pupil of the late Sir Astley Cooper and Mr. J. H. Green, at the then united Hospitals of Guy and St. Thomas. On the separation of the hospitals he joined the classes of Guy's, and continued his medical education there until 1828. He afterwards studied in the medical schools of France, Germany, and Italy, attending the lectures of Gay Lussac, Orfila, Dupuytren, and other distinguished French professors. In March, 1831, he was appointed Lecturer on Medical Jurisprudence at Guy's Hospital, and in the autumn of 1832 he succeeded Mr. Alexander Barry as joint Lecturer on Chemistry with the late Mr. Arthur Aiken. These appointments he still retains. He passed the examination of the Society of Apothecaries in 1828, became a member of the Royal College of Surgeons in 1830, and a Licentiate of the Royal College of Physicians in 1848. He has since been elected a Fellow of the College, and has received from the University of St. Andrews the honorary degree of M.D. At an early period of his career Dr. Taylor devoted himself to one of the most difficult and yet most valuable departments of his profession, that of Medical Jurisprudence, in which he has long held the foremost rank in this country. For many years past he has been called on to undertake the responsibility of *post-mortem* examinations, and chemical analyses in cases of supposed poisoning. Amongst the most remarkable of these, was the trial of William Palmer, in 1856, for poisoning by strychnine, and that of Smethurst, in 1859, who was indicted at the Old Bailey for administering arsenic. In both of these cases Dr. Taylor had to contend with an array of scientific evidence in opposition to his views, which was truly formidable; and although his conclusions were objected to by some chemists, his eminent abilities as an analyst could not be called in question.

TAYLOR, BAYARD, an American author and traveller, was born in the State of Pennsylvania, April, 1825. In his youth he gave early promise of those literary abilities which have rendered him one of the most popular writers in the United States. His first effort of consequence was a long poem founded upon incidents connected with the chivalrous era of the history of Spain. In 1844 he left the New for the Old World, and after visiting England, Switzerland, Germany, Italy, and France, he returned to America, and published an account of his travels, under the title of "Views Afoot; or, Europe seen with the Knapsack and Staff." The work was successful; the young author attracted attention and elicited encomium; and in 1846 he was appointed one of the principal editors of the "New York Tribune," a democratic paper, to which he contributed a series of vigorous sketches of the people, the manners, and the political state of California in the years 1848 and 1849, when he traversed that region on a journey of investigation. In 1851 he made a tour of the Mediterranean shores; and that accomplished, he bent his steps towards the far east, exploring India, China, Japan, subsequently visiting Egypt, Syria, Asia Minor, and Sicily, and penetrating into Central Africa. Concerning all these lands he has written in his naturally straightforward and honest style; and those who have read his "El Dorado," "Life and Landscapes in Egypt," "Japan, India, and China," "Pictures of Palestine," and "Travels in Central Africa," will admit his quick observation and power of description. He has also written a volume entitled "Eastern Poems," but it is not so widely known as his prose works.

TAYLOR, ISAAC, an English writer and essayist, was born at Lavenham, in Suffolk, August, 1787. His education was received at home, and he eventually chose literature as a profession. After his "Natural History of Enthusiasm," the most popular of his productions have been—"Fanaticism," "Spiritual Despotism," and "The Physical Theory of Another Life;" though for calm beauty, and a cheerful hoping tone, he has written nothing superior to "Home Education," "Saturday Evening," and "Spiritual Christianity." His "Ancient Christianity" completely demolished, by its erudition and argumentative power, the position taken by the Tractarians. Besides the works already named, he is the author of "Loyola and Jesuitism," and "Wesley and Methodism." He is somewhat peculiar in his style, but evinces in all his works a great originality and depth of philosophical inquiry.

TAYLOR, ISIDORE JUSTIN SÉVÉRIN, BARON, a French antiquary and traveller, descended from an Irish family naturalized in France, was born at Brussels, on 15th August, 1789. He studied at Paris, and was intended for the École Polytechnique, but his tastes lay more in the direction of art and literature; and after taking lessons from the painter Savé, he wrote some stirring criticisms in the journals of the day. Escaping the conscription in 1810, on account of ill health, he travelled through Germany, Italy, and Belgium, on a tour of artistic nvestigation. Towards the end of 1813 he was enrolled in the army of the Empire, with the rank of sous-lieutenant, and on the Restoration he was chosen to form part of a brigade of artillery of the Gardes du Corps. He entered the Royal Guard as aide-de-camp to General Count d'Orsay, with whose London celebrity most of our readers are familiar. M. Taylor was afterwards attached to the staff of Marshal Lauriston. During the Spanish campaign he was on the staff of General Guilleminot. Though for years employed in arduous, and often difficult and delicate enterprises, he never neglected cultivating literature and the arts, even when promoted to the rank of Chef d'Escadron. On obtaining the latter grade, he retired from the army. Previously, his name had been widely known, especially as a dramatic author, and in 1824 he was appointed Royal Commissioner of the Théâtre Français, having in the interim materially aided in restoring the monuments of the middle ages all over France. As a theatrical superintendent he was a reformer, and therefore not popular with those who knew no distinction between jealousy and rivalry. Under the auspices of Charles X. he proceeded to Egypt to bring the obelisk of Luxor to Paris ; a commission which he executed with perfect success. After the revolution of 1830, Louis-Philippe entrusted M. Taylor with the execution of various missions which came more immediately into the class of his archæological and artistic studies. He was named Inspector-General of the Fine Arts. In connexion with these pursuits he visited Italy and Sicily, Spain, Greece, Turkey, Asia Minor, Egypt, and Africa, and succeeded in gathering together a noble collection of works of art. He has been remarkably active in founding Societies for the support of decayed authors, painters, musicians, &c., and seems to be in reality a genuine, though a modest and unassuming, philanthropist. His works are not very numerous, but they are valuable. Among the best are his "Voyages pittoresques et romantiques dans l'ancienne France," 20 vols. folio ; the "Voyage pittoresque en Espagne," and the "Voyage aux Pyrénées," the "Voyage en Syrie, Palestine, et en Judée," and the "Voyage en Egypte." Baron Taylor has received various honours as a recognition of his learned labours : for some time he has been a Member of the Academy of the Fine Arts, and a Commander of the Legion of Honour.

TAYLOR, Tom, an English dramatist, was born at Sunderland, in Durham, in 1817. His early education was received at the Grange School, at the University of Glasgow, and Trinity College, Cambridge, where his talents and acquirements obtained for him various distinctions. He was subsequently appointed to the chair of English Literature at University College, London. In 1845 he was called to the bar, in 1850 was appointed Assistant-Secretary to the Board of Health, and in 1854 he became Secretary. Since September, 1858, he has held the situation of Secretary to the Local Government Act Office, a branch of the Home Office. During his residence in London, after leaving Cambridge, he was a frequent contributor to "Punch," and became known as a writer of keen observation and pithy humour. His dramatic works are numerous, and always achieve the great end of interesting an audience. "Still Waters run deep," "The Victims," "The Unequal Match," "The Contested Election," and "The Overland Route," are all pictures of real life, and are replete with remarkable dramatic skill. He has also written a careful biography of Haydon, the painter, from the journals of that artist. He is captain of the Whitehall corps of the Civil Service Rifle Volunteers. Mr. Taylor was married in 1855 to Miss Laura Wilson Barker, a lady whose musical compositions are widely known, as combining the qualities of rare originality, science, and sweetness. Her musical adaptation of the "Miller's Daughter," and many other of Tennyson's lyrics, are works of unquestionable merit.

TENERANI, PIETRO, an Italian sculptor, was born at Torano, near Carrara, about the year 1789. His earlier art education was received from Peter Marchetti, his maternal uncle, and in the Academy of Carrara. In 1814 he went to Rome, where he gained the premium awarded by Canova for a statue of the "Risen Saviour." He afterwards studied under Thorwaldsen, and benefited by that sculptor's assistance. Tenerani has risen to the highest place among sculptors ; for his ideas are novel, and he draws his subjects as well from the inspiration of Christianity as from the mythology of the ancients. In 1819 —when but a step or two removed from boyhood—he produced one of his most striking works, "Psyche with the Box of Pandora," which is at present in Florence, a gem in the Lenzoni palace. Other mythological subjects followed with wondrous rapidity from his hand, and each production called forth fresh enthusiasm, from the combination of grace and power which was so definitely manifested. His first great religious work, "Christ on the Cross," was executed in silver, in 1823, for the Church of St. Stephen at Pisa ; this was succeeded by the "Descent from the Cross," a relievo, for the Torlonia Chapel of St. John of Lateran, the "Martyrdom of Eudorus," and other works similarly characterised in style and subject. Many Italian churches possess statues of saints from his chisel, while his monumental statues are very numerous. Tenerani has had commissions from almost all the potentates and nobles of Europe, Queen Victoria being in possession of "Flora," one of his most admirable efforts, and the Duke of Devonshire having in his gallery "Cupid extracting a Thorn from the Foot of Venus." He is Professor of Sculpture at the Academy of St. Luke, in Rome, and member of various academies.

TENNENT, SIR JAMES EMERSON, LL. D., M. P., an English statesman and writer, son of the late William Emerson, Esq., was born at Belfast, in April, 1804, and educated at Trinity College, Dublin. Feeling a strong sympathy with the cause of Greek independence, he visited Greece, and wrote there works entitled "Greece in 1825," "Letters from the Ægean," and subsequently his "History of Modern Greece," all remarkable for research and eloquence of style. In 1831, marrying the daughter and heiress of Mr. William Tennent, he, on that gentleman's death, succeeded to his estates in the counties of Antrim, Sligo, and Fermanagh, assumed the name of Tennent in addition to his own, and took up his abode at the beautiful demesne of Tempè, which was the scene of Miss Edgeworth's tale of "Castle Rackrent." In 1832, and in 1835, he was elected one of the members in Parliament for his native town, and in 1841 was appointed Secretary to the India Board by Sir Robert Peel. In 1845 he became Secretary, and afterwards Lieutenant-Governor, of Ceylon—receiving at the same time the honour of knighthood. In 1851 Sir Emerson was appointed Governor of St. Helena, which he shortly after resigned, without proceeding to the seat of his government. Shortly after he was returned member for Lisburn, and on Lord Derby's accession to power in 1852, he held the office of Secretary to the Poor Law Commission, which he resigned in 1853, to accept that of Joint Secretary to the Board of Trade. His "Belgium" appeared in 1841, and in the same year "A Treatise on the Copyright of Designs for Printed Fabrics" — in 1850 "Christianity in Ceylon" — in 1855

"Wine : its Uses and Taxation," and in 1859 "Ceylon," a work which has already obtained European popularity. His greatest parliamentary achievement was that of carrying the Copyright of Designs Act, for which services the manufacturers of the United Kingdom, in 1843, presented him at Manchester with a magnificent testimonial and service of silver plate, valued at £3,000.

TENNYSON, ALFRED, D.C.L., the poet-laureate, was born in 1809, at Somersby, in Lincolnshire, where his father was rector. The laureate's father, the Rev. George Clayton Tennyson, LL.D., was a man of no inconsiderable ability as a poet, painter, architect, musician, linguist, and mathematician. After some preparatory training at the grammar school of Louth, he returned home, and was educated by his father, being sent, in due time, to Trinity College, Cambridge, where he specially distinguished himself, obtaining the Chancellor's Medal for an English Poem on Timbuctoo. The year following this, "University Success Poems, chiefly Lyrical, by Alfred Tennyson," were published. Three years after this maiden effort, Tennyson published a second volume, which contained "The Miller's Daughter," "A Dream of Fair Woman," "The Palace of Art," and "The May Queen;" and compared with his first volume, was a surprising advance, at once in richness of thought and beauty of imagery. In 1842 he published a collected edition of his works, in two volumes, and at once took the highest rank as a poet. Since then he has published "The Princess," a medley, "In Memoriam," "Maud," an "Ode on the Death of the Duke of Wellington," and the "Idylls of the King," which appeared in the summer of 1859. He is now engaged on a new poem, the subject of which is Boadicea. A few years ago Oxford conferred on him the honour of D.C.L., after he had been appointed poet-laureate. We have not attempted anything more than a bare enumeration of the titles of Mr. Tennyson's poems. The list is, we trust, not yet closed, and it would be out of place to enter, within our narrow limits, on any estimate of the influence which they have already exercised, and are likely to exercise, in the present and the coming age.

THACKERAY, WILLIAM MAKEPEACE, a novelist and essayist, was born at Calcutta, in 1811. His father and grandfather, Mr. W. M. Thackeray, of Hadley, both belonged to the East India Company's civil service. On his arrival in England he was sent to school, and afterwards completed his studies at the University of Cambridge. After having studied art at Rome, with the design of devoting himself to the profession, he returned to London, and gave himself unreservedly to literature. The "Times" is understood to have been one of the earliest of the mediums through which he addressed the public. It was, however, not in the leading journal, but in "Fraser's Magazine," that Thackeray came prominently before the public. His "Paris Sketch Book," "The Second Funeral of Napoleon," and the "Chronicle of the Drum," were published in 1841. The success of these independent publications was not great, the public being slow to appreciate the merit of the new candidate for its favour. But while the higher order of mind was beginning to acknowledge his genius, it was his connexion with "Punch" that first constituted Thackeray a power in English literature, and there "Jeames's Diary," and the "Snob Papers," appeared. In 1846 Thackeray's next separate publication was brought out, entitled "Notes of a Journey from Cornhill to Grand Cairo," by "Michael Angelo Titmarsh," a pseudonym under which he then wrote, and almost simultaneously he commenced the publication of "Vanity Fair," a work which at once placed him in the foremost position as a writer of fiction. "Vanity Fair" was followed, in 1848 and 1849, by two little Christmas volumes. In the latter year also the "History of Pendennis" began to appear; this, again, was followed in 1850, by "Rebecca and Rowena," and in 1851 he wrote the "Kickleburys on the Rhine." In 1852 the finest of his novels, "Esmond," appeared. Thackeray's "Lectures on the English Humorists" is a work which, though slightly marred by mannerism, forms one of the most delightful pieces of biography in the language. The Lectures were first delivered in 1851, in London; they were published in 1853, and recently a cheap re-issue has appeared. The success of the "Lectures on English Humorists" induced Mr. Thackeray to prepare another series, the "Four Georges," which were first delivered in America, during 1855 and 1856, and have since been re-delivered in all the chief cities of England and Scotland, with eminent success, and have appeared in the "Cornhill Magazine." "The Newcomes," and "The Virginians," are the most recent fictions of this eminent novelist. In July, 1857, Mr. Thackeray contested Oxford with Mr. Cardwell, but was unsuccessful. During the last three years, the sketches, ballads, and burlesques written by Mr. Thackeray, while yet unknown to fame, have been in process of republication. These miscellanies give us Thackeray in dishabille—Thackeray in masquerade—and carry us through the entire gamut of his exercises—light or sober—cynical or cheery. The forte of this social satirist has lain among the professional, aristocratic, and would-be aristocratic world, and never has the pitiless daylight been so let in upon the rouge and tinsel of that world's "Vanity Fair." Mr. Thackeray now edits, and confines his literary labours to the "Cornhill Magazine," a new periodical, which already circulates to the large number of 100,000 copies.

THALBERG, SIGISMUND, pianist, was born at Geneva, in January 1812, and received a careful education under the direction of his mother, his father being the Count Dietrichstien. When very young he received lessons from the celebrated Hummel, and surpassed even his master by the firmness of his touch and the grace of his expression. His successes in the concert room began when he was only fifteen, and at sixteen he published his first compositions. In 1830 his name became extensively known, and in 1834 he was appointed Imperial Pianist to the Court of Austria, which laid the foundation of his fame and fortune. He appeared in Paris in 1835, and his reputation being now European, he entered in 1836 on a series of visits to all the cities of the Continent and Great Britain, giving concerts, and acquiring wealth while adding to his celebrity. For some years past he has been professionally engaged in the United States. In 1845 he married a daughter of Signor Lablache. As a composer and pianist M. Thalberg is the founder of a new school, which has had numerous followers, but none, with the exception of Liszt, coming up to the standard of the master.

THIERRY, ALEXANDRE, a French Doctor of Medicine and Surgeon, was born in February, 1803. His father and grandfather having been medical men, he embraced that profession, and studied with the utmost diligence. He received his degree as Doctor in 1828, and afterwards published various learned dissertations on intricate subjects of medicine and surgery. Being on the most friendly terms with Armand Carrel, he wrote for the "National," and became in 1832 Chef d'Escadron of the National Guard. In 1846 he was elected a member of the Municipal Council, and in 1848 he took an active part, as well in stimulating the revolution of February, as in assisting General Cavaignac to maintain the peace of the city. Amid all the chances and changes of government in Paris, M. Thierry has been esteemed as an earnest and yet moderate conservator of public institutions, and has acquired the affections of the people because of his sacrifices on their behalf. Professionally, he is recognised as one of the most skilful operators in France.

THIERRY, AMÉDÉE SIMON DOMINIQUE, a French historian, was born at Blois, on the 2nd of August, 1797. He received a good education in his native town, and afterwards at Paris. Having entered in 1820 the central office of colonial administration, he began his historical studies about the same period. He published in 1824 a short " History of the Province of Guyenne," and four years afterwards, " A History of the Gaulois, or old Celtic Population of France," which has reached a fifth edition. The success of this book induced him to look out for employment in connexion with education. He was appointed Professor of History to the Faculty of Letters of Besançon, where his course of lectures attracted large audiences. In spite of the moderation of opinions and views expressed in his lectures, the government of the day took alarm, the course was suppressed, and M. Thierry was exposed to petty persecutions, which only terminated with the downfall of the Polignac ministry, followed by the revolution of 1830. This revolution completely changed the position of M. Thierry. The new Minister of the Interior, M. Guizot, whose pupil and friend he had been, appointed him Prefect of the Haute-Saône, a situation which he held for eight years. In 1838 he returned to Paris, where he entered the Council of State as Maître des Requêtes, an office which he filled till 1853, when he was named a Councillor of State.

In 1860, the dignity of Senator of the Empire was conferred upon him. Having resumed his literary labours in 1838, and published a " History of Gaul under the Roman Domination," he was in 1842 unanimously elected a member of the Institute, of the section of the moral and political sciences. In 1855 he published his " History of Attila and his Sons and Successors in Europe," a work which was received with favour by the French public, and translated into all the continental languages. He has contributed a number of interesting articles to the " Revue des Deux Mondes." M. Thierry has the merit of having founded in France the study of the " Origines Gauloises," and on this subject his ideas and doctrines are quite in conformity with those of the most competent British authorities.

THIERS, LOUIS ADOLPHE, a French statesman and historian, was born at Marseilles, on 16th April, 1797. Sprung from a poor but respectable parentage, he was first educated at the Marseilles Lyceum, and subsequently studied for the bar, becoming an advocate in 1820. His professional career was, however, by no means encouraging, and at length he resolved to seek his fortune in literary pursuits, and for that purpose removed to Paris. He procured some employment in connexion with the "Constitutionnel," and soon attracted notice by the talents which he exhibited in his contributions to that newspaper. These were characterised by great versatility, and his subjects ranged through politics, theatricals, the fine arts, &c., indicating the possession of a master mind on the part of their author. In the meantime he was engaged on his great work, the " History of the French Revolution," which, on the appearance of the first part, immediately became popular, and has since given to M. Thiers considerable eminence as an historian. In 1830 M. Thiers began to take an active interest in political matters, and held an office in Finance, exchanging it for that of an Under Secretaryship, which he continued in till 1831. Having been returned a deputy, he took a prominent position as a parliamentary speaker, and was successively Minister of the Interior and of Public Works, maintaining the system of protection as essential to the commercial prosperity of France. He held various offices till 1836, when he became President of the Council and Foreign Minister. He occupied the same office in 1840, and in 1848 participated in the misfortunes of the Orleans dynasty, and has since entirely passed away from the platform of political affairs. M. Thiers subsequently occupied himself in historical pursuits, and his "History of the Consulate and the Empire," commenced in 1845, was completed in 1860. Among his other literary productions are some of a minor character, such as his "Law" and his "Financial System," and numerous papers contributed to the "Revue des Deux Mondes," and the "Revue Français," &c.

THIRLWALL, The Right Reverend Connop, D.D., Bishop of St. David's, and historian of Greece, was born at Mile End, Middlesex, in 1797. He was educated at Cambridge, and became a Fellow of Trinity College. He was called to the bar in 1825, but afterwards took orders, and was appointed to a rectory in Yorkshire. He commenced his "History of Greece" in 1835; and in 1840 was elevated to the see of St. David's.

THOLUCK, Friedrich August Gottreu, a German theologian, was born at Breslau, in 1799. He began as a schoolboy to devote himself to the study of Eastern languages, which he prosecuted afterwards in the University of Berlin. He was brought up on principles hostile to Christianity, but having been introduced, in Berlin, into a circle of pious laymen and theologians, among whom was Neander, he changed his views. This took place during the period of a religious enthusiasm which had been awakened by the war of liberation in Germany, and principally in Prussia. The young student felt himself bound in conscience to prefer the theological career to that of Oriental scholarship, and began in 1820, a course of theological study in the University of Berlin. In 1825 he was sent by the Prussian Government on a mission to the libraries of Holland and England, from which he returned with a literary store, part of which he afterwards communicated to the public in his works—"On the Speculative Doctrine of the Trinity in the Philosophical Systems of the East," and his "Poetical Collections from the Mystical Writings of Persian Authors." In 1826 he was transferred by his Government to the University of Halle, the most numerously attended theological faculty in Prussia, the number of divinity students amounting at that time to 950. The rationalistic system having been the prevailing one in this faculty, it was the intention of the Prussian King and the Government of the day, to supplant it by an orthodox theology. Tholuck succeeded in this object. He introduced Christian sentiments, and awakened a Christian spirit in the university. His theological works are mostly exegetical, and consist chiefly of a "Commentary on the Sermon on the Mount," "On the Epistles to the Romans and Hebrews, and the Gospel of St. John," all of which have been translated into English. Of late, M. Tholuck has edited a number of volumes connected with the history of religious ideas in the seventeenth century, preparatory to a work on Rationalism.

THOMPSON, The Rev. R. Anchor, M.A., a divine of the Church of England, was born in Durham in 1821. After being educated at the School and University of Durham, he graduated at

Cambridge. He was Curate of Louth, and of Binbrooke, Lincolnshire, and is now Master of the Hospital of St. Mary the Virgin at Newcastle-upon-Tyne, an ancient foundation in the patronage of the mayor, aldermen, and burgesses of that town. He published a volume of sermons in 1853; "Christian Theism," the Burdett Prize Treatise, in 1855; and "Principles of Natural Theology," in 1857.

THOMPSON, MAJOR-GENERAL THOMAS PERRONET, political reformer and author, was born at Hull in 1783, where his father was a banker, holding a high position as a man of business, and also as a member of the Wesleyan connexion. He was educated at the Grammar School at Hull, and made great progress. From thence he proceeded to Queen's College, Cambridge, and took the degree of B.A. in 1801. In 1803 he entered the navy as midshipman in the "Isis," the flag-ship of Vice-Admiral Gambier, on the Newfoundland station. On returning home he was put on board the "Pomona" frigate, one of the vessels which blockaded the French coast during the war. He remained till 1805 in that service, and during the interval was elected to a Fellowship at Queen's College, Cambridge. He longed, however, for military service, and in the spring of 1806 he entered the Rifle Corps as second lieutenant. He proceeded with his regiment to Buenos Ayres, and was made prisoner in the attack of September, 1807. After his return to England, he was induced to accept the Governorship of Sierra Leone, and one of his first acts was to issue a proclamation for the suppression of the slave-trade in that colony. He found, however, that the slave-dealers were in combination against him; they used every effort to thwart his measures, but he was firm. They then complained to Lord Castlereagh; and though

Governor Thompson had done no more than carry out the acts of the legislature, he was ordered home. He arrived in England in 1810, and two years afterwards was appointed to a lieutenancy in the 7th Fusileers. In 1813 and 1814 he served against the French in Spain; but he was always a student, and he wrote in the camp his treatise on morals and law. In 1814 he composed a work entitled "On a Constitution." In 1814 he became Captain in the 30th Foot, which he afterwards exchanged for the 17th Light Dragoons, then serving in India. He served with honour in the Pindaree campaign, and accompanied Sir William Keir Grant in 1819, as Arabic interpreter in that commander's expedition to the Persian Gulf, drawing up a treaty with the Arab tribes, which declared trading in slaves to be piracy. In 1825 he was promoted to an unattached Majority; in 1829 advanced to the rank of Lieutenant-Colonel unattached; and in 1854 he was gazetted Major-General. Retired from military service, he turned his attention to literature and politics. On the establishment of the "Westminster Review" in 1824, under the auspices of Jeremy Bentham and Dr. Bowring, he contributed a paper on the "Instrument of Exchange." Five years afterwards he became joint proprietor of the "Review" with Dr. Bowring, and wrote regularly in its pages until 1836, when it changed hands. In the meantime his "True Theory of Rent," and the "Corn Law Catechism," appeared. His writings embraced a multitude of subjects, and were at once racy, vigorous, and pointed. Free-trade, Reform, Slavery, Catholic and Jewish Disabilities, Property Tax, Flogging, Music, Mathematics, and various other topics of the day, were treated by him with masterly skill. His friends desiring to see him in Parliament, put him forward before several constituencies, but without success until 1835, when he was returned for Hull, his native town. At the general election of 1837 he was not returned, but afterwards sat for Bradford, and after five years' absence from Parliament was elected again in 1857. He does not sit in the present Parliament. His writings were collected in 1842, and published in six volumes. He has always been regarded as one of the most consistent reformers of the day.

THOMS, WILLIAM, an English antiquary, was born in Westminster, November 16th, 1803. Mr. Thoms has led an official life. Originally placed in the Secretary's office, Chelsea Hospital, he has been for some years clerk of the printed papers in the House of Lords, employing his spare time in writing articles for various periodicals, and publishing works of antiquarian interest. He is a Fellow of the Societies of Antiquaries of London, Edinburgh, and Copenhagen. As the originator and editor of "Notes and Queries," for the last ten years Mr. Thoms has become well known in literary circles, and his paper has been the medium of some most interesting and useful additions to the facts of literature and history.

THORNEYCROFT, MRS. MARY, a sculptor, was born at Thornham, Norfolk, in 1814. Inheriting the tastes and talents of her father, Mr. John Francis, the eminent sculptor, she spent much of her youth in modelling busts and figures. At the age of twenty she exhibited "Penelope," and "Ulysses and his Dog," at the Royal Academy, and subsequently the "Flower Girl," a statue of great beauty and careful execution. Having married in 1840, she afterwards proceeded with her husband to Italy. At Rome she modelled two graceful pieces, "Sappho" and the "Sleeping Child," and through the sculptor Gibson, Mrs. Thorneycroft was recommended to Queen Victoria, as the fittest artist to execute statues of the royal children. So satisfactory were the works which emanated from her chisel that she has ever since enjoyed the patronage of the Court. Mrs. Thorneycroft's productions are characterised by grace, strength, and poetic conception, in her representations of children. A statue lately executed for the Queen, representing the Princess Beatrice floating in the shell of a Nautilus, is probably her best work of this kind, being singularly original in design, and happy in arrangement.

TICKNOR, GEORGE, an American author, was born at Boston, Massachusetts, on 1st August, 1791. After graduating at Dartmouth College, he followed the legal profession, and was called to the bar in 1813; but preferring literature, he determined to abandon the law. He accordingly sailed for Europe, and spent some time in studying at the leading universities, devoting himself chiefly to philology. On arriving in America, in 1819, he was installed Professor of Modern Languages at the Harvard University, a position he held for several years, and one in which he acquired great distinction. In 1835 he paid another visit to Europe, and during his stay devoted special attention to ancient Spanish literature. The results of his investigation were embodied in a work which he published in 1849, entitled "History of Spanish Literature." This production is one of the most valuable that has appeared of its class, and has achieved a high reputation for its author, both in his own and other countries. His other works are of a minor character, but they have, however, in every case, been well received.

TIMBS, JOHN, F.S.A., an English compiler, was born in London, August 17, 1801. He was for many years editor of the "Mirror," one of the first attempts made to establish the now popular cheap press; it was published weekly, at the price of twopence. Mr. Timbs is the author of "The Curiosities of London," a volume of 800 pages, comprising all the information that could be gleaned, historical and statistical, concerning the capital of England, published in 1855, and the produce of many years' labour and research. It has been followed by "Things not Generally Known," a series of five volumes; "The School Days of Eminent Men," "Stories of Inventions and Discoveries," and two volumes of Anecdote Biography. Mr. Timbs has also edited the "Arcana of Science," and "The Year-book of Facts," in 33 volumes. He was for fifteen years one of the editors of the "Illustrated London News," but withdrew from its management in the beginning of 1858.

TITE, WILLIAM, an English architect, M.P., and F.R.S., was born in the city of London early in the present century. He was articled to Mr. Laing, the architect of the new Custom House, and while still his pupil had the entire charge and management of rebuilding the church of St. Dunstan-in-the-East. His next important work was the erection of a very large Gothic church in Regent-square, for the celebrated Edward Irving. His connexion with the railways having commenced, he built the stations in London, Southampton, and Gosport, for the South-Western Railway, and rebuilt the great terminus for the North-Western in Liverpool. He also built the station for the Blackwall Railway. In 1846 he was appointed architect for the new Royal Exchange, and since that time Mr. Tite has had one of the largest architectural connexions in England and France, but principally in London. He was the architect of the Missionary College, Blomfield-street; the Chapel for Mr. Binney, on Fish-street-hill; and many of our largest commercial buildings and establishments. In France he erected the large station at Havre, for the Rouen and Havre line, and all the intermediate stations, up to Rouen. At Rouen he built the two large stations for the Paris and Rouen line. Mr. Tite was elected a F.R.S. and F.S.A. in 1835; and has been on the councils of both societies. He was President of the Architectural Society, until it merged in the Institute. Mr. Tite is also a Fellow of the Geological, Statistical, and other learned societies. In 1854 he was first returned member for Bath, in the place of Mr. Phinn. He has been three times returned for the same constituency, and has exerted himself very much in Parliament on questions connected with lunacy, having obtained the appointment of a select commission on that subject, which has sat for two sessions. His exertions, with reference to the Foreign Office, are well known; particularly on the vexed question of the adoption of the Gothic style for civil buildings, of which he has shown himself a determined opponent. Since his return to Parliament he has been less active in the practice of his profession. His last work is a small memorial church at Gerrard's-cross, in a Romanesque style, which is a bold departure from ordinary types, and has thereby attracted much notice and remark.

TITIENS, TERESA, a vocalist and actress, was born at Hamburgh, in the summer of 1834. Her parents were of Hungarian extraction. During her early years her taste and proficiency in music were so remarkable as to have attracted the notice of her friends; and she was accordingly, at twelve years of age, placed under a professor in her native town, from whom she received a course of preliminary instruction. The brilliancy and compass of voice thus early developed, at once indicated the profession to which she ought to devote herself; and being sent to Vienna, she studied under some of the most eminent masters in that city, and thus prepared herself for a career in which she has become so successful. She made her *début* at Hamburgh, in the *rôle* of "Lucrezia," in 1849, and subsequently spent some time in that city. In 1850 she sang at the Imperial Theatre at Vienna, as "Donna Anna" in "Don Giovanni." In 1858 she made her appearance before an English audience in her Majesty's Theatre, as "Valentine" in "Les Huguenots," and subsequently as "Leonora," in "Il Trovatore." She then returned to Vienna. In 1859 she again visited London, and in the present year (1860) has taken the foremost position in her profession, and is at the present time one of the most popular vocalists connected with the stage.

TODLEBEN, FRANCIS EDWARD, a Russian General of Engineers, was born at Mitau, in Courland, on 8th May, 1818. His father, who was a merchant in easy circumstances, bestowed upon him the advantages of a good education. He entered the engineering school of St. Petersburg at the age of fourteen, and the Grenadier Corps of Sappers, with the rank of Lieutenant. From 1841 to 1848, General de Schilder, a very distinguished artillery officer, employed him specially in preparing projects for the attack and defence of fortifications, which he was afterwards to carry out under the superintendence of the general. Raised to the rank of Captain in 1845, he was sent in 1848 to the Caucasus, to take part in the attacks upon several strongholds among the mountains of Daghestan, where Schamyl, the native general and prophet, offered a determined resistance; and rendered efficient service at the siege of Gherghebil. He was next concerned in the expeditions against the fortresses of Arctati and Tschoch. In 1851 Todleben was named Aide-de-camp to General de Schilder, then at Warsaw. Entering, in 1852, the Engineers of the Guard at St.

Petersburg, he worked incessantly for two years, studying projects of attack and defence against fortresses constructed upon the newest principles of fortification, and superintended, at the same time, the works which the battalions of the Sappers of the Guard executed at the camp of Peterhof. These were inspected by the Emperor Nicholas, who, having been an Officer of Engineers previous to his accession to the throne, took an especial interest in this department of the service. In 1854 Captain Todleben was promoted to the rank of Lieutenant-Colonel, when General de Schilder, then commanding the artillery in the army of the Danube, asked his assistance as the officer in whom he had the greatest confidence. Todleben was present at all the engagements, which at this period took place between the Russian and Turkish troops, and also served at the siege of Silistria. In the month of August, 1854, Prince Gortchakoff, Commander-in-Chief of the army of the Danube, suspecting the projects of the Allies against the Crimea, and alarmed about the fate of Sebastopol, which was extremely weak on the land side, despatched Colonel Todleben, on his own authority, to Prince Menschikoff, recommending him in the warmest manner. Until the disembarkation of the allied army, Lieutenant-Colonel Todleben was not entrusted with any official employment at Sebastopol. He was not idle, however. He studied the character of the ground carefully, at the same time making the acquaintance of the Admirals Nachimoff, Carniloff, and Istomine, who formed a high opinion of his abilities. Prince Menschikoff at length entrusted him with the defence of Sebastopol, and his astonishing success is well known. In the month of September, 1854, on the personal recommendation of Prince Menschikoff, the Emperor Nicholas raised him to the rank of Colonel, and in March, 1855, to that of General of his Military household; and in September of the same year, to the rank of Aide-de-camp General. Recalled to St. Petersburg after the fall of the southern part of Sebastopol, General Todleben was entrusted with new works of defence; in the first place to fortify Nicolaieff, and afterwards to protect Cronstadt from the attack which the prolongation of the war left too much reason to fear would be made. Since the peace, General Todleben has had no active employment. His health has been severely affected by a wound caused by a ball, which passed through his right leg under the knee during the siege of Sebastopol.

TRENCH, VERY REV. RICHARD CHENEVIX, Dean of Westminster, a scholar, poet, and divine, was born at Dublin in September, 1807, and graduated at Cambridge in 1829, after which he spent some years in travelling abroad. While holding the incumbency of Curdridge, Hants, he published in 1838, two volumes of poems. These having been well received by the public, were followed by "Genoveva," "Elegiac Poems," and "Poems from Eastern Sources," which also elicited favourable notices. In 1841 he became Curate to the present Bishop of Oxford, at Alverstoke, and afterwards Rector of Itchinstoke. He was also Hulsean Lecturer at Cambridge, and in 1847 he was appointed to the important office of Theological Professor in King's College, London. On the death of Dr. Buckland, which caused a vacancy in the Deanery of Westminster, he was nominated to that office, which he continues to fill. His sermons are considered eloquent and impressive. Those preached at the special services for the working classes delivered at Westminster Abbey, have been attended by very crowded congregations. He has published several works on theological subjects; among these are, "Notes on the Parables," "Notes on the Miracles," "The Sermon on the Mount," &c.; and his Lectures on the "English Language," and on the "Study of Words," have had a large circulation.

TROLLOPE, MRS. FRANCES, an English authoress, was born in 1791, at Heckfield, Hampshire. The education of the young lady was excellent, and she was naturally gay and thoughtful by turns. At the age of nineteen, she married Mr. Anthony Trollope, barrister-at-law, and a few years afterwards was left a widow. In 1829 she visited America, and prolonged her stay there for about three years. In 1832, Mrs. Trollope published her "Domestic Life of the Americans," a work which caused a sensation in Britain, and created extreme excitement in the United States. Mrs. Trollope continued to write, producing book after book, on a variety of subjects—novels, travels, society, nothing came amiss to her flying pen. A considerable portion of her life was spent in travel, and to this source may be as ascribed numbers of her most vigorous delineations of character and manners. Mrs. Trollope has written and published no fewer than 102 volumes, all of which have been more or less popular according to their groundwork—a sufficient proof of her industry and facility of composition. "The Vicar of Wrexhill," "The Widow Barnaby," "The Widow Married," "The Barnabys in America," "Eustace," "Petticoat Government," and "The Lauringtons," are among the best specimens of her novels; of her travels, the jottings in America, Germany, Paris, and Vienna, are characterised by keen observation and an evident desire to suppress no truth. Mrs. Trollope at present resides abroad.

TROUBRIDGE, COLONEL SIR THOMAS ST. VINCENT HOPE COCHRANE, BART., C.B., was born in 1817, and is the son of Admiral Sir Edward Troubridge, and grandson of the famous Sir

Thomas Troubridge, who served at Aboukir. Joining the army in 1834, he saw comparatively little active service until the war in the Crimea, when, as Major of the 7th Royal Fusileers, he became attached to Sir George Brown's division, and assisted in forcing the passage of the Alma. At Inkermann he commanded the outposts, sustaining the shock of the Russian attack with a heroism which adds to the lustre of the British arms. Even when seriously wounded, he remained on the field; and while his limbs were but partially bandaged, he continued his command. In January, 1855, he returned to England, having, the year before, received the brevet rank of Lieut.-Colonel, and soon after arriving at home, he was promoted to be full Colonel, and honoured with the decoration of C.B.

TULLOCH, THE REV. JOHN, D.D., Principal and Professor of Divinity of St. Mary's College, St. Andrews, was born in 1823, at Dron, Perthshire. He studied at St. Andrews, and was then licensed as a preacher in the Church of Scotland. In 1845 he was appointed to a charge in Dundee, from which he removed in 1849 to the parish of Kettens, in Forfar. As a contributor to the "British Quarterly" and "North British Reviews," he first acquired literary distinction, and in 1854 became Principal of St. Mary's College, at St. Andrews. He obtained the second Burnett prize in 1855, for an essay since published by the Messrs. Blackwood, on the "Being and Attributes of God." In 1859 he published his "Leaders of the Reformation: embracing Sketches of Luther, Calvin, Latimer, and Knox."

TUPPER, MARTIN FARQUHAR, D.C.L., F.R.S., a literary writer, was born in London, 1810. He was educated at the Charter House, and at Christ Church, Oxford, where he graduated in 1831, and was afterwards called to the bar. The first work which brought his name into celebrity, was "Proverbial Philosophy," a book which has reached upwards of forty editions in England alone. It was followed by "The Crock of Gold," "A Modern Pyramid," "An Author's Mind," "A Thousand Lines," "Heart," "The Twins," "Ballads for the Times," "Æsop Smith," "Stephen Langton," "Paterfamilias' Diary," and a multitude of lyrical and national poems, among which the most noticeable for their public influence were those which bore upon our relationships with America, and upon the Rifle movement in England.

TURKEY, SULTAN OF. (See ABDUL MEDJID.)

UHLAND, JOHANN LUDWIG, a German poet, was born at Tübingen, in 1787, educated in its public schools, and adopted law as a profession. Before he entered upon the study of law, Uhland was a poet; and his muse, like the muse of Burns—intensely national—found a fitting theme in the French aggression of the first Napoleon. In a series of soul-stirring lyrics he denounced the Gallic invaders of the Fatherland. The popularity of these patriotic effusions may be guessed from the fact that, before 1846, seventeen editions had been called for. From 1819, he became a member of the Representative Assembly of Wurtemburg, gaining by his superior abilities and varied information, a preponderating influence. In 1830 he was appointed Professor of the German Language and Literature in the university of his native town. In 1844-45 he published a work, doing for German, what Scott had done so well for Scottish, minstrelsy—an admirable collection of ancient High and Low popular German songs. In 1848 he was elected to represent Tübingen in the United German National Assembly, in which he spoke and acted with the democratic party. Uhland, in addition to his poetry, has also given the world some superior prose compositions, chiefly devoted to the elucidation of northern mythology. His songs are, however, the most valuable of his literary productions, and have become highly popular.

ULLMAN, KARL, a German theological writer and historian, was born at Eptenbach, in the neighbourhood of Heidelberg, in 1796. He received the rudiments of his education at Heidelberg, and afterwards continued his more advanced studies in that university, at Tübingen, and Berlin. In 1819 he returned to Heidelberg, and in 1821 was appointed Extraordinary Professor of Theology, and subsequently he obtained a chair as Ordinary Professor. From Heidelberg he was called to the University of Halle, to fill a similar post there, and in this place he continued to lecture to a numerous auditory until 1836, when he returned to Heidelberg as Professor of Theology. In 1857 he was appointed a member of the Church Council, which situation he continues to fill. He is favourable to a Christian union of sects, in conformity with the theological and ecclesiastical views entertained by Neander, J. Müller, and others. Since 1828, he has edited a journal bearing the name of "Theological Expositions and Criticisms." His other works are "The Reformers before the Reformation," "The Sinlessness of Jesus," and several treatises against David Strauss, most of which have been translated into English and other European languages.

URQUHART, DAVID, an English publicist and political writer, was born at Cromarty, in 1805. He studied at Oxford, where he chiefly devoted himself to the Oriental languages and political economy. In 1827 he accompanied Lord Cochrane to Greece, and laboured indefatigably to procure the internal prosperity of that country. After the Peace of Adrianople, he visited Turkey, and on his return to England in 1831, he published his first work on "Turkey and its Resources," which was devoted to administrative questions. He published afterwards another work on "England and Turkey," which was the political complement to his former book. Some time after, he travelled through Germany, Turkey, Persia, and the principal part of Asia, observing and noting the political and commercial influence of Russia in these countries. During his stay at Constantinople, he wrote and published various books and pamphlets directed to the exposure of projects of the Muscovite despotism. These publications attracted attention by the fearless and able manner in which the author developed his views. Appointed Secretary to the Turkish Embassy by Lord Palmerston in 1835, he became still more intimately acquainted with Russian policy. Disagreeing on this subject with our Minister at Constantinople, he resigned his office and returned to England, and, with a hardihood that no man not sure of his ground would venture to display, he accused Lord Palmerston of playing foolishly into the hands of the Czar. In 1840 he published "The Crisis," showing the relation in which the four Great Powers of Europe stood to each other. In 1847 he was elected member for Stafford, but lost his seat in 1852. His strong views in reference to our foreign policy, have tended to alienate many who would otherwise have supported him, and during late years he has rarely appeared in public on political questions.

VANDENHOFF, JOHN, a dramatic performer, was born 31st March, 1790, at Salisbury. He is of Dutch origin, his grandfather having been an Amsterdam merchant. After the ordinary schooling of boys brought up in a city, he was sent to the College of Stonyhurst, Lancashire, at one period entertaining a strong fancy for an ecclesiastical life. He remained at Stonyhurst for about three years, but a change having come over his views, he returned home and thought of other pursuits. For a few months he tried the drudgery of a solicitor's office, but at the age of sixteen he did not much relish that occupation, and he abandoned it for a sub-preceptorship of a grammar school in the Isle of Wight. He remained in that situation for nearly two years. The reading and study of Shakspeare, however, suggested the idea of the stage as a profession more consistent with his tastes than commerce or teaching. His first appearance as an actor was made on the boards of his native city, where he undertook the arduous declamatory character of ' Osmond' in Monk Lewis's "Castle Spectre," a drama of peculiar romantic construction. Mr. Vandenhoff could scarcely have chosen a more trying part; but his success was such, that his friends urged a re-appearance in the following week as ' Octavian' in Colman's "Mountaineers," another part which draws on all the powers of an actor. The theatre was crowded, and the applause was such that the stage was resolved upon as his profession. An old friend and correspondent of Garrick, Mr. James Wickens, was lavish in his approbation of the young actor's efforts. Provincial engagements were at once secured; Cheltenham, Taunton, Exeter, and Weymouth, giving him scope for the exercise of his talents. At Weymouth he acted with Edmund Kean, before that great performer appeared in London; and as Mr. Vandenhoff possessed a versatility which falls to the lot of few performers, he did anything and everything until May, 1814, when he appeared in Liverpool as ' Rolla' in "Pizarro." This was his starting-point on the path of fame; his reception was enthusiastic beyond precedent, and in Liverpool and Manchester he enjoyed, for six seasons, all the honours of a high reputation and as substantial proofs of regard as ever fell to a provincial

actor. In December, 1820, he appeared first in London as ' King Lear,' and played at Covent Garden amid rapturous applause. This part was followed by ' Coriolanus,' in which he has had no competitor since the days of Kemble. Mr. Macready having preceded him in London, he relinquished his engagement and made a tour of the provinces, playing his favourite characters with marked success. In 1834 he re-visited London, and appeared for the second time as ' Coriolanus,' which, after an interval of fourteen years, he played with distinguished ability. Mr. Bunn secured his services for Covent Garden and Drury Lane. His subsequent performance of ' Adrastus,' in the tragedy of "Ion" at the Haymarket, was remarkably fine. In 1837 he visited America, where he met with great success. In September, 1838, he re-appeared at Covent Garden, then under the management of Mr. Macready, afterwards visiting America. In 1841 he accepted an engagement from Charles Kemble, and continued to perform in London and in the provinces, until October 29th, 1858, when he retired finally from the stage, after fulfilling a round of engagements in the principal theatres of the United Kingdom. ·At Liverpool, Edinburgh, and Glasgow, he was always a special favourite, and was received with the respect and esteem due to a gentleman, a scholar, and an accomplished artist.

VAUGHAN, The Rev. Robert, D.D., a Nonconformist divine and critic, editor of the "British Quarterly Review," was born towards the close of the last century. Educated at Bristol, he became Professor of History in the London University, where he remained for several years. In 1842, he removed to Manchester, becoming President of the Lancashire Independent College. He retained the presidency until 1857, when the failing health of his family obliged him to resign. He projected the "British Quarterly Review" in 1844, and has been its editor ever since. He was sneered at originally when starting the "British Quarterly" by some of those who might have been expected to have hailed his disinterested effort to elevate Nonconformist literature. The distinguished success of that review has shown that the powers of its projector are of no common order. He has published numerous works, chiefly on theological and church history matters, and on popular education.

VELPEAU, ALFRED ARMAND LOUIS MARIE, a French surgeon, was born at the little village of Briche, near Tours, in May, 1795, where his father was a country blacksmith and veterinary surgeon. In his early days, young Velpeau assisted at his father's craft, but owing to an accidental circumstance, he attracted the attention of a country gentleman, M. Ducan, who procured the means of sending him to Tours to study. His progress was rapid, though he had to endure many privations, for he was gifted with great decision of character. When admitted to the Hospital of Tours, he studied night and day, passing through the courses of Latin, French, geography, history, anatomy, physiology, and all the medical branches, with such success, that he was soon admitted a pupil in surgery, and then received as an officer of health. In 1818 he achieved the rank of first scholar, and soon after formed the hazardous resolution of repairing to Paris. He carried this resolution into effect; attended the hospitals; received the highest honours from the École Pratique; was named an anatomical assistant; added daily to his reputation; and eventually obtained his diploma as doctor in 1823. After several years of laborious practice, M. Velpeau was named, in 1830, Surgeon to the Hôpital de la Pitié; in 1835 he carried the chair of Clinical Surgery of the Faculty of Medicine at the Hôpital de la Charité; and in 1842, he was called to supply the Academic Chair, left vacant by the decease of the eminent M. Larrey. He has discharged all his public offices with distinguished ability; he holds a first place among the surgeons of Paris, is an admirable operator, and possesses remarkable influence with the profession. He is a very voluminous author in the vast domain of surgery, and his works are received by the faculty as standard authorities.

VERDI, GIUSEPPE, an Italian composer, author of a number of operas, some of which are among the most successful that have been produced during the last twenty years, was born at Roucole, Parma, 9th of October, 1814, and is son of an innkeeper of that town. He received his first lessons from an obscure organist, but soon surpassed his master. From 1833 to 1836 he studied at Milan, under the direction of Lavigna. In 1839 he produced his first work at Milan, a musical drama entitled "Oberto di San Bonifazio," which was tolerably well received; but his next totally failed, and he was so discouraged that for ten months he ceased to write. The year following his "Nabucco," represented at La Scala during the Carnival of 1842, was so successful that he became recognised as a composer. He wrote rapidly afterwards, "Ernani" adding to his reputation. His operas best known in this country are, "Il Rigoletto," "Il Trovatore," and "La Traviata," and he ranks at the present time as one of the most popular of living composers.

VERNET, HORACE, a French historical painter, was born at Paris in 1789. His early days were passed in comparative poverty, and his taste for art was employed in various humble ways in gaining him a bare livelihood. His first exhibition was in 1809, and having chosen military incidents for illustration, the popular taste soon showed its appreciation of his productions. In 1812 he received a medal; in 1814 became a Chevalier of the Legion of Honour; and in 1825 an Officer of the same order. His reputation being now established, he changed his style of painting, and adopted historical subjects. Amongst his productions of this class are his "Judith and Holofernes," "The Arrest of the Princes, by order of Anne of Russia," "The School of Rafaelle," &c. In 1849 he painted his "Taking of Rome by Oudinot;" and in 1855 received a medal of honour at the Exposition Universelle at Paris. Besides the subjects above enumerated, M. Vernet has produced others in various departments of the art, and is one of the most prolific painters of the day.

VÉRON, LOUIS DÉSIRÉ, a French writer and journalist, was born at Paris in April, 1798. He has been by turns a Doctor of Medicine, a writer on the laws of nations, a deputy to the Corps Législatif, and a director of the Opera. He commenced his studies under an ex-priest, and finished them at the Lycée Impérial, in 1816. He first chose the profession of medicine for the exercise of his talents, and having passed the usual course of study he was named, in 1821, a house surgeon to the hospitals. In 1823 he received the degree of Doctor of Medicine, and in 1824 he published at intervals, in a sort of pamphlet form, the results of his medical observations, at the same time that he filled the post of director of the Opera. These publications led to his being noticed by the Duke of Orleans, and in 1824, to his appointment to the office of Médecin des Musées Royaux. For the benefit of the children of a deceased apothecary and chemist, M. Regnauld, Dr. Véron entered into a speculation connected with the once famed *pâte Regnauld*, a pectoral paste bearing the name of the inventor. He embarked his all in the undertaking; his relations with a number of the journals gave notoriety to the *pâte ;* and Dr. Veron, while doing a good action for the children of Regnauld, established the basis of a fortune for himself. In 1828 he relinquished medicine and devoted himself to journalism, first joining the "Quotidienne," afterwards the "Messager des Chambres," and then founding the "Revue de Paris." In 1831 Dr. Véron became the responsible director of the Opera, and superintended the production of a number of the finest works on the modern lyric stage. This situation he abandoned in 1835, but his active spirit could not remain without employment, and he chose political ground. Being defeated in an election he returned once more to the journals, and becoming proprietor of the "Constitutionnel," he imparted new vitality to its columns. He supported the policy of M. Thiers at the revolution of 1848, but in 1849 he broke with the ex-minister, and supported Louis Napoleon. The *coup d'état* of 1851 found an advocate in Dr. Véron, and, as a known government candidate, he was elected to the Corps Législatif for the Arrondissement of Sceaux, and re-elected in 1857. In the mean time he continued to conduct the "Constitutionnel;" but dissenting from some points of the Emperor's policy, he was twice warned. Legal proceedings had also been taken against the journal, but though he was victorious in these conflicts the conjunction of misadventures induced him to close with the most eligible of the offers made for the purchase of his paper. In possession of a handsome fortune acquired by time, ability, and enterprise, Dr. Véron lives tranquilly, and when he does write, writes with a piquancy almost unknown to the present journalists of Paris. He is the author of a few volumes, apart from his newspaper contributions; and since 1852 he has been an officer of the Legion of Honour.

VEUILLOT, Louis, a French author and journalist, was born in 1813, at Boynes en Gatinais. He is the son of a poor working cooper, with whom he went to Paris in 1818, and picked up sufficient reading and writing to enable him, at thirteen years of age, to fill some small place in an attorney's office. Though his education was deficient, his literary instincts were strong, and he entered with courage on the noble work of self-instruction. He was only nineteen when he wrote his first articles for a ministerial journal. His style was so vigorous, and his polemical power so decided, that he was challenged to two duels, one with an actor for a criticism, and the other with a brother journalist of republican sentiments. He subsequently became editor in chief of several newspapers until, in 1837, he was appointed principal editor of "La Paix." His fearless style of writing, and the resolute character of his attacks, were fast drifting him into an untoward and unenviable position when, in 1838, one of his friends suggested a visit to Italy. He arrived in Rome during Holy Week ; his fancy was inflamed by the religious spectacles of the city ; he was presented to the Pope ; and when he returned to Paris he was no longer the same man, having cast aside his semi-scepticism to make way for an ecclesiastical faith. He published several works on the Roman Catholic Church, and accompanied General Bugeaud to Africa, in the capacity of secretary. On his return M. Veuillot was appointed Chief Secretary to the Minister of the Interior, and in 1848 became the chief editor of the "Univers," a journal established for the sole purpose of promoting the interests and progress of the Ultramontane party generally. Fired with zeal, M. Veuillot assailed universities, philosophy, philosophers, revolutionists, socialists, and any or every system not immediately conformable to the dictates of the Vatican. He likewise published a variety of works tending to promote the adoption of his views by those who read them. He conducted the "Univers" until the beginning of the present year, when his language and his method of conducting controversies were found so dangerous to the state, that the Emperor of the French caused a decree to be promulgated suppressing the journal. It is understood that M. Veuillot has removed to Brussels. In matters of church polity M. Veuillot is determined, even to obstinacy ; in his contests he is implacable ; more a theorist than an observer of cause and effect, he believes Ultramontanism to be the only true principle by which the world should be ruled ; but it must not be denied that though his defects are many, he is sincerely religious according to his belief.

VIARDOT, Pauline Garcia, a French vocalist, daughter of Emmanuel Garcia, and sister to Malibran, was born at Paris, in 1821. She exhibited the highest order of musical talent at an early age, and after visiting England and America with her parents, returned to Paris in 1828, and received lessons of Liszt. She afterwards devoted herself to the study of vocal music, and visiting London in 1839, appeared in "Otello" and "Cenerentola." making a most successful *début*. Returning to Paris, she married M. Louis Viardot, Director of the Italian Opera. Again visiting London in 1841, she afterwards proceeded to Madrid, Vienna, St. Petersburg, and Berlin. In 1848 she appeared at Covent Garden. Madame Viardot has attained to the highest position in her profession, and is also one of the most accomplished *cantatrices* of the time, speaking with fluency the Spanish, Italian, French, German, and English languages. Her *repertoire* is very extensive, and she has filled various *rôles* in the compositions of Glück, Mozart, Beethoven, Bellini, Donizetti, Verdi, and Meyerbeer, and has sung most of them in French, German, and Italian.

VICTOR EMMANUEL II., MARIA ALBERTO EUGENIO FERDINANDO TOMASO, KING OF SARDINIA, son of Charles Albert, by a Princess of the House of Hapsburg, was born on the 14th of March, 1820, and until the resignation of the Sardinian crown in his favour, by his father, was known by the title of Duke of Savoy. In 1842 he married the Archduchess Adelaide, of Austria. When Charles-Albert took the field against Austria, the present King of Sardinia took part in the struggle. On the fatal issue of the battle of Novara, his father's abdication gave to him a tottering throne. The hopes of the Piedmontese were by no means high when, after the ruin of the national cause at Novara, they beheld their new King entering Turin. At Genoa, so great was the distrust of the new government, that the republican party rose in rebellion. General Della Marmora, however, crushed the revolt. But, though not disposed to succumb to the republicans, Victor Emmanuel was as little inclined to accept Austrian absolutism. Even with so tempting a bait as Parma, he refused to give up constitutionalism. Peace with Austria was scarcely ratified, when the policy of Rome, which sought to engross temporal, in virtue of its spiritual jurisdiction, found in the Sardinian monarch an uncompromising foe. The assumption of the Church was effectually checked. Time rolled on, and the liberal policy of Victor Emmanuel developed itself. The Crimean war arose— a military convention between France and England was concluded—General Marmora was despatched to the aid of the allied powers, and on the banks of the Tchernaya gave full proof of the valour of Sardinia. The King visited France and England in 1855, receiving in London and Paris the most enthusiastic reception. Since that time he has still further cemented the alliance with France, by giving the hand of his daughter the Princess Clotilde to Prince Napoleon, the cousin of the Emperor; and France and Sardinia successfully combated in 1859, on the ancient battlefields of Italy, against Austrian ascendancy in the Italian peninsula, causing the Austrian Emperor to withdraw his claims to govern in Lombardy, and annexing that state to the Sardinian crown. For this assistance on the part of the Emperor of the French, Victor Emmanuel ceded the territories of Nice and Savoy, a course which has been highly condemned in this and other countries. Since the peace of Villafranca, the Italians have been ready to break out in open insurrection against the Neapolitan and Papal governments, and only required a leader to cause them to throw off their allegiance. They found one in Garibaldi, who, in less than four months previous to this time (October, 1860), has delivered Sicily, Naples, and many provinces of the Papal States. Victor Emmanuel has thought it necessary to enter the Papal dominions with an army, and his general, Cialdini, has succeeded in defeating the forces of the Pope in the north, whilst Garibaldi, simultaneously, has put the King of Naples and his army to flight, near Capua. Victor Emmanuel is just about to enter Naples, and thus to annex the major part of the Italian peninsula to his dominions.

VICTORIA, ALEXANDRINA, QUEEN OF THE UNITED KINGDOM OF GREAT BRITAIN AND IRELAND, AND EMPRESS OF INDIA, was born at Kensington Palace, May the 24th, 1819, and is the only child of Edward, Duke of Kent, the fourth son of George III., and of Maria Louisa Victoria, a daughter of Francis, Duke of Saxe-Coburg Saalfeld, and sister of the King of the Belgians. The Duke of Kent died in 1820, leaving to his widow the care of their infant daughter. Subsequently, the Duchess of Northumberland was associated with her in this charge. As the heiress of the throne advanced in years, she received a careful and complete instruction in all the varied branches of a liberal education. On the 20th of June, 1837, she ascended the throne; and on February the 10th, 1840, 'was married to Prince Albert, second son of the Duke of Saxe - Coburg - Gotha. The family of her Majesty consists of :— 1. The Princess Royal—now Princess of Prussia—born November 21st, 1840; 2. Albert Edward, Prince of Wales, heir apparent, born November 9th, 1841; 3. Princess Alice Maude Mary, born April 25th, 1843; 4. Prince Albert Ernest Albert, born August 6th, 1844; 5. Princess Helena Augusta Victoria, born May 25th, 1846; 6. Princess Louisa Caroline Alberta, born May 18th, 1848; 7. Prince Arthur William Patrick Albert, born May 1st, 1850; 8. Prince Leopold George Duncan Albert, born April 7th, 1853; 9. Princess Beatrice Mary Victoria Feodore, born April 15th, 1857. The constitutional freedom of the people of Great Britain, their parliamentary government, and the strict responsibility of the ministers, whom it is always in the power of the House of Commons to displace, leave but little scope either for the virtues or the vices of the sovereign, whether male or female, unless it be in the example set from so splendid and conspicuous an eminence as the throne to all the families of the kingdom. In this respect Great Britain has been highly fortunate, under the graceful sceptre and mild sway of her present Majesty, a lady who, by the exercise of every domestic and public virtue, has shown herself a model to all her female subjects, as woman, wife, and mother; and who has endeared herself to every man in her dominions, not as a lady alone, but as the excellent painstaking, conscientious chief magistrate of

the widest and noblest empire on the globe. Under the rule of the two preceding monarchs, royalty had become less popular than the friends of the British constitution desired to see it, and there would have been a demur if the Duke of Kent had left no issue, that the sceptre would have passed into a hand which would have still further increased that unpopularity, and prepared the way for commotions and perplexities of no common magnitude. Happily, the auspicious birth of the Princess Victoria averted the evil, and her every act since her accession to the throne has tended to increase, not only the respect, but the love of the people, and to build up the throne on surer foundations than it ever before rested upon. In after periods "The Victorian Era" bids fair to be cited, to the admiration of posterity, as that in which the history of England shines with the fairest lustre, and of which the principal events rival in grandeur, and surpass in fruitfulness of good, those of any previous reign, since that of King Alfred. In 1855 her Majesty and the Prince Consort paid a visit to the Emperor of the French, and at the present date (October, 1860) the Queen and Prince are visiting the relations of his Royal Highness in Coburg, in company with their daughter and son-in-law, the Princess and Prince Frederick William of Prussia.

VIGNY, ALFRED VICTOR, COUNT DE, a French poet, was born at Loches, in March, 1799. In 1814 he entered the Academical Institution of M. Hix in Paris, but, in common with his fellow-students, the passion for war overcame the love of learning. To counteract this influence, the mother of M. de Vigny procured him a private tutor, but no teaching at home could dissipate his dreams of warfare and triumph. When scarcely sixteen, and shortly after the restoration, he was appointed to the household troops of Louis XVIII., and accompanied that monarch to Ghent during the "Hundred Days." In 1816 he joined the Infantry of the Guard, in which he continued for about seven years; afterwards entering the Line, and taking part in the Spanish campaign of that period. In time, the realities of active military life wore away all its romance; and in 1828, having often previously employed his leisure in composition, he relinquished arms and devoted himself to literature. In 1822 he published a volume of poems, and in 1824 and in 1826 other poems appeared, the themes of which were mostly taken from the sacred writings. In 1826 his first historical romance, "Cinq Mars," was given to the world and achieved popularity. In 1832 and 1835 he published his "Stello, ou les Diables Bleus," and "Servitude et Grandeur Militaires." Since the latter date he has written various works, both in prose and poetry, and contributed some successful dramas to the stage. Several of his works were severely criticised, on the ground that he depicted character more from a poetical than an historical point of view, but M. de Viguy silenced hostility by the simple process of showing that a romance is nothing more than its designation proclaims.

VILLEMAIN, ABEL FRANÇOIS, a French author and politician, was born in Paris, June, 1791. He was educated at the Imperial Lyceum, and being appointed Professor of Rhetoric in the Collège Charlemagne, he obtained high reputation as a lecturer. He published two discourses in 1812 and 1814, which gained him so much celebrity, that in 1816 he was made Assistant-Professor of Modern History in the University of Paris, and subsequently became Professor of Eloquence. He had been appointed to an office in the Council of State, but his politics displeased an ultra-legitimist Ministry, and in 1827

he was dismissed from all public employment, and his lectures suspended. He, however, continued authorship. In 1830 he again rose in political favour. In 1833 he was made a Peer of France, and appointed Minister of Instruction, which office he resigned in 1845, owing to the state of his health. He has been Perpetual Secretary to the Academy, of which he became a member in 1821, since 1834. His works, which have been numerous, are on various subjects. His "Life of Cromwell," a new edition of "Pascal's Letters," and "Reminiscences of Historical and Literary Contemporaries," being the most appreciated.

WAAGEN, GUSTAVE FRIEDRICH, a German art critic, was born at Hamburgh, in February, 1794. His father being a painter and his uncle the celebrated Tieck, he received every encouragement to study and cultivate the arts. He was appointed in 1830, Director of the Royal Gallery of Painting, at Berlin; and, while holding this office, he effected a most satisfactory reform —arranging the pictures on a chronological system, so that the development of art could be traced, as far as possible, from the collection. He subsequently visited nearly all the principal galleries of art, both public and private, throughout the Continent and in Great Britain, afterwards publishing works on their distinctive merits. He has written much on his favourite pursuits; but his most elaborate and important production is his "Treatise on the Works of Art and Artists in England and France," published in 1837. An edition of the English section of this work was issued in 1854, under the title of "The Treasures of Art in Great Britain." To this work he has since appended a "Supplement," containing an account of additional works. His most recent publication of importance is a new edition of the "Hand-book of the

History of Painting in Germany and the Low Countries." In his position as a Professor of the Royal University, at Berlin, he delivers annually, a course of lectures on the History of the Fine Arts.

WAGNER, RICHARD, a German composer, was born at Leipsic, May 22, 1813, of an old and honourable family, and received a complete academical education in his native city and at Dresden. His love of music was intense; and he studied, for years, with the greatest assiduity—visiting various cities in a professional capacity, until he reached Paris in 1841; from which city he passed to London. His first important work, "Rienzi," was produced in 1842; and in 1843 he returned to Germany, where he achieved an eminent position, but lost it again in 1848 through mixing himself up with the political disturbances of the time. He was obliged to quit the country, and retired to Zurich. His musical theories—in the exposition of which he has written extensively, and not without considerable ingenuity—have elicited extreme diversities of opinion. It is not within our province to pronounce any judgment on his compositions, which, popular in Germany, are so little known in this country, that, except in a fragmentary state, scarcely any of them have been performed.

WAGNER, RUDOLPH, a German physiologist, was born at Bayreuth, in Bavaria, on the 30th June, 1805. He studied for the medical profession at Erlangen, and also at Wurtzburg, and took his degrees in 1826. He then repaired to Paris; where, under the advice of Cuvier, he commenced the study of Comparative Anatomy, which has literally proved the passion of his life. After a journey made for scientific purposes, through Sardinia and a large portion of France, he returned to Germany, hoping to obtain an Academic chair at Munich; but being disappointed in that object, he settled down as a Doctor of Medicine at Augsburg; in 1829 becoming attached, however, to the University of Erlangen in a subordinate capacity. In 1832 he was named Assistant-Professor; in 1833, Professor of Zoology; and so rapidly did he attain to distinction in this post, that, in 1840, he was invited to Göttingen, to replace Professor Blümenbach in the chair of Physiology. Owing to the state of his health, he was obliged to pass the winters of 1845 and 1846 in Italy. Here he made some of his most interesting experiments in electricity, as connected with the nervous system. He is, perhaps, the most ardent supporter in Germany of an ideal spiritualism, or "double life" in man. He has been a most voluminous writer, publishing papers, tracts, and works, on physiology and psychology, with scarcely any intermission, for upwards of thirty years. M. Wagner's style will always be popular, as it is clear and precise. He is at present occupied with the publication of his "Researches on the Physiology of the Brain, with Special Reference to Psychology," in the Memoirs of the Royal Society of Göttingen.

WALEWSKI, FLORIAN ALEXANDRE JOSEPH COLONNA, late French Minister for Foreign Affairs, is the son of a Polish gentleman, and was born in Poland, May, 1810. Educated in Geneva, he was remarkable for almost precocious intelligence and spirit; and young though he was, he proceeded to London in 1830, to win the statesmen of the day to favour the cause of Poland, after having fought for it at Grochowo. His mission not succeeding, and being on terms of friendship with the Duke of Orleans, he entered the French army, after the revolution of July. After having risen to the rank of Captain in the 4th Regiment of Hussars, and been sent on a special mission to Abd-el-Kader, at

Mascara, he grew wearied of a soldier's life, resigned his commission, and adopted the profession of literature. Being an ardent politician, and knowing much of the world and of society, his position in literature was soon taken; but after writing some *nouvelettes* and a few good plays, in 1840 his career was changed. He was appointed in the beginning of that year to a special mission to Egypt and Constantinople, and under M. Guizot, after having undertaken various missions, he was sent as Minister-Plenipotentiary to Buenos Ayres. Returning to France before the elections of December, 1848, he resolved to follow the fortunes of Louis Napoleon, and had no reason to regret the choice. In January, 1849, he was named Envoy Extraordinary to Florence, from whence he subsequently removed to Naples and Madrid. In 1851 he became Ambassador to the British Court; and in 1855 he was called to fill the place of M. Drouyn de l'Huys, as Minister for Foreign Affairs. He took an active part in the proceedings which preceded and followed the war in the Crimea, and signed the treaty of April, 1856, as President of the Congress of Paris. M. Walewski retained office under Louis Napoleon until 1860, when he resigned in consequence of a difference with the Emperor on Italian policy. He was succeeded as minister by M. Thouvenel.

WALPOLE, The Right Hon. Spencer Horatio, M.P., an English statesman, was born in 1806. He was educated at Eton, and afterwards at Trinity College, Cambridge, where he was highly distinguished by his abilities. He was called to the bar in 1831, and obtained the silk gown of a Queen's Counsel in 1846. Mr. Walpole entered the House of Commons as member for Midhurst; and in various debates of importance has displayed decided power. He accepted the office of Home Minister under Lord Derby. When Lord Derby's administration fell, Mr. Walpole resigned; but on its return to power in 1858, he again took office in the same department. A difference of judgment with his colleagues, on the merits of some clauses in the Conservative Reform Bill of 1859, induced him to relinquish his post as Chief of the Home Office, and on that measure he went into opposition. He is now member for Cambridge University, and is respected by all parties in the House.

WALTER, John, M.P., chief proprietor of the "Times," was born in London, in 1818, and is the son of the late John Walter, the founder of the "Times." He was educated at Eton and Oxford. In 1847 he was called to the bar of Lincoln's Inn, and in the same year he was returned for Nottingham, which he represented till the last general election, when he was returned for the county of Berks, which his late father represented in the parliaments of 1832 and 1834. He is a liberal conservative in politics.

WARD, Edward Matthew, R.A., a painter, was born in London, in 1816. He became a pupil of the Royal Academy in 1834, and had the advantage in his early studies of the advice of Wilkie and Chantrey. He went to Rome in 1836, and while there gained a medal for his picture of "Cimabue and Giotto." He returned to England in 1839, stopping at Munich on his way, to study fresco painting. For two or three years the pictures he exhibited failed to attract the attention to which their artistic merits fairly entitled them, but in 1843 his picture of "Dr. Johnson perusing the Manuscript of the Vicar of Wakefield," exhibited at the Academy, immediately drew public notice to the artist. The story was felicitously told; the drawing faultless; and the style vigorous and painstaking. Next year he produced a "Scene from the Early Life of Oliver Goldsmith," and "Le

Fleur's Departure for Montreuil;" in 1845, "A Scene in Lord Chesterfield's Ante-room, in 1748;" and in 1846, "The Disgrace of Lord Clarendon," each successive work displaying additional power. He has painted several pictures for the New Palace at Westminster, that of "The Last Sleep of Argyle" being considered one of the best works of its class. He was elected an Associate of the Royal Academy in 1847, and Royal Academician in 1855. The following of his pictures are at the South Kensington Museum, namely, "Doctor Johnson in the Ante-room of Lord Chesterfield," "The Disgrace of Lord Clarendon," "The South-Sea Bubble, a Scene in Change Alley, in 1720," and "James II. in his Palace of Whitehall, receiving the News of the Landing of the Prince of Orange in 1688."

WARREN, SAMUEL, a lawyer, legal writer and novelist, Q.C., D.C.L. of Oxford, F.R.S., was born in 1807, in Denbighshire, where his father, at one time a Wesleyan minister, has been for many years a clergyman of the Church of England. He attended classes at the University of Edinburgh, with the view of entering the medical profession, but he abandoned his intentions, and after wavering for a short time between the Church and the Bar, he entered the Middle Temple as a law student. Having practised, for nearly seven years, as a special pleader, he was called to the bar in 1837. In the meantime there appeared in the columns of "Blackwood's Magazine" a series of papers, entitled "Passages from the Diary of a late Physician," which, although somewhat melodramatic, displayed more than ordinary power, and attracted much notice. Of these Mr. Warren was the author; and curiously enough, the opening narrative of the series, entitled "Early Struggles," had been rejected by every leading London periodical as unsuitable, and not calculated to interest the public.

As a last resource, Mr. Warren forwarded his manuscript to the late William Blackwood, of Edinburgh, by whom it was accepted. From this publisher the young author received some valuable literary hints. The "Passages" excited at first some controversy as well as interest in medical circles, the author being even denounced in the "Lancet," on the assumption that the "Diary" was a real record of medical experiences, and for violating the secrets of the sick chamber. In 1839 Mr. Warren commenced the publication, in "Blackwood," of "Ten Thousand a Year," which was some time afterwards followed by "Now and Then," in both of which he displayed high talent as a novelist. After the great English Exhibition, he published a work, "The Lily and the Bee," in commemoration of that event, which has met with much hostile criticism. He is an able pleader, and has besides increased his reputation as a lawyer by the publication of several excellent professional works, the best known of which are his "Introduction to Law Studies," and "Abridgment of Blackstone." He was appointed a Queen's Counsel in 1851, and Recorder of Hull in 1854. Having been returned to Parliament in 1856 for Midhurst, he made several effective speeches in the House, the best received of which, perhaps, was that delivered by him on moving the adjourned debate on the Conspiracy Bill. After Lord Derby's accession to power, Mr. Warren was, early in 1859, appointed one of the Masters in Lunacy, a situation of great responsibility and delicacy. His literary works, including all his contributions to "Blackwood," published in a collected form and issued in a cheap shape, have had a very wide circulation. There are numerous American editions of all his books, and translations of his fictions into most of the modern languages. Even the "Lily and the Bee," the least successful of his works, has been rendered in Italian. His law books have become standard works of reference, both in this country and in America, and in one or two continental universities.

WATT, JAMES HENRY, an engraver, was born in London, in 1799, and at sixteen years of age commenced his artistic education with Mr. Charles Heath, than whom no man then was better calculated to convey instruction. Mr. Watt was an ardent student, but his rapid progress may, to a great extent, be attributed to his inherent love of art and nature. The engraving of Stothard's "Procession of the Flitch of Bacon," now so widely known, was his first great happy effort, and Mr. Watt immediately attained to a high position. Landseer's "Highland Drover's Departure" is familiar to the world by the engraving executed by Mr. Watt. "Horses at a Fountain," "A Court-yard," "May-Day in the Reign of Elizabeth," and "Christ Blessing Little Children," after Landseer, Leslie, and Eastlake, were also engraved by him, besides many other productions, which are as popular as they are pleasing even to the uneducated eye.

WATTS, ALARIC ALEXANDER, poet and journalist, was born in London on the 16th March, 1799. Having been educated at Wye Grammar School and at Ashford, he spent some years in teaching at various schools, and eventually became private tutor in a Manchester family. He first became known to the public in 1822, when he published some poems, under the title of "Poetical Sketches," which proved highly successful. He shortly afterwards became editor of "The Leeds Intelligencer," and distinguished himself by attacking the neglect and inhumanity of the then existing factory system. Some of the suggestions he then made have since been adopted in the Factory Act, and

have become imperative on mill owners. After being some time engaged on the "Manchester Courier," he proceeded to London, and edited the "Literary Souvenir," which was one of the first of the annuals, and contained prose and poetic sketches, intermingled with engravings, of the highest class, from pictures of leading painters. He became connected with the "Standard" newspaper in 1827, and subsequently the "United Service Gazette," established in 1833. Mr. Watts has now been connected with the press for many years, and has published an exquisitely illustrated work, entitled "Lyrics of the Heart," which includes several of his choice poems. He enjoys a pension of £100 per annum from the Civil List.

WEBSTER, THOMAS, R.A., a painter, was born in London, March, 1800. He was originally a chorister at the Chapel Royal, St. James's, but his talents lay in a different direction, and he entered the Royal Academy in 1820, five years afterwards bearing away the first prize for painting. His career as an artist has been one of unbroken success. His first exhibited work, "Rebels shooting a Prisoner," was highly eulogized, as was also his "Gunpowder Plot." He has been a frequent exhibitor in the Academy, the British Institution, and in the Galleries of the Society of British Artists. By 1841 his position was secured with the public, and confirmed with artists, by his election as an Associate of the Royal Academy, and he already struck out a line specially his own. He is remarkable as a genial artist, entering apparently into the frolic of the personages depicted. He was elected a Royal Academician in 1846, and has since produced some of his choicest works, "A Rubber," "See-Saw," "A Slide," "A Cherry Seller," "A Dame's School," and "Hide and Seek," all being of the highest order of merit. Several of his pictures have been engraved, and are widely known through Art Union prints. The admirers of his productions will find the following in the South Kensington Museum at the present time, namely, "Sickness and Health," "Going to the Fair," "Returning from the Fair," "A Village Choir," "Contrary Winds," "Reading the Scriptures," "Going into School," and "A Dame's School."

WENSLEYDALE, JAMES PARKE, BARON, an English lawyer, was born near Liverpool, in 1782. After receiving a preliminary education at the Macclesfield Grammar School he entered Trinity College, Cambridge, where he graduated, and became a wrangler. He eventually adopted the law as his profession, and entered the Inner Temple in 1813. Mr. Parke acquired great success in his professional pursuits, and in 1834 he was appointed a Baron of the Court of Exchequer. For many years Baron Parke held this high position to his own credit and to the satisfaction of all with whom he came in contact. In 1856 he was created Baron Wensleydale, at first only as a life peerage, but eventually, owing to the jealousy shown by the Members of the Upper House against new precedents being introduced, Baron Parke entered that assembly with all the usual privileges of his new rank and station.

WESTMACOTT, RICHARD, R.A., a sculptor, was born in London, in 1799. He is the son and grandson of sculptors, his father being the celebrated Sir Richard Westmacott, from whom he received his early training. He visited Italy, where he remained from 1820 to 1826, neglecting no opportunity of tracing the history and development of ancient classic art. Of late years monumental works and busts have chiefly occupied his attention, and probably his fancy; for to judge of his mind from his productions, he is grave and reflective. In 1827 he first exhibited at the Academy. In 1837 he was elected

F.R.S.; in 1838 an Associate of the Royal Academy; in 1849 a Royal Academician; and, in 1857, Professor of Sculpture to the Academy. Mr. Westmacott has delivered lectures on Art at the Royal and London Institutions, and is otherwise distinguished for literary qualifications. "Venus and Ascanius" (1831); "The Cymbal Player," an admirable work (1832); "Blue Bell" (1836); "Paolo and Francesca" (1838); the statues in the pediment of the Royal Exchange (1842); and "Go and Sin no More" (1850), are among his best known works.

WHATELY, THE RIGHT REV. RICHARD, D.D., Archbishop of Dublin, a theological and economical writer, was born in London, in 1787. The son of a prebendary of Bristol Cathedral, he was educated at Oxford, taking his B.A. degree in 1808, gaining the University Prize for an English essay in 1810, and in 1811 becoming a Fellow of Oriel College. He was Bampton Lecturer in 1822, and also became Rector of Halesworth, Suffolk, in that year. In 1825 he was chosen Principal of St. Alban's Hall, Oxford. In 1831 he was consecrated Archbishop of Dublin, and Bishop of Glendalagh. Dr. Whately took an active part in founding the National System of Education in Ireland, and materially assisted Mr. Stanley, now Lord Derby, then Chief Secretary, in bringing the plan to a successful issue. He remained a member of the Board of Irish Education until 1853, when, believing that undue concessions were being made to the Roman Catholic element, he retired from the Commission, in conjunction with Chief Justice Blackburne, and Baron Greene. As Primate of Ireland, his life has been one of industry and philanthropy, his greatest attention, however, having been directed to the cause of education. The mere titles of a few of his works, which have been very numerous, are sufficient to indicate his views. In 1819 appeared "Historic Doubts relative to Napoleon Bonaparte," a very ingenious attempt to show the fallacy of sceptical criticism, by proving that there never was such a general in existence ; afterwards came the "Elements of Logic," the "Elements of Rhetoric," "Errors of Romanism, traced to their Origin in Human Nature," "Introduction to Political Economy," "Thoughts on Secondary Punishments," and "Remarks on Transportation." He was for a short time Professor of Political Economy in the University of Oxford, and was the principal means of founding a professorship of that science in Trinity College, Dublin. Archbishop Whately has never belonged to any party, political or ecclesiastical, but has carefully kept aloof from all purely political questions, and in what pertains to religion he has always strenuously opposed sectarian feeling, having, in the Bampton Lectures and in other works, laboured to prove it to be unchristian. He is a member of the French Institute.

WHEATSTONE, CHARLES, F.R.S., Professor of Experimental Philosophy in King's College, London, was born at Gloucester, in 1802. In his early days he was engaged in the manufacture of musical instruments, and from studying the laws of sound seemed to have been gradually led to investigate the sciences of light and electricity. The results of some of his researches were presented to the Royal Society in 1833, in a paper on "Acoustic Figures ;" this was followed in 1834 by another "On Experiments to Measure the Velocity of Electricity and the Duration of the Electric Light," and in 1838 he gave the first idea of the stereoscope and the nature of binocular vision in a communication entitled "Contributions to the Physiology of Vision." His scientific abilities were recognised in 1834 by his being appointed Professor of Experimental Philosophy in King's College. Professor Wheatstone has, however, acquired his high reputation by bringing out, in conjunction with Mr. Cooke, that most remarkable instance of the power of mind over matter—the Electric Telegraph. It is no part of our province to say one word on the dispute which has arisen respecting the individual rights of these gentlemen. We will only express our regret that from the time of Sir Isaac Newton to this day, there has scarcely been an instance of a grand discovery which has not been intermingled with *désagrémens*, which every true lover of science for its own sake has had to deplore ; we trust, however, that the day will arrive when the consciousness of having rendered service to our fellow-creatures will be a higher reward than the mere and transient acknowledgment to be obtained by their applause. The first practical application of electricity to telegraphic purposes was made under Messrs. Cooke and Wheatstone's patents, on the Blackwall railway in 1838. The wires employed were made of copper, enclosed in an iron tube, each wire being separated from its neighbour by some non-conducting material. Eventually the present needle-telegraph was perfected, and the wires, now of iron, suspended on poles raised on the banks of railways. To so great an extent has this mode of instantaneous communication been adopted, that at the present time a message may be sent and received in every or any part of Europe in the course of a few minutes, and the total length of wire employed in Europe, India, and America amounts to many thousand miles. Professor Wheatstone has invented some curious optical instruments besides the stereoscope. In 1856 he made an interesting application of his researches on sound, in a mode of conveying music by means of deal rods from one part of a building to any other, between a musical instrument and any diffuser of sound placed in a distant apartment. His merits have been recognised by most of the learned societies of Europe. He was an active member of the London and Paris exhibitions, is a corresponding member of the Institute of France, and Knight of the Legion of Honour.

WHEWELL, THE REV. WILLIAM, D.D., F.R.S., Master of Trinity College, and Vice-Chancellor of the University of Cambridge, was born, in 1795, at Lancaster. His father, who was a joiner, originally intended to bring him up to his own occupation, but the head-master of the grammar school where he was educated, persuaded his parent to send him to Cambridge. After graduating in 1816, and obtaining a Fellowship, he was chosen in 1828 Professor of Mineralogy. In 1838 he obtained the Chair of Moral Philosophy. In 1841 he succeeded to the Mastership of Trinity College, and in 1855 became Vice-Chancellor of the University of Cambridge. Dr. Whewell is a man of an earnest and enthusiastic temperament, and is one of the most generally accomplished men of the present day, his scholarship extending over every department of human knowledge. Dr. Whewell's first publications were mathematical treatises intended chiefly for use among the students of the University. They consist of a work on "Mechanics," in two volumes; an edition of "Newton's Principia," a "Treatise on Conic Sections," and the "Mechanics of Engineering." Dr. Whewell wrote the Bridgewater Treatise on "Astronomy and Physics, considered with reference to Natural Theology." In 1837 he published his "Philosophy of the Inductive Sciences," which has gone through three editions, being expanded in the last into the "History of Scientific Ideas." In the present year he has published the "Philosophy of Discovery." He is the author of several works on Moral Philosophy, of which the principal are—"The Elements of Morality," "Lectures on Systematic Morality," and "Lectures on the History of Moral Philosophy in England." He has published several volumes of sermons, various lectures and papers on university education, &c., and several translations, the most remarkable of which is a version into English hexameters of Goethe's "Hermann and Dorothea."

WHITESIDE, THE RIGHT HON. JAMES, M.P., LL.D., a politician and lawyer, was born at Delgany, county of Wicklow, in the year 1806. He was educated at Trinity College, Dublin, where he took honours and graduated M.A. While prosecuting his studies for the bar, he obtained premiums in the first law class formed in the London University. He was called to the Irish bar in 1830, where he rose rapidly into practice, his powers being so highly valued as a lawyer and forensic orator, that when Mr. O'Connell was tried for political conspiracy in 1843, Mr. Whiteside was chosen one of the leading counsel for the defence. He delivered an address to the jury on that occasion, which was pronounced to be the most brilliant effort of its kind since the days of Curran. During the memorable year of 1848, Mr. Whiteside acted as leading counsel for Smith O'Brien and Meagher. A vivid account of these remarkable trials, with a criticism highly favourable to the eloquence of Mr. Whiteside, will be found in the work of W. C. Townsend, entitled "Modern State Trials." He was returned to Parliament for the borough of Enniskillen in 1851, and continued to hold the seat until 1859, when he resigned it, and then represented the University of Dublin. He was appointed Solicitor-General for Ireland by Lord Derby's Government in 1852, resigning with Ministers in the same year. In 1858, on Lord Derby's return to power, he became Attorney-General, retaining his office until the change of ministry in 1859. He is one of her Majesty's Privy Council. He is the author of "Italy in the Nineteenth Century," and of a book on "Ancient Rome." His parliamentary, not less than his legal career, has been very successful, his style of speaking being such as to please the ear of the House, and he never touches a subject without mastering its details.

WHITTY, EDWARD MICHAEL, a journalist, is son of Mr. M. J. Whitty, proprietor of the "Liverpool Daily Post" and "Liverpool Journal" newspapers, and was born in 1827. He was educated in his native town and in Germany. He has been connected with the press from his earliest days, and after receiving an appointment on the "Times," which he held for three years, he joined in 1849 the "Daily News." He afterwards edited the "Leader," and was for a year or so editor of the "Northern Whig" newspaper, published in Belfast, but left the commercial capital of Ireland, and returned to England in 1858. He has been a contributor to the "Nation," a journal which still supports its character as an advocate of the Repeal of the Union, and the overthrow of the English Church in Ireland.

WHITWORTH, JOSEPH, an engineer, who has lately become so well known through his inventions of improved rifles and ordnance, has for some years been engaged in mechanical pursuits in Manchester. In the Exhibition of 1851 Mr. Whitworth exhibited some splendid specimens of ingenuity in the way of planing machines and other articles intended to facilitate the production of machinery. He subsequently turned his attention to the construction of guns of all calibres, and has been so highly successful, that at the present time (1860) a "Whitworth" rifle is considered one of the best instruments for military and sporting purposes. Mr. Whitworth has also produced some extraordi-

nary cannon of large bore and of great propulsive power. He is still engaged in perfecting those weapons of warfare which seem to promise, by their destructive effects, to put a speedy conclusion to any campaign in which they may be employed.

WILKES, CHARLES, an American traveller, was born about 1805, and becoming early known for his familiarity with maritime affairs and his spirit of inquiry, he was chosen in 1838, by the United States Government, to explore the shores of the Pacific and Southern Seas, as commander of the Expedition, with the rank of captain. Nearly four years were occupied with this voyage, and the result did not disappoint the expectations of the Government, his observations being extensive and valuable. He returned to New York in 1842, when he commenced writing his "Narrative of the United States Exploring Expedition," which appeared in 1845, in five octavo volumes. In 1848 the Geographical Society of London awarded him their gold medal; and in 1849 he brought out a valuable work on "Western America," in which he treats of the capabilities of California and the Oregon territory. Captain Wilkes never pretends to literary excellence, but his few volumes are nevertheless highly descriptive and interesting.

WILKINSON, SIR JOHN GARDNER, KNT., an English archæologist, was born 5th of October, 1797. His education was received at Harrow, and Exeter College, Oxford. On leaving Oxford, his original purpose was to enter the 14th Light Dragoons, but his attention having been directed by Sir William Gell to the study of Egyptian monuments, he determined to devote himself to the study of the antiquities, ruins, and topography of Egypt. In 1827-28, his first work, entitled "Hieroglyphical Extracts and Materia Hieroglyphica," was given to the world; and in 1835 his

"Topography of Thebes, and General View of Egypt." For a topographical work on Thebes he was eminently qualified; he had for a considerable time dwelt in the neighbouring country, and made accurate surveys and drawings of every point of interest in the district. In 1836 he published "The Manners and Customs of the Ancient Egyptians, including their Private Life, Government, Laws, Arts, Manufactures, &c., derived from a Comparison of Paintings, Monuments, and Sculptures still in existence, with Ancient Authors." This work exhibits an extraordinary amount of research and analytical power. The second series appeared in 1841. He published in 1843 his "Modern Egypt and Thebes;" and in 1847 the third edition of his "Ancient Egyptians;" the two series in one revised, with profuse illustrations. In 1848 he published his "Dalmatia and Montenegro," and in 1850 the "Architecture of Ancient Egypt, with Remarks on the Early Progress of Architecture," accompanied by a volume of illustrative plates. In 1851 appeared his "Fragments of the Hieratic Papyrus at Turin;" and in 1854, "A Popular Account of the Ancient Egyptians," being a condensation of his larger works, but containing additional matter derived from a new visit to Egypt. In 1855-56 he again returned to the Nile, and on coming home published a small volume entitled "The Egyptians under the Pharaohs," in which much new matter was introduced, and which serves as a supplement to "The Popular Account" of the same people. In 1858 he published a new edition of his "Handbook of Egypt;" and his work on "Colour, and the General Diffusion of Taste among all Classes;" at the same time completing the notes he contributed to the Rev. G. Rawlinson's "English Version of the History of Herodotus." He has also published papers in the various Proceedings of the Royal Geographical Society, the Royal Society of Literature, the Royal Institute of British Architects, the Archæological Association, &c. His "Plants of the Egyptian Desert," with nearly 200 illustrations coloured on the spot, and his large "Map of Egypt," comprising the valley of the Nile, and the deserts east of the Red Sea, and west of the Oases, unfortunately still remain unpublished. On Oct. 16th, 1856, he married Caroline Catherine, daughter of Henry Lucas, Esq., of Uplands, in the county of Glamorgan. Sir John Gardner Wilkinson, in all his works, exhibits profound learning, accuracy, research, enthusiasm, and genius. He is an honorary D.C.L. of Oxford, a F.R.S., a member of most of the leading literary and scientific societies of Europe, and he received the honour of knighthood in 1839.

WILLIAM III., ALEXANDER PAUL FREDERIC LOUIS, KING OF HOLLAND, PRINCE OF ORANGE, NASSAU, GRAND DUKE OF LUXEMBURG, and DUKE OF LUIBURG, was born on 19th February, 1817, and succeeded to the throne on the death of his father, William II., on 17th March, 1849. He took the constitutional oath to uphold the liberties of the Netherlands at Amsterdam on the 12th of May ensuing. His Majesty married in 1839 the Princess Sophia Frederica Matilda, daughter of William I., King of Wurtemburg, by whom he has a family of two children; William Nicholas Alexander Frederic Charles, Prince of Orange, and heir-apparent to the throne, born in September, 1840, and Prince Alexander of Orange, born in August, 1851. The Prince of Orange has lately made the tour of Great Britain, when a matrimonial connexion between the royal families of England and Holland is said to have been resolved upon. The reign of this king has as yet been quiet, and presenting no events requiring mention.

WILLIAMS, MAJOR-GENERAL SIR

WILLIAM FENWICK, BARONET, K.C.B., a Brigadier-General in the English army, was born at Halifax, Nova Scotia, in 1800. The son of the late Mr. Thomas Williams, Commissary-General at Annapolis Royal, Nova Scotia, and grandson of Edward Amherst, the brother of Jeffrey, the first Lord Amherst, he came to England when young, and his family having extensive military connexions, he was enabled to enter Woolwich Academy. He received a commission in the Artillery in 1825, and was promoted to be Captain in 1840. He served in Ceylon for some years, and was thence sent to Turkey, and assisted to settle the Turkish and Persian frontiers question in 1848, concluding it in 1852. He received for these services the Companionship of the Bath, and was promoted to be Lieut.-Colonel. Shortly after the commencement of the war with Russia in 1854, he was advanced to the rank of Colonel, and then made Brigadier-General, being also her Majesty's Commissioner with the Turkish forces in the East. The defence of Kars is of too recent date to require detailed notice. General Williams was compelled to capitulate, and was sent as a prisoner of war to St. Petersburg. In 1856 he returned to England, was made a Baronet, and a pension of £1,000 a year conferred on him. He also received the freedom of the City of London, having previously obtained the order of K.C.B. He sat for two sessions as Member of Parliament for Calne. At present he is Commander-in-chief of the forces in British North America.

WILLIS, NATHANIEL PARKER, an American author and journalist, who has acquired considerable reputation on both sides of the Atlantic, was born at Portland, State of Maine, January 20, 1807, was educated at Boston, Andover, and Yale College, and graduated in 1827. His first literary occupation was that of editing "The Legendary" and "The Token," and, in 1828, he commenced the "American Monthly Magazine," which was, in 1830, united with the "New York Mirror." Subsequently he travelled through France, Italy, Greece, Asia Minor, and European Turkey, as a member of the American Legation, afterwards reaching England, where he remained for about two years. In his travels Mr. Willis took a keen observation of men, manners, and places, and transmitted his views and impressions to New York, the "Mirror" being his vehicle of publication. His "Pencillings by the Way," as he styled his sketches, were pleasant gossiping papers. Numbers of them were transplanted to the field of British journalism, but his descriptions of the titled society of London, though it has since appeared that they offended nobody but the critics, were very severely handled in the "Quarterly Review," the reviewer being Mr. Lockhart. The description most objected to was Lady Blessington's circle of beaux esprits, which has since been copied by Lord John Russell in his "Memoir." "The Pencillings" were collected and published in London in 1835, and shortly afterwards "Inklings of Adventure," a series of tales, were published in an independent form. Returning to America in 1837, he wrote his "Letters from under a Bridge," and lived in retirement until 1839, when he became editor of the "Corsair," a New York periodical. In the following year he published his "Loiterings of Travel," and an illustrated edition of his Poems, and "Two Ways of Dying for a Husband." He revived the "New York Mirror" in 1843. In 1844 he visited England for the third time; and, in 1845, published "Dashes at Life with a Free Pencil." In 1846 Mr. Willis published all his writings in a complete form, and subsequently undertook the editorship of a literary paper entitled "The Home Journal." His "Health Trip to the

Tropics" is a gallery of pictures arranged from outlines made during a journey to and through the West Indies. His later volumes have been chiefly reprints from the "Journal." He was married in England to the daughter of an English officer, and this lady died in America, leaving one child. He has since married a niece of Mr. Grinnell, whose name is so honourably connected with the expedition in search of Sir John Franklin. He now resides at Idlewild, a romantic and beautiful estate in the Highlands of the Hudson. His prose works are read as extensively as those of any living American author, while his reputation as a writer of sacred poetry is, perhaps, that for which he is most likely to be cherished in the memory of his countrymen.

WILLIS, Rev. Robert, M.A., F.R.S., F.G.S., Jacksonian Professor of Natural and Experimental Philosophy in Cambridge University, was born in London, in 1800. He was educated at Caius College, Cambridge, where he took his degree of B.A. in 1826, and afterwards gained a Fellowship. In 1830 he was elected a Fellow of the Royal Society, and, in 1837, appointed Jacksonian Professor. The range of Professor Willis's investigations is almost unequalled for a single mind's elucidation. Acoustics, language, machinery, mechanism of all kinds, architecture and its history, whether decorative or purely constructive, and numerous cognate subjects, have passed under his review, and are treated with a wonderful application of a rare faculty, that of mathematically demonstrating every position he advances. When the Archæological Institute was founded in 1843, he became one of its most ardent supporters; he was at once its chief and its ornament. At Cambridge he lectures on mechanics, statics, dynamics, and their practical application to manufactures, the steam-engine, and other similar subjects; not,

however, confining himself to these, but giving oral expositions to the Philosophical Society, of which he is a member, to the Royal Institution, to the Royal Institute of British Architects, and to the Archæological Institute. Mr. Willis is the author of a number of works, the titles of which serve to point out the range of his numerous studies. He has published the "Principles of Mechanism," a number of papers on "The Vowel Sounds," the "Mechanism of the Larynx," the "Teeth of Wheels," "On the Pressure produced on a flat Plate when opposed to a Stream of Air," &c., "On the Construction of the Vaults in the Middle Ages," "On the Characteristic Interpenetrations of the Flamboyant Style," "A Description of the Sextry Barn at Ely," "Architectural Nomenclature of the Middle Ages," "The Architectural History of Canterbury Cathedral," "The Architectural History of Winchester Cathedral," "York Cathedral," "On the Conventual Buildings attached to the Cathedral at Canterbury," "Description of the Ancient Plan of the Monastery of St. Gall," "An Architectural History of the Church of the Holy Sepulchre," "Remarks on the Architecture of the Middle Ages." As a lecturer on "Applied Mechanics," a subject widely separated in one sense from archæology, he has no superior, and in all his prelections his varied information is employed in the elucidation of the subject-matter in hand.

WILLS, William Henry, a journalist, was born at Plymouth, January 13th, 1810. He contributed papers to the Penny and Saturday Magazines; wrote many of the articles in Maculloch's Geographical Dictionary, and was for several years one of the editors of "Chambers's Journal." Mr. Wills belonged to the staff of writers who commenced "Punch," was sub-editor and leading contributor of the "Daily News," and was associated with Mr. Charles Dickens in the management of "Household Words," from 1850 till the extinction of that periodical in 1859, when those gentlemen started "All the Year Round." He has recently collected and published his contributions to this periodical (many of them written in conjunction with Mr. Charles Dickens) in a book entitled "Old Leaves Gathered from Household Words." Mr. Wills is Honorary Secretary of the Guild of Literature and Art.

WILMORE, JAMES TIBBITS, an engraver, was born in the parish of Handsworth, Staffordshire, in September, 1800. In the matter of style he is entirely original, having struck out his own method, which renders with unrivalled force the peculiarities of English landscape. His principal plates from Turner are "The Old Téméraire," "Mercury and Argus," "Ancient Italy," "The Golden Bough," "The Doganna," and "Bellini's Picture conveyed to the Church of the Reventore," prints distinguished for their faithful rendering of the chiaroscuro and atmospheric effects. He has also engraved Eastlake's "Byron's Dream," "Calcott's "Rhine," and "Powis Castle;" Stanfield's "Wind against Tide," and "An Italian Town;" Landseer's "Harvest in the Highlands," and "Crossing the Bridge," and numerous other works. In 1843 he was elected Associate Engraver in the Royal Academy.

WINDHAM, MAJOR - GENERAL CHARLES ASHE, C.B., is fourth son of the admiral of that name, and was born in the county of Norfolk, in 1810. He entered the army, as an officer of the Coldstream Guards, in 1826, and became, successively, Captain in 1833, Major in 1846, Lieutenant-Colonel in the same year, and Colonel in June 1854. When the Crimean war broke out he had an opportunity of distinguishing himself, and of exhibiting those qualities which have rendered his name so well known. Both at Balaklava and Inkermann his conduct was signalized by skill and courage worthy of a Picton. At Inkermann, the command of his division devolved on him, and he led his men into action under a tremendous fire, with a devotion unknown to those who are unacquainted with genuine British daring. His star rose at the advance on the Redan, where although the slaughter around him was fearful on every hand, the men being cut down as by a sickle, until at length he had not an officer left, yet, undaunted, he held his ground. His heroism could not be overlooked, and he was immediately gazetted Major - General, appointed Governor of that portion of Sebastopol occupied by the English, and in 1855 he was nominated a Companion of the Bath. On returning to England, he was elected one of the representatives in Parliament for East Norfolk. He again entered the battle-field in India, and became attached to the staff of the Commander-in-chief during the conflicts which are now, happily, at an end. General Windham is a Commander of the Legion of Honour, the cross of the order being presented to him in 1856, by the Emperor of the French.

WINDISCHGRÄTZ, ALFRED, PRINCE DE, an Austrian general, was born at Brussels, May 22, 1787, entered the army as Lieutenant in Schwarzenberg's Lancers in 1804, and took part in the German campaigns against Napoleon. His brilliant conduct at Leipsic gained him the grade of Colonel, and he was not only decorated with orders after the fall of the French Empire, but promoted to the rank of Major-General in 1826, when he took command of a brigade at Prague. In 1833 he became General of Division; and after the popular movements in 1848, he was for some time Military Governor of Vienna, proceeding thence to govern Bohemia. In the war with Hungary, the forces of that country almost invariably gave way before him, but retrieving their sinking fortunes the Austrians were, in their turn, driven back, and the Hungarians became the victors. He certainly had many obstacles to surmount—many difficulties to contend against—but these were not taken into account, and he was removed from his command. Though an able and courageous general, he exercised his authority in such a manner as to draw down a heavy amount of opprobrium on his character. Yet notwithstanding the censure of Europe on his execution of Robert Blüm, he was invited to resume the Governorship of Bohemia, an office which he declined, for reasons best known to himself. He has resided since on his Bohemian estates, and singular as is the paradox, though he was execrated as a public man, he appears to be respected as a private gentleman—though denounced as a governor, he seems to be esteemed as a citizen.

WINSLOW, FORBES, M.D., an English physician, was born in London, in August 1810, and is the youngest son of Captain Thomas Winslow, of her Majesty's 47th Regiment. He received his education for the medical profession, at the London University. Dr. Winslow has devoted his attention to one of the most interesting but painful branches of his profession, namely, that of diseases of the mind. His first work published on the subject was, "An Essay on the Application of the Principles of Phrenology to the Elucidation and Cure of Insanity." He established, some years ago, Sussex House, Hammersmith, an asylum for the reception of the insane, and his intimate acquaintance with the almost infinite variety of the phases of lunacy, has secured him the position of medical referee in most of the leading cases which have come before our law courts during the last few years. Besides the work above mentioned,

Dr. Winslow is the author of "A Synopsis of the Lunacy Act," "The Plea of Insanity in Criminal Cases," "The Preservation of the Health of Body and Mind," &c. He is a Fellow of the Royal College of Physicians, Edinburgh, and had conferred on him the degree of D.C.L. by the University of Oxford, at the installation of the Earl of Derby as Chancellor of the University. He has been President of the Medical Society of London, and was one of the Vice-Presidents of the Juridical Society. He has also been President of the Association of Medical Officers of Asylums for the Insane. The "Anatomy of Suicide" was the first medical treatise published in this country on the subject of suicidal insanity. In 1848 Dr. Winslow established the "Quarterly Journal of Psychological Medicine and Mental Pathology." It has an extensive circulation, and a high reputation in all parts of the world. Dr. Winslow's last work is a voluminous one, on "The Obscure Diseases of the Brain, and Disorders of the Mind." This consists of nearly 800 pages of an elaborate exposition of the incipient symptoms of disease of the brain and disorders of the mind. The first edition of this work was exhausted in less than six months, and a very favourable review of it appeared in the October number of the "Edinburgh Review," 1860.

WINTERHALTER, FRANZ XAVIER, a painter, was born at St. Blasien, in Baden, in 1803. Educated at Carlsruhe, he entered as student at the Munich Academy of Arts in 1823, and passed through the ordinary course of instruction. His earlier works were historic and poetical, but portrait painting being more lucrative, he adopted that line of the profession, and found the most ample patronage. He has painted kings, queens, princes, and nobles, and has been patronized by her Majesty Queen Victoria. His life, however, possesses no incidents of the slightest public interest.

WISEMAN, NICHOLAS, CARDINAL, was born at Seville, August 2nd, 1802. His early education was received at Waterford, and St. Cuthbert's College, near Durham. He was afterwards member of the English College at Rome, where he was created a D.D. in 1824. He became, not long after, Professor of Oriental Languages in the Roman University; and Rector of the English College in 1829. In 1835 he delivered a series of sermons on the "Doctrines and Practices of the Catholic Church," which were afterwards published. His "Lectures on the Connexion between Science and Revealed Religion" were much admired, and gave him great reputation. He was appointed in 1840 Coadjutor to the late Bishop Walsh, and President of St. Mary's College, Oscott. He was chosen in 1850 Vicar Apostolic of the London district; in the following year he was named by the Pope "Archbishop of Westminster," and raised to the dignity of Cardinal. This proceeding gave such offence in England, that Lord John Russell introduced into the House his Ecclesiastical Titles Bill, which need scarcely have been debated, as it is now a dead letter. He has since then delivered numerous lectures on various subjects on behalf of public institutions. He was one of the founders, and for a long time one of the editors of, and a copious contributor to, the "Dublin Review."

WOEHLER, FREDERICK, a German chemist, Professor of Chemistry at the University of Göttingen, was born at the village of Eschersheim, near Frankfort, in July, 1800, and studied for the medical profession at Marburg and Heidelberg. After having obtained the diploma of Doctor of Medicine, he left the profession to devote himself exclusively to chemistry. He was fortunate enough to obtain admission to the laboratory of Berzelius at Stockholm, where he worked for a year. Returning to Germany, he was appointed Professor in the School of Arts and Trades at Berlin, and six years later he obtained the Chair of Chemistry and Technology in the Polytechnic School of Cassel. In 1836 he was appointed Professor of Chemistry and Pharmacy in the University of Göttingen, being entrusted at the same time with the direction of the Chemical Institute, and the general inspection of the apothecaries of the kingdom of Hanover. Of all the German laboratories that of Göttingen is at present much frequented. Among the numerous researches which M. Woehler has conducted, partly with the assistance of his friend Liebig, may be enumerated those resulting in the discovery of aluminium, the metal extracted from clay, and of what has been supposed to be an organic body, under circumstances which seem to have afforded an instance of spontaneous generation. In recognition of his eminence as a chemist he has been admitted a Fellow of various learned bodies, and among others of the Royal Society of London. His works have passed through many editions, besides being translated into several languages.

WOOD, RIGHT HON. SIR CHARLES, G.C.B., M.P. for the borough of Halifax, is eldest son of the late Sir Francis Lindley Wood, and was born at Pontefract, in 1800. He was educated at Oriel College, Oxford, pursuing his studies with a success which enabled him to take a double first-class degree in 1821. He entered Parliament in 1826, as member for Great Grimsby, a seat which he retained until 1831, when he was elected for Wareham. After having been for some time private secretary to Earl Grey, he was appointed Secretary to the Treasury in 1832, an office which he held until the close of 1834. From 1835 to 1836 he discharged the duties of Secretary to the

Admiralty; but the Conservative party coming into power, Sir Charles was out of office until 1846, when, on the resignation of Sir Robert Peel, he became Chancellor of the Exchequer. Though his measures, while discharging the duties of this most onerous of state offices, were sharply censured, and though he felt himself obliged to amend his budget more than once, yet the very principles he advanced then, only to be condemned, are now received with cordiality, and acted upon by the Legislature. Sir Charles Wood's financial schemes had the great merit of being cautious and safe. He retired with the ministry from the Chancellorship of the Exchequer in 1852, being, in the December of that year, appointed President of the Board of Control, an office which he administered for upwards of two years, when he was transferred to the Board of Admiralty, as First Lord of that department. He retained that position until 1858, when ministers resigned on a defeat in the House of Commons, but on the recall of Lord Palmerston to power, Sir Charles Wood took the place of Lord Stanley, as Secretary of State for the Indian Department.

WRANGEL, FERDINAND PETROVICH, BARON VON, a Russian navigator of the Northern Seas, was born in Esthonia, in 1796. After being a pupil in the School for Cadets, at St. Petersburg, he made a number of voyages in the Baltic, and northwards, until 1817, when he went on board the "Kamschatka," Captain Golowin commanding, to circumnavigate the globe. In this expedition he displayed such talent, that after his return he was appointed to explore the Russian Polar Seas, in the discharge of which duty he was occupied for four years. He was required to determine, if possible, the exact position of tracts of land which were rumoured to exist north of the Siberian coast; and he used every exertion towards accomplishing that object; but though making numerous discoveries, the great purpose remained unachieved. In 1825 he again set out on a voyage round the world, this undertaking occupying him about two years. On his return he was appointed Governor of the Russian territory in America, where he remained for five years. On returning again to Russia, he was elevated to the rank of Admiral. In 1836 he was appointed Director of one of the various departments of the Imperial Naval Ministry. At the same time the Russian American Company proposed to him to take the chief direction of that establishment, which he accepted. He managed the affairs of the department of the Naval Ministry, as well as of the Russian American Company, during fourteen years. His health having failed in 1850, he retired from the service, and left St. Petersburg with his family for Esthonia. In 1854 he again entered the Imperial service as Chief Director of the Hydrographical department of the Naval Ministry, and in 1855 was appointed Chief Assistant to the High Admiral Constantine, as a mark of high distinction, being nominated (1856) General-Adjutant to his Imperial Majesty. His health being again totally deranged through very hard duties.-the physicians sent him to the German baths, and to the south of Europe; whence he returned, after a year's absence, in 1858, to be appointed Member of the High Council of the Empire. His northern surveys and adventures are held by the Russians to rank him with Parry, Ross, and Franklin; and his published narratives certainly demonstrate that he is at once an able and well-informed writer, and an adventurous and skilful seaman. The narratives of his northern voyages have been translated into the German, French, and English languages.

WRIGHT, THOMAS, M.A., an English antiquary, was born on the borders of Wales, in 1810, was educated at Ludlow, and afterwards graduated at Cambridge. He early commenced literary pursuits by writing for various magazines, but eventually devoted himself almost exclusively to historical and archæological studies. He was one of the founders of the Camden Society (1838), and of the Percy Society, of which latter he was for some time honorary secretary and treasurer. He assisted to found the British Archæological Association, and for some years edited its journal. He is a Fellow of the Society of Antiquaries, Corresponding Member of the Academy of Inscriptions in the Institute of France, Member of the Societies of Antiquaries of France, Normandy, and Scotland, of the Ethnological Society of Paris, of the Royal Society of Northern Antiquarians of Copenhagen, and of many other learned bodies. Of his untiring labour, some idea may be formed from the circumstance that his works extend to seventy-eight volumes, several of them quartos, all being admitted authorities on the subjects of which they treat. Mr. Wright has lately (1860) taken a deep interest in the excavations which have laid bare the remains of an old Roman town, near Wroxeter, in which numerous relics, illustrating the daily life and occupations of its ancient inhabitants, have been brought to light; and to his exertions, we are thus indebted for many discoveries which have materially added to the stores of the early history of Britain.

W U R T E M B U R G, WILLIAM I., FREDERICK CHARLES, KING OF WURTEMBURG, was born 27th of September, 1781, and succeeded his father Frederick I. on the 30th of October, 1816. In 1816 he married Catherine Paulowna, daughter of Paul late Emperor of Russia, and after her death, Pauline Theresa Louisa, his cousin, daughter of Louis Frederick, Duke of Würtemburg. His Majesty had issue by both marriages. The heir-apparent to the throne, issue of the second marriage, is Prince Charles Frederick Alexander, born on the 6th of March, 1823. The long reign of his Majesty has been quiet and uneventful.

WYATT, MATTHEW DIGBY, an architect, and writer on decorative art, was born at Devizes, in Wiltshire, in 1820. He was educated in his native town, and after being with his brother, the architect of Wilton Church, &c., he entered in 1837 the Royal Academy as a student. In 1844 he travelled on the Continent, and returned home with a large number of architectural and decorative drawings. While engaged in the practice of his profession, he occupied his leisure in writing for the press. Taking a lively interest in the application of art to manufactures, the Society of Arts despatched him to study at the Exhibition of Industry at Paris, in 1849, which mission led to the publication of an able report. In 1851 he took a most active part in organizing the Exhibition, of which he was acting secretary, and superintended the arrangement and architectural details of the Crystal Palace in Hyde Park, receiving His Royal Highness Prince Albert's private gold medal at the close of the exhibition. He has published several valuable works on art, manufactures, and decoration; and has designed the Pompeian and other courts of the Crystal Palace at Sydenham. He was a juror and reporter for the British Government at the Paris Exhibition of 1855, and on that occasion was created a Knight of the Legion of Honour. In the same year he gained with his brother, in whose office he had been brought up, the first premium in the great government competition for cavalry barracks, and was also selected to fill the office of Architect to the Hon. the East India Company. After executing many large works for that body, including their new Museum, on the change in the mode of government, his services were transferred to the Secretary of State for India in council, and he was associated with Mr. G. G. Scott in preparing designs for the proposed new India office. As an architect, his principal works have been, in addition to those already referred to— the Paddington Station of the Great Western Railway Company; the Neeld Memorial for Her Majesty; and several bridges in India. In 1856 Mr. Wyatt, in response to an appeal from the most distinguished men in his own profession, undertook the duties of Honorary Secretary to the Institute of British Architects. He held that office for three years, and gave it up only because his close professional engagements made it impossible for him to fulfil its duties as he desired.

YOUNG, BRIGHAM, the present leader of the Mormons, or Latter-day Saints, was born in Whitingham, Windham county, in the state of Vermont (U.S.), on the 1st June, 1801. He lived with his father, who was a farmer at Whitingham, until he was sixteen. He then learned a mechanical trade, and on the 14th April, 1832, joined the Mormons, or to use a phrase of these sectaries, "was baptized into the Church of Jesus Christ of Latter-day Saints." In 1835, thanks to his superior ability and education, he became a member of the Governing Council, or "Quorum of the Twelve Apostles." He suffered all the tribulations of the Mormons during their stay at Nauvoo, when Joseph Smith was put to death by the riotous inhabitants of Illinois. In June, 1844, Brigham Young, "in accordance with a previous appointment by the prophet, and ordination under his hands," succeeded to the presidency of the Church. Nauvoo had no sooner become a prosperous settlement, than the Mormons were forced to abandon it, in consequence of the strong popular feeling against their creed and

morals in Illinois. In 1846 the President set out from this settlement with a large company of his followers, in search of a locality where they would not be interfered with, either by the mob or the legislature. A prompt compliance, however, with a requisition by the Government of the Union to furnish 500 "Saints" to serve in the war with Mexico, connected with other circumstances, enabled the emigrants to halt on the right bank of the Missouri at a point since called Florence, where they passed the winter of 1846-47, under tents, or on transport waggons, exposed to the ravages of disease and the depredations of the wild Indian tribes of the country. In the spring of 1847, President Young, with a pioneer company of 143 men, left the winter quarters at Florence in quest of the promised land; and crossing the Rocky Mountains, arrived at the Great Salt Lake Valley, between California and Oregon, on the 24th July in the same year. After surveying the site for a city afterwards built and named the Great Salt Lake City, and erecting temporary forts for the reception of companies who were to emigrate that season, the President returned to winter quarters at Florence. With his family, and large additional numbers of the Saints, he returned to the new city in the autumn of 1848. The city rapidly grew in importance. In 1850 it contained 8,000 inhabitants. The colony was shortly afterwards recognized as a territory by the Federal Government, Brigham Young being appointed Governor, with a salary fixed for him at Washington. In 1856, when the population of Utah had increased to 30,000, which, under ordinary circumstances, would have entitled it to be received as a state of the Union, President Pierce refused to acknowledge its claims to admission, on account of the recognition of polygamy, and its prevalence among the Saints. Brigham Young protested against interference, and defied the Government authorities to prove to him by the Bible, that a man is not entitled to take as many wives as he thinks proper. By the laws of the community, six wives are allowed to each Saint, the President only being permitted an unlimited number, a privilege of which he has taken ample advantage, he having some years ago taken unto himself no less than seventy ladies from his flock. According to his disciples, Brigham Young is endowed with great firmness and energy of character, wit, sound practical sense, and good judgment, which, with his natural kindliness and benevolence, admirably fit him to control and influence his followers, and to maintain peace among them.

# ANALYTICAL
# TABLE OF MEMOIRS
## CONTAINED IN THIS VOLUME;

### COMPRISING :—

| | | |
|---|---|---|
| ACTORS. | GEOGRAPHERS. | PHILOLOGISTS. |
| ANTIQUARIANS. | GEOLOGISTS. | PHYSICIANS. |
| ARCHITECTS. | HISTORIANS. | PHYSICISTS. |
| ASTRONOMERS. | JOURNALISTS. | PHYSIOLOGISTS. |
| AUTHORS. | LAWYERS. | POETS. |
| BOTANISTS. | MILITARY OFFICERS. | POLITICAL AND SOCIAL |
| CAPITALISTS. | MUSICAL PROFESSION. | ECONOMISTS. |
| CHEMISTS. | NATURALISTS. | SCHISMATICS. |
| CLERGYMEN. | NAVAL OFFICERS. | SCULPTORS. |
| DIPLOMATISTS. | NOVELISTS. | SOVEREIGNS. |
| ENGINEERS. | PAINTERS. | STATESMEN. |
| ENGRAVERS. | PHILANTHROPISTS. | TRAVELLERS. |

---

### ACTORS.
(See " Musical Profession.")
Alboni, Marietta.
Barnum, Phineas Taylor.
Bishop, Madame Anna.
Buckstone, John Baldwin.
Celeste, Madame.
Cushman, Miss Charlotte.
Forrest, Edwin.
Grisi, Giulia.
Houdin, Robert Jean Eugène.
Kean, Charles.
Kean, Mrs. Charles.
Kemble, Mrs. Fanny.
Macready, William Charles.
Mario, Joseph.
Phelps, Samuel.
Piccolomini, Maria.
Ristori, Madame Adelaide.
Robson, Frederick.
Sedgwick, Amy.
Taglioni, Marie.
Vandenhoff, John.

### ANTIQUARIANS.
Botta, Paul Emile.
Bustamente, General.
Collier, John Payne.
Dyce, Rev. Alexander.
Ellis, Sir Henry.
Gerhard, Edward.
Halliwell, James O.
Laborde, Leon, Count de.
Layard, Austen Henry.
Lepsius, Carl Richard.
Madden, Sir Frederic, K.H.
Nichols, John Gough, F.S.A.
Palgrave, Sir Francis, F.R.S.
Planché, James R.
Rawlinson, Sir Henry.
Saulcy, Louis Caignart de.
Taylor, Isidore, Baron.
Timbs, John, F.S.A.
Thoms, William.
Wilkinson, Sir John Gardner.
Willis, Rev. Robert, F.R.S.
Wright, Thomas, F.R.S.

### ARCHITECTS:

Cockerell, Charles Robert, R. A.
Fergusson, James.
Godwin, George.
Paxton, Sir Joseph, M.P.
Pennethorne, James.
Scott, George Gilbert, A.R.A.
Smirke, Sir Robert.
Tite, William, M.P., F.R.S.
Wyatt, Matthew Digby.

### ASTRONOMERS.

Adams, John Couch.
Airy, George Biddell, F.R.S.
Argelander, Friedrich.
Encke, Johann F.
Herschel, Sir John F.W., Bart.
Hind, John Russell.
Leverrier, Urban Jean Joseph.
Rosse, Earl of.
Santini, Giovanni.
South, Sir James, F.R.S.

### AUTHORS.

(See "Historians," "Journalists,"
"Novelists," and "Poets.")

Abbott, Rev. Jacob.
Abbott, Rev. John.
About, Edmond.
Ampere, Jean Jacques.
Anthon, Charles, LL.D.
Arthur, T. S.
Auerbach, Berthold.
Beecher, Henry Ward.
Beecher, Miss Catherine.
Bell, Robert.
Bohn, Henry G.
Borrow, George.
Bowring, Sir John.
Bray, Mrs. Anna Eliza.
Brooks, Charles Shirley.
Bulwer, Right Hon. Sir Henry.
Bunsen, Chevalier Von.
Carey, Henry C.
Carlyle, Thomas.
Chambers, Robert.
Chambers, William.
Child, Mrs. Lydia Maria.
Clarke, Mrs. Mary Cowden.
Clausen, Henri.

### AUTHORS—(Continued).

Cole, Henry, C.B.
Coleridge, Rev. Derwent.
Collier, John Payne.
Collin de Plancy.
Costello, Miss Louisa Stuart.
Craik, George Lillie, LL.D.
Croly, Rev. George, LL.D.
Crosland, Mrs. Camilla.
Crowe, Mrs. Catherine Stevens.
Cunningham, Peter.
Curtis, Benjamin R.
Curtis, George William.
Dale, Rev. Thomas, M.A.
Dickens, Charles.
Dixon, William Hepworth.
Doran, John, LL.D.
Dyce, Rev. Alexander.
Eadie, John, D.D., LL.D.
Ellis, Mrs. Sarah.
Emerson, Ralph Waldo.
Eotvos, Josef.
Forster, John.
Gerstaecker, Frederic.
Gilfillan, Rev. George.
Gleig, Rev. George Robert.
Gordon, Lady Lucy Duff.
Grimm, Jacob Ludwig.
Hagenbach, Charles Rodolphe.
Haliburton, Hon. Mr. Justice.
Halliwell, John O.
Hawthorne, Nathaniel.
Head, Sir Francis Bond.
Headley, Joel Tyler.
Hengstenberg, Ernest William.
Herzen, or Hertzen, Alexander.
Hildreth, Richard.
Horne, Richard Henry.
Ingersoll, Charles Jared.
Jerrold, William Blanchard.
Jewsbury, Miss Geraldine.
Karr, Jean Baptiste Alphonse.
Kavanagh, Miss Julia.
Kinglake, Alexander William, M.P.
Kingsley, Rev. Charles, M.A.
Kinkel, Gottfried.
Knight, Charles.
Knowles, Sheridan.
Kugler, Franz Theodore.
Lamartine, Alphonse de.

AUTHORS—(*Continued*).

Landor, Walter Savage.
Lee, Mrs. A. Bowdich.
Lewes, George.
Lewis, Sir George Cornewall.
Lucas, Hippolyte Julien Joseph.
M'Culloch, J. R.
Marston, John Westland.
Martineau, Miss Harriet.
Masson, David.
Maurice, Rev. Frederick, M.A.
Mayhew, Henry.
Melville, Herman.
Merimée, Prosper.
Michaud, Louis Gabriel.
Montalembert, Comte de.
Muloch, Miss Dinah M.
Newman, Francis William.
Oliphant, Lawrence.
Oxenford, John.
Pardoe, Miss Julia.
Parton, Mrs. Sara P.
Pepoli, Charles.
Planché, James Robinson.
Pulszky, Madame Ferencz.
Pyat, Felix.
Quinet, Edgar.
Redding, Cyrus.
Ritchie, Leitch.
Rogers, Henry.
Ruskin, John.
Russell, Lord John.
Russell, William Howard, LL.D.
Sala, George Augustus.
Sartorius, Ernest William Christian.
Say, Horace Emile.
Schœlcher, Victor.
Scribe, Eugène.
Sinclair, Miss Catherine.
Stanley, Rev. Arthur.
Stirling, Willam, M.P.
Stowe, Harriet Beecher.
Taylor, Bayard.
Taylor, Isaac.
Taylor, Tom.
Tennent, Sir James E., M.P.
Tholuck, Friedrich Gottren.
Timbs, John, F.S.A.
Trollope, Mrs. Frances.
Tulloch, John, D.D.

AUTHORS—(*Continued*).

Tupper, Martin Farquhar, D.C.L.
Ullman, Karl.
Urquhart, David.
Vaughan, Robert, D.D.
Villemain, Abel.
Waagen, Gustave Friedrich.
Warren, Samuel.
Whatley, the Right Rev. Richard.
Whewell, Rev. William, D.D.
Willis, Nathaniel Parker.

BOTANISTS.

(See "Naturalists.")

CAPITALISTS.

Ashburton, Lord.
Baring, Sir Francis, Bart.
Baring, Thomas.
Brown, William.
Demidov, or Demidoff, Prince.
Overstone, Lord.
Rothschild, Nathan, Baron de, M.P.
Salomons, David, M.P.

CHEMISTS.

Becquerel, Antoine Cesar.
Boussingault, Jean Baptiste.
Brande, William Thomas.
Bunsen, Robert William.
Chevreul, Michel Eugène.
Christison, Robert, M.D.
Dumas, Jean Baptiste.
Faraday, Michael, D.C.L.
Graham, Thomas, F.R.S.
Griffin, John Joseph, F.C.S.
Herapath, William, F.C.S.
Kane, Sir Robert.
Liebig, Justus, Baron.
Mitscherlich, Eilhard.
Niepce, de Saint Victor.
Payen, Anselme.
Pelouze, Theophile Jules.
Playfair, Lyon, C.B.
Poggendorf, John Christian.
Raspail, François Vincent.
Regnault, Henri Victor.
Rose, Heinrich.
Sainte-Claire Deville.
Taylor, Alfred Swaine, M.D.
Woehler, Frederick.

## CLERGYMEN.

Abbott, Rev. Jacob.
Abbott, Rev. John.
Alford, Very Rev. Dean.
Anderson, William, LL.D.
Antonelli, Cardinal.
Barnes, Albert, D.D.
Beecher, Rev. Charles.
Beecher, Rev. Edward, D.D.
Beecher, Lyman, D.D.
Binney, Rev. Thomas.
Caird, John, D.D.
Campbell, John, D.D.
Candlish, Robert, D.D.
Canterbury, Archbishop of.
Cheever, George Burritt, D.D.
Close, Very Rev. Dean.
Coleridge, Rev. Derwent.
Croly, Rev. George, LL.D.
Cullen, Paul, D.D.
Cumming, Rev. John, D.D.
Cunningham, William, D.D.
Dale, Rev. Thomas, M.A.
D'Aubigné, J. H. Merle, D.D.
Dewey, Orville, D.D.
Dublin, Archbishop of.
Duff, Alexander, D.D., LL.D.
Dyce, Rev. Alexander.
Eadie, John, D.D.
Ellis, Rev. William.
Exeter, Bishop of.
Gavazzi, Padre Alessandro.
Gilfillan, Rev. George.
Gleig, Rev. George Robert.
Guthrie, Thomas, D.D.
Hamilton, James, D.D.
Hereford, Bishop of.
Hinds, Right Rev. Samuel.
Hook, Very Rev. Dean.
Keble, Rev. John, M.A.
Kingsley, Rev. Charles, M.A.
Lacordaire, Abbé.
Lee, Robert, D.D.
Liddell, the Very Rev. Henry.
London, Bishop of.
M'Hale, Right Rev. John.
Macleod, Norman, D.D.
M'Neile, Rev. Hugh, D.D.
Maurice, Frederick D., M.A.
Melvill, Henry, B.D.

## CLERGYMEN—(Continued).

Milman, Very Rev. Dean.
Moffat, Rev. Robert.
Newman, John Henry, D.D.
Noel, the Hon. and Rev. Baptist W.
Oxford, Bishop of.
Pius IX., Giovanni Maria Mastai Feretti.
Pusey, Edward Bouverie, D.D.
Raffles, Rev. Thomas, D.D.
Reed, Rev. Andrew, D.D.
Ripon, Bishop of.
St. David's, Bishop of.
Sedgwick, Rev. Adam, M.A.
Spurgeon, Rev. Charles Haddon.
Stanley, Rev. Arthur.
Thompson, Rev. R. Anchor, M.A.
Trench, Very Rev. Dean.
Tulloch, Rev. John, D.D.
Vaughan, Rev. Robert, D.D.
Whewell, William, D.D.
Willis, Rev. Robert, F.R.S.
Wiseman, Nicholas, Cardinal.

## DIPLOMATISTS.

(See "Statesmen.")

## ENGINEERS.

Albert, Martin.
Armstrong, Sir William.
Brunel, Isambard Kingdom.
Burgoyne, Sir John F.
Dargan, William.
Fairbairn, William. -
M'Neill, Sir John, C.E.
Minié, Claude.
Napier, Robert.
Nasmyth, James.
Peto, Sir Samuel Morton.
Rankine, J. W. Macquorn, F.R.S.
Russell, John Scott, F.R.S.
Todleben, General.
Whitworth, Joseph.
Willis, Rev. Robert, F.R.S.

## ENGRAVERS.

Burnet, John.
Doo, George Thomas, R.A.
Goodall, Edward, R.A.
Watt, James Henry.
Wilmore, James Tibbits.

# ANALYTICAL TABLE OF MEMOIRS.

## GEOGRAPHERS.
Berghaus, Henry.
Johnston, Alexander Keith.
Maury, Matthew F.
Munch, Peter Andreas.
Petermann, August Heinrich.

## GEOLOGISTS.
(See "Naturalists.")

## HISTORIANS.
Alison, Sir Archd., Bart.
Bancroft, George.
Bauer, Bruno.
Brougham, Lord.
Buckle, Henry Thomas.
Burton, John Hill.
Campbell, Lord.
Cantu, Cesar.
Capefigue, Jean Baptiste.
Carlyle, Thomas.
Craik, George Lillie, LL.D.
Creasy, Sir Edward.
Dahlmann, Frederick Christopher.
D'Aubigné, J. H. Merle, D.D.
Forster, John.
Gervinus, Georges Godefroid.
Gleig, Rev. John R.
Grote, George, M.P.
Guizot, Francis.
Helps, Arthur.
Jomini, Henri, Baron.
Lamartine, Alphonse.
Liddell, Very Rev. Henry.
Lieber, Francis, LL.D.
Martinez de la Rosa, Francisco.
Menzel, Wolfgang. .
Merimée, Prosper.
Michaud, Louis Gabriel.
Michelet, Jules.
Mignet, François Auguste.
Milman, Very Rev. Henry.
Quinet, Edgar.
Ranke, Leopold.
Raumer, Frederick Von.
Sparks, Jared.
Stanhope, Earl of.
Strickland, Miss Agnes.
Thierry, Amédée.
Thiers, Louis Adolphe.
Thirlwall, Right Rev. Connop, D.D.

## JOURNALISTS.
Arago, Etienne.
Bryant, William Cullen.
Delane, John T.
Dilke, Charles Wentworth.
Dilke, Charles Wentworth, junior.
Dixon, William Hepworth.
Duffy, Charles Gavin.
Fonblanque, Albany.
Forster, John.
Girardin (Emile de).
Greeley, Horace.
Hall, Samuel Carter.
Hannay, James.
Hunt, Thornton.
Janin, Jules Gabriel.
Jerdan, William.
Jerrold, William Blanchard.
Lemon, Mark.
Mackay, Charles, LL.D.
Maclaren, Charles.
Miall, Edward.
Redding, Cyrus.
Ritchie, Leitch.
Russel, Alexander.
Russell, William Howard, LL.D.
Veron, Louis Désiré.
Veuillot, Louis.
Watts, Alaric Alexander.
Whitty, Edward Michael.
Wills, William Henry.

## LAWYERS.
Alison, Sir Archibald, Bt.
Baroche, Pierre Jules.
Bell, Henry Glassford.
Berryer, Pierre Antoine.
Bethell, Sir Richard.
Billault, Auguste.
Brougham, Lord.
Butt, George M. .
Cairns, Sir Hugh M'Calmont.
Campbell, Lord. .
Chambers, Montague.
Chelmsford, Lord.
Cranworth, Baron. .
Creasy, Sir Edward S.
Curtis, Benjamin R.
Glencorse, Lord.
Kelly, Sir Fitzroy.

LAWYERS—(*Continued*).

Lyndhurst, Lord.
Pollock, Sir Frederick.
St. Leonards, Baron.
Senior, Nassau William, M.A.
Warren, Samuel.
Wensleydale, Baron.
Whiteside, Hon. James, M.P.

MILITARY OFFICERS.

Abd-el-Kader.
Alvarez, Juan.
Baraguey, Marshal.
Bedeau, Marie Alphonse.
Bosquet, Pierre François Joseph.
Burgoyne, Sir John Fox.
Bustamente, General.
Cabrera, Don Ramon.
Cambridge, Duke of.
Canrobert, François Certain.
Cardigan, Earl of.
Changarnier, General.
Chesney, Francis Rawdon, D.C.L.
Clyde, Lord.
Codrington, Sir William, K.C.B.
Combermere, Viscount, G.C.B.
Douglas, General Sir Howard, Bart.
Edwardes, Sir Herbert Benj. K.C.B.
Espinasse, Esprit Charles Marie.
Evans, Sir De Lacy.
Garibaldi, Joseph.
Gomm, General Sir William, G.C.B.
Görgei, Arthur.
Gortchakoff, Prince Michael.
Gough, Lord.
Houston, General.
Jellachich, Baron Von.
Klapka, General George.
Kmety, General George.
La Marmora, Marquis de.
Lamoricière, General.
Luders, General.
Macmahon, Marshal.
Magnan, Marshal.
Menschikoff, Prince.
O'Donnell, Marshal.
Omer Pacha.
Oudinot, Marshal.
Outram, General Sir James.
Pelissier, Marshal.

MILITARY OFFICERS—(*Continued*).

Pennefather, Lieutenant-General.
Pepe, Florestan.
Pepe, Gabriel.
Rosas, Don Juan Manuel de.
Sabine, Major-General Edward.
Santa Anna, Don A. Lopez de.
Scarlett, Sir James Yorke.
Schamyl.
Simpson, Gen. Sir James, G.C.B.
Smith, Sir Henry, Bart.
Thompson, Major-General Perronet.
Todleben, General.
Troubridge, Col. Sir Thomas, Bart., C.B.
Williams, Major-General, Sir W. F.
Windham, Major-General Charles, C.B.
Windischgrätz, Alfred Prince de.

MUSICAL PROFESSION.

Alboni, Marietta.
Auber, Daniel F. E.
Balfe, Michael William.
Benedict, Julius.
Bennett, William Sterndale.
Berlioz, Hector.
Bishop, Madame Anna.
David, Felicien.
Goldschmidt, Madame.
Grisi, Giulia.
Halevy, Jacques-Elie-Fromental.
Hayes, Mrs. Catherine.
Hullah, John.
Liszt, Franz.
Mario, Joseph.
Meyerbeer, Giacomo.
Novello, Madame Clara.
Piccolomini, Maria.
Potter, Cipriani.
Roger, Gustave.
Rossini, Joacchino.
Rudersdorff, Madame.
Thalberg, Sigismund.
Titiens, Teresa.
Verdi, Giuseppe.
Viardot, Pauline Garcia.
Wagner, Richard.

NATURALISTS.

(See "Physicians" and "Physiologists.")
Agassiz, Louis Jean.
Bell, Thomas.

## NATURALISTS—(*Continued*).

Burmeister, Hermann.
Dana, James Dwight, LL.D.
Darwin, Charles, M.A.
Ehrenberg, Christian Gottfried.
Eichwald, Edward.
Fortune, Robert.
Gosse, Philip Henry.
Gould, Augustus Addison.
Gould, John, F.R.S.
Gray, Asa, M.D.
Hooker, Sir William Jackson, K.H.
Hooker, Joseph Dalton, M.D.
Junghuhn, Frank Wilhelm.
Kobell, Franz Von.
Kock, Charles Henri Emmanuel.
Lankester, Edwin, M.D.
Latham, Robert Gordon, M.D.
Lindley, John, M.D.
Lyell, Sir Charles, F.R.S.
Martius, Carl Von.
Murchison, Sir Roderick, D.C.L.
Nees, Von Esenbeck.
Orbigny, Charles d'.
Owen, Richard, F.R.S.
Phillips, John, M.A., LL.D.
Reichenbach, Baron de.
Rogers, Henry Darwin, LL.D.
Rose, Gustave.
Schomburgk, Sir Robert Hermann.
Sedgwick, Rev. Adam, M.A.

### NAVAL OFFICERS.

Back, Sir George, D.C.L.
Belcher, Sir Edward.
Constantine, Nicholæwitch.
Deschenes, Admiral Percival.
Dundas, Vice-Admiral.
Dundonald, Earl of.
Du Petit Thouars, Admiral.
Napier, Sir Charles.
Slade, Sir Adolphus.

### NOVELISTS.

(See "Authors" and "Poets.")
Ainsworth, William Harrison.
Andersen, Hans Christian.
Bremer, Miss Frederika.
Carlen, Madame Emilie.
Carleton, William.

## NOVELISTS—(*Continued*).

Collins, Wilkie.
Conscience, Henri.
Dickens, Charles.
Disraeli, Benjamin, Right Hon., M.P.
Dudevant, Madame.
Dumas, Alexandre.
Dumas, Alexandre, jun.
Gaskell, Mrs. L. E.
Gore, Mrs. Catherine Frances.
Grant, James.
Grattan, Thomas Colley.
Hall, Mrs. Anna Maria.
Hawthorne, Nathaniel.
Howitt, Mary.
Howitt, William.
Josika, Nicolas Baron.
Kingsley, Rev. Charles, M.A.
Kock, Charles Paul de.
Lennep, Jacob Van.
Lever, Charles.
Lover, Samuel.
Lytton, Sir Edward Bulwer.
Manzoni, Count.
Marsh, Mrs. Anne.
Miller, Thomas.
Muloch, Miss Dinah.
Musset, Paul Edme de.
Normanby, Marquis of.
Norton, Hon. Mrs.
Reade, Charles.
Reid, Captain Mayne.
Sedgwick, Miss Catherine Maria.
Stowe, Mrs. Beecher.
Thackeray, William Makepeace.
Trollope, Mrs. Frances.
Warren, Samuel.

### PAINTERS.

Adam, Jean Victor.
Bendemann, Edward.
Bonheur, Mlle. Rosa.
Cattermole, George, R.A.
Cooke, Edward W., A.R.A.
Cooper, Thomas Sidney, A.R.A.
Cope, Charles West, R.A.
Corbaux, Miss Fanny.
Corbould, Edward Henry.
Cornelius, Peter Von.
Creswick, Thomas, R.A.

PAINTERS—(*Continued*).

Cruikshank, George.
Danby, Francis, A.R.A.
Delacroix, Eugène.
Delaroche, Paul.
Doyle, Richard.
Dyce, William, R.A.
Eastlake, Sir Charles Lock, P.R.A.
Egg, Augustus, R.A.
Faed, Thomas.
Fraser, Alexander.
Frith, William Powell, R.A.
Frost, William Edward, R.A.
Gavarni, or Paul Chevalier.
Gilbert, John Graham.
Goodall, Frederick, R.A.
Gordon, Sir John Watson, P.R.S.A., R.A.
Grant, Francis, R.A.
Gudin, Théodore.
Haghe, Louis.
Hart, Solomon Alexander, R.A.
Harvey, George, R.S.A.
Hayter, Sir George.
Herbert, John Rogers, R.A.
Herring, John Frederick.
Horsley, John Callcott, R.A.
Hunt, William Holman.
Ingres, Jean Dominique Auguste.
Isabey, Eugène Louis Gabriel.
Kaulbach, William.
Lance, George, R.A.
Landseer, Sir Edwin, R.A.
Lauder, Robert Scott, R.S.A.
Lee, Frederick Richard, R.A.
Leech, John.
Lewis, John Frederick.
Linnell, John.
M'Culloch, Horatio.
Maclise, Daniel, R.A.
Meissonier, Jean Louis Ernest.
Millais, John Everett.
Mulready, William, R.A.
Nash, Joseph.
Overbeck, Friedrich.
Paton, Joseph Noel, R.S.A.
Pickersgill, Fred. Richard, R.A.
Poole, Paul Falconer, A.R.A.
Pyne, James B.
Redgrave, Richard, R.A.
Roberts, David, R.A.

PAINTERS—(*Continued*).

Schnorr, Jules.
Stanfield, Clarkson, R.A.
Vernet, Horace.
Ward, Edward Matthew, R.A.
Webster, Thomas, R.A.
Winterhalter, Franz Xavier.

PHILANTHROPISTS.

(See "Political and Social Economists.")

PHILOLOGISTS.

(See "Antiquarians.")

Allen, William, D.D.
Baehr, John Christian.
Bekker, Emmanuel.
Boeck, Augustus.
Bopp, Franz.
Bosworth, Joseph, D.D., LL.D.
Dindorf, Wilhelm.
Latham, Robert Gordon, M.D.
Panizzi, Antonio.
Ramsay, William, M.A.
Richardson, Charles, LL.D.
Roget, Peter Mark, M.D.
Smith, William, LL.D.
Trench, Very Rev. Dean.

PHYSICIANS.

Andral, Gabriel.
Arnot, Neil, M.D.
Auzoux, Th. Louis.
Blackwell, Elizabeth, M.D.
Brodie, Sir Benjamin, Bart.
Christison, Robert, M.D.
Clark, Sir James, Bart.
Dickson, Samuel Henry, M.D.
Dunglison, Robley, D.D., LL.D.
Elliotson, John, M.D.
Forbes, Sir John, M.D.
Frerichs, Frederic Théodore.
Holland, Sir Henry, M.D.
Langenbeck, Maximilian.
Rokitansky, Charles.
Schönlein, Johann Luk.
Simpson, James Young, M.D.
Skoda, Joseph.
Smith, Thomas Southwood, M.D.
Syme, James, M.D.
Taylor, Alfred Swaine, M.D.
Thierry, Alexandre.

PHYSICIANS—(*Continued*).

Velpeau, Alfred Marie.
Winslow, Forbes, M.D.

PHYSICISTS.

(See "Astronomers.")

Arnot, Neil, M.D.
Babbage, Charles.
Barlow, Peter.
Becquerel, Antoine Cesar.
Biot, Jean Baptiste.
Brewster, Sir David.
Bunsen, Robert William.
Cayley, Arthur.
De-Morgan, Augustus.
Faraday, Michael, D.C.L.
Gould, Benjamin Apthorp.
Harris, Sir William Snow.
Herschell, Sir John, Bart.
Hunt, Robert, F.R.S.
Morse, Samuel Finley Breese.
Olmsted, Denison.
O'Shaughnessy, Sir William B.
Pouillet, Claude.
Roget, Peter Mark, M.D.
Ruhmkorff, N.
Sabine, Major-General Edward.
Somerville, Mrs. Mary.
Wheatstone, Charles, F.R.S.
Whewell, Rev. William, D.D.

PHYSIOLOGISTS.

(See "Physicians" and "Naturalists.")

Bernard, Claude.
Carpenter, William Benjamin, M.D.
Muller, Johannes.
Owen, Richard, F.R.S.
Wagner, Rudolph.

POETS.

(See "Authors" and "Novelists.")

Aird, Thomas.
Andersen, Hans Christian.
Anster, John, D.C.L.
Arnold, Matthew.
Augier, Guillaume Victor.
Aytoun, William Edmondstoune.
Bailey, Philip James.
Barthélémy, Auguste Marseille.
Bell, Henry Glassford.
Brown, Miss Frances.

POETS—(*Continued*).

Browning, Mrs. Elizabeth Barrett.
Browning, Robert.
Bryant, William Cullen.
Carey, Miss Alice.
Clare, John.
Cook, Eliza.
Dana, Richard Henry.
Dobell, Sydney.
Dupont, Pierre.
Fields, James T.
Freiligrath, Ferdinand.
Hahn-Hahn, Countess Von.
Halleck, Fitz-Greene.
Holmes, Oliver Wendell.
Houssaye, Arsène.
Hugo, Victor Marie Vincent.
Ingemann, Bernard Severin.
Jasmin, Jacques.
Keble, Rev. John.
Kobell, Franz Von.
Lamartine, Alphonse.
Landor, Walter Savage.
Longfellow, Henry Wadsworth.
Lover, Samuel.
Lowell, James Russell.
Mackay, Charles, LL.D.
Martinez de la Rosa, Francisco.
Massey, Gerald.
Mery, Joseph.
Milnes, Richard Monckton, M.P.
Norton, the Hon. Mrs.
Patmore, Coventry.
Procter, Bryan W.
Reboul, Jean.
Smith, Alexander.
Swain, Charles.
Tennyson, Alfred, D.C.L.
Uhland, Johann Ludwig.
Vigny, Alfred, Count de.
Watts, Alaric Alexander.
Willis, Nathaniel Parker.

POLITICAL AND SOCIAL ECONOMISTS.

(See "Statesmen.")

Albert, Martin.
Blanc, Louis.
Bright, John.
Brougham, Lord.
Brown, William.

ECONOMISTS—(*Continued*).

Burritt, Elihu.
Carey, Henry C.
Chadwick, Edwin, C.B.
Chevalier, Michel.
Chisholm, Mrs. Caroline.
Cobden, Richard, M.P.
Cousin, Victor.
Coutts, Miss Burdett.
Dawson, George, M.A.
Godwin, George.
Gough, John B.
Guthrie, Thomas, D.D.
Hill, Sir Rowland, K.C.B.
Kingsley, Rev. Charles, M.A.
Lieber, Francis.
M'Culloch, J. R.
Martineau, Miss Harriet.
Maurice, Rev. F. D., M.A.
Metz de, Frederick A.
Mill, John Stuart.
Milnes, Monckton, M.P.
Nightingale, Miss F.
Potter, Louis Joseph.
Proudhon, Pierre Joseph.
Reed, Andrew, D.D.
Rollin, Ledru.
Say, Horace Emile.
Senior, Nassau William.
Shaftesbury, Lord.
Shuttleworth, Sir James Kay.
Smith, Southwood, M.D.
Thompson, Major-General.
Whatley, Archbishop.

SCHISMATICS.

Cabet, Etienne.
Proudhon, Pierre Joseph.
Ronge, Johannes.
Strauss, David Friedrich.
Young, Brigham.

SCULPTORS.

Baily, Edward Hodges, R.A.
Bell, John, R.A.
Foley, John Henry, R.A.
Geefs, Guillaume.
Geefs, Joseph.
Gibson, John, R.A.
Kiss, Augustus.
Lough, John Graham.
Macdowell, Patrick, R.A.

SCULPTORS—(*Continued*).

Marochetti, Baron.
Marshall, William Calder, R.A.
Monte, Raffaelle.
Powers, Hiram.
Rauch, Christian.
Steell, John, R.S.A.
Tenerani, Pietro.
Thorneycroft, Mrs. Mary.
Westmacott, Richard, R.A.

SOVEREIGNS AND PRINCES.

Abdul Medjid Khan, Turkey.
Albert, Prince Consort.
Albert Edward, Prince of Wales.
Alexander II., Russia.
Bonaparte, Jérome, Prince.
Bonaparte, Louis Lucien, Prince.
Bonaparte, Napoleon, Prince.
Buchanan, James, Ex-President U. S.
Chambord, Comte de.
Charles XV., Sweden.
Constantine, Nicholæwitch.
Danilo, Petrovitch, Montenegro.
Eugénie, Empress of the French.
Ferdinand IV., Ex-Duke of Tuscany.
Francis Joseph I., Austria.
Francis II., Naples.
Francis V., Ex-Duke of Modena.
Frederick VIII., Denmark.
Frederick William IV., Prussia.
George V., Hanover.
Ghika, Ex-Hospodar, Wallachia.
Hien Fung, China.
Isabel II., Spain.
Leopold I., Belgium.
Maximilian II. (Joseph), Bavaria.
Napoleon III., France.
Otho I., Greece.
Paris, Comte de.
Pedro V., Portugal.
Pius IX., Pope of Rome.
Soulouque, Ex-Emperor of Hayti.
Victor Emmanuel, Sardinia.
Victoria I., Queen of Great Britain, &c.
William I., Würtemburg.
William III., Holland.

STATESMEN.

(See "Political and Social Economists.")
Aali Pasha.

STATESMEN—*(Continued)*.

Aberdeen, Earl of.
Almodovar, Count of.
Anstey, Thomas Chisholm.
Antonelli, Cardinal.
Argyll, Duke of.
Argyropŏulo, Pericles.
Aristarchi, Nicolas.
Ashburton, Lord.
Azeglio, Marquis d'.
Baines, Edward, M.P.
Barante, Baron de.
Barbès, Armand.
Barrot, Odilon.
Bastide, Jules.
Baxter, William Edward, M.P.
Berkeley, Hon. Francis, M.P.
Bethell, Sir Richard.
Bibesco, George Demetrius.
Black, Adam, M.P.
Blanc, Louis.
Blanqui, Louis Auguste.
Botfield, Beriah, M.P.
Bourqueney, Comte de.
Bowring, Sir John.
Bravo-Murillo, Juan.
Bright, John, M.P.
Broglie, Duc de.
Brooke, Sir James.
Brougham, Lord.
Broughton de Gifford, Lord.
Brunow, Baron Von.
Buccleuch and Queensberry, Duke of.
Buchanan, James.
Bulwer, Sir Henry Lytton.
Bunsen, Chevalier Von.
Buol, Shauenstein, Count.
Buren, Martin Van.
Caballero, Firmin Agosto.
Caird, James, M.P.
Cairns, Sir Hugh M'Calmont.
Campbell, Lord.
Canning, Charles John, Viscount.
Cardwell, Right Hon. Edward.
Carlisle, Earl of.
Carnot, Lazare Hippolite.
Casabianca, Count of.
Cass, General Lewis, LL.D.
Caussidière, Marc.
Cavour, Count.

STATESMEN—*(Continued)*.

Chelmsford, Lord.
Clarendon, Earl of.
Cobden, Richard.
Coningham, William, M.P.
Cormenin, Vicomte de.
Cowley, Lord.
Cranworth, Baron.
Crémieux, Isaac Adolphe.
Dalhousie, Marquis of.
Dallas, George Mifflin.
Decazes, Elie Duc.
Derby, Earl of.
Disraeli, Benjamin, Right Honourable.
Drouyn de Lhuys, Edouard.
Duchâtel, Charles M. T., Count.
Dufaure, Jules Armand Stanislas.
Dufferin and Clandeboye, Lord.
Duffy, Charles G.
Duncombe, Thomas Slingsby, M.P.
Dupin, André-Marie Jean Jacques.
Dupin, Baron.
Dupont de l'Eure, Jacques Charles.
Eglinton and Winton, Earl of.
Elgin and Kincardine, Earl of.
Ellenborough, Earl of.
Enfantin, Barthélémy Prosper.
Espartero, Don Baldomero.
Everett, Edward, D.C.L.
Fazy, Jean J.
Fillmore, Millard.
Fould, Achille.
Fox, W. J., M.P.
Fremont, John Charles.
Garnier Pagès, Louis Antoine.
Gibson, Rt. Hon. Thomas Milner, M.P.
Gladstone, Right Hon. William E., M.P.
Gortchakoff, Prince Alexander.
Graham, Sir James.
Granville, Earl.
Grey, Earl.
Grey, Sir George, M.P.
Grey, Sir George, K.C.B.
Guizot, François.
Haliburton, Mr. Justice, M.P.
Hardwicke, Charles P. Yorke, Earl of.
Henley, Right Hon. Joseph W., M.P.
Herbert, Right Hon. Sidney, M.P.
Hope, George William, M.P.
Isturitz, Don Xavier de.

STATESMEN—(*Continued*).

Jordan, Sylvester.
Kern, J. Conrad.
Kinnaird, Lord.
Kisseleff, Paul Dmitrevitch.
Kossuth, Lajos de Kossuth 'Falva.
Lamartine, Alphonse de.
Lansdowne, Marquis of.
Lawrence, Sir John.
Ledru Rollin.
Lesseps, Ferdinand de.
Lewis, Sir George Cornewall.
Lindsay, Lord.
Lindsay, William Schaw, M.P.
Llanover, Lord.
Lyndhurst, Lord.
Lytton, Sir Edward Lytton Bulwer.
M'Neill, Sir John, G.C.B.
Madoz, Pascal.
Malmesbury, Earl of.
Manteufel, Baron.
Martinez de la Rosa.
Mazzini, Joseph.
Milnes, Richard Monckton, M.P.
Mocquard, Constant.
Montalembert, Comte de.
Monteagle, Lord.
Morny, Comte de.
Narvaez, Don Ramon, Duke.
Nesselrode, Comte de.
Newcastle, Duke of.
Normanby, Marquis of.
O'Brien, William Smith.
O'Donnell, Marshal.
Orloff, Alexis, Prince.
Overstone, Lord.
Pakington, Sir John, G.C.B.
Palmerston, Viscount.
Panmure, Lord.
Peel, Frederick, M.P.
Peel, The Right Hon. Jonathan.
Peel, Sir Robert.
Persigny, Jean Gilbert Victor Fialin.
Poerio, Carlo.
Pulszky, Ferencz.
Remilly, Ovide.
Reschid Pasha.
Ripon and De Grey, Earl of.
Roebuck, John, M.P.

STATESMEN—(*Continued*).

Rosetti, Constantine.
Russell, Lord John, M.P.
Saint Leonards, Baron.
Saldanha, Duke of.
Santa Anna, Don Antonio Lopez de.
Schœlcher, Victor.
Seymour, Sir Geo., G.C.B.
Shaftesbury, Earl of.
Stanhope, Philip H., Earl of.
Stanley, Lord.
Stirling, William, M.P.
Stratford de Redcliffe, Viscount.
Taunton, Lord.
Tennent, Sir James E., M.P.
Thiers, Louis Adolphe.
Urquhart, David.
Villemain, Abel.
Walewski, Comte de.
Walpole, the Right Hon. Spencer, M.P.
Walter, John, M.P.
Whiteside, the Right Hon. James, M.P.
Wood, Sir Chas., M.P.

TRAVELLERS.

Ainsworth, William Francis.
Back, Sir George.
Barth, Sir Henry.
Bartlett, John Russel.
Belcher, Sir Edward.
Borrow, George.
Cailliaud, Frederic.
Chesney, Francis Rawdon, D.C.L.
Davis, Sir John F., Bart., K.C.B.
Franklin, Lady.
Kinglake, Alexander Wm., M.P.
Laborde, Comte de.
Layard, Austen Henry.
Livingston, Rev. David, LL.D.
M'Clintock, Sir Francis.
Maclure, Sir Robert Le Mesurier.
Richardson, Sir John, K.C.B.
Ross, Rear-Admiral Sir James Clark.
Schomburgk, Sir Robert Hermann.
Taylor, Isidore Baron.
Taylor, Bayard.
Wilkes, Charles.
Willis, Nathaniel Parker.
Wrangel, Ferdinand.